DAUGHTER OF TIME

an infinite trilogy

Reader, Writer, Maker

Erec Stebbins

New York, NY, USA

Only one thing is impossible for God: to find any sense in any copyright law on the planet. — Mark Twain

Published 2015 by Twice Pi Press

Cover design by Erec Stebbins. Images used under license from Shutterstock.com, copyrighted artists Vadim Sadovski, Juergen Hofrath, Aleksandar Mijatovic.

ISBN: 9781942360049

TWICE PI PRESS

Contents

EREC STEBBINS

READER

DAUGHTER OF TIME
BOOK 1

READER

Daughter of Time
Book 1

Erec Stebbins

New York, NY, USA

For Ambra:
I did what I could
and enjoyed the company

Time is the fire in which we burn.
—Delmore Schwartz

PART I

Point α

A child's life is like a piece of paper on which every person leaves a mark.

Chinese proverb

Chapter 1

$$\nabla^2 \mathbf{A} - \frac{1}{c^2}\frac{\partial^2 \mathbf{A}}{\partial t^2} = \mu_0 e\psi^\dagger \alpha\psi$$

$$\nabla^2 \varphi - \frac{1}{c^2}\frac{\partial^2 \varphi}{\partial t^2} = \frac{1}{\varepsilon_0} e\psi^\dagger\psi$$

Who sees the future? I am conscious of being only an individual struggling weakly against the stream of time.

Ludwig Boltzmann

The dream always began well.

It was a moist and warm spring afternoon, and a soft breeze blew over the lush grass of our backyard toward the house, carrying the strong smells of the newly tilled earth. The sun partially blinded me as I ran over the grass toward the edge of our corn fields, stumbling on my short legs, yet not falling, my arms stretched out to embrace a tall shadow in the light before me. I could not have been more than five years old.

The sun darkened as my father's broad frame eclipsed its radiance, and the shadow transitioned instantly into his familiar form. I leapt into his outstretched arms squealing, and his soiled hands caught me tightly and swung me around as I giggled, staring into his bright-blue eyes framed under locks of golden-red hair. Then he tossed me upward. The ground below me, half green from grass, half rich brown from the newly plowed field, receded as the blue sky enveloped me, and I felt the thrilling tug of gravity grab my stomach, and pull me back to Earth. Several times he threw me, and I went farther and laughed harder each time. Higher and higher I soared, until the blue turned black and the Earth below became a mere sphere, dotted with continents and oceans, and above the stars shone through the thinning atmosphere.

For a moment I floated, thrown so high I nearly escaped the bonds of gravity tying us to our home world, and the stars seemed to tug at me as well

—beckoning me, luring me with a cold intensity that my child's senses felt as vaguely threatening. My giddiness began to turn to anxiety as I felt something wrong, something impure out there that waited in the diamond-pricked blackness in front of me. Something searching...*for me.*

But then I began to fall again, the air rushing over me, through clouds and air currents, seeing the ground first as a patchwork of squares and rectangles as from an airplane, resolving slowly to the familiar patterns of our neighborhood, and, at last, to that of my own family's farm. Spinning slowly in my downward trajectory, I saw my father from above, patiently waiting for me, arms outstretched with hands held high to catch me. The air whipped my clothes back behind me as I hurtled downward. Wasn't I going too fast, falling without aid from the edges of space? How could he possibly slow my momentum, catch me before I plunged devastatingly like some fiery meteor into the ground?

But he did. With a slight impact, I was caught and safe in his arms, some extra momentum diverted into a swinging motion, once more spinning me in circles until I laughed. Slowly, he came to a stop and set me on the ground, my head a mess and dizzy, my legs wobbly. He smiled down at me, tousled my hair and said, "Only you can go so high, Ambra Dawn. You were meant for more than just this place."

His words were so lovingly spoken, and yet in my heart they echoed ominously. And, as if in answer to my deep fears, his face clouded, and he focused behind me, rising from a partial stoop and gazing across toward our house. My eyes followed him upward, and then my entire body turned to track his gaze.

Standing outside the back door that exited from our kitchen was my mother, her long red hair caught like a sideways waterfall in the breeze. Yet she stood still. *So terribly still.* Her face was frozen in stone: anxiety, fear etched in every line. One arm was raised at ninety degrees to her body, pointing like an arrow in front of the house. She remained pointing, unmoving, like some directional sign indicating the path we must follow.

My awareness sped toward her, stopping in front of her face, then turning and following her arm from the bright light of the day outside and into the dim blackness of the kitchen, through the inside of our house, and then out again from the front door.

Three black cars with tinted windows were parked in front of the house. Out of these cars stepped a troop of tall men in suits and dark sunglasses, several of them very broad and muscular, with earpieces and wires dangling from them. I found myself no longer in a small child's body but now inhabiting that of a preteen of eleven years. They brushed me aside and herded my parents into the house. I followed behind them, feeling ignored and unwanted. A terrible sense of foreboding hung over me, and the darkness of the men's suits seemed deeper than that of the space I had gazed into only moments before.

Short, and yet long separations of time. The way of dreams. For me, the way of life.

They sat around the kitchen table, the smaller men talking to my parents, the larger ones posted like soldiers around the house and out by their cars. My mother was getting very anxious. She spoke with a shrill note in her voice. The small room was so still and quiet after the wind and openness outside.

"I don't understand. We don't know who you are. We can't just turn her over to you without more information, whatever you say."

"Mrs. Dawn," said the smallest man, with a raspy voice that made my skin crawl, "we are a special governmental division, and we have developed unique technologies for the military. One of these is a special type of laser. Army doctors have shown that it can be used to kill cancer cells. We can promise you a full cure, without major side effects. No one else can. But this is top-secret technology. We cannot share this with you or anyone else – not even your doctors. Therefore, her treatment must remain secret."

He took off his dark glasses and stared at my mom, but I was sitting behind him and couldn't see his face. "A doctor in the Omaha unit is a friend of mine. He was direct with me – she won't live past next year with current treatments. We are your only hope."

I saw my mother tear up and my father's jaw become set. "Now you look here. You've got no cause to be speaking like that and upsetting my wife. This is all irregular. Government or not, it ain't my way to trust shadows. If what you're saying is true, we'll work with you. But I've got to know more."

"But Frank, you *heard* him," my mom began.

"Never you mind what he said. I don't like this talk. We ain't shopping for some used car right now."

Just then, I dropped the wooden toy I was holding in my hands. It was a small hand-carved globe, with all the continents embossed on the surface. I can see it now hitting the wooden floor with a thud and rolling out of the kitchen to the living room. My heart constricted. *The Earth! I did not want to lose it!* The man in the dark suit with his back to me turned around, and then I screamed.

I couldn't help it. I was only eleven, and it was too much for me. That demon face – I had seen it before. In another dream. Dreams within dreams. His face was part of a foggy future vision, one I had forgotten and that rushed back through me like nails in my veins. Flashes of future memories whipped through my mind of pain, and fear, and loneliness, and horror – all connected to this face grinning back at me like some fiend from hell.

I ran. I jumped from my seat and ran like I've never run in my life. Behind me I half-heard the shouts of my parents calling my name and the harsh barks of this man to his soldiers. "Get her!" Then the horrible screams of my parents behind. But I could not stop running. That terrible sense in a dream of a monster approaching from behind grew within me, and I could feel its breath and fangs approaching, gaining ground, nearing to grapple at my back and legs.

I ran so hard I thought my chest would explode. Across the manicured green of our backyard, into the high fields of corn that spread out like a sea on all sides, grown thick now near harvest season. The stalks slapped me in the face, on my arms, across my chest as I ran, my breath like deep wheezings from some dying thing. Where was I going? I didn't know. *Away. I had to get away.* "On the other side of the cornfields," something screamed in my mind. There was safety, if I could just get through the fields, to the road, I would find a car, someone to take me to get help and protect me from the monsters following behind. I was close. My panting was like a windstorm in my mind. *So close.*

And then a sharp pain, a bright light like a flash in my eyes, and I was on my back, a dark figure towering over me. Warm liquid trickled down from my nose, and I felt too weak to move.

A second figure stood over me, blocking out the light of the day. In the shadow of his body, I saw that demon face again, smiling, laughing as he stared down at me.

"We've been looking for you for a long time, little girl. Don't think you can escape. Don't *ever* think you can escape from us. We have plans for you."

I couldn't respond: fear, pain, and nausea swept over me, and the world above me shrank to a small point as darkness filled in the sides. In a moment, all was black, and the sky was gone.

The same dream. Experienced countless nights. Memories of the past recreated. But this time it did not end with the darkness.

In that absolute black, I heard voices. *Your* voices. Millions of them, rising like an ocean of sound, a chorus calling to me across the ever-changing fabric of Time. And in that half-asleep state, moments before waking, when inspiration meets the practicality of day, I *knew.*

The answer was clear before my mind.

Chapter 2

$$\forall x(F(x) \leftrightarrow x = n)$$

In the world's audience hall, the simple blade of grass sits on the same carpet with the sunbeams, and the stars of midnight.

Rabindranath Tagore

N othing is ever as it seems or is as it might be.

Stay with me for a while, hear my story, and then you'll understand. Understand just how different everything around you is from how you now believe it to be and maybe come to terms with just how important you are to what might someday come to be.

On the cover of this book you're reading is an author's name. He believes this story is full of his ideas, born from his own mind. It's not. *I* am writing it *through* him. In his reality, it's all part of a clever plot he's stitched together, even down to this very sentence that says he *isn't* writing it. Instead, it is the effort of my mind reaching out, back through what you call Time, and inspiring his mind, shaping his thoughts, convincing him of this reality.

Sounds crazy? It is. I know it is. And *I'm* the one doing it. But you should look down, grab the buckle and fasten your seat belt, because it's just going to get worse.

I don't enjoy doing this, playing puppet master with this citizen of your time. But our need is hopelessly desperate. More than you can imagine has been lost. And we are left with nothing but ashes in the cold of space.

I've done worse. This is dangerous, both for his mind and my own. Already, I have failed many times to send my message, and my efforts wrecked the receiving minds, driving them to madness. At other times, what has come out of the author has been a story so distorted, so warped by his own imaginings, that the message is lost, and can't achieve its purpose. Your libraries hold some of these disasters. I can only hope that this, my last effort, will not fail.

There is so much to explain, so much that you need to understand before you can accept the message, and take the step we so desperately need you to take. So many things— strange things, horrible things. Things that can't possibly be true, but are.

You will also need to understand something about Time. This may be the greatest stumbling block. Alone, it's like a monolithic stone, an arrow marching forward like some godlike unstoppable force, rolling through history. What has happened is frozen in the Past, untouchable and unchangeable, and what will happen, the Future, is determined by the Now. But the Universe laughs at such simplistic ideas.

The first thing you need to let go of is the idea that Time *is* alone. *Space* and time go together, and feed off one another, in grand loops and dances that change both. I know this, because this dance plays before my mind's eye like a rainbow in the mist.

Because of this, you must let go of the idea of the Past as set and the Future as something that does not exist. *Space-time* is an ever-existing clay trapped inside the great bubble we call the Cosmos. Like clay, it can be shaped, changing past, present, and future. Always with rules. But not yet with rules any creature has come to fully understand.

Sadly, these are only abstractions, colorless phrases that teach little and distort much of the living experience. I hope that you will understand more as you hear the story.

But it is only because of these truths that I can even reach you now, and only because of them that I need to. You see, as much as the future can reach back into the past, the *past* can reach *forward* into the future. And in our time of need, we need you of our recent past. You have a part to play in righting a terrible wrong, saving billions of lives, and reversing the horrific fate that has descended upon humanity. Somehow in these pages I must convince you of this. May I be forgiven if I can't.

My parents called me Ambra Dawn, and I am a Reader. But this is *our* story.

Chapter 3

$$S = \int \frac{\dot{x}^2}{2} dt$$

Wisdom leads us back to childhood.

Blaise Pascal

I was born in the yellow-green cornfields of Nebraska.

My father was an independent farmer, one of the last not bought up by the great agribusiness corporations of the twenty-first century. When I knew him, he was a tall and lanky man in his mid-forties of Scottish heritage, his fair skin always reddened and hardly tanned in the long summer seasons. He had crisp blue eyes and large hands that could tear open an ear of corn in a single fluid motion. When I was a small child, before I was taken from my parents, he would hold me in those huge hands like a small ear of corn, often tossing me high into the air as in my dream and laughing until a thousand lines creased his face.

He had a real gift for predicting the weather. Not trained in any meteorological sciences, he was a more accurate forecaster than the US Weather Service, which saved more than one harvest. It was one sign of the terrible genetics that would combine to produce me.

My mother was from a Celtic background too—an Irishwoman new to the United States. She *found* my father more than she met him, with a sense of destiny that she helped make come true. She looked like a stereotype out of a book of fables—a classic lady of the Green Isle, pale and redheaded, fiery in spirit and with her tongue. The recessive genes just keep adding up.

Even more than my father, she *forecast*, but she forecast broadly into many areas of life. Maybe four hundred years ago they would have burned her at the stake for witchcraft, but my mother was a devout Catholic and used no spells or prayers to divine the future. Such things just came to her. As I would learn painfully, they came not from the supernatural but from the all too natural, buried deep within her brain, in a soft spot of unusual tissue and blood vessels that any neurosurgeon, had he taken a look, would have dismissed as a small cyst – an unnatural growth of little significance.

Two years after they were married, I was born.

I got my mother's red hair and green eyes. Both parents' skin seemed to combine in me to the palest white possible outside of albinism. The real kicker, though, was a combination of genes that led to a tumor in my brain in the same place that my mother's small psychic cyst lay. We'll get back to that soon, because without that tumor, none of what I am going to tell you would have happened.

In the beginning, I was just a normal farm girl. Well, maybe *normal* isn't the right word. I was *definitely* a farm girl, though. By the time I could walk, I was playing with the animals, rolling in hay, and happier out in the air with the earth under my feet than anywhere else. How cruel is the irony when I think back on what has happened to me. What I would give now to see the sky again, to feel the earth underneath, or to run through my hands the fresh soil after it was plowed. To even know it was still there, that it existed *somewhere*— that would be enough, more than I would ask for after this terrible journey.

But normal, no, I guess I can't say I was ever really normal. Normal means seeing things and reacting to things like most people. Looking like most people. Being treated like most people. One after the other, I lost all these things.

First to go was seeing things like most people. Even early on, I think my mother knew something was different about me. When I got old enough to notice such things, it seemed that she was always looking at me like someone would an artifact from another world. She loved me, but she sensed there was something *other* about me that even a mother's love couldn't get beyond. Maybe it was her own sixth sense. But somehow, she *knew*.

In a way, that was good, because I never had to worry about surprising her or letting her down. I don't think my dad ever really knew, not even when they came to "cure" me. Which was good in its way, since his love never had to get through any walls and always reached me.

But the first time I realized I was a freak was when my dog died.

When I was eight years old, I was already experiencing many wild and strange dreams. After I described a few to friends and my parents, I learned by their reactions that some of my dreams disturbed them and were best left inside my own head. Crucified unicorns, roaches crawling out of my eyes, light beams causing holes to sprout and blood to pour from my arms—that kind of thing. But I had learned by then the difference between reality and dream. Or so I thought.

One night I dreamed that our sheepdog Matt died. Matt had been with us from a few years before I was born. In the dream, he was running around in a thunderstorm, barking like he does at the deep subsonic roll that drives some dogs crazy, and in a flash of lightning, he seized up, just fell over, dead. In the dream, I could see inside him, saw the clot in his heart, watched the life like some light dim in his mind. I woke up shaking and afraid, but I didn't tell anyone. Another dream to keep to myself. One I could slowly forget.

Three weeks later, a storm front rolled in from the west. When relatives would visit from other parts of the country, my dad would always talk about the weather and make his flat joke (as my mom called it): "Well, it's really flat out here this time of year." Nebraska is *really* flat, and you can see the storms coming for hours in the daylight, an express train made out of dark, gray mountains pushing like a tidal wave across the plains. I started shaking again, not because I am afraid of storms, but because I was afraid of *this* storm. Because I had seen it before.

Then the sun darkened, and the rain poured down on us like syrup, and I watched like I might a horror film on TV the replay of my dog barking and running and falling over dead in the grass. This time I couldn't see through him. But I knew. I knew what was inside.

And I knew I was a freak.

It's hard to be normal when you don't see things like other people. In my case, I saw things that no one else could see. Visions in Time. Not intuitions, not a vague sense of doom or excitement – *visions*. They began in dreams but soon came even in the waking day. Not only visions of the future – for a Reader, it's actually a lot easier to see into the past. Visions of what was and sometimes, what was to be, came more and more frequently, disturbing my days and my nights, pushing me further and further from people, walling me off from the normal world. Believe me, when you have seen your own birth, watched your mother scream in agony as she pushed you into the world like some deformed lump of lasagna, it changes you. When you can't tell anyone around you these things, not even your parents, you are trapped in a prison where you slowly form your own thoughts. *Different* thoughts. Thoughts that shape you inside and out.

And that is when you lose the ability to think like normal people.

By the time I was ten, I was one odd little girl. I couldn't really relate to the kids at school or to any adults. All I had were my own thoughts and, of course, the visions. Like some ghostly companion, they were always with me, playing reels behind my eyes, movies only I could watch. Some boring. Some interesting. Some horrible. Things I knew were somehow real or that I feared would be real someday.

I became ostracized by my peers. My teachers couldn't reach me. My parents became very concerned. Finally, they took me in for evaluation. A few examinations by psychologists, then doctors, and, at last, the neurologists. Brain scans. *Finally,* there was something concrete they could hold onto, something clearly wrong with me, something to explain all the weirdness and problems.

And something that brought me to the attention of those dark forces that really control the fate of our world.

Chapter 4

$$e^{i\pi} = -1$$

Behind the ostensible government sits enthroned an invisible government owing no allegiance and acknowledging no responsibility to the people.

Theodore Roosevelt

I f I could give you any one piece of advice that I think would help you in your time, I would say turn off your TV.

Unplug it, place it on a cart, and roll it into the river. *Never* watch it again. Take your video game console and controllers – build a bonfire. Don't *ever* go online again. I'm completely serious. What I know and what you don't, is that all our digital technology was not the product of our tremendous cleverness like everyone believes. No, it was a gift, *from above*. Or rather, a poison, a drug—electromagnetic narcotics for controlling their human herds. Call them high-tech cattle prods, if you want. To *Them*, you're all just a gene pool with potential, kept docile and reproducing ignorantly while the greatest show on Earth called *human culture* plays out. One giant sham.

Some of you know it. Some of you with half-awake Reader potential. Some of you feel it. Some of you outcasts, those who never fit in and end up on the streets or in the mountains or in institutions—you knew all along much more of the truth than our comfortable and successful herds. You suffered that deep discomfort, afflicting all your thoughts and actions, that sharp sense that something is wrong, deeply wrong with the world and how it is being presented to you. The sense in the back of your mind that things *don't fit*.

Well, they don't. I'll explain more as we go on. Meanwhile, pick up a book, go stare at the stars. *Think.* You're a junkie, strapped into a pleasure tube – a pig ready for the slaughter, or worse. Don't let them control your mind anymore. Advice from a former slave. Take it or leave it.

My journey of bondage was about to begin. The brain scans were very clear. Even at eleven years old I could understand. Also, there were vague visions, like half-glimpsed dreams. In the beginning, Reading the future is like that, more like *remembering the future* than seeing it. The past too is like a memory, slightly out of focus, sometimes wrong, but mostly right. The future, well, that's like a wild dream. Ever woken up from a dream, the details like colors bleeding out from your mind, until several hours later, you can only hold onto the most basic and faded outlines? That's a vision of the future. Most of them, anyway. Sometimes, like a horrid nightmare, the vision will be so strong you remember almost everything. Like a nightmare, these visions, *prophecies* if you want, will shake you out of your normal state of consciousness. It's a psychic slap in the brain. But those are very rare. Mostly, it's half-remembered somethings you can never quite place.

Those were my visions of my own future, of my illness, of the soon-to-be nurtured tumor in the middle of my head. The doctors were amazed I could still see. The mass was the size of a golf ball then – quaint to me now, really. Near the back of my brain, it was lodged, growing, between what neurologists call the occipital and parietal lobes. These are basically big slabs of your brain that do different things. The occipital lobe, at the very *back* of your head, processes visual information from your eyes (which are at the front of your head – God works in mysterious ways, believe me). The parietal lobe does a lot of things, like sensing where you are, navigating, working with numbers, moving objects. No, I'm not a doctor. What I am is a freak with a freaking tumor growing in the middle of all this stuff, so, well, it *matters* to me.

The tumor was mostly growing out towards the occipital lobe like some elliptical golf ball, crashing into all those cells that process information from my eyes. The doctors were amazed I wasn't blind yet. My parents looked sick listening to all of this. I was half-scared, half-remembering some blurry future where all this stuff wasn't nearly the worst that was going to happen to me.

"It appears to be a fast-growing tumor," one of the doctors said. "Many children's tumors are, growing quickly, the cells dividing quickly like the rest of the growing body, but even worse. This is very serious, and very difficult to treat. We recommend you send her to specialists. We can't treat her here."

So began the long search for doctors across the country. Nebraska has some good medical facilities in Omaha, but they still referred me to New York, to Sloan-Kettering Cancer Center. My parents were on the phone for hours and hours to doctors and relatives in the area. By then we'd all seen enough doctors' offices to last a lifetime. And all the time, the brain scans showed the thing inside my head kept getting bigger. We prepared for a long trip to the East Coast.

Then one day, just like in the dream, without a phone call or any kind of warning, three black cars with tinted windows pulled up to our farm. Out of these cars stepped the men of that nightmare that I relive over and over again. They came, they tried to convince my parents to release me into their "care," and when my parents would not, they took me by force.

When I awoke from the blackness, I was being roughly unloaded from the car by one of the burly men in a suit, maybe the very one who knocked me unconscious. He threw me over his shoulder, grunting as he carted me towards a bland building covered in metallic gray like some enormous warehouse. In my foggy vision it seemed so unimportant, so featureless and unreal, yet it would be my home for many years to come. My prison. A place from which, as the man had promised, I would not escape.

Chapter 5

$$\nabla \cdot \mathbf{E} = \frac{\rho}{\varepsilon_0}$$

Madam, I have come from a country where people are hanged if they talk.

Leonhard Euler

While I lived as their prisoner, before I was sold into slavery, I knew in my heart that I had no hope of escaping. I had no hope of living very long. The things they did to me, the conditions of my life convinced me that I had gone to hell, or hell on Earth, and that my time here would be the final years of torture before my death. Because I did not understand anything, had none of the knowledge that I would later slowly piece together, their purposes seemed meaningless, random and obscene – torment without any goal except to drive me mad, to tear all hope from the soul of a young child.

When I lay unconscious on the ground in the cornfields my dad had planted himself – that was my last day in Nebraska. I never returned. Now, returning is impossible. That day was the last time I would ever see my parents. At the time, I didn't know what had happened to them. You might think that ignorance of their fate would have been a curse. I'm sure it would have. But it is also a curse to know exactly the fate of those you love, when that fate is evil. The past is not hidden from me, especially when it concerns me closely. It wasn't a year before I had experienced a vision showing me their murder, the cruelty of the men who visited my house, how they disposed of their bodies without respect, dignity, or care.

I'll spare you details. But I wasn't spared. And even if I suspected, the visions mercilessly gave me no chance to hope or doubt. By the time I was twelve, I knew I was completely alone and in the hands of monsters.

By then my eyesight had started to go, but I was way beyond expecting my captors to care about that. As you'll see, it was just the opposite; they wanted me blind. And they always got what they wanted. During my first year, as my vision started to fade, I was introduced to my new "home" and my new way of life. I learned for the first time how to live in constant fear. When I displeased them, they beat me or starved me for days. For the first few months, for even the slightest infraction of their strange rules, I was beaten. Again and again, until I became what they wanted – so afraid of pain, so living in fear of their cruel police sticks and electric wires that I became like some caged animal, totally responsive to their commands. A well-trained monkey.

Their rules were both simple and strange to me, at least at first. There were the understandable, if awfully harsh, rules about living – where to stand and sleep and eat, how to behave, how to answer questions and commands. Speak out of turn to another child – yes, there were many of us – and the stick might smash across your mouth. Out of your bed in the middle of the night? Maybe because you needed to stand, or pee, or think, or something? The cameras in the rooms would record it, and the next day you might be plugged into the wires, fire sent inside your nerves. Not enough to damage you. They didn't want to devalue their product. But it was more than enough for their purposes.

The other rules were the scariest, because none of us could understand them in the beginning. There is nothing more frightening than being asked to do something you don't understand and being punished when you fail to meet their expectations.

Many days we would be paraded out of our rooms and forced to march down long corridors that looked like hospital wings toward glass encased laboratories with rows of electronic equipment. They would hook us up to the equipment: large helmets with a hundred wires running from the top into computers. Our eyes would be masked by opaque glass in the helmets and our ears covered by headphones that blocked out all noise except the commands of the experimenters. Then they would ask us to describe what we saw, to find our way through labyrinths our eyes could not see. When we failed, they were displeased.

My heart bleeds now looking back at my twelve-year-old self, sitting utterly alone with a giant electronic helmet on my head, surrounded by people who killed my parents, who beat and tortured me, and who asked me to see the universe in a way I did not understand. I feel even worse for the less gifted children, who day after day stumbled and failed to progress, and who day after day were punished.

In this place, I was both lucky and unlucky. Lucky, because it soon became clear that I was special. Even before they realized my progress, I *did* begin to see *something* when other stimulus was removed. As that something became more clear, I was able to more and more confidently find my way through the trials they erected for me, even though I did not understand the purpose. Even if I did not understand *what* it was I was doing. As my eyesight began to fail—so that soon the dark glasses did little to take away what was almost gone—I began to develop a conscious new sense. Patterns, substance, *something* was becoming clear to me, and I gained the power to succeed. At that stage, that was all that mattered, some end to the displeasure and cruelty. I was crushed and nearly broken. It didn't matter why, as long as the pain stopped.

Soon, I became all the rage with the men and women in white coats. How they fawned over me and smiled, happy with their little animal that was performing so well. I was isolated even more from the other children. Around that time, the operations began.

It was good that I met Ricky before they started the long series of surgeries. Ricky was the only kid I knew who seemed able to smile in this sterile place of fluorescent lights and metal corridors. Silly and fat, a few years older than me, and an obsessed Red Sox fan who could name every player and team statistic since 1908, Ricky became my only friend. The others were too hurt, too traumatized and too afraid to open up to anyone, and like shocked lab rats, they huddled to themselves. Ricky braved many beatings showing some sort of life, some sort of humanity in this place. And once or twice he even made me smile. Doesn't sound like much, but in this place, a smile was a miracle.

I asked him once how he had the courage to dare the things he did. He laughed over the lunch food. "My fahther," he said, with the full-mouth "ah" of Boston, "beat me worse than this many nights, after he'd been drinking." He leaned close to me, glancing over his shoulders, and back, looking into my eyes, eyes that saw him only as a blur now. "These whitecoats, they're mean jerks and all, but they ain't nothing compared to a good drunk."

"Ricky, why are we here? What do they want from us?" It was the first time I had asked anything like that since I arrived.

He shook his head. "They won't tell, and we ain't gonna find out. What's important is not them, but *us*. What *we* want, why *we're* here. If we make it all about them, well..." he pointed around to the other kids, "we'll just end up like them. You got to find your reason, Ambra. And hold on to it. Don't let them be your reason, or take yours away."

I didn't really understand what he meant then, but his words stayed with me, circling in my mind. Months later, when things got worse for me and I nearly lost myself to despair, his words landed somewhere deep inside and planted themselves, growing slowly but steadily into a great oak tree. A tree with deep roots and colossal arms, and ten thousand leaves blowing in the wind of my soul. His words imploring me to find my reason, any reason, saved me.

It wasn't much later that they took Ricky away. He knew it was coming. "I can't make heads or tails of these tests," he told me. "I'm not what they want, Ambra. They won't be keeping me long." He sounded sad but not defeated. I always remember that tone in his voice, when you know that you can't win, that the end is there, but no matter what the powers do to you, you won't ever give in or stop being you.

I don't think I would have made it through the next two years without remembering his inspiring words to me that day. Months and years of having monsters cut on you, carve up your skull and brain, and for such a terrible purpose—I would have given up, my soul would have been broken. But even as they did these things, I found my way. I found my reason.

Deep into the past I retreated, and out of the past I slowly stumbled into my future.

Chapter 6

$$\nabla \cdot \mathbf{B} = 0$$

True knowledge comes only through suffering.

Elizabeth Barrett Browning

He was younger than the other whitecoats, with a sparse beard and longish black hair. At least that's how I remembered him from the many times he had worked with me. Now, he was a featureless blur, and I knew him by his voice.

The excitement was too much for him. He bubbled over with words that he should not have been speaking to me.

"You're special, Ambra," he said as he took the helmet off my head. "We've never seen a child like you before. You've mastered all the navigation drills, succeeding in ways we don't even understand. And the other things you are doing...what are you doing in there, Ambra?"

When they ask you a question, you have to answer.

"I don't know, Sir."

He stared at me for a long moment. "No. You probably don't." He sighed and turned away from me. "We haven't had a visit in a year. Soon they will come back, and we will lose you." He sounded genuinely distressed. Not for me, to be sure, but for losing his prize guinea pig. Then something brightened his tone.

"But next week a new phase in your training will begin. Next week is your first surgery!" he said excitedly, seeming to expect me to understand the import of the statement. My expression clearly depressed him.

"You know what the surgeries are for, don't you?"

I was still naive enough to think back to the original excuses these criminals had given my parents before they murdered them.

"No. Maybe...for my tumor?"

His voice lit up. "Yes, Ambra. Very good. For your tumor." Talking to me like I was three years old.

"They will take it out, finally? It's getting hard to see."

There was a long pause. I became very afraid. In my small hope I had spoken without being addressed first, and perhaps I had said something wrong. It had been some time since I had been beaten and a long time since they had shocked me. The thought of either made me start to sweat.

Finally, he spoke. His voice was sad. "Yes, we've noticed your visual impairment. It is not unexpected." He set the helmet down with a thud on the counter. "Come, our time is finished here. I won't see you for a few weeks, not until after your recovery. Over the next few months, we'll see how you progress."

That was the first hint of what they were planning for me, and the first sense I had that what was happening was part of something larger than me, or even this place. *Who* would come soon? What was navigation? And why was what I was experiencing and responding to in their tests so important to them?

But I had little time to learn more. The morning came, and I was whisked into a prep room, shaved bald, and had my scalp drawn on with Magic Markers. I was then wheeled into the operating room under bright lights and the gaze of several blurry figures I assumed were the surgeons. A needle was stuck into my arm, and I saw a shape that must have been a bag of some liquid feeding drops into my veins.

The room shrunk to a point. I was on the outside of the universe. Just as suddenly, it was back to full size. I heard myself say "Wow." Again it happened, and I felt farther away from the universe than ever. The third time ended in blackness, broken by a strange awakening of pain and dizziness that blinked out in a moment and a final return to consciousness lying in a bed.

I could tell that my arm still had a tube wired into it, and my head felt twice its normal size. I reached up to touch it, and it was a large swollen thing, wrapped in bandages. Sitting at my side was a blurry shape, the voice recognizable. It was my talkative scientist friend. *Dr. Talkative.*

"You're awake, Ambra. Good. That's *good*. The operation was a success. Aren't you happy?"

My throat hurt, and I could barely gargle out words. "Is the tumor gone? Why can't I see better?"

"No, Ambra. The tumor is still there. It will *always* be there, growing larger and larger. We've created space for it. We've opened space for further growth inside your brain and opened the back and top portion of your skull. It will grow outward now much faster, so much pressure and hindrance removed. You have a temporary new skull of composite material in place with a greater circumference. It will have to be replaced, of course, as the tumor grows further. And that growth will be aided by the new blood supply. The surgeons are very talented. They routed vessels from the occipital lobe over to the tumor. To better nourish it. Of course, this will accelerate the loss of vision, but that cannot be helped at this point. All that matters is the tumor. Your *gifts* come from it, Ambra. It is your space-time eye!" he chirped out, laughing. "God, you are going to be a star!"

He patted me on the arm and stood up, walking out of the room and leaving me feeling like some terribly twisted form of life.

And sure enough, a month later I was totally blind.

Chapter 7

$$ds^2 = \frac{1}{2\omega^2}\left(-\left(dt + \exp(x)dz\right)^2 + dx^2 + dy^2 + \frac{1}{2}\exp(2x)dz^2\right)$$

I myself am time inexhaustible, and I the creator whose faces are in all directions. I am death who seizes all, and the source of what is to be.

Bhagavad Gita

My dad used to say every cloud has a silver lining. So what do you get for being stricken with a giant, literally head-splitting tumor that destroys your sight and a fake skull and grafted skin to cover the extra surface area of your head that will never grow a hair that leaves you looking like the cross between a bulbous-headed alien and a middle-aged man? You could say I was given extraordinary powers and a central part to play in a power struggle between good and evil. But I never wanted any of that. At the time, I got Ricky's Red Sox hat.

I don't know how he did it. It shouldn't have been possible with all the security and paranoia of this place, but somehow, he managed to smuggle in his Red Sox hat, keep it hidden from them all that time, and then hide it my room, stuffing it inside the metal tube that served as one of the legs of my bed. I was lucky to find it, or maybe it was inevitable. My sight going quickly, I began to use my hands and feet to feel out everything around me. I had to learn to move about on my own to some degree, and I took the first "steps" toward that in my room, touching everything, feeling the walls, furniture, even the air as it changed directions and taste, telling me if a door was open, or a window, or if some machinery had been switched on. As my sight died, my other senses were growing—including my *other* sense, but I'll get to that later.

In the weeks of recovery following my surgery, after being transferred from the medical wing back to my cage, I had lots of time to do nothing. And it seemed that the cameras didn't care anymore what I did. One day, feeling around, I found the cap, stuffed in the tube, rolled up and mashed so that it would never recover its intended form again. But it was Ricky's hat, all right. I knew that from the smell and his description of the 2084 World Series Champions emblazoned in raised letters on the side, as well as the Ricky Hernandez signature scrawled inside in permanent marker that someone described to me later on. Complete with phone and address in Boston.

I think one of the first steps I took away from the pit of madness I was close to falling into, was putting that cap on, and not giving a damn what they would do to me. My head was already too big for a normal human hat, and this was just operation number one. I unsnapped the back, left it open, and it fit. Kind of. The grafted skin was tender and sore, but I wore the hat anyway, and it covered the new addition to my body, giving me an almost normal appearance again. My hair would grow in over time from the part of the scalp that still had hair, slightly above the cap, so that from a distance, if you didn't look too closely, I might just look like a normal redhead wearing a Red Sox cap.

I took to wearing it all the time. At first, the whitecoats sounded slightly disturbed by it, but then—*a miracle!* Since I was now their budding superstar, I got special privileges, and they let me wear it and stopped commenting. I guess they wanted to keep me happy, keep me performing.

The other thing that saved me was retreating into the past. Not psychologically, where I retreat into *my* past memories to hide (even if there was some hiding going on). I mean *everyone's* past, including my own. As I learned later, a Reader's power grows and matures fastest in puberty, and I was right in the middle of that, my whole body changing. It might even have been something I could have obsessed about—my changing body—if it weren't for all the other stuff that pushed it far to the side. But at the same time that I was impressing them more and more in their little examination room, other things were happening to me, things they didn't know about. One of the first I noticed was my growing power to enter the past. I still had future visions, but what obsessed me, what came out clearly, in high-resolution detail, and what I began to be able to *control*, were my visions of what *had* happened. Or, as I like to think of it now, what might *have had* happened. Like I said, past, future – both are fluid.

In the dark and pointless hours in my cell, I began to have these long and grand adventures. Journeys into events of the recent—and sometimes not so recent—past. As I learned to control my path through time, with greater skill and experience, and with greater concentration, I could direct myself back further and further. During the first few years I was able to do this, I explored things that were emotional touchstones for me. My childhood, my parents' lives, my family, important world events that touched me. It wasn't until much later that the usefulness of Reading the past to the present and future dawned on me. Embarrassing that I didn't think of it earlier, but I was only thirteen. And I was really screwed up.

This ability also allowed me to compensate for something that was depressing me—my lack of schooling. Most children would be glad to be free of school, but let me tell you, when they won't let you learn, and years go by and you realize that there is the entire world of human knowledge denied you, passing you by, you might have a different attitude. I became almost traumatized that my captors had not only made my life this hell but that they had also locked me from all the light of humanity, leaving me ignorant, in the dark, powerless. No books to read or music to listen to or art to see. No new ideas or experiences to grow with. Sometimes I felt like panicking, and I would do math problems in my head or try to remember books I had read.

And that of course is what connected things for me. I realized that in the past, I had access to everything humanity had achieved. So, I went looking for it, spending increasing amounts of time pushing myself through past visions, extending them, improving their clarity. As time went on, I actually became able to sit through visions and learn from them, like a student eaves dropping in the shadows of a lecture. Obvious places to linger were schools and libraries, but really, the entire world was open to me as I came to realize. Did I want to learn about great art? I could study at the Louvre. Learn advanced calculus? I could sit at the feet of Newton (not time well spent, let me tell you). The experiences of explorers as they sailed to the New World—I could be there with them or riding in zero-g above the Earth with astronauts. And as the blackness fell down on top of me in all other aspects of life, the visions continued to bring me sight. Through them, I could still see, see as vividly at times as I ever had with my eyes. I was blind, but in a strange way, I was not.

It wasn't always *easy* to find these visions of the past. When the visions first came, I did not control when or what, even if they tended to involve things close to me. As my skills grew over the years, and as I consciously honed them, I could dance through libraries of visions, flipping through them like pages in some ethereal book, finding those of more interest, and expanding those pages of the past into a landscape. I said I was unlucky and lucky. In this way, I was lucky – I achieved an education no human being had ever experienced. But I would have traded it all in a second to be back on my farm with my parents again.

I became so obsessed with the past that I ended up blocking out nearly all possible future visions. Amazingly stupid, I know, considering how useful future visions might have been. Even worse, I never sought out the history of this place, these people, what and who they were, why they were acting as they did. How much I could have learned, perhaps to help me cope, even escape this terrible place. I don't know how to explain my inability to realize these things except to say that I had nearly fallen into a black hole of hopelessness, and through the exploration of the past I had found beauty, hope, and light. It saved me, carried me through the experiments, the surgeries, the inhumanity of the place. I needed this different world too much. I guess that maybe part of me purposefully ignored things closer at hand, however *useful* they might have been. The other things were more useful. They kept me sane in an insane life.

Chapter 8

$$v = \sqrt{\frac{GM}{r}}$$

I took it up, and held it in my hand. I was a trembling, because I'd got to decide, forever, betwixt two things, and I knowed it. I studied a minute, sort of holding my breath, and then says to myself: "All right, then, I'll go to hell" and tore it up.

Mark Twain

They were all happy, happy voices in the glass room.

The giant helmet came off, and the sounds of the place washed over me once more—the faster flits of motion of the team working with me, their excitement in their motions, breaths, and vocal tones. It was strange – as time went on, as I became better and better at their silly games. It became easier and easier for me, and boredom set in, even as their excitement grew. At first it was such relief to know I was pleasing them so much, and I looked forward to each new session. How quickly it all changed when I think back on it.

It became clear that this device they placed on my head had something to do with stimulating the world of my visions. Strap me in, turn it on, and I could "see" things created in front of me, like some magic laser-disco ball in front of a sighted person. A small child is in awe of the disco ball. In a few years it might seem interesting for a few minutes. If you saw it several times a week as a young teen, well, its secrets were all gone.

Their secrets faded fast. As I approached my fifteenth birthday, it had been almost two years and six surgeries —a surgery almost every four months—and a lot of time growing into my new abilities. By now the tumor was as big as a squashed softball, and my head had expanded at the back and top so that even the Red Sox hat barely fit with the strap totally open, even though I had torn the stitching to make more room. At least my hair could finally grow back in all the way. I vowed to myself never to cut it again—in the dream place where I had such control over my life.

My whitecoat entourage had grown to a team of at least ten, headed by Dr. Talkative. He loved to tell me how big the tumor was, updating me on its slowing growth, its stabilization within my brain. He was bragging, boasting of his pet project that he had guided, boasting of my achievements with their stupid, limited little manipulations as if *he* had achieved them.

I had learned over time that, whatever it was that they were doing, they didn't understand much about it. They could set it up, read the output, and know if I was succeeding or not. But they understood nothing beyond that, like people who use a microwave and have no idea what it's all about inside. They didn't know what I was seeing, how simple it was all becoming, and how I was realizing that there was a much, much greater world to be perceived by this dramatic new sense I was developing. They made me into this freak, but they didn't know what they had made.

As I outgrew their disco ball, I was better able to ace those little tests with it. Soon, it became something I could do in the background, while I thought about other things or even explored the past as had become my obsession. That was the case on the day the bad news came.

Just as the team was bubbling over with joy from my latest *bored out of my mind* performance, Dr. Talkative came into the room like a dark cloud. I could sense it in his voice and movements; I could nearly smell the anxiety in his sweat. Everyone else in the room likely figured it out by seeing his face. I bet it looked bad.

"I have some bad news," he overstated the obvious. He walked over to the computer station and paused a minute. "Fantastic performance today, Ambra." He sighed. "I think you've outgrown us."

He placed his clipboard down with a clack and stepped back into the middle of the room to address his staff. "And like all children when they grow up, you must move on."

I heard several audible groans and the shifting sounds of uncomfortable people. One woman spoke up somewhat shrilly. "They can't come now! She's just showing us her potential! They won't care about what she can do, what she could become. They'll strap her into a navslav ship and she'll waste away her life like the rest of them!"

While it wasn't exactly comforting to hear that I was headed for a lifetime of servitude, her outburst opened my eyes, so to speak. Truly startled me for the first time since I had come to this place. To hear them fall from the top of the food chain – it was priceless! *The fear in their voices.* Who were these mysterious *They* that were coming and over which they had no power? After coming to view the whitecoats as my local non-benevolent deities, it was discombobulating, and liberating, to see them shake.

"That's enough, Katie. It doesn't matter what we think or want." He paused a minute and spoke mordantly. "As you know, we have in our enthusiasm...*tampered* with their property. I believe it was a step in the right direction for science, for the potential that lies within the human race. But *They* may be displeased. I don't have to remind you how serious the punishment can be for infractions." There was complete silence. I could hear my own heart beat.

"Nevertheless, as your group leader, I will take full responsibility for these actions. I pray you will maintain your appropriate demeanor when our visitors arrive tomorrow."

"Tomorrow?" someone called out in disbelief.

"Yes. For some reason, we did not receive their long-range communication. They are entering orbit as we speak. Representatives will arrive in the morning."

Chapter 9

$$2^N > N$$

Once upon a time, Zhuangzi was dreaming that he was a butterfly dancing and flying about, joyous and free. He had forgotten that he was Zhuangzi. Then he awoke and felt himself solid and sure. But he didn't know anymore if he was Zhuangzi who had dreamed he was a butterfly, or, a butterfly dreaming that he was Zhuangzi.

Zhuang Zhou

I*n orbit?*
What in the world did this mean? Frankly, in my readings and self-education through the accepted annals of human knowledge, the idea of visitors from outer space was an extremely unlikely and fanciful scenario. Like believing in ghosts. Or little blue elves. Sociology argued that human claims of visitation were the modern extensions of being visited by demons or angels, a "projection of our well-documented, overly active imagination contextualized to the modern mythology," as one lecturer put it. Harvard professor, I think. And science texts, and respected astronomers and astrobiologists had pointed out many clear problems with extraterrestrial visitation. One of the most basic was the fact that the distances between even the closest stars would require centuries of travel. Hyperspace and warp-speed were inventions of science-fiction authors to make their stories possible. How ironic that my future would be intimately tied to hyperspace travel of a very real sort, helping to guide aliens that couldn't possibly be visiting us. It was a sad case of solid thinking being wrong, even if more admirable, and loony thinking being right. Well, I can tell you—life isn't fair.

It took me a while to fall asleep that night. In the early hours of the morning, I awoke and was washed over deeply with a powerful vision. In the vision, I stood in an enormous chamber carved out of some strange and unearthly material, like some cross between marble and the sand of an anthill. Odd patterns in unusual color mixtures decorated the walls and floors. Huge moss-green pillars that seemed to grow like trees with numerous branches erupted from the ground and climbed toward the dome-like ceiling, supporting it in a hundred places. Rows of these led forward to a throne of some kind, on which sat a monstrous form, humanoid yet not human. I watched a young man led forward, obviously in pain, by similar humanoid creatures, their insect-like forms towering over him. As he was dragged to the throne, which sat raised above the rest of the floor by a set of many steps, I realized in horror that there were human shapes chained to the walls on either side of the throne.

I won't describe to you what had happened to them. You might could imagine terrible things, but this would be worse. The creature on the throne turned a set of three eyestalks on what might have been a head toward the man. An artificial sound filled the room as it spoke in a hideous tone. The language was English, if awkward, and clearly translated by some kind of machine, produced in a *basso profundo* with extensive lower frequencies that made the bone and artificial material in my skull vibrate.

"Human Reader—you have lost the time. If you and we cooperate, you to be able to rescue your people. If you do not, these deaths here only a mild beginning will seem."

The young man was exhausted, yet a fire burned deep in his eyes. I watched him clench his jaw. I knew what he would say; I could not believe it. I wanted to grab him and beg him to stop the pain I saw around that throne and that I felt in those metallic, insectoidal words.

"No!" he cried out. "You can do with me as you wish, but the Other will find her way. She will bring an end to you. You cannot hide—she watches even now!"

The words shook me, and I lost the threads of the vision. The room came into focus. I sat on my bed, cradling my knees. Tears came pouring down my face, and I fell asleep crying like a little child.

I awoke to the sound of my door being opened, and heard the rapid footsteps of someone entering the room.

"Ambra, you must dress now. You must come with me *immediately*."

It was one of the women, an aide on the experimental team. Her voice dripped with fear.

Chapter 10

$$G_{\mu\nu} = 8\pi G(T_{\mu\nu} + \rho_\Lambda g_{\mu\nu})$$

In the ordinary theory of relativity, every line that can describe the motion of a material point, i.e., every line consisting only of time-like elements, is necessarily non-closed. An analogous statement cannot be claimed for the theory developed here. Therefore a priori a point motion is conceivable, for which the four-dimensional path of the point would be an almost closed one. In this case one and the same material point could be present in an arbitrarily small space-time region in several seemingly mutually independent exemplars. This runs counter to my physical imagination most vividly.

Albert Einstein

The room was dank and yellow. Dank because they had raised the humidity to some absurd level so that moisture dripped from anything it could condense on—glass from the windows, metal on the walls, and the dark-green material like none I'd ever seen that made up the bulk of the funky alien spacesuit in front of me. Yellow because the lights in the room were only yellow, emitting few other wavelengths, which I assume was another effort to comfort Squidy as he (she? it??) swam in the sea of whatever liquid was inside the suit—likely water, or why the humidity?

Squidy was definitely an alien, or else some mutant octopus that had grown intelligent and been provided with an earthsuit by the U.S. government. There was something like a head, which was a dark brownish-green, oblong and squishy like an octopus's head, but at the same time very different. One difference was the random-seeming patchwork of what I had to conclude were eyes of some sort. The long whiskers extending from many parts of the head gave Squidy the look of a cactus that had forgotten to shave for a few days. The arms were also very octopusesque, with no suckers but tens of very thin tendrils at the end, all of which were dexterous. These "fingers" could manipulate objects that floated inside the suit as well, positioned by some unknown mechanism, composed of materials completely, well, alien.

You are likely asking yourself, "*How does she know all this? She's blind.*" Amazingly, as I saw these things, it did not surprise me at the time. Something about the stress of the situation shoved my brain into survival mode, and in this mode it learned to integrate my powerful new sense into its general scheme of decoding reality. Only later—much later—when I had time aboard the navships to contemplate, did I piece together what had happened in that session and learn to apply it from that point on, to my great empowerment. It was then that I realized that my highly developed abilities to see into the past had a very practical application to the life of the blind.

So bear with me for now and trust me when I tell you, my descriptions of the event are accurate.

Dr. Talkative was there, too. He looked like he had *Salmonella* poisoning. The female aide walked me in and led me to a chair in the middle of the room. This was the scene out of a nightmare or horror movie: a dentist chair that was made out of metal with no cushions or anything to make it comfortable and was, in this case, also dripping wet from all the humidity. It was designed with many restraints for arms, legs, and head. I felt myself sweating in the dampness as she sat me in the chair and clamped the metal restraints over my wrists. My breathing became labored when my ankles were locked in, and I think I actually began to shake when they placed the metal band around my head. As she snapped it in, my neck was jerked backward so that it was like someone was pulling my head back by the hair. But I couldn't move my head. I couldn't move anything. They could do anything to me, and I could not even try to stop them.

"I'm sorry, Ambra," she whispered, her voice shaking with the tones of pity and fear, and I heard her scamper out of the room. The door to the chamber closed with a loud metallic clank.

"Try to relax, Ambra," began Dr. Talkative. "You are property of the Navigation Conglomerate, and a representative of the Sortax is here to examine you. You will speak when spoken to and obey all his requests. Your life and your future depend on his assessment of you today."

Then Squidy took over. There wasn't any doubt that it had been in charge the entire time, of course. The sound that came from it shook me even further, as the artificial voice of a translator, while less heavy in lower frequencies, carried a tone and quality I had heard only hours earlier in my dream. It was the same voice of the insect creatures that had tortured and killed the human beings in their throne room.

"They are that, which they changed?" it croaked and rang out.

I didn't know how to respond.

"He is asking if you are the one that we have worked on. He means our operations with your tumor, Ambra."

"Yes, I guess, I am."

"They are that, which were not authorized." I didn't respond, assuming it was a statement and not a question. Dr. Talkative squirmed in his seat. Squidy only floated about, making little jerky movements every few seconds.

"They will serve in navslav the ships and supervised. They with value, exchanged for with the Dram." A small glowing objected floated into the path of several tendrils inside the suit, and the tentacle holding the device reached out toward me.

My mind exploded.

I screamed in agony. Truly, I had never known pain before. Not the surgeries, not the beatings or electric shocks, nothing prepared me for the fire that was poured inside me. I don't know how to explain to you. You don't have my tumor, my sixth sense. Even with my other senses, I had never known such pain. As a light thousands of times too strong for your eyes flooding all your experience, tied to two red-hot iron knives then driven into your sockets at the same time, my new sense that I had grown into, come to explore and know and integrate into my consciousness became the raw skin over which a new and terrible acid was poured. Every muscle in my body convulsed, and I projectile vomited across the room, coating my visitor and Dr. Talkative in the process.

I could not, of course, process this at the time, but the pain ceased, the world dissolved, and the next thing I knew the sad woman was bent over me calling my name, wiping my face clean, and removing a needle from my arm. She was nearly as pale as me, and sweat beaded on her forehead.

"Ambra, please, talk to me. Are you okay?"

"Mom…I want my mom…" I'm embarrassed now at how weak I became.

The woman had tears in her eyes. "I'm sorry, Ambra. She's not here. Please, you need to wake up, *now*. *They* need to question you further. *They* can't wait for you to get any better," she said, a suppressed anger in her tone.

She wiped a cold, damp cloth over my face. I tried to focus, to bring my concentration back from the pit of hell that still burned around the edge of my consciousness. Slowly, roughly, it came. The dank room, the two forms in front of me, one horrible, from a nightmare, the other the man who had engineered a series of surgeries on my brain that had left me deformed, different, and, I now knew, terribly vulnerable.

"Ambra," started Dr. Talkative as the woman once again walked out of the room. "We are sorry for that…disruption. You were being scanned with a device that is designed to probe your powers of perception. Only it is calibrated for a normal Reader. You are not normal. The signal was too strong," he said, a tone of shock and pity in his voice. Later, when examined by the doctors of the Resistance, I would learn that I had almost died that day.

"Enough," clanged out the voice translator. "We must again scan."

"No…please…" I begged them. I would have done anything at that moment to prevent them from scanning me again. Given them anything. Promised anything, said anything. It would not have mattered what—jump off a cliff to my death? Sure. A thousand times easier than being scanned.

"Ambra, it's ok. We've lowered the signal strength considerably. It will be safe now. You must be conscious for the examination. Please let us know if you are in pain."

"The pain do not constitute," it injected.

"She may be valuable to the Dram," Dr. Talkative noted.

"They may be," it concluded.

It raised the device toward me again. Instinctively I tensed, and while the experience was painful, it was tolerable. If it had not been for the first injury, this scan may have been only uncomfortable, and not painful. Sunlight on a burn hurts, *it burns*, though it does not burn healthy skin. But even as it hurt, it was interesting to some abstract part of my mind. This was the advanced version of the disco ball. Disco-ball 2.0. *The patterns!* The structure and substructure—it was like nothing I had experienced from these artificial devices. When it ended, after images of dancing shapes in multiple dimensions filled my mind, and stayed with me for days.

"Not authorized. They are for the navships," it sounded out as the visions faded.

"No! She is more than that! You can't fry her mind like that and then expect to get a meaningful scan!"

The creature turned its earthsuit-encased form toward Dr. Talkative, who shrank like a shadow when the sun rises. "Not authorized," it spit out as it turned around and lumbered awkwardly toward a door at the other end of the room.

As it left me and the doctor alone, I felt a kind of relief. A relief even in the presence of a man who had made me into the freak I was. Relief because, however traumatized we both were, whatever he had done to me and whatever had been done to him over the years, we were both human. Until you are in the presence of the alien, the truly alien and not simply strange, you can never know the deep meaning of the presence of another human being. Even your tormenter.

I sat there, wet and stinking in my stained clothes, still strapped into the metal chair and unable to move. My entire body hurt.

He looked at me and closed his eyes. His hand reached out and pressed a button on a controller hanging from a string around his neck. Several seconds passed, and then the door behind me opened, and I heard the sound of footsteps.

"You'll leave tonight with the other children."

Chapter 11

$$-2\exp(-x)\partial_t + z\partial_x + \left(\exp(-2x) - z^2/2\right)\partial_z$$

Time is no specific character of being. In relativity theory the temporal relation is like far and near in space. I do not believe in the objectivity of time. The concept of Now never occurs in science itself, and science is supposed to be concerned with the objective.

Kurt Gödel

I'm sure it must be frightening and exciting for kids to leave home for camp, being away from their parents who have always cared for them, living with many strangers, new rules, new dangers and opportunities. Or going off to college, really stepping out for the first time as an adult, even if you have a safety net most of the time to fall back on. *Adventure!*

To hell with adventure. I was scared. Terrified, actually. Just a few years before I had lost a beautiful life —a nice home with parents I loved and who loved and cared for me. I eavesdropped on the past and saw them murdered. I was deformed and tortured by the disciples of the organization that had destroyed my family. Now this terrible place seemed like a haven, a refuge compared to the infinite dark and alien that awaited above. Soon these creatures would take me and some untold number of kids with them like trained animals, take us away from our home planet and away from any sense of security or the familiar.

I didn't know how I would make it. In the coming year I would see many an Earth child *not* make it, grow physically or mentally sick, wasting away or exploding in madness. And the sick were removed efficiently.

For the time being, I sat in my room, wearing the long and featureless robe I had been instructed to put on, my hands in my lap, cold, curled tightly into one another. I had no belongings—no books to read (even if I could read them anymore), no music, no mementos of family, no toys, no evidence of a life of any kind. Only my Red Sox hat, perched on my big head, and I didn't know if it would survive what was coming. I looked out unseeing over my bare room as the minutes dripped slowly by, one unit of time after the other. Waiting.

The door swung open and I jumped. It was Dr. Talkative, which was unusual, as he had never visited my room. He was alone, which was also unusual, since his staff and team nearly always followed him or lurked nearby. The door closed with a click, and I heard the sound of a metal chair being dragged across the stone floor and placed in front of me. With a sigh and disturbance in the air, Dr. Talkative sat down.

"Ambra, we don't have much time. *They* will call soon for the children, and we must deliver you to the docking chamber." His clothes rustled as he shifted his weight, a short silence ensuing as I waited for him to say whatever he was there to say.

"Ambra, it is unfortunate what happened during your examination. Years of work destroyed because that clumsy Sortax representative would not listen to me. I *know* you are capable of so much more."

Tears started flowing down my cheeks. After everything, after all they had done to me, even after the sense of strength and rebellion the last few years that I had found as I mastered their system, it all evaporated. I crumbled into a small ball and could feel only the desperate guilt of a wayward child.

"I'm sorry!" I sobbed uncontrollably. "I really tried." Sobs shook my shoulders, and my breath came in gasps.

Then the strangest thing happened. He rose and sat next to me and placed his arm around my shoulders.

"Ambra, listen to me," he said, and I slowly stifled my sobs. "Humanity is in a terrible place. There is so much you don't know. Cattle, Ambra. We are nothing more than bipedal cattle to these aliens that rule space, that rule us to the ignorance of most of our kind. I'm sorry for what I have done to you. Years ago, before *They* took me, I would have been ashamed of it. Perhaps I am inside, still. But I became a slave. To succeed within the system I found myself in—that was all that mattered. *Don't you make this mistake*. Please, Ambra, because I am going to tell you something only I know, something that is important, I believe, for the human race. Something I have buried inside me, denied, rationalized away for years."

I didn't know what to say. Nothing made sense anymore. Nothing was sane.

"Please, just listen and remember. You can't process it all now, but you will later." He paused and then spoke in a whisper, his sentences strangely inflected. It was like hearing scripture.

"Many years ago, when I first came to this place, still working as a staff member with the young children being brought into the facility, a young boy, not much older than you are now, was preparing to ship out, just as you are tonight. I had given him his last series of shots like you got earlier, and was about to send him off, when he spoke to me. He was a very gifted child, second only to you, Ambra, in what he could do with the space-time matrices. He stared at me with his deep-brown eyes —I'll never forget them or the words that came out of his mouth.

'*Doctor, a woman will come, a young girl. She is the Sunrise, she will see with Truth into the darkest night. She is our hope. She will be the savior of this world in its time of need. You will know her by her sign, and you will understand after you have wronged her. Before the end, you must repeat this to her: Daughter of Time, you must wake, and not fear to gaze forward and walk the path set before you. We are waiting.*' "

He paused and cleared his throat, his voice cracking. "These were his last words before I shipped him off to a life of slavery. I paid them no heed, thought them mad ravings, and pushed them out of my mind. When you came, and my ambition blinded me to everything except your terrible gift, I did not hear his voice, or *would* not hear it. Even as they returned this last year to haunt my dreams." He paused a moment in silence. "Now, I can't stop hearing them."

He cupped my head in his hands: I assume he was also staring into my eyes that could not return the gaze. "I want to say those words again: *Daughter of Time, you must wake, and not fear to gaze forward and walk the path set before you.* Ambra, he meant *you*. He was a powerful Reader, and he forecast your coming. He *saw* you in the fields of Time. Listen to him. He was speaking of you, that you have a part to play for all of us in a possible future. I can't undo what I have done, but I can try to play my part rightly for the first time. Don't be afraid, Ambra. *Survive.* You are important beyond the dreams of men."

He stopped and exhaled, and then stood up and walked to the door. "My actions have doomed me, Ambra. They will make an example of my tampering. My last hours, my last minutes, I have spent giving this message to you." The sounds of scurrying feet and raised voices grew from the hallway, and I heard intermixed with it the chilling echoes of the voice translators. It was beginning. *They* were coming for us.

"You've never even been given the courtesy to know my name—I who have made you what you are. I'm sorry we have been so inhuman. My name is Frank, Ambra. Frank Fields. Forgive what I have done and remember his words."

The door opened and then closed quickly, the air pressure blowing against my face, the swelling sounds outside spiking in intensity and then dropping to a muffled drone.

I felt I was going mad.

Chapter 12

$$\forall n \in {}^* \mathbb{N}, {}^* \sin n\pi = 0$$

A journey of a thousand miles started with a first step.

老子 Lǎozǐ (Lao Tzu)

W hen you first begin to *see* as a Reader, you have no experience, nothing to connect the new sensations to, and your brain works the new information into all its preexisting patterns— images, ideas, emotions. Dreams play things out as your brain tries to process it all. Then, it begins to leak into your days. Visions that are the product of this confusion. That's as far as most have ever gotten in human history – seers, prophets, madmen. A new sense organ in a minority of the population, hardly developed. Granting visions, often loss of sanity.

An irony is that in all other things, we humans are the idiots of the galaxy, the least evolved intelligence, life-forms considered backward, primitive, and enabled in their technology only by the aid of more advanced life.

In this galaxy where we have so little to offer, our only value is in prescience, this poorly developed sense organ, that rivals, and often exceeds, that found in species far more developed in every other way. An accident of evolution that made us the idiot-savants of space-time.

They harvested us through human farmers, picked those with real potential, took some of us to God knows where across the galaxy for breeding programs, cloning attempts, and, of course, for the navships. Scattered about star systems and nebulae, entombed in oppressive and harsh prisons, humans serve the space-faring needs of many creatures that are otherwise disrespectful, even contemptuous, of our very existence and presence among them. We are a necessary evil.

With me, the humans they empowered got carried away, and before they realized, my captors had created a monster. *Me*. A monster for all involved, human and *other*. Because, while I am certainly monstrous to my fellow earthlings, my gift is a terrible threat to the galactic hegemony of the Dram – of them, you will hear much more soon. In me, the organ is beyond developed. It has become my dominant sense, unfathomable even to the most powerful Readers of any species. I no longer can see the light of day, but I can see the energy of tomorrow and yesterday. Even though I can't tell you what it looks like exactly, I can say that it isn't much different in spirit from what I saw with eyes: beauty, horror, and everywhere, *existence*.

As the ship raced through the Earth's atmosphere, taking me for the first time beyond my home planet, I was still, as far as my potential, very much asleep. A sleep that was, as I tried to explain, more emotional than anything else. I wasn't ready to accept what I was becoming or to grasp the power my unique insight offered to me. I had to adapt slowly. But the time was coming, and soon the first real steps would be taken. Frank Field's last words lodged in my mind, buried like lily bulbs waiting for spring.

I suppose a trip into space should be described with lots of vivid images of breaking through the atmosphere, seeing the first blackness and stars, and the sunrise over the edge of the Earth. For me and the fifty or so children onboard, the only thing to describe was the tiny space we were crammed into, turbulence, and the feeling that we were going to asphyxiate.

From the facility on Earth, we were marched in line down a long corridor into a large hangar that opened up to the night sky. The chamber was very large, football field-sized, and in the middle was a spaceship. Now that I know more about these things, it was a surface transport, designed to ferry cargo planet-side from a starship. But at that moment, it was the first time I had seen anything like it, and it was overwhelming. As big as a tanker, shaped like a cross between a flying saucer and the space shuttle, it was ringed with earth-suited Sortax. By the time the chamber was entered, there were no more humans around us. We were alone with monsters from space who were putting us into their ship to take us away.

We all walked quietly in our thin robes, cold and afraid. Several kids could be heard sobbing, and one or two broke down and refused to enter. The response from the Sortax was rapid and harsh. They would extend a dark rod towards the child who would then scream in pain and collapse. The Sortax would command the child to move forward in line, and, after that pain, each did.

Inside, it became clear how alien we actually were. The ship was designed, of course, for its crew, these sea-dwelling Sortax with their many arms and liquid-filled suits. The ship inside was designed with liquid filling nearly all the chambers, and I marvel now at the compensation the Sortax must have used to offset all that extra weight. There were "airlocks" of a kind for the natives (*Them*), that we bypassed without engaging. A short tunnel led to our holding pen, which, once all the children had entered, was sealed off from the rest of the ship.

Sealed off from the rest of the ship. That essentially describes all the interactions of humans with any of the diverse alien species in the galaxy, as compatible environments rarely existed. Some needed liquid medium like the Sortax, others required some kind of gaseous environment. Often these gases were toxic or otherwise incompatible with our survival. One ironic exception turned out to be the Dram, the Romans themselves. who ruled over all the other species and who required a very similar oxygen and nitrogen content to that on Earth, even if their Earthlike planet was on the other side of the Milky Way. The other were the Xix, who needed only a small modification to an Earthlike atmosphere, which they achieved through a device worn around their necks in our presence, if you could describe the Xix as having necks.

So, in nearly every ship I was on, humans were walled off from the host species in our own climate-controlled cells. *Controlled* was always a loose term, as many ships provided air and temperature that was just slightly better than unsuitable for human life. That was my impression when we entered our chamber on the Sortax ship, although now I know that their efforts were slightly better than average.

At the time, once the doors closed and we were at the mercy of their climate system, it was oppressive. The air was acidic, burning our throats and eyes. It stank in a manner that to the human senses was unidentifiable— alien, and it was sickening. With no instructions or warning, we were provided makeshift seats and straps, and soon the ship blasted off into the sky; several children who were not prepared were sent flying to their deaths or suffered serious injury. It made no sense. If they wanted us, why treat us like this and risk our lives? Some sort of demented natural selection for the best slaves?

The ride to the starship was short, and soon after a jarring docking (I bet such dockings weren't so bad for Sortax floating in water) and a long wait (likely for the Sortax to leave the ship and to pump out the water for our exit), our hatch-like door opened and we all looked out to see what awaited us.

Amazingly, standing in the doorway were two human beings. They were dressed in robes not too different from our own—thicker, more worn, with strange markings across the back. They were likely in their twenties, although they looked older. As I was to learn, life for humans in space under alien care was shorter than on Earth, full of many more health problems and complications. Most of us did not live beyond forty years, and by the time we hit our thirties, we looked sixty.

A moment of hope and relief swept through the group of children. It was quickly dashed as the men spoke.

"No words," one barked. "You will do as you are told and prepare to serve the Sortax. This is a training vessel, and you will be instructed in guiding the navships to the Orb portals. Nothing else matters to your existence. If you cannot perform, you will be discarded. You are to report to us or other Human Shepherds. Under no circumstances are you to attempt any contact with non-human residents of any ship. Follow us to your quarters."

They turned, and marched from the door, leaving us stunned and empty. One by one, we stood up, stretched our sore bodies bounced by the trip through Earth's atmosphere, and walked through the door to our new life.

PART II

Point τ

I am become Time, the destroyer of worlds.

Bhagavad Gita

Chapter 13

$$V - E + F = 2$$

To delve into the deepest mysteries of nature and discover the underlying truth has been denied us, but with the right imagination, a hypothesis may explain many phenomena.

Leonhard Euler

So my new life began – a life of military constraints, claustrophobic imprisonment, long training sessions, and a horrible sense of separation from all that I was. In space, without night or day, without clocks or anything to mark the passage of time, it was hard to know how long we had been there, how long the sessions lasted, so that the orderliness we took for granted and depended on vanished, and soon, all sense of normalcy was lost. For many it became too much. As they lost their connection with Earth, its rhythms, its air, its life, they lost their bearings internally, and their minds with them. These were efficiently removed and never seen again. There doesn't need to be much guessing as to what happened to them.

It might have been the same with me, because my being is very tied to the Earth, and even in the harsh metallic and sterile center I had been trapped in before transfer to space, I had suffered for the disconnect from the land. You should remember, I am a farmer's daughter.

In space, it was so much more terrible. I saved myself again by exploring the past, finding some powerful echo of Earth in the lives that had lived before me. When the complete separation in this alien environment would descend on me, I could find some solace in Earth's past.

For the time being, for all of us who could adapt, in whatever ways we found, we kept very busy learning how to eat the terrible material they gave to us as food, learning how to function in the toxic air, sleep on the metal shelves allotted to each of us, disregard our privacy and cleanliness in an environment not designed to comfort human sensibilities. And, above all, learning to pilot along the Strings that spread from the Orbs.

It finally became clear what we had all been gathered for, the reason our Earth masters had taken us from our homes, trained us, evaluated us, sought to hone our other sense for a specific purpose. For such a crude purpose our gift was channeled, but it served a practical need. Amazingly, our unique talent was the backbone of the entire galactic civilization. We were treated, bred, and trained as beasts of burden, but on our backs thousands of worlds depended. Without us, interstellar travel would grind to a halt.

It was initially a shock for many who had been brought on board to have a new kind of helmet set on their head and to see the world as they had never experienced it. For me, it was like walking for the first time into a bright, sunlit city having only seen by moonlight. Whatever these new helmets did, they channeled the "stuff" of my vision, brightened it with great contrast, yet only in a certain color, so to speak, in a single dimension. It was beautiful in its way, and yet only a tiny part of the whole. But within this part was a skill we were required to learn.

In the beginning, we were subjected to simulations. Always, it was the same. From a disembodied point of view, I would see myself approaching a sphere of light of great complexity. To call a real Orb a sphere is a distortion, as the word suffers from the biased view of humans and aliens who cannot see it as I do—the substructure, layers upon layers not unlike an onion, but casting out in independent dimensions beyond the three we perceive with our eyes. My mind's other sense could see in these directions, and the Orbs were more like infinite webs whose projection in three-space was a humble sphere.

The simulations captured only a faint aspect of this— only when we approached a true Orb did its beauty become apparent to me. Our training sims were not focused on the Orbs, however, but on the tendrils, the glowing Strings that spread from them. The Strings extending from a true Orb traveled in many dimensions, but the sims captured only those that were in the visual three dimensions, and it was along these lines that we were to direct the point of view, the ship in reality, when the time came to navigate in earnest.

We would spend hours guiding little simulated spaceships onto the tendrils, one after another after another. What I would find out later is that the galactic hegemony of the Dram was established through using the tendrils to travel through space-time. The Strings could be used as tunnels, shortcuts between any two Orbs, cutting the travel time between stars and planetary systems from eons into days. I did not understand how this happened or why these Orbs had been placed where they had. For the present, all that mattered was mastering the ability to help the ships navigate.

The ships themselves had the technology to exploit the Strings but not the ability to peer into the space-time matrix and navigate. The starships required

Readers for this, some from many of the worlds connected by the Orbs or, increasingly, from the relatively cheap and primitive world of Earth that was enriched in Reader potential and powerless to defend itself from the superior technological development of the aliens that needed our singular talent.

I quickly adapted to the tasks, my unique organ giving me advantages no other human or alien possessed, and which I had not even come to fully appreciate. I was surprised to find that, unlike on Earth, my mastery did not bring me advancement or attention. It was not noticed. It became clear to me after a time that it was not individual humans guiding the navships but the collective, that our overall average effort was being used by the aliens to direct the craft to the appropriate String. In a way it made sense, as individually, not even humans had the skills to perfectly navigate—each person would make too many random errors. But averaged over the whole, the outliers, the mistakes, were smoothed out, and the overall direction was true.

True, but slow, inefficient. I became frustrated as I participated, always sure how to direct the craft, but the overall movement was slow, effective, but not the quickest route through space-time. I was only one of a horde, and no one understood what my potential was.

Increasingly, I was drawn to the Orbs. With them lay much more complexity, something far more interesting and inspiring than hitching rides on Strings. While the sim Orbs displayed little of this, as we progressed in our training we made more frequent approaches to the Orb that lay in orbit between the asteroid belt and Jupiter. It was resplendent, *incandescent* compared to the other objects around us in space. Our bright sun, a ball of radiating energy in the electromagnetic spectrum, was a fairly dim and dull object to me. But the Orb, no larger than a major Earth city in diameter, shrouded a terrible beauty. Within it seemed locked a cosmic potential that called to be reached, explored, tapped.

Soon, in my training sessions, I began to focus more on the Orbs than the purpose they had set for us. I saw these close approaches as a chance to study the Orbs, to engage myself when all else of meaning had been stripped from me. In the Orbs I began to see what seemed to be pathways, like trails in the woods, locked off by iron gates. Roads to the past, the future, *elsewhere*. Was there a latch on the gate? I looked; more and more I looked.

Until one of the group leaders called me aside one day.

"Your scores have dropped. You must raise them or be eliminated."

It seemed that they monitored the individual performances in the horde.

"What are the Orbs?" I dared to ask.

"The Orbs are a mystery. We do not approach them. We use the space-time distortions they leave to travel through hyperspace between Orbs. Stick to your lessons, or you will face elimination."

He walked off like a robot, and I knew he meant what he said. As hard as it was, I tore my attention away from the Orbs and back to the assigned task. Soon, our initial group of nearly one hundred was whittled down to less than twenty, as attrition from madness, illness, and poor performance took its toll. Our group was now as optimized as it would get, as I judged from the performances. It seemed the aliens were happy with our progress. Soon we approached the Earth-Orb for the last time and were instructed to guide to a particular String. As we did so, a power surge went through the ship. We maintained our course and approached the String until the spacecraft lay directly in its flow.

What this looked like to the human eye, with its limited sense of a narrow band of electromagnetic radiation, I don't know. I can guess it was fairly unremarkable. The Orb and Strings would be invisible, and only the slow movement of the starship in the vastness of space would be seen. Then, the ship would accelerate dramatically, vanishing in seconds to a small point as it exited the dimensions we can perceive.

To my "eyes" it was an utterly different experience. In the bright and glowing stream of the String, there was radiance passing through the ship, through me and all around me like a churning stream growing to a broad river. As I began to be mesmerized by this vision, there was a whirl of equipment being engaged, a strange tug deep inside me, and then, while my body felt as if it were being turned inside out, my mind drowning in showers of infinitely complex patterns of light and dark that erupted and flowed around me, the ship plunged through hyperspace toward a distant world.

Chapter 14

$$\ell_P = \sqrt{\frac{\hbar G}{c^3}}$$

Execrable son! so to aspire
Above his brethren, to himself assuming
Authority usurp'd, from God not given.
He gave us only over beast, fish, fowl,
Dominion absolute; that right we hold
By his donation; but man over men
He made not lord; such title to himself
Reserving, human left from human free.

John Milton

I should explain how it was I became able to "see" the events around me. The descriptions of the events to come all depend on this ability I first tapped into on Earth during my first meeting with the Sortax. It was in visiting their home world during our first real navigation that this skill blossomed within me so that I could recognize what I was doing and control it at will. Perhaps being among them again, in the presence of so much that was alien, helped to trigger it. This skill has allowed me to compensate for my blindness.

The power to visit the past, which had not only provided me with an education but also a refuge in which to hide from the painful realities of my life, offered something immediate and practical: the power to form images of things around me. It was as if my mind could weave a tapestry from memories so that my new, strange sense could wrap its impressions in the visual metaphors of my lost sight. These are what *visions* are for a Reader, the blending of our sixth sense with the efforts of our mind and imagination. It is a painting of the impressions of this sense in a manner we can understand. Perhaps if we had developed the ability to Read as infants, we would not need to do this: we would "see" in this new way just as we see with our eyes and smell with our noses without needing to frame the experience with another sense. But our abilities begin near puberty, when the rest of our brain has already been shaped and is far less plastic than it once was.

In the beginning, I had used this sense to learn of things I could not have known any other way. The further from my own personal experience, the harder it was to "see," as if such things were at a greater distance. Naturally, many of those things I was most interested in were very far away and required great concentration, and I had to practice my skill to perceive things in any useful manner. The significance of things very, very close, those things that were very easy to perceive, I had initially failed to comprehend. I had ignored them— things that were obvious to me for many other reasons, and that were also part of the world I was seeking to escape emotionally.

Then the Sortax came to Earth, and in the panic, the fear of being near the truly alien, my survival instincts focused my awareness, focused it tightly to Read moments, milliseconds that were only recently past and that were very close to me. If you Read so close to the present, it is very little different from *seeing* the present, except that you have the power to see not only what you might have seen with eyes, but also beyond that, to all the events you chose to explore through space-time. And so it was and became again as we descended through the turbulent atmosphere of the Sortax home world. My mind focused, and this time I understood what I was doing. This ability served me tremendously from that point on in my life. It was also the starting point for the next obvious step – the exploration of events not only moments past but also short times in the future, and from that, the much harder and powerful deliberate search into the future of events to come.

Once through the clouds, the vastness of the planet became clear. Perhaps three times the size of Earth, the entire surface was covered with purple water, and through a descending orbit that traversed nearly two-thirds of the circumference of the world, no sign of land, not even a small island, was present. It became obvious that there would be nothing to "land" on, and that these creatures lived beneath the waves, and under them we would be going.

The ship soon arced sharply over the sea and then made a swift dive down toward the violet water, shuddering as impact was made. The howling sounds from streaming across the atmosphere were replaced with the churning flow of liquid outside the walls of the ship, and quickly the sounds of pressure on the walls could be heard as a soft groaning as we plunged deeper and deeper into the ocean. The Sortax must have lived terribly deep in these waters, and I wondered how creatures like us of fragile flesh, bone, and air could survive at the depth and pressures of their underwater cities.

After what seemed like hours, the ship, now more a submarine, stopped descending, and the metal-on-metal clunk of our docking rang throughout our small room. Then there were several moments of silence as the terrified breathing of those around me punctured the air. Once again we were placed into the alien and unknown: alone and powerless. This time I was less afraid, assuming that there could hardly be anything worse than what had happened to us so far.

I could not have been more wrong.

The door to our chamber opened, and our human Shepherds instructed us to follow them out. The Sortax must have exited through another location this time, likely one designed for their underwater lifestyle. Our exit was under atmosphere, and we were not given any suits to put on. Instead, the ship had docked with a corridor that led deep into the recesses of our new submerged city, or a small air bubble within it. As we walked down the tunnel and then into the many chambers that were maintained in these Earthlike conditions, I was amazed that these aliens had gone to so much trouble for our survival. I was soon to learn, however, how wrong I was to think this was all for us.

"Into the examination room," barked one of the Shepherds, as he pointed to a large chamber to our right. The architecture was disturbingly unlike anything a human mind could have designed. The walls and supports undulated as they curved toward the domed ceilings; the material was some type of metal never seen on Earth, a pale green that seemed almost to give off the slightest glow. Illumination came from what seemed to be a moss-like substance embedded in the metallic walls themselves. The floor was of a similar metal, but more brown, and it was incredibly slippery so that several children had fallen already.

As we entered the chamber, we had our introduction to the Dram. Tall, insectoidal soldiers that were right from out of my earlier vision. Several stood at what seemed like attention beside large pieces of equipment, carrying long objects that even in their alien form could only be weapons. Smaller Dram, marked with symbols on their thorax regions that I could not decipher, crouched down, adjusting elements of the machines.

One by one, we were led to these clusters, were stripped, forcibly placed onto a square region in the center of the machinery, completely restrained, poked and prodded in every orifice. Skin, hair, blood, saliva, and mucus samples were torn from our bodies, devices run over different parts of our anatomy, and all the while we lay helpless and terrified as these enormous insects appeared ready to dissect us on the spot. As they removed my clothes, I did not resist them, but I held on to the one thing that mattered to me—the Red Sox hat given to me by Ricky. I balled it in my fists, clenching them tightly, willing to suffer whatever might come if they tried to take it away. Lucky for me, they didn't seem to focus, or perhaps didn't care, about the crushed baseball hat in my palm. They were too busy removing all possible dignity from the rest of me.

In all that turmoil, I was unable to recognize the startling fact that the Dram were breathing the same air we were, were living at our pressures and temperatures. If I had noticed, I would have pieced together that these chambers were not for us but had been made long before to comfort the Dram, whose control of all planets in the sphere of the Orbs was near absolute. They ruled with such power over the galaxy that the Sortax had allowed this giant air bubble to be lodged so deep within their undersea civilization.

As they finished with me, a probe came out from the side of the examination equipment. A Dram worker rolled me so that my back faced the probe, and instantly I felt a searing burn across my skin. I cried out, as so many others had, but could not move as the sharp ends of the Dram worker's many arms held me in place. A small chip had been inserted into my skin that held all the relevant data for those who would be in the market for human Readers: my training certification, physiological profile, estimated age, and expiration date.

Then we were marched off into a second chamber that I can only describe as a human market. One by one, we were placed on a small stage and displayed in complete humiliation: alone, naked, cold, and afraid. Small devices that resembled odd cameras whirled about us. A device would also scan the chip in our backs, all the information presumably transmitted to the bidding aliens who needed Reader services. What I didn't know was that, based on a weighted formula of many of our traits, we were each given a score. Those with the highest scores would likely serve in pleasure craft of the rich governmental ships or military vessels. Lower scores meant passenger freighters or, worse, the wild and cheap auction market that attracted any of a number of despicable space travelers. My blindness and deformity lowered my score greatly, and as yet they had no inkling of my gifts, no means by which to assess them.

Afterward, I was led by a robotic drone down several corridors and into the storage room, where we were placed into small, coffin-like containers and packaged for delivery to our new owners. I was doomed to land in the hands of some of the vilest criminals of the space-faring races, of a form I never even saw but whose monstrous cruelty almost killed me. Worse still, through all that they did to us, my spirit was nearly shattered. This is the hardest part to tell you. Even now, I become faint and sick just thinking about it.

I began to shiver. My breath came out fogged, and a gel-like foam spread over my body, injected from the sides of the pod. It was incredibly heavy, and I could not move it, even as I struggled. And it was *cold*. Ice-cold and burning. I started to shiver, but slowly my panic faded. My shivering stopped. I could hardly keep my eyes open. I yawned. Sleep—heavy, deep sleep descended on me like an enormous blanket, blocking out the pod I was in and my fear. I forgot where I was. All light faded as I tightly squeezed the crumpled baseball cap in my numbing right hand.

Chapter 15

$$\frac{\dot{a}^2 + kc^2}{a^2} = \frac{8\pi G\rho + \Lambda c^2}{3}$$

The whole visible world is only an imperceptible atom in the ample bosom of nature. It is an infinite sphere, the center of which is everywhere, the circumference nowhere.

Blaise Pascal

Somehow in that artificial sleep, I dreamed.

I was floating in space. Not in a ship or spacesuit, but floating freely like some child in water, an impossible wind blowing over me from molecules of air that could not exist in this emptiness. I felt no cold despite the fact that it should have been absolute zero around me. The air in my lungs did not rush out into the vacuum and the saliva in my mouth didn't boil. Nitrogen gas didn't bubble in my blood giving me the bends, nor did my eardrums rupture. Despite the lack of oxygen, I didn't get light-headed or pass out. In fact, I felt comfortable. Free. *Was I dead? Was this my spirit?*

I looked around. A yellow star shone at a distance, but even though I stared at it without the filtering of atmosphere or protective glasses, my eyes were unhurt, and the intense ultraviolet radiation had no effect on my china-white skin.

Our sun. Our home star. It was then that I marveled that I could see.

In front of me was a small point of light. Like a magnet it pulled at me, and I felt my body accelerate, slowly at first, and then faster and faster. Slowly the object grew in my field of vision, a small white coin, then a plate, and finally the pocked surface came into focus. *The Moon.* My rate of approach slowed as the white disk began to fill my range of sight.

An unease grew in my stomach. A sense of foreboding, of danger, even of evil lurking on the other side of the disk. Something wrong, something monstrous was hiding behind our Moon, something deadly and murderous. And I felt it, I felt it searching, seeking, trying to peer around the dead ball of rock. *Searching for me.*

I knew it was close, but I could hear voices on the other side. Voices calling out in fear, terrible fear and pain. Voices crying out together, like some nightmare chorus, rising in crescendo and sweeping over me like a tempestuous sea, and then, in one terrible instant, silenced.

What had it done? What had the monster done? Concern for the voices that cried and anger at the monster overcame my fear. I began to gain speed, to drift toward the other side of the Moon. The lunar surface swept past, and my eyes became focused on the horizon, on the edge where I would see the bright-blue of Earthrise. Soon, any moment now, I would see home and find my way to the cries for help. I could hear them echoing in my mind.

They were calling out my name.

Chapter 16

$$Q = 2 - \frac{4}{p}\sin p + \frac{4}{p^2}(1 - \cos p)$$

When I look up at the sky, I somehow feel that this cruelty too shall end, that peace and tranquility will return once more.

Anne Frank

When I awoke from the hibernation the transport pod had induced, the first thing to hit me were the smells. Human odors, not alien odors. Odors of human waste and decay, of sickness and death, of filth from a hundred bodies malnourished, unwashed, and weakened with illness and despair. Right after this stomach-churning stink, small robots grabbed us from the pods and herded us through the entry port into a larger chamber. The simultaneous visual assault of what was left of the human beings on this death boat combined with the smell nearly cause me to vomit—an addition to the room that would hardly be noticed. It took a few moments after that initial revulsion for me to finally look into the deep and hollow sockets of the people in the room, and feel the bone-chilling fear of staring death in the face.

They made no sounds. Standing idly or sitting listlessly, voiceless, bent as with great age, these zombies seemed like cattle in pens, dumb eyes staring yet seeing nothing, hair matted, filthy, even falling out. Sores festered on their legs and buttocks, all too visible through the torn and frayed cloth or, in many cases, the lack of any covering at all. These were people who had lost all sense of personal dignity or sense of self. They were emptied of those things that made them once human, or even animal—they were broken and dying.

I had never seen anything like it in my life, even at the worst of the treatments I had received. There were so many of them staring at us. My entire body shuddered. My soul wanted to scream. What could have done this to them? I took the Red Sox cap and placed it over my bulging head, pulling the bill down over my eyes to shield me from these stumbling horrors. It was a pointless attempt to hide from them.

I had no idea where I was now. After I had been sorted at the Sortax home world, and packaged in the pod, I had been made to sleep. *For how long?* It could have been days or years—there was no way for me to tell. Where had they sent me after that? Who had purchased me? Why? There were questions, but in this place, there were no answers to be found.

Like shepherd dogs, the small robots herded us to the far metallic wall. Small depressions in the floor indicated places to stand, and if we didn't understand, the metallic hounds pushed us around and into place. A loud crash above our heads startled me, and as I glanced upward, a panel slid open to reveal a metal claw with three fingers snaking down toward me. Several people near me screamed, and some tried to run. The robots, merely annoying up to that point, showed that they had a bite along with their bark. They swooped in quickly, zapping anyone out of place with a painful jolt of blue electricity, repeating until we were all back in place. Meanwhile, the claw had descended and clamped around those of us who had not moved, the metal fingers with one hundred joints seemed to morph into a boa constrictor. We were held tightly in its grip.

Once we were all loaded in the claws, they raised us upward into the tube above. Like some part in an assembly line, we were sped along several tubes by the robotic arm, up, sideways, down, and then fitted into place. I was dropped into a hard, wet seat, restraints fixed around my legs and arms, rows of others to my right and left in a similar position. A syringe with a large needle emerged from a small panel to my right, and before I could even react, it had pierced my thigh and injected its contents. To this day, I don't know what was in it, but I assume it was a combination of antibiotics, vitamins, and steroids—something to keep us alive and healthy as long as possible in the conditions I would soon come to know all too well.

Beneath me, the smell of urine and feces. I noticed that the seat I had been strapped to had a hole in the middle. You can guess what that was for, and what the wetness I felt seeping over my skin where I sat must have been. We worked twelve-hour shifts before the claw brought us back to the holding pens where we tried to sleep; nature would call. We were also fed at our stations. Running the length of our row in front of us was a trough that would periodically fill with a green sludge for our consumption. We had to bend forward and slurp the stuff up with our mouths. At first the rancid smell of it prevented me from eating. But after two days, even that nastiness tasted heavenly to a starving body.

After the needle had withdrawn and several of us had screamed or wept or cried out in other ways, the navigation helmets descended and plugged us into the system. It was like the training sessions, almost the same interface for our minds. At first, we were led through a series of drills, clearly not real, as there was no sensation of travel through hyperspace. The crew was not going to take chances on us guiding them through a star or asteroid field. They had lessons to teach as well, harsh ones. For anyone who did not match the correct trajectories, there was an electric shock, a longer punishment than the robots gave, dispensed from the seat. A few in our group screamed on the first run, the pain so terrible that I saw tears in the eyes of a girl next to me. Mentally, a projection of the correct path was emphasized by the machinery from the helmets, and from that all were supposed to learn. Very soon, all in my group had learned, and the shocks and screams stopped. These lessons never ended. Anyone performing poorly could be shocked at any time. Later on, as our physical and mental state deteriorated in this nightmare, our performance dropped. Some lost all ability, and when shocks did not work, the claw descended and removed the offender. We never saw them again.

After those initial test runs and the harsh punishments, the crew brought us online for the first hyperjump. Again, the beautiful Orb came into view, that increasingly seemed to me like some pure thing in a dirty universe. The indicated paths were shown, and we directed the ship to the set course, and then the tug and inversion feeling of the jump passed through me.

Repeat this endlessly, and you have a good idea of our quality of life.

Our time became a drudging monotony. We never saw any of our destinations. We would guide the jumps, wait in position for docking, hear and feel the loud noises of cargo transfer, and then we were back out and headed to the next jump. This would happen perhaps every hour, giving us ten or twelve jumps per shift. For many it was exhausting concentrating under the pressure of pain to guide the ships correctly. At first for me it was quite simple. As my body began to fall apart over the coming months, it became a challenge even for me to focus on the tasks. By then most of those in the group who had come on board with me had disappeared, having ceased to be able to function adequately. They were quickly replaced.

Much later I would learn from the Xix that this had been a smuggler ship, part of an underground black market of traders that often employed human Readers as disposable slaves. These smugglers ran nearly ceaselessly, maximizing transfers, minimizing downtime, and mercilessly running through humans like some obscene form of organic fuel to drive and guide their ships. It was all illegal but tolerated up to a point by most local authorities. We were considered a low form of life, with poor self-awareness, unable to suffer like the more advanced life-forms. Our exploitation and pain was rationalized away. Laws were often ignored, especially when there was wealth to be had.

I still cannot fully reconcile these two perspectives: one, this galaxy presented academically by the Xix and others, an economic truth of an unfortunate nature; and two, the minute-to-minute torture of the hell I lived through. Those things could not possibly be the same. They were from two different universes. In my current life, I choose not to think of it, because I feel madness lurking in trying to reconcile those incongruent truths. Telling you now is harder than you can imagine. But it must be done. It's part of the big picture, understanding the truth about reality that you have been made ignorant of until now.

After our long shift, the claw descended and carried us like used baggage to one of several large and crowded rooms. These holding pens consisted of cold, hard walls and floors—no comforts, no divisions for privacy, no separated areas to take care of bodily functions, no space for a human being to have any sense except for a festering claustrophobia. We packed ourselves together, cold, choking on the poorly conditioned air that made our throats and eyes raw, lying in our own excrement, trying to find some short period of sleep before the next shift. During this time we went without food. Anyone acting out was quickly targeted by robots. As you can imagine, there were many who could not adapt. Some turned violent, some became catatonic. Either way both were removed, never to be seen again.

It all sounds so bland as I read what I have written. I don't have the words to make you smell the stench, feel the oppression of senses, the fear of smothering in others' awful bodies or of the unclean conditions in which we lay. I know of no way to tell you how this state of existence began to rob me of my sense of self, my ability to think or feel or remember what life on our beautiful planet had ever been like. It was as if all that was real was the horror around me, and anything else was only some faded and remote dream of fresh air, green grass, blue skies, and smiling faces. And hope.

But there was no hope in this place. The dream became ever more remote, seeming a cruel delusion to torment me with beauty and kindness and freedom I could never have. Reality was nightmare, a plane of Hades, and we were the tortured souls never again to know decency.

Every few days the room was flooded with a harsh blast of cold water at high pressure. It left abrasions on our skin, but for a short while it washed the filth out of the way. The water tasted awful and smelled of toxic chemicals, no doubt to further disinfect the room. Our owners used these coarse methods to keep us healthy—sanitizing washes, injections of antibiotics—as long as was possible. But they would not care for us individually, and even these efforts left us, one after the other, depending on our constitution and luck, succumbing to infections we had brought with us from Earth. Our weakened immune systems could not keep up. Skin sores and boils, respiratory diseases, and the ever-present diarrhea brought us down. Some labored on, seeming to have infinite willpower, dragging their skeletal forms forward, coughing blood, *trying*. Others seemed to reach a point at which life seemed not to matter, and they just lay down and refused to do more, and were removed.

"Nights" were the worst part of it, if you can identify a period as day or night in a place with no sun, no changing lights. Like fish in a can, squashed together in filth, hearing the moans of the sick, the weeping of the broken.

Their hopelessness was more infectious than anything else. There was no peace, no rest. I almost looked forward to the navigation hours.

And so it went, hour after hour, day after day, for weeks that blurred in my mind until I could no longer keep any kind of count of time. My body began to waste away. I spent several painful sessions with intestinal illnesses that made me wish to die. Soon, I had lost so much weight that my ribs were like an anatomy chart, my pelvic bones jutting sharply from my sides. My clothes were an unwashed, raggedy set of strips that hardly covered anything I normally would have cared to cover. Ricky's hat was still on my head, but it had been soiled, partly torn, stained beyond ever being clean in this awful place. By this point, I didn't care. I can only assume my eyes had begun to take on the hollow look of the creatures I had seen when I first entered the space-ship. Creatures for whom death is a mercy to be welcomed.

Through all this time, I had lost the ability, even the desire, to travel into the past and had forgotten anything to do with the future. I was a zombie stumbling forward, knowing only to perform in the seats or face pain, to eat as much of the green sludge as I could before feeling sick, and dreading the feverish nights in the holding pens.

It was at this point that I discovered a thing that would have quickly led to my death, or to the breaking of my spirit before my death.

As I leaned over one navigation session to slurp up the food from the trough, a woman next to me was crying. I would have ignored her. Most of us who had been there more than a few weeks began to withdraw from emotional and social bonds. We became zombies, numb to everything around us except immediate and sharp concerns. The woman was staring at me, crying, then she began yelling. She called me a monster. Finally, I looked over at her. She was a recent addition, acquired at one of the last stops. She was fat, her clothes intact. Her emotional outburst indicated that she would not last long. This place would break her quickly.

"How can you? How can you eat that? What have they done to you?" she screamed at me as green porridge leaked down the sides of my chin. "Look! Look at what they make it from!"

Slowly, I turned my head and stared at what she was pointing toward. Even more slowly, the blur of green food cleared, and there, in the midst of the awful glop, was a severed human finger. It had the same greenish hue, partially ground up, but it was a finger nonetheless, clear as it could be. Amazingly, I looked back at her, not yet able to process what my eyes had seen.

"Don't you care?" she moaned. "Oh, God, you're eating each other!"

Finally, understanding spread inside me. It was a terrible revelation. In all that had happened, in all the things that had been done to me or that I had seen, I had at least felt detached, a tortured innocent caught in the monstrosity of others. Now, tasting that food in my mouth, understanding what I was eating, I became the monster. For the first time in my life, I felt tainted. I felt evil. I felt as if the devil had transfused my blood with that of a hundred murdered infants. I was eating my own kind.

I threw up. I vomited over the trough, and for the first time since I had come to this place, I wept. I felt my insides melt, felt my sense of myself as a person dissolve. I had become a disease. I spoke nonsense to the woman.

"I'm sorry," I cried hysterically. "I didn't mean to. I'm sorry, I'm sorry, I'm so sorry!"

But she only cursed at me more, and at everyone in the row. She condemned us to hell for our actions. I stopped crying. It was all so clear. The poor woman, she was so lost. Didn't she know that we were in hell? And we were corrupted by it to the uttermost evil?

I stopped eating. I could not clean myself of this stain, but I could at least not continue to debase myself now that I knew. Let me tell you, though, it was the most difficult thing I've ever done in my life. All that I went through, and all that I would go through—tortures, cruelties, sacrifices—none of them compared to the trial of simply not eating that inhuman, human sludge. If you have never starved, you cannot understand. I would lean toward that porridge, weeping, wanting to bring it to my mouth, my body screaming at me, my saliva dripping. Somehow, I stopped myself. Somehow, *a madness*, I forced myself to starve more and more, until my body became a thing almost separate from me, and my thoughts like some mind floating above it, guiding the actions.

But it was not a triumph. Don't ever believe that it was. Because I *wanted* that food. I wanted that food more than anything I had wanted in my life or that I have wanted since. You don't know what it is to starve. I only managed because of my own terrible, terrible need to find my humanity, whatever was left of it. Like some dishonored Samurai plunging a blade into his abdomen, I tortured myself for that. But even now I can feel the terrible hunger I had for that food, and it still dirties me to remember it.

My time was now very limited. Quickly, each hour, I grew much weaker. After three days of not eating, I could barely focus on the navigation and slept little at night for the pangs of hunger in my belly. I am sure that I would have failed the fourth day, been punished several times by the chair, and then been removed, to be sent and processed myself into the green slop.

But on the fourth day, the Xix came.

Chapter 17

$$\hat{\mathbf{L}}_{GR} = p^\alpha \frac{\partial}{\partial x^\alpha} - \Gamma^\alpha{}_{\beta\gamma} p^\beta p^\gamma \frac{\partial}{\partial p^\alpha}$$

The greatness of a nation and its moral progress can be judged by the way its animals are treated.

attributed to Gandhi

I f you were to cross an iridescent and elongated Smurf with a spindly-armed alien from early science fiction films, add sixfold radial body symmetry, and throw in a large dose of ballerina-like elegance of motion, you might get something close to the impression a typical Xixian specimen would give. But you would still be missing the heart of these noble aliens, something that I hope I can show you in my own words in the next few chapters.

When I first encountered the Xix, you must imagine me to be hardly human anymore. I was a dying and wasted thing, starving, skeletal, my gums bleeding, sores all over my body. I no longer cared to live and could barely process the reality around me.

The demon-ship that held us in torment had docked, and the usual sounds of unloading and loading could be heard. In the midst of this routine, an unusual racket erupted over the expected sounds. Perhaps I heard explosions, although my mind was not in the best state to process anything. Then a deep silence fell over the entire ship. Distant at first, and then growing louder, footsteps could be heard outside our entry port. Equipment was placed outside the door, and then with a loud crash, the seal was broken and the door pulled aside.

The long and tall Xixians walked in, carrying devices of some kind in one of their four arms. They were uniformed in unusual garb that resembled robes stitched together at several points along the often highly angular contours of their bodies. The clothes were dark blue, with alien insignia and characters I could not decipher, and their porcelain and faintly iridescent skin contrasted sharply with the dark hues.

Of all the aliens I was actually to observe before I returned to Earth orbit, the Xix were the most humanoid, even more so than the insectoidal Dram. To begin with, they were bipedal: two legs, even if strangely proportioned for the Earth-raised, with six-pointed feet harboring not toes exactly, but protrusions that would have to be compared with toes. The legs were multi-jointed, clearly supported by some kind of muscle and structural elements utterly foreign to Earth physiology. Were an Earth creature's legs to bend in several directions simultaneously, attempting to support weight at those absurd and dangerous-looking angles, the bones would snap, the ligaments tear. Instead, the Xix tolerated those ridiculous bends and just danced to a strange rhythm in their gait. Two very long arms near the midsection of their bodies, as long as yet thinner than the legs, also adopted the multi-jointed angles of their lower body. These arms ended in six-toed "hands" very similar to the protrusions on the feet. Nearer their heads, pulled slightly inward, were another two arms, much shorter and thinner, consisting of only two joints and ending in a set of very different hands. These much finer and smaller hands were also radially symmetric but with twelve elongated fingers of six joints each, so bendable, yet strong, that when they moved they almost appeared as tentacles. These hands held the odd spherical devices, like a weapon.

The top of the torso, fused together like a cone, erupted outward with three sets of six eyestalks. This was what I thought of as the "head." Each set of eyes was also positioned with radial symmetry around an axis running through the middle of the body from top to bottom, so that the Xixians could see very well from all directions. Membranous fibers seemed to span the area between the thick and highly mobile eyestalks, but there was too little mass for any kind of a brain-like organ, which, I was to learn later, was positioned in the center of their large barrel chests.

These quasi-humanoid creatures stormed into the holding pen where I lay dying. After scanning the area carefully, they drew back their weapons and spoke into small communicators around their smaller upper hands. All of us drew back instinctively from these creatures, truly monsters for the human psyche. Within several moments, two Xixians in slightly different uniforms – lighter blue, with different insignias – entered through the door. They appeared to have a highly modified form of the "universal translator" worn by other aliens like the Dram or used by the Sortax from their tanks. It was much sleeker in appearance, also functioning as a kind of gas mask to alter the composition of the air brought into their bodies. Once words began to pour through the devices, it became clear that they were of a far superior and significantly more advanced design to those any other aliens used.

The first sounds from the device worn by the two new Xix sounded suspiciously like Chinese to me, and indeed, several Asian men and women in our room glanced up at the sounds as if they understood them. After an initial burst of Chinese, I heard other languages spoken, foreign, but clearly not alien. Even when unintelligible, they were sounds that touched my heart. Sounds of Earth. Finally, the words were spoken in English.

"Please be calm. We are here to help you, to remove you from the illegal confinement and abuse in this criminal vessel. We are representatives of the Xixian Federation, charged with Life Rights for creatures in this parsec. We will take you to better quarters and provide you with medical assistance. When you are healed, we will help you find appropriate and safe work within the Hegemony. Again, please do not be afraid. We are here to help you. We are a rescue party."

No one moved. We were all beyond the ability to believe or process much intellectually. As we stared forward stupidly at our saviors, several teams of Xix in green uniforms—the medical crew, as I came to think of them—rushed in through the door and began to attend to the worst of us. Others were approached by more light-blue-uniformed nightmares, who spoke soothingly and tried to gather humans together and lead them through to the outside. *How gentle they were!* If there was anything to map between human empathy and the alien psychology, it seemed to me that the Xix *felt our pain*, and genuinely cared for us. My long association with them has taught me only how amazingly true this is.

At the time, however, I could no longer stand. I felt the many-fingered yet delicate hands of two Xixian medics lift me onto a hovering stretcher of some kind. Bobbing up and down in a crazed dream, I saw the snaking eyestalk head of one of them bend over and look at me, passing a strange glowing device over my body. A warmth spread through me, and my pain lessened, and slowly, but irresistibly, I fell down into a deep, deep well of darkness and into a peaceful sleep.

Chapter 18

$$\nabla \times \mathbf{B} = \mu_0 \mathbf{J} + \mu_0 \varepsilon_0 \frac{\partial \mathbf{E}}{\partial t}$$

For after all what is man in nature? A nothing in relation to infinity, all in relation to nothing, a central point between nothing and all and infinitely far from understanding either. The ends of things and their beginnings are impregnably concealed from him in an impenetrable secret.

Blaise Pascal

Again, I dreamed.

I floated through the black of space, a small point of light growing in the distance. Larger and larger, it took on the dimensions of a disk, a great pocked disk of rock rushing toward my disembodied perspective. *The Moon.* I did not recognize the surface patterns. It was the moon, but not the Moon I knew; craters and lines of patterns were unknown. As the Moon rushed past me to the right, now covering most of my vision, the bright blue and white of the Earth peered over the edge of its satellite, and the Moon slowed to a stop to reveal nearly half of the glorious marble set in the black of space.

Home. I felt myself weep, but there was no body to respond, no tears to fall. Slowly, I felt my perspective gain momentum, revolving around the Moon toward the right, the Earth dipping below the disk. *Earthset.* I longed to see it again, and as I spun around toward the other side of the moon, I felt myself straining to catch a glimpse of the edge of the blue disk breaking out over the lifeless surface of the moon. *Earthrise.*

I traveled over the surface, the dark side of the Moon giving way to the patterns I knew. Continuing, flying in orbit across the surface, and still the

Earth did not break over the horizon. *Where was it?* How far around did I have to go to see the Earth? I wanted to go home.

Around and around, peering, straining. A cold chill passed through me, and again I felt the presence of something terrible and wrong. The monster was near. *I had to find the Earth!* I cast my vision across space, straining for a glimpse of anything besides the Moon and this blackness.

A terrible laughter echoed around me. Long and cruel, it pierced my spirit like a poisoned sleet storm, echoing, echoing in the infinite darkness. And I *knew*. I felt it like a knife in my gut. It was gone. *Earth was gone.*

I felt myself scream in silence, my rush around the Moon increasing, spinning faster and faster, seeing remembered patterns of the surface, then back again to the unremembered, around and around, yet everywhere, only darkness. *Only the Moon.* Panic welled inside, I felt as if I were to strain and stretch until I snapped. Around and around until the surface became a blur.

The Earth was gone!

Chapter 19

T proves that if T proves that $(P \rightarrow Q)$
and T proves P then T proves Q.
In other words, T proves that ProvA($\#(P \rightarrow Q)$)
and ProvA($\#(P)$) imply ProvA($\#(Q)$).

Only the shallow know themselves.

Oscar Wilde

I awoke in a soft bed, feeling stiff, as if I had slept for a time uncounted. At first, all was dark, as in my dream, and fear gripped me before I remembered: *I am blind.* Calming myself, I made an effort and scanned the immediate past. From the nothing of darkness, the dream of my past reading became visions of the recent Now, and my location was painted within my mind.

It seemed I was in a small room. A warm light like an early spring morning shone on my face from a kind of lamp overhead, casting earthlike tones to the objects around me. I lay on a small bed, blankets of some strange material draped over me. Next to my head was a blue and red artifact with a stretched and sewn strap in the back, a stained bill and top, stitched lettering across the front—Ricky's hat. It looked like someone had even attempted to clean it. Two broad and strange chairs were in front of my bed. In each chair sat a monstrosity. As my mind cleared, my memory returned, and the months on the deathship flooded back. At the last, when my strength had failed, I remembered the entrance of the strange aliens: the Xix, *our salvation*. Little glimpses, like half-recalled dreams told me I had awakened several times to lose consciousness, that I had been in several places, attended to by these creatures, but no details emerged.

Where am I?

Two tall Xixians, green robes covering their unusual bodies, sat in front of me, their snaking eyestalks and fingers squirming as the rest of their body remained still in their seats. The fear of them had begun to leave me. Somehow, I knew that these creatures had purposefully taken what was left of us off that ship, and that they had cared for me. Why, I did not know. Fear still remained for what they might want with me.

"Welcome back, Ambra Dawn," said one of them before I could muster any courage for interaction. Its translator was strung about its strange head like a necklace, lights flashing across the surface as words were spoken. "Please, do not be afraid. We are medics of the Xix. We have tended you since our forces retrieved you from the smugglers."

"Smugglers?" I managed to croak out. My throat was very sore.

"Barbarians," spoke the other in an identical pitch, identical accent, although a different personality came through the cadenced inflection of the words.

"You were nearly beyond our aid. Many of your companions already were," continued the first one.

"Where are they all?" I asked, afraid to hear the answer.

"Those that survived are well cared for at a rehabilitation facility."

"Rehabilitation?"

"Yes. We are a division of Xixian forces devoted to identifying groups that violate the laws in place ensuring the proper treatment of underdeveloped creatures. Too often more advanced species abuse their power and resort to treating humans in unconscionable ways, simply to maximize profit. Too many do not believe in your ability to suffer, or do not care. Our job is to police such abuses. Your shipmates will be healed as much as we are able to heal them, and then reassigned to more, shall we say, humane, employments."

My mind attached a soft smile to the words. Of course, the Xix had no teeth or mouths that I ever saw. They never dined with us and it was always my theory that they absorbed their food through their rough skin. I'm clueless about how they interfaced with the translators.

"Why am I here?"

The eyestalks swiveled around and settled on me. "Because you are special, Ambra."

"How do you know my name?"

"You have spoken much in your delirium. We have been careful to record and study everything about you once we understood your value. Shortly after we brought you to medical services, our scans of your body identified items of interest beyond the illnesses and damage to your body that we sought to repair."

"My tumor."

"Yes, Ambra. But I don't think you fully appreciate your condition."

"I hate it."

"Yes, that is understandable. But we often hate things we do not understand."

The second one spoke, its many eyes focusing on both me and the other Xix. "Ambra, who modified you? Was it Earthlings? Or others?"

"Modified me? Oh. You mean the surgeries." I turned away from them. For some reason, I felt ashamed. "Humans did it. They wanted the tumor to grow. I think my Reader powers come from it."

"Yes, Ambra, they do. Did you know that many humans have such tumors?"

I turned back around. "They do?"

"They are much smaller. All humans with Reader powers have this growth in the brain. It is a recent alteration of your neural physiology, within the last fifty thousand of your Earth years. In most it is no larger than the tip of your finger."

"But in me?"

"Your genetics combined to create a benign tumor in this tissue, accelerated in growth by hormones at puberty. The surgeries modified your brain tissue, your skull, vasculature – all to allow the tumor to grow uninhibited. It gives you special abilities."

"I don't want to be special."

"But you are, Ambra." I turned away again. Several seconds passed in silence until the first one continued the conversation.

"We know you are blind."

"Yes."

"The scans revealed the damage from the growth to your brain tissues involved in processing visual information. And yet, Ambra, you see."

I remained silent, turned away from them. I didn't know what to say. Most of the conversation had been from the first one that had spoken. The second leaned forward.

"Ambra, I too am a Reader. Readers exist in many of the alien species in the Dram Hegemony. But our talents are weak compared to human Readers. And compared to you – there has never been a Reader like you, Ambra."

"The man who did this to me said there was. He said there was one who predicted me."

There was a long pause. The Xixian Reader then continued. "We will not speak of this right now. But what you say is true. But you have the potential to surpass everything that he has done."

My head was swimming. Already fatigue was catching up to me again. *What did they want with me?*

The first one spoke again. "Ambra, how is it that you are blind and yet you see?"

I shook my head. How was I going to explain all this? I couldn't really even explain it to myself. My trips to the past – where they real? Was I mad? Did I really *see* or did I imagine? After everything that had happened to me –

kidnapped, my parents killed, the surgeries, the aliens, being sold, nearly driven to death, and now this – how did I know I wasn't mad? And if I wasn't, did I even have words to make sense of it all?

"I...I look at things that were...*before*. I can look and see things, many things, that have happened. It's like a web or weaving dancing in my mind... no, I don't know, I don't know how to explain it. Things far and close. If I look close, and at those things near me, I can see what was moments before, which is like seeing what is now. Almost. That's what it is for me."

The two were silent, and their eyestalks darted back and forth between each other. I guess it's what I would call a "knowing look" for these creatures. Something passed between them. The Reader spoke.

"Ambra, you may call me Thel. I have been assigned to you. There are many things we would like to know. We need to know what you can see."

Finally, it was enough for me. The fatigue, the questions, the strangeness of everything around me. I nearly shouted. "Why?! What do you want with me? I just want to be left alone. I don't want this anymore. *Please*...please. Can't you just take me home?"

Thel spoke softly. "No, Ambra. We can't."

I began to cry.

"For your pain, we would. But there is so much you do not understand."

"What? What don't I understand?" I sobbed out between breaths.

"Earth is not safe for you, Ambra. Earth is not what you think it is. You seem to have explored the past, but not thoroughly, or you would have seen that several hundred years ago, Earth was infiltrated by agents of the Dram. In humans, they found a gold mine, herds of humans with powerful Reader potential. They quickly subverted your cultures, your nations, and guided the development of your civilization with the sole goal of breeding, identifying, and selecting humans of the greatest Reader powers. There is no place on Earth where their influence does not extend. Should you return to Earth, very soon you would be back in their hands."

"Like I'm in *your* hands?"

"We believe we are different, Ambra."

"Prove it. Let me go. Take me back!"

"Ambra, we do not wish to use you as the Dram would use you, only for selfish gain. But we need you. Not only the Xix, but many alien species need you. And your own race needs you, too. Quite desperately."

"What can you need me for?"

"The Hegemony of the Dram has ruled our galaxy for too long. There are those underneath their rule that seek what you would call liberation. This Resistance needs you. Only when the Dram are defeated can they be removed from Earth, and your own planet be freed. Nothing on Earth is as it seems. You are not in control of your destiny. You are puppets on strings. Cattle that are bred, raised, and taken for one purpose: slavery."

I was still for several moments. Have you ever had a sudden sense of truth, of something that was hanging over you, but until that moment, you couldn't see it? Right then, hearing those words, a thousand things came together – the searches in the past, my life experience, their words. And like some landscape becoming clear in a fog, I *knew*. I knew it was true. I had felt it all my life, this *wrongness* of our life on Earth. The sense that things were not making sense, were not as they seemed, and that something – something darker – lay behind it, blotting out the real sun.

"Revolution?" The word sounded electric in my ears.

"This is not the time to speak of it, but yes. There is so much for you to learn. But your powers offer a key to unlocking the shackles the Dram have placed on so many."

"Why don't *you* fight them?"

"As Xix, we are poorly suited to this task."

"Why?"

"It is an irony for many in the Resistance. The Xix have surpassed all others in knowledge and technology, yet we are unable to seek the destruction of others, even for the greater good. We of Xix excel in the making of things, in the healing of hurts, in the explaining of what little of the universal mysteries that we can. Violence, the infliction of pain – these are things we recoil from. It is beyond mere morality. It is wired into our tissues."

"You had weapons when you came. I saw them. And there were explosions."

Thel answered. "The explosions were attacks from the smugglers on our forces. Many Xix perished. The objects our forces held that you call weapons can stun attackers, but they cannot kill them. That is as violent as we can be. And only some of us are able to undertake such training."

The other Xixian followed up on those words. "We know this weakness in ourselves yet we cannot alter it. So, we seek other means or the means to empower others to resist. Ambra, we suspect that you may be that means, what our Resistance has been seeking for a long time. Something to turn the tide. The Dram are ruthless, powered by terrible weapons and technology we of Xix shudder to even imagine. They were the first to probe the Orbs to manipulate them, because they wanted the power. All of the Orbs connect, Ambra, and they are all found near the planets of intelligent life. This led the Dram to many worlds, worlds that mostly were not prepared to resist such an aggressive and merciless foe. Galactic wars followed, but soon the Dram over-powered all. Now, the galaxy rots under the tyranny of the Dram. It must end."

The Xixians did that thing again with their eyestalks and then spoke once more to me.

"We see that you are tired. We have said as much or more than we should have. We will let you rest. You have the means to examine the truth of our words. Use it. Come to see that we do not deceive you. Soon, we will return to speak more, and, if you will consent, to begin to try to understand your real potential. For now, we travel toward the next step in your journey."

"Where will we go?"

"Someplace safe. A secret place where you will learn the depth of what awaits you." The two Xixians stood, legs moving at impossible angles, yet the motion was fluid. They strode to the door at the far wall.

"Rest now, Ambra Dawn, *Reader*. There is much yet that you must do."

The door opened and within seconds closed, leaving me alone in the room. Alone with too many thoughts for my exhausted mind to hope to consider.

Chapter 20

$$zz^* = (x + yj)(x - yj) = x^2 - y^2$$

The mind is not a vessel to be filled, but a fire to be kindled.

Plutarch

The next few weeks found my body healing, and my sense of self returning to me once again. I was still thinner than I ever had been, and the sight of food always made me sick to my stomach. Memories of that horror still are with me. I forced myself to eat, because whatever had happened, whatever my life meant anymore from my old perspectives, the words I had heard after waking on the Xixian ship had struck a deep chord. I didn't know who or what I was anymore, nor did I know what I could possibly want from this existence, but if I could make a difference, if I could help *turn the tide* in a universe I felt had indeed gone very wrong, then that is what I wanted to do. Perhaps in that I might find something for myself. But even if I didn't, I had to live and see what my role might be.

Most of the other humans who had been on the smuggler death-ship with me had been removed to another place, off-ship. Only a few remained, I think chosen by the Xix for their Reader powers, as well as to keep me, their prized hope, from being isolated from my own kind. I became more and more grateful for this as time went on. While the Xix were gentle and kind, if always sharp with their probing, they were fundamentally alien. Even their smells offended some deep part of my primitive instincts. To have other humans around in this alien environment helped keep me sane.

We all worked together with the Xix. First, we were used to help pilot this craft. The Xixian ship was so different than those of the smugglers or the

Sortax. Their architectural lines were so elegant, flowing, yet not wasteful. The other ships seemed thrown together by comparison, walls, floors, doors thoughtlessly and crudely assembled, showing signs of decay and impermanence. The Xixian ship seemed ageless, as if it had been made yesterday and would never show sign of wear.

Xixian navigators were onboard, but when we were brought to the navigation pods—small, womb-like boxes as unlike the stalls on the smuggler ship as I could imagine—the native navigators gave way for the humans. We were instructed to help pilot the ship on a strange and roundabout course. Thel, who was ever at my side during my time on the ship, explained that they sought unpredictable and less-traveled paths through the Orb String Tree, as they called the many branching and reconnecting paths of the hyperspace portals. Planets rarely visited by the Dram. Places where their ship would not be searched.

I wondered at this, as I could find no reason why the Dram should be after us. After all, it was only the Xix that had thought me of any value in this alien universe. The Dram had examined me, branded me, and auctioned me off to the lowest of extraterrestrial life. As time went on, I came to understand that it was because of the Resistance. Some of the high-ranking members had to be onboard this ship. That's why they needed such secrecy. Well, the last place I wanted to be was with the Dram again, so I did all I could to help steer us as the Xix wished. And for several months, we never saw signs of any other vessel. The transit times were on the order of several days per hyperspace jump. Unlike the smugglers, we took our time, and the Xix planned each step carefully. They also did not wish to tire us too greatly by using us as navigators, although the work was hardly much compared to what I had known. Instead, they wished us to focus our energies on the training and tests they lined up for us day after day.

Unlike the tests on Earth, or in the Sortax training ship, the Xix tests were much deeper, more challenging, and, as I came to understand, much more instructional in nature. Very soon, I had gone so far beyond the other human Readers that I got my own time, private lessons if you will, with Thel and some of the other Xix Readers and scientists. While I was clearly the subject of their tests, I never felt like a lab rat in their cages. Instead, it felt more like they were my teachers and I their student. I mentioned this to Thel, who seemed surprised that I was confused about something that seemed so obvious to them.

"Ambra, what good will you be to yourself, or us, or others, if you are not nurtured to become truly yourself? We of Xix cannot see an object only as a means to an end, but instead as a seed that must be nourished to become."

"To become what?"

"What it was meant to be."

Sounds cheesy, I admit, but these bizarre-looking things really meant what they said.

For the first time in my life, someone began to try to explain what it was that I was doing, what I was *seeing*, in the way all Readers *saw*. I was constantly amazed at the Xixian translators, which somehow pulled out of thin air the simple human words for ideas in math and physics I knew must be much more complicated in Xixian thought. Thel confirmed this for me.

"I will try to explain, Ambra, but you must remember that human language, even human thought, is far more primitive than Xixian. I don't say this to insult you, but to let you know that the words you hear are simplifications, and because so, distortions of the truth. But it is the best we have at our disposal."

I nodded, sitting patiently in the place I called the Practice Room, where every day, twice a day for several hours, I had my private lessons.

"I was trying yesterday to explain your Reader vision. Calling it *vision* is a good analogy, because like vision, or smell, or hearing, or taste, it is a sense. It is a part of your body interacting with the world around you in a way that gives you information. But it is also a poor word, tying you to a concept that distorts the information you are receiving, just like explaining sight in terms of hearing would be. When you *Read*, Ambra, your neural organ, that growth you call a tumor, is sensitive to particles like your eyes. Not photons, but particles that carry information about space and time. We might call them something like what your physicists call gravitons, if those were real particles that described the physics of our universe. But the gravitons you detect are of a different nature than Earth physics comprehends at present, yet they carry information of the fields of space and time just as photons do of the electromagnetic world."

Physics. I wished I had explored it much more carefully in my searches of the past.

"What is important to understand is that space and time are always changing, in flux, like electricity and magnetism. Your ideas about them are very primitive ones, and your recent physics of the last two hundred years on Earth has only barely scratched the surface of their complexity. But like you once could see the world, what had happened, and what would happen, with your eyes, so you can see such things with your tumor. More directly."

"It doesn't feel like that."

"No, just like it doesn't *feel* like that to *see*. Seeing gravitons isn't like some abstract particle physics diagram. When you were sighted, nearly every moment of your waking day, you were detecting photons, bundles of electromagnetic energy, quanta, wave-particles dualities—light. You didn't see the physics. You *were* the physics, and your mind experienced the powerful green of an Earth plant, the churning froth of flowing water, the diamond pinpricks of stars in the night blackness. These are experiences that shaped your emotions, your thoughts, your actions. Photons. That is something like the way a Reader can *see* gravitons, and yet as different from sight as sight is from smell. But no different in that it is experienced, extending into all areas of our awareness, our creativity, our dreams. We have a sense others don't have and can't really imagine. It's like explaining sight to a person blind from birth."

"Why can't I see the future like I can the past?"

"You can. That is how you navigate the ships, seeing the lines of possible connection."

"But I *can't* see the future like the past! The past I can see in detail. The future—when I do, it's like a dream. So many dreams. I don't even know if they are real."

"And you know the past is real?"

"I learn things that I find out are true."

"And so you will with your future dreams. You must begin to tell us of your dreams, Ambra. They may be very important."

"But I can choose to see into the past, search it, grab details, go where I want."

"We believe that soon you will learn to do this with the future as well."

When they weren't trying to explain what it was about, they were training me to see farther, faster, and with more detail. Most of that work focused on the future. Already, I pretty much could ace anything that they threw at me for reading the past. In fact, I know I could see things that their test couldn't pick up. But I was clumsy with the future, always going forward and then falling back. I was frustrated, and uneasy. As before, it was Thel who helped me understand why.

"You stumble not because you cannot, but because you *will* not."

"I will not what?"

"Ambra, you are afraid."

I sat quietly with this. The truth of it sunk in deep. I knew Thel was right. Always, when I began to peer over the edge of the Now and began to glimpse that giant landscape of what was to come, shimmering like a city at night, I could see the shapes of things I knew, and many I did not. Out there, in the middle of it, were forms of me. Whenever I began to sense them, I felt the landscape snap back and away, my vision darken, and I would lose focus.

"Why am I afraid?"

"You are afraid because you fear what you will see, of what will come to be. But your fear is misplaced."

"But I am afraid, Thel."

"You are afraid to see yourself in the future."

"Yes."

"You cannot."

"But I can! I can see shapes…"

"Shapes. Have you ever tried to focus on those shapes?"

"No, I withdraw before I do, without even thinking of it or realizing."

"Ambra, no matter how hard you try, even if you overcome your fear, you cannot see the details of your future."

"So, the future can only be seen in general terms?"

"No, that is not what I said. We believe that you will be able to see many details, of many lives, just not your own."

"Why not my own?"

"Few Readers have ever been able to see much about the future. Those who have seen the future always failed to see themselves. We of Xix believe we understand why. You have begun to study physics in earnest. Do you know the Uncertainty Principle?"

"Something about not being able to know where something is and how fast it's going?"

"That is an example. The general principle involves the effect of the experimenter on the measured. You cannot detect something with high detail without putting energy into the system, for example, using electromagnetic waves to visualize slides in a microscope or atoms with X-rays. The more precise you try to be, the more detail you seek, the more you disturb the system just by measuring it. Try to determine where an atom is exactly, and you add energy to it and speed it up. Try to measure its speed, and you lose track of exactly where it is. You can't have all the information in the system. Therefore, you can only know facts at a certain level of uncertainty. Information is blurred. A version of this applies when Readers try to determine their own place in space-time."

"Can *you* see my future then, Thel?"

"I have tried, as have other Readers on the ship. We cannot. Your mind casts such strong distortions into space-time that it is impossible to Read too close to you in the future."

"What does that mean?"

"It means, Ambra, that you have powers even we do not yet fully comprehend."

This triggered something in my mind. The Xix didn't understand everything. More than most, or so I was led to believe (and so I was to see verified in my experience and my past searches). But like other creatures, even they did not understand the Orbs. They used them, but like the rest, used only what seemed to be the overflow of power from those mysterious spheres. I had felt the depth and power in them. Something more than anything I had ever experienced. More and more I was drawn to them or, rather, to what lay within them.

"Thel, what are the Orbs?"

Thel was silent for a moment, its eyestalks dancing around. After a few minutes, I thought that it would not answer me, or that perhaps I had offended. When it spoke, it was deeply serious, almost with tones of awe.

"You have made the right connection in this conversation, subconsciously, I am sure. The Orbs. They are great wonders that all species have studied, and still study, and yet which remain mysterious even to us. Do you ever wonder why it is that they are found only near planets with life, and mostly intelligent life?"

I had to admit I had not.

"It is much more than curious, Ambra. The Orbs are not natural objects like stars, nebulae, or planets. They are artificial, built several billion years ago for a purpose which lies locked within them."

"Built? By who?"

"This is a great mystery. We do not know. Whatever intelligence made them is beyond anything that we currently know in our galaxy—far, far more developed than anything within the Hegemony, even more than we Xix." I could almost detect a smile again in the tones of the voice.

"We of Xix believe that they were meant as portals. Not for the crude use we make of them, but for something more profound. And we also believe that their presence near sentient worlds is not coincidence but is causal."

I felt a strange feeling deep inside my stomach. "Causal?"

"The Dram consider this a dangerously threatening line of thought, Ambra. It threatens their rule, their power in the galaxy. But we believe that something far older than all of us, as old as the Orbs, and which made them, also was instrumental in the evolution of life, and intelligent life in particular, on all the worlds near an Orb. Most call them the Ancient Ones. We affectionately call them the Gardeners."

"Gardeners? Like we are their plantings?"

"Exactly, Ambra. I'm glad you seem to understand. Yes, we are the young saplings the Gardeners planted as seeds a long time ago in the little incubators we call solar systems."

My head was swimming. "Thel, what does all this mean?"

"It means the galaxy and the Dram are small things in a much greater Universe, and this should give us hope." Thel paused, and then continued in the smiling tone I had come to recognize. "But you are tired, and have had enough for today. We'll take this and other things up tomorrow."

Chapter 21

$$S^n = \left\{ x \in \mathbb{R}^{n+1} : \| x \| = r \right\}$$

Imagination is more important than knowledge.

Albert Einstein

N othing good ever lasts, someone once said.

I would add that even something that is okay is bound to get snatched away, too. I'm sorry to be such a cynic. I've just seen too much.

My time on the Xixian ship was not pleasant, was not what I wanted, but it was a time to heal, a time during which I learned much, when deep seeds were planted that would soon grow. It also turned out to be a short time, after which decency was once again shattered and evil stamped its ugly print upon everything in its path.

The attack came just as we were preparing for our next hyperjump. I sat in one of the navpods, helmet in place, getting ready to guide the ship as we approached an Orb in orbit around a star system with thirty-three planets, if you can believe that. It was mostly a computer-controlled run through the system of mostly dead worlds, each surrounded by automated mining equipment extracting materials for shipment to systems that supported life. We were maybe ten minutes from close approach to the Orb. I closed my eyes for the moment, resting my mind.

I had been making some progress in my studies the last week. More and more, I was allowing myself to face the visions of the future that lay just in front of my awareness. Mostly, it had been nibbling at the edges, predicting highly controlled events in the context of their measuring devices. But recently

I had begun to reach beyond this. Seeing the future has much in common with seeing the past, but the past is not relived. When you see the future of your surroundings, and then watch it play out in front of you, it is at first extremely unsettling. In fact, if you glance just on the edge of the Now, you can recapture the ability to see the world around you, even in blindness. Almost in phase with the Now, it was useful for me. The further from the current moment I glanced, the more out of phase my vision was with what was happening, and yet the future would quickly become the Now. Like beats of sound when the tuning between two strings is just slightly off, my consciousness was battered by the rhythm of events – seen first in my mind, experienced next in my present. It is hard to explain, but it was fun to play with as I got the hang of it.

Just this day I had found myself creeping even farther forward, discovering events several minutes before they happened. I noted it to Thel, wondering if my knowing could lead me to alter the events I'd seen, and then wondering what I would see when I gazed ahead again.

"Paradox is only evident in a simplistic view of time, a linear view of time. Space-time is decidedly non-linear, recursive in manners your scientists have yet to appreciate. Your visions themselves propagate waves through space-time, Ambra, which themselves alter what you see, like your swimming in the water changes the shape of the water in which you swim."

The memory of it prompted my mind forward again. Part of me was tired from it, like using a muscle unaccustomed to exercise. But I was also a little bit drunk on the wonder of the experience, and this thirst for the experience pushed me past the fatigue. I extended my awareness around us, even outside the ship and forward into the future.

My screams brought several Xix running to me.

"Thel. Where is *Thel*?" I called out, my breathing heavy.

"Ambra, Thel is not in the control center. We may send a message if you wish. What is wrong?"

I could barely speak, the shock of my vision like a blow to the stomach. "Oh God…Danger. Something…coming. The ship…attack! *Thel*…"

"The ship is in danger of attack?" repeated one.

Alarms erupted around the control room, the bright lights of the room went dim as emergency defenses were activated. A Xixian pilot called from one of its stations.

"Dram warship. Armed and closing." The Xix switched to their own alien language for more rapid communication. I still didn't know much about their technology. I assumed that they had some sort of defense shield or the like. But really, as so often in my journey from Earth, I was ignorant and helpless. All I could do was wait.

One of the Xix came up to me. "Ambra, we are trying to make a run for the Orb. Please be ready to make the jump. The Dram ship is firing on us, and we may not make it."

"Firing? I don't feel anything."

"You will not unless our defenses fail. We are absorbing tremendous energy from a determined attack of a fully armed Dram battle cruiser. There is only little hope. Please be ready."

I nodded and slipped the helmet on securely. The ship was dashing madly, flying dangerously through this obstacle course of planets and asteroids, heading directly to the growing presence of the Orb. The String we needed was clearly visible, and it would be easy to guide the ship, even at this speed, into its path. It would only be a few minutes at this rate. I was sure we would make it.

I felt the ship lurch horribly, artificial gravity failing, circuits exploding around us as power surges ran through the system. Our course maintained, however. Only moments to the String.

A Xixian voice spoke through my navpod. "Ambra, it is no use. They have hit the Time Turbines. We have normal mobility, but we cannot make the hyperspace jump."

My heart was stuck in my throat. *The Dram!* What would they do? "Will they destroy us here?"

"No. They hit us there to prevent escape. They could have destroyed us. Now, we are trapped in this system and cannot evade them. They want us alive, Ambra. They will board us."

In my mind the vision of the future I had glimpsed poured through my awareness. "Thel…" *No!* I shut my mind to the terrible visions. I couldn't let them board us. I couldn't let it happen. Thel said I could alter visions by my knowledge. *I would!*

The multifaceted and layered glory of the Orb still approached. I stared at it, drawn by my fascination and my desperation. Thel had said that they were portals, that we used them only in a crude and clumsy way. Portals to be opened how? I probed the layers, focusing all my thought on the Orbs, the layers, the interlocking pieces, tunnels in space-time that mixed and dove and intertwined like some sort of multidimensional maze.

"A labyrinth…"

"What was that Ambra?" the voice asked through the communication system.

"Steer us into the Orb."

"What? Ambra, that is impossible. It is certain death."

"*Please*…trust me. I can see….*doors* in the Orb. There are paths through the labyrinth…"

"Ambra, no one has ever approached an Orb straight on and survived. You have great vision, but this…how can we know?"

"Please! If we don't, many will die! It's the Dram!"

There was a moment of silence. Then Thel's voice spoke over the others. "Ambra, the Dram will have us in minutes. Are you sure about this?"

What could I say? Of course I wasn't sure! I didn't have any idea what I was doing. I only knew I had to do something. I *had* seen *something*—structure in the Orbs, and paths. Only I did not know the end point. Could we be lost in a space-time maze forever?

"Thel – I see through the Orb. I can try to guide us through. Give me control of the ship. Let me try."

"OK, Ambra. Better we die in the Orb than at the hands of the Dram. Or worse. I had hoped for more before death. If only to see Xix a last time."

And then, like understanding a geometry problem for the first time, a light spread from my time-sense image of Thel to me, and from me, to the Orb. The light seemed to set a series of tumble locks in motion, one after the other falling into place. *And I saw!* Clear as a trail in the forest, I saw a way through the maze inside.

Right at that moment, I felt the ship's control pass to me, and with a sudden burst, I plunged us directly into the Orb. The sphere seemed to brighten dramatically, as if some button had been pushed, activating it. And then, like the most insane roller coaster ride you could ever imagine, we hurtled through one space-time wormhole after another, darting through countless dimensions in directions that were impossible, perpendicular to everything, that could not exist in the human mind. Faster and faster, as if the Orb were infinitely deep within its finite spherical enclosure, the ship followed the path I directed, the path illuminated for me through means I did not understand. I could focus on nothing else, I could sense nothing around me, only the diving deeper and deeper into the bowels of light and space, bending around a circle yet finding ourselves somewhere new.

It may have lasted a second or a millennium, I could not tell, but there was a *before* and an *after*. The tunnel of light we followed opened not to another branch point but to a circle of darkness in which were embedded countless bright points of light. The ship erupted from an Orb behind us, the sphere glowing brightly as I have never seen the Orbs glow, and just like that, we were in normal space again. A green star shone before us, and very close, the outlines of a crescent of an orange planet.

I lay back in my navpod, sweat pouring down my face. My breathing was labored. This effort had exhausted me, but I knew I had done something never before believed possible. And I had saved us from the Dram.

"Ambra, are you all right?" The tones were Thel's, not elated, but sober, almost still.

"Yeah. Hey, told you I could do it!"

"Ambra, you did."

"Where are we?"

"You don't know?"

"No…crazy, I brought us here, so I guess I should. But I don't."

"It's Xix, Ambra. My home world. You listened to my last wish. Somehow, you heard it, saw its location. You brought me home."

Chapter 22

$$r_s = \frac{2Gm}{c^2}$$

What is life? It is the flash of a firefly in the night. It is the breath of a buffalo in the wintertime. It is the little shadow that runs across the grass and loses itself in the sunset.

Chief Isapo-Muxika ("Crowfoot")

Thel's words made me smile, and I laughed as I lay back in my navpod. "Hey! How about that? *Home.* That is a good word. Safe at last."

"No, Ambra, not safe."

This caused me to open my eyes and sit up in my seat. "What do you mean?"

Thel sounded tired, almost sad. "We've finally figured out how the Dram found us. They've been tracking you since you left Earth, on the chip they embedded in you. Another blind spot for us Xix, the deviousness of the Dram. The Sortax must have warned them that you had been valued as exceptional on Earth. They didn't believe it, I guess, but they told the Dram anyway, just in case. The Dram, never ones to lose an opportunity, yet unwilling to waste too much energy on a wild goose chase, did not place a standard branding chip within you. They placed a hyperspace tracker, able to send weak signals along the Strings, allowing them to go undetected yet always remain aware of your position. We have just deciphered the signal, as it resonated with the Dram warships."

This didn't make any sense. "But they let me be sold to those monsters! I could have died there! If they were curious about my value, they wouldn't have risked wasting me like that!"

"You don't understand the Dram yet, Ambra. Yes, they would have risked it. In their philosophy, their extreme religious beliefs, strength rises to the top, is manifest in survival. If you had died, it would have proved, to them, your lack of worth, however myopic that viewpoint clearly is. But as we thought ourselves clever in zigzagging our way through the String Tree, the chip was reporting our every jump, and soon it became apparent to the Dram that something highly unusual was going on. We were telegraphing ourselves as suspicious through our clever methods to remain hidden. Finally, they converged on us."

"But we lost them. We are safe now."

"Initially, I had hoped so. But the chip was able to broadcast even through that series of dimensional portals you led us through. We intercepted communications as soon as we entered Xixian space. Dram warships were signaled and will arrive here by hyperspace any moment."

"Can't Xix protect us?" I asked with a growing desperation.

"Not overtly, Ambra. We dare not risk the Dram destroying our home world. And believe me, they can. They can be *terrible*."

My breath came in gasps. I was so tired from the journey that I could hardly think. It took an effort even to scan the near past or future to see around me. "What do we do?"

Thel again sounded sad. "There is nothing to be done. Our ship is without power. The damage from the Dram attack, and even more so the trip through the Orb, has left us floating in space, life support barely functioning. Before Xixian ships can come to our aid, the Dram will be here, right off the String from the Orb. We cannot fight, and we cannot run. We will have to be more clever than that. We will allow ourselves to be captured."

"Why?"

"Don't think that Xix has not been informed. They now know everything about our journey and will study the recordings of the Orb traversal. They will soon be convinced of your powers, Ambra, which are beyond even what I might have expected. But they will help only indirectly, or directly later when the time is ripe."

"Time? We won't have time! The Dram will kill us!"

"Kill us? Perhaps many of us, but not you, Ambra. They have seen what you have done. They will put together the information from the chip and the activation of an Orb. They likely already know that an Earth Reader, of potentially great power that they were tracking, was aboard a ship that traversed through an Orb. Nothing like this has been accomplished before. The Dram will do all that they can to learn this secret, to have this power. They will not kill you, not yet, not until they believe they have exhausted all avenues to gain this power for themselves. They will preserve you, Ambra, although they will not be kind. But you must survive! A little while, no matter what they do to you. I promise you, Xix will come. Somehow, we will come. You are our hope, and the doom of us all if the Dram control you."

"Control me? How?"

"Don't think of such things. Word is out. Xix will come. You must hang on, Ambra."

A sharp rapping on my navpod window shook me out of thought. A Xix pilot was standing outside, motioning for me to exit. I stepped out and looked around. The ship was dark still except for emergency lighting. The crew was mostly gone. The ship did look wounded, at death's door.

The pilot spoke. "Thel is coming. The rest of us are assembling near the entrances. A Dram warship has locked onto us, and we are being pulled into a docking position. They will be here momentarily."

Just then a door beside the elevator opened, and Thel moved in. Thel and the pilot spoke in the Xixian language, and then the pilot walked off to the elevator and disappeared within it. Thel walked over and crouched beside me.

"They are coming, Ambra. The slaughter is merciless. They are killing all Xix and scanning humans for your chip, killing those who do not match. We don't have much time, and I need to tell you something before they arrive."

My mind was swimming. Why couldn't we run? Hide? Something? Sitting, waiting for them to take us, it made no sense to my panicked mind. And something was forcing itself to my awareness, something ominous, something familiar. It felt as if the room were adopting some shape in my mind, a place I had seen before but had not visited. *Déjà vu*. Part of me knew it must be important, but I could not focus.

"Listen to me, Ambra!" Thel had gripped my shoulders, all its eyes bent toward me. "A last physics lesson to take with you."

Physics lesson? Had it gone insane?

"Sentient thought is a *field*. A *physical* field like an electromagnetic field or a gravitational field. This won't make sense to you, but it is a truth of the Cosmos. Now, grand unification theory marries all the forces of physics. Not as your scientists would have hoped, something far grander, and far more subtle. But a consequence of these two things is that sentient thought is coupled to the space-time matrix. The more sentient thought, the more complex it becomes, the more coupling. Advanced civilizations with many billions of hyper-intelligent beings can so distort space-time that this effect can be measured as small perturbations in the orbits of their planets."

I was shaking my head, not understanding. This was all gibberish.

"Ambra, thought *itself* sends ripples through space and time. We of Xix had always wondered if this could lead to communication through the space-time matrix."

I heard explosions and screams, the sounds of conflict and stamping of feet. I would have retreated to a corner and hid, but Thel's strong grip kept me in place.

"Communication?" I could only stammer out.

"Telepathy, you would call it. But nothing mystical or magical. You sense distortions in the space-time fabric, Ambra. Thought contributes to this matrix, hence, with your great sensitivity, you can sense those thought ripples. You can *read* minds."

I shook my head again. "Thel, no, I can't." The sounds were closer, louder. The elevator signaled that it was heading downward. What had called it?

"You can, and you *did*. Ambra, how did you bring us to Xix?"

"I don't know, Thel. I just saw the way."

"You saw a way through the Orb, but to where? You couldn't have known *yourself* where Xix lay. Yet what was the last thing I said to you before we entered the Orb?"

My mind raced. The elevator had stopped below and had begun its ascent. There was no time left. Something was coming. "I don't know! You said you wanted to go home once more!"

"Yes! Don't you see, Ambra? My thoughts were strong for home, and you picked them up, needing a path through which to aim in the Orb. You *read* my thoughts, Ambra, just as you *read* the past and the future. Both are embedded in the space-time matrix."

"It can't be true…"

"Ambra, listen to me. It is. Don't turn away from this! You must develop it and harness your powers. You will need all of them to survive what comes next. *Believe* in yourself, Ambra. *Survive.* You are what we have been waiting for."

Thel shuddered and flung her arms in several directions, one of them striking me. I was driven to the floor in pain. With a crash and a flash of light, Thel fell to the floor, charred and smoking, eyestalks filmed over and gray. Lifeless.

Behind Thel were several Dram infantry, weapons aimed in my direction. One stepped forward, raising a strange device toward me. I crouched lower, tears streaming down my face as I looked at what was left of Thel—alien, *other*, one of *Them*, yet my teacher, my healer, a force in the cold of space that cared for me. Thel was not indifferent or hostile. Thel was another thinking being that had spent its last moments to help me.

Tears for this death, and also for my failure to prevent it, dropped out of my sightless eyes. Now the vision that had been lurking on the edges of my awareness locked mercilessly into focus with the present. Now I remembered. I *had* seen this before, in my terrible vision of the future—a vision where Thel died beside me, the vision that had driven me to warn the Xix, and to find a way to pass through the Orb. I had seen this death and had opened the portal to prevent it as much or more as to escape the Dram warships.

But it had *not* saved Thel. My actions to prevent the future fit into the chain of events leading directly to it. *Why?* Because I had not looked closely enough. Because I had not examined carefully and considered the details of my vision. It did not console me that there had not been time, that the Dram attack was imminent and forced me to act. But in this it was clear that the future and its complexities were not to be taken lightly. I wept bitterly for my naïveté.

I examined the immediate present. The Dram soldiers put down a scanner and spoke in their hideous clicking language. Two armed soldiers raced beside me and lifted me harshly to my feet and dragged me forward in front of the leader.

"They are property of the Dram. Resist not otherwise they are eliminated," came the clumsy sounds of the Dramian translator.

I went limp and was quickly hustled by the soldiers through the Xixian ship and onto the Dram warcraft. Along the way, I stared helplessly down at the bodies of Xix and humans, side by side, gunned down and left to rot by the Dram army. I felt a terrible anger grow inside of me, like I had never felt before, even after everything that had been done to me.

I vowed as their troops tossed me through the ship that I would find a way to avenge those that died, for what the Dram had done to me, to my world, and to all the worlds beneath their savage rule.

Chapter 23

$$ds^2 = -\left(1 - \frac{2M}{r}\right)dt^2 + \frac{1}{1 - 2M/r}dr^2 + r^2 d\Omega^2$$

He who has a why to live can endure almost any how.

Friedrich Nietzsche

I t wasn't long before they came to question me.

I had been thrown harshly into some sort of holding cell, which, like the rest of the Dram warship, had been made simply, efficiently, and with such a harsh sense of purpose that it bordered on architectural cruelty. Like the underwater chamber on the Sortax home world, the same strange metals and luminescence embedded inside the materials characterized the construction. Armed guards were posted outside my cell, which was surprisingly open. There were only three walls, the fourth some sort of invisible force field that let in light and air but resisted firmly any attempts to press against it. The harder one pushed, the harder the invisible wall became. I managed to slowly press a few fingertips half an inch or so through the resistance, but that was all I could manage.

The guards never glanced in my direction with their eyestalks. They seemed to have no fears of my escape. I suppose dumb humans don't score very highly in the "escape risk" column. And that pretty much was the reality for me. Soon I gave up and sat down in a corner facing the invisible wall, knees pulled up to my chest and my arms wrapped around them. But I didn't cry. Something else was inside me. So much anger and determination.

A Dram officer appeared from nowhere, clicking to the guards, who deactivated the shield wall. The officer entered with a guard alongside. It was shorter than the guards, dressed in a less militaristic outfit, and it carried no weapons. Its eyestalks were surrounded with small bubbles that seemed to float around the central eyeballs but without touching them. *Hi-tech alien glasses?* I wondered to myself. The insect bent its body nearly in half, the lower abdomen and its legs parallel with the floor, the upper part of its body and "head" at nearly a ninety-degree angle to the rest, the eyestalks and little bubbles pointed toward me.

"They are it, which opened the Orb?" it began as the translator barked the broken English at me.

Thel had admonished me to survive, but I could not bring myself to reply to these killers. The insect head tilted left, then right, seeming to seek a better view of me and my silence.

"They are it, which opened the Orb?" it repeated. Still I said nothing.

Then it began saying what I assumed was the same thing over and over in one Earth language after another. After ten or fifteen of these repetitions, it began to get irritating, and I figured speaking to this thing was better than getting a tour of badly translated Dram in all of Earth's tongues.

"English," I spat out angrily. "I speak English."

The insect was quiet, just staring at me.

"They are it, which opened the Orb?" it rang out again.

"Yes, for God's sake. Now, can we move on beyond this?"

The insect pulled out a small device, horribly reminiscent of the one the Sortax representative on Earth had nearly killed me with. Before it could activate the scanner I shouted out loudly, startling the bug and causing several of its many back feet to retreat slightly. The guard partially raised its weapon.

"Careful! You have to use the *lowest* setting on that thing or you'll kill me, and then I won't be any use to you. I am a powerful Reader, and I am far more sensitive to the space-time matrix than others."

"Applicable is this?" it asked.

"Yes! Try the low setting. You'll see."

The Dram officer adjusted the device and aimed it at me. I tensed, but it was not painful. A bit like having several different-colored laser beams flit over your eyes at very low levels. Compared to the Orbs, such simple, boring patterns.

"They are much highly cannot be measured." The Dram turned off the machine. "Why negative the Sortax explain rather to us?"

"Because they are stupid squid-heads," I added helpfully.

"Yes, they are stupid. To be punished." The officer tapped several things into a small device it removed and then replaced it on a belt around its upper abdomen. The thing then just stared at me, silently, for several moments.

Thel's words came back to me then, those mad words about me reading minds. The Xix had said it was real and that I could not turn away from it, but that I would need all my skills to survive. I decided to trust Thel's final words, to believe in them with all that I had. If they were true, then I would find out now and probe my captors.

I closed my eyes as the Dram creature observed me silently. Being blind, it didn't do that much, but it was long habit from sighted years when trying to focus. Slowly, using all my concentration and the meditative techniques Thel had taught me, I scanned with my unique organ, my sixth sense. Past and future spilled back and forth over me, but I ignored them, seeking for something different, something tied to the creature in front of me.

And then it happened, like seeing an optical illusion play out its different visuals in front of you. A subtle, so subtle and effervescent shimmering of a glow beside me came slowly into focus, and I knew, I could *feel* that it came from the presence of the two Dram in the cell with me. One was simpler, far more angular and hard. *The soldier*. The other was still harsh, as all Dram would turn out to be, but more complex, layered. There was a deeper intelligence and complexity in this one that was not in the other. Its thoughts disturbed the space-time matrix in several dimensions at once.

But also so much fear. *That* I could recognize even in this alien creature. A deep fear that was totally absent from the mind of the guard. This intrigued me and gave me a sense of my own power in this place. This Dram officer sought something from me that was terribly important.

My eyes opened. "Why do you fear me?" I probed, deciding to offer a wild opening gambit.

The insect once again recoiled, taking several steps back, then stopped. "They are an intelligent," it finally responded. It decided to resort to a lie. "The Dram fear nothing! But we are we try to we include, what you to be have made."

"You mean opening the Orb?"

"Yes! How human creatures, a nothing member of Hegemony, is in position so that does make such a thing? Which secrecy did you learn of Holy Orbs?"

Holy Orbs? This was getting weird. Since when did aliens get religion?

"Are you a priest?"

I felt a surge of anger from the consciousness of the creature.

"No! Never! I do not grasp the idiots of those superstitions! I besides the fact that power in the Orbs, it seems I and like me, understand those respect in order to control, seeking those."

Control? Power? A technologist! A scientist, perhaps. This made sense, and many of my readings of its mind now fell into place giving me a much clearer image of the personality and motivations of the creature I was dealing with. Motivations to be exploited, perhaps.

"I can control them. You wish me to give you my secret?"

The insect's feet padded up quickly, bringing its hideous face close to mine.

"When Dram wish, they take," it said ominously. I had to be careful.

"If you make a mistake, and you harm me, you may damage my mind, and you will never learn the secret. Do you dare take that risk now, alone? What will your punishment be if you fail?"

The wash of anxiety from the creature was like a prismatic spray. Again it retreated several steps. "They are a human intelligent, yes. Special. But in Dram is skillful large number very with persuasion. The Emperor thinks, is grasped that we consume this you-power; It orders. Then this word of you has not importance. Until time, enjoy the existence."

The officer clicked toward the guard who escorted the creature through the door and re-engaged the force field, leaving me alone, and for the moment, free from their probes.

But for how long? I could feel the time-tugs of hyperspace jumps—we had made at least four since I was brought onboard. The Dram could not go directly to the destination they wished as I had done by activating the Orbs. They were limited to the off-shooting Strings, and had to follow the indirect routes of the String Tree, heading eventually, I presumed, to their home world. The nexus of the Dram Hegemony, with their Emperor, and all their numbers "very with persuasion." Soon, I would be in their hands, and while I doubted that they could learn how I controlled the Orbs – I didn't even know – I knew that they very well might kill me in trying to find out. Or worse. I had to find a way out of this, for so many, not just myself.

Every expansion of my abilities has been centered on life crisis, and it was no different this time. I sat down in the cell, crossing my legs, closing my eyes, and throwing out everything that had been a part of my hiding from the future. I decided to take my potential seriously. I decided to risk anything, even my sanity, to cross over the planes of possibility and look the future square in the face. More than my life might depend on me becoming what I was meant to be, to let the seed finally sprout. If the Xix were right, perhaps the Resistance and freedom for so many in the galaxy rested upon it. Yes, it was megalomaniacal. But you can't let humility get in the way of the truth.

Nothing in my life or training prepared me for what was about to happen. I sank into a deep trance, my awareness focusing inward until I could count each heartbeat, analyze each slow breath as my lungs drew in the air and then forced it out. The universe around me became infinitely distant. But the secret in meditation is finding without seeking, and at this terrible distance, it became microscopically close to me. Slowly, one by one, the obstacles my psychology had placed in the way of my vision were toppled over by the force of my will. Each felt like a rush of panic, screaming to go no further, my soul terrified of what lay on the other side. But now I was filled with purpose greater than my fears, and I knocked them down.

Did you ever put a bottle in the freezer, super-cool it, pull it out hours later unfrozen, then tap it hard? It freezes all at once before your amazed eyes. That's how my sixth sense finally awakened fully within me. That enormous organ, grown to grotesqueness at the hands of my fellow humans, opened its odd eyes from a long slumber. It was like the sledgehammer striking the surface of the dam over and over, until the small cracks became fissures, trickling water, and then, with one fateful blow, the concrete shattered, and the water gushed forth with terrible force. I pushed through my fears and weakness, and the future burst over me so that it could not be stopped; a thousand visions flooded my mind, and continued to do so over the next few days so that I could not hope to even process them all.

I fought a strange battle to stay focused, to hold these visions at bay, to integrate the Now and the coming times. Present, Past, and the enormous Future churned and mixed within me so that one blurred into the other in a confused fashion—future events gave birth to past ones, the Past to both the Future and the Now. Cause and effect became meaningless, and it was as if I stepped out of Time and saw a giant ocean of events, tossing and twisting before me, waves undulating and splashing and morphing. There was no center from which to observe, no arrow of time, only the ever-churning currents of an infinite ocean.

I lost myself in this sea, set adrift never to find a place on which to stand. During this trance, I responded to nothing, even as, I later discovered, Dram medics and scientists tried to revive me. For three weeks of travel through the String Tree, and two more weeks in a hospital on the Dram home world, I lay unmoving, unresponsive in a deep coma. Fed intravenously, my captors, and representatives from several other species, watched with great anxiety my condition.

But I found my way home. The meaning of how it happened, I do not know. Somewhere, as the mists cleared before my eyes over the tempestuous sea, I saw Ricky smiling and laughing in the distance. I followed his voice, swimming against the raging currents, to some place within me where there was only me and the love I had. And there the sound of his laughter was full and loud, spanning my awareness.

I had finally understood what he tried to tell me that day.

Chapter 24

We do not rest satisfied with the present. We anticipate the future as too slow in coming, as if in order to hasten its course; or we recall the past, to stop its too rapid flight. So imprudent are we that we wander in the times which are not ours, and do not think of the only one which belongs to us; and so idle are we that we dream of those times which are no more, and thoughtlessly overlook that which alone exists.

Blaise Pascal

I drifted in space once again.

Space was terribly still. Uncountable patterns of stars lit the darkness around me. Behind, the golden light of the sun pushed forward, and, like a giant sail, I drew speed from the solar wind. Slowly, irresistibly, I accelerated, gaining speed past Mercury. Then past the sulfurous clouds of greenhouse Venus. In front of me, the Moon appeared once more, yet behind it, like a quarter surrounding a dime, the blue, white, and green-brown of Earth captured my vision.

Earth! There she hung in the blackness, in all her glory. After the violet seas of the Sortax home world, the alien structures of the Dram, the orange deserts of Xix, and the countless sterile and horrible things I had seen, even the saint-like Xix that still caused primal discomfort in my simian brain, here before me was that one place in all the expanse of seeming infinity that was right for me. For all human beings. *Home.*

I felt myself crying and smiling broadly at the same time. I rushed like some gleeful child into the arms of her mother, dashing past the lifeless Moon, arms outstretched and encompassing the blue marble as it approached me. *I was finally going home.*

My smile foundered, broke and faded like clouds on a mountainside. A terrible mask of horror replaced it as I watched in near madness as the planet I held in my arms began to dissolve. From pole to pole, sea to land, the sphere shattered like some stained-glass window, the separate fragments blurring and melting in my hands. Frantically, I worked my fingers and palms, trying to reshape the thing as if it were some melting snowball on a warm spring day. But there was nothing to stop the merciless process. Dripping right through my clasped fingers like flowing blue-brown ink, the Earth *melted*, and I cried out in anguish as the liquid poured through, then into the blackness of space, only to dissipate, evaporate into a faint mist and then to nothingness.

My scream echoed through empty space like some wolf's howl in a stone cathedral, reverberating and interfering, wailing for a soul abandoned and trapped forever in the cold of space, unable to perish, unable to escape, and forever unable to find its way home again.

Chapter 25

$$r_{\pm} = \mu \pm (\mu^2 - a^2)^{1/2}$$

No visiting angel, or explorer from another planet could have guessed that this bland orb teemed with vermin, with world-mastering, self-torturing, incipiently angelic beasts.

Olaf Stapledon

The first thing I saw when I awoke was the monstrous form of a Xixian medic. For a moment, I thought I was back on the ship with Thel. A false relief spread over me that the nightmare of the Dram attack and Thel's death, and the nightmare that was a dream of the dying Earth, were both unreal. Then I saw the Dram workers standing around the medic, and the doom and dread of reality struck me solidly in the stomach. Along with it came a resurgence in the grim determination I had developed since becoming a captive of the Dram.

"You are awake," said the Xixian medic. The Dram insects crowded around behind the Xix observing, their many hands and fingers tapping against each other loudly yet not interfering.

"Why does a Xix work with the Dram?" I wondered aloud.

"The Xix serve everywhere within the Hegemony," it chirped. "Especially in the medical sciences, where our talents and technology cannot be perverted so easily to actions that run counter to our being. We often prove quite useful," it said, with some seeming emphasis. I wondered if it meant something more than it seemed to be saying. Thel had said the Xix would know about me, would work to help me. Was this medic communicating this?

There was no time to find out. A Dram military officer stormed into the room, its composite armor clicking nearly as loudly as its many feet and the communication to other Dram in the room. It turned toward the Xixian medic. With several bursts of clicking sounds between them, the Xix bowed and left the room. The Dram officer turned to me.

"Depending upon us the best efforts employed, had in order to maintain human, its life. They must better prove the Emperor their worth."

"And if I don't?" I rebelliously replied.

"Then, they will end." It signaled to other officers who came in and began to wheel my bed out of the room.

"No, wait," I interrupted, pushing myself up and swinging my legs over the side. "I am well enough to walk."

The officer signaled to them to release the bed, and I walked of my own accord. The trance had weakened me, and my muscles had not been used for weeks while I was in the deep coma. But I had not been ill or injured, and I found the walk, while stiff and shaky, very much within my powers. Down several hallways and to an adjoining building filled with prison cells, I finally was stopped in front of a cell similar to the one I had been held in on the Dram warship. The force field was deactivated, and the Dram soldiers pushed me inside, reactivating the screen.

The officer stared across the barrier at me. "This health, it is good therefore to be maintained. That we being expected from directly, makes that trial is begun possible. The tomorrow supporter, the Advocate, is to be allotted. That it cooperates to investigation, is best your, with of everything where you are required is made clear."

Yes, best that I make *everything* clear to them, I'm sure. With that hardly veiled threat, it turned and hustled out of the corridor, leaving me to my thoughts and the silence of the Dram prison ward. I shook my head, wondering what this trial would be like, and what an Advocate could be in this system of justice with the Dram.

I was not left alone for long. Within a few hours, a group of four or five Dram that I now easily identified as members of the Technologists—as I liked to think of them—came tramping into my cell. The guards felt to me less than pleased to allow the entrance, clearly far preferring to obey the military wing in the Dram power structure, whatever it might be.

The Techies positioned themselves in a semicircle around me. Already, I had probed enough of the immediate future to anticipate their first actions, and I spoke to prevent any unpleasant scans of my brain.

"Before you pull out your scanners and fry my brain, please turn them down to the lowest setting. I am very sensitive, and can easily respond to your weakest signals."

The Techies nervously twitched and exchanged glances. Finally, one in the middle of the semi-circle revealed itself to be the leader and spoke.

"You expect our energies well."

I decided just to unload on them early. "I *read* your actions. I saw it in my immediate future."

"You are so much powerful Reader?" it asked.

"I can do this and many more things."

"You have then the open of the Orbs," it said, even the lousy translator somehow getting across in tone the awe behind the question.

"Yes."

"This possible with from Ancient Ones?"

"It comes from me!"

This elicited a lot of excited clicking between them.

"It should they are sharing these informations with us, that we can present to the Emperor!"

"I will not do that."

"It should! They will suffer in the hands of Emperor if there is not! And they will be in the danger of partisans that will seek death before they attend to what is known or can made be. For them, you gestate the Heresy, that contaminating the Holy Orbs. They will not allow in it in order to they will live. Only death given with them. It should there is saving and it say to us how this thing is made!"

Decoding their longer translations was always a headache. "The *partisans*? Oh, I see. The Priests." I didn't care if the term was appropriate; getting tangled in the petty politics of this murderous society was the least of my worries. I had seen too much. I decided not to break the news to this thing gently.

"Let me tell you something, insect. In exactly thirty seconds, an angry group of your priestly friends is going to show up here. You will have a screaming fight with them, and their guards will shout at the guards here, and you will be promptly thrown out on your exo-skeletoned asses. I doubt after that you'll get the chance to be alone with me again. So, there won't be a chance for me to tell you anything." I leaned forward, so angry I nearly spit in his eyestalks. "But even if there were, I wouldn't tell you a thing, you murderous piece of Dram vermin. You have enslaved my species. It is because of you that my parents were gunned down in cold blood and thrown into the sea. Because of your power-hungry rule, the galaxy is in bondage. I've watched Dram soldiers murder the innocent and brave. I will die before giving you the key to more power than you already have. And you might as well calm down. Here are your priest friends."

The anger radiating from the group was so great, I feared that they might harm me. But I had vision they did not, and as I spoke my last sentence, the priestly delegation stormed into the cell area, and the shouting (or clicking) match began. Soon, the guards forcibly removed the Techies to great waves of gloating from the Priests. They exchanged angry clicks all the way down the hallway until they were out of earshot. Finally, for the night, I was offered some peace.

But peace would not come. I began to shift through the visions of the future that had nearly consumed me, and that, at a moment's notice, if I did not hold them back, could flood over me again, blocking out consciousness. To stay within the Now, I had to exert enormous control, letting only small streams of information through, holding back the flood with willpower like a dam. Slowly, I was mapping out the near future, and more and more, what lay beyond. This conscious sifting through the events to come was controlled, logical, progressive, and exhausting.

The parade of visions loomed in my consciousness, so many to consider, too many to count, but I was beginning to separate the meaningless, the inconsequential, from those that were important to my life and to the lives of those I might one day affect. Imagine being blind, and then granted sight, opening your eyes at the top of a high peak, staring down over lower peaks, valleys, rivers, cities with bustling people and, in the distance, the glint of a great sea. Then imagine that you had never processed visual information, so that even the details of a falling leaf or the drops from melting snow could grab your mind's attention for hours if you were not careful to focus. Finally, mix in the fact that, down there below you, people you care for were in danger, and you had to find out where and how. This was something like my problem – so much vision, so little experience, and nearly no time.

Inspiration was found only in the world of dreams. Finally, completely drained, I would find sleep overtaking me, and in dreams I would make imaginative leaps to future events of more significance. And dominating everything, over and over again the next few weeks, was my vision of the melting Earth. It hung in my psyche like some bomb waiting to explode. *What was its meaning?* To know, I could not rely on the imagery of dreams. I would have to find my way to that point in the future consciously, and that would likely require a great effort to forge ahead, skipping careful deliberation, risking the dam breaking over me again.

The time was coming, I knew, when I would have to take this risk. But not tonight! I would have to face a lot tomorrow, and I had to face it sane and controlled. The dream would come.

Yes, I remembered, very soon, it would come.

Chapter 26

$$G = (H \otimes I) \, C_N$$

The single biggest problem in communication is the illusion that it has taken place.

George Bernard Shaw

A day lasts thirty-six hours on the Dram home world, which throws the human biological clock pretty out of whack. We can reset at different start points on a twenty-four-hour clock, but we don't do very well when the duration moves far beyond twenty-four hours in either direction. Here you remain in a constant state of surreal suspension, your body never able to adjust. Never completely awake, never restful in sleep.

The star in this system is a hideous red. Not the blending and warm red before nightfall of a sunset on Earth, but a constant, powerful red that bled into everything, washed out all other colors of human perception, even in my reconstructed memories of color. A giant star, already having burned through its store of hydrogen, ballooned up upon fusing the heavier helium. The Dram had evolved fairly rapidly from simple organisms that had made little headway in the cold, pre-red giant phase of this solar system. With the expansion of the star, their more distant planet had warmed dramatically, becoming a hothouse jungle for many hundreds of millions of years, and then, slowly, a desert world. The Dram were tough, harsh and unforgiving like the desert, capable of flowering at times, but all too often bringing death to those they encountered.

When the door opened the next morning, it was hard for me to know how long it had truly been since I lay down. In many ways, it didn't matter. I hadn't slept—like some feverish convalescent, I had bobbed up and down the entire night on an ocean of visions. The hard reality of my prison was a bracing contrast.

In walked a small guard of Dram, few in numbers, armored and towering insectoidal forms. I loathed them. Behind them entered a Xix with its absurd elegance. A captain of the guard clicked to the Xix, and its troop strode menacingly out of the room. The Xix paused a moment as the shield was reactivated, then bowed to me politely and seated itself on the ground across from my bed shelf.

I had slowly detached from the vision processing as the guards entered and raised my head slightly as the Xixian creature had entered. Now I pulled myself up and sat on the bed shelf with my feet on the floor, half in a trance still, waiting patiently for the Xix to speak.

"Greetings, Ambra Dawn! I am Waythrel of Xix, your Advocate for the Tribunal."

My *Advocate*. Well, this was exciting and unexpected. A Xix! "I am very honored and pleased to find that you are here on my behalf, Waythrel," I began formally, yet brimming with joy. "I feared one of these hideous bugs would be charged with the half-hearted attempt at defending me."

"The Dram often use Xix in official roles. We are masters of their language and laws, and are constantly updated with new tools from Xix itself. We are granted many privileges for our loyal and useful service. Your tone with the Dram shows that you are reckless and do not fully understand your hosts."

It's warning me. These Xix, always teaching! My mind raced, remembering the riddle games I played with Thel. "Updated from Xix" – it knows about me like Thel said! "Privileges for loyalty" – its position as my Advocate will be compromised if becomes clear to the Dram that the Xix are in a conspiracy to help me. "Reckless and not understanding"….what did it matter what I said? Unless here confidentiality meant nothing. Yes, that was it. The Dram were listening to everything! We had to be very careful.

"My teacher was Thel of Xix before my journey here," I began, hoping to convey that I was still a student and would do my best to learn. "I am ignorant of many things. Please be patient with me."

Waythrel removed strange devices from pockets in its robe. As these were activated, several opened to project visual information in discrete planes in the room, as if invisible screens had been lowered from the ceiling. Others opened like semicircular keyboards, one for each upper arm, with hundreds of keys for their many digits, and Waythrel began to type at what seemed like the speed of light.

"Good, then we may begin. You have much to learn before the Tribunal, and now only two Dramian days, or four of your Earth days, to prepare. Your very life is at stake, Ambra. I hope everything I have learned of you is true, because you will need all of your talents before the Tribunal."

Was it saying that I would need to forecast? As a Xix, it must know that I could not see myself clearly in any future.

"Not for points of law and theology – I will handle those myself, as much as that is allowed. But for your own questioning, you will need to understand the context in which you are being examined, Ambra. I will need to communicate this and much more with you, and you will need to understand me very thoroughly." It paused. "Sometimes, I think that these translators we make, however powerful, are almost useless. If only there were more direct ways to communicate these difficult things without the errors of language conversion."

Telepathy. It was telling me to use telepathy! Of course! How else to talk openly about important yet dangerous topics when the Dram were listening in? Somehow Thel had communicated this power to Xix. And somehow, I had to make this work. I had now read minds and feelings on several occasions, but had never tried to read details or send information. Could that be done? Or would I have to speak in this coded way Waythrel did? Could I do that without revealing to the Dram what I was doing? I doubted *that* very much.

"Yes, Waythrel, I think I understand what you mean. I am only an Earth creature, please, put these concepts to me simply, strongly, focusing on the key elements so that I might understand." If this was going to work, Waythrel would have to concentrate on the ideas intensely, and not in a complicated Xixian way, so that hopefully I could grasp them. I closed my eyes and focused inwardly again, breathing deeply. Slowly, sensing the glow of its awareness in front of me, I reached out to the mind of my Advocate.

I momentarily recoiled from the complexity. The mind of a Xix made the Dram seem so simplistic. Like crystalline spider webs, its maze of thought dangled all around me, as I peered deeply and gravitated toward a brighter glow within. There were ideas I could sense but not understand. Others were accessible to me, and my mind clothed them in images, short memories playing in front of me like a video.

Amazed, I watched as Waythrel opened a memory to me and strangely did so through the eyes of another Xix as it exited a hidden chamber in the ship that I had piloted through the Orb. The Dram warriors had left the craft taking me back to their warship. This Xixian crew member had run to the bridge and found Thel just after the attack. The Xixian had bent down and touched the fibrous material between what had once been Thel's animated eyestalks. When their membranes met, images poured from Thel's dying mind, now only a faint light but still with a last contribution to make. Visions of the final few weeks on the ship, up through the activation of the Orb and the final conversation with Thel, entered the mind of this Xix. It was like a life download. Now this Waythrel had acquired the memories.

You see, part of Thel is within me now, Ambra. With all the Xix. And I know much of what you are and have done. Many in Xix do. We have distributed these memories.

I heard these thoughts! How would I reach back?

"I'm calmer now, Waythrel," I said out loud, "and ready to learn what you have to teach me. I feel that a part of Thel is with me in you."

I knew I had reached my mark by the long pause that followed. When it spoke next, I realized that our conversation today would be unlike any I had ever had.

"In what I say about the Dram law and custom, Ambra, you must listen at two levels," Waythrel began, "doing your best to understand each. I'll need you to let me know from time to time that you have understood all meanings in this complicated discussion."

The Xix's words echoed in my mind. *I mean hearing me here as well, Ambra. Please answer affirmative and nod your head three times if you do.*

"Yes, I understand," I said, following the instructions.

"Good. To begin, you must understand that historically, there has been a balance between the religious caste and the naturalistic caste here on Dram. This division has caused many conflicts, at times creating deadly wars, but it has been preserved through the ancient times of pre-technological civilization throughout the establishment of the Hegemony."

It is in this division of faith and reason that the Dram are at their most superficially powerful, but in truth at their weakest. In the long term, such an artificial separation of the undivided light of revelation is a sickness of the mind and soul, only too obvious in the myopia and brutality of the Hegemony. Societies that cannot believe are sterile. Societies that cannot doubt are arrogant fools driving over a cliff. The Dram sway between them in violence, tearing apart what must be united.

My mind was spinning. It was like hearing a conversation in one ear and a commentary in the other. I concentrated and tried to integrate these two streams of information.

"The Holy Orbs are at a nexus in this conflict. To the religious caste, the Believers, they represent a revelation in a spiritual dimension and must be approached in a purified and humble state before the Creator of the universe. The scientific caste, the Naturalists, sees them as primarily physical manifestations and seek to harness their power. Such actions are viewed as sacrilege by the Believers, who consider profiteering from the Holy Orbs to be a sin against God. Several millennia ago, when the Dram first encountered the Holy Orbs, and earlier Naturalists spoke of making use of the Strings, the dispute erupted into a civil war that exterminated nearly one-fourth of the Dram population."

Remember, Ambra, any species that can so viciously turn on its own kind will, with much less deliberation, become murderous toward those very different from them.

Part of me squirmed thinking about the actions of my own species, of Earth's numerous descents into slaughter. Were we any better than the Dram?

We must focus on the Orbs, Ambra. The Tribunal will make a decision about your life, and the manner of your death, based on how they view your manipulation of the Orbs. We of Xix feel that there is no safe judgment for you. If the Believers prevail, it will be torture and execution for heresy and sacrilege. If the Naturalists win the day, it will be mental enslavement to harness your power. We are convinced of your worth to the Resistance. Therefore, we are planning a terrible risk, to intervene on your behalf and subject ourselves to the wrath of the Dram. Please nod three times that you have heard these last thoughts and understand them.

Even though I was very shaken by what Waythrel said, stunned to hear that an entire species would risk themselves for a single alien creature, I managed to nod my head and to even respond with words.

"Such extermination in the Dram wars is something I would never wish to see, Waythrel."

The Xixian Advocate bowed slightly toward me. "In all such sacrifice, there is the belief that a higher purpose is being served. In this motivation, you may understand many choices, many actions."

I cannot yet tell you what we will do. We are placed in numerous positions of power across Dram and can therefore manipulate much to our designs. But this must be planned thoroughly, because for so many reasons, we cannot fail.

"At the Tribunal, you will be questioned by Advocates from both castes, who will then debate your fate before the High Inquisitor."

"Who is this?"

"The Inquisitor holds an office created many thousands of years ago to aid in mediation between the castes. The position, second in power only to the Emperor, is entrusted to an individual who must balance law and Dram culture between the Believers and Naturalists. This individual must come from one of the Isolation Zones, neutral ground in which the teachings of both castes are withheld until the Dram pass the age of maturity—roughly thirty Earth years. This is to ensure no bias in judgments."

And therefore this position is one of the most corrupt in the system. Enormous bribes are the norm, and those that climb to this position of power too often are hungry for such benefits. Beware the High Inquisitor!

"Tomorrow, you will be brought before the Inquisitor for an assessment in advance of the Tribunal. Here, you may receive offers of clemency should you acquiesce to the Emperor's will."

So much information! Information that I should be internalizing and thinking about. But I couldn't. I was still reeling from the offer of the Xix to risk so much to save me. I knew they were going to do this because they hoped I might provide a way out of the bondage to the Dram. But I also knew that it would mean certain death for the Xix, whether or not I was what they hoped. In my mind, I wouldn't be a hero, I'd be a murderer, responsible for the destruction of an entire species, the brightest and kindest and wisest I had encountered. I didn't know what to do. Something inside me rebelled against it. It couldn't be right. And my mind dashed forward in space-time like some mad thing, heedless of getting caught in those infinitely complex folds that had nearly killed me the last time. I *had* to see enough of the right possible future to know what to do!

Ambra, we of Xix will risk much. All. We need you to promise us that you will do all within your power to follow our plan when it is developed. Soon, I will come back with instructions. I need you to tell me now that you understand, and commit to this to us and our plan.

What could I do? I could not lie, not to the Xix, not in this situation. But I could not let them do this. I steeled myself. What I *could* do was go along with their plan until I developed a better one. I had at least seventy-two hours until the Tribunal. I had to find a way out of this nightmare, just like I did with the Orb. Only this time I would look closely enough not to jump from one trap into another. This time, there would be no mistakes.

Ambra? Did you hear me? Please respond.

I was so full of emotion, that what happened next was over before I realized it had begun, and yet it opened the final door to the destiny that awaited me.

Before I could formulate a response in words, I felt myself emotionally reach out and answer Waythrel. In that instant, I watched it recoil slightly, its mental web showing some disorganization, and I sensed anxiety, surprise, and then awe as the webs reassembled into new and delicate patterns.

Ambra Dawn, what have you done?

What *had* I done? I didn't know how to answer. Its reaction – had I caused it? How? I looked in confusion over toward the alien creature.

You have entered my mind. Your thoughts were impressed in my consciousness. There was another pause. *We never expected this. Even Thel underestimated your potential.*

"Waythrel, please. I am not sure I have understood everything that you have told me today."

"You have understood much, I am sure. And we will speak more tomorrow."

Its thoughts continued to sound in my consciousness. *What has just happened is as important as your power with the Orbs, Ambra. I must report this immediately and seek advice. It makes you far more dangerous, even to us, than anyone could have imagined.* Waythrel paused in thought, concentrating on me with its alien senses that displayed odd and confusing images in my mind. Its next thoughts shocked me.

It means you not only Read, Ambra, you also do something few have even dared suggest might someday be possible. You touched my mind, its thoughts—my consciousness. This goes far beyond merely altering my mind, because of what it means to do that. Remember your lessons with Thel! To alter my mind means that you can modify space-time itself. This is unprecedented. It is terrifying. No one knows where such power could lead. Ambra, you are not just a Reader. You are a Writer. The first Writer.

"Until tomorrow, Ambra Dawn. Think about what I have told you."

Waythrel signaled to the guards, who disarmed the shield, and let the lanky Xixian past. I curled up once more on my bed, exhausted from today's efforts and now stunned by this recent exchange. *A Writer?*

Things were moving too fast.

Chapter 27

$$S(\Psi) = \tfrac{1}{2}\langle \Psi \mid Y(i)Y(-i)Q_B \mid \Psi \rangle + \tfrac{1}{3}\langle \Psi \mid Y(i)Y(-i) \mid \Psi * \Psi \rangle$$

Nothing is more despicable than respect based on fear.

Albert Camus

T he red starlight waxed and waned, forcing its relentless way through my room across the small force field–buttressed window on the far wall. But I was becoming increasingly abstracted, diving into future memories and sifting, beginning to see the patterns of possible futures, of paths through them toward the goals I sought—escape, freedom, and ways of preserving the lives of the innocent who sought to help me. Waythrel returned several times over the next day and, noticing my withdrawal, questioned me. But while my ability to penetrate minds and use telepathy increased at a frightening rate, my focus was elsewhere, and, as yet, I dared not explain why to my Advocate. I absorbed the lessons to some degree, but, increasingly, as I worked my way through the future's maze, it became less important. Many of the details around my future self I could not see, and those that I could, many I ignored to find my way to a path that led home with the least suffering for all.

I did learn that my alterations of Waythrel's mind, the imprint of my own thoughts in its own, hadn't done any damage. The Xixian medics had performed scans of the brain-like organ in Waythrel's chest and had seen nothing unusual. Apparently, this telepathic communication I used was something like an external stimulus. But Waythrel was uneasy, voicing concerns that it need not be that way. And with the ability to modify space-time itself, all the Xix were very concerned about how my powers would develop.

All that mattered to me was that I got us all out of this. I had seen enough to know that, in the paths where I did nothing, where others took the lead, even the Xix, there would be untold carnage and chaos. Genocidal fires would smolder across many worlds in a galactic war.

Not that way. I began to see another future in the jungle of time. A safer path. *Safe for many.* A great tragedy loomed over the time horizon in my consciousness, but it was spatially distant and not dependent on what I could do. At that time it was bigger than my own abilities. I would face it as I had to.

As I struggled to find an answer, the hour arrived for me to be brought before the High Inquisitor. An unusually large and formally attired troop of Dram escorted Waythrel and me through the detention zone, via ground transports to another building, and finally into the chambers of the Inquisitor.

The office was held by a surprisingly unimposing Dram. One might call it a runt if it weren't still over six feet tall. From what I had learned of these creatures, it was old, its slow movements the best giveaway – at least to an alien life-form like me who had trouble distinguishing the signs of aging in other species. The Inquisitor was perched more than ten feet above us behind a green and gold counter, like some too-tall judge's bench. It looked down on us —no doubt literally and figuratively—from above during this short but very informative *assessment*.

Waythrel and I were marched in front of the bench, allowed a small but still claustrophobic space by the Dram guard. Everything was taller than me – the seven-foot-high Dram guards, the elevated Inquisitor, and even my Advocate. What did it matter? I had my own strengths.

Waythrel and the Inquisitor clicked back and forth for at least ten minutes. The Xix had told me that it would try to have the Tribunal abolished but had little faith that this could be achieved. There was clear documentation of my manipulation of the Orbs, and this made me a center of questions for power and religion in the Hegemony. After the discussion swayed back and forth between them, the High Inquisitor waved off Waythrel and addressed me.

"You have been informed of the charges?" The translator was of Xixian manufacture, an unusual choice for the Dram who were so suspicious of foreign devices that they most often chose to use their own, far inferior machines. Unless they were dying and needed Xixian medics, of course. Or, in this case, when a member was less intimidated. Waythrel had told me this mentally early on in the assessment.

Whatever it pretends to be, this one is a Naturalist. Only one very comfortable with technology would wear one of our translators. He will seek to make a deal with you to reveal your powers over the Orbs.

"Yes," I responded to the Dram above me.

"Would you repeat them for the Inquisitor."

"I am charged with High Sacrilege in the contamination of the Holy Orbs by an impure species."

"And do you know the penalty for such a crime."

"Purification, and then death." Meaning torture and then death if the torture didn't kill me first.

"There are other ways, human."

Ambra, here comes the offer. Please hear my thoughts on this before you answer.

The giant insect pressed a button, and lights dimmed as a cone of energy came around the three of us, leaving the guards and others outside of it.

A cloaking shield, Ambra. No one can overhear or record what happens inside. The Inquisitor is protecting itself from what it is about to say.

"The Emperor is very keen that the Hegemony possess the power you have revealed. I and the Emperor share a more enlightened view of your deeds than others on our world. While they may prevail in the Tribunal, we would have it otherwise. And if you will agree to the Emperor's terms, the Holy Office of the Emperor has the authority to annul the Tribunal."

"And if I refuse?"

Ambra! Wait, I said!

"Then you will find yourself at the mercy of the Tribunal," said the insect, an anger radiating from its consciousness. "And should the Naturalists prevail, you will find less kindness in your service to them."

The stupid fool. Already I could sense all the lies in it. I would suffer no matter what they said or promised. They would enslave me and recoil from no indecency to my person in attempting to extract the knowledge they desired.

Ambra, this is an important political turning point. If we can bypass the Tribunal, it will buy us considerable time and likely the momentary facade of better treatment. I suggest that you accept its offer. Let me express this to the Dram.

No! I shouted into its mind, and I saw my Advocate momentarily disoriented from the impact of my thoughts. I stepped forward and spoke angrily to the Inquisitor.

"Should I accept your offer, so that you will place me in better conditions for a time before ripping my mind apart? Turning me into an experimental subject on which you will work and likely fail to extract the secret you desire? No! I will risk a better death in torture before that! I will not work with the galaxy's fiends and murderers! Tell your Emperor that a lowly creature from Earth spits in his face!"

Waythrel had recovered by that point, and I sensed the overwhelming shock and panic in its mind. The anxious Xix thought the High Inquisitor would have me executed on the spot for this. That was nearly right, so much anger boiled out of the Inquisitor from my outburst. But I had seen the bright path to safety, and it did not end here. Poor Waythrel, it would be so hard to explain. *Soon, Waythrel, soon you'll understand.*

The High Inquisitor clicked angrily and soon the guards were ushering us back to my cell. Even as it spoke those commands, I had begun to withdraw. Seeing the bright path, I understood more and more what was required. Waythrel was speaking animatedly to me on the return trip. Little of it entered my consciousness, and surprising even myself, I began speaking out loud in the relative safety of the noisy ground car, a stream of consciousness as my mind's eye stopped seeing things around me but glimpsed the coming futures.

"They will fight over me, Waythrel, and the Naturalists will prevail."

"Ambra, what are you talking about?" it asked incredulously.

"Not even religious dogma can win over the chance for new power. I see them, conniving, backbiting fools. Scheming and drunk on power. But it will only be a prelude to a greater movement; and then, a crescendo of joy and sadness."

"Ambra, please, what…"

I turned my face toward my Advocate, tears trickling softly down my face. I didn't see the alien next to me. My mind was overflowing with the vast horror before my unique sense in time. "I can't *look*, Waythrel, I can't let myself look at the sadness, even though I know what I will see!"

We sat in silence for the rest of the trip to my cell. Just as well—I was somewhere else anyway.

Chapter 28

$$S = \tfrac{1}{2}\langle e^{-\Phi}Q_B e^{\Phi} \mid e^{-\Phi}\eta_0 e^{\Phi}\rangle - \tfrac{1}{2}\int_0^1 dt \langle e^{-\Phi}\partial_t e^{\Phi} \mid \{e^{-\Phi}Q_B e^{\Phi}, e^{-\Phi}\eta_0 e^{\Phi}\}\rangle$$

In this playhouse of infinite forms I have had my play, and here have I caught sight of him that is formless.

Rabindranath Tagore

When Waythrel next visited, it was a while before I could be roused. I lay on my bed shelf with open eyes and a slack-jawed expression. At first Waythrel misunderstood, as the tender skin where the laser had sealed the surgical incision had leaked some blood, staining my clothes quite visibly from the outside.

"Ambra, wake up! What have they done to you? Are you drugged? Have they tampered with your mind? Ambra, answer me!" The distressed Xix shook me with its smaller arms, eyestalks darting about in a panic. Some detached part of my mind watched it speak into a communicator, and within what seemed like seconds, although it was much longer, Xixian medics were surrounding me.

"She is not drugged currently," I understood one to say, but whether through a translator or through my telepathy, I don't know. "Remnants of a human chemistry narcotic are present, but at such low levels, they cannot be affecting her now. Furthermore, there is no intervention anywhere else except the abdomen. Her brain is untouched."

"Why is she like this then? She has to be at the Tribunal in four hours!"

"The visions," I whispered hoarsely, "they have never opened up to me like this before, Waythrel." I swallowed, my throat dry, my words croaking out.

"Infinite layers and webs inside of membranes….I must learn to better control my exploration; it is too easy to be lost in it."

"Ambra, what are you talking about? What have they done to you?"

I felt more tears in my eyes. For myself, for the others I had seen, for the history and future of pain and injustices that cannot possibly seem to be balanced even by all the love in the universe.

"My eggs, Waythrel," I said, turning my head toward them. "You didn't think that they would risk losing me if things go badly at the Tribunal or afterwards."

"Your eggs." A statement. I could *sense* the wheels turning in its mind.

"Last night, they came, threw me on a table, cut me open, and took them. My possible children, taken from me before they could ever be." I felt a few sobs spasm through me. I had never thought that much about having children, especially with my deformity. I mean, really, what man would have this? But I had never thought I would be invaded and robbed like this. With this act, something primal in me had been violated by these monsters, and my soul cried out. My soul cried out to the heavens, wondering what else would be taken from me.

The Xixian medics scanned the areas where my ovaries were and confirmed the results.

"I am sorry, Ambra," Waythrel began. "We did not anticipate this. Once again, we have been overly naïve in imagining what the Dram might conspire to. It is obvious upon reflection. They wanted more genetic material to breed out your powers again. They could not clone you – human chromosomal instability has yet to be solved by the Dram. But your eggs – they could inseminate them with diverse sperm from males similar to your father. They have been plotting far ahead." Waythrel paused and only repeated, "I am very sorry."

"Waythrel, there was nothing we could have done to stop it," I moaned, trying to sit up comfortably. "Not now, not when larger things must be done."

"What larger things, Ambra?"

"It's all becoming clear to me now, Waythrel. A straight path home." I laughed bitterly, almost a cry, really. "No! Oh, *God*, no. Not home. Never home. But escape."

"Have you seen this? The Xixian Council is formulating a final escape plan. We suspect the worst for us, and are evacuating many of our kind as secretly as possible. But if you have seen our future, Ambra, you must tell us!"

I smiled toward the lanky alien. "It's okay, Waythrel. It will be okay. I'm seeing to it."

"You're seeing to it? Ambra, please, these stakes are too high for such riddles!"

I was beginning to fade again. "Don't rush me, Waythrel. Just a few loose strands left to tie up now, and the path is sure. Can't…rush like …. before. Must see…..*all* the paths." I floated in and out of a trance for the next few hours with Waythrel and the other Xix anxiously flitting about me.

Time marched slowly in my cell, yet danced maniacally before my consciousness as events rushed past me. I don't know how it happened, but finally, at a single point, these two different melodies of time met, and out of the myriad strings of the *perhaps* emerged a single thread of *destiny*. I know it sounds absurd, but that is the best way I can describe it. I opened my eyes, seeing the future and my present, superimposed like counterpoint, just as the Dram guard entered. We were silently marched to the Holy Tribunal.

Along the way, I continued speaking in stream-of-consciousness manner. I'm sure it sounded like nonsense to Waythrel, and the poor Xix likely thought I had gone mad at the most inopportune time, minutes before trial, hours before the Xixian plan that might lead to their destruction was set in motion, both of us trapped on a hostile and ugly world at the center of the Hegemony.

"It will never be the same," I spoke as the blasted landscape, cooked as if in a red furnace, devoid of greens, or blues, or even yellows, blurred by us in the ground vehicle. "A fetus as a single grain of sand; twenty billion souls burned, ruptured in a moment of time; all gravity; it was so simple; only *gravity*; space-time that bends thoughts, and kills; eons only it sat there, one long orbit after another; a stupid planet wannabe; but it would slay an entire world. These bastards, Waythrel—they will debate their creed while slitting a baby's throat."

Waythrel tried to have the Tribunal postponed, but the Dram would hear nothing of it. Of course, my mental state was not really of interest in these proceedings. It wasn't about truth or fairness to me. It was about their power struggle, laws, and creeds. There would hardly be a part for me to play in the entire farce besides showing up. My poor Advocate would be reduced to listening to the blowhards debate.

"I'm ready, Waythrel. This toy Tribunal is a proud gasp in the face of the infinite. The only thing I dread is the awful waste of time it all is. I wish that I could replace one piece of time with another…"

Waythrel simply stared in my direction with its many eyes. I was too engrossed in thought to bother even trying to sense its state of mind. I'm sure it was pretty bad.

Chapter 29

$$S(\Psi) = \hbar \sum_{g \geq 0} (\hbar g_c)^{g-1} \sum_{n \geq 0} \frac{1}{n!} \{\Psi^n\}_g$$

Men never do evil so completely and cheerfully as when they do it from religious conviction.

Blaise Pascal

The audience in front of the High Inquisitor was impressive, but nothing prepared me for the Tribunal itself. Even as we pulled up outside the giant dome in which the trial would occur, it was obvious this would be something that had Galactic Empire written all over it.

The dome was incredible. Easily the size of a small city on Earth, it had been covered with that disturbing metallic marble-like substance the Dram loved to build with, yet it was polished in what must have been a million facets, each focused slightly differently so that they reflected the red light of the star upward and outward from the center of the sphere, radially like a giant incandescent bulb. I suppose this was to give it the appearance of power radiating from within, but I found it hideous and tacky, astounding me only in the force with which these aliens pressed upon all things that they encountered.

We were led through an enormous corridor on levitation flats, small rectangular devices with guardrails that traveled a few feet above the ground back and forth between the entrance and the inner chamber of the dome. Of course, these were designed for the Dram, and even a normal human would have trouble holding onto the rails. At my height of five foot two, there was really only a post to secure myself to, although the devices were almost completely bump-free. Still, they moved pretty fast, and instinct made me hold on tightly.

Soon, the cylindrical tunnel opened up into a mini-dome within the main dome, yet still the size of a football field. It was completely absurd. In the center was an elevated platform, perhaps two hundred feet in the air, on which Waythrel and I would stand for the entire ordeal. Hovering from above, several hundred feet in length, was an enormous platform for the seats of the Tribunal members, arrayed in a semicircle around a second platform opposite the entrance. The far walls were hardly lit, and light was focused down on the smaller platform, leaving most of the Tribunal in dim illumination. The only exceptions were the seat of the High Inquisitor, and next to that, towering above him, the grand throne on which the Dram Emperor sat.

It was all created to have an effect on the accused, and to bolster the Dram inherent sense of their own superiority, I guess. It had the opposite effect on me. It was in some ways the final sign of how mad these aliens were. At that point I lost whatever hope I had that there could be any way besides my plan to escape this situation. Even more, it had the effect of increasing my confidence. These Dram were so unbalanced, it would not be hard to defeat them now. This room was the proof. They sacrificed anything of practical value for show. The scale of the thing was so large that it was impossible to see the members of the Tribunal from the platform, and therefore they could not see us. So, they had rigged giant suspended holograms to display things, like monitors in Times Square or something. I nearly laughed at the ridiculousness of the entire farce. I suppose that I should have been more respectful. They were smarter than me, much more powerful than any other species, and, of course, very willing to do terrible things. But it wasn't me that was blind now. I had sight in a world where the rest were blind.

The Emperor dangled ten feet in front of me, blown up to ten times its already large size in the projection, its form and clothing familiar from my vision on Earth, from a time in my life that seemed a thousand years ago. It clicked out sounds as Waythrel and I settled onto the platform, bathed in light. The clicks rocked against my ears, amplified by Dram technology. The Tribunal was in session.

It lasted nearly four hours, and I will spare you the details. Most of it was taken up with a constant religious and legal back-and-forth between the High Inquisitor and appointed Advocates of the Naturalists and Believers. The Believers presented their case, showing evidence recorded by Dram sensors of my manipulation of the Orbs, the original notes from Earth about my abilities, and a brief questioning of Waythrel and me about whether or not I had indeed done these things. Honestly, it seemed that many in the Believer camp had a lot of trouble *believing* that a lowly human could have power over the "Holy Orbs." They spent a lot of time arguing the impossibility of an impure creature having such power, focusing on my deformity. "This human is even a monster among its own kind!" one particularly empathetic Believer Advocate exclaimed at one point.

Their case was pretty easy to understand – I was an instrument of evil, a vile creature empowered by dark forces to sacrilege. Seriously, how could an impure, lowly and deformed piece of humanity have any legitimate power over the Holy Orbs? There could be no cooperation with me, nothing good to come from my actions. I should be purified of the evil that possessed me and sent to death for my sins in punishment, and to prevent any further desecration of the Orbs.

The Naturalists then took up their position. They countered immediately the words of my deformity by casting it in a positive light, saying that the Creator had no doubt endowed me with special gifts, a new organ of vision. They played up a false respect for the Believers' faith. Who was to say whom God had chosen as the instrument of revelation? Did not the scriptures claim that even the lowest would see God? Had I not opened a Portal? How could evil ever have done so? How could God have allowed it? They argued for a break from what they called barbaric interpretations of the Believers and a more progressive, modern view. They argued that I was sent from God, and must have been put in their presence for a purpose. The Dram should make use of this instrument of God and discover that purpose.

On and on it went, back and forth, until I frankly stopped caring and finalized in my mind what would be done in the next few days. The dancing futures in my mind – these were real, while the bickering insects around me, their power struggles and ancient superstitions, were the true dream. Deep in thought, ignored during the long debates, I lost track of the time around me until Waythrel shook me back into the present. Apparently, they were nearing an end. The Advocates had been ordered to sit. The High Inquisitor stood before us, its face hovering in space.

"Finally. Let him spit it out at last," I muttered to Waythrel. Through the Xixian translator I wore, the Dram clicks morphed into English in my ears.

"The Emperor has signaled closure. The debate has ended. All hail the Judge and receive Judgment!"

The High Inquisitor sat down, and the projection flicked to the form of the Emperor. Even I could tell the Emperor was old. The bent legs, the poor posture, the discolorations in the exoskeleton, and the aids to vision that surrounded the three eyestalks – this was a creature that had been worn down by many years. Yet there was a sharpness in its words, even through translation. Sharp in essence, but not in effect. I sighed; I had heard them so many times already.

"The evidence and arguments have been presented. But there is still too much mystery. A primitive creature is said to have power over the Holy Orbs and yet shows no sign of the faith, no knowledge of the Ancient Ones. How can such power have come to such a lowly creature? How can we know it was this Earth creature that opened the Portal, and not another force that lays the blame on it to divert attention?"

I felt Waythrel stiffen beside me. The Xix had not anticipated this paranoia in the Dram. To blame the Xix because of their superior technology – it was classic Dram. But deadly serious.

"We need further proof!" Soft clicking could be heard around the chamber. "I command that this creature provide the core Tribunal with a demonstration! In four days we mark the end of the Sun Spot Cycle. It is a Holy omen. We will travel to the Dram Sacred Orb, and this creature will show us the truth of its power, or perish in torment for its heresy!"

Several in the Believer camp broke out in some kind of protest, while I felt the Naturalists smile with pleasure inwardly. The Emperor was clever. It would test that I did hold this power, and at the same time establish a use of it by the Dram. It would make its task easier to insist upon my exploitation to the Believer caste.

"Silence!" the Emperor thundered, pounding a clawed hand upon the throne. "I am empowered by the Holy Powers and rule with their authority! I *command* it. In four days, this creature will be brought before the Holy Orb! Take them away!"

And then it was over. The guards entered, hurried us out of the chamber and out of the absurd dome toward the ground transports. I saw Waythrel shield its many eyes from the outdoor light, bright and searing after our hours in the dome. The noise of the Dram city filled the spaces around us. I leaned over towards the very exhausted-looking Xix and whispered, "Now that we've endured their hot air, we have plans to set in motion."

"Plans?" Waythrel asked.

"Yes, Waythrel." I smiled and sighed at the same time. It was good to finally open up about this.

"Soon, we will escape, and there is a lot we need to arrange. We must make sure it is as I have fore-planned."

"Ambra, you will tell me now what you have seen?"

"Oh, Waythrel, that would take more than our lifetimes. But a local corner of it all, yes, I'll tell you. These arrogant bugs, they are going to lead us right to the exit."

Chapter 30

$$r_c = \frac{\text{arccosh}(3)}{\sqrt{2}\omega}$$

It is incomprehensible that God should exist, and it is incomprehensible that He should not exist; that the soul should be joined to the body, and that we should have no soul; that the world should be created, and that it should not be created.

Blaise Pascal

The path through the labyrinth was clear now. Like some luminescent highway in my mind, composed of a thousand different threads of time from possible futures woven together, it dominated my visions. In my present, I helped lay each new thread, and knew those that must be stitched in the near future. It all was within what I could do. Only by choice now would I not be able to follow the bright road. But only through that path could we escape, could the Xix survive, and could I finally return to where my journey had begun. It was the right path for so many, even as I could hardly face what waited for me at its end.

I told Waythrel that we needed a chance to speak more openly together, without the Dram overhearing. While the sounds and movements outside between the Tribunal and my cell masked our conversation, there was not enough time to explain what the Xix had to know. I told Waythrel to ready all of the Xix on Dram, and all of those that could exchange information and service with their home world, to prepare for what I would ask of them. I felt the resignation within Waythrel. The Xix assumed I would ask something similar to their own plan to endanger themselves. Deferring to my visions, Waythrel felt a growing helplessness as I took over the planning of our escape.

The next day, Waythrel and several Xixian medics entered my cell.

Pretending to examine me, one injected something into my arm. It wasn't painful and barely left a mark. I made no sound and waited until they left the room. Waythrel spoke.

"We have implanted in your skin a small device that will mask our conversation from the Dram. I have a similar device in me. The device will mimic malfunctioning Dram eavesdropping equipment, which will give us a short time to speak openly. The device is organic, and will dissolve and be absorbed within your tissues in thirty minutes – undetectable. Speak quickly, all that must be said."

I closed my eyes, the bright path in my consciousness.

"When they bring me to the Orb, the Emperor will ask me to activate it, planning for me to guide the ship to Earth. A measure of the cruelty of the Dram," I said without further clarification. "But this will not happen. The Resistance will swing into Dram space and hit the escort ships. They have been moving into near jump space the last few days."

"Ambra, I have no word of such plans, what are you saying? Why would the Emperor demand that you bring them to Earth?"

I ignored its words and continued. "At that time, a delegation of Xixian scientists will be revealed to be Xixian defenders, and will begin to immobilize Dram soldiers."

"Ambra, please…"

"Listen to me, Waythrel. " I shook my head. There wasn't time to explain it all. The alien would have to trust my visions. "The Dram have too many numbers, and such terrible weapons, the Xix cannot stop them all." I smiled, thinking of my gentle friends. "These others I will stop."

"*You* will stop? How, Ambra?"

There was only one way to convince the Xix of this. I concentrated on the pulsing waves of thought that emanated from Waythrel. Such complex lines, such beautiful webs within webs. So much more refined and deep than my thoughts, and yet even the Xix were blind where I could see. Only I could see these thoughts. And only I could touch them. I reached out, kindly but firmly, and plucked the web.

Waythrel recoiled as if struck. The elegant web of thought became scrambled for a moment, and it used its many arms to balance along the walls of my cell. The eyestalks rotated wildly around the room, unhinged, disoriented. Slowly, the web reformed, and the long alien body relaxed, the eyestalks calming and turning slowly toward me. I lowered my head.

"I'm sorry, Waythrel. You would not have believed me otherwise."

"You frighten me, Ambra."

"I know. It's too much power for an Earth mind. I *feel* that inside. Seeing our history, I *know* it—we are not wise enough. But this power *is* mine, good or bad. Perhaps both." I raised my head and leveled my sightless eyes toward my Advocate. "And I was gentle, Waythrel. I don't have to be so gentle." I could feel Waythrel recoil instinctively from the implication of my words. "The Dram will be helpless, at least the number around us on the ship. I can handle that number. They will not understand what is happening and will not target me before I have incapacitated them all."

I shook my head in disbelief at where things had brought me. "I have seen it all, Waythrel. You must trust me. Report my words back to the Resistance. The Dram will want Xixian scientists there to try to explain and capture the mystery of my power over the Orbs. Irony—they need you even as they don't trust you! Fill their ranks with fighters. Tell the human who plans with you what I have said."

"The human?" Waythrel asked with astonishment. "How do you know?"

"I can *see* him, Waythrel. I can see him in my future, and I can see him as a distortion in the matrices of space-time. Thel's little seeds are sprouting so quickly, I can't even keep track of them as they grow within me. Soon, we will go to him and to the heart of the Resistance. I will meet him before the end."

"The end?"

"The end of many things. The beginning of the end of the Dram."

"If these things are true, then my heart will rejoice."

"Stop being silly, Waythrel," I smiled. "You don't even have a heart! Your translators are too poetic."

"The sentiment is the same."

"Yes, but it will be mixed with grief. Terrible grief. Tomorrow we head for Earth, but we will not find it."

Chapter 31

$$\zeta(s) = \sum_{n=1}^{\infty} \frac{1}{n^s} = \frac{1}{1^s} + \frac{1}{2^s} + \frac{1}{3^s} + \cdots$$

We must admit with humility that, while number is purely a product of our minds, space has a reality outside our minds, so that we cannot completely prescribe its properties a priori.

Carl Friedrich Gauss

The trip into space was far grander than anything I had known or would know again. After the Sortax introduction to space, followed by the nightmare in the smugglers death holds, and most recently the detention cell in the Dram warship, the Emperor's ship was majestic. It was the largest spacecraft I had ever been on, easily twenty times the size of the Sortax training craft. The energy needed to bring that thing out of the Dram world gravity must have been colossal. It was also finely crafted, at least for the Dram, and certainly compared to the warship they used to kidnap me. Inside it seemed that no effort had been spared in creating a luxury ship for the ruler of the galaxy. Spacious corridors of plush fabrics led to high ceilings in rooms that housed the most complex technology and the finest materials and decorations. Dram-style art hung from the walls, typically their favored weavings of desert plants into carpet-like hangings and floor coverings painted with images from their histories and mythologies. They meant little to me, and often were hard to even decipher. I suppose human images would be equal nonsense to alien life.

We weren't given long to observe. The guards firmly escorted us to the bridge where the Emperor and its entourage awaited us. By the time we reached it, the ship had already ascended into space, using some sort of artificial gravity, I suppose, to keep things from being pushed vertically during liftoff, and keeping everything normal now that we were technically in zero-g. When we entered the enormous command center, I was struck by the panoramic windows built into the walls, now showing nothing but the blackness of space interspersed with the pinpricks of white starlight. I marveled at the engineering, the materials science that allowed windows to be placed there under the incredible pressure from inside pushing against the vacuum of space. Whatever the material was, it was tough or perhaps was aided by some sort of energy field that lessened the outward forces on the windows. It sure made for a spectacular sight, almost like floating out in front of the ship in the darkness.

The windows dimmed dramatically as the system's star swung into view, its oppressive red now confined by the blackness of space around us. Its light was still intense, in fact, more intense now that the atmosphere didn't absorb the radiation, and there was an automatic filtering of the light by the windows to protect those within the ship. The starship continued its arced course, and the red sun moved across the viewing area, as shadows shifted sharply from one side to the other around me.

Waythrel and I were brought forward to a small raised platform at the foot of the Emperor's throne. I suppose this was where those granted audience with the Emperor were placed. I looked around and noticed the fifteen or so Xixian scientists hunched over various pieces of equipment. I hoped these were not true scientists but a Xixian team trained for combat. I glanced toward Waythrel and probed its mind. Waythrel seemed to understand my concern and clearly formed the answers to my question.

The forces are in place as you have requested, Ambra. So are the Dram troops, as you have noticed. There are at least forty of their elite guard. I hope you are up to this.

I impressed upon its mind that I was.

The Resistance will be here upon my signal through the Dram Orb string, after which they will make the jump to this system. We will have only minutes to escape from this ship and board a Resistance freighter. At any moment we could be destroyed by a Dram warship. It will be perilous. And finally, what of the Emperor? We dare not risk injury to the Emperor. It could mean terrible retaliation.

I smiled, and spoke out loud. "Don't worry, Waythrel. It won't be pretty, but we'll be okay."

Waythrel acknowledged me only by bending several eyestalks in my direction. Alien sarcasm! Well, I couldn't blame the poor Xix. I was the one-eyed woman leading the blind.

I sensed it before anyone else in the room stirred. There is nothing in the galaxy like an Orb. Not even the complexities of the Xixian mind matched the convoluted and intricate maze of space-time that churned just beneath the surface of those spheres. My sensitivities let me feel the local space-time distortions from the Orb acutely. The Orbs reached out and touched so much in the star system. I had noticed it off-handedly before, but now it was so much more clear. It was as if the extruding and receding tendrils of power from the Orb had a purpose: tending, *gardening*, the majority of their efforts reaching out to the Dram home planet. Thel had spoken of it. *Gardeners*. Could it be true? I felt the energies reach through my body, and a tremor ran through me. What were those tendrils *doing*?

Waythrel sensed my reaction. "What is it, Ambra?"

"We are close," I managed to get out through a dry throat.

Several Dram officers clicked to the Emperor, and soon the Orb became visible to all through the viewing windows. In the visual realm, how boring the sphere seemed! But whatever effect the Orbs had on the sight of those around me, I could sense within their minds the stirring of awe. Some religious, some exclusively scientific, but all knew the power in what we approached. The portals through time and space planted around the galaxy by the mysterious Ancient Ones, left for billions of years to be discovered by species too primitive to understand how they even functioned, or why.

My translator echoed the Emperor's tones. "We have reached the Sacred Orb of the Dram! It is now time for the heretic to prove its truth and worth, to open the Orb and reveal the power of the divine, or to fail and expose itself to be a fraud of the Evil Force."

How I hated these dramatic moments of voodoo, made worse by the fact that the Emperor was a hypocrite who sided with the Naturalists anyway. Sanctimonious hypocrisy mixed with extreme power – nothing was worse, especially when the authorities could soon be deciding exactly how to torture you.

The Emperor turned to Waythrel. "Your client is ordered to open the portal."

"Ambra, obey the Emperor's command."

I sighed and inhaled deeply, closing my eyes. *Okay, buddy, get ready, 'cause here it comes!*

I went deep inside myself, to that place where my unique sense opened up to me and occupied all my consciousness. To my sixth sense, the Orb flared like a supernova. I felt its energies as nearly overpowering. I held steady, focused, and reached toward it.

This time it was more straightforward. The pressures are far weaker without a Dram warship chasing you through space. And my powers had grown in so many ways even in the short time since I had opened the last Orb. Add to that my confidence that I could do it, and that in my bright path I had seen it happen. All I had to do was dance with destiny.

I felt the equivalent of gasps from those surrounding me, even from Waythrel, as I unlocked the Orb. Visually, it was quite a light show. The dark surface rippled into a multidimensional maze of lasers, a many-layered tunnel in space erupting before us, seeming ready to swallow the ship whole. *As indeed it was.* It took some concentration to configure the Orb to remain open without drawing the ship inside, and even so, I think everyone on board felt the space-time tugs. A subtle anxiety seemed to sit deep within all.

I opened my eyes and glared at the ugly cockroach on the throne. "There, *your majesty*," I spat out. "Is that what you were looking for?"

The Emperor and other Dram were too transfixed to hear me. Even the guards were staring up at the heavenly-hell of the endless and structured light of the Orb. I noticed with satisfaction, however, that the Xixian team was not. I spoke mentally to Waythrel to send the signal. It nodded, pressed a device on the translator and breathing device around its neck, and transmitted both to the Resistance forces and the Xixian team below.

And that's when everything went nuts.

Chapter 32

$$|\Psi\rangle = \int d^{26}p\left(T(p)c_1 e^{ipX}|0\rangle + A_\mu(p)\partial X^\mu c_1 e^{ipX}|0\rangle + \chi(p)c_0 e^{ipX}|0\rangle + \ldots\right)$$

Battle not with monsters, lest you become a monster, and if you gaze into the abyss, the abyss gazes also into you.

Friedrich Nietzsche

I
t was a few seconds before the Dram realized what was happening.

The Xixian scientists immediately began to immobilize, but not kill, Dram warriors with special devices they had concealed. As the giant insects began dropping to the ground, a cry went up from crew monitoring space. I'm not sure whether they had detected Waythrel's signal or were responding to the small fleet of Resistance ships materializing from the Orb String and opening fire on surrounding Dram warships escorting the Emperor's vessel. Whatever the reason, I had to act quickly, before they turned the firepower of the ship on the emerging craft. The Resistance had been instructed not to fire on the Emperor's ship. How could they? I was onboard, and I was the only reason that they were here. They had to get me off this ship and safely away.

I spun and faced the rows of ship technicians, pilots, and weapons staff. Their intense thoughts in the midst of combat struck my awareness harshly. How quickly they revealed their presence to my mind! *If they only knew.* One by one, I struck them. Focusing thoughts tightly, it was a mental slap the likes of which these creatures had never known. A second or two for each, and then the next, and the next, on and on like dominoes I dropped them. When I had incapacitated those at the consoles, I took on the soldiers, who were now in a deadly fight with the Xixian team. The Xix had done well, and piles of soldiers lay in front of them. But the insects were like ants from a nest, pouring in through the many doors along the walls of the room. The Xix were being overwhelmed: two had already fallen to Dram weapons, lying charred and twitching in a growing wreckage caused by the Drams' less elegant weapons.

I found myself improvising, and in a giant mental sweep, like summoning a wave from a quiescent sea, I sent a burst of mental distortion across the hordes of Dram soldiers. I was in some strange hyperkinetic state, and the power I let forth caused scores to drop instantly, some, I am sure, permanently. Seeing another horde coming through the main entrance, I recalibrated and released another burst, sending all but a handful down on their faces. Those remaining looked stunned, unable to function, and they wandered aimlessly around the room for several minutes before falling down, staring vacantly, and doing nothing. I don't know if these were permanently brain damaged.

I felt a powerful swell of anger and realization rise behind me, and a venomous urge strike toward me. *The Emperor.* I read its mind all too easily. The monster who had directed the pain of so many aliens and humans filled my consciousness, and I sensed its thrusting of a deadly weapon in my direction. *It knew.* It would seek no Tribunal to decide my fate. Funny, I had not seen this in the visions! Too close to my person, I suppose.

Waythrel screamed, "Ambra! Behind you!"

Poor Waythrel, so worried! By the time I turned to face the Emperor, Waythrel sent out thoughts of shock and awe, and stared at the Dram ruler. The beast stood still, its upraised claw clutching a weapon aimed in my direction. The creature gasped for air, yet could not move, trembling in a tremendous effort to break free of the invisible bonds holding it in place.

I walked slowly up to the insect, staring into its many eyes.

"Emperor of all Dram!" I shouted at it. "Now you will hear *me.*" And then, I let thunder in its mind: *One way or the other!*

The Emperor tensed as my anger slapped at its consciousness, and fear flowed toward me like a cold river.

"You are right to be afraid," I said. "You have a debt to pay for all the souls you have tortured, murdered; the light you have extinguished."

I could not help myself, I felt my thoughts squeezing, tightening in their fury. The Dram began to make wheezing sounds, pitiful throaty wails of an alien physiology, yet no less desperate than a human being strangled.

I slapped its mind hard. *I know what you have done.* I felt desperate cries of pain and fear from the creature, but in response I gave no pity or mercy, but played out in its mind the scenes of my visions. The Dram Emperor recoiled in shock at my knowledge, and my power, seeing now that its executioner was near.

"Ambra," Waythrel whispered near me, but the Xix was only a butterfly near the hurricane of my vengeance.

"See them scream, Emperor? See the billions boil and burn? I've seen them.

Day after day, night after night, I have seen them, and I know you decreed their deaths."

Tighter and tighter I squeezed. The creature could no longer stand on its own power and began to sag to the ground.

"You gave your victims in your dungeons no rest! Up with you!" I felt myself invade its mind further, and, overpowering the normal biology, I diverted energy from other vital life processes and strengthened the signal to the legs, forcing the Dram to stand, turning its eyes that flailed vainly for help or escape, turning them toward me. I filled its mind with my image, my anger, and its imminent demise.

"Ambra, you must stop!" Waythrel cried more strongly.

"Know now the helplessness of those you have tormented and murdered. Feel their histories drown you." I opened the valve of vision and directed the terrible currents through my mind into that of the Dram Emperor. I watched as the captive consciousness was battered in the visions of other lives, other worlds, other dreams and hopes that could not be processed. The insect began a terrible trembling across its body, the legs, even under my tyrannical control, losing strength, the creature's body near the breaking point.

"Ambra, don't become a monster!" a voice pleaded with me. "Release it! Don't let your own power consume you!"

There was a pause, a breath in Time. Only my awareness was mobile. In that moment, somehow, some part of me heard the plea. Some part of me looked and saw the mad she-god I had become, summoning a deathly storm of power around me.

I stepped back from the edge of my own damnation. I can't analyze how it happened or why, but like waking from a dream, I shook off the crazed mood and released the Dram Emperor. It fell unconscious to the floor. Alive, yet forever wounded, always to remember and experience the suffering it had created.

Waythrel grabbed my shoulders with its spidery arms. "Down to the airlock. A ship is docked."

We raced through the Dram ship, the surviving members of the Xixian team loping like crazed ballet-dancing spiders, incapacitating the stray Dram that got in our way. We reached the airlock, entered the chamber, and transferred to the connected ship of the Resistance.

Within seconds, our ship and the remaining Resistance craft that had not been blown out of the sky converged near the Orb. Crew members screamed that an armada of Dram death boats was headed our way and would be within firing range in minutes.

"Ambra, please, get us out of here."

I looked over at Waythrel, not even sure I was really sane yet—from what I had seen, and done, to what I would see, and do. It all blurred together. Time —it was churning through past, present, and future. It was hard to know which way was forward.

"Sure, Waythrel. Got an express ticket."

"To where?" it asked.

"Home, and nowhere, Waythrel." I shook my head. "You can never go home, they say."

I fixed my mind on the destination and flexed my thought to open the Orb. And it opened, filling my mind with radiance, filling the eyes of all around with a different light. We dashed through a million dimensions of nowhere and everywhere, leaving behind the red of Dram, filling the windows of our ship with the golden rays of Sol.

Chapter 33

$$z_{n+1} = z_n^2 + c$$

Nothing we can do outrages Nature directly. Our acts of destruction give her new vigour and feed her energy, but none of our wreckings can weaken her power.

Marquis de Sade

Without willing it consciously, my mind darted back in time, deep into the recesses of the past.

For nearly three billion years this cratered rock had waited for its day. Circling endlessly, cold, silent, an outcast from the warmer rock huddled around a blue star, the largest of millions, yet failed. Orbit after orbit, the stars whirled across the rocky horizon, and yet it did not lose patience. It did not count the eons. Without promise, without hope, without thought, it held pregnant within its core a fate unguessed. And then, in the wink of an eye to this ancient entity, moving at the rapid pace of life, hundreds of small metallic gnats buzzed around it. Each nudged softly, surely, augmenting each other, until a crescendo built, and the old path was discarded. It latched upon the seemingly infinite energies of the tendril of an Orb, slingshot toward another star system, guided by malevolence, erupting from hyperspace with a swarm of demons blackening its outline. Inward toward the bright golden light it rushed, gathering frightening speed, aimed like an arrow with terrible purpose. Gravity. *Only gravity.* Slight alterations in gravity, then an exploitation of ancient and mysterious powers, leading to terrible accelerations and flight toward its final fate.

The cool morning breeze blew through a young woman's auburn hair. A vivid blue sky welcomed a new spring day, and she watched the children run across the concrete playground in London. Other mothers sat nearby, or walked shepherding their young. All familiar to her, many known well. She squinted into the bright sunlight and made out the form of her three-year-old stumbling forward and pointing to the sky.

"Look, Mummy, there's a falling star up in the sky!"

She followed her daughter's finger into the cloudless day. A bright speck, as if it really were a small star, shone brightly in the west.

"Yes, darling, it must be a falling star. I've never seen one in the daytime before." She smiled as the toddler grinned upward.

"Mummy, mummy, I'll make my wish! I'll make my wish!"

"Make it a good one!"

The little girl closed her eyes tightly, frowning in concentration. With a squeal she opened them again and hopped into the air.

"Mummy, I can't tell you. It's a *secret*, or it won't come true!"

The young woman smiled and glanced up into the sky once again. Her smile froze a moment, then faded as several lines formed on her forehead.

"Look at it. It's so bright."

High in the atmosphere of Earth, where each day thirty tons of material the size of sand grains enter and burn up in the atmosphere, something horribly larger ignited. One thousand miles away from London, a deep shadow darkened the capital of Iceland. Vendors on the street looked upward, people in office buildings glanced out of their windows, and frantic calls on military and national security lines screamed in urgency at the completely unexpected calamity set to befall. The Sun was blotted out, yet a second star now shone, moving like some crazed thing across the sky, erupting into a brilliance so terrible it could not be viewed by the creatures on the ground without causing blindness.

The atmosphere of Earth exploded over Canada. The energy of one hundred trillion megatons of TNT from the rushing object began its conversion into diverse forms of energy on the Earth. A fireball nearly two hundred times as bright as the Sun was born, igniting everything within its growing radius. As the Earth's surface absorbed the impact, the thin outer layer of crust was peeled off in a growing wave from the center of impact, like the skin off an apple, thrown with tremendous power high into the atmosphere. On this skin were the world's oceans, its land masses, every town, city, and state. Every living form on Earth. Underneath, and also ejected high into the now burning air was an ocean of magma. For all of human history, hidden from view by the cooled crust except for rare volcanic eruptions, enormous volumes now were poured over the Earth's surface and into its skies. In front of the growing impact crater that spread like some yawning maw across the planet, a hypersonic pressure wave of compressed atmosphere rushed away from the impact, carrying the equivalent of winds blowing at over eight thousand miles per hour. Everything in its path was flattened and then set aflame by the fireball that followed. Earthquakes of magnitude fourteen on the Richter scale threw down anything else that somehow remained standing.

Within hours, the playground in London had been lifted off the Earth's surface and thrown into space. Along with all the remaining crust ejected, it would then fall back to Earth as fiery meteors to rain destruction on the rest of a dying planet. There was no chance for any reaction, no ability of the small creatures dotting the planet to take any course of action that could protect them in any way. Those within several thousand miles of the impact were vaporized almost immediately. Ten billion souls cried out into the blackness of space, and then were silent.

Within a day, the entire surface of the Earth was a raging inferno, where the oceans boiled to nothing, all vegetation was reduced to ash, and every sign of life was wiped clean from the molten landscape. The once blue and white marble in the solar system became utterly black, lifeless, and still. The third planet from the star was now sterilized.

The Emperor's will had been done.

Chapter 34

$$H(X) = -\sum_{x \in \mathcal{X}} p(x) \log_b p(x)$$

The choice before human beings, is not, as a rule, between good and evil but between two evils.

George Orwell

From the infinite maze of light, the starship plunged into the blackness of space. The glowing Orb behind us burned brightly for several moments, and then, as if a switch had been thrown, went dark. The Sun radiated at the center of mass of the small system of nine worlds and asteroids, its disk large in the field of vision near the third planet from the star. The Xix at the controls on the bridge exchanged rapid conversation. I could sense them three floors up.

Waythrel rushed down the corridor to my room. It signaled outside the door, and I pressed a panel to allow entrance. The door slid open, and a very frazzled-looking Xix stepped inside—if you can ever really describe a disturbing alien life form with such a human term. I looked up from the over-large chair I was sitting in and waited for it to tell me what I already knew.

"Ambra," the Xix began hesitantly. "We have come upon the coordinates of Earth."

The weight of the unspoken was heavy in the air. I simply nodded and waited. My emotions were both drained and repressed. I had cried inside one thousand times for the future that had become my present.

"There is something wrong. We need you on the bridge."

Again, I nodded. I stood slowly, feeling no weakness or fatigue in my limbs. Only a terrible stillness deep inside.

I followed the alien through the ship and up to the bridge. The Xixian pilots and crew were silent, almost still before their instruments. I had chosen a black robe from the clothes provided to me. Xixian make, overly large and oddly proportioned for my human dimensions, it lay draped around me like an odd funeral garment. The robe was fashioned of some strange material never imagined on Earth, and it seemed to drink the light and then somehow subtly reflect it in hints of iridescence in the midst of darkness. On my head was Ricky's Red Sox hat. Ricky, murdered in another age of my mind, cremated only hours ago.

Waythrel spoke. "Ambra, the coordinates are correct. There is a rocky satellite of a mass and distance as specified. The planet must be Earth. But..."

Tears streamed down my face as I finally spoke, the words unlocking something deep within me. "It burns before us still, my alien friends. My home world, where my roots would have found soil again to end the withering of my soul. Spirits like dust are riding on the solar wind, blowing over our ship's shields. I hear their voices, *billions* of them crying out. I've heard them again and again. Can you feel the wind of their *souls*?"

I walked forward to the view screen and stared at the blackened sphere, rivers of magma a dull red like bloodshot eyes crisscrossing the surface. Across nearly the entire Northern Hemisphere, an enormous orange pool of lava, boiling like some eye of the Devil.

"The Dram have left by now; their work is finished."

"Why?" Waythrel whispered. I felt a terrible shudder from it and the other Xix. Alien, all of them, and yet they all cared. More than so many humans I had known. If any creatures carried the torch of divine love in our galaxy, it was the Xix.

I looked across the control room. "They have my eggs and many human captives for sperm. They believe I can be recreated. They desire a monopoly on my power." It was all so logical, so coldly calculated. "The gene pool of Earth, waiting to produce more Ambra Dawns, and who knows what else of Reader power, was a threat to their Hegemony. So they removed the threat. And so Earth has been put to death."

"Ambra, I don't have words for you," Waythrel began and then paused. "You have known this?"

"Since my arrival at Dram."

There was a stunned silence. "Ambra, why? Why didn't you tell us? We could have stopped it!"

"No, Waythrel!" I cried out, the alien's words cutting deep inside me. "I have seen all the threads. The possible futures, Waythrel, there are not infinitely many, not in the short term. There was only one path out of the Dram home world, one possible hope for me to survive." My tears came heavily now, and it took all I could to stop myself from sobbing beyond the ability to speak.

I stared out at my blackened home, where my bare feet would never touch the soil again. Where so many innocent lives had been extinguished. "I chose the most horrible choice. That the lives of many should be sacrificed for the life of one. Because others had foretold and foreseen hope for many more worlds than Earth. A hope in me."

Waythrel and the other Xix were silent and still as stones. I could feel their churning emotions at my words. I turned to Waythrel. "I chose to let my world die, so that we might save so many more, now, and for the years to come." Wiping tears from my eyes I choked out words at all these monstrous forms around me. "I hope we will not make their sacrifice a vain one."

And I turned away from them, my form the most monstrous of them all, the greatest mass murderer of all time fleeing in her dark robes like Death into the bowels of Hell.

Chapter 35

$$\int_{\mathcal{R}} d\omega = \int_{\partial\mathcal{R}} \omega$$

The Tao that can be expressed is not the eternal Tao;
The name that is spoken is not the unchanging name.
That without name is the beginning of heaven and earth.

老子 Lǎozǐ (Lao Tzu)

We landed on the Moon three hours later.

The Resistance had established a base there years before, on the dark side, tunneled into the lunar rock several miles to shield it from Dram scans. It was, of course, one of many such secret bases throughout the inhabited worlds, but being close to Earth, the Earth that was, had a special significance. Earth had been the source of all Readers of importance, and the greatest supply of Readers in general. Now only the Dram in their human stockyards would breed more of us, as slaves, programmed to do their bidding.

We passed over the barren lunar landscape, pocket-marked with impact craters – the longtime evidence of celestial violence never erased on a body that had no wind, or rain, or tectonic plate movements of any kind. The Xixian ship descended into one of the larger craters, and a channel appeared in the rock. We entered this tunnel that dove straight toward the heart of the Moon, the light from above quickly dimming, and only the ship's navigation beams eerily illuminating the sharp edges of the drilled rock.

Soon a dim glow arose from underneath us, and grew in intensity until it seemed bright after the relative darkness of the tunnel shaft. The passageway opened into a large chamber in which numerous ships were docked. We taxied to a free space, and the large vessel came to a stop on a landing pad hewn out of the lunar rock. Once we had Earth and gazed to the lifeless Moon. Now life stirred only on the moon, as Earth smoldered a quarter-million miles away.

A small group was there to greet us, both Xix and humans somber, the members of my species pale and burdened. A young man with a blond beard led them forward and stopped before Waythrel.

"We received your transmission, and your codes match those smuggled to us yesterday," he said gravely. His eyes darted towards me. "*She* is with you?"

Waythrel gestured in my direction. "Michael, let me introduce to you Ambra Dawn. She led us through the Orbs and defeated the Dram Emperor herself. She is our great hope."

This Michael eyed me cautiously. "Hope," he muttered. "There is not much of that left. We are left in darkness after yesterday." He glanced at me again, looking over my dark and loose-fitting robes, baseball hat, my absurd skull. "She will be brought before Richard. He will continue to guide us, and tell us what value this girl may have now."

"Then, he still lives?" Waythrel asked.

Michael bristled at the question, a fire in his eyes hidden only poorly by his attempts to control his anger. "Yes, although the medics cannot say for how much longer. The cursed Dram poisons continue to degrade his tissues, but he has lost none of his powers!"

Waythrel spoke softly. "Of course, Michael, we expected nothing less. Please forgive me if my question seemed insensitive. You know we of Xix are doing all we can to preserve his life."

The man lowered his gaze. "Yes, and we are thankful. You know as well as I that his Visions have made the Resistance possible." At his last words, he glanced once more in my direction and then turned to the rest of the party that had accompanied him.

"See that they are housed and attended to. Afterward," he added, turning to Waythrel, "we may arrange a meeting between these two Readers. Richard has waited long for this day."

With that, he turned and strode out of the docking chamber, leaving us alone with the remainder of our hosts. I questioned Waythrel with my mind.

"A complicated politics, Ambra. Michael is loyal and attached to his leader, who lies dying after his torture at the hands of the Dram. You come here with the rumor of greatness, beyond even Richard's powers. Michael resents this, and you will need to walk carefully in the beginning. Don't worry for now, there is much to learn. With your powers, I have no doubt you will know all there is to know soon."

We exited the docking chamber and entered an elevator that sped us even deeper into the Moon. The last stage of my journey had begun.

PART III

Point ɣ

First the Cosmos, then the gods.
So, who can say from where the creation arose?
Perhaps, it created itself.
Perhaps, it did not.
The Being, the first Origin of Creation
Who looks down on it:
Only He knows.
Or perhaps, He does not.

Rig Veda, Creation Hymn

Chapter 36

$$r = \cos(k\theta)$$

The flower which is single need not envy the thorns that are numerous.

Rabindranath Tagore

We were quickly led to our quarters within the hidden Moon base. Waythrel and I insisted that we be housed together. There was too much of great importance happening, and we both wished to have the time to discuss matters when needed. It was strange to be in chambers designed by humans, even if the Xix had aided their efforts. The personality of a species can be felt even in its architecture, and just that small piece of humanity comforted me.

The base was still not completely made for humans, however, and many concessions had been made for the Xix that also lived there. The humans probably outnumbered the Xix twenty to one, a ratio only to be found in the Resistance base so close to Earth. Waythrel spent half an hour in an ultrasound Xixian chamber in the room, a strange device that bombards the occupant with high-frequency sound waves. The Xix find this soothing in a way humans cannot understand and certainly cannot experience. I took the human equivalent, a long, hot shower, hoping the steam and temperature would somehow burn away all the horror of my life. Of course, I stepped out merely numbed for the moment and had hardly finished dressing when we were pinged by a messenger outside our door.

It turned out to be an aide of the leader they called Michael, and he asked us to accompany him to meet with Michael and be taken to their great Reader. Waythrel insisted on accompanying me, even though the aide was firm that the initial meeting with Richard would be private, only with me. With that understood, we marched through the tunnel-like corridors of the Moon base, descending several more levels in the process on elevators, which opened into a large medical ward.

Waiting for us there was Michael. With my mind somewhat recovered from the shock of seeing the dead Earth of my nightmares, I was able to study him more closely. Of average height and stocky build, he looked like he could have played football for some Midwest college team. Yet there was a crispness to his blue eyes, a trimness to his beard and hair that spoke of great discipline and scholarship. Whoever he was, he appeared formidable as a leader.

At his side was a white-coated woman, Asian features, long midnight hair tied up in a bun. She was likely an attending physician. It was clear that Richard was a dying man.

"Waythrel will need to wait outside," he began. "Richard insisted on meeting Ambra alone this first time. He wishes to commune with her as a Reader. Human to human."

"It is understood," answered Waythrel, although its translator conveyed an annoyed tone.

The doctor interrupted. "I'm Emily Chan," she began, "I am the ranking human physician in the medical wing and have been overseeing care of Richard Cross. We apologize for this inconvenience," she said, gazing between Michael and Waythrel. "In the medical unit, we are only too aware of the aid the Xix have given in all our efforts."

Michael glanced with some annoyance toward the doctor but then motioned for me to follow. I walked behind them, down the hallway, nearly to the end of the medical wing, where we stopped in front of a set of double automatic doors. He turned to me and looked me gravely.

"Behind those doors you will meet the most powerful Reader in the Resistance. He has guided our strategies, risked his life, his health, his very sanity to serve our cause. Don't underestimate his vision."

Dr. Chan twitched uncomfortably at my side. "Michael, stop antagonizing her! This is *Ambra Dawn*. She unlocked an *Orb*, faced down the Dram, and has been brought to us by the Xix. She has the potential to surpass anything any Reader has yet done, if she has not done so already. We *need* her!"

Michael set his jaw, his anger plainly visible on his face. "Whatever rumors you have heard of this girl, until she has served the Resistance as Richard has served, she is nothing more than another lost Reader who has been found."

"So, why is she here? Why has Richard desired to see her?"

"The Council believed in her potential."

"Which means you don't, I suppose."

"What I believe is not of consequence."

This back-and-forth about which freak would win in a throw down reminded me too much of what was juvenile in our species, arguing about our heroes, superheroes, our gods. All I could think about was that behind these doors was someone who could finally understand me, someone who maybe had enough of my experiences to have some clue about what life was like inside my head. Maybe, in this seemingly indifferent universe, I might not be completely alone.

My frustrations boiled over. "We don't have time for this! I've come a long and horrible way under knife and death and madness. Now I stand near the blackened Earth to listen to your bickering?" I nearly shouted. "Richard has asked to see me, and I *will* see him before he passes." I held up my hand as Michael began to protest. "Yes, he will pass. And it will be soon. I can see it even in the distortions of space-time he causes. Just like I can feel your anger at this future you do not wish to accept."

"I don't care who you are!" shouted Michael. "I won't have you speak like this!"

He took a step toward me, but before he could follow through or the doctor stop him, I sent a hard thought into his mind. Not enough to hurt him, but enough to stun him momentarily and shake his anger out in surprise. Plenty of surprise, as well as a little fear.

I will meet with your Richard. I have hoped to meet him for some time. I will not let you stop me. I have too much I need to learn and share with him.

Michael stepped backward, his eyes swimming, an awed look on his face.

"Michael, what is it? Are you okay?" Dr. Chan asked as she glanced with concern at the paleness spreading over his face.

"I'm fine, Emily," he said hoarsely. "Just…just let her through."

Both stepped aside, opening the space between me and the doors. I took a deep breath and walked forward. The sensors detected my presence and set the machinery in motion.

The doors opened.

Chapter 37

$$\int_{-\infty}^{\infty} e^{-x^2}\, dx = \sqrt{\pi}$$

While God waits for his temple to be built of love, men bring stones.

Rabindranath Tagore

I walked into a dark room. The lights were off except for a few that dimly illuminated a countertop directly across from me. Between me and the counter was a hospital bed surrounded by numerous instruments of human and Xixian design. Many wires and tubes from these machines led towards the bed, and converged on a prone figure: Richard. As I drew nearer, I could see that his back had been opened up, revealing his spinal column, into which numerous tubes and wires entered. These invaders of his flesh were surrounded by an odd plastic, likely of Xixian manufacture, coating everything and sealing it off from exposure. Likewise, a number of tubes and wires also entered into his skull, giving him a look of some nightmarish dreadlocked singer. His lungs breathed regularly, too much so, so that it was clear that they were aided by machinery as well. I felt a great sense of pity swell in me. Here was another who had paid a great price for his talents and his choices.

Out of some indefinable respect for this price, I withheld any probing of his mind. Slowly, I made my way around the machine to a chair that had been placed at the front of the bed, likely used by those who wished to speak with him. As I approached, his features became more clear. A black man, tall and thin, perhaps once of athletic shape now shriveled to near-skeletal form. His eyes were closed, and yet still I did not probe to see if he still had conscious thoughts. I sat quietly and waited. After a few moments, his eyes fluttered open, and he spoke.

"I knew you were here before you even landed on this barren rock," he croaked out. "It's amazing. You distort the very space you move within."

I smiled. "So they tell me."

"I apologize. I cannot give you a better welcome. I can hardly look you in the eye. But then again, you see so much, and not with your eyes, am I right?"

"You are right. I am blind."

"And yet not blind," he continued, and a short coughing fit took him. "Ah, that hurts. The Xix have been so helpful. I know it looks horrific, but all this, it keeps my mind as free from the Dram poisons as possible, while also maintaining my life functions. Without all this," he gestured with his eyebrows and a slight motion of his head, "I would have been in the throes of dementia and death months ago."

"The Dram have little mercy."

"No doubt, you know too well. You have seen it, I suppose, my capture, my torment, and escape from their dungeons."

"Yes," I said, feeling a tear in my eye. "In dreams long ago, and in visions more recently. The Xix were never suspected in your escape, although many humans died."

"Yes, our greatest burden, Ambra. That so many would die, that we might live."

I could say nothing. My pain was too great.

"And yet I did not see it coming. This greatest of calamities. I have waited to speak to you for so long, while fate kept us apart. I had so much to tell you, to inform you, of this universe, of Earth occupied, of our long plans to set it free. Now, after what has happened, I don't know what to tell you. I have no more words of wisdom. Only the question of why this terrible thing never revealed itself to me."

He began coughing again and motioning to his throat, indicated that he could no longer speak.

That will not keep us apart, Richard.

His eyes widened, and then closed, and I allowed myself to fully enter his mind.

This is more than I could have imagined, his thoughts relayed. *You have grown powerful beyond the dreams of even the Dram.*

It is a power that is limited, as you can see. Earth is reduced to ashes despite all I can do.

Why, Ambra? You had foreseen it. Why didn't you stop it?

I can't explain, Richard. But I could show you. Do you have the strength?

I don't know. But I would rather die knowing and also experiencing even a small piece of your vision, than live a few more hours in ignorance.

So be it. I focused my thoughts, stripping away all that was not necessary. I had to show him the bright path through the maze of destruction, so that he could understand. Whether he could accept humanity's sacrifice for the rest of the galaxy, I did not know.

I reached out as gently as I could, and joined our minds, letting the flow of visions enter his. His strength was barely up to the task, and the machines blinked and beeped in consternation as his vital signs approached dangerous levels. His body shook, trembling softly as the shock roiled through him.

And then it was over. I withdrew from his mind to give him time to recover, keeping a tendril of contact to know when he was voicing his thoughts again.

I am sorry this had to be placed on you, Ambra. So much you have had to endure and carry. So alone. At least I can tell you, I can feel more than anyone the toxins you have swallowed.

I felt tears well up in my eyes. I reached out with my hand and touched his head. "And I know yours, Richard, in seeing your broken body and in communing with your mind," I spoke aloud. *I only wish our parting would not come so soon. I don't wish to be so alone again.*

Yes, soon. Even my visions are fading, which means the poison has finally reached my central neurons. I am fortunate that the Xixian treatments have slowed the progress so much, that the rest of my body is nearly destroyed and will fail before I go completely mad. But it grows dim, even dark at times. And yet, I believe I still can see something you cannot.

Tell me.

I can't see you, Ambra, because you twist all space-time around you. But I can see your form, like a glacier crushing everything in its path, carving out a new landscape by your power. Your form is constantly being made and unmade. But now I understand why I did not see Earth's destruction. In my mind, Earth still exists in our future, even though it does not now. How can this be?

His thoughts faded as the machines began complaining again. His body was truly dying now.

Richard? Please, are you there?

I reached deep into the recesses of his blurring mind. His consciousness was now fluid, trapped at sea, bobbing above and below, knowing thoughts only in those moments of breaking through to the air and taking a breath before plunging downward into near oblivion.

Fading…Ambra…You are turbulence in the path…Blinded me…

Dr. Chan came springing into the room, followed closely by Michael. She glanced at the monitors and called a code to other nurses in the medical wing. I closed out their efforts. Time was short. I focused on his dying thoughts.

Ambra…events are fluid…like the sea…turbulence…can't see into it…but I can see—after. A miracle. So much light…the voices of heaven singing…

I didn't know if he was sane any longer. True visions? Or hallucinations of his dying mind?

Fingers of Divinity, Ambra….through you they will speak…you only need to touch it, and the course of everything is new.

There was a team of Xix and human medics standing around him now. Waythrel turned toward me.

"Ambra! You must stop! The strain is too much for him! He's dying!"

Don't listen to them, Ambra...better I die now than live empty and only for suffering. Goodbye, Reader. It has been my privilege to know you...so much light...

His thoughts became silent, lost in a more primitive boiling of mental functions, and I didn't know if he had lost all consciousness. I glanced up at Waythrel.

"It is his wish to share with me before he dies."

Michael looked over at me in horror and back to his leader with pain etched on his face.

"I'm sorry," was all I could offer him.

Ambra.... The thoughts came as if from far way, deep within the cave of his mind. *Ambra, change the course...they will help you...you...must...change...its course.*

His mind went completely dark, and the machinery became ominously silent. The frantic activity around me stalled, and for a moment, everything was as still as empty space.

"He's dead," said Dr. Chan. "There's nothing we can do."

I heard Michael weeping as he knelt beside his leader, burying his head next to his fallen friend. I also felt a palpable sadness in the Xixian minds. They mourned the passing of a friend and a powerful force in their fight against the Dram.

Even so, I felt their hopes reorient and turn toward me, however unsure and directionless in their uncertainty of my abilities to take up that role. The hopes of entire species, and the remains of a massacred human race, all became set on Ambra Dawn. It felt like the weight of a star.

Even that was secondary as I stared off into space. I had lost the only person who could remotely understand me, someone with whom I could relate fully as a Reader and as a human being. Richard had left his last thoughts with me, urgent thoughts that conveyed something he had seen that I could not, something about me that he had strained to convey as his mind died.

And I had absolutely no idea what he was trying to tell me.

Chapter 38

$$\sigma_x \sigma_p \geq \frac{\hbar}{2}$$

I don't think of all the misery, but of the beauty that still remains.

Anne Frank

I sat still in the guest room with Waythrel, partially nauseous from the low gravity on the satellite. The Moon base had been hastily constructed in great secrecy even as the agents of the Dram herded our clueless kind on nearby Earth. There had been no time to be sophisticated, no time for gravitational enhancements or even a crude rotating design to increase average gravity. I had refused lunch, sick from the odd gravity, sick from watching Richard Cross die, sick from watching Earth die one hundred times in my visions, and sick from a long and empty conversation with Waythrel about a dying man's thoughts.

"I am sorry, Ambra," it spoke after a long silence. "For all we know, those words were spoken in a decaying brain state and perhaps have no meaning. He may have been speaking nonsense."

"I don't believe it," I whispered softly. "I could feel him fighting to maintain focus, to convey to me something he finally understood. If so, it's important, and I need to find the answer. If it's nonsense, then it doesn't matter."

"Except that it will drain your energies from other tasks."

I felt like screaming. "What other tasks, Waythrel? I may have found the strength to do what I did, but I am wounded to the core. Would you feel any differently had Xix been destroyed? How can any creature ever thrive without their home world, even if it is just the knowledge that it is there to return to? We are like limbs cut off from the tree, and we will wither."

165

"Ambra! You must not! Or else this sacrifice will be in vain! You are now our best hope for defeating the Dram. You must find strength in that!"

I sighed heavily. "Waythrel, I will try. And that is why I hope to find the meaning of Richard's last words. I felt a hope in them, a hope specific for my kind. I wish he could have told me more. But that hope is what keeps me going now."

"Then may it not be a false hope."

"Take my mind somewhere else, Waythrel. I am too exhausted to seek answers. What has happened since our escape? What do the other worlds know of Earth?"

"The Dram have reverted to full militaristic mode. Their aggression has increased a thousand-fold, and all are harshly reminded once again of how terrible they can be. Information from Dram is censored, but of course we of Xix are able to elude their crude technology and transmit. The Emperor is in critical care. His mind is wrecked by your actions. He babbles nonsense and cries out for protection from humans. The High Inquisitor has followed succession rights and assumed interim control of the Empire until a new Emperor is chosen – an archaic and barbaric ritual of the noble houses that I will save for another time. In the meantime, the military has orders to violently suppress even the hint of any insurrection in the Hegemony. Many innocents are paying with their lives."

"Yes, I had seen this. So much pain. Even in hope for victory, so much pain."

"Word of Earth has spread throughout the Hegemony. I am sad to say not so much in concern for Earthlings, but much more for the implications. Firstly, reminders that the Dram are more than willing to slaughter entire worlds, as if this could have been forgotten. Secondly, that the greatest well of Readers to supply the galaxy has been destroyed. I am sorry to make it so clear what worth humans have been to the Hegemony, but this is the hard truth. You have been a resource, a necessary resource, and a great fear is sweeping through the galaxy that this resources has been destroyed."

"It's okay, Waythrel. My experiences have made this clear to me, in ways far more painful than your words."

"Yes. I can't doubt that. Now, all worlds see that the Dram hold whatever humans may be left, that they fully control all aspects of a scarce resource, without which interstellar travel will cease. The Dram tighten their control of all space with this slaughter."

Waythrel stood up and began the strange Xixian tap dance as it paced back and forth across the room.

"But one thing the Dram did not suspect – that word of you and your actions would escape. We of Xix have secretly seen to that. Word of one who has opened the Orbs now grows and takes shape. Word that this human also escaped the clutches of the Dram Emperor. Like a spark dropped in a parched land, a fire has kindled and is spreading wildly from world to world. I have never seen anything like it. The Dram strike out mercilessly to stop the blaze, only to find their actions testify to its veracity – they feed the fire in their clumsy efforts to snuff it out."

Waythrel stopped pacing. "Ambra, you are fast becoming legend."

I just shook my head. I hardly had the spirit to laugh at this absurdity I had also foreseen. "From slave-freak to legend in a blink of an eye. Waythrel, all I have done is watch passively as my home world was charred black. Do you know if I close my eyes, I hear their screams? Billions of them." I began trembling as the voices passed over my consciousness again. I fought them back and pushed the vision aside.

"Ambra, legends seldom earn their status, even if you are a heroine in your own way."

"No."

"I will not argue with you over your sacrifice, or theirs," it gestured upward, indicating Earth. "What I mean to say is that legends serve a purpose for those who nurture them and spread them to willing ears. They need hope, Ambra. This oppressed galaxy crushed under the tyranny of the Dram has lost the capacity to believe in victory. Only something larger than themselves, that they can believe is larger than the Dram, can give it back to them. Your feelings in this matter are irrelevant. Your legend grows because they need it, Ambra."

"Then I will need to find a way to live up to it."

"You have said it. So I can only believe it will be."

We didn't speak anymore that night. I was exhausted, even if Waythrel required nothing resembling sleep. I had to rest. I prepared for bed, told my alien roommate goodnight, and collapsed on my mattress, falling instantly to sleep.

Some legend.

Chapter 39

$$\left[M \frac{\partial}{\partial M} + \beta(g) \frac{\partial}{\partial g} + n\gamma \right] G^{(n)}(x_1, x_2, \ldots, x_n; M, g) = 0$$

We cannot define these things without obscuring them, while we speak of them with all assurance. ...our doubts cannot take away all the clearness, nor our own natural lights chase away all the darkness.

Blaise Pascal

And the dream came.

I flew through the heavens, launched by my father's arms. I saw the cold indifference of the distant stars and sensed the evil that lay hidden among them. I passed through my past and sat at my family's kitchen table to see the demon-man. I ran through the high corn to feel the blow of his henchmen, who dragged me off to be butchered and altered.

But in the darkness, as I lay on my back, staring up the high stalks to the green of the ears of corn, then to the blue canvas of the sky, the sunlight blocked out by the shadow of evil standing over me, as the light faded and blackness closed about me, I did not wake up screaming. Not this time. Not like all the other times.

This time, I floated in the blank emptiness, without light, without sound, without smell. Madness lurked in this sensationless null, yet it sharpened my awareness as I approached the abyss of sanity. I reached desperately out into the nothingness for contact.

Then came a disturbance. So soft at first, I could not tell which sense was being engaged – was it sight, a soft light growing in front of me? Or touch, a cool breeze, a ripple of air like a whisper over my skin? Or did it stir faint memories of cold winters in the plains, when one could barely discern the hint of a smell, that taste of wood smoke from a fire that resonated with ancestral memories of safety in the ice?

None of these. As the sensation grew, it was as if a thousand voices came to be recognized, as some celestial choir, a melody growing in the darkness around me. But this sound was more than sound, it came from the force of personality of the chanters, not from their mouths but from another place deep within. A place I knew more than any human who had ever lived. Their song painted the emptiness around me in a beautiful light, a light I knew, a light I could touch. And as I reached out to this light, it became not just a song I might listen to but a water I could swim within. A clay I could shape.

And then *I knew. I understood,* and the voices around me seemed to laugh with joy. From all directions, their energies came to me. I had only to reach out and embrace them.

Then—cold, hard, irregular. I felt it before I saw it. Turning around in this directionless place, seeking, I found a new disturbance. Slowly, a shape unblurred before me. And like a net with infinite dimensions, the light around me bent and surrounded it, enveloped it, and waited.

Everything was still, all the energies potential, like the taut string of a bow with the arrow notched.

I needed only to aim and release the shot.

Chapter 40

3:2

δῶς μοι πᾶ στῶ καὶ τὰν γᾶν κινάσω:
Give me the place to stand, and I shall move the earth.

Archimedes of Syracuse

I don't understand," Waythrel said again, as we raced up the corridor to meet with the Xixian physicists.

"Waythrel, I don't have the words, the understanding. I don't even know if you and the Xix do, so how can I hope to explain rightly?" I gasped out in frustration, as we approached the Xixian wing of the Moon base. "I only have intuition. Like Thel once told me, before I was blind, I didn't understand the physics of seeing, and yet *I saw*. I don't know how this can be, or what it means, or how to say it. I only know I believe it and can do it. But I will need *help*."

Waythrel was silent until reached the doors to the makeshift laboratory. "Then we will try to explain to our scientists. Of course we don't have the best of them here, or even the best representation of the areas that you need. Only a handful of Xixian technologists spared from other needed activities, sent to this Resistance base to serve multiple functions, mostly as engineers. I hope this will serve."

The doors opened, and we walked inside. Several Xixian scientists were waiting for us at Waythrel's request. I could sense the curiosity, expectation, even as I was unable to venture into the complexity of the Xixian thoughts.

"Go ahead, Ambra. It's your show." Waythrel stepped slightly to the side, and I was left in front of about five other Xix.

I took a deep breath. I might as well just get to it. They were the experts. They would have to figure out what I meant.

"Thel once told me that space-time is like a gel, an ever-changing fluid where events of past, present, and future depended on the shape of the gel itself."

One of the scientists spoke up. "A crude description, even in your simple language."

"Yes, okay," I said, not wanting to lose their trust in me. "Humans can understand simple causality— events now creating future states. The gel is squeezed one way, and reshaped in future dimensions."

They were silent, waiting, likely demoralized at my conceptualization of it all. But I had to try. "So, why isn't it possible for the future to reshape the past?"

There was some exchange of conversation between the alien creatures, and I felt an intense concentration from Waythrel. The one that had spoken to me stepped slightly forward, in shape slightly larger than Waythrel, its coloration a greenish-blue with iridescent stripes, contrasting sharply with Waythrel's deep-purple spots.

"You distinguish falsely between past, present, and future, so that it is difficult to communicate with you on this topic without distortion. Within these constraints, however, it is something considered long possible, but which has been untried."

"Why untried?" I asked.

"Because we have lacked an understanding of how to proceed technically, and because it has been considered unwise to enter recursive space."

"Recursive space?"

"It is difficult to explain in this limited language. Should you alter the events of the past from the future, you also alter the future, perhaps impacting even your actions to reach into the past. A circular chain of events, which, simplistically, appears to lead to paradox."

"Like killing your mother before you were born, so that you would never have been born to kill her."

"In general terms, yes. These are effects within effects, like procedures in a computer program that call on themselves, potentially looping infinitely in causality. Such loops cannot be followed until they resolve."

"What does that mean?" I wondered out loud.

"That we cannot predict the consequences of such actions. Why do you ask us this?"

I looked at Waythrel. I had to come clean, tell them my hopes. I knew I couldn't do it without them.

"Because I think I can save Earth."

"Save Earth," asked Waythrel incredulously. "You mean by altering the past?"

"Yes."

"How, Ambra? Even we of Xix cannot do this."

"I don't know exactly how, but I know enough of what I can do that I am hoping with your help I can succeed." I walked around, almost aimlessly, as I tried to explain the vision, tried to put into words what were insights beyond any words I had. "There is power, Waythrel, enormous power beyond anything you have ever imagined in the millions of latent Readers of Earth. *Earth Before.* Readers that were, but who are no more."

"I don't understand, Ambra."

"They are also *Writers*. Blind Writers, but with latent Writer potential. Some more, some less. I can shape space-time, you know this. So can they, but they cannot direct it. Their prescient organ is too undeveloped. But they can be channeled, Waythrel! Their power refocused!"

"To what end?"

"I can *read* the past. I can *write* in the present. You must see the next step."

One of the scientists spoke up, excitement radiating from her thoughts. "You believe you can alter the space-time of the past."

"Yes!" I nearly shouted. "But there are at least two problems that I can see. And probably more I can't. First—it needs too much energy. Much more than I'll ever have. To reach backward in time and pull the strings of space-time as we need is beyond me. I know this. That is why I need them."

"The Earth Readers of the past?"

"Yes! Together we have the strength. Our energies can be combined, guided by me, like a chorus singing together. Tens of thousands. So much more powerful than one voice."

"What is the second obstacle you mentioned?" Waythrel asked.

"The second—I'll need a lens to focus this power. Even if I can direct it, the power is still too weak, dispersed like a mist or fog. It must be focused like the light of a star through a child's glass, a bright spot that sets a piece of paper on fire!"

"What kind of lens? How do you focus such power?" asked another of the scientists.

"You can't guess? What is the most powerful distorter of space-time known to us in the galaxy?"

I felt the dawning of understanding in the Xixian group, a sense of the audacity of my ideas. Waythrel whispered out. "The Orbs."

"Yes," I nodded. "And I know them and how to travel through them. We have thought of them only as tunnels between different spatial points in the Now. But they are... *more*. I have seen infinite doors in the Orbs, opening one behind the other. Not only in space, but also in time."

One of the Xixian scientists spoke up with agitation. "But each Orb leads to another, either indirectly on the Strings, or, as you have shown, directly, when the Orbs are opened. How can you direct through time what is forced through space? How do the Orbs connect to each other through time?"

This was the part I didn't know if I understood myself. *And yet I saw.* Maybe I didn't need to understand. These alien geniuses could figure it out. I would speak simply of what I could see.

"The Orbs do not connect to each other."

"Ambra," began Waythrel as I hesitated, "of course they do."

"No, it seems so, but you cannot *see.* Your instruments cannot probe. They don't *connect.* I don't know how it can be, but I have seen it. All those Orbs *do not exist,* not as you believe. There are not many Orbs: there is only *one.*"

"Only one?" whispered Waythrel.

"Yes, only one, and it is in all these places at the same time, an infinite door opening to infinite spaces, infinite times. Spaces far beyond those of the String Tree, the worlds you have discovered the Strings to connect. A door opening to spaces so much farther than we can imagine, galaxies half a universe away...."

Astonished thoughts passed through the group around me. "Not only distant spaces, but also *times,* near and far. The Orb here, the opening of the door in this space, will do as well as any to focus the power of Readers past."

"And where will you focus this power, Ambra Dawn?"

I looked over to the Xixian scientist who asked the question, awe and fear in his voice as he contemplated the possibilities of my words.

"On that which murdered my people," I said calmly, firmly. "Richard Cross asked me to change its course. So I will."

Chapter 41

$$m\Psi - i\gamma^{a} e_{a}^{\mu} D_{\mu} \Psi = 0$$

Where there is sorrow there is holy ground.

Oscar Wilde

M onths of research followed this conversation. Soon, the best of Xixian minds had transported to the Moon base, and I was introduced to the intellectual stars of their species, minds even many Xix could not fathom.

It didn't matter to me. I was a simple rodent to these developed creatures, but a rat with a power and insight they did not have, who had stimulated a cascade of ideas in their science never seen before. And I gave them a "humanitarian" reason to pursue these ideas—a chance to save an entire planet and perhaps its dominant species, with all the Reader potential held within it.

So they imported minds and equipment, and experiment after experiment was performed. How they did this without discovery by the Dram amazed me. For several weeks, I spoke to Xixian scientific delegations. They listened to my words and questioned me again and again, and developed their theories for making this bold attempt succeed.

Then, for an entire month, I was left alone, as they pursued the implications of my ideas independently. Only Waythrel would keep me updated, telling me of successes and failures, using the simple terms my poor human mind could work with. In the meantime, I fought off the terrible chill that was creeping over me.

You who read this are sitting somewhere on beautiful Earth, surrounded by an ocean of life—humans, other animals, insects, even the bacteria in your gut and on every surface of your body. In some ways you are a small cell in a giant living body scientists called the biosphere—that tiny shell of air and sea and life, paper-thin floating on a lake of magma.

But that lake will be set loose. It has poured over field and stream, peak and valley, sea and city. Burning. Burning them all to ash. You cannot feel what it is like when the great organism of Earth has died, and you, a single, small cell, are cast into the cold of space. Cut off. *Dying.*

That is the feeling I had, the feeling I sensed from the other humans around me. We were dying some kind of death never before cataloged. A death of having the planet to which we belonged murdered. So different from traveling away from it. Traveling, you are cut off as well, but there is some kind of psychic link, some connection, that is like an umbilical cord keeping you alive, feeding you, calming you, until you make your return. Now, Mother Earth was truly, utterly dead. And for those of us who were left, it was getting terribly cold in space.

Expeditions went regularly to that horror around which we revolved each month. Some even ventured to the surface, searching places where the fires had been less fierce, where perhaps some life might still remain. But nothing. Even near the deep-sea vents, where bacteria had thrived near geothermal springs at temperatures near boiling, there was only cooling lava.

And all of it was so pointless. Even if some form of life survived, the biosphere could not be re-created, not in a million years, not in one hundred million. It had taken several hundred million years the first time, and four billion for life intelligent enough to think about itself to evolve. As far as humans or animals or plants were concerned, our planet was gone. The charred cinder we still called Earth might start over, with perhaps something evolving to consider the universe again in another five billion years. By this time, our sun would die, would blow up to a red giant like the one in the Dram system, cooking the Earth beyond salvage. Cheering thoughts.

Only once did I join the surveyors and travel to Earth. We left the Moon base on a Xixian spacecraft, circling around from the dark side of the Moon until we witnessed Earthrise. Not the Earthrise from NASA images, those stirring photographs of a crescent blue-white marble hanging in the blackness of space. Instead, a cinder-shrouded ash heap decorated with rivers and lakes of lava peered like some monster's eye over the lunar horizon.

Within hours the powerful ship had put us in orbit around Earth, from which we then descended to examine the landscape. Our home was unrecognizable. It was impossible to see very much through the clouds of smoke and ash and the constant yet diminishing plunge of debris from space back to the planet. Things were extremely hazardous as well, and Waythrel and others had strongly protested my traveling. But at different wavelengths the Xixian instruments could cut through the smoke and reveal the ravaged landscape beneath. Without the oceans, the continents were difficult to discern. No polar caps, and it became easy to lose orientation of north and south. And nowhere could be spotted even a single reminder that we had ever been there. Even space had been swept clean of our satellites and space junk by the material hurled into orbit, much of it still waiting to return to Earth and bring more fire in its fall.

A few hours were enough, more than I could bear, and nearly shaking with horror we returned to the equally desolate surface of the Moon. *Equally lifeless.* But Earth was more desolate for what it had once been, for what had been lost and burned or buried in that cataclysm.

Afterward, sitting in my room trying to purge my mind of those images, I remembered visions from my travels into human history. Germany, 1940. The slaughter of millions. Ashes sent into the skies. The word they used years later, that ended up in the history books, came to me. A two-part word, from the ancient Greek: *holos*, "completely" and *kaustos*, "burnt." *Completely burnt.* The word haunted my mind.

Holocaust.

Chapter 42

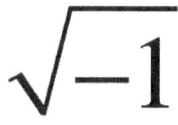

All great truths begin as blasphemies.

George Bernard Shaw

In the meantime, the experiments continued. Even as I fought off the terrible chill threatening to freeze my soul and render me helpless, there was that one small seed of hope trying to germinate as the Xix found their way through the maze of science and technology. After a series of experiments performed without my input, they began to include me in the process. At first it was simple things, reaching into the recent past to modify space-time in small ways that they could detect and quantify. Nothing related to the big task at hand, no manipulation of forces through the Orbs or channeling of other Readers to a common task. I guess they wanted to get a sense that I could do even these simple things, and how well I could do them, before they moved on to more difficult, and more dangerous, experiments.

The second phase was working with other Readers. There was, of course, a high proportion of Readers among the humans on the Moon base, and many of them eagerly agreed to work on the project once they had been briefed about our hopes. A few of the most powerful Xixian Readers also participated to flesh out the chorus of power at our disposal. In all, I would estimate that in these secondary experiments, several hundred human and Xixian Readers were employed.

At first, our success was limited. While I could sense the Reader Fields, it was almost impossible to develop any sort of method to organize the energies, to channel the forces in a productive way. Their latent Writer potential was so diffuse, so weak, that it was like trying to pick up a radio signal from Earth in the Andromeda Galaxy, and to focus those radio waves into a laser beam to burn through a sheet of steel. Of course, the final plan was to focus these weak and diffuse manipulations of space-time through the Orbs, but some kind of initial lens was needed. One not so powerful, but that could take a much more diffuse signal and compact it to send to the greater lens. It was like building some kind of telepathic telescope.

It took a long time to solve this problem, months until it was realized that I could not be this lens, that my own power could not solve this problem. While I could focus my thoughts, I could not focus those of the other Readers. Only *they* could do this, but there seemed to be no way to teach them how. The Xix tried as they had trained me, but all efforts failed. Perhaps because my abilities were so great to begin with, the Xixian training was productive. But not here. Not with the average human Reader. We were stalled and getting nowhere.

I had begun to despair when the monk came.

He was an old man, Tibetan, white eyebrows and a bald head perched atop a crimson and orange robe that draped to the ground. The monk stood at the door Waythrel had opened to our chamber, looking neither toward me nor the Xix beside him. His eyes seemed distant, a soft smile always on the edge of his expression. I sensed hesitancy in my Xixian friend.

"Ask him in, Waythrel," I said, and it invited him inside.

The monk bowed and entered. He walked up to me and knelt, taking the hem of my black robes. I was getting used to this, my gradual deification in the eyes of my species. For whatever reason, they did not brand me with the guilt of my choices, and my abilities appeared almost magical to them. I suppose my strange appearance only added to the mystique. After Waythrel's words about my becoming a legend, I realized there was little I could do, even if it seemed ridiculous to me. So, I let him prostrate himself.

"I am Chodak, Daughter of Time," he began.

I gasped. "Where did you hear that name?"

Visions of that terrible dream returned, as did the last words I spoke with Richard. Outside of my visions, I had only heard one other person use that title: the scientist who had helped make me the abomination I was.

"Forgive me, Sighted One," he said, bowing further, his face nearly touching the ground, his strong accent garbling the words. "It was spoken to me in a dream."

I took his hands and raised him up. "Please, sit with me. Tell me about your vision." He nodded solemnly and I thanked him. "And call me Ambra. No titles, please."

The old monk limped over to the couch in the chamber. We sat side by side as he spoke intensely, the entire time never releasing my hand. His constant smile was blissful.

"It was in my meditations, Ambra Dawn. Always, I see most clearly when in the deepest meditation."

Waythrel danced over and stood across from us. I sensed a deep concentration in the alien, but could not focus on its thoughts.

"Always, I seek to find you, to find how your Light will deliver us and save us from this darkness. But you are too hard to see, and the light is too bright." He shook his head, smiling. "Until last night. Then I found my mind *inside* the mind of another. It was difficult to understand how this could happen, but I traveled across the entire galaxy in a single moment and entered. Then I saw you with his eyes."

Waythrel interrupted. "You entered the consciousness of another?"

The monk shook his head in the negative. "No, truly only his brain. A flesh in which his mind abided. Or so it felt."

I didn't know what to think of this. "And what did you see?" I asked.

The old man closed his eyes and was silent for a moment. "A lifetime's worth of experience in the time of a butterfly's breath."

"And did these experiences show you how Ambra prevails?" asked Waythrel.

"No," he said, opening his eyes, the smile still there. "It was of a different time, a different place. One that made little sense to my small soul."

I squeezed his hands tightly. "Then why are you here, Chodak? There are many visions. Many futures and many pasts."

"Because he loved you, Ambra Dawn," he said simply, his eyes shining. When I did not speak for several moments, he continued. "Not only as we love the One who has become our Light in this dark time. This and more. He loved you also as a man loves a woman in the flesh, and he attended to your every movement. And through his eyes, I saw this. I saw the deepest meditation of a lover for whom all time stops as his beloved simply turns her head to the side or takes a step. Focus and concentration on each detail, each hair strand, each breath. And always filled with adoration. Through his eyes, I also saw *your* eyes. Deep, blind green eyes of sadness, but with the joy of him in them. You were to be married."

I could hardly breathe. Was this vision a metaphor? Or had this monk seen into a future where some human man might dare care for me? As I have told you, the reality of my deformity, my blindness, the monstrosity of my actions had shut down most normal human thoughts. And there had been no time, no chance to examine the idea of my womanhood. Not a single moment to exist in that human dimension. To shine this light onto it was disorienting. It hurt.

I couldn't help myself, my thoughts leapt over to his mind, and breaking a privacy I always try to respect, I looked and saw that it was true. He spoke the truth of his vision. In his mind I could witness the adoration of a lover from a time yet to be. My own face stared back at me through the memories of the eyes of a possible future.

The monk smiled and patted my hand several times. "He loves and serves, and he awaits you. I came to tell you this, to tell you so that you would know that in a future I found, you will be loved in this way."

The universe is cruel. More than anyone, I know that there will be no single future, and that even what has been could *unbe*. Was it better to know that there existed the possibility of such love, even knowing it was unlikely to be realized? Or better to never have known, never have felt the imaginative stirrings of affection in a dying life? How could I sit there infatuated with the cyst-inspired hallucinations of an old Buddhist monk?

Waythrel interrupted my thoughts. "Chodak, you said that you see more clearly in your deepest meditations."

The monk nodded. "It is so."

"We of Xix understand the focus of consciousness, the stepping out of it and becoming more even as you become less. We trained Ambra in our ways as best we could an alien mind. But you are human," it said, in a tone I had come to imagine as it smirking, "and a professional."

"Devotion is not a trade for us."

"I understand," it said, continuing to probe. "How did you find this man's mind in your dream?"

The monk glanced upward and to his left. "I searched for Ambra Dawn and could not see for the light. But there was a tunnel, a path that seemed to lead toward her. One that I might follow without becoming blinded by the light. I turned toward this path, and it took me to him."

"You *chose* this path? You *directed* your Read?"

And suddenly, I understood. My emotions leapt over toward Waythrel. *Yes, Ambra. Here, we may find our answer.*

"Yes," he nodded. "But only with a great stillness."

Chapter 43

$$E_k = m_0(\gamma - 1)c^2 = \frac{m_0 c^2}{\sqrt{1 - \dfrac{v^2}{c^2}}} - m_0 c^2$$

It is by logic that we prove, but by intuition that we discover. To know how to criticize is good, to know how to create is better.

Henri Poincaré

And so we stumbled on the process of prayer.

Yes, you heard me right. *Prayer*: An idea from a Buddhist monk who was part of our Reader cohort. You may not know it, but before Earth died, there was a good bit of scientific research that showed that meditation, prayer, whatever you want to call it, has a remarkable ability to alter brain states, focus consciousness, even improve health. Jesus said: "Pray, and it will be as you believe." Yeah, I know that's not quite like the Bible has it. But I heard it from the Rabbi's mouth, so trust me on this one. And he had a good-sized cyst, in case you were wondering.

What seemed to be passed down from generations, and what science seemed to be measuring, was that *prayer* affected the *mind* and the world around the mind. Given the human Writer potential, it should have been obvious what was really going on. Prayer focused and stilled the mind, cut it off from the five senses of the world around it, and allowed our sixth sense the stillness and quiet, the resources it needed to function optimally. And that's where the magic of humanity is born. "Be still and know that I am God." In some strange way, we've always known the truth.

Our monk had delivered to us an answer to the misdirected energies of our Readers. Waythrel saw the answer before we could ever have hoped to on our own, and that very night we began an intense training in the thousand-year-old practice of Tibetan meditation.

Chodak and I worked together to direct this giant, prophetic prayer group. I had discovered an alien form of meditation with the Xix, but he taught the Earthlings among us a more *human* way. It was far, far more effective, even for me, than the Xixian training. We performed basic meditation practices throughout the day at first over several weeks. But the results were so immediately measurable that we were motivated to continue the arduous hours of stillness for months. I could see the energies brightening. Instead of the diffuse fog around me from this Reader chorus, now there were little will-o'-the-wisp shimmers dancing around each of them.

It felt crazy even to me, despite all the miracles and madness I had seen, but it worked. Intense sessions of meditation and feedback snowballed, and I was soon able to drive the space-time distortions of the Readers into a much more organized and malleable form. You have to understand, individually, each of them was so much weaker than me. They could affect little in the space-time fields. Even groups of ten or twenty had little power. But these focused *prayers* of hundreds of Readers actually registered as a blip on the instruments and became like some congealing blob in a lava lamp to my vision, a clay that I could reach out and touch, tug – *shape*. Saints we weren't, but we sure began to spike the detectors of the Xix.

Now we were getting close. We had a means to bring together and integrate the power of many Readers in a way that I could channel and control. But still, that wasn't enough. Not *near* enough, even should the Xix and I succeed in using the Orb to focus the energies one thousand times. It was the combination of moving through time and space that made it so difficult. It wasn't like adding the difficulties of one to the other. To reach back into the past and alter space-time in a major way was like multiplying the energies involved – thousands, tens of thousands of Readers would be needed. There were not enough left in the galaxy for such a deed, or if there were, gathering them all together would be impossible under the eyes of the Dram and the needs of interstellar travel.

But the numbers *were* there. Waiting, if I could reach them. And so, when the Xix finally came to me and said that they believed they could use the Orb to channel the energies (with my help, of course), all that remained was the little task of getting those tens of thousands onboard with the plan. Tens of thousands who lived decades, hundreds of years ago, on an Earth that no longer existed, in times and cultures diverse and distant. I had to find a way to reach them and convince them all to *pray* for our deliverance.

Thank God, I had an idea. Unfortunately, we first had to deal with an unfriendly visit from our insectoidal hunters.

Chapter 44

$$| \delta \mathbf{Z}(t) | \approx e^{\lambda t} | \delta \mathbf{Z}_0 |$$

You need chaos in your soul to give birth to a dancing star.

Friedrich Nietzsche

Michael came bursting into our room without knocking. Waythrel and I stood unmoving, deep in telepathic communication over our recent progress with the Reader groups, and had to shake ourselves out of the trance. To help us along, the entire base was plunged into red emergency power lighting as alarms began to sound.

"Dram warships," he gasped, nearly out of breath. "Five of them surfing off the Orb String."

"*Five?*" I had seen the damage one of them could do.

"They know we're here," he continued. "I don't know how they discovered, but that doesn't matter. We were too optimistic. It was bound to happen."

Waythrel danced around in that impossible Xixian fashion. "Ambra, we have to get you off this moon! Michael, what ships are available?"

"No time! They set this up perfectly and were detected only minutes ago. They came off the Orb Tree at a tremendous velocity, aimed right at us. Already their longer-range weapons have disabled our sensor ships, and we can only track them from Moon systems. The Xix team has taken over, redirected all power to defenses, but it won't last long."

I sensed a deep anxiety within Waythrel that was only partially focused on me. "We had no advanced warning, even through our Time Tree relays. This can only mean one thing."

Michael nodded. "Word came in shortly after the ships appeared. There has been a mass purging of Xix on Dram, and spreading to Dram-controlled worlds."

"And Xix itself?" I could feel the creature nearly dissolving. Its mental patterns were much simpler now, less complex, primitive emotional-like states dominating the structure.

"No word of any attack. Yet. Maybe, they don't have the evidence to suspect that much. Maybe, they are just purging Dram in case."

Waythrel moved quickly. "Michael, there must be a ship we can use to try an escape!"

"You'll be blown out of the skies in seconds. You know nothing will get by."

I couldn't stand it anymore. "Or should we just sit here until they liquefy the base? Is that better?"

He shouted. "I don't have a plan! We're helpless!"

My mind raced. I began to feel the first tremors of explosions, likely the initial impacts of Dram weapons on the lunar surface. At that distance, with the generators we had, it would likely be a few minutes before they could effectively target the base. But only a few minutes.

"Michael, assemble the Readers in the meditation chamber." He stood there quietly, perplexed. I shouted. "Michael! Get all the Readers down there, now!"

I felt a dawning awareness spread across Waythrel's mental web. "Ambra, no, it is much too dangerous."

"What is too dangerous? Why do we need the Readers?" His face was completely blank.

I pushed past him, beginning to sprint down the hallway, a blind woman dashing through narrow corridors, feeling with my hands along the walls, feeling with my mind along the Strings. "Waythrel, gather the Xix techs and fire the damn machines up. We've only got minutes!"

By the time we had critical numbers, we were starting to take damage. The entire base was rocking with the explosions and impacts. *Five warships!* It was probably enough firepower to destroy an entire metropolis ten times over. They wouldn't even have to kill us directly—just knock out the life support on this airless and frigid rock. Of course, the Dram would make sure and boil the base away as well.

Waythrel and the Xixian scientists had already powered up the amplifiers or whatever they were that would aid in channeling our space-time manipulations. They performed coolly under pressure, much better than my human brethren.

"Everyone!" I shouted over the din of war and human panic. "Listen to me!"

But it was no use. People were shouting, running around, clutching each other. My voice could not penetrate the cacophony. So I closed my eyes and resorted to more brutal means.

It was a brief burst, but harsh. There were several cries as everyone in the room simultaneously grabbed their skulls, shutting their eyes tightly in pain. Several fell to the floor and slowly stood up again. One did not rise and remained motionless on the floor. They looked at me in dawning understanding. Some looked betrayed.

"I'm sorry!" I screamed, as much to stop my own thoughts of what I had done as to focus their attention. "Listen to me! The Dram will destroy this base in minutes! We can't beat them in a fight. We can't stop or repel their weapons." The room was utterly quiet except for the rumbling from above. I swallowed and pressed on. "We have *one* chance to stop them. When the Orbs are opened, there is a terrible distortion of space-time around them. Unless tightly controlled, there is so much curvature, the Orbs will draw into themselves anything nearby. Even warships."

I heard Waythrel in my mind. *Ambra, hurry! Time is running out!*

"I can open the Orbs, but I can only do it if I'm close to them. And I don't know if I can control them from this distance. Not without your help! This is the time to use all that we have been practicing for. Right now, I need you to quiet yourselves and harmonize, and reach out with me. Together, maybe we can open the Orb and draw the Dram warships into it!"

"What if you can't open it from here, even with our help?" a woman called out.

"Then we die as we surely will anyway," cried Waythrel.

The monk stepped forward, his smile only a weak shadow. "And if you cannot control the Orb?"

I looked at Waythrel and its thoughts echoed my own. "I don't know. I think it could consume the entire system."

There was a second or two of buzzing, but a strong earthquake shook the room, and dust rained down on us. Waythrel cried out, "Unless you survive, your star system is already dead! The only risk is delay. Take your positions! Calm yourselves. Find your focus and direct it to Ambra!"

They listened. The Readers crouched and sat. As a group they frantically tried to reach a Zen-like calm. Have you ever tried to reach a Zen-like calm frantically? The ultimate irony: in order to save our lives, we were forced in panic to reach an enlightened state of calmness in which we no longer feared for our lives. It wasn't working.

Sensing the inability to focus, the old monk called out reminders of his teachings, stepping among the Readers calmly, trying to coax them to relinquish their attachments to themselves. To safety. To life itself. To seek a state of detachment where death does not matter in order that we might save our hides. That wasn't working, either.

I became desperate as more explosions rocked the base. Once again, survival drove me to actions I never would have imagined in saner moments. I thought back to my invasion of the other Readers' minds, my mental slap to calm them down. I had stunned them all, possibly damaged the mind of one, in order to get their attention. Was my only option disturbance? If I could cause such damage, couldn't I also heal? I decided that I would try, even if it meant in the end a form of mind control. I sent my thoughts out over the Readers before me, waves of intricate space-time distortions that interacted with their mental fields. At first, everything was out of phase, clashing. As I adapted and sought to know each personality that I touched, one by one, my calming thoughts began to resonate with them. One by one, I drove out the thoughts of fear and panic, and the Readers were freed of them. They could then focus as they had been trained, inwardly seeking to concentrate and redirect their own force fields towards me.

I felt Waythrel's thoughts from across the room as it deduced what was happening. *I love you, Ambra Dawn, but I fear you. Now you control even the thoughts of others.*

I didn't have the luxury to question the ethics of what I was doing. This was the only way I knew to save our lives. And it was probably not even going to work.

Chapter 45

$$2^{\aleph_\alpha} = \aleph_{\alpha+1}$$

A set is a Many that allows itself to be thought of as a One.

Georg Cantor

I floated midway between the approaching Dram warships and the lunar base.

Like in the dreams of Earth from before, I had no body, no damage suffered from the vacuum of space or the scalding radiation of the sun. I was a disembodied sentient knot of space-time, projected from inside the lunar surface, the product of my own mental structure and efforts and the amplification of hundreds of Readers and Xixian space-time modulators.

I didn't have time to examine how this had happened or what had truly happened to me. Not only to me—but to the entire Reader chorus that strove and connected with me. This projected, multi-dimensional knot of consciousness, the product of the mind-space-time field that Thel had introduced my inadequate human intelligence to, was something new. My consciousness dominated the matrix. I shaped and held it together. But there were hundreds of threads, thousands even, from the thoughts of the other Readers entwined. Not only entwined, but *interwoven* so that we became something more than simply a chorus in harmony. It was almost like the birth of a unified, newborn synergistic mind greater than our individuality. Formed of the combined strength and power of multiple minds, augmented by the advanced technology of the Xix, but like ice melting, transitioning into a new state beyond all that had been known before. *We* had become something *Else*. It was like waking up, except that the being that awoke had just been born.

Some portion of me was still inside, meditating with the others inside Earth's Moon. But what it was of me, of all of us, that was outside, I to this day do not know. The Xix do not know. It was me but only a part of me. A "me" projected and concentrated, but that could dissolve leaving no damage to the rest of us sitting quietly in lotus position in the middle of a dust-choked room entombed on Earth's satellite.

The Dram energy weapons passed through me without effect, and their explosive missiles did not detonate. Nor did they impact the base. Already, I had left sharp warpings of space behind me, between me and the base, so that, as the Dram radiation and solid weaponry followed available paths in space-time, they curved, seemingly repelled by the base itself, and scattered harmlessly around the remaining surface of the Moon. It was an intuitive "shield" I constructed, in my efforts to will their weapons away from the base. It was also draining, but I knew I could keep it up longer than they could.

Their inability to target us only fueled the Dram soldiers to anger, and they unleashed a bombardment the likes of which I had never seen, even in the space battles I had witnessed before in my journey. Five powerful Dram warcraft unloaded on the little lunar base and, like some prismatic spray impacting a wall, exploded in light of a thousand colors casting shadows on the Moon's surface. Part of my mind rejoiced: they were draining their energy supplies dramatically, and when the gravitational vortex came, they would have that much less with which to resist it. I could maintain this shield long enough to debilitate them. I was not in a hurry. In fact, I felt strangely calm.

Ambra, open the Orb!

I discerned the intricate threads of Waythrel's consciousness calling from within.

Ambra, now! There isn't time!

It was hard to feel the same desperation out here. Without the full flood of my body's limbic soup—its adrenaline, cortisol, hormones, oxygen, sugar—I felt a strange form of detached peace. And what was the hurry? The stupid Dram army was just draining its batteries, anyway.

It's okay, Waythrel. I've blocked them. Let them empty their ammunition.

Ambra, please! It's not about them, it's about you! Your body—something is wrong. It is losing temperature. Your heart rate is slowing dangerously. You must return! Open the Orb!

Strange. *My body.* Yes, I could still sense it. Back there, linked weakly by a thread to this new me. I guess I would need my body. If I were to continue my journey, end the Dram war, I would need to survive, would I not? Was this motivating? I wasn't sure that it was. In this new state of being, all my ideas of what was and wasn't important took on new forms. Eons seemed to shrink to ages, parsecs seemed to be only short trips. Matter and energy and time mixed and spun and transformed in millions of fashions.

So what if my body died? How imprisoned we fleshly creatures were! So blind to the vastness, the openness, the *possibilities* of the universe. Our vision myopic, tunneled by bone and blood and limited mental horizons. What I had become was something very different. I was not unhappy or harmed in this state. To the contrary, I felt empowered, strangely free. I could explore the universe. Perhaps forever.

Ambra! Please, no! We can feel your thoughts. Please, please don't leave us. Ambra, I am only a Xix, but...I...we...we love you.

The Orb fluxed brightly in my mind's eye. It was a pulse of power, a flash, blinding like a detonation, and it had not been part of our plan. I had not reached out to it as yet. This was not my doing. Instead, I felt *it* reaching out, reaching out to *me*. A tendril of radiance sped at greater than light speeds and targeted me like a missile. I could not move or escape its approach. It struck me as a mental blow and enveloped me. I was surrounded, enfolded into an energy field not of cold indifference, not of some mechanical production, but of something that felt much more organic. Something that felt *alive*. Something that felt more than alive and that had a will of its own: *The Orb was conscious.*

And, it spoke to me.

Chapter 46

$$\phi = 1 + (1/\phi) = 1 + (1/(1+(1/(1+1/...))))$$

In love all the contradictions of existence merge themselves and are lost. Only in love, are unity and duality not at variance. Love must be one and two at the same time.

Rabindranath Tagore

Once again, I awoke after a long sleep to stare up at the alien form of a Xixian medic. Detectors were positioned around my body, data collected, vital signs examined by the wonders of Xixian technology. The room was dim, and even so the weak light hurt my blind eyes. The occipital lobe at the back of my oblong head may have been obliterated, but my retina could still very much feel pain.

I felt sore and cold, and I blinked several times. Slowly, an awareness beyond the five senses grew, and the consciousness of many creatures washed over me—human and Xixian. And of *another* in the distance. Now that I had experienced it, I would never again lose the sense of its presence. Powerful. Quiescent. Alien and yet more human than myself. I knew something was different. Something profound had happened. I just could not remember.

Close at hand, I felt the mind of Waythrel. I reached out to it.

Hello again, my dear Xix.

The room burst into applause. With my prescience, I scanned the immediate past and saw that a crowd was gathered around my hospital bed, cheering and crying, smiles and melting anxiety washing the room like a rainstorm. I couldn't help but also smile.

"Were my thoughts so loud?" I asked through a croaked voice.

There was laughter and more tears. Waythrel touched my forehead with one of its many tendrilled fingers. "We are tightly bound now and sense each other as never before. We nearly lost you, foolish human child."

My sleep had been dreamless, empty, and my memory was a torn patchwork. "What happened, Waythrel? My last memories—they are of you calling for me to open the Orb, and of...something else."

The entire room was silent. Waythrel continued to stroke my forehead. "You are our prophet, Ambra. Your mind was traumatized, and you can't remember right now, but a higher power spoke through you."

"A higher power? What do you mean? What of the Dram? What *happened*?"

"The Dram are gone—where, we don't know. You opened the Orb, or, perhaps as we understand better now, the Orb opened *for* you. The ships were dragged into the wormholes and sent to some distant place. Even a distant time, perhaps. There is no record of them appearing in any system. The base is secure. As soon as you recover fully, we will return to our training. To our plan." I felt it reach out to the others with a fluidity and skill I had never sensed in it before. "I think that you will find our performance will improve dramatically."

I processed this wonderful victory quickly, its other words disturbing me. "What do you mean the Orb opened *for* me?"

"Do you remember nothing, young one? Nothing of the personality that embraced you in the emptiness of space? That brought you back to us because not only our love called out, but because it loved us?"

I sat up straight in the bed and pulled my knees to my chest, wrapping my arms around them. Like some dream reawakening, I felt a golden warmth surround me, a caress of light and gravity penetrating my consciousness. "The Orb," I whispered as the events came streaming back: the detachment as I was projected into space and encountered the Dram, the emotional call of Waythrel and the other Readers for me to return, and the sudden response to that call from...*the Orb*?

"Yes!" said Waythrel, a happiness, nearly giddiness, spilling from its mind. "The Orb! We were all linked together as your body was dying, as you began to detach from your fleshly form—from us. It came when our breaking hearts cried to you, and it answered our prayers. It spoke to you, and you listened. The Orb opened, the ships were scattered. And you returned."

"What did it say to me?" My memories were still blocked.

Waythrel was silent. I sensed the smiles around the room, the hundreds of humans and aliens that in joy knew something that I could not yet recall.

I can't explain it. Not even in the Xixian language. Read, Ambra. Read my mind.

When you first learn a new language, after you have studied for some time the syntax and grammar and begun to spend the necessary days and months immersed in the spoken reality of the tongue, you reach a first important threshold of progress. At this point, you can understand a great deal of what is said to you, sometimes nearly a fluent comprehension. But your speech will lag, flounder, and fail. You will stumble to match the fluency of your understanding with words from your own mind and mouth. So it was here.

Waythrel's thoughts opened up to me, and poured an experience I cannot describe in this shallow book with these empty and clumsy words. I understood it, I understand it, but I cannot express it. I can only say that all the vague prophecies and poems and scriptures in human history that spoke of the divine were made mute by this vision. It was a singular interaction between a cosmic space-time anomaly and my enhanced and projected consciousness. It was a revelation from the Orb to hundreds of Reader minds interwoven like counterpoint with mine. An entity that scores of alien species had crudely manipulated for gain, so far beneath its true purpose, that it was like ants walking across a discarded telescope to bridge a small stream. *The Orb had spoken*. In this revelation were shards of cosmic truths that even in our enhanced state we could not understand, and in our separated individuality we grasped even less. The divine had entered the room, and we could not even comprehend the dust it scattered. We could only stand in awe.

The visions flooded me from Waythrel and stimulated at last the full release of my own memories. It was beautiful. It was terrible. It was so vast in space and time, and simultaneously so localized and intimately personal, that it generated mental vertigo. It's as if you went deep inside yourself to that point of the sharp awareness of existence, and at that dimensionless singularity, from that single point exploded all of universal creation. Trillions of galaxies, their billions of star systems, planets, living forms, civilizations, culture, science, religion blasted like a fire hose through your mind. And at the center of it all, in the middle of a thousand dimensions of complexity was a singularity simple and impenetrable. Eternal. Indestructible. A unified force that bound everything else together, that gave it structure, and that generated the very laws of mathematics and physics underscoring existence.

Of all the words I have in my own language for this thing, there is only one that comes close. It fails badly, it distorts, it lacks—but it is the distant echo of a dream whispered across infinity. It is not God, for the idea of God is too human, too finite. It is not faith or hope, for in the end these fail before the darkness.

The only word I know that I dare use—is Love.

Chapter 47

$$dt_E^2 = \left(1 - \frac{2GM_i}{r_i c^2}\right) dt_c^2 - \left(1 - \frac{2GM_i}{r_i c^2}\right)^{-1} \frac{dx^2 + dy^2 + dz^2}{c^2}$$

The child ever dwells in the mystery of ageless time, unobscured by the dust of history.

Rabindranath Tagore

So, the hunt began for human Readers of the past, and you won't believe where we ended up the first time we launched ourselves backward in time.

Maybe we were all a little cocky now that the group had become some Orb-integrated, psychic, Dram-warship-trashing space-time commando team. Maybe it was because we were just completely new and clueless to this bizarre new occupation of communal-mind time travel. Or maybe we were a sad collection of broken mortals slowly dying off near our grilled home world, and this was just the best we could manage the first time.

Whatever the reason, none of us, not even the Xix, anticipated the wee little problem of my focusing into the past and zeroing in on the strongest Reader signals I could perceive. It was enough trying to move through the Orb Time Tree, navigate its labyrinths with my hundreds of fellow intellects, discern in the space-time fabric the lights and undulations that bore the unmistakable stamp of humanity, and surf the strings to those points in space-time. Our naive logic sent us straight to the brightest collections of these past Readers. Surely, they would be the ones we needed to persuade to spread the message and form the massive trans-chronological prayer group we envisioned.

Our multidimensional knot of consciousness erupted over the beautiful landscape of an older Earth. An Earth before magma had spilled over its surface. An Earth before concrete and human industrial pollutants had tarnished our solar system's gem. An Earth radiating life and potential. It was the more primal Earth of our ancestors, and every human mind that I carried with me nearly swooned to drink in the beauty of our planet once again. The azure skies dotted with puffy white, the breezes stirring smells no longer alien, but of home. Green of leaf, brown of branch and soil. Bird's song. If a disembodied group mind could weep, ours did.

Even the Xix were moved. Sharing our consciousness, they were exposed in an intimate, direct manner to human experiences, memories, and sensations in a way that was only fleeting by the more unconscious space-time telepathy of a standard Reader. Although I could sample the minds of humans and aliens alike by myself, even the most powerful Readers of the Xix were as unconscious in their abilities to Read as any human. But with my mind stitching all the others together, they *saw*. And they felt what it was like to be human. These shared experiences more tightly bound our consciousness.

After a few moments of wonder, we forced ourselves to attend to the business at hand. There was some surprise that we were in an earlier age of human history. Most of us had assumed that we would encounter the most powerful Reader concentrations in the modern age, which provided the additional benefit of many more numbers and the technology to spread our message widely and quickly. But perhaps it was not so strange. Weren't the faith and devotion of the inhabitants of earlier epochs unique? Maybe their prayers would make up in their intensity for what they lacked in numbers.

I focused our mind more intently. A very strong source of human space-time distortion was near, and I followed the warped pathways through a forest and up a steep slope. There was smoke spilling up to the sky, and the indistinct sounds of voices ahead. With increasing anticipation, our little thought matrix sped upward and broke through the trees and came out into a clearing. It was rocky, the tree line beginning to fail. There was snow and ice covering the ground and a large fire burning in the middle of a rock-lined pit. A loud chanting was underway, rhythmic, accompanied by a strange music.

Banging on animal-hide drums and piping on animal-bone flutes, a group of short men wrapped in wolf hides danced. They were unkempt, bearded, heavily muscled and tanned, even in the cold weather. In the middle, a group of very hardy-looking women presided over some sort of ritual slaughter. A deer lay in the middle of the concentric circles, tied with ropes to the ground, its eyes wide with fear. A woman knelt down beside it and lay a jagged white blade to its neck. She let out a long and sustained howl, and as one, with a final crescendo in the chanting and single powerful drum beat, the music ceased.

Then she slit its throat.

So, after searching the past for the most powerful groups of Readers we could find, we followed their signal, landing in the middle of the religious rites of our prehistoric ancestors.

Thinking back on it, it should have been obvious that this would happen. The human mutations that led to our sixth sense occurred tens of thousands of years prior to the age I lived in. In fact, I was to discover many years later that the individual mutations and tissue alterations had already begun in our hominid forebearers before *Homo sapiens* had arisen. What singled us out, what gave us the edge over the other hominids, the wild animals, even nature itself, was the rapid development of that organ in the middle of our brains that allowed us to forecast.

Becoming sensitive to the space-time matrix, seeing the future and the dangers and opportunities it presented, even if only in the vague manner of dreams and visions, was to become the one-eyed species in an ecosystem of the blind. Like the other senses that had conferred tremendous survival advantages in a dangerous universe, being able to Read changed everything. Once again, we were to learn that it was not our grand intelligence—as we so often thought of it—that made us king of the hill. Did you know dolphins are actually smarter than us? Well, they are. No, what truly made us special was a pre-cancerous neural growth.

There is nothing like having a sense that a mountain lion is coming around the bend, or that dangerous weather is approaching, or that food can be found *that way*. Nothing like the sense that mating with so and so seems to produce a better future. When we forecast, when we Read the world, we had a power over it no other living thing did. We *chose* from the strands of possible futures.

And nature selected for this trait very strongly. In a harsher age before we had mastered everything, those who could Read, and Read well, were much less likely to get killed before they passed on their special genes. They were much more likely to survive. Give that several thousand generations, and by the age in which we found ourselves, nearly *every* human present was as strong a Reader as I had ever met from the modern age. Every one of them. No wonder they had produced such a powerful and localized Reader signal. Our technical mastery of the Earth—aided in large part in later ages by the alien races who discovered our Reader abilities—removed that harsh selective pressure. Humans in whom the genes produce no psychic cyst could survive every bit as well as the Readers. Better actually, because the Reader genes extract many prices both physically and psychologically. By the time I was born, Readers were rare. Rare and prized like bluefin tuna, and treated about as well.

Not with the cave folks. They were each bright with it and sensitive. In fact, they even detected our presence. Within seconds of the dying animal's drowning cry, as the blood poured over some ritualistic rock carved with strange symbols, the entire group become distracted. They stood up, one after the other, and *turned toward* us! I could feel their minds reaching out, the tendrils of our thought matrix like a warm fire that their hands approached cautiously and pulled back from, so that they would not be burned. They knew we were there. *They felt us.*

I don't know what they thought we were. Something elemental. Divine.

The matriarch stood on a rock and held toward us a strange relic—thorned branches of some bush, pruned and adorned with animal bones and rocks. She cried out to the skies with some new chant, and the other women and men knelt down and prostrated themselves, bowing in our direction. It would have sent chills down my spine if I had one.

But what was there to do? With the purest optimism, we tried to interact with them. It was a disaster. Their minds had never encountered something so strong, so abstract or complex. We could give them images of simple things, sensations and conceptions of a life that they had known and understood. These they could grasp without distress. But there was no hope to explain our errand, our need, or what we hoped they might accomplish. All such attempts led at first to frustration, and then fear and even madness in our contacts.

After several days of trying, the group left the cave terrified, conducting ritual after ritual when exiting, marking off the territory with crafted artifacts and drawings in the dirt. It was like some prehistoric occult protection spell from the demonic forces. After several hours, they were gone, and we had no desire to follow them. The most powerful and concentrated Readers in human history were utterly useless to saving humanity.

So, we withdrew from this Earth history having failed completely. Our first efforts, our powerful cohort of human and alien Readers coming off a high in thwarting the attack of the galaxy's most powerful military, had reached out to the past, to the most powerful Readers in our past, and had nothing to show for it.

Nothing but the distinction of having created a haunted mountain in the depths of humanity's past.

Chapter 48

$$\lim_{x \to \infty} \frac{\pi(x)}{x / \ln(x)} = 1$$

It is very hard to find a black cat in a dark room,
especially when there is no cat.

Proverb

O ur next attempts were also failures, and for similar reasons, even if the minds and cultures we encountered were more advanced.

It turns out that most, if not all, of the great advancements in human civilization occurred from a coupling of the randomness of genetic recombination and the arbitrariness of human climate, disease, and resource availability. For the world's great civilizations of India, China, Central and South America, and, finally, the European enlightenments of Greece and Western Europe, prolonged periods of plenty and general lack of disease, along with specific availability of resources (either local or imported), set the foundation. But we also discovered that was not enough.

As we scanned through the past, our community repeatedly discovered that the significant aggregations of Readers were nearly always present at these cultural zeniths. Because mastery of agriculture had reduced the selective pressures for survival, the Reader genes were less significant and could be lost with less impact. Therefore, they became more diffuse in the human population, and only when the genes combined in a lucky fashion to enhance the relative number of Readers did we see the effects.

From my explorations of history in human thought, it had always been somewhat of a mystery why there would be these random epochs of such great cultural and intellectual progress and energy. Historians knew that the resources and stability of the environment had to be there, but that did not explain why some cultures with all they needed went nowhere. Often the explanations were centered on racial theories that had more to do with justifying the superiority of the historian's race than with facts. And that's because the critical facts were missing to all of them.

When the density of Readers was high enough in a closely knit group, their combined sixth sense kindled their awareness, opened their minds and stimulated exploration and creativity. You could maybe imagine it if you thought of the world's peoples as being blind but for a few "Seers" who could perceive a blurred fog of the visual spectrum. Just this different and additional stimulus to the neurological structure of the brain set things moving that wouldn't otherwise have moved. New ideas, new perspectives, faith in a bigger universe beyond simple "sound." I can tell you as someone who has seen so much more than anyone else, you have no idea of how deep, how multilayered, how *different* reality is than you imagine it without a space-time perceiving organ. It is so obvious in retrospect, but these random concentrations of Readers in the right places at the right times were bound to drive human cultural development.

It also explained the equally strange tendency of cultures to lose the "spark," to drift for a few generations, and then for the civilization to become something far less dynamic and creative, or even to fall into decay. Always, there was the sense in these cultures that they could not live up to their forebearers. The reasons were mysterious and usually explained by moralistic historians as being due to lax morals or other aspects of the culture or world events. Sometimes, this was true. Usually, however, it was simply that the Reader genes were bred out, mixed in a way that the individuals with developed organs in their brains became fewer, and critical mass was lost. The culture stagnated.

Of course, the Xix were the first to perceive this and to explain it to us. As alien anthropologists, they dissected the development of our species without the biases that we brought to the process. Once we understood, we became excited. We could almost count on the fact that the locations and times in history where we would find the highest local concentrations of Readers would be in ages where humanity made intellectual and cultural leaps, and, most importantly, where their minds were most open to new ideas. And we had a heck of a message to bring them.

But our enthusiasm was misguided. In tragic encounter after tragic encounter, we dove joyously into these bubbling cultures and sought out the powerful Readers. We communed with them. We explained reality and our terrible plight.

And we flooded them.

What we came to learn after numerous disappointments was that even when open to new ideas, there is only so far the human mind can stretch effectively. In ages where the Earth was the center of the universe, where atoms were unknown, where spirits spoke from stones and souls were reincarnated, our hyper-modern, even alien narrative was composed of too many threads for which their minds were not ready. I say "effectively," because there were individuals who could accept our message, even spread it, but they tended to be viewed as mystics or madmen, and sometimes we indeed drove them mad with the visions we shared. We were even the stimulus for several human religious and philosophical movements. We triggered suicides. We helped spawn persecutions like the Salem witch trials. We walked with Jesus and Buddha.

All of this was amazing, unexpected, and useless to the only task that mattered. No matter how much we tried to convey the important essence of our story, we failed. People were encouraged to pray for the salvation of humanity, but the idea of altering space-time as we needed them to was too abstract. Their prayers were misguided. Finally, after emotionally and physically draining months of engaging the brightest eras in human history, we gave up.

We then turned to the only other option left: what we couldn't achieve with the brilliant few of past ages, we would seek to accomplish with the far more dim, but numerous, populations of the modern era. Mediocrity with multiplication would reign supreme.

The final straw was that the Xix had run the numbers. Even if we had managed to get the brightest Readers of the past to understand what we needed them to do, it wasn't going to be enough. There weren't any other Ambra Dawns, and even the strongest Readers of the past were not present in sufficient numbers to alter history as we needed.

The equations told a simple tale: only in the modern era, when the world's population soared to unprecedented levels, stabilizing around ten billion, would there be the number of Readers we required. More than enough, actually. But only if we could get them onboard. Only if our message could reach them effectively. Only if enough of them took action.

And that really was the problem. Even in modern times, after Einstein, after quantum mechanics, when science fiction novels and films had introduced millions, perhaps billions to the ideas of relative time, curved space, multi-universes—in an era where such crazy ideas were not necessarily tied to a religion or dogma but could lead to further scientific thoughts about cause and effect—even then, how to convince them that *this story* was real enough to take that vulnerable plunge? In an age of cynicism, of the loss of previous cultural values and meaning, when church and state had become objects of distrust, how do you reach out from the future and convince people that they had to do something so humbling, so silly as to pray to save humanity—without driving them to madness?

Some of us argued for creating a new religion, convinced that only through the devotion of religious certainty could we focus the minds as we would need. Despite misgivings from many, we made several attempts to achieve this very end. All were spectacular failures. Those people open to the idea of *revela-*

tion also were the least inclined to be rigorous in thought, and often creatively modified our visions to suit their own emotional needs. Cults were formed, even scientific religions, but they all distorted the message, often so severely that it would have been a comedy if it weren't so tragic. We were especially good at creating doomsday cults.

The idea of creating new religions had failed, and so we moved on. We explored the manipulation of political movements, nation-states, cultural fads, and philosophy. All had certain attractive features to achieving our goals, but all suffered from one or numerous fatal flaws that quickly became apparent. In the end, after we had moved from the best and brightest Readers to the average in order to get the numbers required, we also abandoned the elevated routes of religion, philosophy, and culture. We decided upon the lowest common denominator, the one commonality across cultures that attracted the largest numbers, the greatest resources, and had the longest staying power: entertainment.

In the modern era, nothing could move people and resources faster than a great story told well. We knew we had a great story, but storytellers we were not. So we looked for them. We sought out poets and playwrights, novelists and musicians. We engaged with those who seemed receptive to initial probes. We sought to help them bring about the telling of their future in a way that would capture hearts and move the narrative across the world. To find Readers. To convince them.

You know how this ends. You are holding the resulting artifact right now. After everything in this long and insane journey, this book is how we have reached you.

Chapter 49

$$C_0 = 1, \ C_{n+1} = (4n+2)C_n / (n+2)$$

Nothing that is worth knowing can be taught.

Oscar Wilde

O n a base dug into the surface of the Moon, you might not expect to find a sequestered garden where light and shade, marble and trees, life and death are so balanced, so respectfully interlaced, that you feel you are in a holy place.

Yet, there it lies still. The designers must have been both human and Xixian. There was too much there from the human heart – the quiet fountains, the overhanging branches, the marbled columns approached by grass-shrouded marbled footpaths – this could not be from the alien souls of the Xix. But the realization of the place, the amazing simulation of Earth's atmosphere-filtered sunlight, the acceleration of growth in the towering beeches that could only have been planted a few years before, the slight increase in gravity that spoke of alien technology used sparingly in this base – these had the fingerprints of the Xix all over them.

It was perhaps the most beautiful synergy of human and alien work that I had ever seen. Soft shadows from a spring morning dappled the green grass in front of me with intertwined patterns from the branches and leaves. I stepped softly on the overgrown marbled path, walking silently, solemnly toward a single raised platform of stone. Resting on top and in the center of a marble slab that capped the polished granite was a golden bowl filled with fragrant oil. Floating on the oil was a wick embedded in a light material, perhaps cork sandwiched between two golden pieces of metal in a circular shape. The wick burned softly and steadily over the sea of hydrocarbons.

I knelt down and bowed my head. Using my second sight, I read the words my blind eyes could not: Richard Cross, 2060-2094, *His Memory is Eternal*. So simple, and all the more powerful for it.

"It's time, Richard." I was whispering. "We're going to try once more today. I've found him. He'll tell our story right."

With the work of the Xixian scientists finished, our new experiences with the Orb stitching us more tightly together, and our clumsy apprenticeship in exploring minds of the past, we were ready. Limited time and danger had focused our efforts. Already we had repelled two more Dram warship attacks. From newly deployed Xixian sentries hidden from the Dram, reports spoke of a third armada being amassed—the largest one yet. They were determined to destroy us on the Moon. Even if they did not know what we plotted, they suspected I was here, and that was enough.

I was not so concerned about the Dram ships and weapons—I knew how to handle those with the power of the Orb. Something more nebulous was eating at my mind. The last attack had been different. I had more trouble altering space-time to block the attacks. There was interference, and I could localize the source to the Dram ships. *Something* was fighting me at this new level, in the arena of space and time. But I had no knowledge of my enemy. Creature or machine? One or many? Destroyed or returning? Right now, I held the upper hand. But would it last? What was this new challenge from the Dram? Would I soon be overwhelmed? I didn't know how much time we had left.

We needed a catalyst, a place where a small initial input of energy into Earth Before would turn into a chain reaction. This was where we would push the first domino, be the butterfly wings in America that cause a typhoon in Australia. If there were an America or Australia left. If there were left even a single, elegant butterfly still in existence.

Even after we settled on finding a few *receptive* minds, we were still so clumsy that we tread very lightly. We remembered the problems of our first attempts. We stumbled around lightly, breaking through barriers of space and time, trying to focus on the minds and energies in the shadows of *before* that flitted past our awareness. Initially, we barely made contact.

But then, *such disasters*. Like a bull in a china shop, we smashed and broke and cut ourselves and others in the process. The dangers to my mind were real, and I spent one week in a coma when our efforts went awry, when I entered too deeply into the wrong mind and was nearly consumed. It took the concerted efforts of the Reader ensemble to call me back again. Slowly, painfully, we increased our mastery. Soon I could visit and enter the past minds, interact with them, and return with my health and sanity intact. *But the minds of those I reached!*

My first serious contacts were still so crude. My skills in this work, and, as importantly, my knowledge and intuition of human psychology, were only very rudimentary. Here I was, a seventeen-year-old girl whose life experiences consisted of the absurd tale you have read, trying to mentally contact minds in the human past that were as different and diverse from her own as could be imagined. As in human antiquity, many believed themselves insane when I spoke to them. Many times my thoughts were twisted and garbled by these minds or rejected as voices, demons, or stray thoughts and never pursued. And some minds shattered with the impact, leaving institutionalized wrecks behind, or human vegetables in place of once-whole persons.

I did this. *I* risked them, wrecked them, and wrecked them again and again in my efforts to find a way. Slowly, I learned. I learned the subtleties of human thought, human internal deliberation, inspirations, belief, and motivation. I learned when to sense the fragility of a mind, to know when it was strong enough to handle what I had to give it and when it was not. In the end as I perfected my skills, I learned how to direct these minds toward the course I desired, and to do so in a way that left them completely unaware that I had been there at all.

Now I must finish what I left unexplained in the beginning of this book. Now I must tie together what I have done and what I am trying to do. Now everything must come together.

The sounds of the fountains floated above the soft whispering of the leaves as an artificial breeze blew through the beeches. Water trickling, trees quietly speaking, everything still before the monument to the Reader who had helped guide the Resistance, who had given up his life for that cause. I felt the grass on either side of me, breathed in deep the fresh air. The echo of Earth through space and time.

Prayerful.

Chapter 50

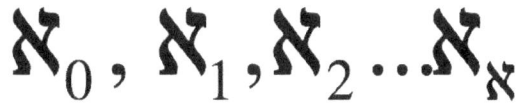

The eternal silence of these infinite spaces terrifies me.

Blaise Pascal

The fear of infinity is a form of myopia that destroys the possibility of seeing the actual infinite, even though it in its highest form has created and sustains us, and in its secondary transfinite forms occurs all around us and even inhabits our minds.

Georg Cantor

In the end, it was so iconic, that it almost made me laugh.

I walked down the corridor to the new wing built onto the Moon base by the Xixian crews. An area the size of what was once Brooklyn devoted to the power plants and equipment required for this grand experiment. Waythrel opened the door and I stepped in, looking around in shock. Really, it was almost funny.

Imagine an ancient Greek amphitheater, you know, the ones where there are rows and rows of curved benches ascending. The room was like that, with layers of a strange material rising from a center point, like a great satellite dish. At the focus of the room, maybe one hundred feet carved deeply into the Moon, was a chair. And boy, what a chair!

As if going for the greatest stylistic contrast, the chair, a composite of enormous amounts of instrumentation of Xixian design, wires and circuitry, even organic technology, was pitch-black. This showed up wonderfully against the nearly pure white of the material used to build the amphitheater. I didn't ask why.

I was led down to the focal point and strapped in. It gave me shivers remembering my torture at the hands of the Sortax representative on Earth Before, at a time that seemed centuries ago after all that had happened to me. Initially, I did argue with them about my Red Sox hat. They said it had to come off, as special sensors were to be placed on the giant bald patch, the great ostrich egg-sized protrusion from my tumor in the back of my head. The hat would interfere. Finally, I gave in and let them place the bowl-like device over my head with numerous cords running out of it and into the machinery. My hat I held in my lap.

So, there I was, a seventeen-year-old freak of nature, sitting in an obsidian chair in the center of a giant dish designed to amplify and focus gravitons from and to my tumor. Bowl on head, hat clutched like a teddy bear in hands, my porcelain-white skin shining next to the black chair and black robes I still wore. My flaming red hair, now long and halfway down my back, hung loosely, appearing to extend out from the black bowl and wires, cascading over my shoulders and arms. This is what I had come to—child of nearby charred Earth, growing legend in a galaxy, centered in a seat of strange power of alien design.

I had traveled from my parents' farm, under knife, through space and torture and dungeons and violence. I had seen the universe as no one had ever seen it. I had become blind and deformed. I had opened the Orb. But even as I was to join with hundreds of other Readers and form that strange, communal consciousness that empowered our travel through space and time, in my heart, I still felt alone. So alone that I still clung to the hat of a boy I knew only briefly before he died.

How could I let anyone near? I had no family. My own kind had betrayed me, mutilated me, and then I had eaten them in return to stay alive. Finally, I had sacrificed all of them that I might live, all to save aliens often so hideous I still shuddered when I looked at them. I was the corrupted Messiah. The anti-Christ. The alien human. Always, to the end, the freak of nature.

So, here I sat, at the bottom of this technological marvel of a hole. Group mind notwithstanding, I was its homunculus, its center, and without me it could not be. Bright orange and white me in a black chair. Ready to reach out to the universe through space and time and literally change history. If I could.

But as alone as I felt, I could not do this alone. The final players had yet to make their appearance. Finally, they must take hold of this dream and make it real and play their necessary part. The time had come for them to fully understand. The ranks of our choir to be massively filled.

It is now *your* time, Reader.

Chapter 51

$$\dot{x}_i = \sum_j w_{ij} x_j - x_i \sum_{ij} w_{ij} x_j$$

The future needed service, not pity, not piety; but in the past lay darkness, confusion, waste, and all the cramped primitive minds, bewildered, torturing one another in their stupidity, yet one and all in some unique manner, beautiful.

Olaf Stapledon

I have lived in the mind of this author for a while now. It's taken *forever* to get him to write this story, to listen to me, to stop putting it off, to neglect his other duties and tell this crazy tale. I'm bone-tired of massaging his mind, dealing with his personality quirks, his dreadful insecurity problems. But it is done.

After destroying many minds, and after many minds destroyed my words by taking the threads of my story and spinning them into books and films of shapes glorious or ghastly, yet all distortions, I finally found a mind that could survive my manipulations and tell my story effectively.

Of course, *effectively* is different from *accurately*. Looking over the words here, I am aghast at the absurdities that have crept into the story, the distortions of ideas, events, alien worlds and beings, chronology. But the main message is here, the terrible loss of Earth, the power of Readers, and the plan we have to save our planet—here, for the first time, the story in essence *is true*.

And that is the only point. I could never reach all the Readers of the past one at a time. But if I could find a medium to spread the story so that many Readers over time would come to know it, and if I could use this author of your time to make you believe, then perhaps, *just perhaps*, you might take that final step.

And you must. You *must* remember my story, my pain, my struggle, the terrible place humanity finds itself in, both in your time as slaves, and in mine, as nearly extinct. Please, I have never begged for anything like I am begging you now – *believe in me.*

I know it seems impossible. *Ridiculous.* The author himself does not really believe it at all. But *you* must. Even for a few moments, you must believe and channel that belief into prayer. If you don't like "prayer," then meditate, think deeply, focus – your energies must be channeled, you latent Readers.

I'm sure that you've never had a book beg you to believe its story before, let alone ask you to pray with conviction with all your heart and mind towards the future. *But you must.* Only if enough of you do so can the handful of Readers among you become a large enough number to provide us with the power we need to change history.

What history will we change? This is the object of your prayer, the place you must focus all your thought toward. The Dram altered the course of a large asteroid and sent it plunging to Earth. You must seek to change that event, to push the asteroid off the course the Dram had calculated so that it will fly by and miss Earth. That is all we need from you. A little push, and the belief, the trust, to focus your thoughts toward that reality. Your energies will be channeled to me by the Xix, and I will spin them into a force that will bridge time and space and impact momentum.

It doesn't matter when this happens. You could pray earnestly tonight, next month, three years from now. Others could pray in ten or twenty years. The threads of time do not need to come from the same spool. We only need to collect them and weave them together to create a force to warp the space-time in front of a rushing asteroid and send it harmlessly off course, sparing billions of lives and giving the human species, and all of life on Earth, another chance.

I nearly despair to convince you. I must plead my case through the mind of another person who imperfectly transfers my words to print, who himself has not lived through our time of terrible tragedy. How can I touch your heart so that you will be moved? Had you seen it all, experienced it, and stood before me in this instant, I know many of you would fall on your knees and pray that we may be delivered from this nightmare. Just a single viewing of Earth, the charred and lava-stained mutilation alongside our Moon, would forever change you. But here, in the pages of this sterile book that can be tossed aside with no repercussions to you or your life – *how do I reach you?*

My life, my losses, my pains, my dreams, my hopes—you have walked with me through them to this point. You have shared in the wonder and horror of a universe that exists right outside your ability to see it. *Faith is the confidence in things not seen.* Belief reaches across the finite, limited powers of our senses and minds to cross the chasm between what we can't see and what is *true.*

If your heart has been touched by our pain and our love, then what isn't seen has been made real to you, and we exist within the awareness of your soul. You can *feel* me. If you do, and know within yourself who I am, I now ask you to *believe* me and take this final, crucial step. If you cannot, all will be lost.

The story must spread for there to be any hope. We need you. This is my last attempt. There will be no more minds touched, no more stories or plays or films inspired by my efforts. The cold is creeping over me at last. It is covering all of us. One by one, we are falling into listlessness. Perhaps it is simply an understandable depression. But I feel otherwise. I feel it deep within. *The withering of the branches.* We don't have the heart to continue anymore. Our love binds us together, but together still we are ill. Our end comes.

Don't let us die. Don't let Earth fall into fire and final darkness. We have this grand Xixian machine set to receive. *Send to us, please.*

Can it hurt you to reach out with faith, just this once? The cause is just. Our fate, terrible. Our need, more than desperate.

Reader, *dare to believe*. There is nothing more to say, no story left to tell. Our fate is in your hands.

The final step in this journey—*is yours.*

This is not the end.
It is not even the beginning of the end.
But it is, perhaps, the end of the beginning.

Winston Churchill, 1942

WRITER

DAUGHTER OF TIME: BOOK 2

EREC STEBBINS

WRITER

Daughter of Time
Book 2

Erec Stebbins

New York, NY, USA

for Ambra & Nitin

never two part

When one being comes to know and love another, a new and beautiful thing is created, namely the love. The cosmos is thus far and at that date enhanced.

—Olaf Stapledon, *Last and First Men*

Prologue

I have seen a face whose sheen I could look through to the ugliness beneath, and a face whose sheen I had to lift to see how beautiful it was.

The Madman of Gibran

How do you make love to a goddess?

Not to a divinity; this is not a myth. Well, maybe it is a myth. Or rather, the beginning of a myth, where facts and hopes and dreams and the madnesses of humanity and its desperations maniacally shape the story of the past and future like some child's clay. Maybe it's the beginning of a legend. The birth of a new Divine. After all that has happened, all that I have seen, I understand why it may seem so.

I come from a land where religion soaks into the very soil, where one thousand ragas encompass every mood and expression of our species, where a million theologies were born, copulated, and recombined like genomes to produce monotheists, polytheists, thirty-three and ten million divines, and the number zero. Where the stories of the gods and goddesses never ended and a child had no need of a superhero—with charming Krishna, dancing Shiva, and beautiful Parvati, there were stories uncounted. Perhaps, then, it is no wonder that we so easily worshiped her. The real wonder is that nearly all do, every nation across this blue-and-white marble pulled from the ashes.

Even these monstrosities, these aliens now positioned across our world with their own godlike technologies and cities—they hold her in awe. In the erased fragments of time, a shattered Earth she made whole. The tyranny of the Dram trembles across the galaxy as her power sweeps outward like a tide washing clean a tainted shore. She communes with the Orbs, summons their power, opens their portals. She is a Cosmic Messiah, writing anew the story of our universe.

But not to me. To me, this is only a beginning.

Standing here as the soft morning sunlight of New Earth streams through our bedroom window, I look down on her sleeping. The white sheets are nearly blinding, wrapped tightly around her seductive curves. Her naked shoulder has slipped out of the fabric. It is nearly as white as the sheets—such a contrast to my dark copper. The entire blank canvas is dramatically altered by waterfalls of red curls streaming down to her waist.

She is beautiful enough to be a goddess.

But *not* a mere goddess to me. She may be all these things, but to me she is a woman. My lover. She is my dearest, Ambra Dawn.

I was born to love Ambra. I know this from my heartbeat to the deep ache in my bones. It was my destiny made possible only by the miracle of her powers, born when she turned the first Dram fleets to dust. Had she been a normal woman, we would have never met. Never loved. Never walked hand in hand on the beaches of New Earth to feel the waves lap our ankles in the reddening sunset. Never made love on a distant world overlooking the colossus of our own galaxy as it painted the night sky like a frozen explosion.

But Ambra is no normal woman, and I, no normal man. I am abnormal in the ways I knew from childhood. Now, in this terrible darkness at the end, I see that my abnormality is deeper than could ever have been suspected. But it cannot be helped. It is not my doing. Can we who are made from the dust and the clay reshape our Maker?

As I look at the swollen—some would say grotesque—form of her skull resting on the soft pillow, I feel a deep attraction, a pull to touch, to caress. Her Writer powers churn there in the benign tumor that has changed the fate of the universe and given her insight into the inner workings of space and time. Insight into the minds of any she chooses to probe.

This every schoolchild knows and so also I was taught, but this does not explain my childhood obsession with that deformed, beautiful head. Nor how I melt to see those sensual red locks, stopped two-thirds of the way up her scalp, where her skin shines white and scarred, the hair removed by countless surgeries from a time long ago when she lived in bondage and pain.

I pause even now to dwell on the artificial bone around the enormous, grapefruit-sized bulge, sculpted, implanted by twisted scientists of Earth in thralldom to the Dram. The brain tissue inside altered to feed the tumor in her adolescence until it grew beyond anything anyone could have predicted. It gave her a sixth sense and stole from her the ability to see as we do, leaving her totally blind with perfectly healthy eyes.

My Ambra's bright-green eyes see nothing. And yet, they see everything. They haunt the corridors of Time.

Other schoolmates learned the story of New Earth's Mother by rote. I plunged my mind into the codified years like a warm sea. I took those lessons —words of her parents' death at the hands of monsters, her abuse, deformation, torture, escape with the help of the angelic Xix, her turning back of the powerful Dram, and even of time itself—I took them deep into the core of my consciousness.

There, she impaled my heart. I memorized every event, each line on her unchanging face from countless holographs, every lilt and tone and nuance of her voice from audio recordings. Before I had the hormones to be in love, I *loved* Ambra Dawn as no man, no human, no saintly Xixian has ever loved another. In the truest sense, I had no choice. At this terrible end, I see the inevitability of it.

And so now, as I walk to the nightstand and open the drawer, it is only in a state of unreal detachment that I remove the weapon. The composite metal should feel cold in my hand, but it does not. I feel nothing. The muscles tighten around the handle of the pistol, but I give no commands, feel no responses, and sense no contractions or tightness in my skin. I can only see as if from a distance, from a vantage point I cannot define in space or in time.

And this automaton, my body—or now rather some alien form that is no longer mine—pulls that weapon out, unlocks the safety, and turns toward the bed, raising the barrel to the elongated head of my beloved, nearly touching the scarred edges near her hairline.

And before anxiety or understanding can even rise within me, she opens those blind, green eyes with adoration, turning to stare directly into my own, tears trickling down her white cheeks. I hear her voice in my mind.

Don't be afraid, Nitin. I love you.

I pull the trigger.

Part I

And I saw a new Heaven and a New Earth:
for the first heaven and the first earth
were passed away.

Apocalypse of John

Chapter 1

Courage is resistance to fear, mastery of fear—not absence of fear.

Mark Twain

Without warning, the HUD pixelated, froze, and went dark. The view screen was blank. I was screwed.

I thought I heard a popping sound from my headset, but I couldn't be sure, and there was no time for diagnostics. Three Dram sandworms were bearing down on my team, and now I was blind.

"Control, this is MECHcore Lieutenant Nitin Ratava reporting emergency tactical failure! Display and all telemetry are down. Repeat: Enhanced combat mode is down."

There was a heartbeat of static and then a response.

"Roger that, Lieutenant. Situation critical." An American voice. It would be the new instructor. "The drill's live, son, and those captured Dram don't know time out. Switch to manual and optical mode. Continue theater." There was another brief pause. "Life through action!"

Life through action. Our motto, and likely the best advice for me in the middle of the Thar without backup and with live bugs bearing down on us. I was going to need *a lot* of action.

"Ratava, got your position. We'll try to draw hostiles until you can engage. Thirty seconds, max. Get rolling, metalhead!" *Suresh.* He would make the best captain if I didn't make it out of this, which I likely wouldn't. I was sure there were examples of soldiers whose suits shorted out on them and who made it through a triad. I just hadn't heard of any.

Triads were a nightmare. The Dram's smallest infantry modules, they were designed for close quarters, with three bugs per worm and three worms per group. The sandworms were a cross between a hovercraft tank and a flying drill bit—boring under the sand, flying over it, accelerating so fast your eyes barely kept up.

The real danger came from the firepower. The beam weapons usually weren't our worry—too much energy. The bugs would risk draining their power source with those only if they had a clear and important kill or were sure of victory. It was the flechettes that struck fear into our hearts. Ever since the Dram War began over two hundred years ago, on the surfaces of a hundred planets and moons, even with the Xix to help us develop countermeasures, those flechette canons firing out thousands of supersonic metal needles in a three-dimensional spray wrecked our most fortified attack units. Our armor couldn't stop them. A bed of nails would be comfortable compared to being filleted alive by those things.

Thank Dawn that the hydraulics on my suit were still functioning. I rolled onto my back, the thick metal of the combat chassis scraping across the desert sands like sandpaper on marble. I felt a slight pull in my stomach from acceleration, and I began sliding down the dune. At least I was on the right side and this would hide me from the coming Dram for a few more seconds.

I slowed my breathing and focused to remember my MECHcore training. It wasn't often that a suit failed like this, but it was known to happen, and it was something we all had to prepare for. Reaching over my head, I felt around with the nanofiber gloves and located the control box. Muscle memory of one hundred drills took over, and I disengaged the digital controller and flipped the latchkey to manual. Light streamed in, momentarily blinding me, as the plasma screen rolled back to reveal the Xixian glass faceplate. As my naked eyes adjusted to real light, the swirling sands of the Thar came into focus around me. That and black smoke rising from the other side of the dune.

Static broke out on my communicator. Suresh's voice was strained and I could hear the sounds of explosions and cries of other MECHcore infantry.

"Sandworms engaged! Repeat, MECHcore platoon 3351 engaging Dram sandworm triad. Sergeant Suresh Murli for Lieutenant Ratava. Commencing dance!"

The Xixian Dance Maneuver. It was programmed into each of our suits. It confused the sandworm AI and was promising to become the best tactic for defeating them. The suits did the dance, soldiers carried along for the stochastic pattern, the drivers firing weapons and dropping out if targeted. It had a 77 percent success rate from our trials. If all went well, the worms would die.

All wasn't going well.

I flipped to my feet and charged up the dune. The sounds of battle—sonic booms of flechette canons, ionization crackle of our Xixian ion guns, cries and static over the COM—assaulted me as I crested the sand. Below me the dance was on; two worms were down, plowed into the sand and burning.

But the nightmare was just beginning. The third had found a node. That was what we called it, a place in the random-walk dance of the MECHcore suits that prevented us from effectively engaging the worm. Angles were wrong. Friendly fire was a real danger. We were exposed, and it was all happening so fast that human eyes couldn't track it, let alone fix the problem. Already I could see two suits down, glints of light from the thousands of silver needles embedded in the MECHs' armor. Whoever was inside those units was dead, sliced into hundreds of pieces.

"This is Command! You're in a death node, Sergeant! Break and reinitiate. Repeat, reinitiate dance sequence!"

Shit. In the time it would take to break off the formation and form a new pattern, we could lose most of the team to that remaining worm. I had to do something.

I charged down the dune, firing up my ion slingers, but before I got halfway down, I launched my two shoulder-mounted rockets. It was a pretty hopeless tactic. Without telemetry, without AI to parse the blindingly fast darting of the worm and the soldiers, I was risking their lives as much as I was chancing a hit on the Dram. But hitting them wasn't my goal. I needed to throw a wrench into the Dram AI, sop up some critical computing power with an attack out of nowhere before they could lock onto any more of my team.

And I sure as hell got their attention.

The next thing I knew, I was airborne, a thunderclap behind me from the superheated air exploding where their beam weapon had narrowly missed melting me into my suit. The combination of that explosion and my previous dash down the dune propelled me forward almost directly toward the worm. As I hurtled toward the Dram, crazy instinct took over.

Fifteen years of gymnastics training had left a set of reflexes I hadn't lost. Reflexes, it should be noted, that were honed for my body alone—not my body encased in several tons of advanced battle armor. I was going to see how well that training could be transferred.

Tucking, I somersaulted near the bottom of the dune, the impact even through the MECH suit knocking the wind out of me. I planted my feet at the end of the roll, felt the powerful hydraulics engage, and channeled the momentum into a leap that took me over twenty feet into the air. There was a sonic boom of flechette needles behind me as the worm tried to adjust to my unorthodox attack, and then I plunged down, firing the small positional thrusters on the suit. Intended for more controlled maneuvers—floating over chasms, jumping over obstacles—it wasn't much. But it was enough to steer me directly onto the worm itself. Or rather, *crash* me on it. As I plunged, I fired several ion pulses into the bulk of the craft and then momentarily lost consciousness as I slammed into the outer casing of the Dram warcraft.

I think I only lost a few seconds, coming to with the sounds of my COM screaming in my ear.

"Ratava! What the hell are you doing! Get off that boat!"

My face shield was cracked, and I could taste the soot and sand blowing up around me like some demonic tornado. My hands grasped the sandworm, or rather the edges of the metal that had been blown apart by my ion blasts and suit impact. The worm was careening to the side, the Dram navigation momentarily disoriented, flechettes firing off wildly in several directions at once. I was being jerked roughly along with it. Now was the time!

"Reform the dance, Sergeant! Low complexity; no time! Dance, dance, dance!"

They listened. The remaining platoon synced and began jetting through another set of randomized Xixian movements. The worm was reorienting, the Dram recovering. But the bugs were too late.

"Lieutenant, abandon that vehicle!" barked Command. "They can't engage with you on it."

"Hell they can't!" I yelled. "Suresh, blast this thing back to Naraka."

"Ratava..." Suresh began.

"Do it! Fore and aft! Before you lose the chance!"

Maybe I'll get lucky in the middle. The worm shuddered as the Xixian ion shots slammed into the hull. They did as I asked, centering on the front and back of the worm. Now, I would complete the job. I detached two plasma grenades from the suit's side and engaged the magnets. The grenades jumped away from my suit and slammed into the sides of the worm, holding tightly.

"Plasgrens attached and activated! Clear! Everyone clear!"

The dancing MECHs broke formation and fired escape rockets, blasting out and away from the sandworm. I did the same, only without telemetry, I was going to have to rely on pure guesswork for the burn.

I angled upward and fired the rockets. I let them go just two seconds, or what seemed like two seconds to me. Firing manually in the adrenaline rush of combat, where time was as distorted as it was around the Daughter, was a recipe for putting your suit in orbit or through a canyon wall. My stomach was yanked to my feet, the g-forces causing my mind to blank. I heard the deafening explosions of the plasma grenades, confident that the hull-breached worm was not going to survive their discharge, and turned my attention to the ground now rushing up to greet me.

My suit was descending quickly. Way, way too fast. I had one shot before impact: to counterfire the front thrusters. But without the AI there was no way I was going to get it right. So I hit them for a full burn. Maybe too much, but then I'd gain a little height and maybe the second bounce wouldn't be so bad.

I was right about the first, painfully wrong about the second. The front thrusters fired and drained. My momentum stopped in a snap, reversed, and threw me thirty feet up. Then gravity took over. I had nothing left to stop it.

I smashed onto the desert floor.

Chapter 2

Not the wind, not the flag; mind is moving.

Kōan 29, The Gateless Gate

I stood in the middle of a cornfield.

The smell of the earth and thick growth around me was overpowering. My awareness seemed oddly distorted, slowed, unreal as I stared out over row upon row of shoots blasting into the clear, blue sky above, bright-green leaves in the sunlight sprouting out from nodes in the stems, husks large and pregnant, seemingly perched to release an avalanche of seed to flood the world.

I felt dizzy and I swayed, catching myself on one of the nearby shoots, the hard stem providing enough support as I tried to steady myself. The sounds from my mouth were ragged, quick. I tried to slow it, exhaling long breaths, inhaling in short spurts. *Where am I?*

The sky and corn gave no answer. In the distance there was the squawk of a large bird.

I began to walk, aimlessly at first, the warmth of the sun becoming a heat bath. I stumbled through the field of tasseled giants. I should have become lost in this sea of maize, but I never circled, never redoubled my position. It felt as if a soft pull was leading me forward, coaxing me to turn ninety degrees at this point, stopping me from backtracking when I felt confused. From nowhere and everywhere, I felt a gentle *guide*.

The soil was moist from frequent irrigation. Looking down, I was surprised to see bare feet, my toes squelching the mud where water had pooled. *I'm completely naked.* Part of my awareness, some distant chamber of my mind, whispered that I was now dreaming. But for all the rest of me, it was completely real.

I broke out of the corn ranks and stepped onto a manicured lawn. A small farmhouse stood across a glowing patch of grass. A cool breeze stirred, causing the corn to whisper behind me.

In the middle of the field was a tall and lanky man, his short hair hidden underneath a broad hat, his pale skin nonetheless reddened from exposure to the sun. His back to me, he crouched and lifted a bundle in his hands, which he then tossed into the air. Across the grass, I heard the high-pitched burst of a child's laughter as a red comet rose into the sky and fell back into his arms. Over and over he tossed the bundle, and again and again the little child squealed.

I stepped forward as in a trance. As I approached the pair, the farmer turned around and furrowed his brows at me. The little girl pressed his arms downward with impatience.

"Daddy, Daddy, down! Put me down. *He's* here!"

Her father acquiesced, a look of confusion and surprise on his face. The little girl turned her glowing green eyes to me and stepped cautiously forward. Red hair swirled around her head in the breeze as she looked me over. Then she smiled.

"Nitin."

The sound of my name ran through me like warm water. I found myself kneeling on the grass, equaling the level of our gazes, staring at the figure before me but unable to speak to her.

"You really came!" she said, her smile growing to span her entire face. "I missed you *so much.*"

My mouth began to form a word. "Ambra?"

But before the girl could answer, the air between us began to distort, warp tangentially to the planes of space around us. The light faded—the blue and green, the red of her hair inches from my face. The wind and smells all disappeared. The figures disappeared. Time seemed to stop.

I was in the dark.

Even with my eyes open, I could see nothing. I tried to breathe, but no air would enter my lungs. Again and again I struggled. *Breathe. Breathe, damn you!* My mind panicked.

My body did not react. I did not suffocate. Absolutely nothing happened despite my frantic efforts to draw in air. Not for minutes. Not for hours. Days of struggle.

Or were they years?

Time had no meaning here.

It almost seemed that I floated unbound by the pull of mass. No planet. No starship. Only—emptiness.

Where am I?

Did I have a body? I did not know. I could not see it; all was black. I had a phantom sense of limbs, yet to move them gave only the sensation of paddling through molasses.

Is this hell?

I felt, rather than heard, a hum. A deep buzzing like some chainsaw in my teeth, rattling my skull, my spine, my phantom limbs. Soon, it felt as if I would burst from the terrible resonance.

And then—*light*.

Finally, light. At a great and terrible distance, a tunnel of light appeared, the walls iridescent. Undulating. Vibrating.

Pulling.

Pulling at me, deep inside me. And I felt myself ripped from the strange molasses, torn as from a womb, yanked through a passageway now blinding with radiance that seemed to stretch endlessly. Bent and twisted and crammed into a merciless tube of burning incandescence.

I was dragged helplessly across a forest of lights. Millions and millions of lights burning and winking and dying and being born in shrouds of hydrogen.

They were stars.

Chapter 3

Life is short, and Art long; the crisis fleeting; experience perilous, and decision difficult. The physician must not only be prepared to do what is right himself, but also to make the patient, the attendants, and externals cooperate.

Aphorisms of Hippocrates

"Welcome back, Lieutenant Ratava."

The lights continued to burn my eyes. I squinted, blinking repeatedly, trying to adapt to the brilliance around me. I could barely croak out my questions.

"Where am I? What happened?"

A calm yet otherworldly voice responded. "It is natural to be disoriented after such trauma, Lieutenant."

Slowly the lights dimmed enough that I could begin to focus on the objects around me. A strange shape occupied my field of vision, blurred so that I could not quite discern its nature. The soothing voice came from it.

"You suffered a severe concussion, multiple broken limbs, and third-degree burns across much of your back. Fortunately, all was well within the medical skills of your Xixian medics, both onsite and here."

Xixian. The tall shape came into better focus. Six-fold symmetry, four arms, two legs, forty-eight appendages including their twelve highly dexterous fingers on each of the upper "short arms," eighteen visual organs perched on darting eyestalks at the top of a conical protrusion at the top of the glimmering, multicolored torso. I could only find relief in recognizing the monstrous form of our galaxy's greatest benefactors.

The Xix. Dedicated to nearly every higher ideal humanity had ever imagined and succeeding in living those ideals to a level I could only find miraculous. Without the Xix, New Earth would still be ash, the Dram would control the galaxy, and the Hegemony would remain intact. Without the Xix, Ambra Dawn would have perished centuries ago in a smuggler's death boat.

And so I loved them. For me, everything returned to her.

"What do you remember, Lieutenant?"

I felt a stabbing pain in my scalp as my brows furrowed. "I'm not sure. Kidnapped Dram triad training session—went bad. They found a node. Had to improvise." The images washed across my thoughts almost uncontrollably. "My suit was FUBAR. Had to do a manual escape burn to clear the plasgrens. Guess it didn't go so well."

The eyestalks bounced over closer to me. "Considering you worked without AI, you are lucky to be alive."

I laughed. Or tried to, but the sudden movements made me gasp in pain. *"By the Daughter.* Maybe we should just go full drone. Not sure the point of organics out there. Too bloody fast."

"We need organics for the improvisation you mentioned, Lieutenant. AI is certainly artificial, but *intelligent* is still under debate."

Did these Xix have a sense of humor? I was never sure. All these years, trusting and dependent on them, and they were still as alien as alien could be to humanity. I certainly didn't understand them.

It continued. "A fully drone troop would have been annihilated in that engagement. We've seen it happen in the military's trials to remove organics from combat. Only your creative randomness saved your team."

For a moment it surprised me that a medic would know such things, and then I remembered that the Xix had some sort of group memory, something like the experience the Readers shared through the Daughter, that gave them access to everything that happened to their species.

"How many did we lose?"

"Three in the end," said the medic, flitting around the instrumentation in that bizarre bouncing choreography that so typified the Xixian movements.

Half my team. "Dear God."

"Two more are seriously wounded and under care here. You were all flown out after triage to Delhi, and from there to Tokyo, to the Xixian village outside the city."

Uchujin. A city created after the rise of New Earth, after the Unmade Calamity. Following the first few years of war on New Earth to remove the Dram and their agents, the Xix had settled in several locations across the globe. San Francisco, Paris, Auckland, Shanghai. *Tokyo.* Always outside the major human cities, building their own separate cities optimized for their living on an alien world. Always with the permission and collaboration of local governments.

But *not* always with the approval of the populace. That was for sure. I'd never forget my first engagement with the Earth First terrorists. Hatred for humans who looked or speak a little differently could be intense enough. Imagine the hatred toward the truly alien.

Over the last two hundred years, Uchujin had grown to a size nearly to rival Tokyo itself and served as the de facto center of Xixian governance of their population on Earth. It was the center of their technological contributions to humanity in engineering and medicine. They had taken me to the best facilities on the planet.

Which worried me.

"Why am I here?"

The Xix stopped bouncing and attending the medical equipment. Its eyestalks nearly to a one centered on me. "Lieutenant Ratava, do you remember nothing else?"

"Nothing from the engagement, I'm sorry."

The eyestalks didn't move. It was a little unnerving. "Anything *not* from the engagement, but after it?"

The dream. How could it know? Perhaps it had been monitoring my brain functions. But why would some injury-induced REM chaos be of any interest to this thing?

"Just…dreams."

"What sort of dreams?"

"Vague dreams, of being trapped, paralyzed, flying through space. Typical nonsense dream stuff. Why?"

"Your brain activity after your concussion was highly unusual."

"Wouldn't it be?"

The Xix turned a host of eyestalks back to monitors and equipment, keeping several on me. "In predictable ways, yes. Your brain scans were not like anything we have ever seen."

"I'm not a Reader, doctor, if you are wondering. Tested three times. Believe me, my parents hoped so much I'd turn out to be one like my cousins. Since the Calamity, the only thing better than a doctor for Indian parents is becoming a Reader." My smiled faded, the humor apparently lost on the alien.

"We need to understand as much as we can about you, Lieutenant. Your heroics have made quite an impression. I have been informed that you are in consideration for a special transfer."

My heart nearly stopped. *Could it be?* After two years of failed applications? After devoting myself to the MECHcore, training with a passion matched only by that of my dearest hope—*had I succeeded?*

"Do you mean…?"

"Appointment to the Temple Guardians." The Xix seemed to know what was in my heart. A few moments passed in silence. "You will receive a visit from your superiors as soon as I clear you medically. As soon as we are satisfied that your vitals are acceptable."

"And are they?" Now I really *was* worried about those stupid brain scans. I cursed the dreams and the threat that my overactive subconscious might derail my greatest hopes.

The eyestalks jumped back toward me, a small set remaining glued to the output of a floating 3D projection of my brain lit up in multiple colors.

"Probationary, Lieutenant. You will continue to have monitoring. The Temple Guards protect our most precious resource, as you know. They are screened as no one else. In two hundred years, we have never had an incident, never an unstable personality, never a traitor, an embezzler, anyone devoid of anything except the highest functionality and devotion to the Daughter. In this age of increasing threat from outside and within, I hope that you can understand our vigilance."

I did. And maybe had I been the one doing the screening, I would have rejected such an appointment— seen my rashness, my impulsiveness. Perhaps even my obsession was too much.

But I wasn't anyone else. I knew in all the galaxy, they would never find anyone so devoted to her as I.

"Continued monitoring," it repeated. "But cleared for service."

Cleared for service! The room seemed to swim. An elation wanted to explode from me. I wanted to shout, sing, dance! To serve her, so close, each day!

But I had to compose myself. Especially being *on probation*. I had to appear for all the world to be the stable, capable, and trustworthy soldier they were looking for.

"Should the Core find me worthy, I would be honored."

The alien medic stared at me in silence.

Chapter 4

Be ye therefore wise as serpents, and harmless as doves.

Jesus of Nazareth

"Kavita, please; he is not a child."

My father scolded my mother again as she practically touched the holographic projector in their apartment in Delhi. Her brandy eyes were enhanced by the crimson sari she wore, and her long and elegant fingers danced and gesticulated in the center of my Japanese quarters. The Tokyo MECHcore base was small but well outfitted. The reception from India was crystal clear—I could even see the garnets on her bangles.

I was struck once more by the combination of genes that had produced me. My mother, petite from northern India, lighter of complexion with a beautiful smile. My father, from the southern continent, nearly dark as an African, tall, thin, with a bristling mustache. I was painted in hue somewhere between the two, with my father's height and build, my mother's face and smile, and a psychology that had kept the entire family in turmoil since I was a child.

"He is *my* child, Sriram, and I will tell him when he is acting a fool!"

The anguish on her face was all too clear in the projection before me. My father simply stared upward. He knew all he could do was to wait this out.

"Are you deliberately trying to kill your own mother?"

"Amma, please…"

"First you join this army, full of these aliens and these low-life men. Just listen to you speak! Your language is foul like some American soldier! Then, you are nearly killed because of it and lay in a hospital thousands of miles away! We cannot even come to see you!"

Great. She was crying.

"Now? You tell me that you will go to the *Temple,* a place where powers from outer space will gather. A place of war with monsters. To risk your own life! Why, Nitin? Why? Because of some childish sense of romance for some woman who isn't even human anymore!"

"Amma, stop!" I had to control myself. Hot flashes of anger swelled across my cheeks. I knew she would attack her; it always came to that. Years and years, since I had been a child, growing in vehemence when I was an adolescent, and now, desperate as I made my choices as a grown man.

Grown, yet still a child. Still unable to free myself from childish fears. What was childish was not my love of Ambra Dawn, but the way my mother could still tie me in knots!

"Do you know what I have done?" her face was firm with that expression when she punished me as a child for coming home with my uniform soiled. "I have torn down the projections in your room! Yes? Do you hear? On the walls, the ceilings! I have thrown out the crystals, all the videos and images! There is now just a bed and desk. A proper room for a proper child, not some mad shrine to a freak!"

"Kavita, enough!" My father whispered, shaking his head. I was grateful for his intervention, however small it would be. It was not that he was on my side or ever understood these feelings, but he at least understood that he did not understand. In his universe, there was at least some space for his son to be something different, someone he could love and worry for and yet not control. Not so with Amma.

I tried a different approach. "Amma, this is a great honor."

She almost shrieked. "It is a shame! Your cousins are doctors or Readers! You? A *soldier.* Chasing a mad goddess!"

"I am determined, Amma!"

I don't know where my clarity of mind came, but despite all the inner turmoil of feeling my mother's harsh disapproval, hearing her ugly words about me and about her, a peace intervened through all the hurt. I can only think it was a gift of the higher powers. Suddenly, I was calm, sure of myself, of my life, of the path I was taking. I had always known where I had to be. For the first time, that surety gave me confidence before her.

"Amma, I will go to the Sahara. I will stand guard at the Temple. There are only a handful of people from across the world allowed there. The gods have chosen me. I have felt their call all my life. I know where I must be. And it is with her."

She sobbed, my father holding her shoulders, but she glanced toward me. She had heard the tone in my voice, and there was a resignation in her eyes. The sudden surety inside me gave way to insight, and I saw a path to salve her pain.

You see, while my father was a lapsed Catholic, Amma was a devout Hindu. She went to temple frequently, was faithful with Nitya at home, and was particularly devoted to Kali, the goddess whose name means Time. My mother had a special prayer shrine, rarely visited by my skeptic father, built as an addition to the house. A floor-to-ceiling icon of Kali, the Bhavatārini form of the goddess—literally "redeemer of the universe"—dominates that space.

"Amma," I said gently, staring into her projected eyes floating in front of me, her face as large as my body, "do you not see? The Daughter is an *avatar*. She is the Bhavatārini of the goddess here and now. They call her the Daughter of *Time*—can it be anything else? She delivered the world! Go and ask her icon. What better place can there be for your son?"

Her eyes widened, and I couldn't tell whether it was from fear that I was mad or fear that I might be right. Perhaps both. She buried her face in my father's chest.

"Nitin," he said, his voice rough, "We will talk later. I...I am happy you are well. We are thinking of you." And just like that, he switched off the connection.

I let out a long breath. It was never easy with parents.

An hour later, there was an alert tone from the house AI. "Visitor at the front door. Please advise."

The colonel. 6:25 p.m. He was early, as was his habit.

"Visual—external view, front door."

The holoprojector flashed back on, and the giant form of Lieutenant Colonel Brad Snowden appeared to invade my living room. Six foot five, 245 pounds, and even at fifty-seven he looked more like a boxer than a paper pusher. And he had lived up to his appearance with the distinction of being one of only three humans ever known to defeat a Dram warrior in hand-to-hand combat. For that badge of honor, he had lost an eye and gained a six-inch scar across his face. Most significantly of all, he was Texan.

"Son, you gonna ogle my old ass all day or let me the hell in?" At least he was in a good mood.

This is it. Nothing short of a court-martial or major promotion would warrant the personal visit of our regiment's leader. After the words of the overly talkative Xixian medic, I was counting on the latter.

"Allow entry."

I walked over toward the door, my limp almost gone. The bolt locks on the door retracted with loud click, and the magnetic latch reversed polarity. The door swung inward and Snowden marched in.

I stood at attention with a salute. These Americans were hard to predict. One day a superior officer would have a beer with you and the next dress you down for a sloppy salute. Best just to go overly formal and play it safe.

"Colonel Snowden, sir."

He shot back a salute. "At ease, son. You got any bourbon?"

So it was going to be informal. I shook my head. "No sir, but I've got sake."

"With ice; none of that warm shit." I tried not to make a face. *Texans.*

He paced around the room, looking it up and down while cocking his head for his good eye, and let out a low whistle. I understood. The Japanese did things well. The room was spacious, three times the size of standard quarters. There were couches and tables sized to fit Westerners' expectations. There was that top-flight holoprojector. I even had my own modernized kitchen complete with nutrient synth.

"Didn't have such fancy digs back in my day. Least not in the desert."

I gripped the sake bottle tightly. "You were there?" I finished pouring the drink and handed it over to him. The ice cubes rang like small bells as he gestured.

His drawl thickened. "Sit down, Ratava. We need to talk."

The colonel pulled up a seat at the kitchen table, and I sat across from him. He took a sip of the sake and rubbed his temples, leaning back in his chair.

"You know why I'm here."

"My request for transfer."

"Son, I've had three—*three* soldiers over thirty years under my command who have been selected for the desert. It was always unpredictable. They weren't usually the toughest, the smartest, or the best. Don't get me wrong; they were always *good*, but that Witch has her ways of seeing things."

I suppressed a grimace. There were many names for the Daughter, not all of them kind. I had heard this one used by a lot of skeptics and rebel prisoners. And hard-asses who had seen too much to believe in fairies. Snowden wasn't a rebel—of this I was sure. He was certainly a hard-ass and probably a skeptic. It didn't matter. I'd dealt with many of those in the MECHcore. But it meant this conversation might be very difficult.

His one eye glared at me shrewdly, sizing me up. "Ratava, I understand that you have a certain fondness for the Witch."

"I prefer to call her the Daughter, but—yes. I don't suppose there's anyone in MECHcore who doesn't know. The military can't block all the anom networking."

"Pinups on your walls ain't gonna prep you for what's waiting in the desert. At the *Temple*. All your pretty schoolbooks, the propaganda in the media—that's all a fairy tale designed to keep fifteen billion souls in line."

"You sound like the extremists."

Snowden laughed. "One thing you'll learn is that what makes any rebel cause a contender is a foundation of *truth*. That I can see it doesn't make me a traitor or give me desires to be one. It makes me a better leader. If you're going to survive down there, you've got to grow up, son."

I felt my jaw clenching, my molars grinding against each other. "Yes, sir. What do I need to know?"

He waved his hand dismissively. "Way more than I've got time to tell you.

Like I said, they snatch my people rarely and always unpredictably. Your *fondness* for the...*Daughter,"* he said, pausing with a smile, "made you the least likely to be selected, from the analysis of many. Hell, son, I thought it was pretty unbalanced myself when I reviewed your requests for transfer."

"I don't understand."

He sighed and leaned forward, resting his massive arms on his knees. "There's too much to learn now. And it's all in flux anyway." He shook his head, an anxious look clouding his face as he gazed past me. "And times are changing. The war's goin' bad."

"We've had setbacks. The Dram are resilient."

"Setbacks? You've got to read *between* the lines of the official reports. We're *losing* this war, Ratava." He looked me in the eye. "The Dram have breached the galactic center."

My stomach dropped. The center was our defensive nexus. If the galaxy were a wheel, the center gave the most direct access to any location through the Orb Time Tree. To take back the center—it was inconceivable. It was a disaster.

"There are no reports—"

"Of course not! Do you know the panic that would result?"

"But the Daughter! She controls the Orbs and the Time Tree! How can they use the Strings to jump if she prevents it?"

"Well, that *is* where things get interesting. If they could jump willy-nilly, they'd be turning us on a spit for those damn spider pets they keep. But they haven't shown up on our doorstep, and I can only assume the Witch is the reason. But the center *isn't* holding. More and more they are gaining access, making raids. It's all hush-hush but the writing's on the wall. Ambra Dawn, even if she won't die, ain't God. And her powers are failing."

I couldn't believe what I was hearing. "Then there is something you don't understand about all this. Her powers don't fail! She reached back through time and saved us all!"

"So the story goes. But even if you believe that myth, she didn't do it alone. She's not all-powerful. She needed *Them*, these aliens. Saintly aliens we're all led to believe, and so they seem." He laughed glancing across my body. "They sure as hell fixed you up fast—three weeks after that crash? Yeah, that's alien meds for you."

"They treated me well."

"I'm sure they did. They always do. But do we really know them? Has anyone ever penetrated their culture, understood their motivations? Their *real* plans? Two hundred years on Earth now, building cities, giving us tech, plotting who knows what, and we are none the wiser!"

"They helped free us from the tyranny of the Dram!"

"Words right out of a textbook. A-plus, son." He downed the rest of his drink. "Sure, there's enough military history of the Emancipation to convince even me that it happened. But did we trade one alien tyranny for another?"

Now he was really edging dangerously close to treason. "Sir, we can't understand them. They are too advanced for us."

Again he waved his hand. "Perhaps, or perhaps that's just more smoke and mirrors to keep us from questioning."

I was feeling dizzy, lost at sea in this frightening conversation. This was my commanding officer! "Colonel, what are you trying to tell me?"

Snowden stood up and walked over to the window overlooking Tokyo. The sun was setting behind the forest of skyscrapers, their windows giving the wall of buildings the appearance of an endless checkered light board. Spacecraft darted back and forth across the darkening skies. Off to the left, the eerie green glow of Uchujin and the Xix. Snowden shook the ice cubes in his glass with one hand, his other arm behind his back. He nearly stood at attention.

"We're at a turning point, Ratava. As they used to say, 'The game is afoot.' Call it soldier's intuition, but after surviving a hell of a lot of death holes, you might want to take mine seriously. Something's gonna happen. Not today. Not tomorrow. Maybe not this year. But it's close. There's something big growing out there in between those stars, and when it comes, there's gonna be a fire raining down on that Temple in the desert."

Ambra. "With all due respect, sir, then I need to be there. Now."

Snowden turned around and stared at me. "Have you heard a goddamn thing I've said?"

I stood up as well and set my shoulders. "I've heard all of it. And if I've been chosen, then what I most need to do right now is get on a transport for the Sahara. ASAP."

His single eye bored into mine. "I don't know whether you're the biggest damn fool I've ever met or a fucking apostle."

I swallowed as he continued to stare at me. "Neither, sir, I hope. I just know where I have to be."

He shook his head again and put his glass down on the table. "They weren't shitting me when they said you were a believer." He walked toward the door and pressed the touchpad to exit. As the door swung open, he turned back to me.

"Report tomorrow at the hoverport, 0600. Pack lightly; you'll get new gear on arrival. And a new team, *Captain*."

"Captain?"

"And, Ratava, keep your eyes open. Innocent doves end up sacrificed in the sands. The animal for the desert—it's a snake."

He stepped through the portal and it whisked shut, the bolts slamming into place.

Chapter 5

I am always wandering around in enigmas.

M.C. Escher

I didn't sleep much that night.

What little I got was plagued by parades of dreams, foggy narratives that slipped through my mind—training, childhood, Xixian medics hovering over me. In the end, I remembered almost nothing.

Except for the last one. A flashback to primary school in Delhi, standing in front of a projection of the Daughter as some angry teacher called out my name repeatedly.

"Ratava. Nitin Ratava! Answer the question!"

It was a dream reliving the first time I had seen a holo of Ambra Dawn. There she was, a life-size projection in three dimensions, the shimmer of a poor-quality lamp giving a ghostly appearance to the form. I almost felt as if I could reach out and touch the red curls cascading down her shoulders. Her eyes glowed like giant pools of fluorescent water.

I was to answer some question about her, the instructor calling on different children to recite the lessons. But I only stood there frozen, transfixed—struck dumb by her beauty and majesty. A boy of six utterly overwhelmed and unmade in an instant.

But in the dream, the memory changed. The static holograph animated and turned to me. Her bright eyes locked with mine, and I was bathed in a warm radiance. All else dimmed—the school, the instructor, the world. Only she was left. I looked up into those green pools, felt them draw me in like some wormhole in space toward another universe. I felt a slow acceleration, rotating faster and faster around her, the center of my experience those beautiful, unblinking eyes. She opened her lips and whispered.

"Nitin."

I awoke shaking to the blaring of my alarm.

I dressed quickly in my travel uniform. I still had my lieutenant bar and would have to see if the colonel's last words would include gaining another bar to the rank of captain. But the promotion wasn't so important to me. The destination was all that mattered.

I packed lightly, as instructed. My standard issue firearm, a Xixian gyrostabilized slug thrower, Hertz 744. All-carbon composite, grid synchronized workhorse of the MECHcore. As a rule, since we served most of our time suited up, they didn't get much use. But old traditions died hard. Otherwise, one uniform change, grooming gear, and a single zettabyte crystal. Small, not much for holoviewing. It carried graphs of my parents, a few of my cousins. All the rest of her.

I rushed out the door.

The hovercraft was impressive. As I walked into the hangar, barely settling my stomach after a poorly calibrated drone transport hurtled me from the barracks, I had to marvel. The size of one of Old Earth's airships, this was the classic image of an alien spacecraft to our precontact ancestors. Disc-shaped with a protruding spherical dome on the top, it could handle a thousand troops at capacity. Not to mention cargo. Ring-bands of magneto-thrusters lined the bottom, powerful enough to accelerate the ship into orbit if needed.

Troops were already marching onboard. Most were infantry to be deployed at one of the Six Cities surrounding the Temple in the middle of the Sahara. Six Cities to house the human and alien engineers operating the massive network of power plants and more esoteric equipment used by the Daughter to commune with the Orbs. Six Cities over the six ancient aquifers below the sands, necessary water sources built up during older geological periods when the desert was a jungle. So went the textbooks, anyway. Mostly, it was a mystery that few had seen. Those who had rarely spoke of it.

Only a handful would continue from the outer circle toward the Temple. The Temple wasn't like the other cities. Shrouded in the deepest mystery of all, it was rumored to be dominated by a single large structure that served primarily to house the Dish, the great antenna that focused Ambra Dawn's psychic space-time powers. The Dish was thought to be buried under the Temple structure, deep below the sands in the bedrock. There were no holos, few reports, and more contradictions than established fact. Whatever was there, it was kept under the strictest secrecy.

Some of those lucky few who were to be granted access to the inner palace of the Daughter were waiting for me near the hovercraft. Colonel Snowden stood with his hands on his hips, a black scowl on his face that would likely turn a sandworm around. His eyes were hidden behind reflective shades. I half expected cowboy boots to complete the picture and was disappointed to find regular shoes.

"Captain Ratava. About goddamned time."

He shoved a small latched box toward me. I took it, popped it open, and saw the gleaming captain's bars.

Snowden smirked. "No time for formalities. Paperwork was cleared at light speed. Not that it will mean a rat's ass down there. They have a whole *other* way of doing things." He turned toward three other soldiers, two men and a woman, and swept his arm outward, as if to the sands and Temple. "Which all of you will be learning of soon enough. This is Captain Nitin Ratava. You've been briefed, but until you land and are put under Temple command, you'll be taking orders from him. Introduce yourselves."

The colonel stepped back, his body language suggesting I engage for the introductions. I stepped forward, coming to a stop a few feet from the three. The male leftmost from my perspective saluted.

"Master Sergeant David Kim, sir! Operations!" Our team sergeant. Korean from the name and accent, short, five foot six, stocky with thick quads that stretched his fatigues. Eager beaver.

I saluted back and turned to the middle soldier. She was tall, an inch or so taller than I at five foot eleven inches. Her eyes were sharp and intelligent, her skin a shade darker than my own. Her salute was swift and hard.

"Warrant Officer Aisha Williams, sir."

She would be my second in command in the MECH team, basically my alter ego. I would need to get to know her well.

I pivoted slightly to meet the third, a Caucasian male around my height and of moderate build. I caught a glint from contact lenses.

"Sergeant First Class Ryan Marshall, sir," he said, the most reserved of the three. "Medical."

I turned to the colonel. "What about the rest of the team?"

"Coming from other corners of the globe, Captain. They will rendezvous outside the Six Cities for your info briefing prior to your journey to the Temple."

I nodded. There was going to be a lot to learn.

The Texan jerked his head toward the hovercraft. "Why don't you three saddle up before this wagon leaves without you. Ratava, a few words before I leave you."

The three grabbed their duffels and darted off, jogging onto the transport. The pad was nearly empty now but for the service staff prepping the saucer. I turned toward Snowden.

"Colonel, I don't understand. You aren't coming with us? I thought—"

"Command and Control gets a reboot a hundred miles outside of the Six Cities. They've got their own way of doing things, and you'll get your commanding officer there. Besides, there's no way in hell I'm setting foot in the desert again. They know that."

I nodded without understanding, beginning to feel a bit isolated. New commanders, brand-new team. New rules. There was going to be *a lot* to learn.

"Last bit of intel for you, Captain." He waited as several dock workers rushed past, lugging crates and loading them into the hull.

A voice blared out over the speakers announcing the departure of our flight: "*All nonessential personnel clear the hovercraft pad. Liftoff in five minutes.*"

He didn't raise his voice, and I had to concentrate to understand his words over the noise. "I'm under the strictest orders not to be telling you any of it, but you need to know. This has *not* been a normal recruitment—hell, if any of them are normal."

"What do you mean, sir?"

"*Shuttle A58L departing in five minutes. All nonessential personnel clear the hovercraft pad.*"

"You had a special visitor during your coma, son."

"Visitor?"

"*Liftoff in five minutes.*"

The colonel almost looked awed. "Never happened before. Damnedest thing. Shuttle landed two days after you came in. I was summoned, and it was requested that I meet an envoy from the desert at the hospital. *Your* room."

"My room? From the desert?"

Snowden looked away. He actually seemed afraid, and his voice fell to a whisper. Fortunately, there was a brief lull in the announcements, and I could hear him clearly. "Spent hours with you, didn't say a goddamn thing. Just sat there by your bed, staring with those terrible eyes." He barked out a staccato laugh, glancing hesitantly at me. "That's why I left, you see. Put in for a transfer my third year. I couldn't take those damn eyes anymore. How do you stand in front of blind eyes that see *into* you?"

"Sir, *who* was there?" My hands were trembling.

"Isn't it obvious, son?"

"*Shuttle A58L departing in two minutes. Clear the hovercraft pad.*"

I couldn't say anything. My brain didn't seem to work.

"Now, you think on that as you break atmo."

Chapter 6

The liftoff was what I had come to expect from the magthrusters— deceptively smooth acceleration that lulls you into gawking at the alien tech, followed by a whiplash onset of nausea around the time the ship reaches escape velocity.

My partial team was isolated from the rest of the passengers on the transport, tucked away toward the middle of the saucer in a private lounge outfitted for the brass or moneyed. Even the five-point restraints were plush, and you could almost enjoy it until you needed to revisit your breakfast.

The ride affects each person differently. Some find the initial acceleration disorienting—*too smooth* and unlike any natural or human technology made to get from A to B. For others, it's the switch when breaking atmo, several minutes of zero-g before the plunge back to the destination. And others find that plunge disturbing, physiologically or psychologically—if those things can be separated—and that's when the barf bags come out.

For me, it was the switch to weightlessness. I had the palpable sense that my stomach was lurching independently of the rest of my body, and my brain didn't like that sense one bit. I knew how to control it. I knew to eat little in the morning. I just needed to concentrate. Of course, it was just at this point in the journey that my warrant officer decided to get chatty.

"Not looking so good, Captain," said Williams, a half-hidden smirk dancing at the corners of her mouth.

I decided to change the topic by going on the offensive. "How much combat experience do you have, Williams?"

The smirk was gone. "Standard basic and advanced infantry M, sir. Plus four live skirmishes on Freinzel."

"I hear that moon was pretty damn infested."

I could see the glow of pride on her face. "Yes, sir. Two thousand Dram grunts with some allied species. Three triads protecting a central hive."

"How'd you take it on?"

She paused, a shocked expression on her face. "Air support, sir. Drones. We cleaned up the soldiers. Standard procedure."

"I see." I let the silence do its job.

Williams looked toward me sharply. The wheels were turning. "But I've heard some teams are taking on triads directly."

Kim and Marshall woke up at her words and glanced over. I was going to have their full attention.

I nodded. "It's new. The Xix have developed a partially randomized movement pattern for the MECHs. It's a little scary—you hand over complete control to the AI—and your suit just flies around in ways you can't predict. Confuses the hell out of the triads—operators too. You do it right, you get lucky, they're sitting ducks, and you vaporize them."

Williams was studying me intently. "You've done this."

"I have. That's why I'm here. You're all going to learn, and I'm going to train the core troops at the Temple. Or so the plan goes."

Kim shook his head. "I don't know, man. Full AI control? Why do they even need us, then?"

I corrected my assessment—Korean American. With English the default in the New Earth forces, training ensured fluency in just about everyone. The Chinese resisted a little, but with India, Europe, and America onboard, it was a done deal. But that standard fluency could mask origins, at least until you engaged the speaker for some real conversation. Kim wasn't a native English speaker. Likely an immigrant to America. I hoped I would get dossiers on all of them in the desert. This entire redeployment was being rushed like hell.

"Because the AIs are as dumb as they are smart. When the patterns fail, they still need us to think on our feet. Improvise."

"Improvise? Sounds like a good way to get yourself killed," said Kim.

"It's dangerous," I agreed.

"We've heard the rumors." It was the medic, Marshall.

"What rumors?" I asked.

Williams only stared. Again I sensed the wheels spinning. *She's a careful one.*

Marshall continued. "Tokyo General. They brought wounded from India, only there a few hours before they transferred them to *Uchujin*. That was you, wasn't it?"

I nodded.

Williams cut in. "Word was the team got into trouble. Training exercises with *live* Dram. A fucking *triad*."

"On *Earth*?" Kim asked. I nodded. He laughed. "How'd you sign the bugs up for that?"

"The Daughter," I said. "That's what we hear, anyway. She grabs them, somehow, from somewhere. Maybe even from Dram."

Kim's jaw hung open. "*Grabs* them? What the fuck?"

I shook my head. "Wormhole snatch? Xixian raid? No idea. But they're Dram all right. Sandworm triad. Right in the deserts of India."

"That's fucking *crazy*," said Kim again. "*Jesus*. What the hell are we getting ourselves into down there?" He gestured toward the continent of Africa, now growing in size on the blue marble as we commenced our decent from Earth orbit. The Sahara was obvious even from this altitude—like a tan brush stroke across northern Africa.

I spoke firmly. "We are getting ourselves into the most important service in this war. We are learning the most advanced techniques, training against the enemy themselves to prepare, because our job will be to protect what is most important."

"The Daughter," said Williams, her smile returning slightly as she looked at me.

"Yes, of course."

The two men nodded, seeming to become absorbed in their own thoughts.

"You speak of her with awe, Captain." Williams studied me. It was uncomfortable, but I knew all this would come out, if they didn't already know from the grapevine.

"Go on, let's get this over with," I said, noticing the other two reengage. And it was Marshall who continued the conversation, as if he had never tuned out.

"You have quite the reputation as a member of the faithful, Captain. What denomination are you—not Orthodox—you don't sport the gear. Chrono Reformed?"

I looked across them. "Special forces are worse than the tabloids."

"That's part of how we stay alive, Captain," said Williams.

I sighed. Now came the part that wouldn't make sense to them. "None. No denomination. It's a…personal relationship."

"Sounds Next Agey," said Kim.

"It's *personal*. Since I was a kid. Now look, every team I've been on worries about this until they get used to it. I can tell you it's no different from any other personal beliefs or feelings every one of us has. You have nothing to worry about. I do my job, better than most."

"Except that our job's all about her now, isn't it?" noted Williams. "This isn't like any other old job. You've got stakes."

I locked eyes with her. "We've *all* got stakes. Our planet has stakes. She's what freed us and keeps us free still. Everyone on this planet, everyone in this transport—each of you—owes your life and freedom to the Daughter. Protecting her is protecting Earth. Whatever else I or anyone else feels doesn't figure in. Those are the hard facts. That's why we wear the uniform."

There was a silence. The muffled sounds of rushing atmosphere filled it awkwardly. I glanced at the floating view screen, its image of a rapidly growing northern Africa shining brightly in the darkness of the room.

Kim laughed. "Hell, Captain, what people do on their own time is their business. Local tail, boy-girl-alien threesome, bingo—not my concern. All I need to know is where those bastards are and when I need to start shooting."

Marshall laughed softly, and I smiled. Kim aimed his hand as if it were in a suit, angling imaginary ion slingers, a hard smile on his face. One thing about the MECHcore: to a one, they lived for combat. It was an addiction, perhaps, an age-old primitive drive augmented wildly by the speed and feedback of the machine enhancement. The thrill of life-and-death performance at light speed was a hell of a high.

Williams looked amused but didn't smile. She just stared at me.

Chapter 7

Thoroughly conscious ignorance is the prelude to every real advance in science.

James Clerk Maxwell

The Thar is hot, but even my training there did not prepare me for our planet's largest desert. As the transport doors opened, we were met by three things: First, a blast of sandy wind that felt like a blowtorch. Next, a tan radiance bright enough to hurt through our smartglasses. And finally, an ensemble of human and Xixian handlers who would shepherd us for the remainder of the trip.

The transfer of power was immediate and obvious. Where once we were the soldiers of the New Earth Force, our infantry and officers now stood surrounded by members of the Six Cities. These humans and Xix did not wear Force uniforms and answered themselves only to the Daughter. But they did not hold themselves like commanders. As rumored, they carried themselves more like the members of a religious caste.

The humans dressed in accordance with their personal traditions and the necessities of desert life. Over time, their clothes increasingly resembled the garb of the long-term nomads of the regions nearby, the Berber Arabs and other tribes that had long ago optimized their lifestyle under the sun and over the stinging sands. Full-body coverings were the norm, modernized with reflective fabrics that allowed thermal radiation to escape in the day, but they were temperature toggled to internally reflect infrared after sunset during the cold desert nights. It wasn't unusual to get a swing from one hundred degrees to freezing across a single evening. Clothing needed special properties if you weren't indoors with climate control.

The Xix required no coverings. Their homeworld was basically one large Sahara, nearly a complete desert, and they seemed to feel most at their element on New Earth with two of their six-toed feet in the sand. Their metabolism seemed to handle extreme heat and extreme cold effortlessly. Their skin was impervious to everything except the most violent sandstorms.

Towering over the group waiting for us as we exited was a Xix that did wear a thin covering, a cyan robe that was partially transparent when viewed at certain angles, as if it had been polarized. The robe opened near the cone of tissue that erupted upward from the midsection of the alien and was held in place by a blue-green organic-looking metal band that I recognized as their universal translator. Underneath the robe I could see across its body a spray of deep-purple spots, some large, some small, in patterns dizzying and hard to follow. Many of its eyestalks sprouting from the cone were trained on me, and I could feel the burn of its gaze, hotter than the air around us.

Standing alongside the Xix were several humans in the white robes of the Temple servants. Directly in front of them all were two uniformed soldiers, Special Forces, a man and a woman. By the MECHcore insignias, I knew they must be the remainder of my team.

Williams, Kim, and Marshall instinctively fell into a line a half step behind me as we approached the group. They were dressed as I was, advanced Force desert gear sized and provided in the saucer. Brown-and-tan camouflage clothing and hats, combat boots, and the dark smartglasses. I dialed the brightness down on the latter to better make out the faces in front of me as we approached. I stopped in front of the three new soldiers and saluted.

"Captain Nitin Ratava of New Earth Force reporting for duty. This is part of ODA 111, my assigned M-team for service at the Temple. Sergeants Marshall and Kim," I said, gesturing. "Warrant Officer Williams. Requesting permission to enter and be received into the Six Cities."

There was a long and awkward pause. The desert wind whistled around us, the robes in front of me dancing to some turbulent pattern. It was a little unnerving stepping into this bubble of governance on New Earth. Who actually held authority here? Not my team, that was for sure. One of the humans? I scanned their faces but saw only blank stares.

The eyes of the Xix drew my attention. Instinct told me the seat of authority lay with the alien. I took off my glasses and, momentarily blinded by the light and grit, squinted toward the monster.

"Is permission granted?"

The Xix spoke through the translator clasped about its neck like a necklace. "Indeed, Captain," came the fluid accent of the device. The voice was genderless but warm, the tones sharp with intelligence. "Both you and your team. Two you have not met and stand before you: Weapons Sergeant Grant Moore and Sergeant Erica Fox, your engineer."

It was odd to hear the alien speak the military jargon so effortlessly. But I had to remind myself to take the Xix very seriously and not underestimate them. They could likely handle all of our human areas of expertise and thought without breaking a sweat. Well, almost all of them. Humans could still *Read* better than any. That was why they were living on New Earth. That was why my team and I were here.

I made the introductions within the team. The two last members looked as capable as the rest. Fox was a small woman, of mixed heritage, possibly Chinese and European. There was a slight detachment in her demeanor I had come to expect from the techs. Moore looked every bit the stereotypical Force officer from a recruitment poster: tall, muscled, and tattooed. As I would find out frequently later, also a tongue loose and salty. His lowbrow British twang gave his speech a memorable character. Both instinctively grouped with the rest of the team, and we were now facing the Xix and its greeting party.

"Captain Ratava, I am called Waythrel, and I serve Ambra Dawn at the Temple."

My throat went dry. *Waythrel?* This was a figure out of the history books. This was the Xixian spy on Dram who had helped free Ambra Dawn from their dungeons, who had accompanied her on her mission to save Earth. For more than two hundred years, the alien had been her closest and most trusted advisor. By the Daughter, what was it doing here?

"Waythrel of the Xix, I am honored that you have chosen to welcome us." I spoke formally, trying to employ half-forgotten exocultural protocols from our basic Force training.

The eyestalks darted around impishly. "It is we who are honored. We have a special assignment for you waiting at the Temple, and Ambra desires that we get to it quickly. We will rest tonight and depart first thing in the morning. My assistants here will lead you to housing that has been prepared."

I could sense the members of my team stealing glances in my direction. They were likely dying to know what was behind this unprecedented visit of one of the Temple's most legendary residents.

They were also likely curious as hell about the meaning of a *special assignment*. MECH teams usually played an important if unexciting role at the Temple. Ours was to have been one of several that were charged with handling security and personal safety of the populace. Nothing like Special Forces flying around encased in alien-metal suits to make an impression. But I couldn't focus on the broader picture. My pulse had spiked. Waythrel's words were spinning in my mind.

Ambra desires.

My team was to be used for something unusual, and that plan was tied closely to the wishes of Ambra Dawn herself! We were not going to serve as some standard MECHcore unit. We were going to be used for something special, something *she* was planning. We might even soon be in her presence.

I could barely breathe.

"Welcome to the Fourth City, Captain."

Chapter 8

There is one disease which is widespread, and from which men rarely escape: that every person thinks his mind more clever and more learned than it is. I have found that this disease has attacked many an intelligent person.

Maimonides

Williams stood in front of the group with her hands on her hips. "Captain, what the hell's going on?"

We were gathered in a makeshift quarters. Despite their age, the buildings appeared ultra-modern, half Xixian design common in the Six Cities. The walls were *dynamic* inside the structure, composed of some field that could be altered for appearance, texture, and position. Need a bigger room to house a special forces team? No problem! Reprogram the damn walls. You could select anything from wood to marble to unearthly materials preferred by the aliens. Incredibly realistic.

The external structure was more permanent—some concrete composite material that performed a similar service as the high-tech clothing: heat stayed out in the day but was retained at night. It was also hard as hell too, and I didn't see a single scratch on the gleaming surface despite hundreds of years of sandstorms. The Xix knew how to build.

"Calm down, Williams."

Her eyes flashed at me.

That was the problem with elite forces, maybe especially the ones the Temple had selected. They were bright. They asked questions. They had attitude. That was what gave them the edge the ordinary soldier lacked, what made them the creative destroyers you needed to handle the hard cases.

And what made them such giant pains in the ass to command. The meeting hadn't even begun before the questions erupted.

"Captain, I'm calm, but I signed up for Guardian duty. I know what that requires. I'm prepared. But I didn't sign up for any *special assignment*. I want to know what we're getting into."

"Take a seat, Williams," I said firmly, motioning to the set of chairs set up in the center. I had a smartholo floating in the middle of the space, but I didn't know if I'd even get to use it. I'd planned to begin going over the new MECH AI that they would employ to engage the Dram. For now, that was on hold.

Williams eyed me for a moment and let out a curt breath, turning and taking a seat alongside the others. If one could passive-aggressively sit, she had it down.

The five were in a single line in front of me, Williams on the far left, my right-hand side for my second-in-command. Kim was next to her, followed by Fox and Marshall. Off slightly on his own a few feet from the others was the muscled tower of Moore, keeping to himself.

"I know as much as you all do about this, which is *nothing*. Colonel Snowden warned us that once we landed, we'd be under new management. Previous orders and protocols don't necessarily apply here. You signed on knowing this. That means we adapt or get back on that transport and bug out."

"Bugger out, mate. Maybe!" Moore laughed. "Squids ordering us to fight bugs for that lady who runs the damn world."

"Moore, you're welcome to fly back tonight," I said.

He just smiled.

Marshall interjected, "Then how do we prepare for a mystery assignment?"

I sighed and ran my fingers through my hair. "By staying flexible, informed, in shape, and ready. The bugs don't play by any rules, so there isn't any certainty in any engagement." I gestured to the holoscreen. "Not even in the new attack plans I was going to introduce tonight. That's true for standard Temple duty or for whatever they have planned."

"But you can't know that, sir," said Kim.

"Look, I don't see why we're that worried," interrupted Fox. "There's never been as much as a shot fired at the Temple. Or even in the Cities. Not in two hundred years. We go in, march where they say, do our time, and we're out with benefits. Meanwhile, just think of where we *are*."

"Maybe a tour there was simple before, Fox, but things might be changing. I suppose you've heard some of the rumors."

There was a short silence as glances were stolen back and forth. Williams spoke first.

"Losses on the five fronts. Dram raids. Supply lines cut."

"Worse," I said. *They needed to know.*

Moore looked up with a sharp expression. "So, what are the bloody bastards not telling us now?"

"The Center's been compromised."

Several sat upright. Williams hissed under her breath. "Those mother—"

"I know," I said, feeling that betrayal as well. "Some very bad news from Colonel Snowden."

Kim started waving his arms. "Whoa—time the fuck out! Compromised the Center? What does that mean? Hit and runs? Occupation? Are we going to get Dram war fleets pouring out of the Orb toward New Earth?"

"*I don't know!* I don't have access to field reports, and Snowden said it's all being hushed up to prevent a panic!" I tried to slow this down. "It can't be that it's been significantly occupied, or we *would* have bugs crawling out of the sewers here. But it's got to be bad, maybe significant penetration with intermittent access to the central time point."

Williams whistled. "Well, that ain't good, man."

"Fucking got that right," laughed Moore.

"That's why I'm telling you this. We're not part of Force anymore. We're cut off from the leadership and any communications by the Xixian defense fields. We're on our own. Maybe there hasn't been an attack here since the Temple was built, but we can't take that for granted anymore. I think Snowden was trying to tell me that. Don't assume. Don't take anything for granted."

Kim spoke anxiously. "Maybe they know something Snowden didn't. Maybe there *is* an invasion force on the way. Maybe *that's* our special assignment! A fucking meat grinder."

Great. He's panicking.

"Calm down, Sergeant," I said. "Don't you think there would be a Force mobilization the likes of which we haven't seen since the early days of the Dram War?"

I let that sink in. "We might have had some setbacks in the War, setbacks the brass don't want advertised on every wave across the allied net, but it's not that bad yet. We need to trust the Daughter. Ambra Dawn has never let us down. Let's keep our heads on straight and not lose touch with her."

Kim wasn't onboard. "Maybe you're the one a little too touched with her."

Fox looked at him sharply. "What the hell does that mean?"

"Means everyone knows the captain's a true believer."

Fox reached inside her shirt and pulled out a pendant. It was New Earth with a sunrise breaking over the edge of the planet. One of the main religious symbols of the Dawnists.

"He's not the only one, asshole."

Kim stared back. "Well, maybe you two are ready to die for her, see whatever heaven they promised you. Maybe he already knows what's coming and welcomes it. Maybe I don't."

Before I could respond, Moore cut in. "Or, maybe our new Capt's interested in more 'an being touched by the power of the bald lady. Maybe he's some touching of his own in mind—eh, Capt?"

Fox murmured something I couldn't hear. I was momentarily flatfooted by the radical shift in the conversation.

Moore continued. "I been watchin' you, sir, cause I wasn't goin' into this bloody assignment with some nutter prayin' to that Witch half the night."

There were a few gasps from the team. Fox cut in icily. "You ought to learn how to bite that fat tongue of yours, Moore."

Moore smiled. "You blokes make me laugh. Sure, yeah, *The Daughter* an' all 'at. Keep your pendants, fine with me. But for our DC—all those rumors about him weren't *resting* well with me."

"Yeah? *You're* starting not to rest well with me, Moore," said Fox.

This was a tough balancing act. Moore was edging up to the line of insubordination. And then pissing right next to it. But if I cut in too soon, I'd look weak for taking the bait. Too late, and we might have a brawl.

"But all's good, mates." He smiled broadly. *Mischievously.* "Been watchin' him. All that talk 'bout Ambra Dawn: our Capt ain't no choirboy. He ain't longing to take a needle blast for her. He's longing for something else! Arse over tits or I'm blind. I know when a man's 'bout to pitch his tent!"

From India, I knew the British slang, and felt my cheeks flush. I was glad I was dark enough in this light for it to go unnoticed.

"And she *is* fit, mate, long's you don't mind that head."

Fox stood up, but before she could engage Moore, he was in front of me, up in my face, and I sensed the other team members tense. I stood still in front of his bulk and didn't flinch, looking him in the eye.

He saluted. "Religion of heavenly bodies, sir! Sign me up!"

There was a pause, and some laughter followed. I smiled out of one side of my mouth. *That bastard!* This bruiser was sharp as a tack, and had with one short diversion derailed Kim's panic and lessened any threat from my personal feelings.

It was an acceptable trade, a little embarrassment for some humanization and team bonding. But I'd have to watch him and Fox. That looked like a bad mix brewing.

"You're enlisted," I said. "Now, sit your ass down, soldier."

"Yes, sir!" Moore grinned back and turned around, taking a seat. The other soldiers visibly relaxed. Even Kim let out a sigh. Fox sat down as well, her eyes smoldering.

Williams shook her head. "*Shit.* Looks like I'm in deep with a bunch of crazy-ass motherfuckers. Okay then, Capt. Why don't you light up that board and show us all this new shit the squids have handed down. Sounds like we might be needing it."

Chapter 9

Any sufficiently advanced technology is indistinguishable from magic.

Clarke's Third Law

We were nearly packed when Waythrel entered our quarters. The humans subconsciously made a semicircle with the alien at the center, the presence of a creature so viscerally strange and unsettling always eliciting primitive responses that were hard to completely suppress.

And Waythrel did make an impression. Towering over us, limbs moving at angles impossible to the human body, the presence of a great intelligence unmistakable—the creature commanded our attention without a word.

"The caravan is prepared for you," Waythrel spoke. "There is a military-grade sandglider that will hold all of you and your items."

I stepped forward. "I was led to understand that our suits will be waiting for us at the Temple?"

"This is correct. However, these will be new suits, not those you had shipped. We have built enhanced versions of the MECHcore standard suits that are optimized both for the desert and for our latest battle training. Part of your initial exercises will be to learn to integrate with the suits and understand their full potential."

I heard some quiet grumbling behind me. New suits. Even more new training. *Don't move a soldier's cheese, Xixian!*

"The suit improvements are significant. Ambra wishes for her Guardians that they be outfitted in the best gear available."

I nodded. It was hard to argue with that. The alien gestured outside our quarters, and we followed it out into the blazing sun.

The glider was hovering silently in front of us, the only evidence of its propulsion system the undulating ripples in the sand. It was shaped like one of those old-time computer mice, but nearly as big as a bus, a sleek Xixian design with the upper portion completely transparent. It wasn't glass. Some other material the aliens had produced that was strong, more resistant to erosion than human material science could produce, and that had embedded in it numerous touch displays and control features.

We tossed our bags into the back, hopped into the central portion, took our seats, and buckled in. The cab consisted of seats appropriate for humans and Xix, and Waythrel occupied one of the larger seats for the aliens. Within moments, I felt the lurch of acceleration, and the glider darted like an arrow from the city.

These desert ships reached a maximum velocity of around four hundred miles per hour, the air displacement leaving a tunnel of swirling sand behind us. As we sped inward from the ring of the Six Cities toward the Temple, within minutes the structures of civilization receded to a blur and we were surrounded only by the colors and shapes of the deep desert.

The transport darted effortlessly over the colossal dunes, some reaching heights of several hundred feet. The glider would fly up the long windward side of the dune and then dart back down on the slip face to cruise within the valleys formed between the sand mountains. With the morning sun low on the horizon, those valleys would often plunge us into darkness and shadow, only to burst into blinding light again climbing another dune. All this happened at speeds of several hundred miles an hour. Now I understood why the Xix had designed the gliders with the viewport. It was stunning.

Gradually, even the dunes began to give way as we flew over an extended sand sheet of hundreds of miles. We were close to the middle of the Sahara, nearly equidistant from all inhabited regions outside the ring of the Six Cities. Basically, we were about as in the middle of nowhere as anyone could be on Earth outside of an ocean.

As the craft accelerated over the flat terrain, I could begin to make out the blurred outlines of a structure ahead. From my geography lessons, I knew it wasn't giant dunes or mountains—until two hundred years ago, there had been only flat sand in this region of the desert. It was something intelligence had thrown up from the desert floor. Thrown up very, very high.

"There it is, Captain," came the voice of Williams, her neck stretched to look toward the growing forms in front of us. "There's your Temple."

All my team stared at the marvel before us. As the dark shape took form, I felt a growing sense of awe. Not only for its sheer size and location, but for what this place meant to humanity. Here was the focal point in our war against cosmic forces that should have consumed us and continued to enslave our primitive species. If not for the help of the alien Xix. If not for the unexpected wild card in the history of our galaxy that was Ambra Dawn.

The medic Marshall whispered, "All that power in the middle of nothing."

Many of Waythrel's eyes turned toward us. "Many have wondered why we chose to build so deeply in the desert." The tones from the translator seemed to grow in mystery as we approached the Temple.

"Because the Xix want sand between their toes is what I heard," came the voice of Moore. He was slumped next to Williams, his chin on his massive chest, seemingly bored with the sightseeing, impervious to the spectacle before him. His eyes were hidden behind dark smartglasses.

"Yes, Sergeant Moore," came the unfazed voice of the alien. "We are certainly partial to such locations. But we do earnestly seek to work with our human hosts, and we understand that such climates are extreme for your organism."

Moore flipped his shades up and smiled. "Extreme for our organism. I like that."

"If not for Xixian comfort, then what?" Williams asked.

Waythrel's many eyes scanned my team, a few of them never leaving their focus on me. "From the beginning, after the recursive time alteration of the Calamity, New Earth has been in great danger. Greater danger than most humans have appreciated. Especially in the early years, there was the constant threat of attack by the Dram. In fact, there were several attempts—major, planetary-level assaults—to achieve again what had been undone."

This had my team's attention. This was definitely *not* textbook material. Kim broke in.

"You mean like the asteroid? They shot more at us?"

"Yes, there were multiple attempts through various strategies to destroy New Earth or render it inhospitable. Similar assaults on my homeworld of Xix as well as several other worlds harboring species important to our war effort. These were all effectively countered."

"The Daughter?" I asked.

Waythrel gestured with its hands moving oppositely from the center out. "Of course, Captain Ratava. Only by the powers of Ambra Dawn have we been constantly shielded from certain destruction."

"So, why didn't we ever hear about this?" asked Kim.

"Representatives of your many governments begged Ambra to keep silent. They feared that word of the continuing efforts of the Dram could instill a planetwide panic."

These facts sat quietly with each of us. While we all had learned as children about the Calamity—the alternative history of the planet in which the Dram had reduced it to slag by hurling a giant asteroid through an Orb—there were no such stories about additional, world-threatening attempts. Only stories of the alliances against the Dram, the long hundred years of continuous war— victorious war—in which we had broken the Hegemony, pushed the Dram back to a few systems near their home world. And of course the long work to create a safer galaxy for humans and aliens. It was a nice myth. Told across the globe in every schoolhouse perhaps for some of the same reasons the recent setbacks against the Dram were withheld.

"But because of these threats, Ambra insisted that we place the Temple as far from human habitation as possible. That way, should an attack succeed, even a minor one, the carnage to life on Earth would be minimized as much as could be managed."

"So why not just leave the bloody thing on the moon where it was built?" asked Moore.

"Indeed, that was Ambra's wish. But we had seen what isolation from your planet had done to individuals of your species, and to Ambra in particular. We convinced her that it was in the interests of our struggle that she relocate to her homeworld. The desert was her compromise." The Xix paused, its smaller fingers darting around. "In addition, we needed to build a new device to amplify her powers and integrate the Reader groups. The one on your moon was effective, but only a first draft, as you say. A prototype. We learned much from its building and use and put that knowledge into practice here in your world's largest desert."

"The Dish," I said.

"Yes. The Dish is an engineering feat that dwarfs the efforts on your satellite. Most of the mass of the Temple is contained in the device, which spans the size of some of your larger cities."

The dark blur in front of us had begun to come into focus. It was like approaching Manhattan in a low-flying airplane, seeing the expanse of the city across the entire field of one's peripheral vision. Instead of randomly placed skyscrapers, however, there was a striking order to the monolithic structure that grew toward the sky from the desert floor.

"My God," gasped Kim as he nearly stood up in his seat against the restraints.

"They said it was tall. I've seen the numbers, but nothing is going to prepare you for *that*," said Williams, her mouth agape.

Rising out of the desert sands like some webbed volcano was the great antenna of the Dish. Of course the Xix had built it; there wasn't anything close to the scale of the structure in human engineering. It was impossibly tall, and it was impossible to grasp the size with human intuition. It dwarfed anything on New Earth. Staring up at it, I lost my sense of scale completely.

"It reaches to nearly fifty thousand feet," said Waythrel. "More than five times the height of your tallest mountain."

Even Moore perked up a little and had a look. "How'd you keep that giant todger from falling down?" he asked.

Waythrel pointed to the lower portion of the structure. "Do you see how wide the base is? It is difficult to appreciate from this distance, but it is more than five miles in diameter and anchored three hundred feet into the desert floor, which provides considerable support. The rods that curve up from the base like parabolic spokes—some one hundred feet in diameter—are fashioned from our strongest and most lightweight materials, millions of times stronger per unit mass than your best composites. Had it been necessary, the structure could have been several times its current height."

Extending radially from the huge base were much smaller buildings of recognizable height—likely living quarters and other constructions serving the needs of the Temple. But it was hard to focus on them. The antenna seized all attention.

The ground below us transformed from the tan and rough sands of the desert to a black gloss. I recognized the planet's largest solar array in the giant circular mat that flowed out across the desert. The term *array* was archaic, as the material was more a continuous sheet rather than thousands of individual solar panels. The glider seemed to be speeding over a dark and utterly still sea.

"It's beautiful," said Fox, her eyes watery.

"Amazing," I said marveling as well. "This is what powers the Dish?"

"No," said Waythrel. "The Dish requires much more energy than that."

"It looks like those astronomy dishes," said Kim, staring up at the tall structure. "Focuses all her power like radio waves or something?"

Waythrel gestured in an oddly inhuman manner. "This is difficult to explain. While there is a superficial similarity with your radio dishes, the operating principle is very different. Your dishes are designed to handle electromagnetic waves of specific energies, or wavelengths. Ambra's manipulations of space and time occur through different physical means. That is why the Dish is so large, and also why it requires so much power to operate. In fact, to focus her powers on New Earth requires a gravitational lens that can be achieved only through the presence of a micro black hole."

"You're shitting us!" explained Kim, a nervous smile on his face. "You've got a damn black hole in there?"

Waythrel responded patiently, "Four."

"Holy *shit!* Well, I'm with you on the vote for the desert location now for sure."

"The black holes are located in strategic positions," added the alien. "One is in fact at the top of the tower, nearly ten miles above the desert surface. The space-time distortions the four create are channeled and focused by other devices to a multi-dimensional location, a three-space cross-section of which is located in structures beneath the sands, embedded in the bedrock. It is there that Ambra goes when she requires a great amplification of her powers."

"And how do you juice all that?" asked Moore. He had flipped his glasses back down.

"If you mean the energetics, Sergeant, we have an array of twenty fusion reactors built around the Temple."

"*Twenty?*" exclaimed Williams. "So why do you need all the solar panels?"

"The fusion cores are devoted exclusively to the powering of the Dish and the maintenance of the black-hole amplituhedron. Both require enormous energy expenditures. The solar sea is in place to provide energy for all the organism-related activities at the Temple: life support, communications, standard military defenses."

The antenna now towered above us, so high one would need to lie flat to stare up at it. If there was a black hole at the apex, we were going to have to take the alien's word for it. The top was so high as to be invisible.

The glider began to decelerate, and we plunged into shadow again as we pulled alongside the buildings of the Temple. Small in comparison to the central tower, they were still many stories high, blocking out the rising sun of the early morning.

The craft came to a stop in front of a large courtyard. A broad street extended from it and the outer desert into the walls of the Temple city itself. For the first time, we saw green in the Sahara. The courtyard was lined with olive and palm trees, and even some thorny bushes bearing flowers. While the plants were certainly arid species, significant irrigation was undoubtedly required to keep them alive here in this wasteland.

We released our restraints and assembled, filing out to the cargo section to grab our gear. I hoisted my duffel bag over my shoulder, waited until the rest of my team had secured their items, and then led a march in the direction Waythrel had taken.

We stepped alongside the sandglider, its bulk rising above our heads on the right. Waythrel had turned around the front of the ship and was lost from sight, a trail in the sand marking its path. I picked up the pace to keep close to the alien.

We made the same turn around the nose of the craft and ran right into a greeting party. This one was far larger and more diverse than that which met us at the Fourth City. Thirty to forty humans and half as many Xix awaited our approach. They were clothed in flowing desert garments of diverse colors, the fabrics reflecting the sunlight strongly. The alien eye-stalk clusters danced here and there above the short sea of human heads.

Waythrel had reached the crowd and had stopped, speaking to a central figure. The sun crested over the tops of the buildings, and the courtyard was bathed in light. My smartglasses automatically engaged and reduced the glare.

Compulsively, I stepped forward, my thoughts relegated to some distant portion of my consciousness. A mindless moth to the flame, I was drawn irresistibly to the figure underneath the height of the alien. Step by drunken step, I approached, oblivious to everything else.

It was a young woman, clothed in long robes of black, her skin seeming as bright as the white walls lit by the morning sun. The top of her head was bald and swollen to obscene proportions. Rivers of red curls fell from a midpoint in her scalp down her shoulders and nearly to her waist.

"*Daughter of Time,*" I whispered.

It was Ambra Dawn.

Chapter 10

What then is time? If no one asks me, I know what it is. If I wish to explain it to him who asks, I do not know.

Augustine of Hippo

ime.

Whatever that idea represents, if anything at all in the reality of our universe, it stopped. There was no sound. No movement. The sand particles were suspended in midair, and it seemed that my own heart no longer beat its rhythm in my chest.

Only the eyes. Blind eyes. Bright-green emeralds glowing before me. Only they seemed able to move. While everything else stood impossibly still, her eyes turned to me and focused, looking deeply into my own. It was like falling into warm water, a subtle impact rippling through my awareness, as if she had entered into my very consciousness.

It is said that time is distorted around the Daughter. The textbooks, physics lessons I hardly understood. The science-fiction serials waved through the datasphere—they all said something about it. She stopped time. She slowed time. She stood outside of time in some undefined *elsewhere*. While none of the writings agreed on what she did to time, it was clear to me now that those stories were much more than legends.

Standing before me, commanding all my attention and thoughts in the midst of all these creatures, was a human being who was over two hundred years old. But she did not look a day older than seventeen. No age lines, no skin discoloration, no gray hair or sagging posture. Ambra Dawn was the same biological age she had been when she came into full use of her powers.

I didn't understand it. None of my fellow students at the academy had understood the explanations of cyclically warped space-time that left chemistry intact yet her body unaged, that stopped time but permitted the formation of memories, that led her consciousness to loop in and out of her carbon-based flesh into hyperknots of space-time strings.

For me, it was all gibberish. Right now, with her gaze entering me like some vulnerable lover, the nonsense of understanding mattered little. I only wished to stay in this place, to forever have her dive into me, to be consumed by her, to experience her, endlessly in this impossible place with no time.

Right now—whatever *now* meant in this strange stasis—I only wished to tell Ambra that I loved her.

Be patient, Nitin. This is not the place.

The words rang in my mind as if I had thought them, but the voice was not my own. Her eyes held me a moment longer, and I felt tears trickle down the side of my face.

Like a blow to the stomach, Time leaped forward again. The noises and smells returned, the sand grains rasping across my skin. Voices, footsteps. A murmuring crowd.

I stood halfway between my team and the crowd. The blowing sand had already begun to crust the tear paths on my cheeks. Everyone was staring at me, and Ambra smiled.

"Captain Ratava, please bring your team forward," she cried over the wind, motioning elegantly with her hand. The murmurs died down at the sound of her voice. The stares lingered.

I turned to look behind me and was greeted with shocked expressions from the members of my team. They seemed stunned but walked forward with me, and we came to a halt in front of the Daughter and Waythrel.

"We welcome you to the Temple," Ambra said. "For everyone at the Temple, I want to say to you all that we appreciate your service, your sacrifice for our common mission to protect New Earth."

I looked around at the crowd. Their faces—the many smiles and steady gazes—it felt as if this were not simply some political platitude, but that her words were true for everyone around us. It was the first realization I had of the earnestness of the people who served the Daughter. There was something different—*they* were different from almost any group of people I had ever encountered. The closest I could place them was with the Hindu monks I had known in my youth, but even that was a pale comparison.

Her blind eyes crossed over my form as a lightning strike, sending shivers through me, and then scanned across my team.

"I am needed urgently within, so I will not be able to be with you as you enter our city. Instead, I will turn you over to the capable hands of my counselor, Sepehr Mazandarani, who will serve as your guide. He will be your point of contact for the next few weeks as you prepare for Guardian service." She gestured behind her, and a short, thin man in dark-blue robes stepped forward.

His complexion was dark, his eyes a deep brown with a dagger's gaze, and a trimmed and sharp goatee accentuated his diabolical appearance. He shuffled forward with a casual confidence until he was beside the Daughter.

"Sepehr." Ambra nodded to him and turned around, walking beside Waythrel on the road into the Temple city.

"Hello. From me as well, a welcome to the city." He looked across my team, resting lastly on me. I felt a suspicion, a hostility in his gaze completely at odds with the welcome we had just received. He quickly looked away.

"You will be staying at the south end of the city, near the military training fields. There you will find housing, your new battle suits, and trained Earth Force soldiers who will work with you to get you up to speed. Inside the city, we walk whenever possible—it keeps us well adapted to the climate. Please follow me. Your quarters are about a half hour away."

With that he smiled an unsettling grin and turned to walk down the same entry road the Daughter had just taken. Ambra and Waythrel were now out of sight, and it was unclear where they had gone.

I turned to my team and smiled. "Okay, here we go." There was a pause, and no one moved. My smile faded. "Problem?"

They each looked from one to the other incredulously. Moore grinned and let out a bark of a laugh.

"Yeah. You might say."

I turned to Williams. "Warrant Officer Williams, would you kindly report on what is the damn problem with my team, and why we aren't marching inside?"

"Yes, sir," she said, bringing her face close to mine. "That is, if you can explain what the hell just happened."

"What happened? We were met by Ambra Dawn herself and assigned to her representative. We are following him to begin our required duties."

"No, sir. I don't mean that." She just stared at me. The others stared as well, Fox with a look of religious awe on her face.

Moore spoke. "She's a bit put out from your shimmering disappearing act."

My throat felt dry. "My what?"

He laughed again. "You know, the part where you blink in and out of existence and seem to teleport halfway to that would-be girlfriend of yours." He looked around at the others. "That about it?"

No one said anything. Their eyes were wide.

Moore nodded. "Yeah, see lads, we've not all gone bloody barmy in the heat. We all saw it." He hoisted his duffel. "But, I think we'd all like to hear your thoughts on the matter, Capt."

I just stared back at them.

Chapter 11

The easy confidence with which I know another man's religion is folly teaches me to suspect that my own is also.

Mark Twain

I t was three weeks before I saw Ambra Dawn again.

I threw myself into the training and drills. My team members were hardworking soldiers, but I outworked them all. My energies burned with a zeal no one else could match, and the team worked that much harder because of my example. Because of what we would soon face, it was critical that we did.

And it was only the fire hose of information and training my team and I withstood that preserved my sanity, that allowed me to continue, to hold myself back from seeking her out after what had occurred before the gates of the Temple City. Part of the problem was that I did not even understand myself what had happened. Even after a few conversations with my team—each of which left them and me very unsatisfied—nothing was clarified.

"So, now," said Fox, staring around at us. "Now do you believe?" Half her torso was encased in the battle suit, her black hair blowing wildly behind her in the scalding wind. The composite chassis drank the sunlight, charging power reserves in the battery cluster planted in the back.

We had just finished an exhausting training session. Sweat poured down our faces and ran in rivulets into our suits, which sopped it up, filtered it, and stored the potable constituents for later use. The wind did little to cool us.

The team stood in a tight group. A wasted sandworm triad lay smoking before us. The new suits were incredible. A jump in technology of four or five generations. They combined new general battle features with eco-survival adaptations for the desert. The new AI for the worms was far more sophisticated, and my team had mastered the interface quickly. With the more powerful ion slingers, it almost made taking on the worms fun.

Kim shuffled his feet, nodding uncertainly. "Yeah," he exhaled, his fatigue evident. "Yeah, Fox. I guess so."

I could see in the eyes of the others that he wasn't the only one. But there was acceptance of the event, and then there was interpretation.

"Well, it's not anything new to hear that she can pull out her magic wand," spat Moore. "That don't mean I'm getting baptized."

Fox shook her head. She nearly chanted, "And in that age were great signs, but many disbelieved. And the Daughter said, 'If you believed not in Moses and Jesus, then you will believe not in Me.'"

Moore burst out laughing. "You think that witch actually said any of that shit?"

Fox stepped toward him.

"That's enough!" I said, engaging the hydraulics of my suit to push them apart. "Keep your beliefs and critiques private! We have one fight we need to focus on, and it's not with our species!"

"Yeah, Captain, but, you know, there's been an *event*. With the Daughter." It was Kim. I heard a growing awe in his voice. "We saw it. *You* were part of it. It's like all the legends, man."

Strange things had happened that seemed to defy the common-sense laws of nature we took for granted. But this event had centered not on New Earth or the Great War with the Dram, or some other textbook-worthy crisis concerning the Daughter and humanity's survival. It had focused on a single person out of all the swarm of humanity. *On me.*

Williams nodded. "It was one thing when you were such a fanboy, Captain. Now…what is it with you and her?"

I looked at the ground as they all focused on me. "I don't know, Williams. Nothing about her is normal, right? Well, I'm part of that. And maybe I'm the least strange part of it. Millions worship her."

"Yeah, but you don't," said Moore. Fox eyed me closely.

"Sergeant, I don't know what people should call it. I know what I feel. I'm not a Dawnist. I'm not a skeptic. But I know where I have to be, and that's here. With her."

Fox nodded her head. "I understand. You're like a monk. You're devoted to her."

"He ain't no monk," smirked Moore.

Fox glared at him. "I bet he's never been with another woman. Never been in love. He's waiting for *her*."

Kim looked straight at me. "That true, sir? Not to be too personal, but we're all getting past that line, I think. Is this thing with her so extreme? Have you ever even kissed a girl?"

It was strange. Of all the unusual aspects of my devotion to the Daughter, it was always sex that riled people up the most. I could have painted myself up like the wildest Hindu priest and chanted into the night on the top of a pillar, and it would go down better than abstinence. Or the perception of it.

"No, I've kissed girls. I've even slept with them. Once, I was engaged to be married. And I even loved her." I inhaled sharply, trying to dampen my emotions.

There was a silence broken by the smooth alto of Williams. "What happened?"

I stared out over the desert, unable to look directly at the others. "My parents arranged it all. They'd been trying to marry me off for a while. Maybe you can imagine how they felt with my long focus on the Daughter. These things were usually very awkward, pointless, and over before the dinner was finished." I suppressed a sigh. "But not the last one."

I could still picture her face clearly. Delicately boned with a Persian nose and rich black hair like a strong river, she was petite, barely five feet, absurdly elegant in her motions, and quick with her wit.

"She was a professional dancer. Classical Indian style. Her eyes caught me instantly and we had a very powerful mutual chemistry. Body, mind, all that. So, for the first and only time in my life, I abandoned the idea of that destiny with Ambra Dawn." I laughed. "Of course, I had a lot of help from my parents. They were beyond overjoyed to recognize that I was moved by this woman."

"So what *happened?*" pressed Fox.

"I broke it off."

"Why?" asked Kim.

"Because, while I had convinced myself to grow up, move beyond my life-long dream, I was fooling myself. I could not let go of Ambra Dawn. While I made love to this beautiful woman and planned a life with her, my mind, my heart was not pure, not devoted as it should have been to my wife-to-be. And she deserved so much more than that. As time went on, I saw that I would forever be haunted by another. Nothing I could do would change it. It wasn't fair to anyone, but it was more unfair to pretend. I knew that later it would cause even more pain than were I to end it early."

"Didn't peg you for a heart-breaker, Captain," said Williams.

I still stared into the distance. "It might not make sense, but there is love, and then there is another kind of love. A kind of love that seems bigger than even the two involved. And yes, maybe it's madness."

It is one thing to feel that reality within yourself, and quite another to have the external world dramatically verify it. And yet another to lead a military assault squad with massive doubts about all that was taking place.

"Well, she *did* single you out, Captain," said Kim.

Marshall agreed. "Maybe there is some strange destiny going on."

And I heard her voice. This was something I could not share even with my team. Psychologists and skeptics could roll off one hundred theories and reasons why I had been delusional. Perhaps it would be simple enough to explain the entire episode as a cognitive reaction to the time distortion around her.

But I believed differently. More than that, I *knew* in my heart that Ambra Dawn had spoken directly to me. The experience was as real—more real—than many events in my life, even my own thoughts. Perhaps it was the beginning of a split personality disorder. But the Daughter was thought to be telepathic, to be able to enter the minds and even control the thoughts of others. I believed strongly that she had touched my mind.

With that conviction, and longing to receive more and to see how my own mad purpose in life was truly to be fulfilled, I felt her absence like a terrible vacuum in a space that had not existed before. She entered me, touched me, spoke to me, and in the fertile landscape of my love for her, had formed a nascent mini-universe. Yet it was empty! Only the displacement of reality around it to testify that it was there. What would it become?

And when?

I needed to get the team to move on from this. "So we've gotten some real-world confirmation of everything we've been taught about her. Not on a holo, not from our elders, but right in our faces. In the sands in front of us."

I looked around, holding each momentarily with my gaze.

"Things a lot bigger than us are going on. Let's take that to heart and let's get serious about why we're here. The myths are real."

The team looked sobered. Even Moore's smirk was gone for the moment. Of course, it returned quickly.

"Right, Captain. And you can hope to get a little more *serious* with the girl yourself, now that you've moved up to teleporting with her."

I looked away and put my helmet back on. More worms were coming.

Chapter 12

All warfare is based on deception. Hence, when we are able to attack, we must seem unable; when using our forces, we must appear inactive; when we are near, we must make the enemy believe we are far away; when far away, we must make him believe we are near.

The Art of War, Sun Tzu 孫子

The first information we received concerning our unusual assignment came at the end of the first week of training. We had just finished a particularly grueling skirmish. A captured triad was released on us in the sands, but that wasn't the challenge. We were to begin testing in combat the most powerful new feature of the redesigned MECHcore battle suits: space-time neutralizers. We were given no explanation for why we would even need such countermeasures, but the design of them into the suits had our minds racing.

As the worms were released, accompanying them were field distortions in space and time. Left uncountered, they slowed us down, sometimes dramatically, or displaced us physically or temporally. It didn't need to be much in the heat of battle to be lethal. Our suits would constantly counter the fields automatically, but it required a change in our combat style, a strange rhythm, pulse in our movements, actions, even thoughts, that really can't be described. When time and space are being jerked around, the sensations and responses are very counterintuitive.

We spent an entire day in drills to master it and had just finished our first live combat experience with the technology when Mazandarani came to escort us back to the military barracks. We followed, cleaned up, and were immediately brought to a briefing room in a nearby building. There we were introduced to Major Tomoko Mizoguchi.

Major Mizoguchi was a hard-asses' hard-ass, and she seemed to step out of some ancient war holo. The older Japanese warrior was clipped in cadence, full of bluster and drama, and eager to put fools in their place. Her short salt-and-pepper hair was nearly spiked, and she wore a uniform that was pressed until the edges seemed sharpened like a knife. We had gathered from Mazandarani that the major had been at the Temple for over a decade and had personally run military engagements involving the Daughter and Xixian forces at various points in the galaxy during this time. But these roles had been kept at a very low profile outside of the Temple. None of my team had even heard of her. But over the next three weeks, we heard a lot from her. The voice that erupted from her short frame resonated through the room.

"You may *think* you know what you are up against. But let me tell you, you don't."

This was how Mizoguchi began our briefing on the first day. For a group of highly trained MECHcore special forces, most of whom had seen combat with the Dram, this was something to say.

"The tide of the war has changed," she said grimly. "We are no longer on the offensive but are now in a full-scale retreat across most of the galaxy."

There was a long silence. We sat there stunned. *Full-scale retreat?* This was far, far worse than anything Colonel Snowden had hinted at. *What the hell was happening?*

"As of last month, we no longer control the Time Tree. Dram forces have occupied the central Orb projection, and have begun to launch attacks against the more weakly defended worlds in the alliance. Most of those attacks have been devastating."

I glanced at Williams, who sat on my right side. Her eyes told the story—disbelief, shock, and fear. She held my gaze a moment and shook her head, returning her attention to the major.

"It is obvious that something has catalyzed this phase transition in the war, and what that catalyst is has become the focus of much of our current efforts. It is in this respect that you have been recruited here."

She paused dramatically, casting a withering gaze across each of us. Her eyes stopped last and longest on me.

"After you complete your training, which we expect will occur before the end of the month, there will be a special announcement during the Festival of Rebirth. The Daughter will address the faithful of the Temple City and broadcast the message throughout the world. We have notified all the major political and media leaders to expect this transmission."

She paused again, and I couldn't stop myself from interrupting her narrative. "And what will she say?"

The major nodded and turned to her right, motioning to a projection holo of the galaxy. Several bright points appeared across its expanse, and I recognized them as the location of extra-solar system Orbs. Or rather, as the Daughter had revealed and our books taught, the locations of projections of the one and only Orb. Many of the Orb locations turned from white to red.

"In red, you see those locations now occupied by Dram forces."

There were gasps. It is difficult to explain to you of another time what this meant. You, who have struggled only with the maps of Old Earth, the distances and meanings of national borders, you cannot grasp the size of the galaxy. You were not raised on the now-hundred-year-old charts that outlined the Dram Quarantine around their home planet. That galactic map had been burned into the consciousness of generations. We knew the Dram homeworld and the handful of satellite worlds that remained under their control. It was a small percentage of the systems with an Orb, a testament to our victory in the Great War.

But no longer. In the holo presented by the major, fully half the galaxy was red. She flicked her hand, and the map rotated around us, the viewpoint zooming into the galactic center, New Earth shooting behind me and to the back portion of the room. She zoomed to the central Orb.

"Their attack has been long planned. Once they seized the central Time Point, multiple attacks across the Time Tree occurred simultaneously. Nearly every system targeted has fallen."

"Oh, my God," whispered Kim behind me.

"Our forces find themselves unable to repel the attacks and hardly able to communicate anything useful about them. We only have strange reports, contradictory statements that even the Xix do not know how to interpret."

"What reports?" I asked. "What do they say?"

"You all will have provided to you the recordings and data streams we have been able to obtain. We want you to study those. To brainstorm. To prepare for the completely unexpected."

She touched several floating buttons on the holopanel and the projection filled with a poor-quality holovid. White noise and audio static clouded the projection, but the scene was one of battle. A human communications officer spoke with a look of desperation on her face in the midst of the chaos of explosions and screams.

"Freighter Centari 2-11658. Mayday, mayday, mayday. Escort battalion has been destroyed. We are defenseless and taking fire from Dram forces."

There was a bright light and deep sound, and the image disintegrated into random pixels. It flickered back, and the woman spoke from in front of a raging fire.

"Freighter Centari 2-11658. Mayday. Life support is failing. Condition unsalvageable. Initiating terminal data squirt."

A *TDS*. When your ship was going down, when it was clear that there might not be anything to recover or no way to recover it, if you had the presence of mind to send all information to relay beacons—to inform and warn—you could spend your last few moments firing off a squirt. It would likely drain whatever you had left in the ship's batteries—the signal was designed to reach the relays. It would render you helpless. It was a final act. The officer knew she was going to die and that it was imminent. It was on her face, the steely determination in her eyes.

Her hand paused in the air. She had not yet sent the signal. She had something she needed to say directly and set her jaw, her expression grim.

"This is Operations Specialist Emma Sung. Look for the *shadows*. The *ghosts*. I can't explain any better. They are coming."

Her finger moved. The image froze.

Mizoguchi gestured to the holo. "This is the TDS from a transport convoy destroyed three weeks ago by Dram forces. Data recovery confirms the visuals. The ship was seconds away from coming apart. Sung was one cool customer."

"Or delusional and psychotic," said Marshall. "*Ghosts?*"

The major eyed the medic harshly. "Yes, it would seem. Except for the fact that we have multiple TDS from the last month, all from devastating attacks on our forces, and in several of them are reports that sound a lot like this one."

"What do you mean?" asked Williams.

"All report strange events. Creatures or forces penetrating all their defenses, wreaking destruction on their personnel and machinery. Forces *not* Dram."

"Not Dram?" asked Moore, his lip a sneer. "*Ghosts?*"

"Ghosts, Sergeant. Or shadows. Gas clouds. Force fields. Whatever you want. Different terms for the same phenomenon, it would appear."

Moore continued. "So, you're saying that what has suddenly made us lose most of our positions across the galaxy, maybe about to lose the whole fucking war, is a bunch of evil spirits attacking our forces?"

Mizoguchi shook her head. "What I'm saying is that something has changed, and the Dram have a new weapon that we do not understand and cannot counter."

"And that is why we are here?" I hardly knew what to expect.

The major nodded curtly. "We have a crisis. One that must be addressed immediately, or we may lose everything. The Daughter and her advisors have devised a plan. It is not a large-scale military engagement—we now know that such efforts would be futile until we can understand the threat."

"Then what?" asked Fox, her eyes narrowing.

"Guerrilla tactics. We will transport elite special forces teams to several key locations in the Time Tree. These teams will be charged with two missions. The first is recon: find out what the hell we are up against and how to respond."

"And the second?" I asked.

The map reappeared, the Dram-controlled red sea of points ominous in the darkness. Several of these points grew in size and brightness.

"Sabotage. The Daughter has determined a set of three nodes in the Tree that, if impeded, can effectively seal off the majority of the accessible hyperspace routes to the regions we still control."

Thin blue lines connecting the Orbs appeared on the screen, showing the possible routes through the Time Tree. When Mizoguchi pressed the bright Orbs highlighted, the web of interconnections fell apart, isolating the Dram-controlled regions from the majority of those the alliance still held.

"Without access to the Orb strings, the Dram and whatever new forces they have brought into this conflict are effectively isolated through the vast interstellar distances."

"Won't this cut off many worlds that depend on our protection?" asked Fox, her expression horrified.

"Yes," said the major. "It cannot be avoided."

"What will happen to them?" asked Marshall.

"We don't know. They could be attacked. Or perhaps with them cut off from us, they will be ignored as the Dram focus on how to deal with the setback. But losing contact with intergalactic trade might mean that some of them will face food and energy catastrophes."

I probed further. "And we have to hit all three of those points? Does the order matter?"

"The order is unimportant. However, doing them in sequence and not simultaneously could result in the Dram deducing our purpose. This could lead to fortifications of the Orb projections in those systems."

"So we hit them with the teams at the same time?"

"No," said the major. "There will be a single team."

"But if they will fortify the last two, that doesn't make sense!" said Kim.

"It makes sense if you understand the limitations of the engagement," said Mizoguchi harshly. "We can't send normal forces."

"Why not?" I asked.

"We have tried to. We performed seven missions to various Orbs early on. None of them returned."

"Jesus," whistled Moore. "So this is a death mission."

"Perhaps not. Because those other teams lacked a critical element that you will have."

No, they can't. My stomach lurched. "And what is that critical element, sir?"

"Ambra Dawn."

Fox gasped. *"The Daughter?"*

The major nodded.

Moore slapped his hands together. "Now that's worth signing up for! This whole *assignment* just got a hell of a lot more interesting!"

"Wait. We're missing something here," said Kim. "How are we supposed to get back once we take those nodes out? We'll be cut off, too!"

Mizoguchi turned from him dismissively. "You forget that the Daughter doesn't need to travel through the Time Tree. She can open the Orbs."

Ancient history was becoming our very practical reality. The major continued. "This decision is not a light one. Our safety has depended on her for two centuries. Our greatest battles have been fought through her. Now we have learned to lock her behind the walls we think are protective. But those walls keep her from fighting now where she is needed. And those walls are no longer as safe as we once thought."

"What do you mean?" I asked.

"In addition to the nebulous threat our reports have brought to us, there is a far, far less nebulous one. A threat we have anticipated. One that was sure to occur, although the day on which it would was unknown."

"*What threat?*" I nearly shouted.

"False Dawns, Captain Ratava." We all exchanged confused looks. "Biological clones of the Daughter, constructed from the eggs stolen from her when she was a prisoner of the Dram two hundred years ago. Eggs that have been used to create, to breed, to engineer—we don't know exactly what has been done—a number of *replicas* that have been raised effectively to recapitulate many of her powers."

"Is this for real?" asked Kim, his expression disbelieving.

"Reports and documentation of those attacks have now surfaced from several battle fronts. Images of a young woman, looking remarkably like the Daughter, opening space-time wormholes and entering combat against our forces."

"*False Dawns?*" I repeated numbly, the world spinning around me.

"How many do they have?" asked Williams, her voice still and quiet.

"We don't know."

"You don't *know?*" asked Kim incredulously. "You mean they could have an army of them?"

"Unlikely. What they have achieved is technically very difficult. The Xix claim it is beyond their current technology given the instability of human chromosomes during manipulation and the even harder problem of randomness in neurological development. It's hard enough to clone an Ambra Dawn. Then you have to raise one. There is psychology, tumor growth, and many variables that an alien race would have extreme difficulty with."

Moore shook his head. "Unlikely, but not unlikely enough, it seems."

"They may have had help," said the major.

"From who?" Moore asked.

"Again, this is speculation. But consider the facts: suddenly after centuries of devastating losses, the Dram counter with two breakthroughs in this war that seem beyond anything they have ever done."

Fox cut in. "If so, then you are talking about aliens with tech better than the Xix. There's nothing like that in our galaxy. Who are they? Where are they coming from?"

"Another galaxy?" offered Kim.

"No," I said. "As far as we know, only ours has the Orbs. We're cut off from other galaxies completely. There's no intergalactic travel."

"So far as we know," added Moore.

"Again, this is all speculation," said Mizoguchi, "but it is the leading theory in the Daughter's advisory circles. The Xix are convinced the Dram cannot have achieved these advances by themselves."

Williams sat back in her chair. "*Shadows* and *ghosts* tearing apart our ships, and now, the Dram have replicated the powers of Ambra Dawn." She shook her head. There was a long silence.

Mizoguchi looked grimly at us and closed the holo, the room lights switching on automatically. We were transported from the depths of space to our small briefing room, from existential darkness to a mundane light. She spoke coldly.

"We no longer have a monopoly on manipulating space and time."

Chapter 13

We only have to look at ourselves to see how intelligent life might develop into something we wouldn't want to meet.

Stephen Hawking

It was a clear day for the festival, and the Temple crowds were large. Most were from the Six Cities and Temple City itself, devoted pilgrims who had dedicated their lives to the service of the Daughter. In addition, there were several thousand visitors from around the world, those fortunate souls who had received clearance and visitation visas for the event. In all, there were likely fifty thousand people gathered to celebrate the salvation of New Earth. It was a security nightmare.

Special mission or not, we were still assigned to the standard Temple patrol alongside numerous MECHcore teams but were singled out from the others by being placed at the Temple gate where the Daughter would speak to the crowds. It was a duty of some prestige that sat uncomfortably with other teams that had greater seniority. Our unusual suits also marked us as different from the others charged with patrolling the area. While these suits were designed for another, much more dangerous purpose, I still didn't mind having one on me. After what we had learned recently, paranoia was at an all-time high.

I tried to keep a lighter heart and not think about the dark facts of the war. The Festival of Rebirth was the anniversary of the beginning of the Great War, the salvation of our planet and emancipation from the tyranny of our alien masters. It was the education of the entire Earth. After the Calamity was reversed, a New Earth really was born, one of a different time path, a parallel universe in which the planet was not destroyed by the Dram. Humanity now shared a vague vision of death and destruction, of horror unmade. Like waking up from a strange dream, our ancestors discerned for the first time the reality of their slavery, their libraries full of books and warnings. A world war was sparked to purge the Dram and their agents.

We won. We pressed our war with the help of Ambra and the Xix throughout the galaxy. A terrible dictatorship based on fear and death was removed and hundreds of worlds freed.

The Festival of Rebirth was still raw and real to humanity. It was the greatest holiday on the planet. Few just went through the motions. Many would make the pilgrimage to the Temple at least once in their lifetimes. And billions would watch the proceedings live as it was broadcast to every grid-point on the globe. Dawnists would worship. Skeptics would mock. Separatists would protest, and some would cross the line into terrorism. It was the same every year.

Except we knew this year things were not going to be the same.

How would the masses react—on this day of all days —to the news that the world might actually be ending after all, and what's more, at the hands of the Dram? Would there be panic? Would we come together? Would the separatists feel the threat from outside and put down their arms and join the rest of humanity and the allied aliens? Or would they just ramp up their claims of the Calamity hoax and the invasion of Earth by the Xix? I couldn't see the Earth First diehards converting over a broadcast by the Daughter. They immediately assumed everything she said was a lie.

But the stakes were high, and emotions would be rattled. So our patrol was not an ordinary one at the Temple. We all felt the weight of events hanging over us. In the middle of all those feelings, it was difficult to feel the joy of the festival. But I tried. There were hundreds of memories from my childhood and adolescence to bring to bear. Nights watching the Diwali lights relit for the Rebirth. A field trip to Dawn's Eyes, that great Indian monument built by devout Hindus who took her as our contemporary avatar of God. Seeing her face projected across the world during the Communion, when she reached out from the Temple and shared her mind with all the Readers of Earth. Staring at the stars at night after the fireworks, dreaming of her, imagining countless ways in which we would meet. How could I know that our actual meeting would be far more magical?

Most exciting was that she would come to speak. I would be in her presence again. That thought alone sent a wave of energy through me.

"MECHcore captains, this is Sepehr Mazandarani. Waythrel is now moving to the platform to introduce the Daughter. Please assume your secondary positions."

All the teams called back their affirmatives. On our select band, I made sure my group was moving. We were to be in front of the dignitaries and the largest crowds. The last thing I wanted was to miss any signs of terrorist activity or for my team to respond to an attack ineffectively.

"Roger that, Captain," came Williams. "We're already there. Fox removed three civilians from the crowd earlier. Scans found weapons. Don't know how they got those in. Nothing in the databases about them. Don't think they were here to cause trouble, but they're eighty-sixed."

"Noted. Moore, how's that desert look?"

"As fit for our bloody bones as it ever was, sir," he reported back. "Nothing growing, nothing moving."

"Roger. Marshall, status?"

"In position. Aid stations are operational and staffed. We've got a full triage unit as well. Ready for anything except a land war."

"Copy." I picked up a growing murmur from the crowd on the other communications bands. "Looks like Waythrel is moving to the podium."

Cheers went up from the crowd for New Earth's most popular, and most despised, alien life-form. A large stand had been erected between the entrance garden we had stepped into on our arrival and the barren desert. It stood twenty feet above the ground, with the crowds in front of it. A ramp from the main road into the Temple City was placed on the back end of the stage. The towering Xix bounced forward from the road onto the ramp, and with its strange dexterity and speed, it was soon at the podium. Hologens were placed around it to capture the speaker and beam it to projectors around the globe.

"Greetings, citizens of New Earth," it began, the amplification systems producing localized holosound around the crowd. A full minute of cheers and applause flooded the sands around us. When it had died down considerably, the alien continued.

"We celebrate this New Year—233 AD. After Dawn. After a young Earth woman stepped into a machine. It was a machine built not by members of her species, but by creatures strange, even frightening to her. With great vulnerability, she placed her body into that large device. She opened her mind to share the consciousness of hundreds of others—humans and nonhumans—and worked together in trust with them to achieve a great purpose: the unmaking of a terrible evil, and the beginning of a new timeline in the history of our galaxy."

Again, the cheers and cries. The Xix were not naive. I had no doubt that the translator was imbuing its tones and words with exactly the kind of charisma needed for this speech. But it didn't matter. It was not false because it spoke the truth, however artfully. I felt my own heart stirred. This truth is part of what drew me into the military in the first place: to defend our world, our lives, and that which was most precious.

"Captain?" It was Fox. "Unusual readings coming out of my tensor field monitors."

"Say again?" I asked.

"Space-time distortions flickering nearby, localizing to…the desert. You're not seeing this?"

Waythrel continued. "In those early days, New Earth united to fight a common foe, and we achieved great things together."

"Negative, Fox. I'm not reading anything."

The alien paused, its eyestalks scanning in multiple directions at once. "For two hundred years, we have worked together to keep a great peace in our galaxy."

"I'm getting it too, Capt," said Moore. "It's behind the crowd, centered several hundred yards in the desert."

Maybe I was too far from the source. I raced forward toward the crowd, my movements in the gleaming MECHcore suit drawing stares. "What the hell is it?"

"Not sure, Captain," said Fox. "But the signal's growing off the charts."

I felt a knot form in my stomach. Intuition took over. "M-teams, this is Captain Ratava. All available suits to the Temple entrance—immediately!"

I lowered the volume from the nonmilitary channels, Waythrel's voice becoming a soft whisper. "And now, the Daughter needs you once again to achieve that unity, that commitment, that devotion to a cause."

I reached the crowd and continued around behind. My instruments were definitely picking it up now. Most of my team had assembled nearby, and the other M-teams were closing.

"You see *that*?" yelled Kim, pointing forward.

I stopped completely, staring forward. "By the Daughter…."

The desert sands, the air above it, the dunes in the distance—all was becoming distorted. It was as if we had been embedded in crystal-clear rubber and some giant's hand was pulling on the material in front of us. I could continue to hear Waythrel speak through the broadcast, but no longer could focus on the words.

"Call this in, Kim, now!" I switched to a broader transmission band. "All M-teams, *combat alert*. I repeat, combat alert! Possible security breach at alpha point 7." I switched to my team directly. "We may not have long."

I was right. As I spoke those words and heard the acknowledgements from the other M-core teams, the distortions became a vortex. The clear rubber imploded and dove into itself as if it were being sucked in a direction perpendicular to everything else: a dimension beyond those we could access even mentally.

"It's a portal," said Williams flatly.

The vortex morphed into a whirlpool and the diameter increased fivefold, spanning three to four hundred feet. The clarity of the portal faded, and it took on a hideous black-and-violet hue. A depth became apparent to the structure making it look more like a tunnel than door.

A blast of air struck us, kicking up a wave of dust that accelerated outward and rained across the crowds. An electromagnetic pulse nearly shorted out our suits. The hologens weren't so lucky: they exploded. The broadcast failed; Waythrel's voice was cut off in midsentence. Through the thick chassis of my battle suit, I could hear the faint sounds of people screaming.

On several smaller picture-in-picture streams from suit cams displayed in the corners of my view screen, I could see the crowds turning toward us and the growing disturbance. But what held my gaze was the portal itself. The entrance turned pitch black. Out of that darkness poured a battalion of Dram troops like a plague of locusts.

The chaos began.

Chapter 14

There is an urge and rage in people to destroy, to kill, to murder, and until all mankind, without exception, undergoes a great change, wars will be waged, everything that has been built up, cultivated and grown, will be destroyed and disfigured, after which mankind will have to begin all over again.

Anne Frank

We were outnumbered one hundred to one, but our fifty MECHcore soldiers held their own. All the suits were outfitted with the new AI modules of the Xix, and we brought considerable firepower to bear as well. But we were not prepared for this. A terrorist attack, a core of trained assassins, perhaps. But not an invasion force. In all our combat drills, in all the sims and imagined encounters, none of them involved the opening of a wormhole at our feet.

And out of the wormhole came the worms. Ten or twelve triads and the escorting company of insectoidal Dram infantry—we never could nail down the exact number in the end from all the carnage. They flooded the sand plains in front of us with weapons blazing. Assigned to the front of the festival activities, it was up to me to organize the response, and I had to respond quickly.

"Equispaced grid assignments! All MECHcore units prepare for triad pairings. Commence AI dance immediately!"

Williams fired back. "Captain, we have a lock—two triads!"

"*Two?*" We'd never engaged two. What was the crazy computer doing? But there was no time to think. "Dance!"

Flechette rounds sprayed near us, but we managed to stay out of the way.

Our team locked into the dance, centering on a pair of triads—six worms in all —situated close to each other. It was one thing to buzz around with our thrusters orbiting one triad, but with two, it seemed like some crazed multi-star system with planets dancing between each ball of hydrogen. A wrong move and we'd be vaporized.

It quickly became a blinding geometrical nightmare. In our suits, at these speeds, the infantry was a nuisance, but we could handle those for the most part. As we spun about the triad pair, we blasted through their ranks with the ion slingers. Their charred forms began to litter the desert sands.

But most of our attention was on the worms. Amazingly, we held the advantage. The new AI was incredible. Just when it seemed they'd gotten a lock on one of our team, blasting a flechette round, there would be a complicated choreography that would leave their guns off target. We closed in and readied the missiles.

"Confidence level reached, Captain," called Williams, her tone strained. A data read on my view screen told me that her suit was damaged.

"Damage report, Officer."

"I've got a few minutes, sir. Give the order!"

"Take them down!"

Darting back and forth, in and out like a mad amusement park ride, it seems like the height of insanity to simultaneously launch missile strikes from multiple directions. But until you have seen the dance, watched the blinding intricacies of the movement, your ideas of what is sane in combat are out of date.

We fired. Old-school chemistry-based-propellant, dual-EMP/solid-explosive warheads. The EMP drilled a hole in any field defenses they set up; the explosives were a very modernized version of some of the best twenty-first-century weapons. Twelve missiles fired, two per worm, and we rocketed outward to avoid the debris field. The triads were down in seconds. We spun back and quickly mopped up the infantry cohort.

"I'm out, metalheads," said Williams. Her suit was venting black fumes and flying irregularly.

"Copy that. Get your ass down on the ground." We needed a battlefield perspective now. "Status report, Kim."

There was a brief pause as my team sergeant plowed through the tactical. We reoriented, forming a tight circle facing outward. "Eight triads down, sir! Minimal casualties for our forces. Wait. Yes, four down, two confirmed fatalities. The civilian situation is FUBAR. A bloodbath."

Dear God. "Okay. Status on that wormhole."

"Empty of hostiles, sir. Looks like we got this under control."

"Not even close, Sergeant! We need to shut that door. Get Central Command on the line. We need the Daughter out here! She's the only one who has a chance of closing it."

"Yes, sir!"

"As long as that portal's open, *anything* could come through."

And then—something did.

The first sign that we were in trouble was the screams from several MECH-core transmissions. Then five or six suits were flung past us.

"What the hell?"

Kim broke in. "Gamma-3 team, sir. They danced past us toward the hole during the battle. Life signs have flatlined. They're all dead."

We had been pushed to the left of the platform, nearly up against the city walls when we downed our triads. We couldn't see what was going on in front for the mayhem. But I had a very bad feeling about the situation.

"Alpha team—power up the space-time countermeasures! Power them up now!"

Then it came, a cry over the COM, the chaos too wild to figure out from which team. "False Dawn!"

"False Dawn, False Dawn!" And then screams.

"To the wormhole!" I shouted to my team. "We're the only ones who can hope to engage!" We fired our thrusters and blasted toward the spinning vortex.

And there she was.

A nightmare I could never have imagined, standing at the base of that hell-tunnel was the small figure of a woman in a white robe. She walked forward slowly, her arms upraised in front of her. MECHcore soldiers were thrown away from her like debris in a cyclone. The sand in front of her was matted and compressed, heat waves rising from the ground, darkening and reflective pools forming in places from the heat and pressure that glassified the grains. Red hair fell from the sides of her partially bald and bulbous head. Her green eyes were clear in my magnified view screen. It was Ambra Dawn.

And yet it was not.

Her gait spoke of a different personality, her features similar but not identical to those of the Daughter. Her expression vile, devoid of the depth and empathy I had come to associate with that face. Hideous cables and wires sprouted from regions of her skull to embed themselves at others—of medical or mechanical nature, I couldn't tell. This was a demon's fashioning of Ambra Dawn, a fiend's torturing of an already tortured life.

And I was going to destroy it.

"Semicircle around that thing!" I yelled, arming my final missiles. "Full tensor deflection on! Burn the batteries dead! We'll only get one shot at her!"

My team responded. I detected the field activations, the warheads armed in other suits, and they struck the formation in seconds. The countermeasures allowed us to resist the space-time warping that had doomed the other MECH-core teams.

"Launch!" Ten birds blasted toward the creature from multiple directions, closing in at several times the speed of sound.

All for nothing. Before impact, all the missiles veered away sharply, flying harmlessly off into the scorching desert. Several seconds later, their explosions could be felt. But we didn't have several seconds to contemplate events.

My suit exploded. The chassis was blown off my body, the material ripped off cleanly like some discarded exoskeleton. I was thrown to the ground with a terrible impact. I screamed as I felt my right leg snap. The bone ripped out from the thigh through the muscle, blood spurting and running down my shattered leg to wet the sand below.

I don't know how much time passed. I couldn't move, the pain blinding me, distorting all my senses. I was half naked, stunned, cut off from my team and all communication.

I have failed to protect her.

A shadow dimmed the sun, and a figure stood over me. It was the demon girl. That impostor with red hair and green eyes who dared violate the sacred image of the Daughter. I tried to reach up to grab the vile form, to beat the false life out of it, but I couldn't lift my arms. Some force from that thing had paralyzed me.

Then she entered my mind.

Her thoughts were a knife driven into my skull. Inward they drove against my will, pushing, tearing, groping their way through my consciousness, my thoughts. My life, my memories, my feelings, my dreams—she sampled them all harshly, holding me in contempt at every moment. Completely vulnerable, broken in body, and now my mind lay supine, her corrupt Reader organ digging deeper into my being than even I had ever gone.

The False Dawn paused a moment, seeming to grasp some structure of my consciousness within the tentacles of its thought. And that monster smiled. It smiled down at me with a hideous glare and began to laugh short barks that sliced me like razors.

I screamed. I screamed as I never had from any pain, any injury I had ever suffered. Like a child trapped in a nightmare that he cannot escape, my soul cried out for salvation from this torment.

Suddenly, the universe *shifted*. I don't know how else to explain it. A seismic event in space-time. Nothing that could be seen or touched or felt except in some deep, primitive place. The air around us undulated. Time stopped and started, events hopping from point to point discretely without meaning. A deep, infrasonic throb within the center of my consciousness.

The False Dawn stood up. In an instant, the agonizing probes were gone, its hellish mind removed from my own. My body shook. I could not help myself; I wept. Tears flowed madly from sobs in profound relief and personal devastation.

But greater events were unfolding. The remaining Dram triads imploded, crushed into objects hardly larger than a suitcase and slung to the side. The remaining infantry collapsed, bodies intact, forms dropping to the ground as if they had suffered some terrible stroke.

The False Dawn stared grimly around her and then turned to look behind me, toward the Temple. Weakly, pathetically, I arched my neck to look as well.

The Daughter had come. She floated—*floated*—like some goddess descended from on high, the rubber matrix of reality around her puckered and warped and appearing to strain to the breaking point. She glided forward toward her clone, her expression furious, her eyes nearly glowing like emerald lanterns in a sea of white and red.

The False Dawn threw her hands forward. Ripples of distorted space exploded between her and the Daughter. Unfortunate souls between them were pulverized, torn inside out, and most bizarrely, aged or returned to fetal forms of themselves. It was like some sort of space-time bomb.

And it hit a wall of nothing in front of Ambra Dawn. As if space itself were made of water, the air seemed to refract everything around it like spray from a hose impacting a crystal sphere. *Space* and *time* splattered, bounced, and danced in multiple directions. Droplets of reality congealed in the air and floated, events and places locked within them, winking out of existence in a miniature vortex. Rivers of the universe cascaded in all directions away from the Daughter, ignoring gravity, repelled by some incomprehensible force.

The False Dawn's jaw slackened. She appeared momentarily stunned.

The Daughter drew her hands together slowly, like someone raising up a precious package, and the False Dawn screamed. It was a hateful cry, a furious rejection of the events occurring around her. She was lifted off the ground, her arms and legs thrashing, her eyes wild. Ripples formed around her and then turned into cords and ropes of transparent nothing, wrapping her in a cocoon of solid emptiness.

The Daughter eased up in front of her. The False Dawn was helpless, trapped twenty feet above the desert floor, staring forward maniacally at her near mirror image. Then Ambra closed her eyes.

The False Dawn arched her back in midair, her green eyes rolling back in her head, her body turning rigid like the onset of rigor mortis. It remained that way for several seconds, and then her body began to shake. At first barely detectable tremors, and then progressing to visible convulsions.

Yet Ambra did not let her go. The Daughter's eyes remained closed, her expression firm but focused. Given what had just happened to me, I knew what was occurring. She had entered her enemy's mind.

Ambra's eyes flew open, and at that moment from the corners of my eyes, I saw shapes. *Shadows*. Forms indescribable, their edges seeming to burn the essence of reality around their shapes. As a viscous smoke they flowed from the wormhole, extending black projections toward the False Dawn, wrapping tendrils around the imprisoned creature.

Initially, they began to pull her back toward them, the wormhole narrowing. *They're trying to rescue her!* The Daughter watched their efforts silently, seeming to study the situation carefully.

As the shadows seemed to take control of the False Dawn, Ambra closed her eyes again.

The effect was like nothing I had ever known. Everything before, from the military engagement to the powers of these two Readers distorting reality around me, paled in comparison. From a center near the shadowed entities, from some point of nothingness, a force radiated outward that seemed to impact me like an explosion as well as a hallucinogen. Time and space —*meaning itself* was thrown down, obliterated, in whatever way these things exist. I cannot explain any better. I have no words for it.

The result in front of me was dramatic. The creatures melted, blended, and like some chaotic ink were driven back into the tunnel. My mind felt struck by what I could only characterize as screams from these creatures. But their screams did not take place in the medium of sound. I don't know what I was experiencing.

The Daughter stepped forward, and her hand plunged through the distorted rubber prison around the False Dawn. She touched the creature's forehead with the flat of her palm, and the woman's head whipped backward. The False Dawn floated limp in the cocoon, blood dripping from the insertion points of some of the larger cables in her skull. Ambra waved both hands toward the woman, and the bubble and figure within flew violently backward into the tunnel. They disappeared from sight.

Staring forward, her glare fierce and disgusted, the Daughter closed both fists. The portal slammed shut. A powerful blast of sand burst out from where it had existed and rained quietly about us.

A terrible silence fell. I had not realized that there had been such a great noise until the portal shut. In this relative quiet, I began to hear the moans and cries of the wounded.

She turned to me and glided over beside my form, her feet lowering and then gently resting on the sands by my chest. I could see tears in her eyes as she knelt down and stroked my forehead.

"I'm so sorry, Nitin. Rest. It will be okay." Her voice was the most beautiful music I had ever heard.

An enveloping warmth flooded through me, a profound sense of safety and belonging. And fatigue. Deep, deep fatigue. I could not keep my eyes open and felt myself losing consciousness.

I slept.

Chapter 15

A thing is, according to the mode
in which one looks at it.

Oscar Wilde

The tunnel never seemed to end.

I was passed through it, backward and forward, like some package in a delivery system, until I couldn't tell which direction was which anymore. Stars surrounded me, peered brightly through the distorting walls of the tube. They were so silent. So still. Unconcerned.

I could not speak. I could not scream. I had no voice or sense of my form. Back and forth, again and again, stars blurring during my acceleration or just staring back at me callously during lifetimes of stillness.

What am I?

The tunnel seemed polarized. I began to sense opposite charges, feelings, purposes. *Beings*. At one end there was light and warmth. A terrible and wonderful love that I could hardly face without being reborn by it.

At the other end, an opposite force. A darkness. An anger and need to unmake. Manipulation. *Antipathy*.

From both ends, green eyes stared back at me through this endless space.

Green eyes in blackness, cold darkness. Laughing. Green eyes in sunlight. Weeping. Calling my name.

Nitin. Come to me, Nitin.

Ambra, how do I come to you? I can't come. I can't move! Help me!

Then I will come to you, my love.

Green and blue.

The green swayed in the blue, golden crowns dancing at the tops of towers. My eyelids twitched open and shut in the bright light. My shoulders felt weighted down, my entire body pressed into a clay mold.

Soil. My hands opened and closed, my fingers scratching through dirt. The towers came into focus. *Corn.* Adrenaline coursed through me. *I know this place.*

Weakly, painfully, I pulled myself to a sitting position. I sat in the middle of a giant cornfield once again. My body naked. My mind muddled and sloppy. Part of me was afraid. Afraid of this strangeness, this vulnerability. Afraid for my sanity.

But Ambra is here.

I stood up. It was as if I had left only recently. I remembered the way. Limping forward at first, then nearly bringing myself to a run, I dashed through the maze of cornstalks, my heart racing, a powerful hope of seeing her driving me on.

I crashed outward from the corn and stumbled onto the grassy lawn. The farmhouse loomed before me. A figure stood in front of it.

"Nitin." Her voice traveled undiminished across the yard.

Tears welled in my eyes. So much horror seemed lodged in the back of my mind, threatening to grow and consume me. My body felt ransacked. Broken. I was lost.

But here is my haven. Standing before me was a woman not yet twenty. The image of the Daughter I had known and gazed on my entire life. Pale like china. Red like fire. Green like emeralds. Light seemed to dance around her.

Yet different. Alive in a way I could never feel from holos. Transcendent in a manner only this dream could create. And centered in a universe without other distractions. Without other worries. Focused on me alone.

And I on her. "Ambra?"

She too stood naked, my eyes darting across the lines and curves of her body. There was desire. There was stunned awe at the depth of her beauty. She walked toward me.

"Do you know where we are?"

I blinked at her words. "No. A farm?"

"*My farm,* Nitin," she said, taking my arm in hers and smiling more broadly. She pulled me forward gently and led me toward the house. "I was born here, spent eleven years here." Her voice began to lilt and dance as though she were reciting a magical tale. "You came out from my father's cornfields. They go on and on until it seems like the world will end before you get out of them. He used to work so hard out there. The big companies always wanted to swallow us up, but he was determined to stay independent. He hated them and how they killed the plains."

We were about halfway across the backyard when she turned and pointed to an open expanse of land between the tall cornfields and the house.

"Isn't it beautiful?"

The land continued, seemingly forever, nearly flat but for a very slight slope that enhanced the view from our position. Browns and greens and houses dotted the endless plain until it faded into the horizon. The blue above and around us faded toward that end, turning first gray, then black as it crashed into a bubbling mountain range of clouds. Lightning flashed in front of me a million miles away.

"A storm is coming," I said.

"Many," said Ambra solemnly. "But they are not here yet. We have a short time."

I turned to her and spoke, the wild creativity of a dream releasing my thoughts. "Please don't go away this time." I was remembering the other dream. *Memories of dreams in a dream.* I tried to suppress tears, but so much emotion flowed over me that I was overcome. "Please let me stay here with you, Ambra. There is a hole. It eats away at me. My whole life. No one understands. I can't face that hurricane of emptiness." I trailed off, a nightmare lurking just behind my conscious thoughts. I tried to push it away.

"I understand, Nitin," she said, placing her hand on my face.

"But here," I said, "here it's safe with you. It's right. Please, can we stay?"

She shook her head sadly. "I'm sorry, Nitin. We can't."

"So, I am dreaming? This is all a lie?"

"Dreams are not lies, Nitin. Dreams are other spaces. Other times. But spaces and times within larger places. Bubbles within seas. Sometimes a person can stay in the bubble and ride out the storms. Never leave the dream."

I looked back at the dark clouds, seemingly no closer yet no less threatening. "But we can't."

"No Nitin, we can't. And that is my fault." She sighed.

Just then a tan-and-white blur sped around the corner of the house. Before I could process it, Ambra let go of my arm, and the blur leaped into the air. She caught it and embraced an enormous pile of hair. I recognized it as some sort of sheepdog.

The animal licked her face and seemed beside itself. Its fur was copious, thick, and silky, giving the dog an appearance of being overweight.

Ambra laughed as she cradled the dog. "This is Matt, Nitin." She turned the dog toward me.

Dogs do not have the popularity in India that they do in Western nations, so my experience was more with street strays than manicured breeds. The strays were usually diseased beggars or even aggressive ones. Hesitant, I reached out my hand.

"Turn your palm down and bring it below his nose."

I did so, and the dog sniffed me and looked me over. Satisfied, but not much taken with me, he returned his attention to Ambra.

"I saw him die, you know," she said. "First in a vision. It was horrible." Her face clouded as she squeezed the animal a little too tightly, and the dog started twitching its paws. "I couldn't stop it then. I didn't even know it was a vision at that age. And then later, even when I understood my powers, I had to let Earth die."

"But you did it to save so much more. So many worlds! And in the end, you brought us back!"

"That success doesn't change the choice. Or the damage it does, Nitin."

"Don't blame yourself."

She shook her head. "If you could only know and see. I am a frightening nexus of cause and effect. It was my fault my parents died. Servants of the Dram killed them, butchered them to get to me. My fault an entire planet full of life boiled. And it's my fault that we can't stay here." She touched my cheek again and smiled. "Where it's safe."

I reached out and held her hand, the porcelain hue like a beam of light in my palm. "It's okay; I knew that we couldn't. Felt it. But I can't explain how much I need you. Need to be with you in a place that is safe."

She looked into my eyes. "You are the handsomest man I'll ever not see." I was taken aback slightly as she laughed. "Do you know what is most powerful about being close to you? Warmth and *smell*. You know I can see in my weird way. I can see your features. I've *seen* them in ways and times you don't even know. And you *are* handsome to me, Nitin. I've had crushes and infatuations, but the first time I saw you—the many times I've seen you—always such power! It's underneath conscious thought. But I do not see you with my true eyes. All those pathways in my brain are atrophied now. All to the great service of my tumor."

"You speak like it's evil."

"It is."

"It's what has saved us!"

"And killed so many." She looked out across the plains again toward the storm. The dog jumped down and, nose to the ground, began an indecipherable olfactory quest across the grass. "You grew up with the powers of this thing in my skull as a force for liberation. But living with it, what it has done to me and others, what it will do—nothing is ever as it seems."

It was unsettling to hear her pain in those words. History lessons are one thing—imagining the difficult life of another is an important exercise, but so limited. A five-minute conversation in the middle of a dream conveyed infinitely more. Seeing the lines in her face, the tension in her muscles, and sadness in her blind eyes.

"I want to understand, Ambra. I want to know everything about you."

"I know you do. And you will. A few steps at a time, Nitin. That's how we climb to the Temple. Hand in hand."

She breathed in deeply, closing her eyes. "*Smell*. Waythrel said something about immune receptors and genetics and mate selection, but it's all a blur.

Biology. Isn't it strange how so much of everything we are and know and feel is biology?"

"We are what we are."

"Yes! But even the Readers don't know what that is."

She inhaled again, dipping her head close to my neck, sending involuntary shudders through me. "I could eat you up!" She paused there a second as my body tensed like a bow.

She pulled away. "Walk with me, Nitin, away from the storm for a time, or I'll want to entangle us right here and now. But it's the wrong time. And the wrong place."

My throat was dry, and my hairs stood on end. I felt things stirring below and was momentarily embarrassed. But she pulled me toward the side of the house, the growing thunderheads at our backs and a bright sun halfway to noon before us.

"It *is* beautiful," I managed. I had never seen America's Great Plains before. I had imagined that the sameness, the flatness, and the agricultural devotion of the land would be monotonous. Boring. In a way it was, until you drank in the enormity of it, the fields like a sea with different colored crops cresting here and there, houses like small boats afloat. Even the storm we had turned our backs on was majestic in a terrible kind of way as it poured forward like lava from a volcano.

"This is what imprinted me," she said wistfully, "shaped and programed the impressionable mind of a little girl. I guess I was born learning to see into great distances. But I can never go back to this place, as much for where I must go as for what terrible things happened here."

The land she loved, and yet the land that was stained with the spilled blood of her parents. Why were we here? And where was she going that she couldn't stay?

We came because you approach my heart, its light and darkness, Nitin. We came as you search with me to return from the darkness that clone monster threw you into. We came because existence is layer upon layer of dream within dream.

At the mention of the clone, that nightmare I had pushed aside threatened to rage into my consciousness. I shook slightly, and Ambra held my hand firmly.

"But look, Nitin! There is so much light!"

She waved her hand across the fields before us, and the air shimmered and swayed, and space opened. In the middle of the bright daylight, a necklace of gemstone stars exploded.

She pulled me forward into the breach of space, and we stepped through the day on Earth onto the sands of an alien beach. Strange seas crashed in front of me, and above was a churning miracle of radiance: an entire galaxy painted across the night sky.

Ambra pressed her naked form against mine and kissed me gently, staring deeply into my eyes. She placed her hand on my chest, near my heart. My breathing deepened and quickened. She whispered softly into my ear.

"I am with you, Nitin. Always. Never forget. Follow my voice as you did to get here. Feel my love. And you will find your way home."

"Is this home?" I asked stupidly.

"One of many," she said, smiling. "A place we will soon visit in another dream. Here we will love each other on these very sands."

Chapter 16

There is always some madness in love.
But there is also always some reason in madness.

Friedrich Nietzsche

Once again, I woke from trauma in a hospital bed, staring up into the forest of eyestalks of a Xixian medic.

I was completely disoriented. I didn't know where I was, where I had been, what day I had woken into. The room was strange; I did not know it. The medic was a Xix, but not one I recognized. I was thankful I could recall my own name.

There was a tunnel. I remembered a long and endless tunnel. There were worm triads in the Thar. Japanese nurses. *No, that was before.* The Sahara. A new team. *Yes!* A special mission to salvage the war.

A wormhole.

I shuddered and closed my eyes. It came back to me. The monster came back to me. I could still feel it, feel her thought tendrils in my mind, probing my inner person. I felt sullied. Unclean. *Used.*

A warm sensation pressed against my hand. I opened my eyes, turning my sore neck to the right, and stared into green, blind eyes once again. But not the clone. Eyes that embraced and did not wound.

"It's okay, Nitin," she said. "Don't think of her." Her hand squeezed mine more tightly.

"Daughter of Time," I whispered. I did not know what else to say. Echoes of a dream washed over me. *Was it real? Is this real?*

"I am more than that to you, my Nitin." She smiled; it was soft and lined with sorrow. I had never felt so much love poured toward me. "Say my name."

I choked out the word, hardly suppressing the tears.

"Ambra."

I was in no state of mind to analyze what was happening, what had happened. There could be no sequence of events that I could imagine leading to this moment. Nothing I could conjure in my imagination that would place Ambra Dawn at my bedside. Holding my hand. Speaking impossible words.

"My love," she said, the smile large and radiant. *You don't have to understand, Nitin.* The words in my mind again. *Just accept what you know is true. There will be a time soon to talk more.*

"Yes. Please." I closed my eyes as emotion overcame me. I could not process these events. Then other memories came flooding back. "What happened…to my team?"

A familiar voice spoke. "They are recovering nearby." It was Waythrel. I shifted my gaze to my left side to see the huge bulk of the alien. "Most of the injuries were moderate, like your leg."

Moderate? I looked down to see my thigh. There was little evidence of damage, only a hairline scar where the bone had torn through.

"Most of the injuries?"

"Medical Sergeant Ryan Marshall died before we could reach him. He spent his last moments tending to the others. He saved their lives." Waythrel paused a moment. "The rest of your team is stationed back at the barracks. They recommenced training yesterday."

"Yesterday? Why am I still here?"

The medic cut in. "Because your injuries were more severe." I glanced down at my leg, but it corrected me. "Not to your body. To your mind."

Ambra reached over and brushed her fingers against my forehead. A thrill ran through me. "She had done terrible things to you, Nitin." Her face was pained. "An act of violence and power that was as unnecessary as it was cruel."

"The mind, and the neurological support framework that gives birth to the epiphenomenon, is fragile, Captain Ratava," said the alien medic. "We had to act quickly, or much of the damage would have become permanent."

"Damage."

"Psychological damage, and through that, physical damage," said Waythrel. "The matter of the brain and the field of the mind are like a particle and a wave in quantum theory. Two aspects of a greater whole. Damage to one is damage to the other. There was some work that could be done at the level of your organism, but for the sentience field that is your mind, we needed a different kind of doctor."

"Ambra." I turned back to her and looked into her eyes. They had turned to green pools filling with water.

Waythrel spoke. "Ambra did not leave your side for a week."

"Until I knew I could do no more," she said.

A week? I wasn't sure what was harder to believe: that the Daughter had devoted herself to my sickbed for an entire week as the war effort collapsed around us, or that she needed to. I shuddered involuntarily. "I can still feel that thing in my head."

"Even with Ambra's ministrations, it was impossible that you would suffer no lasting effects from such a mind probe," said the medic. "But we can assure you that your cognitive functions are unharmed. Psychologically, there will be residual pain."

I turned to Ambra. "Thank you." I spoke to the others as well. "Thank you, all." I couldn't convey how grateful I felt to have that horrible mind erased, even incompletely, from my own. Had it not been, I'm sure I would have gone mad.

I felt fatigue creeping over me again, but there were questions bubbling underneath the surface that began to break through to my consciousness.

"I saw...*shadows*. Were they real?"

Ambra spoke firmly. "Yes."

"What are they?"

"Nothing that we have encountered in this galaxy," said Waythrel. "But by showing themselves here, they have revealed much to us. Ambra herself as well as the monitoring equipment that survived the battle have provided enough information for us to begin piecing together what we are dealing with."

"Why did they come?" I asked.

"We don't think they meant to," said Ambra. "They were overconfident in their red-headed Frankenstein. The clone was not supposed to fail so completely, to be taken prisoner."

Waythrel picked up the thread. "At the least they probably assumed their Reader could retreat and return. When it was clear that she could not escape from Ambra, they sought to intervene."

"So, they were close. Waiting."

"Yes," said Ambra. "Hiding in the corners of space-time. Whatever they are, they have extremely advanced technology, as we could have guessed from what is going on. Not advanced enough to control a wormhole—they still needed their Reader clone. But enough to know how to exploit them, cache themselves unseen within them."

"But you defeated them," I said, a note of pride in my voice I didn't mean to let escape.

"They aren't supernatural creatures, Nitin. They are made of the basic components of matter in this universe, just like everything else."

"With one exception," finished Waythrel.

An exception to material existence? "What do you mean?"

"They are creatures wholly composed of antimatter."

"Antimatter? *How?* Wouldn't they just explode or something in our atmosphere?"

"We aren't sure how they manage to shield themselves, but they expend enormous energy to do so," said Waythrel. "But because they are very much natural creatures, Ambra was able to deal with them."

"Then, we have a chance," I said, finding myself slipping into sleep. "The mission. There is hope."

"Yes," said Ambra, smiling. "We'll talk more when you are stronger." She bent over and kissed my cheek, whispering in my ear. Her breath was warm and raised goose bumps over my body. "Soon, we will walk among the stars together, Nitin Ratava. And for a time, you will experience how beautiful they are."

Her words spun around me like poetry, beautiful and comforting, and I felt myself smile even as I drifted off again into a deep sleep.

Chapter 17

Jealousy does not wait for reasons.

Gandhi

The clinic staff had turned in for the evening, and I was alone with the flashing monitors and night-shift nurse at her station in the hallway. Tomorrow, I would be released and allowed to rejoin my team, as we were to meet with Ambra and her advisors to finalize the mission plans.

Several days of intensive rehab had proven to me that the Xixian medical technology was nothing short of miraculous. My shattered leg was as good as new, and my basic physical performance, as well as short drills in my suit, showed absolutely no degradation of function. There were some attention-deficit red flags. Apparently, it would take a lot more time to smooth out the mental damage that monster had inflicted on my psyche.

I couldn't notice it in my daily actions and thoughts. But nights were another story completely. I dreaded them and began to fear my own dreams. I needed to get this thing out of my head completely, or the sleep deprivation was going to end up making me dysfunctional.

It was on this last evening in the hospital, later into hours after midnight, that he came. I wasn't sleeping. Another nightmare had startled me awake. I was wiping the sweat from my forehead when I heard footsteps in the corridor outside my room. Not the soft padding of the night nurse, but a heavier, more assertive gait.

Curious, I propped myself up in the bed and listened more carefully. At least this gave me something concrete, something tangible to consider instead of the ghostly remnants of a mental assault. The steps stopped outside my door and a tone sounded, indicating that the touchpad outside had been activated. The door dissolved as a male figure stepped into the room.

"I understand that you sleep poorly at night."

It was Sepehr Mazandarani, the advisor to Ambra Dawn. In this moonlit dark, his devilish features were only caricatured, and it was with some apprehension that I watched him pull a chair over to my bedside.

"News travels broadly here," I said, a sense of threat palpable from this man.

He smiled sharply, waving away my words. "I am the Daughter's closest advisor. *Human* advisor, anyway. Her thoughts are rarely hidden from me."

"You are a Reader? Do you commune with her?"

I saw his face tighten. "No. Ambra employs me for other talents that I can offer."

He seemed to enjoy playing with words for my discomfort. "What talents?"

Again that smile. "Analysis. Logic. Strategy. She relies heavily on my counsel."

"Yes, you are an important man."

He cocked his head slightly to the side and laughed. "I did not come here to monkey dance with you, Ratava."

"Good. Just why are you here, then?"

He eyed me harshly. "I don't dance, Captain. I act when I have the data to act. Right now I don't have that data, except for circumstantial evidence. But that evidence has me concerned greatly for the safety and well-being of the Daughter."

I pushed myself to an upright position. "What do you mean?"

"In your desert heroics at the Rebirth, you were present at an event that has never occurred before. *Never* has there been an attack at the Temple. Not in two hundred years."

"Yes, I know."

"Furthermore," he continued, cutting me off, "in order for that clone to have breached the Xixian defense fields, they would have needed help from within. The three-space location of the Temple is scrambled to any Reader of space-time, and opening a wormhole at the perfect location and time to attempt an assassination would require a device, a beacon of some sort, to be placed to transmit our real location."

"What are you saying?"

He locked eyes with me. "That we have a traitor in our midst, Captain."

In the Temple? It was impossible to believe. I had seen the devotion of the people here. I couldn't imagine any of them aiding our enemies—the enemies not just of Ambra Dawn but of the entire human species. Not even the terrorist groups. They might hate the Daughter, but they hated the aliens even more.

And besides, how could they get a spy past the Daughter? She could read minds. She could read the future!

"What do the Xix say? What does Waythrel say?"

"It was *their* hypothesis. They know the nature of the defenses they have established—which now they are modifying to prevent a repeat event."

"Who could possibly do such a thing?"

"We don't know. But I will tell you, Captain—I am going to find out." His face poorly concealed an anger bubbling beneath.

My thoughts were troubled. Something felt wrong. His visit with this information in this manner made little sense. "Why are you telling me this now?"

"The Daughter has developed a particular empathy toward you. At best, I hope to persuade you to take this threat seriously and to do all that you can to protect her."

"And at worst?"

He stood up and grasped the neckline of his black desert robes, looking down on me with contempt. "I don't like anomalies, Captain Ratava. Unexplainable events or people. Your resume as it concerns Ambra Dawn is strange beyond explanation. You have single-mindedly aimed your career trajectory like a missile to place yourself just in this location. You offer this seeming unconditional emotion to her, immediately winning her attention and confidence. And it is only just after you arrive, after centuries of peace in the desert, that our defenses are breached from within and the Daughter attacked."

I felt the blood run out of my face. "You can't be serious."

"Circumstantial evidence, Captain. But rest assured, if it ever becomes more than that, I will be the first one with a gun to your head."

With that, he turned sharply on his heels and marched out of the room.

Chapter 18

W e entered an enormous room located directly below the gargantuan tower reaching toward space.

The four remaining members of my team had been escorted by a still-suspicious Mazandarani across the Temple City. The tower loomed above us constantly, impossible to grasp in its height, and our path soon within the five-mile radius of the supporting base.

We passed the massive columns of a strange Xixian metal that plunged underneath the desert sands. The base supports themselves were as wide as buildings. The webbed shadows of the structure fell across our path from the setting sun. We came to rest at the entrance to a beautiful building, some well-realized combination of human and Xixian tastes blended harmoniously.

The structure rose to a height of seven or eight stories like some strange plant or deep-sea creature. The largest portion was at the top, a toroidal curvilinear solid that looked something like a sphere that had been pressed in deeply from the top. It seemed to float above the desert sands but in fact was supported at six points by tapering columns that became ellipsoids at their apex. The larger top portion was therefore resting on smaller round objects that appeared to almost flow into the desert floor. The material seemed to be the same indestructible concrete found in the buildings in the Six Cities, the tan color blending into the sands around us.

Most strikingly, the walls seemed almost porous in places, complex, flower-like geometrical patterns of different sizes arrayed across the surfaces of the bulbous toroid. As our local star dipped below the horizon, the day faded quickly in the Sahara, and a golden light radiated outward from those thinner regions of the walls. It was like looking at some enormous Japanese lantern, or perhaps some strange bioluminescent jellyfish from the depths.

The Temple. There had never been a holo to emerge from the Sahara. Here the Daughter met with some of New Earth's most powerful Readers along with those from many alien species. Here they entered into a group trance, their minds connecting through the medium of space and time. Many claimed they formed a powerful community mind greater than the sum of its individuals. This mind had once traveled back in time and unmade history. This was the epicenter of our power in the galaxy.

As we walked up the thirty broad steps below the entrance, we passed beneath a high arch decorated with symbols of both alien and human origin. We entered a cavernous space, the curved walls appearing far larger than they could possibly have been from the outside. What had appeared as human-sized geometric patterns on the outside now took on dimensions many times that span.

But what stole my eye was the light source that gave the glow that seeped through the patterns on the outside. In the middle of this vast space undulated a brightness that I can only compare to a plasma. Like some superheated state of matter, its iridescence was formed from multiple colors flowing and merging in constant motion. Its shape was hard to fathom. From a distance, with a brief glance, I assumed it was a spherical object. But the longer I looked, the closer I approached, it seemed as if there were some solid structure present beyond anything I could grasp, but that only part of it was in this space. As its shape altered, I felt as if I were seeing pieces, projections, sides of the full shape that came into view and then disappeared. It was dizzying.

As if that were not enough, in the middle of that terrible and unearthly energy was a dais. I identified it from legend—the dimensions of a small table, obsidian, connected to the pulsing energy field by numerous extensions, many of which appeared alive like slick tree roots. This was the Xixian-designed seat of power for Ambra Dawn. This was where she sat, connected to the powerful devices that amplified her modulations of the space-time matrix. Placed radially around this central point were several hundred small depressions—additional seats built into the Temple floor.

Despite the presence of that powerful energy source, I felt nothing. No disorienting sickness as I felt when the Daughter had battled the False Dawn, no sense of electricity or heat. The air was mostly still except near the entrance where the Sahara winds entered feebly and died. There was no sand anywhere in the Temple.

"They sure don't mess around," said Moore. He and the other members of the team gawked at the vision before them.

"There's some kind of geometrical distortion here," said Fox. "Space-time funkiness. It's bigger inside than out."

"Yeah, noticed that," said Williams. "What do you suppose that glowing glob is there in the middle?"

A voice answered from in front of us. "A doorway that opens to the Orb." It was Ambra Dawn.

Seeming to step out of fog and darkness, the Daughter appeared flanked by Waythrel on her right and Major Mizoguchi on her left. They walked toward us slowly as Mazandarani left our side and took a place beside Mizoguchi.

"The Orb?" asked Kim. "How is that possible? We're on New Earth."

"The geometry of time and space is not intuitive, Sergeant," said Waythrel. "We could give you more detailed explanations, but we are here to discuss more pressing matters."

"Why in here?" I asked.

Ambra smiled. "That will become apparent soon. Please, take a seat." She gestured at the floor space in front of her and elegantly crouched into a crossed-legged sitting position. Her advisors, including the alien, also sat. I looked across my team and shrugged. We sat.

"With their victories in space, our enemies grow more bold," said Mizoguchi. "Although with the compete destruction of their recent attack force, they will perhaps be more cautious for the time being."

"In addition, Ambra has sent them a message," said Waythrel. "She cast back at them the dead body of the clone prior to closing the wormhole."

"Yes," I said remembering. "What did you do to her?"

Ambra looked sad. "I tried to look into her mind, to understand what she was, what had motivated her. But there was so much darkness. The Dram can apparently program their human cattle to harbor extreme hatred toward us— so much that there was little hope to reach out to that pitiable thing." She shook her head. "There was no saving her, no hope to keep her prisoner. And I could not let her return. So, I wiped her mind."

Moore leaned forward, his long legs uncomfortably splayed in his seated position. "You did what?"

Ambra sighed. "It was a telepathic overload, a destruction of her mental space-time matrix that scrambles all coherence."

"The biological portion of her mind was reduced to pulp," said Mazandarani. "You can think of it as *frying* her neurons."

"What this means," said Waythrel, "is that our enemies will learn nothing from her, nothing from their attack except that we hold a power that they do not yet know how to counter. Even a cohort of their new allies was destroyed."

Mizoguchi cut to the chase. "But because of the recent attacks, we have decided to accelerate the covert mission. You will be leaving today for your first target node."

"Today?" I had just stepped out of the hospital!

"Whoa, wait a minute! Time out!" cried Kim. "What about recon? Mission prep? Stuff we like to do to stay alive."

Williams cut in. "We're not just going to jump to some random system today and engage without knowing anything about it."

Mizoguchi answered. "Of course not. Do not insult me with such a concern."

"Then what?" Kim asked.

Mizoguchi looked toward the Daughter and Ambra picked up the conversation. "If you are willing, you can learn all you need to know about the locations right now, in there next few minutes. We can cut through hours of briefings and holocrystals."

"And just how might we do that?" asked Moore.

"By opening your mind to me. With your permission, I can share the information telepathically without the need for any slower and more cumbersome methods."

"Hold it right there, princess," said Moore. "No one's crawling up inside my noggin—you got that?"

"Sergeant—," I began.

"Sorry, sir, but no fucking way."

Mazandarani looked sharply at Moore. "There is nothing to fear unless you have something to hide."

"Yeah, I got a lot of things to hide," said Moore, leaning back and smirking at the counselor. "Like what me and that mechanic girl were doing under the engine hoist the other night. Or what I think of that minger growing on your chin."

"The Daughter is discrete," said Waythrel. "Such sharing is a daily experience with the Xix. It unifies us, eases misunderstandings, and grants us an efficiency and group memory we would not otherwise possess. Ambra has now brought this gift to your species. Already, the Readers of New Earth have begun to be united in this way, especially those who have taken part in the great sharings here at the Temple."

"It sounds amazing," said Fox. Moore eyed them all suspiciously.

"What do you mean discrete?" Williams asked.

Ambra spoke. "She means that I am careful to touch only those aspects of your consciousness that I am required to. I will not pry into your thoughts or memories. I will learn from you only that which you want to share with me. Also, none of you are Readers, so you cannot through me invade one another's minds. Only I can reach out to each of you."

My heart was racing. I couldn't believe the privilege we were being offered. While I could understand the concerns of Moore and Williams, my heart responded like Fox's. I wanted nothing more than to have her mind share with me. But I dared not speak of it, or speak anything. I feared my eagerness would spook the members of my team.

Kim raised his hand. "You said that we could share what we wanted. What do you mean? Are we going to hear your voice in our heads and point thoughts at it? See your face? Exactly what the hell's going to happen?"

Ambra smiled. "It is a different experience for every person, and not one that has a simple physical correlate like those you mention."

"I think I can answer this," said Mazandarani, still keeping an eye on Moore. "I'm not a Reader, but I have shared like this many times with the Daughter. If you have ever had a sense of another's personality—their soul, for lack of a better word—that understanding of their nature that is not tightly bound to their appearance or voice or words. *That* is the experience. You will be given the experience of the Daughter's personality without having to do all the work of really getting to know her. It will just be there, filling your awareness, more completely and clearly than in any way I've ever known."

"By the Dawn," said Fox.

"Exactly," quipped Mazandarani. "Through Ambra Dawn."

Moore ignored him and turned to Ambra. "Well, what if I don't want to get to know you that badly?"

Ambra nodded. "I respect that. I respect any of you who refuse."

"If we refuse, then what? We're out?" asked Williams.

"No," said Ambra. "You can be briefed by the others en route and at the site. Only they will know far more, and you will be playing catch-up."

Moore didn't hesitate. "Count me the hell out, then." He leaned back on his elbows.

"Williams?" I asked. She didn't look as if she was too keen on the idea either.

My warrant officer stared straight at Ambra for fully half a minute. I didn't know what her internal battle was, but in the end she nodded and accepted the sharing.

"Risk assessment," she answered when Moore asked her why. "I calculate that the gains outweigh the losses."

Mazandarani spoke. "Am I to assume that the rest of you are in favor? Except for Sergeant Moore, of course."

Kim, Fox, and I nodded. Moore stood up. "So, what, I go wait outside or something?"

"Not necessary," said Ambra. "But please don't disturb us until we wake."

"Wake?" asked Kim.

"From the trance," said Mazandarani. "You don't think the Daughter will enter your mind and download a week's worth of material and you'll continue to chat?"

Kim and the others took this in silently. Waythrel spoke. "Please, then. Try to calm your thoughts and feelings. It usually helps for humans to close their eyes."

I closed my eyes. I tried to calm myself by imagining the forms around me. My mind moved to the rip in the fabric of space that had embedded a segment of the Orb in this very chamber, the colors of the thing spinning in their bizarre paths and hypnotizing me. For a few minutes, I heard nothing but the soft breathing of those around me and the faint, dying howls of the winds outside —haunting cries of a tortured land.

It grew quieter and quieter, until I began to hear my own heartbeat, feel it throbbing in my ears. The pounding grew louder and began to take on shapes. Shapes of the heart muscle, vessels straining under the pressure, blood coursing in spurts through my body. Blue to red. Lung to heart. Webs of alveoli opening, growing in size, until I could see the cells themselves take on the form of vast continents stretching before me to the horizon. And regularly, like clockwork, the pulse and pound. Each beat brought a wave of gray particles, molecules of oxygen, which were trapped, held, and fed to contorted monsters, bands of chained atoms with a central core not unlike the dais of Ambra Dawn.

Inward and inward I sank. Past protein molecules, to amino acids, carbon-carbon bonds. Electrons danced around me, nebulous, unreal and alive. Inward, crossing thousands of times the distance before, toward a glowing center like the heart of a star. The nucleus exploded to reveal quarks and strings and elements I had no words for. They danced and danced around me in confusing motions.

And then everything reversed. The bizarre strings took on the shapes of atoms again. Simple structures of the simplest element: hydrogen. And at speeds I had never experienced, I raced out from this microscopic labyrinth into the very depths of space.

A nebula. A nearby star lighting the colors of the gas cloud. A band of diamonds coating the space opposite me. Thousands of stars.

An ocean world, blue and reflective in the blackness of space, devoid of land. It spun about the star.

Between them, the dancing colors I had seen in the Temple in their full context: the Orb.

Chapter 19

The more you see how strangely Nature behaves, the harder it is to make a model that explains how even the simplest phenomena actually work. One does not, by knowing all the physical laws as we know them today, immediately obtain an understanding of anything much.

Richard Feynman

Three star systems, their planets, the location of the Orb in each system. It was as if I had lived multiple lives in those distant spaces, ages flowing through me, images and cultures and locales. It was like no learning experience I had ever known.

I was passive in the beginning, letting the Daughter do whatever it was she had to do in order to plant this information in my mind. The flood of information was all-consuming. Detail upon detail of places and times and events. Entire histories of other worlds and planets—somehow it was all hers to share, as if she had lived eons across every point in space. Her vision was with the eyes of a god. Sometimes so much would pour through me, things that made no sense and bordered on surreal, that I cannot explain how that experience translated into concrete information about the place. I was not conscious of any learning—only endless experience.

But learn I did. Later on, when I woke from the trance, I knew all I needed to know about each target to complete our mission. Much more than I needed. I had become a citizen of each world, a historian and anthropologist. An organic library.

By the experience of the third system, the third Orb projection, I began to become accustomed to the process. The mind is an adaptation machine, and already mine was finding an equilibrium with the impossible. I found myself restless. Searching. Reaching out into the blackness for that which truly held my heart.

Nitin.

Her voice whispered my name. I experienced the warmth and love I had sensed lying in the hospital bed when she tended me, but a thousandfold more strongly.

Follow my voice, Nitin. Come to me.

There was an Orb. All space was black, the star systems gone, the background of the galaxy missing. The information flow stopped in an instant.

There was only the Orb. It grew in size, or I approached it at reckless speed. I could not tell which. Without any reference points, size and motion were relative.

Patterns, colors, *passages* rippled across the enormous surface—which I discovered was not a surface but like the reflective ocean skin, an illusion blanketing fathoms of mystery. I sensed the power of the thing, a terrible, monstrous depth and abstraction that nearly froze my heart. Cold, dark, like the bottom of the deepest chasm in the sea.

Yet warmth. At the same time, in the midst of the alien and transcendent that I could not comprehend, there was empathy. A vibrational resonance connecting me and the Orb. Pure. Guileless. Limitless *affection*.

By now the object had grown to span the width of my peripheral vision, the multidimensional corridors frothing beneath the surface of the entity transforming into enormous rivers that dwarfed me.

Nitin, come.

She called from within the god-sphere. I felt her, felt her person like a presence in my own flesh, that barely remembered flesh that once sat in the Temple in the center of the Sahara. I hesitated one instant—a heartbeat staring at that anomaly—and then I steeled my courage, willing myself to her.

I felt a terrible acceleration pull from deep inside me. A madness of dimensional mazes darted around me, through me, all the while sensing her presence grow stronger and stronger. It seemed that the entire Orb was becoming one with her.

And then screams. Panicked cries around me. Not my voice. I was yanked back and forth. *Stars stars stars stars in this endless tunnel.*

My dream? I felt that nontube that held me bend and twist and form hyperspace knots and burn at the very fabric of space. The stars took on hideous rainbows of distorted color.

And cold hands, cruel hands pulling, pulling, tearing at me, seeking control, breaking my form, remaking it, demanding pounds and pounds of my flesh.

The pain was excruciating. I had no body, but I felt my teeth grind, my body spasm, my back arch, the very skin across my ghost form stretching and tearing and yielding to the merciless strain.

Now, I screamed. I screamed down this Orb hole and tunnel of hell where time spiraled and spun and completed a circle to re-become.

Full circle in multiple dimensions, I crashed screaming face first into the onrushing madness of my own torment.

Chapter 20

My heart, the bird of the wilderness, has found its sky in your eyes.

The Gardener of Tagore

There were waves.

Waves crashing, the sounds of their foam bubbling across my consciousness. Waves and wind. Water over rocks while a breeze stirred refreshingly across my face.

"Nitin, wake up."

I opened my eyes. For a moment, all I could see was green. The green of the evening glow of the vegetation. Of a forest of bizarre trees climbing around me, their fluorescent light glinting off the ocean to my left.

And her eyes.

I lay on my back, a rough sand underneath me. As I stared upward, the sky was an explosion of shape and form. Something like the aurora borealis danced madly through the atmosphere. Behind it, roiling like some vortex of light, was a sea of stars, an entire spiral galaxy splayed out across the night sky. The atmosphere rendered the stars in multiple winking hues of gold, crimson, and purple. Like gemstones.

Like the two emeralds above me.

Ambra stared down into my eyes, her knees in the sand beside me, the water lapping the black robes that trailed behind her. Her hands held mine over my chest.

"My Nitin." She smiled.

For some time, I could not respond. Could not move. The shock of my experiences, the devastating beauty of the planet around me, her body alongside mine as she looked into my eyes—I was powerless. Once again unmade by her.

Finally, she reached one hand behind my neck and pulled me to sit up. It seemed that I weighed four tons, and my body was sore in all the muscles and joints. I grunted, breathing in shallow gasps as she helped me sit, her right arm around my shoulders, the left still holding my hand.

"It will pass soon."

I looked into her face. "What happened, Ambra? Where is the Temple? What has happened to me?"

"Too many things that should not have," she said. "The Temple is where and when we left it. We will return to rejoin the others soon."

I breathed shallowly through the pain. "Was the journey so difficult for you?" She seemed unharmed.

Ambra shook her head. "No. And it should not have been for you. Travel through the Orbs can be disorienting, especially the first time. But it is not painful." She sighed. "Unless there is interference."

"How can there be interference?"

"I am no longer the only one who manipulates space-time in our galaxy."

"The False Dawns."

"Yes. Their numbers grow, and so does the recklessness of their attacks."

"They are created that quickly? Don't they have to be raised like a normal person?"

"Yes, but not all in just one era. Our enemies have been patient. They *will* be patient. And their successors have sent back an army to destroy us in our time."

"An *army?* How many?"

She shrugged. "They can hide much from me now. I see only the warped edges of string-space where they have vandalized the Mind."

I didn't understand what she was saying. "Ambra, please, what do you mean?"

She frowned and pressed her body into mine, her arm looped now around mine. "These wormholes. These cloaking efforts. They are *obscene*. Because space-time and sentience are a unified field. Where there is one, there is the other. Where there is great intelligence, or a mass of minds, space-time is altered. Where there are great alterations in space-time, dynamic and structured—can you guess?"

I could, but the implications were insane. I caught my breath a moment, thinking through her words. But I felt so unafraid to speak to her. I did not fear her judgment, even in my stupidity and blindness. I felt only acceptance.

"There is...a *mind?*"

"Yes, Nitin!" she squeezed my arm again. "Of a kind. The very fabric of our universe is constantly stirring, cogitating, becoming. From its chaotic birth pangs to the great structures of our era until the singularity of equilibrium, it will grow and become in ways we will not understand for billions of years. Only at a time when our far descendants have grown together with the rest of intelligent life into a form that can communicate and understand this much more alien and powerful thought."

"But you understand it now?" Part of my mind wondered why I was even accepting this bizarre idea.

"To recognize it, to feel its living soul is very different from understanding it. But these reckless acts are wounding the structure of this mind. Creating lesions in the cosmic cortex."

"Why do they do it then?"

"Because they are like children. They cannot see, born and bred as instruments of war. They are horrible, but I pity them. I know what it is to be an object, Nitin, with no other value other than what purpose you can be to another. To be helpless while altered as others see fit, never understanding. Only knowing pain, fear, and self-loathing."

I felt my arms tighten around her waist. Her past was rote history for most of us. But not to her. I could see the pain of her enslavement etched in her face. "I'm sorry, Ambra."

The corners of her mouth twitched. "But what's driving them is something different. Much *darker*. Even the Dram do not understand the bargain that they have made to acquire this new power."

"The shadow forces?"

"The *Anti*. We pull them now, Nitin. Pull at them terribly for our ordering and our great growth through time. Our bias of the cosmic background. They will do all that they can to destroy us."

"Why? What are they?"

"Our inverses, Nitin. And no more. The shadow of our light, as for them, we are the shadow of theirs. Creatures we know little about. But now they have revealed themselves." She sighed and shook her head. "At least it is still small. Still localized. These clones are clumsy and stupid. Raised without love. Taught without wisdom. But there are so many."

My thoughts were racing around, trying to process the implications of these confusing words. "What about the Orbs? Don't they also damage this Mind?"

"That is what makes them so special. They don't. The Orbs *synergize* with it. They harmonize with it. They have been made with a purpose commingled with the cosmic mind. They are meant for far greater things than our simplistic use of them." She sighed and looked around the green seaside. Shadows from the alien trees danced across her face as the aurora undulated. The wind tasted fresh. "Even if that is what brought us here."

I looked around again. "Where are we?"

She smiled. "One of my favorite places in all the galaxy, dearest. We are orbiting a star on the outskirts of the Large Magellanic Cloud, a satellite galaxy of our Milky Way."

My mind searched through the extensive astronomical training required by the MECHcore. "That's hundreds of thousands of light years from Earth."

She nodded. "Fifty kiloparsecs."

"Ambra, how?"

"The Cloud is teeming with life. Some intelligent. So, there are also Orbs here." She smiled and gazed up at the swirling cornucopia of colors. Our Milky Way. "Isn't it beautiful, Nitin? I have come here many times over the last two centuries. It has been a place to escape the burden of all that I must do. All that is asked. A place to forget, if only for a moment, all the terrible destinies. But I grew tired of witnessing it alone. It grew harder and harder to wait for you, even in this heaven."

"Wait for me? You knew…" I stopped myself. Of course she knew. She was the Daughter. "You called my name in dreams," I whispered, memories flooding back. "You had never met me, but you called me *love* in the Temple hospital. You speak as if we have already lived our life together. You have seen everything already?"

She shook her red curls at me. "Not like you think. The broad outlines, the truth that one day you would come, yes, I knew. But the closer events come to me, in space, time, or heart—the more poorly I see. Blame quantum mechanics."

"I don't understand."

"Better to ask Waythrel. I don't understand the physics either. What's important is that I did not know when or what form you would take. I only knew you would come. But I could sense you, Nitin. Once you were born, I knew you had come. I sought you out and watched over you as you grew in India. I came to love you as a child at your grandmother's country home, as a young adult studying late into the nights to pass the Force entrance exams, as a grown man—brave, honest, and determined to find me."

I stared at her in wonder. She had seen my entire life. She had known about me for centuries.

"I came to you in Japan. And in the Sahara, I tended your bruised mind and learned to love every one of its imperfect contours."

"But Ambra—why? Yes, I was searching for you! If you knew this, why did you wait? Why make me search? Why have we wasted so much time?" The idea that I was alone—yet not alone—that so much of my life had passed by when we could have been together—it sent a wave of panic through me.

"It's not that simple, Nitin," she said, sadness in her eyes. "You are blind in ways I am not. If certain futures are altered, the ripples can become tsunamis. The fates of our galaxy always rest on my choices. I am never free of that. Even when—especially when—it concerns what is most dear to me. I've known nothing more painful than watching you in silence for decades, longing to reach out to you, play with you as a child, speak to you as a man. Feel your love for me openly." She looked into my eyes and squeezed my arm. A wistful look clouded her face. "It's funny. Chodak saw this two hundred years ago and shared his vision. I saw myself through *your* eyes. It was then that I knew the depth of your love, felt your soul adore me as I had never witnessed a man love a woman."

I swallowed. "Who was Chodak?"

She smiled sadly. "Someone long dead. A monk and powerful Reader. He forecast your coming to me. He told me we would be married."

My head was swimming even as my heart raced. "Ambra, please. *Please.* Everything with you is a mystery. Every time you speak with me, it is like the universe changes and I cannot keep up."

She pouted. "So you are saying that you do not want to marry me, Captain Ratava?" Her brows were wrinkled, her expression ridiculously charming.

"Ambra, I…" She continued to stare at me. I felt as if I were leaping into the dark. "Yes. Yes, in fact I do. But this is not exactly how I had pictured the subject coming up."

She threw her head back and laughed. Her shoulders shook as she brought it back down and nestled into my chest. I smelled her hair, and it was like a revelation. A thousand pathways in my brain must have lit to this simple olfaction. My eyes drank in the orange surrounding me, and instinctively, I reached up and stroked it, caressing the enormous bulge of skin over the top and back of her skull.

"Yes, my heart," she said, her laughter subsiding. Tears filled her blind eyes, and I knew from her face that they were tears of both joy and sadness. "You love even that. That deformity that no human animal should carry before her mate. Who would love such ugliness? And yet, you do."

I placed my hand on her face, softly stroking the left cheek with my hand. I stared into her eyes. I knew those eyes could not see into my own, yet her mind could Read the deepest place in my person. Her breath was warm in the cool air, tendrils of fog extending from her lips. My hand appeared nearly black alongside the whiteness of her skin. I cupped my hand and pulled her mouth to mine.

Kissing a goddess is to open not only your body to another, but also your soul. As our lips met, and the limbic thrill shot through my veins, a much stronger electricity rushed through my consciousness. As we held each other in this embrace on a distant world, our hands wild, exploring, our lips and tongues caressing, I felt the fingers of her mind pass gently over the contours of my consciousness.

Love should always a mixture of body and soul. But when you kiss a goddess, the greater ecstasy is in the soul.

I pulled back after a few moments. "Daughter. Of Time."

She did not laugh at my clumsy exclamation. A flame of passion possessed her features, but they were also imbued with sorrow. "Nitin, wait. You must know."

I ached as I stared into her eyes. "Know what, Ambra?" I only wanted to kiss her again.

Tears ran down her cheeks. "Our time together can only be short."

I nodded. "That's okay. We have an important mission. I understand." I found myself reaching for her again.

She pushed me back gently but firmly. "No. I don't mean now or here. Not because of the mission. Together, all paths end in darkness."

"What do you mean?"

"I can't see the details, but the broad form is all too clear." Her face was twisted in agony. "If you choose to be with me, it will set in motion events that cannot but end in tragedy."

"What tragedy?"

"Your certain death, my love." She was now perfectly still.

I looked away from her, my hands still on her shoulders. *My certain death?* As many times as I had faced death in battle or seen it in the casualties around me, it was hard to imagine my own death, my own nonexistence. And yet these words came from the Daughter. I looked back at her.

"And if we are not together?"

Her face tightened. "There are many futures on that path. But in most you will live a long life."

"Without you?"

She nodded. "Yes."

My words poured out instantly from deep within me. "Then it will be a long and empty torture. It will be living in the darkest prison." She looked at me with a strange pity. But my choice was easy. The easiest choice for death that I could imagine making. "So then—how long do we have?"

"Oh, Nitin." She held me tightly for a moment. "Do you want to know?"

I thought about this. If I knew, I might only focus on that date. Yes, I would obsess on that fate as the clock ticked down to the exclusion of what occurred around me. She was right. It was better that I not know the hour and live in the moment. With her.

"How will I die?"

"I don't know, Nitin. I can't see so near to myself—and you are as close as my own soul." She touched her fingertips to my temple. "But it will be terrible, my love. And it will be at the hands of our enemies. We will be shattered by betrayal. In the end, our humanity stolen forever. In return for this terrible price, I can give you so little. A short time, but a time when we will love as none have ever loved."

She drew her face near mine. Our lips brushed as she spoke. "One short and beautiful dream for all the horror. I had to tell you. You must choose."

My throat caught. "My only horror is to leave you. If I am torn from you, tortured, killed—I can only die once. But to walk away, to live each moment alone, apart from you—that is a choice I can't make even once. And certainly not every moment of my life. That life is hell."

She wept and smiled. Her hands cupped my face, her fingers slipping over my scalp sending waves through me. Her body pressed against mine. I felt the swell of her breasts, the warmth of the life within her. I was surrounded by a sea of red.

"Then love me now and until our time ends."

Chapter 21

I submit to you that if a man has not discovered something that he will die for, he isn't fit to live.

Martin Luther King, Jr.

We stepped out of the Orb projection into the Temple center.

Again I was disoriented. Again the pain racked my form. Ambra had tried to minimize the discomfort, and while I suffered, it was far less than before. I didn't ask why, as I was sure to misunderstand it. I was just happy I was not to end up screaming in agony and half dead on the ground again.

In fact, overall I felt better than I had in a long time. Alive. Even *fulfilled*. To kiss a goddess is one thing. To make love with her, something entirely different. Our bodies were remarkably attuned to each other. I had no explanation for it. Few couples find such physical harmony so early on. Part of the joy and pain of coming to know another person is just in this adapting to and learning of another's body, communicating in intimately personal and sensitive ways. Perhaps because of how we had already entwined our consciousness, perhaps for reasons I would only discover later, that harmony of body was already present between us. If sex can be a religious experience purely on physical terms, then I had been born again.

But the physical ecstasy was the lesser of our oneness. I cannot tell you much about how our souls met, how her telepathic powers brought our consciousnesses together, and as we joined our bodies, joined our minds. It seemed an eon. A place beyond time. We met in a thousand memories, hers and mine. We bathed in a million desires and fears. Images. Music. Smells. We shuttled through the labyrinth of cognition like some ray of light through an evanescent maze, the walls painted in flickering ideas, until they mixed and touched so that the resonance began to remake the essence of each independent consciousness.

I was one person when I journeyed to that alien world overlooking the Milky Way. I left as someone else. In the process, my mind had been healed, purged of the lingering damage brought on by her clone, and continually remade in ways I would slowly come to understand.

We stepped out of the swirling colors and into the relative darkness of the Temple hand in hand.

Astonished faces greeted us.

The members of my team were talking animatedly with Waythrel and Mazandarani. Slowly, one by one, they noticed our presence from afar and turned to face us. It took a full minute for us to walk the distance across the Temple floor. In that time, none of the others uttered a sound.

We stopped in front of the group. "It is time," said Ambra.

"Wait a moment!" said Williams, her expression flabbergasted. "What the hell just happened? My brain is about to explode from drowning in a sea of information, and then I wake up, see the rest of these bozos waking up with me, but you two are *gone*. Vanished like magic. Then you reappear coming out of that *thing*?"

Moore laughed. "Holding hands like lovers in the park."

Waythrel was silent at the outburst. Mazandarani stared at our clasped hands, his expression devastated. I didn't know what to say.

Ambra took the lead. "You should be happy—Nitin can report back to you about travel through the Orbs. He has successfully completed the test flight." She smiled at the confused expressions around her. "You didn't think that we were going to travel by strings, did you?"

No one answered. Waythrel spoke. "It is far less efficient, and dangerous now that the Dram control much of the Time Tree. But Ambra can access the Orbs directly."

"Right," said Kim. "We just have to teleport through that thing." He stared wide-eyed at the kaleidoscope in the center of the chamber.

"It would be an honor, a great privilege, Daughter of Time," said Fox, and bowed her head.

"So, Captain, hell of a ride?" Moore asked.

I couldn't suppress a laugh. I nodded. "You have no idea."

"Wicked. I'm game. Don't even know where I'm going, but I'm not going to miss out on surfing that baby."

Ambra looked over the others. "The rest of you? You have the information. You know the purpose."

Williams nodded. "Something else, all that *sharing*. We should be using that at all the schools."

"Someday we will," said Ambra. "Most people aren't ready for it yet. But New Earth's Readers are learning from the Xix. Our planet is in the early stages of a group memory, soon to be a group awareness. A sum far greater than its parts that is slowly waking up."

"I remember," said Kim. "You're going to seal the Orbs!"

Moore looked over. "Seal them? What does that mean?"

Kim looked at a loss for words. "I saw it, but I'll be damned if I can explain it."

The alien spoke. "Ambra will reconfigure the local projections. The hyperspace filaments will be retracted. There will be no string on which to navigate. The node will be dead." Waythrel paused. "And while we are there, we will find out what we can about our enemies. If we are lucky, we might even run into them, or lure them to us."

"We?" asked Fox. "You're coming, too?"

"Your team seems to be short one member," said Ambra. "I have chosen Waythrel to fill the gap."

Williams objected. "Waythrel would not complete a team. The exercises are tuned for six soldiers. She would be an outlier."

Waythrel addressed her doubts. "In what will come, your previous training will have little relevance. We will not be a special forces operation. We will be a unique delegation serving as much or more as detectives than as soldiers, even if fighting may become necessary. I will fit well into this construction."

"Detectives?" asked Williams. "So why us? You don't need soldiers. Especially not with her." She gestured to Ambra.

"It's not about that, is it?" said Moore, his eyes squinted and sharp. "It's about *him* and about her. We're part of that puzzle. Part of the *vision*."

"You are fated," said Ambra. "There is no other word for it. No other way to explain it."

"So can we choose to change our fate? Is that some kind of paradox?" asked Kim.

Ambra smiled. "Only because your minds limit what you can see. Each of your choices is free *and* preordained. The distinction between the two is artificial, like describing a tree as either soaring into the air or digging into the ground. Contradictory—yet both true, because a tree is much more than either conception. Each choice you make is really a family of choices that propagate through space and time to sum to your final reality. If you could see, truly see the essence of the fabric around us, you would understand that you actually will make *every* possible choice available to you. You are infinite even as you create finitude."

Williams shook her head. "I shoulda never put my name down for this crazy assignment." Fox beamed.

Ambra prodded me with a look. I turned to my team. "Suit up, metalheads!"

We donned our gear, the Xixian skins layering over our forms like some self-aware organism groping its way forward. The process took several minutes, with pauses to examine fit to check specs and performance.

Meanwhile, I watched Mazandarani walk up to Ambra. They were some ten feet away, but I could hear the exchange. The counselor paused in front of her, seeming at a loss for words.

"This fate is cruel, Sepehr," she said.

He didn't raise his head, but looked down at the ground. "You know my heart, Daughter of Time, so I can only be honest and agree." He seemed to move his mind to another topic. "But you also know my thoughts. Why do you take this risk?"

"I trust him, Sepehr. I *know* him. He will never hurt me."

"I only wish that you had omniscience. A little prescience is a dangerous thing."

She kissed his cheek. For a moment a wave of jealousy flowed through me, but it was quickly dissipated. Her expression was not desire. It was love. An affection and concern that I realized was even deeper than what I had feared. I felt ashamed.

"I will return, Sepehr. And he will be with me. I need you to prepare for our return and for the ceremony to follow."

"Why do you ask me for this?"

"Because you must walk this path or never be free. I am cruel, perhaps. But I care for you too much to have you enslaved anymore."

He nodded. "My fear is that I will disappoint you, Daughter. But your disappointment will not be from my failure to try. It will be as you asked." He stepped away.

Fox appeared before me, blocking my view to the conversation. "We're ready, Captain!"

I nodded, looking over my team. After what I had seen and experienced, I realized how ridiculous we were. Our little special forces crew wasn't much of a match for even a well-armed Dram attack force. What were a bunch of metal-heads thinking to accomplish stepping through an Orb? Traveling through space and time? Perhaps meeting an enemy that even Ambra feared and none of us understood?

Waythrel had joined Ambra at the edge of the long pathway to the Orb projection. They motioned, and we followed. The walkway was lined on both sides with the creature-sized depressions. After our sharing with the Daughter, we knew that these were the seats of the other Readers who would telepathically connect with Ambra during the long meditation sessions when they formed a group mind of some nature.

Ambra had tried to share this experience with me during our unexplained absence, but I had understood little, even when she shared it telepathically. She had even admitted that it was hard for her to understand. The combined mentality of the group exceeded her own consciousness by such a degree that even she could grasp only bits and pieces of the insights when separated. I understood nothing, not even bits or pieces.

We reached the Orb. Ambra gestured toward it. "Step inside; it is perfectly safe." We walked inside followed by the alien and Ambra. "If you are ready, I will open the Orb."

I nodded, and the members of my group gave their assent in various ways. All looked nervous. All seemed excited.

Fox smiled. "Get ready for the trip of your life."

"Or the trip to our death," said Moore.

Ambra stared solemnly at them. "Both futures have already occurred."

And then, infinity exploded around us.

Part II

Until you grasp the limitations of Entropy, you cannot understand the possibilities of Time.

Wisdom of the Six Cities

Chapter 22

How on earth did Descartes, who could not on prima facie evidence accept his existence as real, believe that his thinking was? This was the beginning of the dark ages of European philosophy.

Yin Yutang

Water.

It dripped. It began in a plastic bag, puffed out, gleaming. A drop traveled through a valve, down clear tubing approaching a bedside, and there dove into an adaptor with a sharp needle at the end. The needle plunged into the pale skin of an arm.

Ambra's arm.

I sat at her bedside. Her eyes were glassy, the sedative beginning to dull her senses. I held her hand. It was very cold.

"Nitin, I'm so glad you're here. I'm scared."

I looked around at all the hospital equipment, dumbfounded. "Where are we?"

She sighed with sleepiness. "Dreaming. We're dreaming again. Walking layers of awareness and walking and walking..." She trailed off.

As my thoughts began to clear, I studied her closely. She was younger. My mind slowly ground into gear, and I pieced together the facts from her life.

"This is when you were a prisoner on Earth. These are your surgeries, the ones that changed you forever."

The early teenager smiled wanly. "Yes, Nitin. My second surgery. The most terrible."

"The first wasn't?"

She shook her head slowly. Her words were slurred. "Nope. Nope. I thought they were going to *cure* me then. Take it out like they promised—right before they killed mom and dad. I was starting to go blind. That scared me. Nope. First surgery was fear and hope."

"The second?"

"Then I knew. Bastard *told* me. 'Making it bigger. You'll be blind soon; isn't this sooooooo cool?' Freaks R Us. Freaks R Us. Freaks R Us."

I waited for her to calm down. "So this time, you knew they weren't curing you. They were destroying you."

"Yeah. Sucks, huh?" She looked up at me and smiled. "You look *really* good. Well, almost blind here, but the me visiting this me knows. So many of me. Me, me, me clone me. Mmmmm, you smell good, too. Sound good. Bet you taste good."

"Ambra...."

"Going to fall *off* the world, Nitin. Drugs pushing me under the water and outside the universe. And I'll be just meat meat meat to them again. Cut, drill, screws, slice. I'm falling to black and sick at my stomach, and they are going to come with saws and drills and screws..."

Tears trickled down the sides of her face as she shook it back and forth. I squeezed her hand tightly and kissed it. "It's okay, Ambra. I promise you'll be okay. I'm here with you. I'm here with you the whole time."

Her green eyes flashed open. She gripped my arm tightly. "You promise?"

"Yes, of course I promise."

She relaxed and sank back into the pillow. "Then I'll sleep. And we'll go away. To a new place. I just don't know where..."

She closed her eyes again and began to breathe deeply. The breaths became rhythmic, louder, pulsing and grasping my attention so completely that before I could realize it, everything had faded around me. The hospital room, Ambra, even her hand.

Only that constant rhythm.

I had thought it was her breath—but she wasn't here. But the rhythm was here still. Pulsing. Beating.

Rushing.

—

Water.

It sounded like a giant waterfall or storm wind through the trees. White noise. Deafening. The sound was focused in front of me. The blurring was decreasing. I was seeing.

Masses of naked men and women cowering against a wall. Robots darting about blasting high-pressure water against them. People struggling to get in front of someone to ward off the pain.

Those who could. Many just lay there on the floor or crawled slowly away from the machines. These were hardly people anymore.

It was the smuggler's ship where the Daughter had almost died. Interstellar merchants who drove their human cattle until they dropped. They bought those who had scored poorly in the Dram sorting. My Ambra's deformity had not been recognized for what it was, and she was scored poorly. She was defective, cheap goods. Bought by smugglers who nearly killed her before the Xix raided the ship.

I scanned the row of screaming and blistered slaves. *There*. Near the far corner crouching into a ball. A mass of red, unkempt, tangled hair that ran down from a bald top.

I rushed over, the water not touching me, the robots unconcerned. "Ambra!"

I knelt down beside her. I hardly recognized her face. She was shivering badly. Her pale skin was so thin that the blood vessels decorated her like some demonic henna art. Muscles and fat were gone. Only transparent skin over a skeleton.

This was what happened to Ambra from the history books and in the art of our age. But all that didn't prepare me for what it was like to be in the presence of near-death starvation. It was horrible.

"Go, Nitin," she whispered faintly. I bent closer to hear. "Don't see me like this. Let me die."

Dreams within dreams. She had said I experienced her childhood home because it was close to her heart. I was in the hospital because she was deathly afraid and called to me. And now I was here.

"I won't go. I love you, and you are going to survive this. You know you do. I know you do. Remember that. I don't know where in time and space or your memories we are, but I'm going to stay with you."

She was too weak to answer verbally, but as I cradled her, the fingers of the sticklike hand on my shoulder pressed meekly.

"Good. Don't talk, Ambra. Just feel me here. I'm here I'm here I'm here," I said, rocking her in my arms.

"Don't stop," she managed to mouth silently.

"I won't."

And I sat there on that floor filthy with human waste and dirt, rocking the wrecked form of my beloved, over and over through what seemed to be an ever-slowing rate of the passage of time. Rocking her nearly weightless body pressed to me like a crumbled paper bag. Rocking back and forth, stronger and stronger, until we drowned out the screams around us, silenced the roar of water.

They became muffled sounds. Beeping of equipment. Darkness in the rocking. Or was it floating?

Yes, floating in a dark sea. Water everywhere.

—

Water.

The older dreams. Back in this awful place. But these dreams had never had water before. Even when I was floating, there was only darkness. Numbness. Emptiness.

And stars.

But now I could see it. *Water.* A faint light seemed to grow from the giant sea around me. It was a faded color, pulsing. Inorganic. Without life or sense of purpose. Just—rhythm.

But it shone through water. Of this I was sure. I knew I should be seeing the maze of the Orb light. I was traveling somewhere. There were all these facts and truths and things just beyond my ability to grasp them, hold them, focus on them before they bled out in a rainbow of colors and dissolved into the green.

My mind thrashed wildly trying to hold onto...*what?* I was a soldier. I was on a mission. I had loved a woman, the only woman, the only woman in the universe centering my life and hopes. I held her hands and I rocked her to peace and she is red and white and soared through the clouds of a nebula and a beach where I made love to her looking up at our galaxy in a night breeze.

Things that must be true but now gone and only existing as belief in my devolving memory of dream, fading in this throbbing greenness, this water of death.

I tried to move. *I saw!* Motion. Blurred. A hand! I had a hand! Again I flailed my arm, but it only achieved a weak waving, a sickly motion in the mossy ocean. But I saw it again. There was form. *I had form.* Form in water.

But there was no exit, no way to wake from this nightmare. Nothing but stasis and wetness and flailing, feeble limbs. Endless green water.

Nitin, come back.

Ambra? I called in my thoughts. *Ambra, please. I'm lost!*

Beside my chest, there was a brightness. A vortex of light spun in the middle of the water. I peered into its center, the point elongating from the edges, drilling deep into a third dimension. Soon, it seemed that I was looking down a long tunnel.

You aren't lost. Only displaced.

The tunnel pulled me. I felt myself drawn slowly through the green water, the vortex growing, the light from another space flowing into the dark sea around me, brightening. Soon I felt myself spinning, following the strange undulations of the turbulent light, accelerating to greater and greater velocities. Around and around and around until there were only star trails of radiance.

I left the sea and entered the swirling tunnel, buffeted, flipped, stretched, and pulled forward relentlessly, a billion suns and years and parsecs flying by my awareness.

Plunging through the light and out of the tunnel. Free. *Free!* Floating free above a great and terrible world of blue. Horizon to horizon blue. Enormous. Endless.

Water.

Chapter 23

Innumerable suns exist; innumerable earths revolve around these suns in a manner similar to the way the seven planets revolve around our sun. Living beings inhabit these worlds.

a heresy of Giordano Bruno, burned at the stake in 1600

So much water.

I lay on my side, my breath coming in shivering gasps. The floor below me, the walls pressing against my forehead—were invisible. Like perfectly clear glass without back reflection, absorbing no moisture from my breath in condensation, never smudging from the oils of my skin. A technology that did not exist.

Underneath me was—nothing. Darkness and stars. Behind me, I felt the warm pressure of light. Because of the planet before me, I knew it must be from a star. We had arrived at Orferlin: planet without land.

I rolled slowly onto my back and gazed up at a group of faces. The alien, Waythrel, monstrous and still. The members of my team. And Ambra. She knelt down beside me.

"Welcome back, love."

I pulled myself up to a sitting position, the low friction in this strange bubble disconcerting. I felt unsure of my motions. I rubbed my temples. "I thought you said this wouldn't happen again."

"I know." She sounded apologetic. "It was a massive problem, interference from our enemies. I was prepared for something, but nothing so intense."

"They knew we were coming," said Waythrel.

I looked around at my team. They seemed okay, but I needed to make sure.

"What happened? Anyone else hurt?" I pulled into a ball, and placing my hand on the nonexistent wall, pushed myself up. I could stand in the bubble. My feet appeared to be planted on nothing. But that nothing held me up.

"No," said Waythrel. "You are the only one who suffered any deleterious effects."

"That doesn't make sense."

"Captain's a little soft, is all," laughed Moore.

"It's not the first time," said Ambra. "He's being targeted. Because of me."

Waythrel looked on in silence. Williams stepped toward us. "And just *who* is targeting us? More of those clones?"

"Thousands of them," said Ambra, her expression troubled.

"*Thousands?*" asked Kim.

"Their numbers have risen considerably."

"How can there be more? Where are they coming from?" asked Fox.

Waythrel spoke. "From many spaces and many times. There is a growing convergence. A massing of the troops, if you will."

"I'm sorry, Nitin," said Ambra. "It was more than I was ready for. An ambush."

"So how the hell did they know we were coming?" asked Williams.

"The same way they found us in the desert," answered Waythrel. "We have been infiltrated. There is a spy among us."

"Whoa—*us*? Time out, okay?" said Kim. "Others besides us knew we were coming. What about that counselor? He seemed pretty unhappy with the group. Especially the captain."

"Or even Major Mizoguchi," said Williams. "She's not Force. She works for the Temple only now. That's unusual. Maybe she's there for a purpose. Don't turn on us just because we're the new recruits!"

"Sergeant Moore refused to share with the Daughter," said Waythrel.

The sounds of ion chargers filled the space as Moore's suit lit up. "You look here, squid-head. I didn't watch my mates torn apart by Dram soldiers on Dworn to listen to this shit. Put up or shut up."

Ambra shook her head, staring at Waythrel. "Enough. There are many possibilities, including many we haven't likely thought of. Mazandarani and Waythrel suspect a mole. But there are forces gathering with powers I haven't yet probed fully. Moore is right. We have no reason to doubt one another. More importantly—we are going to need one another if we are to complete this mission. Distrust will poison us."

Purge your minds of it.

I felt it as a mental slap. So did the others. Ambra was angry, and it was the first time I had felt that anger. It was frightening as much for her power as for how much she was holding back.

"I said I don't want anyone in my head!" shouted Moore.

"Then power down your weapons unless you are going to engage our enemies," said Ambra forcefully.

I saw his mouth tighten, and he eyed her harshly. But it wasn't a look of hatred. He was sizing her up. There was respect in his eyes. The humming ceased as his suit switched off.

"Now we have a task to complete," she said.

"Ambra, where are we?" I asked. Too much was unexplained.

"Orferlin," cut in Williams. "You shared, right? Dolphin world."

"I know the planet and the facts. I remember," I said with some annoyance. I gestured to the invisible bubble around us. "I mean *this*. What is this? An advanced ship? Is it from the Xix?"

Waythrel spoke. "No, Captain. This is beyond the ingenuity of the Xix."

"It's my doing," said Ambra. "A distortion and warping of space-time. There is in three-space room to carry us and also the ability to expand or contract in multiple hidden dimensions, providing volume enough for weeks of air, munitions, food. Anything we need we have brought with us from New Earth."

"Toilets?" asked Moore.

"With privacy, Sergeant, in case you are shy," answered Ambra with a grin. Moore smiled back.

"Also, quite defensive," said Waythrel. "Outside of an overpowering clone attack, there are no weapons the Dram possess that can harm us."

"And what of those *Anti*?" asked Fox.

"We will see," said Ambra. "For now, we need to find out what we can from the inhabitants. Once we've investigated, we seal this node of the Time Tree. We have two more stops to go before we are done."

Chapter 24

What makes planets go around the sun? At the time of Kepler some people answered this problem by saying that there were angels behind them beating their wings and pushing the planets around an orbit. As you will see, the answer is not very far from the truth. The only difference is that the angels sit in a different direction and their wings push inward.

Richard Feynman

The descent to the planet surface was unlike anything I had ever experienced. Without a view screen, a hologram—*without walls*—it was as if we were falling freely from the edge of space. The enormous expanse of water grew before us until it eclipsed our peripheral vision. I instinctively pressed against the invisible walls of the bubble, the unnecessary pressure providing some feedback to my anxious nervous system that we were stable, that we weren't pitching forward through the atmosphere with nothing to support us. I noticed several members of my team doing the same thing.

The ride was also disturbingly smooth. As we broke into the atmosphere, there was no shudder. No turbulence. Nothing to indicate we were in fact moving relative to the planet at all. Only that the darkness of space receded, the clouds swam over us, and the water continued to expand before our eyes.

We even plunged into a gigantic storm dwarfing anything that occurred on New Earth. Orferlin was at least three times the size of our planet, with more than ten times the surface water. So much moisture and a tropical temperature cooked up some continent-sized tempests. Straight into the heart of one of these beasts we flew, all light quickly disappearing, the new night interrupted by colossal bursts of lightning. It seemed like the innards of a nuclear explosion.

Yet, silent. Eerily silent and still. The rain poured over our enclosure without the sound of a drop. The lightning was never accompanied by thunder. The bubble had not a single tremor in the midst of this powerful display of nature.

"It is so quiet," I whispered.

"You wish to hear it, Nitin?" asked Ambra.

"Yes. Can you do that?"

She nodded.

I looked around to the others. "If that's okay with everyone."

No one protested. I looked at Ambra, and she smiled. *Then listen!*

The bubble exploded in sound. Howling winds were accompanied by stunning crackles of lightning that were swallowed by the deepest bone-rattling bass ripples of thunder I had ever heard. The bubble was still moving peacefully through this, but somehow, Ambra had allowed the sound to penetrate. It made the worst thunderstorm on New Earth seem like a drizzle.

"By the Daughter," whispered Fox, her eyes wide.

"Beats anything I've ever seen," echoed Kim.

The tempest roared around our little bubble as we continued our rapid descent. The trajectory was angular, so as we neared the bottom of the storm system, we cleared its shadow and left it seething to our left and behind us. A blinding light exploded, bathing us in the alien blue of the local star. The ocean lay beneath us, extending in all directions to the horizon. As we decreased our altitude, the crests of waves became visible to our eyes. At first they were seemingly no different from those of Earth's seas, but as we neared the surface of the water and could use ourselves as a reference point, the true size of these giants became apparent. Larger than the greatest Pacific waves, these on Orferlin were like small mountains that loomed before our bubble, often blocking out the light and then breaking over us with great noise and drama outside, yet causing no disturbance to us at all.

This planetary ocean was *loud*. Everything you might expect from an Earth ocean multiplied by one hundred. Like small mice in a storm at sea, we stood speechless before the power of it.

"So, we go swim with the dolphins, huh?" asked Moore.

Ambra smiled. "I wish we could. The Brax aren't really very much like our world's sea mammals. They have something more like gills than lungs. Theirs is such a strange and rich culture; it stems from a distributed nervous system with more than ten brain-nodes across their bodies. Makes it almost impossible to damage them in such a way as to render their mental faculties deeply impaired. And the brain-nodes recombine in space-time to form the most beautiful patterns of thought. Their Readers are second only to the Xix of the aliens in our galaxy." She seemed to be lost a moment, as if remembering or searching the planet for signals from the sea creatures. "I wish we had the time to spend..." Her face clouded.

"Ambra, what's wrong?" I asked. She almost looked to be in pain.

She took my hand. "Something's wrong here." She stared off into space, trembling. "Something has happened to Orferlin."

"What?" asked Williams. We all stared toward the bright, blue world in front of us.

"Something terrible."

We hovered over a scene of destruction. The Brax inhabited underwater cities engineered from coral-like substances that they had long ago learned to modify and employ as building materials. Depending on the density of the coral, they were able to build to various depths. These floating, submerged metropolises had housed billions of their kind, their entire civilization powered by solar, water, and fusion energies. My mind had strong images from the sharing with Ambra of the intricacy and beauty of their curvilinear constructions, tunnels, and filigree spanning miles and dwarfing our largest land-based cities.

Now all I saw was ruin. Floating on the surface were the blasted remains of the coral masterpieces. Fragments floated like a snowstorm of shattered china from a distance. Diving below the sea, we saw other structures that had sunk to varying depths. Ambra sped the bubble around the globe at blinding velocities, verifying that this carnage was not isolated but planetwide. Nowhere was there any sign of life, any sign that the Brax were anything but utterly exterminated.

"Looks like the Dram, all right," said Williams. "Fuckers like nothing better than a good genocide to make a point."

"But they usually just like to roast the whole planet," said Fox. "But Orferlin is fine."

"Not exactly fine," said Moore.

Waythrel spoke. Its voice was subdued. "Ambra, is there nothing you can detect? No sign of the Brax at all?"

Ambra was crouched in a meditative position, her legs crossed with her arms on her knees. Her eyes were closed.

"There is more than an absence, Waythrel," she said, her concentration unwavering. "There is an interference. A poison in space and time."

"Wait, what does that mean?" asked Kim.

"I don't know," said Ambra. "I've never felt anything like it. Just to be here is to feel it sickening my thoughts."

Waythrel spoke. "Then maybe this is not the Dram."

"No, Waythrel, it isn't. This is something else. We shouldn't stay here very long unless we can undo what is causing this. But first I will need to understand it."

"Well, if supergirl here doesn't know what's going on, I agree," said Moore. "Let's pull back until we have some idea what we're dealing with."

"Not yet!" cut in Ambra. Her face was strained. "In this poisonous cloud, there is a signal. Faint. Fading." A sorrow came over her face. "*Caga*. I hear her."

"Caga?" I asked.

Waythrel answered. "A powerful Reader of the Brax. We often communed with her from the Temple."

"*From* New Earth?" asked Fox with awe.

"Distance is deceptive," said Waythrel.

The bubble accelerated out of the sea and burst over the water's surface, darting like a missile toward the northern regions. We were moving so quickly that I soon could not process the images outside, which had blurred into a single, multicolored brushstroke on either side of us. In front and behind were small circles in focus.

"She is calling us," Ambra whispered. "And she is dying."

Chapter 25

I hear the approaching thunder that, one day, will destroy us too. I feel the suffering of millions.

Anne Frank

We found Caga near the pole of the planet.

The destruction seemed complete here, as well, but somehow the creature had survived within a spacecraft. The ship was floating without power on the waves, and Ambra had brought our bubble up to it. Nestled alongside a craft as big as an island, she projected a bizarre filament toward the walls of the ship. To our complete amazement, the tunnel passed right through the walls, and as we looked down the passageway, it was clear—the wall did not cross into the space, although Ambra insisted it had not been destroyed.

"The tunnel is outside of the space of the wall," she explained as we followed her down the corridor, the walls completely transparent, the inside of the ship open to us.

The reverse of a human ship, the chambers inside were all water filled for these sea creatures, except for a few rooms where damage had occurred and air flowed in. However, our tunnel created no damage. No air flowed in along our path. We were surrounded by water and a water-functional technology that glowed faintly around us.

We walked for ten minutes until we came to a central cavity in the ship, a giant chamber that appeared to be some gathering place the size of a sports stadium. Thousands of bizarre sea creatures floated randomly about.

The best a human mind could do was map their form to New Earth's sea creatures. The physics of water flow dictated streamlined forms, fins of some kind, but within those design constraints, evolution had a lot of room to operate. The "fins" of the Brax were more like webbed tentacles, making the creatures seem as much like squid or octopuses as dolphins. They possessed visual and auditory organs across their bodies. Without the centering of the neural system at one end of the body, their forms were free to house them around the many brain-nodes spread throughout their elongated torso. Without a directionality, their appendages could easily accelerate them in any direction. I imagined that it would have been amazing to watch them swim.

But there was no motion here. All were lifeless and floated along the currents and turbulence in the dead ship. All but one.

The tunnel Ambra had constructed ended at a medical pod, and a single Braxian creature was suspended with numerous tubes penetrating its body. The visual organs, looking like multifaceted gem faces, moved slowly and tracked our approach.

"Caga," whispered Ambra as the tunnel stopped directly in front of the dying creature. She placed her hand against the side of the bubble, and the bubble flowed outward. She extended her arm until the surface of the spacetime distortion fit it like a tight glove or skin, and she stroked the side of the creature. Ambra closed her eyes, and Waythrel stood strangely still, its eyestalks wrapped around themselves like a braid.

"I can speak with her telepathically. She has consented for me to share with you as I do so, if you wish to participate."

I looked across my team as we each traded glances. Finally, all our eyes settled on Moore.

"Ah, fuck it. Okay," he said. "There isn't going to be anything but fucked up on this trip. Blast away, girl."

Suddenly, it was as if viewports were opened in my mind, and through them I could see—or rather sense—the thoughts of others: my team, the incomprehensible images from Waythrel, the partially understandable thoughts of the creature, Caga, and of course, dominating all impressions, Ambra herself.

You must leave our world. It is not safe.

The creature's thoughts were foggy, whether because I had trouble parsing them or because of its decaying physical state.

Ambra responded. *I know. We are okay for now. Whatever is happening, I can deflect its effects for a time.*

You will grow weary, Ambra.

Yes. And you do not have much time, dear Caga. Please, tell us what you can so that we may begin to understand.

The creature's eyes swam across its body, but its thoughts were strong.

The Dram came. Once to claim the Orb strings and guard them. The Time Tree is compromised. We thought we were spared worse. But five Orferlin cycles ago—several weeks your time—they returned. They laid waste to everything.

Images of the terrible Dram armada flashed through my mind—explosions, the deaths of billions, and the emotions of a species watching itself die. A cataclysm. It was nearly too much. So much horror and pain. I tried to block it out but could not. I'm not sure how much time passed as the images ran through me, but it was likely only a moment.

But of course they could not kill all of us. But the Dram armada departed. Then the Anti came.

The shadowed ships flowed out from the Orb strings like a polluted tide. Black spots like flies separated from the main contingent of ships and stationed themselves equidistant across the planet. Then the madness came.

The Anti left these drones, and returned to the strings and were gone. There is something dark in those machines.

The poison. Ambra's thoughts were a warm light in this sea of strangeness.

Yes. As we tried to salvage our people, all things began to fail. Technology decayed. We lost our power, our machines. Everything. Within days, nothing functioned. Then, our minds. The weakest-minded of us went first. Forgetfulness. Unreason. Finally, madness. As Readers, a few of us could defend our minds longer from the ravages. I lasted the longest, because my ship returned from space and was in orbit for the assault. I landed after the slaughter, lucky to have escaped immediate destruction. A last group of medics sought to lessen the effects by trial and error and have me attached to numerous therapies. They are all dead. They only have delayed the inevitable. I am so glad that you have come.

I felt a terrible sadness flow from Ambra. *Caga, no.*

You must, Ambra, or you will condemn me to the same terrible fate. There is no time to save my world or to save me. You and Waythrel have my memories. You must take them, use *them, and find a way. You must leave before this poison overwhelms you.*

I felt the seemingly infinite complexity of Waythrel's mind engage. *Ambra, Caga is right. We cannot risk staying here any longer. She cannot be moved. She will be enveloped in madness by tomorrow.*

I don't know how Waythrel knew this, but I couldn't process most of the thoughts and images coming from its mind. Just trying to read its thoughts was painful. But I saw Ambra's shoulders slump.

Then there was a human thought interspersed.

What if we can destroy the drones in orbit?

It was Fox. I could sense it from the personality. I felt her mind racing, an empathy for both the dying alien and the pain of the Daughter driving her thoughts like a whip.

Caga responded. *It is likely impossible. We tried to send what forces we had left. They did not return.*

I could feel Fox's mind dismiss the objection. *But you were weakened, your technology decaying. Ambra can protect us. We are soldiers. We can send a small team, to avoid risk to the others, and try.*

I don't know if I can protect you. It was Ambra. *The toxicity becomes stronger nearer the source. I can see it in the odd patterns in space-time. Almost the erasing of patterns.*

But Fox was undeterred. *But maybe we can! Then it would stop, and we might be able to save her!*

Unlikely, responded Waythrel.

We have to try!

"I'll go," spoke Kim out loud. His thoughts also conveyed his determination.

I looked over at the two. "Are you both sure of this?"

Waythrel spoke. "It is too dangerous."

Caga's thoughts were strong. *It is too late for me. I am sure of it. But for you, for others—the risk may be worthwhile. To know if there can be an engagement with these devices. Even if the answer is negative, you can take that answer and the details of the failure with you to devise countermeasures.*

Waythrel's eyestalks uncoiled, and several eyes pivoted toward Fox and Kim. "It is probable that you both will die."

Kim's suit powered up. A second later, Fox's did as well. Kim smiled. "Well, the Daughter has protected us from equipment failure so far. Guns still good."

Fox spoke. "Besides, every engagement has probabilities of death in this war. And I have faith in Ambra Dawn."

You have love for me, Erica Fox. And trust. I thank you, but you have more trust in me than I deserve.

"Humble to the end," Fox said, smiling.

"There is a last consideration," said Waythrel. "Caga spoke that the Dram returned to destroy the world when initially they had spared it. Orferlin poses no risks to the Dram—it has always been a peaceful world riding the currents of the galactic struggles. Why destroy it? The node was secure. Why even spend the resources? And why in a time frame nearly identical to when we ourselves planned this mission?"

There was a long silence. Williams ended it. "The traitor again? You think details of the mission were leaked. You think this is sabotage."

"I am raising the possibility," said Waythrel.

"If so, then it could also be a trap," I said.

"There's no way to know, and meanwhile, this world is dying." Kim looked at me. "Sir, do we have permission?"

And now I had to make a choice: whether to send them to a likely death that they ignored in their bravado or to deny them their bravery and the chance for us to know more about our enemy's terrible weapons. If something happened to them, I would be the one responsible for their deaths.

"Permission granted, soldiers. Ambra, can you take us up to one of them?"

I felt a resignation in Ambra. She broke off the sharing and paused several minutes. She seemed to be communing in private with the aliens. Then she opened her eyes, stood up, and walked toward my team.

"We will try, then."

The tunnel wrapped about us closely like plastic wrap and pulled itself out of the alien ship at high speeds. We merged with the main bubble again and the enclosure rocketed upward faster than a starship toward the blackness and stars.

Chapter 26

I know there is a God because in Rwanda I shook hands with the devil. I have seen him, I have smelled him and I have touched him.

Lieutenant-General Roméo Dallaire

We could all feel it as the dark object came into view.

It came on as a combination of fatigue and disorientation, like a flu without the fever. Moore expressed it best with his distinctive flair.

"Feels like the worst fucking hangover I've ever had."

Ambra piloted the bubble purely on her sense of the thing. We had no equipment, no scanners, *no ship*, but I doubt that any technology we or our allies had could measure and detect this thing. It was like a hole in the night. At this distance, it appeared to be a sphere of unlight at least twice the size of our bubble.

Ambra looked over at Moore. "There is an essence to this thing that is against everything I understand. It's like the very nature of the object is antithetical to understanding itself. I don't dare go any closer. I may not be able to protect all of us if this gets much stronger."

I looked over toward Fox and Kim, who stood together, gazing into the emptiness. "This thing looks bad. No shame in dropping the mission."

I could see fear in their eyes but also determination. Fox spoke for them. "Hell there isn't. Since when do we back down from the enemy?"

"When there is nothing to be won. We outthink it, come back better prepared."

"But that's just it, Captain," said Kim. "We don't even know enough to run away yet. Time we found out more."

They were set on it. I nodded. "Ambra, can you make separate bubbles for Kim and Fox, maintain a link like that tunnel on Orferlin and pull them back if things get bad?"

Ambra shook her head. "I can try. But it might be that this force will sever the connection. I might not be able to bring them back."

"Well, then we'd better make sure we kick its ass," said Kim, the pitch-changing hum of his ion slingers sounding. Waythrel made no comment.

"I don't like this," said Moore. "Very bad feeling. Whatever this thing does, it's like some fucking crime against the universe."

Ambra startled and looked at him. "Yes, sergeant. That is *exactly* how it feels to me. A crime not against us, not fundamentally. But against the very structure of our existence. Against anything that could possibly be us."

"Don't mess with it." Moore stared fixedly at Fox and Kim.

"Damn, Moore, never figured you to be the one to chicken out," said Kim.

"I think he's right," echoed Williams, nodding toward Moore.

Fox rolled her eyes. "Now you, too."

Williams turned to me. "It's the wrong call, Captain. Gut tells me so."

The weight of this decision was becoming enormous. "Waythrel, you were cautioning us before. What is your feeling now that you see it?"

The tall alien seemed to shudder. "There is death in that thing. An unlife, perhaps is a better phrase. It has killed a world. But Caga was not wrong. If we are to face this challenge, we need information. There is only one way to obtain it."

Kim nodded. "Right on! Then it's settled, yeah? 'Cause I'm getting a little nuts debating this here."

"Ambra?" I was desperate for surety.

"My vision is obscured beside this thing. I cannot follow the possible paths. But the endings hold more death than life."

Fox engaged the helmet, and the mechanism grasped her skull and assembled over it. Her words came out from the speakers, amplified and artificial. "Life through action!" Kim followed suit.

"Okay, but we're yanking you back at the first sign of trouble." Little did I know, we would never get that chance.

They lined up against the wall facing the death drone, and Ambra carved out a separate space for each of them. Two bubbles detached from the main enclosure and floated out toward the device. Every hundred meters or so, Ambra would test the connection and pull them backward to ensure that she still had control over their capsules.

Fox and Kim were continuously reporting back. Their sense of sickness in body and mind increased, but they reported that it was manageable.

"Might need to hurl soon," said Kim, "but otherwise okay."

"I'm having some visual problems," Fox said. "Can't focus on the thing. Can't keep it centered in my vision either."

"Yeah, me too," said Kim. "Don't know how we're going to shoot it like this. Telemetry's gone all funky." There was a pause. "Hell, the whole HUD is flanking out on me."

"Then we pull you back," I said, looking at Ambra. She was sitting again, focusing intensely on maintaining the projections despite the disturbances from the drone.

"Wait, not yet," said Kim. "Hard to see, but I'm making out some structure, finally. It looks like—"

And then, it was like a switch was thrown. A harsh static sounded over my communications and I saw both their suits darken. It looked like a total loss of power, even though they carried their own mini reactors embedded in the chassis. Simultaneously, both bodies dropped to the bottom of their enclosures. Neither moved.

Ambra cried out, "A pulse!" She gasped. Then I felt it too, as if my eyes were being driven into my skull with knives. I crouched to one knee and tried to stay conscious.

"Ambra, get us out of here!" shouted Waythrel.

Through eyes squinting in pain, I looked out of the bubble and saw that we were indeed speeding away from the thing. I was glad to see that Kim and Fox were still in tow.

The destructive power of the device definitely decreased with distance, but there was more to it than that. Off to my right, the Orb grew bright. As bright as the system's star from this distance. As the radiation bathed us, it countered the effects. Ambra steered the bubble closer to the Orb, and soon things were back to normal. Or so it seemed until we pulled Fox and Kim back into the enclosure.

I've seen horrors on the battlefield. Flechette injuries and deaths that are almost inconceivable—something your mind can't envision and only direct experience can convey. But I wasn't prepared for what we brought in.

Kim and Fox—they were dead. More than dead, gutted. Dissolved. *Unmade* in a fashion that no weapon I had experienced could achieve. The MECHcore suits, these highly designed products of superior Xixian technology—they looked like ancient artifacts discovered in some tomb aged ten thousand years. The very structure of the metals and plastics seemed to be coming apart. Disintegrating. There weren't words for it. Matter just didn't behave this way.

As for the human bodies, the effects were grisly. Decayed metal and plastic is one thing, flesh and bodies something else. Their remains oozed out of the pocked holes in the wrecked suits like a tomato purée. The biochemical bonds holding tissues, bone, and cells together seemed to have failed completely. There was nothing recognizably human in their appearance at all. That demonic device had removed all semblance of an organism from them and reduced the two members of my team to a homogenized form of their constituent ingredients.

"Captain, what the *fuck*?" hissed Moore, his face strained, green and sick looking. The smell began to hit us.

Williams looked away and held her hand to her mouth. We all instinctively stepped back from the sight. Several moments passed as we stood in shock.

I was gobsmacked. I found myself stammering. "Dear God. I don't know." I felt Ambra wrap her arms around me from behind.

"I'm so sorry, Nitin. I'm sorry I was right and could not stop it."

I held her hands tightly. I felt like a child comforted simply by the warmth and physical presence of another. I had seen that monsters were real in this universe, but I had never seen something so monstrous occur in it.

Waythrel alone seemed composed. "We will have to deal with your sorrow and examine these developments later. We have more urgent matters to attend to."

"Jesus, squid!" yelled Moore, flashing a wild look at the alien. "The Orb strings can wait a few minutes!"

"Yes, I'm sure that they can," answered Waythrel. "But I don't think that the Dram warship approaching us will."

Chapter 27

The observed macroscopic irreversibility is not a consequence of the fundamental laws of physics, it's a consequence of the particular configuration in which the universe finds itself. In particular, the unusual low-entropy conditions in the very early universe, near the Big Bang. Understanding the arrow of time is a matter of understanding the origin of the universe.

Sean Carroll

W e followed the alien's outstretched arm, the twelve digits pointing into space twitching with a suppressed anxiety. The warship was Dram all right. Huge, rendering our small bubble an ant beside an elephant. And ugly in that way all the Dram warcraft appeared to me. Possessed of an inherent malice from even the point of design, the sharp edges seemed more like blades, the terraced, bulky levels like prison floors, the surface pitted and etched as if from acid. The weapons arrayed fore and aft required no hateful intention to convey their purpose.

"A trap!" yelled Williams.

"Looks like it," I said.

I turned to Ambra. She had gone to kneel over the bodies, the pool of remains spreading and nearly wetting her black robes. But the seeping sludge slowed and then stopped. Then the two forms seemed to float away from the main enclosure in their own external bubble.

"Ambra, we need to do something."

She stood up and nodded. "The bodies are in a time stasis that will preserve them until we can examine carefully what has happened." She walked forward and stood beside Waythrel. "Only this ship?"

"Yes," said the alien. "It should not pose a danger."

"Unless they are employing the technology that destroyed Orferlin and killed Nitin's soldiers."

"Do you think that's possible?" I asked. Everyone looked anxiously toward Ambra.

"I am unsure of everything, now," she said. "But something tells me that it would be as deadly to the Dram as to us. For now, we assume they are armed as usual."

Bright trails erupted from the ship. Waythrel spoke. "And so far, they respond predictably. Incoming missiles!"

We were sitting ducks. As soldiers, nearly useless. We could only stand there and watch.

Ambra raised her arms, her bright green eyes disappearing behind closing lids. "Then we respond to them as always."

The Orb flashed. Tendrils of light erupted from the sphere and crossed the distance to us before I could blink. They wrapped themselves around the missiles and detonated them harmlessly before they arrived. Before I could process what happened next, the Dram fired beam weapons, unloading on us nearly everything that they had. At least ten different rays were aimed at our bubble, the coherent light dizzying only meters from my face, yet stopped in their tracks by offshoots of the light tendrils from the Orb.

After nearly twenty seconds of full burn, the Dram wised up and decided not to completely drain their power supplies. They had thrown everything at us, enough firepower to blow up and melt down entire cities on New Earth. We were not scratched. The ship arced violently away from us.

"Chickenshit bastards!" cried Williams.

"They're rabbiting, all right," laughed Moore. "Damn, I've heard what you could do with those things, sister, but, well, *damn!*"

"We're going to board them," said Ambra. "And find out what the hell is going on around here."

"Board them?" asked Williams. The ship was already aligning its panel of engines toward us, readying for a string jump. "Well, first you gotta *stop* it!"

The large tendrils opened into sheets of light. The membranes flowed around the Dram warship, surrounded it. The engines fired, the ion blasts distorting the light around the hull. But it went nowhere. The monstrosity belching forth more power than half the New Earth navy couldn't move.

Williams shook her head. "Guess I had that one coming."

Ambra opened her eyes. I have to say that for the first time, even after that battle in the Sahara, I nearly felt the religious awe so many knew. The raw power of what she controlled almost compelled worship in feeble creatures of flesh and blood. But as I looked into those eyes, that awe was eclipsed by love.

That all-consuming worship not of her divinity, but of her person. My lover. My beautiful and terrible and sad Ambra Dawn.

The bubble sped toward the paralyzed Dram war boat. Her plan was a good one. She had been able to read the minds of the Dram even from the first recognitions of her powers centuries ago. They could not hide anything from her, provided they did not commit suicide. If we moved quickly enough, with the power she demonstrated, they would be helpless before her. Maybe we could find out what the Anti were up to and how to defeat them.

Only the Anti had no plans of letting that happen. As we approached, Ambra darted her head to the side and gasped. I followed her gaze, and beside the Dram ship, a crack seemed to appear in space itself. A massive shadow erupted through the fissure, its form cloaked from light and difficult to discern. I felt in my stomach the same unease I had experienced at the death drone.

"Ambra! An Anti ship!"

Ambra knew, but it was too late. The powerful folds engulfing the warship shimmered, faded, and dissolved like silk unraveling. But the Dram did not flee. Before they could move, a spray of particles came from the shadow ship aimed at the warcraft. The impact was pure energy.

It seemed like a nova. Ambra screamed. "Close your eyes, everyone! Turn away!"

I did as I was told. The bubble turned pitch black as Ambra sought to shut out all radiation. Even so, enough penetrated to make the interior bright enough to blind. The temperature inside increased dramatically, and within seconds, I began to sweat even through the climate control of the MECI Icore suit. I didn't think we could last long in this radiation flux.

But suddenly, it was over. I looked around the bubble. Everyone seemed okay. Even Ambra standing and facing the explosion without protection was unharmed. I ran to her side.

"I'm okay, Nitin."

I looked into her eyes and kissed her, holding her body tightly to mine.

"What happened?" asked Moore, his face pale.

"We lost our catch," said Waythrel. "The Dram ship is destroyed."

"How? Why?" asked Williams. "Where's the wreckage?"

"Annihilated," said Ambra. "Converted to pure energy by an interaction with antimatter."

It seemed that she was right. There was no sign of the Dram warcraft, and an enormous amount of energy had been released. It was exactly what one might expect in a matter-antimatter collision that converted both to pure radiation.

But we were not alone. The shadow ship hovered beside us. Ambra set her mouth into a thin line.

"Let's see how they respond to the full power of the Orb."

She closed her eyes once more. For a moment, nothing happened. There was a total silence in the bubble. The shadow ship didn't move. Finally, a dim light glowed from the Orb. The light slowly intensified, broadened into multiple wavelengths, and then flashed more brightly than the exploding Dram warship. But the light was directed. It sped forward at a speed that I could follow, like some glowing fist thrown at the body of the enemy. I couldn't imagine what it was going to do.

The shadow ship didn't wait around to find out. The inky disturbance kept toward the side of the Orb. The fist of light followed and nearly impacted the dark shape. But the Anti were prepared. They had prepped a jump on a local string. The very Orb that lashed out at the ship provided through its discarded energies a door to the Time Tree, and our enemies stepped through it. The darkness vanished, leaving the star-filled dark of regular space in its place.

"No!" Ambra cried. She looked furious. "I should have sealed the Orb and then dealt with them. Stupid pride! I was too ready to show them justice! Now I've let them escape."

Waythrel moved forward and stood before Ambra. "The good news is that they were afraid of you, Ambra. Whatever technology they possess, they were not willing to go up against you and the Orb."

"Yeah, but they were clever enough to take out that Dram boat," said Moore. "Didn't defend the ugly bugs from us, you'll notice. Not much love there. But they didn't want us getting them, getting any information."

Again Waythrel commented. "Which is another good sign. They fear knowledge falling into our hands. That means they are vulnerable."

Ambra looked toward the alien and smiled. "Yes."

"And this means there is far more hope for our cause than we might have had before the Dram attacked," finished the alien.

Hope? Perhaps. But it was all abstract. I looked out of the enclosure behind us to the smaller bubble holding the time-frozen remains of two members of my team. A feeling of failure swept over me, of responsibility mismanaged. *I* had allowed that mission to occur. Their deaths were in my ledger.

I thought over what had just happened. A world brutally slain and then devilishly poisoned. An enemy with terrible weapons we hardly understood and could not counter. Yet an enemy that feared us, that fled before the Daughter in her wrath, that murdered its allies rather than let us interrogate them.

As we moved toward the Orb and Ambra began the process of sealing the Time Tree strings to shut down this first of three nodes, those last thoughts comforted me some. In the midst of my sadness and revulsion, despite the fear and uncertainty, there did seem to be a ray of sunlight. A hope.

And as always, that hope depended on Ambra Dawn.

Chapter 28

The atoms or elementary particles themselves are not real; they form a world of potentialities or possibilities rather than one of things or facts.

Werner Heisenberg

We left without doing anything more with the death drones surrounding the planet. Because we feared our mission might have been betrayed, time seemed of the essence. Also, the world had already perished, the Dram and the shadow device having destroyed all hope of reviving it. What sealed our decision was the death of Caga. After the shadow ship escaped, we returned to the surface, only to find the creature dead. The last of her kind on a sterilized world.

Ambra stood silently staring at the planet as she guided us toward the Orb for transit. Her expression was inscrutable—sadness, guilt, fear, and expectation were turbulent waves passing over her features. I leaned softly against her arm, holding her cold hand. How was I to comfort her when she gazed on the death of an entire world? A world she had communed with, known intimately in ways I now had begun to understand after our sharing.

Waythrel too stood at her side gazing backward and spoke sorrowfully. "So much waste. So many beautiful creatures. Beautiful minds. So much unmade and lost."

Ambra spoke so softly that I strained to catch the words. "Not lost. Never wasted." She looked between the alien and me with tears in her eyes. "Waiting for a time of harvest."

I waited for an explanation, but Ambra said nothing more, and Waythrel did not probe. I let Ambra have the space she needed to mourn. I had never seen her so heavy with loss.

Meanwhile, the presence of a possible traitor at the highest levels of our group had put the rest of us on edge. Despite Ambra's efforts to persuade us not to second-guess one another, that was becoming more and more difficult as the dangers increased and the Dram seemed ready and waiting to pounce even at what should have been arbitrary star systems for them, places they should have never thought to set an ambush. Combined with the penetration of the False Dawn in the desert, I had to admit that there was a little too much coincidence going on.

But which of us to suspect? If it was to be one of our group on this strange mission, it couldn't be the Daughter or her closest advisor. A Xix betraying the cause? It was beyond unthinkable. That left only the two remaining members of my team. While it was true that I had only just met them, serving together in combat reveals a lot about a person. There is something raw and unfiltered about placing your life on the line in front of others. It's hard to hold a lie in your eyes when your death is staring you in the face. I had been with Moore and Williams. I had seen them face death. I trusted them. Moore had even relinquished his dislike of mental sharing, and Ambra had reported nothing about that. His mind must have been clear of betrayal.

So that only left the other members of Ambra's inner circle. My mind immediately focused on Mazandarani. I knew it was partly jealously as well as anger at his own suspicions of me that biased my judgment. But that very suspicion itself became suspect in this growing paranoia. Did he do it to cast eyes off himself and onto an innocent? Had his hatred of me because of Ambra's love turned him? Men had turned traitors for less than that. But it seemed unlikely that Ambra would have missed such thoughts in him. He too had shared with the Readers, even if he was not one. Finally, there was the major. Mizoguchi hardly seemed the type, but now I questioned everything. Of course, could she have hidden such intentions from Ambra and the other Readers any better than Mazandarani? Could anyone? Spies would seem to be impossible in the presence of the galaxy's most powerful psychic.

None of the potential traitors held up under scrutiny. It was a mystery. I began to feel that either it was someone whom none of us suspected, or perhaps we were imagining a threat that didn't exist. Perhaps the Dram and their new, mysterious allies had ways of obtaining information that we didn't know. We certainly were stymied by some of their technology, and that lack of understanding had cost the lives of two of my team.

It was a quiet, far less adventurous transit through the Orb to our second destination. Everyone was consumed with his or her thoughts and doubts and the mourning of two of our members, whose bodies we carried with us like some surreal baggage. I was also anxious about the transit and once again became ill from it to the point of almost passing out. But the effects were somewhat lessened, and Ambra told me that she worked hard to shield us from the vulnerabilities inherent in the process. I remembered no dream this time.

When we exited the Orb and I had recovered enough to process my environment, our small bubble was orbiting an enormous violet-green gas giant that humbled Jupiter. It had no name from its inhabitants; they were creatures so different from us that even language was a very artificial construct for them, developed only after years of mental communion with the Readers led by Ambra—a concession in order to help very different forms of life communicate. The Xix named the world Gyl, and so we called it.

My mind played over the reams of data I had absorbed from the sharing. Gyl was so large as to possess enough mass and gravitational force to fuse deuterium in it core. It was as much a failed star as a planet. Its star system was located on one of the spiral arms of the galaxy near the center. That explained the bright and dense star field around us, making the night skies of New Earth seem so pale and dim. It was also located a good bit closer to the system's star than our Jupiter, causing the planet to be much warmer. The weather was exceedingly violent in the upper layers of the atmosphere.

Like most gas giants, it was primarily composed of hydrogen and smaller amounts of helium. These elements began as gases in the hard-to-define surface of the planet's outer atmosphere but then transitioned deeper into the world to multiple alternative states in layers as the pressure and temperature increased beyond anything humans could really intuit. At the center of the world was a core resembling in many ways the rocky inner planets of our star system. Trace amounts of the larger elements that make up our planet—those nuclei once formed in the death throes of giant stars—sank to the bottom of Gyl because of their relative density to form the core. Only this core was many times larger than New Earth and under tremendous pressure and temperature, so the atoms adopted states bizarre and outside the modeling of our science.

The layers directly above the rocky core were the heart of the world, however. In those layers brooded a sentience that I found almost impossible to consider *alive*. The hydrogen atoms at this pressure and temperature were forced into a bizarre form of matter that New Earth science had only a foggy grasp of. The Xix understood more, but the explanations were beyond my comprehension. There was a crystalline form of hydrogen, not exactly a solid, not a liquid, but an ordered structure. It was from this order and the interactions with other quasi-crystalline elements that a completely different form of atomic organization occurred. From that organization evolved a form of life so different that it called into question my conceptions of life itself.

Truly thinking about my existence for the first time brought on a disorientation. What were we, exactly? Atoms that on their own have no will, no purpose, nothing but constraints based on "laws" of physics (whatever those really are ultimately). Somehow, under the conditions of New Earth—temperature, radiation impact from the sun and cosmic rays, composition, pressure—these atomic entities can form organized structures that at one point obtained the power to replicate. Then the process of "survival of the stable" took over, and evolution produced increasingly complex molecules, cells, bodies—*minds*. That love and the ideals of beauty and wonder all come from the arbitrary dance of molecules like carbon chains and water is extremely strange when you really think about it. In fact, it makes no sense at all to me.

Given our exposure to the aliens in our galaxy and the powers of Ambra Dawn, I should have been more open to the idea of what life and especially *mind* could be in this universe. But we were produced over millions of years in a very specific (and, by the standards of the cosmos, *strange* environment), and that has shaped our mental framework. It limits our thoughts, places assumptions and obstacles before our minds. *Obvious, logical,* and *reasonable* have meanings we have evolved toward, but they are truly relative. I was now faced with the reality of that relativity as I never had been before.

The atoms of hydrogen, helium, and the trace elements did not form the direct substrate for life on Gyl. The quasi-crystalline lattices *themselves* did. A poor and likely distorting analogy might be that the atoms and chemical bonds that form the basis of our bodies could be mapped to the lattices and interlattice interactions of different crystals in the Gyl planetary layers. There was a higher-level crystal-chemistry that sat above the basic atomic interactions.

Even more bizarrely, the sharing with Ambra revealed that these structures were only partially crystals across the space of these layers. More fundamentally, and critical to the evolution of intelligence on this world, they were also *crystals in time*. New Earth scientists had only recently begun to appreciate the existence and properties of time crystals—where repeated arrays occurred in cyclic time points and not necessarily in space. In the sharing, Waythrel's mind had noted that our theories were embryonic and based on a lot of incorrect thinking, but they were the beginning of a step in the right direction. So my lessons went. On Gyl there existed a wonderland for experimentalists wishing to study the full potential of this form of matter. I would have normally left them to it. But nothing was normal in our mission.

The end result on Gyl was an evolved form of life in a state that had no analogy to our minds, which used the great heat energy of the world from gravity and weak fusion to produce higher and higher order and structure. And finally, millions of years ago, intelligence. The creatures of Gyl were far older than we, and yet, because of their extreme differences, both more and less advanced than other forms of life in the galaxy. Their technology was primitive, their mental reach into science and mathematics profound.

All these thoughts raced through my mind as I stood in our space-time bubble before this enormous world. But before we could begin any attempt to communicate with the creatures of Gyl, there was an unexpected Dram welcoming party for us to deal with.

Chapter 29

The doctrine that the world is made up of objects whose existence is independent of human consciousness turns out to be in conflict with quantum mechanics and with facts established by experiment.

Bernard d'Espagnat

"*Shit!*" Williams whistled. "There must be four or five squadrons."

"And look!" said Moore, pointing to dark patches in the bright local star field. "Shadow ships. Maybe half as many."

My stomach dropped. One Dram cruiser and a single of those devil ships was enough. This time, there were likely twenty or thirty starships between us and Gyl. The balance of power in this standoff was much less clear to me.

Waythrel spoke ominously. "Gyl has no obvious strategic importance to this war. We are here only because of the critical node point Orb that rests next to their world."

"Someone's selling us out." Moore scowled. "They knew we were coming."

"And likely knew about the last engagement. Look at these numbers!" said Williams. "We chased off one of their ghost ships. Can we scare off ten of them?"

The case for the spy seemed to grow stronger. But there wasn't time to think about that. As I looked across the waiting group of starships, my mind raced through stratagems, tactics, scenarios. But something was bothering me. "Why aren't they engaging? Moving? They're just sitting there."

"Maybe they haven't picked us up yet," said Williams.

Ambra responded coldly. "No. They are closing the noose."

Instinctively I spun around. She *was right!* Another twenty or thirty ships were approaching behind us, spreading out to the sides and above, cutting off all avenues of escape. We were completely surrounded, cut off from the Orb and the planet.

"An ambush!" cried Williams.

I turned to Ambra and placed my hand on her shoulder. "Ambra?"

"You must do something soon," said Waythrel.

Ambra smiled at Waythrel. "Dear Waythrel, you should know that time is also an illusion."

And then she was gone.

We all startled. Williams gasped, and Moore let out a short bark. One moment I was touching my beloved gently with concern, the next I was holding only air. We all stared at one another in confusion. And then the explosions of light began.

Afterward, Ambra would explain to me what happened, but all we could see at the time was a sudden, massive, and broad attack on the enemy ships from every position. Those in front of us nearest the planet, those behind us, and those that completed a sphere entombing us in a net of ships—from every location of a Dram and shadow ship, there came light.

The Orb had become bright, as bright as we had seen in the attack around Orferlin, but there was no buildup as before, no period of time to observe the flaming arms of energy extend from the object—they simply appeared around us.

The carnage was spectacular. Where once we were surrounded by a spherical lattice of ships, now a fiery globe encased us. The Dram war boats vaporized, the shadow ships exploded with the powerful energies of annihilation. Before we could even fully process the destruction, a gargantuan cyclone was born in the midst of it, a hurricane of light and debris swirling down to a vortex as large as a great moon, the tunnel of radiance extending back toward the Orb. The great sphere of power controlled by the Daughter lit up brighter than the local star.

We shielded our eyes, and I engaged my suit helmet. As it fastened itself around my head, I toggled the view screen to filter out nearly all incoming radiation. Even so, I squinted as I looked toward the Orb. I watched the remains of a fleet of enemy ships pour into the multidimensional portal and then disappear.

The light winked out. Its disappearance was like a thunderous sound that had been suddenly muted. My senses responded similarly, relief sweeping over me, a long breath escaping my mouth.

"You cannot win a battle if you focus on winning space alone."

It was Ambra's voice. She stood in the middle of the enclosure, a tired look on her face. "One must understand that the universe moves in more than three dimensions."

I opened the faceplate of my suit, ran to her, and enveloped her body in my hard exoskeleton, the nanofiber gloves retracted so that I could feel the softness and warmth of her flesh. Only after I had held her for a moment did I realize how terrified I had been at her disappearance. The irrational fear of losing her swept over me now in waves.

"Ambra, don't do that to me again, please," I blurted out incomprehensibly, my face pressed tightly into her shoulder and neck. "I can't lose you. Not after finding you."

You will never lose me, Nitin. Even if it might seem so for a time. Like distance, time is an illusion.

"I'll be buggered!" shouted Moore. "That all by itself makes this trip worth whatever shit we're going to see."

Williams stared open-mouthed and said nothing. Waythrel walked to the middle of the bubble and stood next to Ambra. "And once more, our Daughter of Time teaches her teacher a lesson." I think if a Xix had a mouth, it would have been smiling.

I pulled back enough to look into her eyes but held her shoulders. She felt cold. "Are you okay?"

"Yes. Tired, Nitin. I will sit." She lowered herself into a cross-legged position on the floor of the enclosure and closed her eyes. I knelt with her, continuing to hold her hands as she sat, as if she were a fragile piece of china that could slip and shatter. Then I instinctively began to stroke her hair, drawing a smile from her lips. "I wish I could sleep right now," she finished, resting her head on my shoulder.

"Okay, so are we going to get an explanation for that Dram navy Armageddon we just saw?" asked Williams.

"I think I can tell you and spare Ambra the energy," said Waythrel. "The simplest explanation is that using the Orb, Ambra can travel through both space and time. Such travel normally requires tremendous energies. But we are in close proximity to the Orb, and she did not need to travel far in any dimension. She was able to access several different three-space locations at the same time."

"Run that by me again," said Williams.

"She accessed the same temporal location repeatedly, but each repetition changing the position." I thought that I heard a slight impatience in the alien's translator. Her words must have been the Xixian version of *Physics for Poets*.

"Went to different places but all at the same time?" asked Moore, his brow furrowed.

Williams nodded. "Right. That's why we saw everything happening everywhere but all at once."

"And if you could have seen with better eyes at higher resolution, you would have seen Ambra—tens, maybe hundreds of Ambra Dawns—positioned near the enemy ships and simultaneously inducing their destruction," said Waythrel.

"That's good enough for now," sighed Ambra taking my hands. She opened her eyes. "But further explanations have to wait. We need to see what is left of the Gyl for us to speak to. And speaking with them will not be easy." She stood up and kissed my hands. "Walk with me, Nitin?"

I followed her to the edge of the enclosure. Even now, in the midst of this insanity, I found myself distracted, stunned by her beauty. Uncountable numbers of stars carpeted the background around us, shining undiminished and without distortion through the space-time compartment she had fashioned for us. The stars framed her form, her red locks bouncing slightly with each step. Still reeling from the sudden sense of her disappearance, the reality of her physical presence before me felt infinitely valuable, precious, and vulnerable. Had I understood our ultimate fates, I would have treasured that physicality even more.

I am yours and you are mine, Nitin. In flesh and in spirit.

"I feel them," she spoke out loud to everyone. The rest drew near, hanging on her words. "You can't see them, but the entire planet is ringed with poisonous seeds."

"The death drones," I said, involuntarily shuddering. The memory of the one around Brax was still very raw. I had to stop myself from looking out toward the bodies of Kim and Fox suspended in time outside our bubble.

"Yes, but the Anti have not achieved their goal here. Not fully. Not yet."

"How do you know?" I asked.

Waythrel responded. "Because we can sense the mind of the Gyl below. It has not been destroyed."

I felt relief. "Then they are okay."

"No," said Ambra. "They are weakening. But it will be much slower with them than with the Brax. I will speak with them now, find out what I can. And then, if we conclude it is safe to do so, I will purge these drones from the system."

Chapter 30

*In the beginning there were only probabilities. The universe could only come into
existence if someone observed it. It does not matter that the observers turned up several
billion years later. The universe exists because we are aware of it.*

Martin Rees

A mbra parked the bubble outside of the planetary atmosphere, but
close enough that the huge world spanned our entire field of vision.
Churning bands of clouds encircled the disk before us, their hues
spanning a range of colors from blue to violet. Monstrous storms the size of
entire worlds spun in tight knots at various locations. I could see perhaps
seven moons on this face of the world, and my memory from the sharing told
me that there should be another five obscured from view.

The Gyl were beings whose form was composed of the very planetary
layers themselves, and to enter the atmosphere was to violate their personal
being in some strange sense. Not the outer layers, as the substrates for the
quasi-crystalline life were buried deep within the gas giant, but Ambra wished
to cause no offense. The crystalline mind of the world was strange beyond
prediction, and she proceeded with great caution.

Immediately there was a problem: the members of my team and I wished to
partake of the communication, but Ambra and the other Readers on New
Earth had only spoken with the Gyl through the telepathic medium, those
fields of space and time that were the substrate and the enzymes of mentality.
While we could have shared as we did with Caga of the Brax, Waythrel
warned that it would not likely be productive. It might very well be deadly.

"You must understand," the alien said. "The thoughts of the Gyl will not be like any thoughts of creatures like us. Only through the deepest meditations, only through the greater insight of the Group Mind were we able to establish contact at all. Here, devoid of the horde of Readers, that mind does not exist. We may not be able to communicate at all."

Ambra explained further. "And if we do, we will only be able to understand them because of that memory, of the lessons our minds learned through the Group Mind experience." Her gaze was serious and concerned. "You have none of that experience. The presence of the Gyl mind may even be dangerous, threatening to your consciousness in its terrible alienness."

"How can some crystal brain in there hurt mine out here?" asked Moore.

"Ambra can kill with her thoughts, Sergeant," said Waythrel. "I've seen her drop entire Dram infantries to the ground without lifting her finger. The brain creates a field. That field can be modified by a Writer, one space-time field modifying another. Those modifications can be beneficial, healing, educational. Or they can be destructive. The interaction of two extremely different mental fields is very unpredictable. You are one small mind in front of a planetary brain of proportions and a nature that would frighten you if you could see it, understand it."

Ambra nodded in agreement. "It will be dangerous even for Waythrel and me, even with the power of the Orb. That is because to communicate, I will have to open myself to them. To become vulnerable."

"Are they potentially violent?" I asked.

Ambra seemed lost for words. "It is difficult to answer that without distorting what is true. Could they damage me? Yes. Would it be violence? Is the radiation that burns your skin violent? Or is violent a word suitable for creatures like us but not for other things in this universe?"

"Lost me, sister," said Moore. "But I'm good to stay out of this sharing. Wasn't keen on the other one except that I was tired of being left out."

Williams agreed. "It sounds like too big a risk. Count me out."

"But there may be a way for you to partake of the conversation, even if it will be strange," said Waythrel.

Ambra looked over to the alien with confusion. "What do you mean?"

"The MECHcore suits," it said. "There is a powerful AI embedded within. It has scaled several levels of proto-sentience."

Ambra nodded, a pained expression on her face. I was immediately concerned. "What does this mean?"

"Sentience. Intelligence. A space-time field, Nitin. I Read and Write. I can begin to interact with the artificial intelligences of the more advanced systems the Xix have developed. Simple minds. Ugly in many ways. But real. And growing more complex with their science, with each generation of the technology."

"And before we left, Ambra had begun serious efforts to interface with our

AI," said Waythrel, "achieving remarkable results with the more developed versions that have progressed much further in consciousness than the more simple minds in your suits."

"Is this bad?" I asked. Ambra's face seemed strained. "You look troubled."

Now is not the time, Nitin. Trust me. I will explain everything later.

"No, it's not bad at all. It means Waythrel is right. I can work through your suits, funnel the fields of thought through them and the Xixian translator." She nodded as if seeing the alien's plan come together in her mind. "Yes. Suit up, turn on your COM, and you'll hear their speech come through the speakers."

"Mangled as it might be by our understanding and Ambra's interface with the AI," completed Waythrel.

Moore laughed and shook his head. "I swear everything that happens on this trip has got to be weirder than a peyote cactus ceremony."

"Cactus ceremony?" asked Williams, an eyebrow arched.

"Yeah, you know, American Indians? Mescaline?" Williams shook her head and shrugged. Moore smiled. "Never mind. Sounds wicked, sister. I'm onboard."

Williams nodded. "Me, too."

"Okay, then let's suit up," I said, grabbing for my headgear before remembering I had already put it on during the attack. I engaged the COM. "Ready whenever you are, Ambra."

We watched Ambra and Waythrel sit together in the middle of the bubble, the alien's long arms reaching out toward her. Ambra held the many-fingered ends of the Xixian extremities and closed her eyes. They sat there silent for more than thirty minutes. The bubble was quiet except for the shallow breathing of the humans and the strange respiration sound of the Xix—a noise like some rhythmic steam leak from a radiator.

I knew that there must be something powerful happening. Something amazing involving the galaxy's greatest Reader, the Orb, and a bizarre crystalline intelligence inhabiting a planet dominating my field of vision.

But I felt nothing. Sensed nothing. Never before had I felt so strongly the difference between Ambra and me. The woman I loved, whom I had loved since my birth, with whom I had shared flesh and heart and mind—right now in this place and time, in this state, she was something very distinct from me. Something I could not reach or understand. I was blind in a sensory world in which she had the greatest vision of all. I felt much more than inadequate—I felt alone. And for the first time, I yearned, longed with a hungry desperation, to be able to share her experience.

I strained. I tried to activate some latent power within me. Like a blind mole, I tried to conjure organs of vision to pierce the darkness. If desire alone could remake the fabric of the universe, I would have succeeded. Of course, it was laughable. The darkness remained, and all I succeeded in doing was to give myself a tension headache. Ambra and Waythrel remained in a place I could not access—would never access. And the realization of that finality brought a weight of sadness on me.

As I waited with that new burden on my heart, our COM units crackled. Static bursts and garbled noises. Then words came out.

The Voice of Gyl.

Chapter 31

What do we know of the world and the universe about us? Our means of receiving impressions are absurdly few, and our notions of surrounding objects infinitely narrow. We see things only as we are constructed to see them, and can gain no idea of their absolute nature. With five feeble senses we pretend to comprehend the boundlessly complex cosmos, yet other beings with wider, stronger, or different range of senses might not only see very differently the things we see, but might see and study whole worlds of matter, energy, and life which lie close at hand yet can never be detected with the senses we have.

H.P. Lovecraft

W*e are the having been becoming to the invader uncreation deathling approaching reaching hydrogen oxygen carbon netting summation broken crystal seed."*

The genderless voice of the AI stopped abruptly, leaving only static flowing over the COM. I looked over to Ambra and Waythrel—they remained motionless in their deep meditation. I locked eyes with Moore and Williams.

Moore shook his head. "What the fuck?"

We didn't have any chance to consider the opening greeting. The conversation continued and cut us off.

"We are a seed of the Sol Mind, the seven-kilo parsec three-dimensioned pathway."

This came through Waythrel's translator, but it hardly seemed the alien's voice. Some combination of the thoughts of Ambra and the Xix, perhaps, relayed through whatever cybernetic linkage Ambra had established between their minds and the equipment. The response in our COMs was even stranger.

"The nucleation event corrected being devoid of augmentation. Understanding through other complexities passes inside solvent channels."

"No other pathways are open," rang out Waythrel's device. "But paths must be taken. Gyl dissolves."

"Gyl dissolves."

"Well, I'm glad we've established *that*," said Williams, rolling her eyes. "Maybe we should have just sat this conversation out. Makes no sense."

Moore nodded. "It's like listening to a malfunctioning translator."

"Then switch off and shut up," I said testily. "I want to hear this!"

"...with the time infinite crowd-mind gate. Gyl lacks the interference projections to unmake the dissolving."

"Carbon crystal seeds dissolve upon breaching radial separations."

"We will maintain a safe distance."

"Acceleration achieving possible state spaces augmentation is the lattice drivings the asymmetry breaking."

There was a long pause after this statement. Several minutes passed while Moore and Williams impatiently paced the bubble and talked together. I ignored them. I was staring intently at Ambra's lined face. There was a lot of tension in the muscles, her pale skin hardly covering the veins bulging from pressure within. Stress was building up within her at whatever the Gyl had said or at her efforts to understand it.

"Yes. The disorder is understood now," came a response at last. "Molecular organization is reversed."

"Surface defects in the lattice only are your thoughts failing assembly of divergent structural integrations. Maximum extensionings through all available states to render the end the beginning sameness."

Ambra's back stiffened. "The symmetry will be unbroken."

"The final first through crystal will was now always healed wounding killing all lattices built from broken order. Earth shards prolong Gyl thankfulness anxiety universal erasure."

"We understand."

Moore laughed. "Yeah, that sure cleared it up." I placed my finger over my mouth to indicate quiet as Williams just shook her head.

Waythrel's translator spoke a final statement. "The symmetry induction for Gyl will be halted."

And the rest was static. After five minutes of it, we shut off our COMs. The two Readers still did not move, and we waited nearly half an hour until Ambra finally stirred. She opened her eyes slowly, like someone who had slept far too long or under the influence of narcotics.

"Waythrel?" she asked softly. The alien did not respond. Ambra reached over and placed her hands across the midsection of the creature, the location of the brain-like structure of the Xix. "Waythrel, come back. Follow me, follow my voice!"

She sat in that position unmoving, repeating the commands for the alien to follow her call. Over and over, her expression pained and concerned, she called the creature's name. Minutes passed. Half an hour.

"This isn't looking good," said Moore after some time, turning toward us and whispering. "Maybe that Gyl-thing lobotomized the squid. If that's even possible with one of those things."

I dared not interfere, even to ask a question to learn what was happening. The minutes dragged by without a sound other than Ambra's repeated calls. Her voice had become quieter, softer, her eyes closing as if her mind were traveling some great distance. Finally, after an hour of effort, which the rest of us had begun to assume was in vain, Waythrel stirred. And promptly fell over on its side unmoving.

"Ambra! What happened?" I leaped across the bubble and crouched down, trying to lift the alien. Even with the hydraulics of my suit, the Xix was a struggle to move.

"Easy, Nitin," said Ambra. "The worst of it has passed. Waythrel's in a recovery state unique to its kind. We won't get a response for a few hours. You can let the body lie down—no need to hold it up."

I lowered the body gently back to the surface of the bubble, the bright and dense star field staring up at me and surrounding the body of the Xix. Having no exobiology training, I could not tell whether Waythrel was even alive.

"Then how do you know it's okay?" asked Williams, both her and Moore also now gathered alongside the alien.

Ambra leaned forward, placing her face into her hands. The enormous bulge from her skull protruded from the tips of her fingers, the veins still protruding and strained. Her fingers were like a mask surrounded by a red halo. The words came out muffled.

"We could connect mentally. Only at the end." She massaged her temples a moment and then placed her hands on the ground behind her for support. "At first, Waythrel's mind had become detached, the Gyl mental field breaking the connection to the physical space-time incarnation. I had to reintegrate them. There was some damage, but it's hard for me to know exactly what. The Xix minds are too complex for me."

"Damage?" I asked. "Permanent? Memory? Cognitive function? What?"

"I said I don't know, Nitin!" Ambra cried. I recoiled slightly, never having been the object of her anger. Her face quickly softened, and she reached out and took my hand. "I'm sorry. This has been extremely difficult. This whole damn day. We'll just have to wait and see."

Ambra stood up and stretched her arms, bending her body in different yoga positions. Waythrel remained unmoving on the floor. Moore and Williams looked back and forth between Ambra and me. Finally, Moore cursed and stood up as well.

"So, while we're waiting to see what happened, can you tell us what the hell all that conversation meant? Because as far as the three of us could tell, it was all just gibberish."

Ambra sighed. "We told you it would be hard to understand. What we experienced in the direct communication was far more difficult."

Williams probed further. "But it sounded like you learned something important at the end, and that you were going to destroy the drones or something."

"Yes," said Ambra. "On the last part, it is easy to explain. The Gyl are unable to remove the drones and were happy for us to do so. It represented no danger to them to simply destroy the devices, and in fact doing so will save them. But what they explained to us about the drones, what they had perceived was happening to them and the planet—that was something very troubling, if we have actually understood it correctly."

The strange words kept floating through my mind. "Something about fixing *broken symmetries* and *achieving all states*. You said that you understood. What did it mean?"

Ambra turned around to face us, her expression serious. "The Anti are not allies of the Dram. The Dram may think so, but if Waythrel and I have under-stood the Gyl, the Anti are the enemies of everything in this galaxy. In fact, of all the known galaxies. Of nearly all the matter that exists in the universe."

Moore looked between us and Ambra. "That's ridiculous sounding. How can you wage war on the universe?"

"I don't know," said Ambra. Her words sounded bone weary. "But these devices are the clue. The first real clue to what is happening. I'm anxious now to reach Hola, our last node. There we may be able to examine the effects of the drones in light of this revelation with a species that is at least *slightly* more comprehensible than the Gyl. Assuming the Anti have placed the drones there as well." She stared out into the surrounding star field. "But I have a feeling that they have."

"So what do they *do?*" asked Moore.

"Entropy," said Ambra. "But in a far deeper sense than it is usually understood."

"Entropy?" asked Williams. "You mean like the second law of thermody-namics, everything becomes disordered?"

"Yes, although *disorder* is a loaded, human word. Things moving to greater *freedom* might be a more insightful phrase, but Waythrel is the better one to talk to. I'm no physicist, and the physics of New Earth is primitive compared to the Xix. But entropy is why when you have order, it becomes disordered. Why you have to keep cleaning your room but it never needs to be messed up. Why when you pop a balloon full of helium that it mixes with all the other gases in the room, doesn't stay separated. Why things break down. Why energy transfer is always with a loss. All possible states are accessed." She paused a moment and nodded as if to an unseen voice. "It's why time appears to flow in one direction. Space, time, order, disorder, freedoms, constraints—they are all tied together in a very deep sense. The ultimate structure of reality is like a chord whose quality depends on the notes sounded by each of these."

I had no idea what she was talking about. "So, if these drones accelerate entropy, things would break down, lose structure, become disordered more quickly?"

"In some sense, yes," said Ambra, looking out toward the remains of my team. "At a terrible level, that was unimaginable until now. The Gyl understood it best because of the highly structured crystalline nature of their being. They possess a unique perspective as well as form in our galaxy."

"Form that these things are breaking down even now, right?" asked Williams.

"Yes," replied Ambra, nodding toward my warrant officer as if receiving a reprimand. "So the time for talk is over. We have some orbiting drones to destroy."

Chapter 32

The total disorder in the universe, as measured by the quantity that physicists call entropy, increases steadily over time. Also, the total order in the universe, as measured by the complexity and permanence of organized structures, also increases steadily over time.

Freeman Dyson

And destroy them she did.

There were over three hundred of them spread around the surface of the planet, just outside of the atmosphere. First we approached them one at a time, and Ambra summoned the full power of the Orbs to grant us maximum protection—a kind of wall of energy—as she crushed the devices by severely warping space around them. There was no form of retaliation from the drones at this activity, and the other drones did not seem to learn from the attack and mount a response. Perhaps the Anti had never encountered anyone who could effectively approach and destroy the objects. Perhaps it happened too quickly for any useful information to be transmitted.

Whatever the reason, the end result was dramatic. After the drones were crushed, they tended to fail in some aspect of dealing with the matter-anti-matter shielding the Anti had employed for themselves and their devices. The drones made contact with the edges of the Gyl atmosphere, and a light show erupted. As the low-density matter impacted the crushed remains of anti-matter of the drones, there was a building glow. Soon, gravity or some random explosion in the annihilation would drive the drone carcass faster into Gyl, and the equivalent of a thermonuclear explosion of epic proportions would occur.

Not enough to be a problem for a planet the size of Gyl, but gigantic, moon-sized explosions.

Three hundred was a large number, and after encountering many of them, Ambra began to sense their locations. She claimed to be able to detect them by the strange effects the devices had on space-time, but also it became apparent after several had been located that they were spaced equidistant around the world.

Once it was clear where they were, Ambra summoned a tidal wave of power from the Orb, and in a burst of flame, all the drones were hit with a blast of energy. Once again, a giant vortex in space formed and drank down the refuse of her wrath and sucked it into the Orb.

It was shortly after this fireworks display that Waythrel woke. A stirring in the eyestalks was the first sign, and soon the individual eyes were pointing in various directions in that way the Xix have to quickly survey their surroundings. Ambra knelt down beside the alien and held its arm.

"Waythrel," she said.

The alien spoke, almost robotically. "We are about Gyl. I have been injured. Deductions suggest that you have destroyed the drones, but I have no memory of such a conversation, or any communion, with the Gyl. The contact must have been too much for me."

Ambra nodded as the alien's legs moved at bizarre angles and miraculously raised it to a standing position. "Yes, the drones are destroyed, and Gyl is free of their poison. You were displaced, Waythrel. I did my best to help. I'm sorry for where I failed."

"We will have to see how much you have failed. And I know you did all you could, Ambra. I knew all the risks." The Xix seemed to be trying to comfort her.

"But there are important things you must know of the communion," said Ambra. "Things too complicated for me to explain. Do you feel ready to share?"

The alien reached out for Ambra's hands. "Yes, but go slowly, Daughter of Time."

Once again the rest of us waited in silence as the Readers functioned in that plane of existence that we could not access. But it was much shorter than the interaction with the Gyl. After little more than five minutes, their hands separated, and Ambra opened her eyes.

"This is frightening information," said Waythrel. The alien began a strange pacing inside the enclosure. Of course, every movement of the Xix appeared strange to human eyes, their body composition and design so completely different than our own. I always expected them to snap their limbs as they supported their bodies at those impossible angles, dangling the midsection bulk by thin legs far off the center of mass.

"I'm not sure that I have understood it correctly," responded Ambra.

"Perhaps not, and I cannot access my memories to compare. But as you noted, we can test the creatures at Hola. We also have the suspended bodies of the MECHcore team of Captain Ratava. There may be critical evidence there that scientific equipment can detect."

It was a little disturbing to hear Waythrel refer to the butchered forms of two of my team in such clinical terms, but I knew that the alien was right. Whatever dignity one could have thought to preserve for their bodies in death had been taken away by the hideous tools of the Anti. If we could learn something about those tools by examining whatever was left of them, at least they would not have died in vain.

"Anyway," began Ambra, "we are nearly finished here. We need to seal the Time Tree node and then continue to Hola. But this time, I think we will make sure we are early."

"Early?" I asked. "What do you mean?"

Waythrel seemed to understand immediately, which indicated to me that the alien had not lost much of its cognitive power. "The Time Tree lattice places all the star systems with Orbs on a synchronized clock. A *time frame* relative to the rest of the galaxy but absolute within the member worlds. Ambra doesn't want any more surprises."

Seeing our confused expressions, Ambra explained further. "We have to assume that our plans have been leaked to our enemies. The Dram and Anti, they expect us to travel to Hola next, and because they are locked with the time frame of the Tree, they can only move forward or beside us in time. They may be waiting now, perhaps setting up a trap days or weeks ago when the spy first betrayed our mission. But not several weeks ago. Not months ago. If we go far enough back in time, after the Dram took the node, but before we made these plans, they cannot touch us."

"Aye, yeah, but there's a hole in all that," said Moore. "What if it's one of us blokes who's that traitor, eh? Then he or she will send a signal to the Dram, and they'll adjust their schedule."

"They can't go back in time on the strings," said Williams.

"What's that?" asked Moore.

"Have you forgotten all your basic training? The strings the Readers navigate on connect physical points, *but at the same time.* That's what she means by a clock. If we go back in time, they can't do anything."

"She is correct," said Waythrel. "Only Ambra, who has far greater access to the dimensional doorways in the Orb, can do so. Not even the False Dawns have yet opened an Orb—as far as we know. If we go earlier, we will be far less likely to find unpleasant visitors."

"So the traitor—if he or she exists," said Moore, eyeing all of us with a sharp smile, "will just have to stew in it."

"Yes," said Ambra. "But we will pick a fairly random time point. We don't know what might be waiting. Probably nothing, but perhaps the whole Dram armada." She raised her hands palms up. "So, what will it be?"

"Fucking life through action!" cried Moore with a broad grin. "Let's go through time, baby!"

"Fine with me," said Williams. "Long as we don't have to talk to any more crystal minds. The Hola, wait, I remember—they're primitive, right? Low-level mind, so maybe no talking at all?"

Waythrel answered. "Communication will not be fruitful. But mental monitoring will be. More significantly, they are a hive mind, and the structure of that mind was studied in detail by a Xixian scientist hundreds of years ago."

I spoke up finally. "I remember from the sharing. But I didn't understand anything of that analysis."

"Me either," echoed Williams.

"Then we will discuss it more," said Waythrel. "But the hive mind now can be analyzed and compared to the data from before. If the Anti devices are increasing disorder, even to the realm of mentality, there should be very specific effects on that mind. A signature, if you will. It will be important proof to this hypothesis."

"And if Ambra's right?" I asked.

The eyestalks danced around. "Then we should be very afraid, Captain."

Chapter 33

In all the laws of physics that we have found so far there does not seem to be any distinction between the past and the future. The moving picture should work the same going both ways, and the physicist who looks at it should not laugh.

Richard Feynman

Once again Ambra stood before the Orb node and sealed it shut. It was something I had to assume was happening. I could not see the strings. I was no Reader. Her efforts left no visible change in the Time Sphere that I could perceive. But as with so much I was being introduced to in the universe during this mission, I would have to get used to being in the dark.

Then we left Gyl through the Orb, and I again was racked with pains and lost consciousness. Once again, to my continued embarrassment, I was the only one affected. The faded outlines of a disturbing dream ate at my subconscious, but I pushed it to the side. I didn't feel like getting up, but I did. I mustered all my strength, denied the presence of the nausea and headache, and announced myself fully ready to continue the mission. Ambra looked skeptically at me but said nothing. I was just happy that I was able to maintain my composure and avoid passing out for the first few hours.

Another large gas giant waited in front of us. The knowledge learned in sharing with Ambra poured through my mind. Several hundred years ago, when astronomers on Old Earth began the first cataloguing of extrasolar planets, those interested in extraterrestrial life were disappointed to find that most star systems did not possess small, rocky, water-covered Earth-like planets.

Instead, the predominant form of star system involved one or more large gas giants. Some at the time spun this to believe that moons around the gas giant could perhaps be habitable enough to support life as they imagined it. This indeed is the case in hundreds of systems. Much more common, however, is that the gas giants themselves would harbor life very much *not* like what the earlier scientists were imagining.

The radiant orange Hola was a member of this common set of worlds. The planet was about twice the size of our Jupiter, much smaller than the enormity that was Gyl. Yet for a creature of New Earth, it still seemed gigantic. Twenty moons circled the world, none of them with life. Life aplenty filled the upper atmosphere of the gas giant.

As we approached, Ambra announced that she had detected the death drones. As on Gyl, they were positioned across the surface of the planet doing their dirty work. So Waythrel's experiment was on. We would examine the creatures of Hola for any evidence of "entropic acceleration." Then, we would destroy the drones and seal the final node.

We descended through the atmosphere in the bubble enclosure, choosing a location equidistant from the drones. The gas layers were highly structured. The cloud formations were beautiful, colorful, titanic, and multilayered. They seemed almost like mountains or towers built out of the vapors of the planet. Light dimmed slightly as we entered more deeply, soon passing a distance several times the depth of New Earth's paper-thin atmosphere. It was here that we first saw signs of life.

Our search was for the more developed Holaians, but our first contact with living beings was with the more primitive cloudhoppers of this Jovian world. Giant bags of gas, they floated in the relatively safer upper layers of Hola by controlling the mixture of hydrogen and helium within them, as well as the temperature of the gases. More hydrogen, higher temperature meant they rose. More helium, colder gases, and they descended. Like everything about this world, the creatures were monstrous. Easily several thousand feet in length, they resembled ellipsoidal jellyfish. Strange projections came from several ends of the creatures, and a complicated internal structure seemed to exist partially visible through the somewhat translucent outer membrane.

There were millions of them, rising and falling across the skies, able to dart with surprising speed in different directions. As we wandered through this biolayer of the planet, my eyes began to discern subtle differences in what at first seemed creatures that were identical. There were in fact hundreds of different "balloon" species mixed together in the air. Some were even predators that chased and at times consumed their prey. Others seemed to move in what I could only describe as "herds." It was all mesmerizing. Like a kid at a zoo for the first time, I felt that I could stare through the invisible barrier and watch these things all day long.

"Amazing, aren't they?" asked Ambra, smiling toward me.

"Yes. They're beautiful," I said.

"Creepy as hell," said Williams, shivering with a chill. "Sorry, I'm sure that there is all kind of astrobiology fun here, but these things are right out of some of my nightmares as a kid."

"Wait, you had dreams of aircraft carrier-sized floating gas bags as a kid?" smirked Moore.

"Not exactly, smartass," said Williams. Her glare was icy. "But close enough."

"I just had dreams of bonking the mail girl," said Moore.

Williams nodded. "Not surprised."

"Where are the Holaians?" I asked.

Waythrel answered. "They are the most developed species on Hola, but their numbers to date are low. With their intelligence, it is forecast that in several hundred thousand years, they could develop a technological civilization and populate the world. But for now, Ambra will have to find them by homing in on their sentient signal."

"Okay Waythrel," Ambra said with a sigh. "It was nice to relax a bit. But point taken."

For the next hour or so, Ambra sat in her meditative position in a deep trance. Most of the time, the bubble simply sat still as the rest of us paced, watched the bizarre animals outside, or discussed our fears of the war. Waythrel remained quiet, seemingly focused on its own thoughts. Every now and then, the enclosure would move—accelerate in some direction rapidly and then slow down, finally coming to a stop. This occurred five or six times. After a few instances, we assumed it was simply Ambra finding a "scent" but losing it.

Eventually, the bubble accelerated again, and this time did not slow down for some time. Williams and Moore moved toward the end of the enclosure facing the direction in which we were moving. We were flying quickly through the giant cloud formations now. I understood how Ambra felt—it would have been nice to let go of the pressing dangers and worries of our mission and enjoy this journey through Hola. There was something soothing about the endless airscape of cloud form, the herds of dirigible life, the orange light, warm and calming, that filled the space of this atmospheric layer.

Ambra stood up and opened her eyes, moving beside the two members of my team. I followed her, staring over her head toward the rising star of the system. It would be early morning in this portion of the planet, whatever morning meant here. Ahead, there was a cloud that looked different from anything we had seen before. To begin, it was small. And black, as well as porous seeming. It also drifted strangely, often at odds to the prevailing air currents.

But it was clear that the cloud was the destination to which Ambra was steering the bubble. As we neared it, the partly solid nature of the cloud disintegrated, and we could see that it seemed to be comprised of thousands and thousands of smaller objects. The individual objects were quite small relative to the lumbering air beasts that we had encountered. But they were much faster, darting here and there with speed, yet constantly maintaining a structured form to the cloud.

"Looks like a flock of birds," I said.

"Or a school of minnows," replied Williams.

"Or some ugly bunch of angry hornets," said Moore.

Ambra laughed, and just like that, the hornets attacked us.

Chapter 34

The second law of thermodynamics is, without a doubt, one of the most perfect laws in physics. Not even Maxwell's laws of electricity or Newton's law of gravitation are so sacrosanct, for each has measurable corrections coming from quantum effects or general relativity. The law has caught the attention of poets and philosophers and has been called the greatest scientific achievement of the nineteenth century.

Ivan P. Bazarov

Protected within Ambra's space-time field, we were never in any real danger, but it was still disconcerting as tens of thousands of angry Holaians threw themselves at our enclosure. Of course, their efforts achieved nothing, but it was amazing to watch. The cloud almost seemed to grow arms and hands, extend those extremities toward us, and try to grab us individually or altogether. Apparently they couldn't perceive the bubble.

"Notice the coordinated projections," said Waythrel, as if the alien had read my mind. "The Holaians are a hive-mind, the simpler individual members of the hive working in unison to create a much greater whole. The cloud, as a whole, functions as a superindividual, far more intelligent and capable than the individuals or even smaller coordinated groups. Only when the cloud has enough members, a threshold, and those members have worked together for decades, diversifying, harmonizing, can the cloud step into this higher level of consciousness."

I had remembered some of this from the sharing. It was like a developing human with our much larger brains. We have billions of neurons that have to work together. It takes us years and years of interacting with the world and being taught to function at the levels of adults. I said as much to the others.

"So also with the Xix," added Waythrel. "For life-forms with large brains like ours, individuals can achieve a higher level of functioning, even if reaching the full potential of the individual requires a larger social mind—a culture—to be involved. The Holaians, however, cannot achieve such mentality unless they have large numbers of individuals. The individual minds are much simpler."

"So its like a bunch of stupid bees together that get smarter when they are part of a hive?" asked Moore.

"Similar," said the alien. "The Holaian individuals are much smarter than your individual insects, and therefore their mentality in a hive-like state is far greater."

"So, hive mind. Got it. What's the plan then?" asked Williams. "How do we know if the drones are getting to them?"

"Waythrel and I will monitor them," said Ambra.

"I have within my species-memory the patterns of their mind-forms from scans of Readers who researched on Hola years before. Ambra and I will compare what we see now and look for evidence of drone effects."

In this manner we spent the next five days. Chasing one cloud mind after another, Waythrel and Ambra in their Reader trance would probe the hives. The process was arduous and long, the hive minds difficult for the two bipedal life-forms to understand. But they posed far less danger than the efforts at Gyl.

Always when they woke from the trance, it was with sorrow. One after the other, each of the hive-minds we encountered showed signs of a terrible mental deterioration. Proximity to the drones increased the decay. It didn't take long for the pattern to be incontrovertible. The Holaian minds were dying.

"They had been on the cusp of an organized civilization," said Waythrel after one grueling session. "The reports from Xixians detailed the progress of the hives hundreds of years ago. Rudimentary versions of social structure and generational learning had taken root. In a manner simpler and yet very different from human and Xixian technological civilization, they had begun to fashion advanced cultural building blocks. Now, they have been set back millennia. At the rate of decay we are witnessing, in several decades they will even begin to lose hive integrity."

"What are these terrible drones, then?" I asked, revolted by the destruction they were describing.

Ambra shook her head. "The deeper purpose is unclear, but we have all but confirmed the entropic manipulation. The antiorder. The higher-level sentient structures are affected first, but the Gyl were even finding evidence that the lower-level structures of chemistry, even atomic physics, are affected."

"We will need much more evidence to confirm that," said Waythrel. "But the possibilities are frightening."

"Atomic physics?" asked Williams. "You mean like atoms falling apart, now?"

"We don't know," said Ambra. "The Gyl were hard to understand."

"But we know enough now to move on," said Waythrel. "With the information we have, and critically the bodies that were subjected to the powerful pro-entropic fields, we may begin to find a way to develop countermeasures."

"So, that's it?" said Moore. "Mission accomplished, and we bug out of here?"

"Yes," said Ambra, standing up from her crossed-legged position. "First we destroy these drones. Then we seal the third and final node and seal off New Earth from the Dram."

"And return to plan the next stage in this conflict," concluded Waythrel.

And so it would have gone, likely to far less sorrow and tragedy, if only we had left a day earlier. Such are the random chances in time. So proceeds the cosmic play in ways that often seem more capricious than purposeful.

We left the decorative atmosphere of Hola, and Ambra set course for the Orb. It was a strange feeling to be thinking that this mad mission was coming to an end and that we would soon be walking on the sands of New Earth again. Of course, I dreaded the transit through the Orb and was beginning to develop a phobia of it. But I could face a last trip without undue anxiety. And there was the satisfaction that we had achieved a critical goal in protecting not only our homeworld, but thousands of star systems that would have been vulnerable to invasion. I knew that Fox and Kim both would have considered their sacrifice worth that end. That was why they had signed on in the first place.

As the Orb grew in size before our approaching bubble, there was a bright flash next to it. I immediately recognized both the phenomenon and the object materializing. An adrenaline spike coursed through my system, causing my heart to race. Coming off a Time Tree string was a Dram warboat. It materialized nearly right upon us.

In the end, despite my reaction, it would not pose any risk to us in and of itself. Ambra would disable it and in fact exploit the seemingly useful opportunity to interrogate its crew.

But what we learned would set in motion a series of events that would long traumatize both Ambra and me.

Chapter 35

Let us draw an arrow arbitrarily. If as we follow the arrow we find more and more of the random element in the state of the world, then the arrow is pointing towards the future; if the random element decreases the arrow points towards the past. I shall use the phrase 'time's arrow' to express this one-way property of time which has no analogue in space.

Sir Arthur Stanley Eddington

L ooks like we have guests," said Moore.

The warship didn't waste any time with pleasantries. There were a few moments of inaction as the Dram likely tried to figure out what exactly this floating group of travelers could be that they saw on their visuals. Unable to do anything but verify the composition of our party, they did what the Dram do best. They immediately opened fire on us.

This surely elicited a second round of confusion in the enemy ship. Even the most shielded Xixian starships collapsed under the focused firepower of the Dram military. Here was a gaggle of only four individuals with a strange cargo—apparently encased in some mysterious and transparent craft—who just stood before the bulk of one of their most feared battle cruisers and took the full fury of their assault.

Ambra didn't give them much time to seek a more analytic mode. She steered the bubble quickly toward the craft, the beam weapons and missiles deflected away from us as the Dram tracked our motion, and parked it outside the hull.

"Time to talk to some bugs," she said impishly.

Unlike our entrance to the Braxian starship where we encountered Caga,

Ambra didn't spare the Dram hull. It began to bend inward, the metal soon buckling and then ripping as she forced her way in. As on Brax, some kind of extension to the bubble was projected forward, and we entered into the belly of the warboat. Air didn't rush out of the breach, so Ambra must have sealed off the ship as much as she shaped a tunnel of nothing for us to walk down. Since the Dram coincidentally breathed an atmosphere very similar to our own, it would have been simpler to exit the bubble once inside in order to engage them. Of course, once the insectoidal monsters started blasting at us inside the ship, I understood the usefulness of the enclosure in a very up-close and personal manner.

The engagement was surreal. The Dram threw everything they had at us short of blowing up the entire ship. Williams had cautioned that they might even try that, remembering what had happened around Brax. But Waythrel disagreed.

"It was the Anti ship that destroyed the Dram. The Dram culture disdains suicide and will always fight to their own or their opponent's death."

"But if a shadow ship comes into the system?" I asked. "Then what? We don't know what their plans were for Hola."

"I'm monitoring the Orb. We'll know," said Ambra. "In the meantime, I've shut down their ship's ability to navigate or send external communications. They are paralyzed and cut off from everything."

Moore laughed. "I do like this new way of fighting."

And so we continued to watch the fireworks. By now we had overcome our instinctual concern about standing in front of Dram warriors unloading their weapons on us. The scene became comical. The bugs were frustrated by now, scampering around the finger-like field of emptiness that prevented even their best weapons from achieving anything.

Ambra sat cross-legged in front of the mayhem, the Dram ship and crew in front of her and the starlit backdrop with Hola behind. From all appearances, there was absolutely nothing between her and the attacking Dram. Seeing the Daughter here, the soldiers were eager to grab or kill her. With their razored hands and weapons, they tried over and over to accomplish either of those goals. Ambra had closed her eyes and seemed not to notice the crazed efforts.

Finally, several began to try to study the phenomenon. Soon the weapons were silenced, and we were surrounded by a semicircle of what must have been exhausted and confused bugs. A few smaller-sized Dram had entered the area near the breach. They brought instruments and set them around us. *Scientists*, I assumed. After a good while of that, some figures with considerable authority entered the chamber and were arguing with the others. I could hear the interminable clicking speech of the insects.

Waythrel spoke. "Ambra?"

"Yes, this one will do," she said, her eyes remaining closed.

Suddenly the figure was inside our bubble. The transition was undetectable except that the other Dram were banging on the outside trying to get to it. The officer inside moved to attack, but Ambra overrode its own mental control of its body, and the creature sat there paralyzed.

"Allow me released or there falls destruction overall complete!" it shrieked through their horrid translators.

"Waythrel, would you like to start?" asked Ambra.

Waythrel approached the creature. The two aliens couldn't be more different in mentality and appearance. The tribal, warlike Dram, who seemed to excel mostly in the creation of devices of conflict, next to the peaceful and contemplative Xix. An insect-like frame towered next to us yet was matched by the bulk and height of Waythrel.

"These devices you plant around the worlds—what is their purpose?" the Xix began.

The Dram officer said nothing. Its many legs twitched in anxiety within Ambra's web.

"We know they are destroying the minds and societies present. But this is not of Dram. The Dram preserve function. The Dram destroy in combat, with honor, or enslave. What has changed? Who controls the Dram and why?"

"The Dram never to be withheld," it spat.

"Then why are you placing these devices for others?"

The bug clammed up again. Moore shook his head and folded his hands over his chest. "Fucker isn't going to talk. Maybe if we start ripping segments off that exoskeleton."

"I'm afraid he's right, Ambra," said Waythrel. "We will need another probe." Several of the eyestalks flipped over toward Moore. "One not involving torture."

Ambra sighed. "Mind probes are at best unpleasant, Waythrel, and being within the mind of a Dram still brings bad memories." She stared directly at the officer. "Listen to me. You know who I am. If you do not answer our questions to our satisfaction, I will enter your mind and take those answers from you. Is this what you wish?"

The officer twitched madly, trying to find some way to escape the invisible bonds holding it in place. Outside, the creatures had returned to a frantic mode, firing weapons at us, one even setting off an explosive device that killed several of their crew yet left us unharmed.

Ambra lowered her head for a moment and then raised it with her eyes closed. The creature stiffened, its purposeful movements subdued. It was clear she had reached within it in some profound way. Even the warriors outside the enclosure paused in a curiosity that got the better of them for a moment.

"Fogged light ships usurp and control," came the strange words from the Dram in front of Ambra. "The appearance from nothing to something in zero. Burnings provide us with the right, as we know it. Performance in the war. The power of life. Shadow promises Dram war triumph."

"The Anti," whispered Williams.

The creature stopped any discernible speech, and the sounds became weak with abortive attempts at clicking. Ambra remained focused as minutes dragged by. But she was unable to coax anything else out of the bug. Eventually the creature began to slump backward and then collapsed on the ground, suddenly outside the enclosure. The Dram dragged the immobile body out of our sight.

Ambra opened her eyes, and I saw a fire in them. "We need to go to Dram."

Moore and Williams approached quickly in shock. Even Waythrel seemed surprised.

"Ambra, we can't go to Dram," I said. The idea was surely suicide.

"We can and we must," she said, beginning to pace.

Waythrel spoke. "What did you see in its mind?"

"First, slavery. The Dram are no longer in control of their own destiny. The Anti have taken over."

Moore scoffed. "So what? Serves the bugs right. Let 'em rot."

Ambra ignored him. "The entire planet is transformed. They have been organized into factory centers, entire populations displaced. Manufacturing cities have sprung up from the wastelands of the planet."

"So these drones, the growing armada—it's all being made on Dram for the war?"

"Beyond anything we could have imagined. And there are clones. Thousands of them. Something enormous is being planned. A long-term industry."

Waythrel stepped forward. "A work with the Anti that will proceed far into the future." The two Readers looked at each other knowingly. Many eyestalks turned to the rest of us. "Ambra may have a point. If only for a reconnaissance mission, there may be important information we could glean given what I have heard."

"And just how do you suppose that we are going to do this?" said Williams. "Just waltz onto the Dram homeworld and start taking holos? Won't the entire planet of Dram warriors and their new shadow friends have something to say about that?"

Ambra nodded. "Yes, they would. But they won't see us. Watch!"

The Dram outside our enclosure startled. Their heads darted around in a panic, several walking forward toward us and then crashing into nothing.

"We're invisible," I said.

"I can block various forms of matter from reaching us here, and I can modify the path of photons. I can make it appear that nothing is inside."

Moore placed his hands on his hips. "Might have been useful earlier, sister, you think?"

Ambra shook her head. "It leaves us vulnerable." The Dram outside seemed aware of our presence again. Ambra gestured toward the soldiers. "They could have shot us just now. Blurring where and what we are prevents me from maintaining the structure for a shield. We didn't know exactly what we'd face before. Now we do. We can't walk into Dram openly."

Moore continued. "So then, you do your magic cloak act, we transport to

Dram, have a look-see, find out what they're up to that's so important, and then get out?"

"That's basically my plan, yes," said Ambra. "The more I think about it, the more it makes sense. We've come across too many disturbing things on this mission that we don't understand. Now I know where the Anti are holed up. It's on Dram, and they are planning big things. We add one more stop on the trip. Maybe the most important one."

I nodded. It made sense to me. It still seemed incredibly risky, but the payoff could be very high. I turned to Moore and Williams. "Waythrel's onboard, it seems. Me too."

"I'm not sure how I'm going to stop myself from opening fire on those bastards," said Moore. "I've watched too many good soldiers killed by those bugs. But okay. I'm there. I wouldn't mind standing under their antenna and pulling out their dearest secrets."

Williams nodded. "I would have had to see this to believe it," she said, gesturing to the Dram around us, who still seemed perplexed. "But that's starting to be my new normal. Never thought I'd set foot on Dram."

"I was there once, many years ago," said Ambra. Her face was pained. "It is not something I do again lightly."

"Then let us finish the mission and seal the last Orb node," said Waythrel. "And then, we set an unexpected course."

"For the Dram homeworld," I said, shaking my head.

As I gazed toward the quiescent Orb, a feeling of dread took hold within me. The Time Sphere looked different somehow. Of course it wasn't. Objectively it had the same appearance I had always seen on the inactive Orb—a grayness not exactly black, a reflection not exactly true, a hidden depth that could not quite be perceived. But it *felt* different. It projected something different to my paranoid eyes.

It looked almost hostile.

Chapter 36

The bright sun was extinguish'd, and the stars
Did wander darkling in the eternal space.

George Gordon Byron

This last trip was the worst for me.

It began as a terrible torture, pain assaulting my body, my mind. Nausea struck me the moment Ambra engaged the Orb. That stomach churning sickness was followed quickly by a splitting headache. I remember falling to the floor of the enclosure and grabbing my head between my hands. I'm embarrassed to say that I think I screamed. It is hard to explain how the physiological reactions occur without one's will when placed in extremis.

After that, I passed out—or that is rather how I understand it. Whether a coma or some trance, I don't know. Maybe it is better that I don't know.

In my nightmarish awareness, I was no longer with the group. This time there was no tunnel. No water. No shapes or stars or competing Ambra eyes.

There was only the devil Ambra. A demon child.

Once more, I was lying in a field of corn. A region around me had been flattened into a circle extending perhaps twenty feet radially. I was at the center, my head swimming, my body aching. The sky overhead was clear and blue.

Then I heard laughter. It floated on the soft breeze, spinning around my dizzy head. A child's laughter, high pitched, playful, without guile or cynicism. *Pure.*

To my left, I heard the sound of cornstalks rustling. I turned toward it, the motion making me seasick. A little girl, perhaps eight years old, walked into the circle.

It was Ambra, yet it was not Ambra.

Her hair was red and long, but she was bald in patches from points at which hideous machinery had been inserted into her skull. Like the Ambra in the desert, she was flesh and machine, natural and artificial. Enhanced. Degraded. *Altered.*

She looked down on me, smiled, and began to skip around the outside of the corn circle, her hands slapping the upright stalks to the rhythm of a song she was humming. I didn't know the tune. It was a strange melody, disturbing in its unusual scales and note resolutions, like some unhealthy inversion of all the musical rules I had grown to know. I tried to follow her as she danced, but I couldn't move my head fast enough to track her movements.

I tried to sit up. My attempt ended dismally with my head and shoulders slamming back down to the ground. The headache returned, momentarily blinding me, and I had to squint to look into the sky again.

The girl was standing over me. Her long red hair hanging down like limbs from a willow tree set on fire, the tips of the hairs nearly touching my face. I could see the enormous expansion of her skull where the tumor lay, the tubes and wires exiting and entering it appearing vile and gleaming. Her eyes were bright green.

"We will have to take it," the thing said.

I tried to clear my head. *Take what?*

"It's all part of a bigger plan. All the gods, they always have their *bigger* plans. She can't know, of course. She's not ready. She won't be ready for a long, long time. I'm afraid she will resist."

I tried to sit up again, more carefully this time, but the effort was too much.

"Do you want a hand?" the girl asked, cocking her head to one side. She offered her arm.

I didn't know whether I should trust her, but I was helpless enough for her to have harmed me by now. That she hadn't gave me a small amount of confidence. I reached out my hand.

"It's safe. I'm all walled off from you."

Walled off? I grasped her hand and with help rose to a sit. The hand felt strangely slick and featureless. "I think I'll just stop here for now," I said as the pain returned.

"Good idea," she said. "You fell hard."

"Fell where? Where am I? How did I get here?"

The clone looked into the sky and around to the horizon as if searching. "She brought you, I think, but I don't really know." She shook her head and shrugged.

"Who brought me where?"

"The answers won't make sense. And words don't help much. Only in the very end will they all make sense. And then there won't be words."

She sat down and crossed her legs in front of me, staring directly into my eyes. I assumed that like Ambra, the clones were blind and used their visions of the past and future to "see" around them. Maybe as cyborgs they had found a way to let the tumor grow uninhibited and still spare the visual regions of the brain. But I actually didn't know.

"Please, why am I here?"

I don't know, Nitin Ratava.

"Please don't do that!" I said. Having a clone inside my mind again nearly made me panic.

"You have mind scars," the girl spoke aloud.

She's reading my mind! "Yes, one of *your* kind attacked me."

"My kind? No, you don't know my kind. And I'm not my kind, really. I'm brokenly fixed."

"Yes, I do!" I nearly yelled. "I know them too well."

The clone in front of me was quiet for a moment. Then she nodded her head. "Oh, I see. Most of it is erased in your mind—she did this, yes? She didn't want it to hurt you anymore. Anyway, I can see enough still there. Yes, they hurt you. They are made to hurt you, as I am."

My heart raced, and I instinctively began to push myself backward from her.

"But if I want to hurt you, you can't run away, Nitin."

My mouth was dry. "What do you want with me?"

"I don't want anything with you. She wants something to happen. *They* do." She looked into the skies again. "But maybe they found what they are looking for. It feels like we are almost out of time."

I shook my head and squeezed it with my palms. "I don't understand *any* of this!"

"I know. I don't either. There is so much for me to learn. Every step is a *lesson*, Nitin. That's the other reason why we're here. Not for you, I'm sorry. But for me."

"We are here for you to learn something? About me?"

"No. We've known about you for a thousand years. The Daughter's consort is an important lesson taught to everyone. Especially for strategy. Many think that you are the flaw, the weakness to find a way to destroy her."

"To destroy Ambra?"

"Yes. And once she is destroyed, they believe the Orbs will fail."

I sat there dumbfounded. "I won't hurt Ambra."

The clone eyed me knowingly. "But the lesson is not to know you but better understand her. At least I think it is. There can be no healing of the crystal without truly understanding her, just as she seeks to understand me. That is why we are here. That is why I can coexist with you now, and even touch you!"

Before I could move, she placed her index finger right between my eyes. I jumped backward and almost fell over.

She giggled. "So fun! They have such power in the deep future." She beamed. "It will be strange to destroy them."

A fierce wind picked up. The clone's hair flew around us, the standing cornstalks swaying madly in the gusts. She started humming that weird tune again and then stopped, looking back at me solemnly.

"Time. Not enough time to know all of you. There are other holes in your mind, Nitin Ratava," she said, closing her eyes and looking upward. "Remember, I will take it soon."

The fabric of space split open before me. The figure of the girl, the green stalks, the blue sky ripped like some aged cloth to reveal a backdrop of stars. The previous vision I had fell into one thousand fragments and scattered into a howling wind.

I floated in the silence of space.

Chapter 37

What I am going to tell you about is what we teach our physics students in the third or fourth year of graduate school. It is my task to convince you not to turn away because you don't understand it. You see my physics students don't understand it. That is because I don't understand it. Nobody does.

Richard Feynman

I awoke feeling as sick as I had remembered in the dream. Ambra was kneeling next to me, her hand on my forehead.

"His fever broke," she said to others outside my field of vision. I could only see her and the seemingly endless star field above me. I remember thinking that this was all I really needed to see, anyway.

"This is becoming dangerous for him, Ambra," came the voice of Waythrel.

"I know," she said softly, concern on her features. "Only one more. I will be much more careful. I was too eager to get here and see what was happening."

I was down for two more days. Meanwhile, the group and I floated outside of the Dram homeworld in our now-invisible enclosure. While I had heard stories and seen holos of the red giant star at the center of the system, it was something else entirely to be close to it, "in the flesh," to appreciate its size and the strange effect that living in a colorspace lacking most of the higher wavelengths has on one. Everything appeared washed out, tanned, and faded. Even living in the deserts of New Earth seemed to bring more vitality.

And yet the busy world of our enemies was below. When I had recovered sufficiently to work my suit, we planned our approach to the planet surface. Ambra wanted to go straight to the seat of power, to the emperor's palace. She believed that we could enter undetected yet observe everything that went on. The prime strategies and plans of the Dram would be revealed to us. We could learn much to help our efforts in the war.

Even more important, there could be much revealed about the Anti and what they were actually up to. Ambra seemed to be holding something back, but I got the sense that her visions had convinced her that those answers would indeed be forthcoming on Dram. From her words of what she had seen in the Dram officer's mind, we might even find the Anti there.

Williams and Moore were concerned that the Anti might be able to detect our approach. I shared that concern, but my level of trust in Ambra was high. Too high, as I would discover soon.

"I mean, we don't know their technology. Even if the Dram couldn't see us, couldn't stop us, maybe those monsters have something that can," said Williams as we debated.

"It is possible," said Ambra, "but I think unlikely."

"Why?" asked Moore. His face was stern, and it was clear he wanted to hear reasoned arguments.

Waythrel interjected. "The Anti aren't magical, Sergeant. They may be composed of particles that are inverted in specific characteristics from ours, but the same laws of physics apply to them. In fact, in their own antimatter galaxies, they could appear as close copies of any life-form in our galaxy. Imagine looking into a mirror of a kind, and everything is inverted in some ways but still basically looks the same. Atomic physics, chemistry, etc., while not compatible with us, would still be entirely recognizable. Life would likely look very much the same."

"Well, they still have tech we don't understand. Purposes we don't understand," said Moore.

Ambra nodded. "Yes. Any advanced alien technology could baffle us for a while, so your worries are legitimate. But so far, they have not been able to counter my effects on space-time. Nothing makes me think that this will be different for cloaking us on Dram. I think it's a risk worth taking."

We finally reached an agreement. We would take an initial risk and descend into Dram, ready to rocket out of there quickly at the first sign of discovery. First we would enter the atmosphere and test their long-range scanning abilities. Next, we would hover over the central city of Gred, where the emperor's palace was located. If things went well to that point, we would proceed to the palace itself and find out what we could.

Ambra assured us that she could make a very fast run for the Orb. From what I had seen in our adventures so far, I had no doubts. What I didn't know and would soon find out was just how fast she could actually go.

We left the bodies of Kim and Fox orbiting Dram in their private enclosure and descended slowly, Ambra monitoring all that she could of the mental states around us. Despite the thickness of the atmosphere, the enormous luminosity of the red giant hardly faded as we descended while the space around us took on a reddish hue so that it nearly seemed that rust leaked out of the very sky itself. For a human to spend much time on Dram would be psychologically challenging.

Ambra was explaining. "Mostly it's too much noise, too many inputs from the billions," she said. "But if we are detected, there will be a synchronized meshing of thoughts with a spike in focus and energy. *That* I can likely sense. As they would organize to respond, such activities would be even more outside the random noise."

Nothing happened. Ambra didn't sense anything and no warships or ground-based defenses responded to our penetration of the atmosphere. The deep desert of Dram began to fill all my vision—a red-and-orange sea of sand dwarfing the Sahara, spanning the entire planet, to human eyes colored nearly monochromatically by that swollen sun. To avoid being overwhelmed visually by the expanse, I focused on the shape of Gred taking form as we approached.

It was a gigantic city, spanning four to five times the largest metropolis on New Earth. The buildings were a stark contrast to human design. There were few sharp edges, little glass. The materials were strange and the shapes curvilinear. It almost appeared as if one were to take Manhattan and multiply it by a factor of one thousand, in width and height, and then turn it to sand and spray just enough water to melt the edges of the structures but have them retain their structural integrity. *That* would be an echo of the alienness of Gred. But really, when presented with the truly alien, my mind could only map it to the most similar memories of New Earth. Usually, there was a lot of distortion in that comparison.

Soon, we were flying over Gred in our bubble. Part of me felt vulnerable. There we were, perched over the largest city of our deadliest foes, with no discernible walls, a collection of three soldiers, one alien, and the wildcard that was Ambra Dawn. Of course, she was the reason the bubble existed, that it withstood without complaint the full discharge of a Dram warship, that it allowed us to see everything around us in protection yet hid us from enemy eyes. I should have been calm. But I wasn't.

"The city appears almost deserted," said Waythrel. "And the sky traffic is minimal."

"Look—that's where the tribunal was held," said Ambra quietly. It was an enormous dome, hewn out of the commonplace metallic, marble-like substance found across Dram architecture, cut with facets reflecting the red starlight. It matched in near-perfect detail the descriptions in the history books. But Ambra turned away from it and pointed to some much smaller buildings nearby. "That's where they held me prisoner. Where they took my eggs to make their abominations."

Her tone sounded loaded to me. I began to wonder if her obsession with coming had something to do with the clones. We would find out soon.

The emperor's palace sprang out of the cityscape in front of us. Unlike the town-sized dome of the Tribunal, the palace rose like an obscene termite construction towering over all other structures in Gred. Military craft darted around it, laying out a protective radial grid of hovercraft with stunning amounts of firepower. One thing about the Dram, they sure knew how to militarize the hell out of anything.

"The emperor is housed at the very top of the structure," said Ambra. "It gives the creature a god's-eye view of Gred and Dram, feeding no doubt into the monumental egos they always seem to have."

Williams laughed. "Except for the one you nearly destroyed centuries ago, right? When you escaped? Unless the history books lie. *That* emperor must have been a bit humbled!"

Ambra looked away. "What happened then is not something I'm proud of." There was an awkward silence.

The sea of guarding spacecraft ignored us, and we passed through their ranks undetected. It was a tense few minutes, and as MECHcore soldiers we were the most tense in this potentially explosive environment. Waythrel and Ambra seemed to remain calm, although Ambra retained a sharp focus that had descended on her since she had looked into the captured officer's mind. Perhaps it was just returning to Dram. I could not imagine how disturbing it would be for her. But it felt like more, as if she suspected something terrible and was only waiting to confirm it.

We approached the enormous tower that gleamed in the ruby light. Ambra did not slow down. Just as I thought that we would smash ourselves to pieces on the hard walls, they *bent*. Where they bent to I cannot describe because my mind can't grasp it. But a kind of hole appeared in the wall that again only we seemed able to perceive. Our little invisible pod entered through it.

Chapter 38

All that we see or seem
Is but a dream within a dream.

Edgar Allen Poe

We haunted the emperor's palace like some aggregated poltergeist. The four of us hovered near the tops of the enormous ceilings, watching and listening as the creatures obliviously went about their activities underneath. It did not take us long to confirm Ambra's worst suspicions.

The floor that housed the emperor was constructed like a throne room. A grand hallway led from an elevator of sorts to a central chamber, domed on the inside, in the center of which was a reclining chair-like piece of furniture designed for the Dram insectoidal bodies. But this was clearly a special version. Even through the alienness of it all it was easy to connect the human desire to aggrandize its rulers with something similar in the Dram. The more I saw of Dram, the more uncomfortable I felt at the similarities between them and us that kept surfacing. Some part of me began to suspect that humanity shared more with this warlike species than with the peace-loving Xix.

The emperor was in its chambers. There was the expected flurry of activity around the ruler as orders were given, problems were raised, deals were negotiated, and strategies were plotted.

Waythrel's translator converted the speech before us almost in real time, casting each speaker's tones with different human voices, allowing us to easily follow the conversation. A subject of the emperor was explaining something to the ruler.

"Dram is suffering, Holy One," came a pleading voice inside our bubble. "Crops are neglected. Power and resources are being diverted to the Project. The alien harvests are consuming all that we have. We cannot continue like this. Dissent is growing. There is talk of rebellion."

The emperor's voice was robotic. "Is that all?"

I watched the many legs of the petitioner dance around at this response. "Yes, emperor."

"Then take this message back to the local governors. The Project is all that matters. Defeat of the human Reader is the highest priority. The war cannot be won without it. Suffering births strength. Any resistance to the Divine Orders will be met with death. The fields will continue to expand."

The giant bug in front of the throne straightened its long torso, lowering its head before the Emperor. It turned and scampered out of the throne room.

"The Emperor looks drugged," said Ambra.

Waythrel agreed. "We have both spent enough time on Dram to know the personalities and character of these creatures. Ambra is right—something is wrong."

"Let's get closer," said Ambra. "There's a lot of room behind the throne, and no traffic."

Our bubble descended. It also turned out to be a fortuitous location. Nestled behind the throne, we were able to observe the comings and goings without becoming an obstacle. More importantly, we were given a view of the back of the Dram emperor's head.

"What the hell is that on its head?" asked Moore.

"A crown," said Waythrel. "Of a kind."

But Moore didn't mean the cap-like crown with its multi-threaded braids hanging half a foot below the head of the creature. He pointed to something else.

"No, look—underneath the braids. That thing in its head. I don't think I've ever seen that in my readings or meeting with the Dram."

"It's embedded in its brain," said Williams, a scowl on her face.

"Ambra, can you allow me to approach?" asked Waythrel.

"Yes. Just walk," she said. "But be careful. If you get too close, and it moves and hits you, it will feel a disturbance from the enclosure. Remember, all of you, while we are cloaked we are vulnerable."

Waythrel walked forward. To my eye, it seemed that the alien stepped away from us toward the throne without anything around it or between us. Of course, I knew intellectually that Ambra had encased us all in this invisible barrier. But it required an imaginative focus to continue to believe in it without any sensorial feedback about its existence. Part of me wished the Dram would start shooting at us again, only so that I'd have the sense that *something* was actually around us and doing something. Of course, with the thing cloaked, those shots might actually do us some harm.

Waythrel approached within several feet, its eyestalks moving forward together to inspect the black box seemingly stuck inside the glistening exoskeleton of the Dram ruler. After a minute or two, the alien returned.

"I have never seen it before," it said. "Five decades on Dram, and nothing like it existed."

"Maybe it's new," said Moore. "Been a few hundred years since you visited."

"Or maybe it's reserved for the rulers," I added.

"The technology is not from Dram—that was clear on inspection," said Waythrel. "It appears to be constructed of raw materials from the planet, however. I have studied Dram physiology and possess a renewed memory of it from my species-sharing. The device is located precisely in the region of the mental organ that controls conscious choice in the Dram. The only reason to embed a machine there is to override or modify the will of the emperor."

"Wait," said Williams. "That box is controlling its mind? And the Dram didn't make it?"

"The Anti," said Moore.

Ambra nodded. "You heard the words they spoke. The emperor is killing Dram, working it to exhaustion and stealing the resources of the planet for some grand project. Some of this I saw in the mind of the Dram soldier. But to see it at this level is something else."

"What are these fields? What are they harvesting?" I asked.

"Not food," said Waythrel. "The reports of starvation and rebellion indicate that."

"Whatever it is, it has to do with *you*," said Moore, pointing at Ambra. "The project is to build something that kills *you*."

"Agreed," said Ambra. "So, you'll excuse me if I am motivated to go find these fields and look for myself."

"Find them—how?" I asked.

"They can't be far," said Waythrel. "If they are diverting power and resources to them from Gred, they are likely on the outskirts of the city."

"Wait—shouldn't we listen in and find out more?" asked Williams.

"Perhaps," said Waythrel. "But I can't think of anything more pressing than determining how they are working to kill Ambra Dawn."

"I agree," I blurted out.

Moore cocked his head to one side. "Fields for harvesting. To kill Ambra. I think I know what they're growing."

I caught my breath. I thought I could guess too.

Waythrel's eyes swiveled and stared at all of us. "We need to go find these fields."

Chapter 39

Close your eyes and listen. Listen to the silent screams of terrified mothers, the prayers of anguished old men and women. Listen to the tears of children.

Eli Wiesel

W e found the fields.

Take the giant AgriCom farms from Ambra's youth in the Midwest, replace them with humans instead of corn or cattle, multiply by a factor of one hundred, and drop the entire thing into the oven-baked landscape of Dram, and you would have some idea of what spread out before us. Mile after mile. Housing, pens, birthing factories, biotech. Square after square of parceled land marked repeating installations in an industrialized assembly line to manufacture people. To manufacture copies of a single person. To the horizon a sea of copy after copy of buildings, workers, and Ambra Dawn.

At first we just flew over the fields, scanning the layout, noticing the absurd lengths to which the Dram and Anti had gone. It was only when we descended to enter the compounds themselves that the disturbing nature of the enterprise really kicked us in the teeth.

I could spend five books detailing everything we witnessed, swooping down into buildings, entering the labs and factories, following the clones. We spied on the workers, Ambra pilfered information from their thoughts, and much was simply obvious as function followed form. But a summary is sufficient. It sickens me to even remember it now, and the briefer I can be, the better.

The biotech labs were staffed by Dram technicians, but it was clear that they did not drive the research. Several other alien species that neither Ambra nor Waythrel had encountered directed the efforts. Imports from locations distant and strange, perhaps, brought in to perform highly specialized work. And behind them in every location, pulling every string and setting each course, were representatives of the Anti. They were housed in energy-gulping protective containers that shielded them from the matter surrounding them. But the seat of power was clear as the unknown aliens took instructions from these shadowed boxes and relayed the research protocols to the subordinate Dram techs.

The labs had obviously been in operation for hundreds of years, likely opening soon after the Great Calamity was reversed. And what had they been working toward for so long and with such dedication? That became obvious in the birthing wards—or more accurately, birthing factories.

The human slaves of the Dram, and the descendants of those slaves, were paying a terrible price for existence. They became the experimental animals on which the Anti applied their dark technology. How many had suffered and died at the hands of these sociopathic monsters, I didn't know. But I could begin to guess some of it when I saw the current products of the R&D.

Women had been converted into fetus-production units of a hellish nature. Each woman in the birthing rooms had become a demonic fusion of flesh and machine, a cybernetic organism invaded and controlled by hundreds of wires and tubes. Their midsection was distended beyond recognition, the womb augmented in size ten times what it should have been. The rest of the body had reversed, atrophied, shrunken to the point that it was clear that everything about these warped creatures was designed for one thing: producing fetuses.

And produce them they did. Artificially inseminated as well as directly implanted with embryos (it depended on the facility—the Anti were trying many approaches), these womb-sacks, human only in ancestry, gestated at many times the normal rate. We didn't have time to find out whether it was due to specialized nutrition, hormones, genetic changes, or other approaches we had not imagined, but it wasn't relevant in some broader sense. Suffice it to say, the Anti with their Dram pawns had found a way to take the initial stock of eggs stolen from Ambra and create an industrial production line for growing clones of her.

Within weeks, each birther would be harvested for offspring. Robotic implements would insert into the exaggerated vaginas and remove upwards of ten fetuses. These fetuses were hardly developed enough to survive outside the womb, but the machines plunged them into artificial wombs for a second round of growth. How they had optimized this—the timing, design, hormone and nutrient balancing—was as unclear as it was astounding. But it worked with horrible efficiency.

From our cloaked enclosure, Ambra discovered more shocking information from the minds of the techs. In the span of two months, they had crawling infants. Within a year, prepubescent girls. Within five years, fully functional adult clones that could speak and manipulate the fabric of space and time. An investment that required extraordinary patience, but at the end, they had succeeded in industrializing the production of the ultimate bioweapons.

The process was centered on the acceleration of human development. We examined several different sites and determined that as newer technology was created, they simply built more locations with cutting-edge methods but allowed the older plants to continue operating—likely until the product was so inferior that they shut them down.

Herds of little Ambra Dawns were penned together, a sea of orange hair covering the landscape like some strange crop. Here and there we could see humans shepherding them, putting them through trials, teaching them lessons that seemed odd to our eyes but functioned within the artificial program to produce these weaponized humans.

How much experimentation in human mental development had they performed? The standard human cattle that they kept at every site were constantly studied and probed. Rudimentary cultures were allowed to develop within their prisons so that they could be observed and mimicked in the raising of their prized breeds.

The rejected failures of their efforts were one of the saddest parts of this terrible story. Deformed, brain damaged, emotionally traumatized—they were the most plentiful population everywhere. But they didn't live long. Studied, tested, tortured—the Anti tried to find what they had done wrong. Once a given failed clone had given them what information they needed, it was killed and discarded.

The scope of the monstrous plan was in this way revealed to us. Now we knew where the False Dawns were coming from. And it was clear that the Anti were just getting warmed up. They were in it for a very long haul. I shuddered to think of the suffering on Dram and across the galaxy their continued efforts and progress would produce. One of those things in the desert had been enough. *An army?*

Soon Ambra zeroed in on the newest fields. These were clustered toward the northernmost position from Gred. She was able to identify them because the clone development in these locations was far superior. The minds of the False Dawns were more intact, more powerful, their signature and distortion of space-time extreme.

And there were thousands of them. Tens of thousands in the largest complex alone. It was at this site of greatest progress where events took a terrible turn and our time on Dram ended.

Chapter 40

Those who understand evil pardon it.

George Bernard Shaw

"I want to speak with one of them."

I could see that she was worked up. Gone was the usual distant tranquility I had come to associate with her knowledge of time through her visions. Her face was strained. Her hands clenched at her sides. I suppose that had we been under less stressful conditions, it would have been easier to understand and forgive her. But I couldn't stop myself from protesting.

"Ambra, no!" I said. "We got what we came for. We've pushed our luck far enough! Let's take what we know, get the hell out of here, and put together a plan of action when we have time! When we can summon resources. *Armies.*"

"He's right, Ambra," said Waythrel. "The risks outweigh the benefits in this."

But Ambra had a wild look in her eyes. "I said I want to speak to one of them. And I will, whatever any of you say."

"Look, sister," said Moore, "what you say we have a wee vote on this? When did this become a dictatorship?"

"When everything that has happened has been possible because of me!" she shouted. "I got us to every world. I protected us from the Dram. I uncovered this information. I'm only asking that we speak to *one* of the clones. *Just one.* I can handle that."

Williams stood in front of Ambra. "And you're losing your mind on this one, girl. In case you missed some important things, we've got two human purée waiting for us in orbit. You didn't see *that* coming. You didn't stop it. So, how about you back off from the almighty god thing and stop ordering us around."

"Ambra, please—" I began.

"Do you know what it must be like for these girls? Do you have any idea what it's like to grow up as a guinea pig in a hostile lab? Where they starve you, beat you, shock you, and cut on you? Turn you slowly, steadily into a monster, a dark, twisted form of what you should have been? Where your worth is found only in their approvals?" She waited as if we would answer. "Well, *I* do!"

Waythrel tried to intervene. "Ambra, whatever pain these clones have endured cannot be—"

"Look at them!" Ambra shouted, gesturing in front of our bubble at the sea of orange hair beneath us. "Thousands of them! At least I had a few years of love from my parents. I grew at some human pace. These things—their mothers are nightmares. They have no fathers. They have no normal development. You want proof of hell? You don't have to look any further."

I saw tears dripping down the sides of her cheeks. I walked up and put my hand on her shoulder. "Okay, Ambra. I'll come with you."

"Ah, shit," cursed Moore, turning away in frustration.

"Look!" I shouted. "Ambra can send the rest of you away, back through the Orb or something. You don't have to be involved."

"For myself," said Waythrel, "I am not concerned. My primary fear is for the Daughter. To engage these highly developed clones could risk much. You don't know their powers."

"I easily defeated the one in the desert, Waythrel," said Ambra. "I will be careful. I will choose one and bring it inside the enclosure, sealed away, unseen by the others. If we are attacked, I will kill it."

"Why don't we just kill it now?" said Moore. "You remember what that thing did in the Sahara, right?"

Ambra looked at Moore but touched my cheek with her palm. "I remember. But I didn't know about this. I hadn't *seen* this. I hated them before—the very idea of them, even. Now…now I feel pity."

"And what do you think you will accomplish speaking with one of them?" asked Waythrel.

"I don't know, but I need to look," she said. "I need to look and find out if there is any hope."

"Hope for what?" asked Moore with exasperation.

"That they can be saved. That there is something inside them that can be saved."

Chapter 41

Everything you do reverberates throughout a thousand destinies.

Nikos Kazantzakis

In the end, everyone signed on to the crazy idea. Signed their death warrants. All because deep down, we were all somehow committed to Ambra, and this was something that she had to do. I saw it first, but the others came to accept it. Foolish or not, it was impossible to stop her. We were either with her, or we would abandon her to this fate.

Ambra floated the invisible space-time bubble over the enormous compound, past the birthing warehouses, the labs, the pens of hundreds and hundreds of tiny Ambra Dawns. For me, it was hardest to see the child clones. I didn't know when in the process of their brainwashing they would be turned into the creatures that would seek to kill us, to kill Ambra, to destroy the planet of their origins. But seeing the small ones, it was almost as if I could detect remaining innocence in their eyes. Children's eyes. And this more than anything gave me empathy to the pain Ambra felt. I could feel deeply why she wanted to save them even if I believed the cause hopeless.

We slowed around the demented "schools" where the older children were instructed. Preteens, early teens—the age when the tumor and its powers developed and flourished. All had been modified surgically. All sported the invasive machine technology embedded in their bodies. All had lost some aspect of their humanity. Most had probably already lost their free will.

They never slept. Instead, unconscious, they would be attached to machines that sent electrochemical signals through their brains. What it accomplished we didn't have the time to determine, but Waythrel guessed that it was an accelerated learning and maturation program. Part of the long research program that had culminated in the ability to produce human clones like so many items on an assembly line, ready to be shipped into battle.

When awake, they were subjected to tests. Attached to machines or out in open fields, their powers over space-time were examined, challenged, and augmented ruthlessly by Dram and human trainers. Some of the older clones served as advanced teachers as well. The Anti had learned to preserve extensive features of human culture, hierarchy, and social bonding even in such a dysfunctional form. They had perfected the madness and addiction of cult attachment.

Ambra found a smaller group of younger teens who were moving from one of the sleeping chambers to a practice field. One of the girls was several steps behind the others.

"She will do," said Ambra, the enclosure swooping down beside the clone. "They likely won't miss her for a few minutes."

The girl stumbled, bumping into an invisible wall. Disoriented, she tried to walk forward but could not. I realized that Ambra had enveloped the clone in the bubble.

"Don't panic," said Ambra. "They can't see her, and she can't reach us. But she can see us."

The clone turned around.

"Ah, shit, here we go," muttered Moore, charging up his ion-slingers. Williams followed in short order.

Ambra walked up to the clone and spoke. "What is your name?"

The girl—no more than twelve or thirteen—looked confused and frightened, but determined. "A4552, Teacher."

"You are blocking your mind from me," said Ambra.

"Yes, Teacher. Lesson 22. Never lower defenses in the field."

"I want you to disregard Lesson 22 right now, please."

The clone appeared anxious. "That is illegal. Is this a new test?"

"Yes," said Ambra. "I want you to share your mind with me."

"I live to kill the Originator," the clone nearly chanted. "I do not break the laws."

"You will not share with me?" asked Ambra.

"I will not break the laws." There was a short silence. "Do I pass this test, Teacher?" The clone's breathing had increased dramatically. It was terrified.

"Sit down," said Ambra. The clone sat, and Ambra followed suit. "If you will not open your mind, I will have to enter it myself."

"I will defend."

"Yes, I thought you would."

The clone screamed. She grabbed her head as her eyes opened maniacally.

Ambra appeared tense. Her eyes were closed, her mouth set as a thin line. The clone began to moan, rocking back and forth, holding her head, the pitch of her voice rising and falling like some tortured animal.

The sounds were terrible to hear. I looked at Moore and Williams. Both shook their heads. The eyestalks of Waythrel danced around, but the alien did not intervene.

"No! Liar!" cried the False Dawn. "It's not *true! Stop!*" Blood began to trickle from the inserted tubes in her skull. "*Liar!*"

"Ambra, you're killing it!" I whispered harshly.

Ambra stiffened, and simultaneously the clone's eyes opened. It spoke in a demonic voice that seemed to project like some loudspeaker. "The Originator. She is here. She is here. Come. Kill. She is here!"

Ambra's face was strained. The space around us began to undulate. The bubble seemed to lose some kind of integrity as waves propagated outward from the clone.

"She's losing control of the thing!" yelled Williams. She stepped forward and sighted the clone in her targeting system, raising her arms to fire.

And then she was torn apart. Blood sprayed across my face, and tissue exploded in all directions. Body parts were slung against the walls of the enclosure.

"*No!*" Ambra shouted. "Nitin! Waythrel! They're programmed! Automatic!" her breathing was labored. "I can't stop it! It will reach them."

And then I grasped my temples. The sound of its voice exploded in my mind.

She is here. She is here. She is here. She is here.

I managed to look around. Moore was kneeling, his hands to his head. Waythrel's eyestalks were darting around wildly and the alien swayed as if it might topple over.

She is here. She is here. She is here. She is here.

Ambra cried again and stood up, a terrible strain in her features. "*No!*"

The clone arched its back, the tubes exploding out of its skull along with blood and bone. A red paint seemed to splash against the invisible barrier behind it and drip slowly downward. The False Dawn swayed backward, its eyes rolling up in its head.

The voice in my mind stopped. The clone fell over and didn't move. I slowly got to my feet, dizzy, unsteady, and stepped beside Ambra. The enclosure smelled of blood. A metallic taste coated my mouth.

I sensed movement in my peripheral vision. A fog of orange seemed to be rising around us, becoming denser, congealing and choking out the other shapes and colors around us. I placed my hand on Ambra's shoulder.

"Are you okay?" I asked.

"Oh, Nitin." Her desperate eyes looked outside the enclosure. I followed her gaze and focused. A swarming herd of shapes converged on our position.

421

Red hair. Green eyes. Thousands of clones. And they knew where we were. They saw us now.

Waythrel spoke. "The dead clone triggered them. They know *you* are here, Ambra! They are coming for you. Uncloak us! Harden the enclosure, now!"

Ambra shook her head. "What have I done?"

Chapter 42

By a route obscure and lonely,
Haunted by ill angels only,
Where an Eidolon, named NIGHT,
On a black throne reigns upright,
I have reached these lands but newly
From an ultimate dim Thule—
From a wild weird clime that lieth, sublime,
Out of SPACE—out of TIME.

Edgar Allen Poe

The entire compound turned on us. I don't know how many there were. Likely thousands in all. Certainly hundreds of the power Ambra had fought in the desert and just killed in front of us. I know that she couldn't have repelled them on her own. There were just too many. She must have tapped into the power of the Orb, which, after everything, brings this part of the story to a most ironic conclusion.

"Kill as many as you can!" Ambra cried.

The contrast to the empathic hurt she had felt only hours before couldn't have been greater. But we didn't need convincing. We'd seen that thing rip our warrant officer to shreds in front of us. Ambra had seen its mind, felt its thoughts and feelings. That she had now jettisoned all concern for their well-being said a lot.

"I don't know what we can do!" I shouted. "We're only two!"

We began firing. At first we created considerable carnage. The clones had no battle armor. They were standing in front of us like ducks on a pond. With our missiles and ion slingers, we likely downed a hundred or more in half a minute.

No doubt Ambra was a big part of that success story. She had semipermeabilized the enclosure. Our little bubble allowed our weapons to escape but still presented a formidable shield for us inside. Even though the clones didn't raise any weapons, this still came in handy when the Dram military showed up and began firing on us, which happened about a minute into this insanity.

Soon piles of slaughtered clones encircled us. But the real battle took place in a realm that only Ambra could access. Waythrel sat with her in the center of the bubble clasping her hands, deep in that Reader trance like the one we had seen around Gyl. But this was far worse. I could see in Ambra's face the tension, the fatigue as her energies were quickly depleted. I didn't know how long we could hold out.

There were massive disturbances around us. The ground itself heaved and buckled, space contorted, and time and again our enclosure suffered assault that seemed to bend the air around us and then pop back. Meanwhile, as our weapons became increasingly useless—the missiles now spent, the ion rays deflected by the clones who had zeroed in on our efforts—even greater chaos erupted outside. In a large-scale replay of the death of Williams, the clones were being shredded. It was literally a meat grinder out there, and the only reason I didn't turn away from the visceral horror of it was that I was caught like a deer in the headlights. I was stunned by the sheer fleshly decimation progressing around us. Only the shield of the enclosure Ambra continued to maintain kept us from drowning in blood.

I began to become seasick, as much from the time distortion as the physical carnage. Back and forth the pace of events seemed to rock—slow, fast, skipping moments, backtracking to create repeated experiences of déjà vu. Holes opened and closed around us, tunnels to nowhere and from nothing. The veins bulged on Ambra's brow, and the alien had changed to a deep shade of purple. This was going to kill them.

"Ambra, just punch a hole in all this and get us up and out!" I shouted.

I'm trying, Nitin. They have cast nets around us, came a voice pounding my consciousness.

Moore looked at me grimly. "We're not going to make it out of this one, Capt. Look! These roaches are just pouring out of the woodwork."

He was right. More and more clones approached. They ignored the horrific fates of the mangled bodies surrounding us. They were fanatical, devoted completely to destroying us. If Ambra didn't get through whatever they were doing soon, we were dead.

A bright light flashed in my eyes and I fell backward, stumbling to my knees. *Flash bomb?* I could see; it wasn't a device. Instead, standing behind Waythrel was an apparition from my nightmares.

It was the little demon girl from the cornfields. Somehow, in the midst of all these identical clones, I recognized her. Something about her movements, the sparkle in her eye, and the slight twitch at the corners of her mouth when she noticed I was staring at her.

"*You?*" I gasped. But Ambra's cry interrupted me. I looked away from the devil girl and saw that Ambra was flat on her back, a stunned expression on her face.

The young clone grabbed Waythrel's upper arm, and the alien cried out and collapsed.

Ambra sat up and screamed. "Stop! Nitin, help me! I can't move! Please, stop her!"

The thing smiled. It looked right at me knowingly and winked. *It winked at me!* Another flash blinded me temporarily. When I looked back, there was nothing. The child was gone. Waythrel was gone. There was only empty space where they had been a second ago.

Ambra sprang forward with a cry toward where they had been. She landed on her knees grasping only air, tears on her face, a wild, mad look burning in her eyes.

"*Waythrel!*"

The agony of her scream cut deep inside me, and I nearly stumbled from the impact of it. But I couldn't focus on her pain. The disappearance of Waythrel had done what ten thousand attacking clones could not: broken her power and focus. The bubble around us collapsed.

Into the breach, a False Dawn clone flew like some possessed witch. Red hair billowing behind it, arms upraised like claws and a homicidal death mask on its face. Ambra didn't respond. She didn't move. She sat there holding herself, her empty arms that had missed grabbing Waythrel wrapped around her chest as she rocked.

I launched my suit forward, but I knew that I could not make the distance in time.

The impact was both metallic and fleshy. Moore's suit blasted upward, his shoulder set as it smashed into the stomach of the clone. I could hear the creature's spine snap as its body was bent from the impact, and the two of them rocketed high into the air.

"Moore!" I screamed, watching as a red cloud of clones darted upward in pursuit.

Moore's actions shocked Ambra out of her state. She stood up quickly, the remaining clones once again boxed out by a wall. Looking into the air, however, she saw what I did. It was too late to save Moore. The clones had already ripped him apart.

"Ambra—"

She held up her hand to silence me. I could sense her concentration. She closed her eyes. Outside the clones redoubled their assaults on the enclosure. But their progress was reversed. The inroads before were turned around.

I began to see them pushed back, struggling against unseen forces. I felt as if I were hallucinating. Many began to age horribly, their skin drying and peeling off their bones, the bodies that seconds ago were attacking us bursting into a cloud of dust. Crawling around in the dust were tens, then hundreds of infants. The structures outside began to sway. The warehouses and laboratories rippled around me. Newly arriving Dram military craft disassembled and rained fragments onto the sands.

"They're still here," said Ambra.

"Who?" I said, my eyes wide at the impossible things I was seeing.

"Waythrel is in the system! We have to hurry. They're heading to the Orb!"

Ambra stared upward and grasped my hand harshly. Two things happened. We blasted off the ground in our enclosure, the surface of Dram quickly receding. Below, it was as if a nuclear weapon had gone off. The entire clone field was flattened, circular ripples extending outward and leveling everything in their path. All the clones, the buildings, perhaps large regions of Gred itself were annihilated in the destruction.

But I didn't watch very long. I turned my eyes upward as we ascended toward the heavens.

And so a doomed pursuit began.

Chapter 43

Madness rides the star-wind...claws and teeth sharpened on centuries of corpses...dripping death astride a bacchanale of bats from nigh-black ruins of buried temples of Belial.

H.P. Lovecraft

W e rocketed upward through the Dram atmosphere. I don't know whether the remaining hordes of clones tried to follow and were held back or were so incapacitated by Ambra's wild destruction that they couldn't. Whichever, I did not see anyone following. All I knew was that I was traveling faster than I had ever experienced with a mad goddess, her eyes flaming green, shockwaves exploding outward from the atmosphere around us as we blasted into space like some meteor in reverse.

She had let go of my hand and placed her own near head level against the enclosure walls. The speed made me want to hold on as well, although the need was illusory. As before, everything within the bubble she created remained stable and unperturbed, sealed off from the chaos around us. In a few short seconds, we were thrust into the blackness of space, a darkness punctuated only by the Dram world receding behind us, its two moons, the red giant star of their system, and straight ahead of us—growing closer at a shocking rate—the incandescent shape of the Orb.

But I had never seen the Orb like this. Even when Ambra had summoned such breathtaking power from them in the battles we had fought, what I saw now was a supernova to a nova. The local star was eclipsed in brightness. And inside the Orb was a churning chromatic cyclone that seemed more hostile than transcendent. For the first time, I began to truly fear the thing.

Ambra focused only ahead in its direction, speaking nothing, her entire body tense like a rod. Following her gaze, I was amazed to see another pair of bodies between us and the flaming sphere, the distance slowly closing. It was not hard to guess that it was the False Dawn and Waythrel. They were heading straight for the Orb as well, and something told me that somehow, impossible as it should have seemed, the creature that had kidnapped Ambra's dearest friend had the power to use the portal as well.

We continued to gain on them, but it was clear that it was a hopeless chase. They would reach it before we could. If the clone could activate the Orb, it could transport to whatever place and whatever time it desired. We would lose Waythrel.

No! We won't lose them! The thoughts from Ambra exploded into my mind. *We will follow them through any pathway to any place or time!*

You can do this?

Watch me!

The Orb storm—I had no other phrase for it—seemed only to intensify, as if responding to her words. The bright light was now also offset with black clouds, vortexes, tunnels, and membranes that seemed to enter and leave our space as portions of a higher dimensional whole. The light almost felt like thunder—so bright it was an assault on the senses. The darkness pulled at something deep within me, something primal, so that every irrational fear that I had ever felt came alive. I was stunned, overwhelmed by the cataclysm brewing within the cauldron before us. My feet felt rooted, unable to move as I stared dumbly ahead. Had I needed to act quickly to save our lives, I don't know what I could have done.

The pair in front of us vanished into the Orb. We were only seconds from entering the maelstrom ourselves.

I still see you, clone. You can't get away!

She was not even speaking to me, yet I heard those words in my mind. She was screaming to the universe, or perhaps toward the shapes that we were pursuing. My mind just happened to be in the blast radius. Ambra was determined to follow that thing to hell and back if necessary.

I remembered the horrible trips through the Orbs that I had experienced. All of them sickening, several reaching levels of pain I had never known. Now Ambra was about to enter the thing when both she and the Orb were in a state of such turmoil that space itself seemed to be seething. She was going to chase through those labyrinths of space-time another being that appeared adroit as well. This would be no prepared journey, no stroll to the edges of the galaxy. This would be a wild chase on a rocket through the fire. I closed my eyes and prepared for the worst.

But it was Ambra who screamed.

I opened my eyes and couldn't believe what I was seeing. Before me, the

Orb had reached some sort of mad climax, the frothing currents of space and time, light and darkness, wonder and fear, like some enormous maw opening to swallow us. But that epic background to my vision meant nothing.

Arms outstretched, her face contorted in rage and pain, Ambra rose before me. She seemed increasingly paralyzed, flattened against an invisible slab, chained to it and unable to move even to turn her head. She thrashed back and forth, staring wild-eyed into the devouring mouth before us.

She screamed again. Her arms moved slightly, her back arching, and the surface of the Orb rippled before her like the sea underneath a squall. Lightning erupted from the dark clouds, rays of light splintered the space around us until I could not keep my eyes open except in a squint. Blood began to leak from her nose, and her body convulsed.

"Ambra, no!" *You're killing yourself!*

I tried to grab her legs, but the second I touched them, an electric charge threw me across the enclosure. My hands burned and went completely numb. My vision blurred, and I had to strain to focus. I tried to stand—my legs no longer functioned. I could not move. Crumpled and helpless on the transparent floor of the enclosure, I looked on this terrible sight in growing horror like some broken and castaway trinket.

Ambra continued to rise like some terrible statue, her form now completely frozen. There was nothing between her and the Orb. The bubble was perfectly transparent, and in this numbness consuming me, it began to feel as if it were nothing more than an illusion. Reality had become the Orb alone, that Titan raging in anger, and it had grasped my beloved and ripped her from me.

Still she rose, now fifty feet above me, still paralyzed, still unmoving. There was no sign of the False Dawn or Waythrel. By now I had to assume they were long gone, and I guessed that Ambra did as well. I could see the muscles across her body straining, twitching, trying to find some way out of this invisible prison. All her efforts failed to move even a finger.

And then the ascension stopped. For minutes that passed like hours, she floated there alone, a fleshly form dangled in the midst of space before the door to heaven or hell, I didn't know. I tried several more times to move, but it was fruitless. Something had damaged me badly, and I would not be able to reach out to my lover. I was helpless to intervene, if there were anything I could have done anyway. Looking on this madness, I knew that I was a fool for even trying, arrogant for thinking that a lowly soldier could involve himself in such affairs. This was an arena for gods.

It was at this moment of resignation and despair that I began to hallucinate. The electrical discharge that had wrecked my nervous system in my extremities must have damaged my mind as well. This is the only explanation I can find for what I next witnessed, but you can judge my memory as you will.

As I gazed through tears toward my beloved, shapes began to form in the churning broth of the Orb. Indistinct at first, small spheres that could be viewed as mini-cyclones in the greater chaos, they took structure. Definition.

Recognizable patterns. Chills swept through me. The Orb surface was forming *faces*.

A few at first, large, the size of cities. Then thousands. *Millions*. Uncountable numbers of faces that bubbled in and out of the broth like some witch's horrible brew. Many of the faces were recognizably human. Most were not.

And then the faces began to chant.

It was like no music I have ever heard or experienced since. I'm not sure that *music* is the right word to describe it, but I have no other. More complex than the greatest symphony, as pure and clear as a temple chant, currents and sounds that were distinctly human were wrapped and mixed with ten thousand that could only have come from the orthogonal mentalities of the truly alien.

The chorus swelled. The faces continued to materialize, the harmonies increase, the sound seeming to fill the very emptiness of space itself. The Orb ceased to churn, the surface of the hypersphere calmed like a placid lake. Only the disembodied faces moved, chanting, creating a music that seemed to have more substance than the sparse matter of the universe itself.

It was beautiful. And it was terrible. It was so much beyond what I could grasp and appreciate, what I could internalize without drowning in it. Being consumed by it, I began to withdraw. A survival instinct perhaps. My paralyzed body began to shut down, and I felt myself slipping away. The edges of my vision darkened, blurred, and I could not focus. Like a drowning shipwreck victim, I flailed madly to tread water and breathe. Frantically I thrashed to stay awake.

As my consciousness bobbed above the chanting currents for a moment, the visions entered the truly bizarre. Now there were two Ambras. Still, my beloved hung as a hazy outline before me. But before her, larger, spanning the size of continents, a form bubbled out from the space-time surface of the Orb. Tendrils of light and cloud clung to it and then fell back into the infinite sphere.

It was Ambra, but not Ambra as I would ever wish to see her. Mirroring the paralyzed position of the Daughter, this titanic apparition floated toward her with arms outstretched to the side, frozen in place and unmoving. But not whole. The hands were mutilated, the flesh ripped and jagged. Worms or tubes or cables or something crawled into the skin of its hands and feet. Blood flowed outward and seemed to stain the fabric of space itself.

But the horror had only begun. The body materializing before us was further desecrated. The skull was cut open, removed, the brain spilling out in layers across a black slime. A giant tumor, some mountainous mimic of my dear Ambra's neural growth, lay like an obscene egg in its own depression of the reflective darkness. Living cables of dark material slithered into those mental tissues and merged with them, the entire form becoming some nightmarish mixture of flesh and machine.

And for a third and last time, Ambra screamed.

Somehow she broke through the forces holding her. Her mouth opened, and a cry of such devastating pain ripped through the cosmos that I was convinced that the geometry of space-time would be shattered and unrecoverable. Her cry did not die but wailed into the void ceaselessly, the waves of sound beating through me, the sense of her pain and torture unbearable.

And then she fell.

A second electric shock coursed through my flesh. And then, I could move. I could see clearly. I leaped forward, my suit granting me a speed and power that made it just possible for me to catch her as she entered the enclosure. Ambra landed roughly in my arms.

The lights from the Orb were gone, and it had turned a deep black. There were no faces, no chanting, no chorus of the gods. The monstrous apparition of Ambra was nowhere to be seen. There was a stillness and powerful silence that felt thick like fog.

And stars. Stars all around, softly shining through the transparency of our journey's bubble.

I sensed the softness of her flesh even through the suit and longed to hold her without this artificial barrier between us. Her eyes were closed. Red hair cascaded down my arms. Her porcelain skin nearly glowed against the black of her robe and the darkness of space.

I raised her closer to my face and bent my neck, bringing my lips to hers. I kissed her but pulled my head back sharply, listening.

She wasn't breathing.

Part III

Parasitism is the birth pang of symbiosis.

The Book of Xix

Chapter 44

The other gods! The gods of the outer hells that guard the feeble gods of earth!...Look away...Go back...Do not see! Do not see! The vengeance of the infinite abysses... That cursed, that damnable pit...Merciful gods of earth, I am falling into the sky!

H.P. Lovecraft

F*alling.*

Holding Ambra, falling to my knees. Struggling to remain conscious. Swimming through images, voices.

Songs.

Endless echoing chants of limitless gods forming shapes and patterns and realities before me.

The dark sphere approached, the surface enveloping us, the universe behind disappearing. Still I held her, tightly, refusing to give in to the call for sleep.

Peaceful sleep. To rest, finally. For this terrible and long struggle to end. The voices spoke of tranquility. I only had to close my eyes, to stop resisting, to trust them to bring us out of danger and into safety.

They knew my name. They knew my heart. And I knew them. Faces of family and friends and enemies. My parents. My slain comrades-in-arms. Fox and her starry-eyed faith. Kim and his childlike energies and enthusiasm. Moore with his rough and loyal mouth. Williams and her blunt analysis. Marshall and his abstracted duty.

Waythrel. The one we chased. She too was here. Beside her another Xix. Waythrel nodded toward it. "You will meet soon."

And then Ambra's face. She spoke to me. I felt her arms around me. "I hold you now as you hold me. Let go, Nitin. It will be easier this time. Don't be afraid. Just let go."

The space before me was spinning, the light labyrinth glowing and beginning to burn brightly. A million passageways through space and time and song. I didn't want to go down those painful roads again. I feared them.

"A last trip. This time, there will be no pain."

My own voice.

It spoke to me from outside of me. My madness and hallucination were complete. Dreaming or imagining, I didn't know. Or were they different? Which was waking and which was dreaming? In this impossible universe, what was truly real? How could such limited forms of flesh discern?

It was too much. I felt myself falling. I placed Ambra down on the surface as a glowing vortex built around us. I lay down next to her as the bubble dropped, plunged down into the bottomless, rotating well of light. I closed my eyes.

We fell.

Chapter 45

I measured the skies, now the shadows I measure.
Skybound was the mind, earthbound the body rests.

Johannes Kepler, self-authored epitaph

I awoke to the sound and scratching of blowing sand.

A fierce heat beat down on me as I tried to open my eyes. Stuck together, the lids refused to part. I reached up and tried to clean them but only managed to spray sand into my face and mouth. I coughed and spit it out, using the spittle to lubricate my eyes. The sand and spit made a mud, and it was rough to rub it across my skin, but it worked.

I cracked the lids open and squinted at the blinding sunlight. Two seas, orange and blue, faced off below and above me. I was disoriented but also comforted in some strange way by something familiar. After a few seconds, I understood. I was back on New Earth.

Ambra!

I sat up and looked around me frantically. Her body was beside mine, face up, eyes closed in the sand. I crawled to her quickly and placed my face over her mouth. *There was no breath!* I grabbed her wrist but could not find a pulse. I forced myself not to panic, to think, to act professionally. My emotions would only doom her, if she was not already.

I powered up my suit, relieved that it was fully charged. I engaged the medapp and diagnostics unit on the side of the suit, and needles and probes extended into her arm, taking samples. The AI reported promptly.

"Asystole diagnosed without discernible trauma. No serious internal injuries, body temperature normal."

No obvious harm! But no heartbeat. No respiration! Normal temperature— then it could not have happened very long ago! There was still a chance!

"Immediate CPR recommended with intravenous vasopressor."

It had been over a year since I had refreshed my CPR training, but there was no choice.

"What's an intravenous vasopressor?"

"Medkit epinephrine syringe is provided to all MECHcore battle units."

Adrenaline! I reached around and detached the medkit, pressing the keypad to open the box. There was a large syringe labeled Epinephrine. I grabbed it, removed the safety cap, and plunged the end into her arm, keeping it there for about ten seconds for the solution to drain.

I tossed it to the side and rose over her on my knees, the sand scraping beneath the metal of my suit. Sweat began to bead over my eyebrows, and I had to wipe my hand over them just to see. I placed my hands above her sternum as I remembered and began the rhythmic compressions, squeezing her heart, forcing blood through her body. Life liquid of cells and oxygen and nutrients and now adrenaline.

I pressed hard, as I was taught, and after six, I heard the first rib break. *No!* I couldn't let it distract me! It happened, I remembered from the training. I tried not to think about breaking her bones.

I continued through fifteen, twenty, and then stopped at thirty. I put my palm on her forehead and gently tilted her head back. Then I lifted her chin forward with my other hand to open the airway. I listened. *Still no breath!* I pinched the nostrils shut and covered her mouth with mine. The contrast to our loving embraces was an offense. A crime so horrible and clinical and desperate. But I made a seal and began breathing into Ambra's lungs.

Back to the chest. Fifteen more compressions, another crack occurring in the middle. *Dear God!* Another breath. Salt water flowed down my face, stinging my eyes. It was almost impossible to keep my vision clear.

"Please, Ambra! Please!" My words were hissed out through the compressions of her chest. Again and again and again I pressed. I didn't know how long I could keep this up in the heat.

In the middle of the fourth cycle, Ambra gasped for air.

"Ambra!" I screamed at her, but she didn't respond. But she was breathing! Her chest shuddered and fell in haphazard movements.

I attached the diagnostic device, and the AI spoke in monotone. "Ventricular fibrillation detected. Recommend defibrillation with current unit. Confirm, please."

"Confirmed!"

"Please clear contact with patient."

I pulled back, and the device hummed to a charge and sent current through

Ambra's sputtering heart. The muscles around the chest wall tightened and striated. Then they relaxed.

"Normal cardiac rhythm established."

I didn't hear anything else it said as the AI rolled out numbers that were much more useful for a doctor to hear. I bent down and felt a regular breath from her lips. Her chest rose and fell. *My Ambra was alive!*

"Recommend immediate evacuation to medical facilities."

For the first time in this insanity, I looked around the desert. It was familiar. A sand plane of enormous length ran in all directions, decorated in the distance by a tower that seemed to rise into the heavens. The Sahara. *The Temple.* How we had gotten here, I didn't know. But I knew we were within communications range.

I stood up and engaged the transmitter on full power and broadcast on all emergency frequencies. "MAYDAY, MAYDAY, MAYDAY. This is Nitin Ratava, Captain of the Special Temple Guardians unit. I am outside the Temple City within sight of the antenna. Ambra Dawn is seriously injured. Repeat, Ambra Dawn is with me, and she needs immediate medical evac. Please respond."

My COM shot back only static. I tried to boost the signal and ramped all the power to communications. "MAYDAY, MAYDAY, MAYDAY. This is Captain Nitin Ratava—"

"Captain Ratava, roger your transmission. We are locating your position. Please confirm again your message."

"I have Ambra Dawn with me. She is critically wounded."

There was a sharp crackle in the static and then a different voice. "Captain, this is Major Mizoguchi linking in. Where is the rest of your party?"

"Dead, sir." Just saying this was a gut punch. "They're all dead. Correction: Waythrel of the Xix was kidnapped. Whereabouts, unknown. Status, unknown."

There was a short pause on the COM before Mizoguchi continued. "And the goals of your mission?"

"A success, sir, but I don't give a damn right now! Ambra's hurt!"

"We have medical on route to your position and have a high resolution visual on you."

"Tell them to burn through their thrusters," I said, seeing a thin line of blood trickle from the corner of her mouth. "I don't know how long she has."

Chapter 46

A man is a god in ruins.

—Emerson's "Nature"

I stayed beside her on the wild flight back to the Temple City. After I had told them all I knew, the medical crew asked me to move to another part of the ship, but I refused. They saw my eyes. I stayed out of their way, and they seemed to ignore my presence.

From their conversation, I gathered that her condition was serious but stable. I had indeed broken ribs in my efforts to revive her, even puncturing a lung in the process. But her vital signs were strong, and they believed that with proper Xixian care back in the city, she would recover quickly.

It was a tremendous relief to hear, and for the first time in many days, I relaxed and let others take on the burden of crisis. I was exhausted both in mind and body. So much had happened, so many losses, so many impossible revelations and events—my mind was still in shock. I leaned back against the walls of the hovercraft and closed my eyes.

The opening of the bay doors startled me awake. They took Ambra quickly off the ship and moved her to the medical unit. I stayed out of their way and decided against causing any more interference. She was stable. She was going to be okay. With that knowledge, I could let them do their jobs.

Mizoguchi, Mazandarani, and several others awaited me as I exited the craft. I sighed, much too tired to want to deal with anyone right now. But I knew they wanted answers. It was only right that I try to provide them.

I stopped in my tracks. A Xix stood with the others, its eyestalks a tower above the humans. I stared at its black and phosphorescent colors shimmering through the color spectrum in curved lines across its body. I had seen it before. In the last dream.

"Synphel," I whispered.

The others looked from me to the Xix in surprise. The Xix walked forward and stood in front of me.

"How do you know my name?" it asked me.

"Waythrel told me."

"Waythrel spoke to you of our mating groups?"

Mating groups? "No." *How do I explain this?* I put my hand to my forehead. I was so tired. "Until I saw you, I would have said Waythrel never spoke of anything like…mating groups. Or your name. But once I saw you, I recognized you from…an experience I had before I transitioned here."

"What was this experience?"

"I don't know. Another strange dream. I always get dreams when I go through those damn Orbs. I heard voices. So many of them. So strange. At the end of it, Waythrel spoke to me. *You* were standing next to Waythrel. Waythrel said that I would meet you soon." I looked over the alien and shook my head. "And here you are."

By this point Mizoguchi and Mazandarani had stepped forward, listening in to the conversation. Synphel bowed to me.

"I am pleased to make your acquaintance, Captain Ratava. You clearly have been blessed with profound experiences in your travels."

"Or cursed."

"Yes, such powerful events are hard to distinguish and are often both." The alien's many eyes looked me up and down. "I recognize that you are weary, but Waythrel is important to me. Please tell me all you know about what happened."

"You are Waythrel's mate?"

"One of them."

"So, you have marriages, divorces? Or multiple spouses?"

"Closer to the latter, Captain. We tend to keep our social behavior to ourselves, but because you are so intimately involved in our stories, I will explain something few humans have heard." The Xix let that sink in. It did, but I had no idea what to do with it. "You may have noticed that we do not use gendered terms when speaking about ourselves."

I nodded. "Yes. It's a strange hiccup in your translators."

"Not a hiccup, Captain. It is intentional, because to do so would distort our natures. Humans have a bisexual genetic and phenotypic biological mating structure: male and female. Of course, there are spectrums of behaviors and physiology associated with this basic average sexuality, as in any biological system, but that is the general structure of your reproductive and culture norms. We of the Xix do not possess two genders."

"You are asexual?" I offered, wondering if they budded like yeast or impregnated themselves. I needed to lie down.

"No. We have six genders."

"*Six?*" I *really* didn't know what to do with that. Even Mizoguchi and Mazandarani looked surprised. This obviously was rare information.

"Yes, with the associated physiological and genetic differences. You have male and female, each with very different bodies and character. Sexual organs. Biochemistry. We have six, and a successful reproductive mating event can only occur when all six copulate simultaneously. Of course, sexual partnership can occur in binary, ternary, and other combinations for the pleasure and companionship of the mating group members, but reproduction requires all six."

Now my head was swimming. "I'm not sure I want to learn much more."

"I will spare you the details. But Waythrel and I were different genders in one such group. In fact, we were a very closely associated pair in the combined sexual event, and somewhat similarly to your mostly monogamous interactions, had lived extended portions of our lives in each other's presence."

"Married?"

"Not precisely, but the term will do. Does this help you understand why I care so much to learn what befell?"

I nodded, thinking of Ambra. "It does. Thank you. Let's go to the hospital, and I will tell you what I can on the way."

The Xix bowed again and stepped to the side. I began to walk toward the entrance of the medical wing.

Suddenly Mazandarani was in front of me. I nearly crashed into him. My temper flared. "Excuse me, yes?"

"You are a fortunate man," he said, remaining where he was. "The only one of your team to survive the mission. It's as if certain fates are shaping your destiny." There was a fire in his eyes.

I couldn't believe I had to deal with this. "Sepehr, *not now*. Just get out of my way and let me go see Ambra."

"Yes. Your only failure was that she lived. Do you go to finish the job?"

I weighed my options in an instant. Possible statements or silences as a response to this. After a half second of consideration, I threw all pretense of maturity to the wayside and hit him.

I smashed my fist across his jaw, and the Iranian sprawled upon the floor. There was a collective intake of breath from bystanders around me, followed by a natural parting of the waters as people cleared out from around me. But Mazandarani wasn't the fighting type. He just held his face and the trickling blood coming from his mouth while scowling at me.

So then I did more than hit him. My suit was still activated. I reached down, and with the full power of the hydraulics, grasped him by the robes and lifted him into the air. His feet dangled inches off the ground, a shocked but unbowed expression on his face.

"Captain Ratava!" came the imperial voice of Major Mizoguchi. "Put down the counselor now!"

But I was in a state. Blame fatigue, loss, mental trauma, or the ugly insinuations of Mazandarani, but I had simply had enough.

He spoke through clenched teeth. "And did they pay you to kill me, too?"

I glared at him. "They wouldn't have to."

I felt a steady but very firm grip on my shoulder. The towering form of Synphel loomed over me like a shadow. "Captain, there is nothing that would pain Ambra more than for us to hurt one another."

And like that, my will for violence was gone. I put Mazandarani down, perhaps somewhat roughly, but the alien had rebooted my emotions. It had known exactly what to say.

Mazandarani straightened his robes and looked at Synphel with some semblance of shame. I simply turned on my heel and strode out of the docking area without a word or a second glance toward anyone.

Chapter 47

No one is as capable of gratitude as one who has emerged from the kingdom of night.

Eli Wiesel

"Y ou saved my life, Nitin."

She looked beautiful. Hair in disarray, eyes bloodshot with dark circles like a raccoon—it didn't matter. It's hard to describe the overwhelming feeling of joy and wonder that ran through me to see her open her eyes and smile. Speak. Gesture with her hands in that elegant way she had. *My Ambra is alive! And I love her!*

"I guess that's fifty to one, now. I'm still deep in the red." I tried to maintain a soldier's composure. It was difficult. "I'm sorry about the ribs."

"They'll heal, love," she said, smiling again.

I sat in a chair holding her hand, gazing upon her face like the first time I had seen it as a child in school. Synphel was present. Mazandarani stood opposite me on the other side of Ambra's hospital bed. After our altercation a few days ago, the two of us did our best to avoid each other.

"Thank you for speaking with Synphel, Nitin. I have shared with her now. All the details that we have are passed on to the Xix. They will do what they can, but there is little hope to find Waythrel now. The clone could have gone to any place at any time through the Orb."

"And the bodies of Fox and Kim? They were not in the desert?"

"No," said Mazandarani. "A thorough search turned up nothing."

Ambra spoke. "It's my fault. I left them on Dram in my chase after Waythrel. The Orb may have brought us back, but it didn't pick up after us."

The Orb. I had a distinct ambivalence about the object now. All my life, I had learned the mythology of the Time Spheres. I had memorized the legends because they were central in the story of Ambra Dawn. Always awe and goodness, always hope when the subject was presented. After the terrible events at the Dram homeworld node, I would never see them in quite the same way again.

"How could the Orb have turned against you?"

Ambra's smile faded. "Oh, Nitin, there is so much I wish I could explain. The Orb is something far greater than I, and it has a mind of its own. I have always known this, but because my will and that of the Orb had always aligned, it was somewhat abstract. But things changed near Dram when they took Waythrel." Ambra sighed. "The truth is that the Orb did not turn against me—I turned against myself."

"What are you talking about?" How could she blame herself for this?

"You see, I had worked a lifetime to accept and plan for our losses, those terrible losses to come that you believe in abstractly because you trust my words, but which I have witnessed time and again. In vision after vision. Never able to escape them, their pain, living daily the loss. I didn't understand how much I had repressed of it. The anger. A deep bitterness. Especially after meeting you and you turned out to be everything I had envisioned. My heart was lost to you. To think about that terrible future—I barely held myself together, Nitin."

I felt embarrassed as she shared such personal feelings. Synphel was one thing—no doubt the alien knew much from the Reader sharings. But Waythrel's mate was still very alien and that provided a distancing. With another human, it was different. With Mazandarani—I didn't like his hearing about our relationship, and I am sure he didn't like it either. A quick glance at his face established it beyond a doubt.

"You seemed so strong. I didn't understand," I said.

She touched my cheek. "I didn't either, or you would have seen it when we shared. But when that thing took Waythrel, something shattered inside me. I had *not* seen this in visions—it was hidden from me by greater powers. A total surprise—something that happens less and less frequently to me. But it was another terrible loss. One I had not prepared for." She nodded, as if explaining the entire thing to herself as much as to me. "I lost control, Nitin. I flew into a mad rage. I abandoned all my efforts in this long struggle, refused to listen to my visions and the calls of the Orb. The clone had opened the Orb. The *Orb* had allowed this. I should have recognized this, accepted it, *understood* the significance. But I was too crazed, too rebellious, too *arrogant* in my hurt to let go and take my rightful place. I'm afraid that I was beginning to believe in my own mythology." She shook her head. "As I tried to change what should not have been changed, the Orb intervened. It showed me my mistakes. It reminded me of my path."

"What path?" I asked, horrified, remembering the terrible visions.

She glanced away from me. "My path is still unfolding, and even I can't see all ends. What happened there is beyond fully understanding. For now, at least. Until events reach completion."

Synphel interrupted. "I am very grateful to Captain Ratava for sharing his experience in the Orb transit. It may not seem to make sense, but I believe that you heard the voice of Waythrel, Captain. How, I don't know. But somehow, through the Orb, Waythrel reached out to you, and to me, to connect us in our future struggles. I will remember this."

I was unsure how to respond. I certainly did not feel I deserved such commitment and connection to Synphel. As always, the Xix left me slightly in awe. But I bowed my head and tried to accept the offer.

"We all loved Waythrel. Ambra most of all."

"Not more than Synphel, Nitin." Her face dropped. "But yes, I miss Waythrel terribly, already."

Mazandarani cleared his throat. "Daughter of Time, I have completed the preparations as you have requested. I only need your go-ahead for the ceremony." His face was terribly strained.

"What ceremony?" I asked.

Ambra's demeanor brightened considerably, and she squeezed my hand. "A marriage ceremony, Nitin. One that will take place here in the Temple, before all the Readers during a Great Sharing. The Group Mind will be formed to preside over the sacrament. The Readers are en route from across the world right now!"

I looked around in confusion. "What wedding? Who's getting married?"

Synphel spoke. "The Daughter of Time, of course."

I looked at Ambra in shock. She smiled impishly at me. I stared at Synphel, who was unreadable, and then at Mazandarani. "Is this true? Ambra is getting married?" It seemed as if the floor was about to give out underneath me.

"Yes. Even though I sought to prevent it."

"Counselor, you have yet to overcome your possessiveness," spoke Synphel. "Until you do, you will have no peace."

I didn't give a damn about Mazandarani or his peace at this moment. *Ambra to be married?* It couldn't be! How?

"Ambra, I don't understand. Married, to whom?"

"Why to *you*, Captain Ratava," answered Synphel.

Ambra laughed. "Nitin, I will not ask you a third time: will you marry me?"

Chapter 48

I dive down into the depth of the ocean of forms, hoping to gain the perfect pearl of the formless.

The Gitanjali of Tagore

But the first ceremony we attended was to pay respects to those who had recently fallen in our struggle. There were now no bodies, no remains, nothing but the memories we carried with us for the five who had died serving humanity. Serving more than our species—giving their lives for thousands of sentient worlds across our galaxy that fought this long and often dark conflict to free themselves from the tyranny of the Dram.

A few of us gathered in the desert, near the spot where Ambra and I had awakened only a few weeks ago. A collection of Xix and humans gazed upon a makeshift memorial hewn from the bedrock, orange and marbled, polished to a gleaming finish, with the names engraved:

Erica Fox
David Kim
Ryan Marshall
Grant Moore
Aisha Williams

Only Waythrel's name was withheld, at the request of Synphel and the Xix. They refused to commit the kidnapped alien to the casualty list, holding out hope that someday Ambra's beloved advisor would be found.

In homage to ancient rituals of Old Earth, a flame was lit in an oil-filled bowl beneath the names. A protective field was set around the memorial, shielding the slab from wind and sand. The oil was to be refilled weekly by servants of the Temple who would trek the distance in the heat to pay respects.

Ambra stood by my side in the winds, her robes billowing and her hair dancing. She smiled and turned to the rest of the group.

"Until we join them again," she said. I was too consumed with conflicting emotions to parse what she meant. Too often, her metaphysical pronouncements escaped my understanding. For the time being, I struggled to accept the loss of my team, my inescapable responsibility for their deaths. Command carried terrible burdens. Sometimes there was a debt that could never be repaid.

We returned to the Temple City, and the Temple proper, by hovercraft. Ambra said that the truest way to honor their deaths was to fully live, and she insisted that our ceremony proceed that very evening. I began to sense that she truly possessed a unique view of death, and therefore of life as well. She seemed to speak as if the dead were not truly departed. Perhaps in her special sense of time they were not. Perhaps she was always able to access their existence from a place outside of time, viewing life and death as eternal elements in the fabric of existence. Try as I might, I could not share her combined joy and sadness, nor could I understand the far-flung gaze she possessed when speaking of and to the dead. I was left with my struggles.

Whatever I thought of Mazandarani, he had somehow pushed aside his jealousy and pain at losing Ambra to me. The marriage ceremony was planned as grandly as the Festival of Rebirth. As we approached the Temple, the streets were lined with forms. Xix and human, as well as the odd other alien species— some in environmental suits, some remaining in protective craft. Tens of thousands had come from every corner of the planet and from star systems distant. It was a gathering like no other I had ever seen.

I wore my military dress uniform. Black coat and pants, the red beret with the MECHcore gear train insignia stitched in gold thread emblazoned on the front. My captain's bars gleamed along with honor badges and medals from numerous combat operations. It was an oven in the suit, but I tried to appear relaxed.

We disembarked from the hovercraft directly in front of the long stairway to the Temple. Ambra and I walked together in the lead up the stairs, Synphel and Mazandarani behind us, and then a pack of dignitaries. Behind them, the crowd quietly fell into line and followed us into the enormous structure.

The mood was festive yet serious. Many of the most powerful Readers of our galaxy were present, and their combined experience and wisdom in perception and repeated sharings produced a crowd personality unlike any I had experienced. Perhaps it was a weak echo of the Group Mind that Ambra often spoke about, now reflected even in the demeanors of its constitutive elements, these individual Readers. There was no randomness of disconnected strangers, nor was there the empty-headed mob mind. It was something else, something more than alien. It seemed to permeate the space around us.

We entered the open expanse of the central chamber and walked straight toward the swirling chromatographic projection of the Orb into our local space. The Orb projection reflected the mood I sensed from the crowd of Readers now spilling into the chamber. Gone were the storm clouds present in the terrible conflict with Ambra at the Dram homeworld. The colors seemed alive with potential and anticipation. The patterns somehow suggested in my mind future possibility and a strange sense of hope. I wondered, somewhat amazed, that this abstract-seeming display could shape my thoughts so.

Onward we walked, hand in hand, and neared the central dais within the color swarm. Thousands and thousands of Readers poured like a river through the entrance behind us, flowing over the surface of the chamber and pooling into their individual depressions. They did so nearly soundlessly, without speaking, the only noise their footsteps and the friction of the fabrics of their clothing.

We entered the prismatic nexus. Ambra turned us around, holding up our clasped hands into the air as the remainder of the Readers entered. I looked at my beloved, as much because I longed to as to calm the anxiety at this strange display of a power I could only sense subconsciously. She was more beautiful than I had ever remembered seeing her. She wore a special black robe, the material finer than anything I had ever seen, partly reflective of the glowing walls of the Temple building. She had recovered under the care of the Xix, her skin radiating in startling white, green eyes like luminous emeralds beyond valuing. I wanted so much to reach over and run my hands through her long curls of red but we remained still in the statuesque position she had chosen to greet the incoming Readers.

It took some time before they were all settled, but once the last Readers had entered, the door to the Sahara outside was shut. The sounds of the desert were completely silenced. The Readers assumed positions of meditation. Most were reminiscent of Indian yoga positions, although there was a wide variety, especially in the alien species that were present and visible.

Ambra lowered our arms and stared out over the landscape of meditating Readers, seeming to enter a trance along with the rest. For a moment, I felt strangely alone in this giant crowd, the only one excluded from the communion of their minds. A simple soldier without great talents placed in the center of a process that he could not understand or partake in.

But it was short lived. I began to feel strange. A vertigo began to unbalance my sense of position and reality, and it almost seemed that I could sense a deep rumble, some barely detectable bass hum that flowed around and diffused through everything. Something unusual was happening, beyond my experience. The passage of time seemed to alter.

I began to feel an irrational sense of presence. It reminded me of the intuition one has in the dark that one is not alone or a soldier feels in combat when a life-threatening event is near. Except this was not a fearful feeling. On the contrary, it was a calming one, but a sense of a presence nonetheless. Of something deep, greater than I. And it was everywhere, unlocalized, pervasive. Had I not known better, had I been alone in the desert with no education and nothing to hang this powerful sensation on, I have no doubt that I would have ascribed it to the presence of divinity.

We form the Mind.

A voice from everywhere and nowhere. I looked at Ambra. She had turned her gaze on me, her eyes penetrating into my own. The voice was not hers. It was not an individual. It was something much larger. It seemed to radiate from deep inside me.

We are the Mind.

I felt waves of warmth and electricity pass through me. I saw Ambra's face flush and her pupils dilate. My breath became stronger, more rhythmic. I felt as if I were being consumed, that tendrils of power were reaching into me from outside, entering my nervous system, stirring up a fire. Then I understood. I was becoming aroused.

The many have become One. Now two will be one and of One.

My breathing was heavy. Goosebumps covered my forearms and legs. My mouth went dry. I felt an erection stir. Waves of life seemed to flow through me, summoning all my energies. It was frightening. It was a hunger I could not possibly refuse.

"Ambra..." My voice was hoarse.

She whispered softly, "And shall I show you marital bliss, my husband?" She came close to me, her lips barely parted and engorged with blood, her body brushing against mine.

I gasped out, panting. "Haven't we already known it?" I wondered, remembering our time outside the galaxy on the sands.

"Not like this."

She began to undo the gold buttons on the front of my dress coat. I saw a bright passion in her eyes. Her fingers explored my chest through the spaces in my shirt buttons, her nails scraping against my taut nipples. I moaned, wanting to explode, my eyes beginning to swim, catching sight of her breasts, the glowing Temple walls, the flashing colors of the Orb, the sea of Readers deep in trances.

"Ambra—*here?* With all of them?" But I knew there was no resisting. No desire to resist. There was only full, complete, utterly consuming *desire.*

"Yes, love," she said, her mouth on mine, her tongue teasing my lips and a warm breath flowing into my mouth. She pulled my coat and shirt down around my elbows and ran her hands over my swelling chest. "A great sharing. And a Mind greater than any you have known outside the Orb will watch over us. And it will bless our love. Even as it partakes and augments it."

She pulled me down on top of her.

Chapter 49

His left hand should be under my head,
and his right hand should embrace me.

Song of Solomon 8:3

S he was right. It was not like before.

There was a swelling in the deep chanting, until it became a true Voice. A voice composed of many voices, low and high, human and alien, spanning notes and scales and qualities I could not have imagined existed and that in a transcendental harmony was multiple yet undivided.

The waves of that chanting washed over us, fueled our mutual desire, drove it higher and higher as we lay down upon the dais. My hands worked hungrily, tearing off her robes, coursing themselves over her naked form. My fingers caressed and scratched, exploring her legs, the red pubic hair, moving across her stomach to the ripe nipples atop her breasts, through her locks, and over the giant and bald skull. She sighed deeply and grasped my erection, stroking, enflaming me, guiding it into herself.

We merged. My hips thrust firmly, a cry escaped both our lips. I looked into her eyes, and they swallowed me whole. Biology commanded, the limbic broth overflowed, and I thrust into her again and again, my lips resting on hers, our breaths shared, her eyes drawing me deeper and deeper into a whirlpool of green scintillations.

The Temple disappeared. Fading to black, our naked forms were entwined as a single organism dangling within the color explosion of a nebula. My mind

—both consumed in the mating act and by her eyes—was enhanced and freed to soar within this cosmic artwork as well. I felt my hands underneath her, grasping the flesh of her buttocks, pushing her pelvis toward me as my heart raced. Before me, the light of stars painted the dusts of space toward infinity.

I love you, Nitin. Always. Remember.

I came. I exploded within her as that life-purpose surged through my form. Again and again I thrust as she cried, her own reaction a perfectly timed orgasm. As before on the beaches of that alien world, our bodies were utterly in tune and in perfect rhythm.

But *not* like before. The tendrils of power flowed even more strongly through me. I felt a charge, and the usual collapse after climax was transformed. The hunger returned, my physiology altered. The arousal did not decrease but ascended to greater intensity.

Her eyes held me. I sensed the question, the request for permission to enter into this frightening and uncharted physical space. The biology of sex is raw power. It can wreak destruction in its intensity to create. I was being asked to play with a fire I only dimly appreciated.

I gave in wholeheartedly, not only from the burning desire churning within me, but also to connect, to become, to merge with the one I loved beyond anything I had known.

And so the waves became storms. The power flowed through us. Again and again our bodies cycled from arousal to climax, gentleness to wild passion. In myriad locations in space we made love over and again—before a star igniting its nuclear fuel, floating over a frozen sea of methane on an ice world, watching the dance of a multiple star system in accelerated time, flying through a dense star field until the points of light became elongated streaks of brightness speeding around us.

All the while in the company of a presence that looked down upon us, enhanced us, observed us, transported us, and loved us in some fashion that I could not completely understand. Beyond any kind of love I had known. Almost to the point of a dispassionate passion, an otherness that transformed the simple affections that creatures like us could possess and understand into something a godlike being would feel.

I was Ambra and Ambra was me and we were part of something *other*. Even I, devoid of Reader talents, felt it distinctly. Whatever vestige of that sensory organ I possessed in my brain, the power of this Being was so great that even I could appreciate it. I could not begin to imagine what it was like for the Readers themselves.

My body was now a portion of a greater organism. In this union, our passions continued, and my emotions were completely unrestrained. Freed by the overwhelming power of the experience, stripped of all semblance of artifice, social inhibition, personal restraint—I wept. And I laughed. I did both with such freedom and completeness that the mystery of how tears and laughter often seemed separated twins was resolved as they integrated and became one. Joy and sadness as much of a harmony as two human bodies becoming one flesh or ten thousand brains becoming a single Mind.

To describe more is impossible. As part of this multipartite creature, my experiences were of a nature I can now only faintly recall. Afterward, they dissolved to faded colors of vivid dreams, ideas that would seem hopelessly in conflict or impossible to be stated or grasped.

But during those moments, the universe itself seemed to drift before my awareness.

Eons passed.

And then we were alone together in her room. The Temple was gone. The Readers were gone. The powerful Mind was a blurring memory.

Ambra lay asleep on the bed, a faint moonlight spilling over the white skin of her bare shoulder protruding from the bedsheets. I was standing, suddenly returning to my senses, as if exiting a trance. I placed my clothes on the chair by a table against the wall.

I was exhausted. I needed to sleep as I had never known. I folded my dress pants, hung my coat, and left my beret on the table. I placed my medals and bars in their boxes and took the holster with my side arm and removed the Hertz, closing it within a drawer in the bedside stand.

I lay down on the bed. As my head touched the pillow, I felt as if the mattress were rising upward and enveloping me. Bone tired, yet at peace. Remade with a powerful emotion that was stronger than any I had ever known yet for which I had no word.

I closed my eyes.

Chapter 50

Men of broader intellect know that there is no sharp distinction betwixt the real and the unreal; that all things appear as they do only by virtue of the delicate individual physical and mental media through which we are made conscious of them; but the prosaic materialism of the majority condemns as madness the flashes of super-sight which penetrate the common veil of obvious empiricism.

H.P. Lovecraft

I *feel myself drown again in dream.*

Standing here as the soft morning sunlight of New Earth streams through our bedroom window, I look down on her sleeping. The white sheets are nearly blinding, wrapped tightly around her seductive curves. Her naked shoulder has slipped out of the fabric. It is nearly as white as the sheets, such a contrast to my dark copper. The entire blank canvas is dramatically altered by waterfalls of red curls streaming down to her waist.

As I look at the swollen—some would say grotesque—form of her skull resting on the soft pillow, I feel a deep attraction, a pull to touch, to caress.

As I walk to the nightstand and open the drawer, it is only in a state of unreal detachment that I remove the weapon. The composite metal should feel cold in my hand, but it does not. I feel nothing. The muscles tighten around the handle of the pistol, but I give no commands, feel no responses, sense no contractions or tightness in my skin. I can only see as if from a distance, from a vantage point I cannot define in space or in time.

And this automaton, my body, or now rather some ghostly form that is no longer mine, pulls that weapon out, unlocks the safety, and turns toward the bed, raising the barrel to the elongated head of my beloved, nearly touching the scarred edges near her hairline.

And before anxiety or understanding can even rise within me, she opens those blind green eyes with adoration, turning to stare directly into my own, tears trickling down her cheeks. I hear her voice in my mind.

Don't be afraid, Nitin. I love you.

I pull the trigger.

Chapter 51

My friend, I am not what I seem. Seeming is but a garment I wear. The "I" in me, my friend, dwells in the house of silence. I would not have thee believe in what I say nor trust in what I do.

The Madman of Gibran

The gun did not fire. My hand pulled the trigger over and over, and nothing happened.

Ambra sat up in the bed, her hair spilling over her chest and the sheets. She looked at me with a terrible coldness.

"We have anticipated you."

My mouth screamed, and my body lurched forward with my hands stretched outward to grasp her throat. But I got nowhere. I was paralyzed, frozen in space. She rose and slipped a robe over her naked body, straightening the beautiful locks above the hood after it passed over her head. The sound of running footsteps filled my ears, and I caught the outlines of several shapes entering the room through my peripheral vision. But I could not turn to see them. I continued to remain suspended.

"You are unhurt?" I heard one of them say. A male voice. Accented. *Mazandarani.*

"Yes," she said, staring across my field of vision to the door. "Sepehr, put the weapon down." There was a short pause, and she spoke with more force. "*Sepehr!* Now. Put it down!"

"He would have killed you." The words were spoken with such venom.

Synphel spoke from the same direction. "Remember not to condemn an innocent, Sepehr. Nitin is as much a victim as Ambra nearly was. More so. He has lived in ignorance because of our machinations. Show pity, counselor."

Ambra watched intently for a few seconds, and then I saw her face relax. "Thank you, Sepehr. Now, place him in restraints and put him in that chair."

My paralyzed and suspended arms were pulled behind me, and there was a buzzing sound as field restraints were used to bind them. Several sets of arms lifted me and moved my body backward, placing it down on a seat, my legs also restrained and bent to a sitting position.

"He is secure?" she asked. I could see them all in front of me now. Mazandarani nodded.

The paralysis ended. My mouth erupted in a string of vile curses aimed at the Daughter. I watched this happen as in a dream. I was possessed. I was mad. I was a split personality, and I watched helplessly as I cursed my dearest love. I wished to shout, to weep, but I could do nothing. I was a mind trapped in the prison of my own rebellious body.

Ambra held up her hands and my mouth closed, the sewage of profanities stopped. "That's enough." She knelt down in front of me, and my body spasmed vainly to get at her, to attack and spill the lifeblood of my lover. She stared fixedly into my eyes. "Nitin, it's okay. This will be over soon. Hold on."

Mazandarani shouted. "Be careful, Ambra! You don't know where he is or what will be waiting for you."

She placed one hand on each side of my skull and closed her eyes. My body was shaking so violently that I thought it might be having a seizure. "No, Sepehr, *they* don't know what is *coming*."

What happened next I can only tell you through analogy and metaphor. I clothe it in visual images and archetypes because this is all my mind can do with the experience. As for what truly happened, only Ambra Dawn knows.

Like some supersonic freight train, the entirety of her consciousness as I had known it blasted into my mind, or rather into some now-enlarged space that contained what I once thought of as myself. Only now, I was not alone. Inside this place, anchored in some way as fundamentally as I was, there lurked *another*. It seemed that it stood in the back of my awareness by a doorway that I had never perceived before. Like a fading shadow, it slipped behind the portal and disappeared.

And the fury of Ambra was a billowing fire that rushed after him. As some phoenix or incandescent dragon, her soul flew past my awareness, through the door, and was gone in an instant, leaving me utterly alone in this strange, new space. Once my mind. Now, some insane house of mirrors.

I found I could move my body under my own will once again. I found that I could speak. I opened my eyes. Ambra was still there, still holding my head in her hands, her eyes closed, focused, and in some trance. The others in the room stared downward anxiously.

"Synphel. *Help me*," I whispered.

The tall Xixian approached. "Captain. It is not safe to remove the restraints yet. Do not disturb her."

"Why?" I asked. "Where has Ambra gone?"

"To kill an assassin."

"What assassin?"

"The one that has lurked within you since the day you were born," said Mazandarani.

"The Anti have been busy for centuries, Captain Ratava," said Synphel, "and not only training the Dram to create clones of Ambra Dawn. Equally audacious has been their plan to infiltrate Ambra's inner circle. To place spies. And among them, to bring to life the perfect assassin. One who could win the heart and mind of the target, who would be placed next to her in moments of extreme vulnerability. One who could be activated at precisely that point when the probabilities of success were highest."

I was trembling, not from the foreign murderous impulses I had felt before, but from my own horror and fear. "What are you saying?"

Mazandarani spoke. "That you are a deadly pawn, Captain. An experiment in murder. A monster designed by enemies so vile that nothing is sacred to them. You were *engineered* to kill Ambra Dawn. And had she not see through it, you would have succeeded."

"No."

"*Yes*," he spat. "A chimeric Frankenstein composed of three bodies and two souls, harboring malice and murder behind a veil of love."

Synphel interrupted. "*Careful*, Sepehr. You are letting your emotions cloud your thoughts. In what is to come, we will need your mind." The counselor lowered his head.

My words were spoken through a parched throat. "Synphel, what does this mean? What is he talking about?"

"A horror, Captain. A diabolic cleverness. You see, somewhere on the other side of the galaxy, in a future several hundred—perhaps thousands—of years from now, there is a ring of power plants not too different from what you have seen here. Except within the bowels of that place, deep underground, there are two bodies floating in a stasis medium. These human bodies are connected to feeding tubes and waste management systems, their skulls sliced open and the brains embedded in a dark technology. Surrounding those brains are a score of False Dawn clones, themselves chained to the room, their fate to maintain a long-term manipulation of space and time."

I felt a growing darkness encroaching on me. My vision seemed to be narrowing from the corners. "How do you know this?"

"The Group Mind has seen it, penetrated the layers of deception woven around the place," said Synphel. "In one of those tanks is your brain, Nitin Ratava, or rather, the proto-organic component of your mind. An advanced projection system of technology combined with the efforts from the clones opens a wormhole connecting a future time and another space with our here and now. This projection brought your highly engineered mind to be embedded in a developing fetus in India. Through a process honed by centuries of experimentation and aid from the shadows of the Anti, this process *worked*. You are that creature torn between flesh and space, brain and time."

"*Why?*" Horror flowed through me.

"Because there is a back door in your mind, Captain. A second body, a second mind projected within you, hidden for all of your life, yet *watching*. Seeing everything that has happened to you and transmitting that back to his masters."

"A spy?"

"Yes, but much more. If the time came, if the opportunity presented itself, this back door could open fully and this second mind seize control of your body. And so today it has happened, nearly to the death of Ambra Dawn."

I stared at the face of my beloved, my horror complete.

"I'm the assassin."

Chapter 52

I know faces, because I look through the fabric my own eye weaves, and behold the reality beneath.

The Madman of Gibran

S o much crystallized in my tainted mind. Many things that had made little sense fell into place. But I took no pleasure in finally understanding the puzzle.

"She *knew*. She knew all along, didn't she? From the moment we met. That's why she came to the hospital in Japan."

Synphel paused a moment. "Yes, Captain. We have all known for some time. Despite our enemies' best efforts to conceal what they had done through space and time, employing the powers of their monstrous clones to do so, they underestimated Ambra's vision. They especially underestimated what the Group Mind could achieve."

"How long has she known?"

"Since you were born," said Mazandarani, "although some of us have only learned of this recently." His expression was sour.

"Because you were too much in love with Ambra not to take matters into your own hands, Sepehr," said Synphel. "You would have wrecked our careful plans."

I felt a bitter seed sprout inside me. I felt used. My Ambra had used me, knowing for decades. She had said *nothing*. "A plan for me."

Synphel continued. "Yes, or rather, for the weapon of the enemy that was your body. We have played them, Captain, feeding them just enough truth to give them a false impression of our strategy."

I stared forward at the face I loved. Her expression was peaceful. Detached. *Cold?* How calculating had she been? How had she hidden from me this truth while we seemingly shared our souls? My head swam. Nothing seemed real anymore.

"You see, we knew that everything you heard and saw was reported back. *Everything.* Knowing you were a spy, however, presented us with an opportunity. So we led them to believe that we planned to shut them out with the closure of the Orbs. But what we did not tell you is that this is impossible. There is no way to fully wall off any portion of the Time Tree."

"Then those missions were a hoax? My team died for *nothing?*" Cold. Calculating.

"We were all to die if this clone army could not be defeated, Captain. Their deaths were not for nothing. They helped you and Ambra set the bait."

"What bait?" I felt sick.

"Once the Dram figured it out, that they could access the New Earth Orb despite what we did, they were exposed to a terrible temptation."

I understood. The military training spelled out the strategy in an instant. "A final hammer stroke."

"Yes," said Synphel. "Thinking that we had miscalculated, they would be tempted to breach our defenses with overwhelming force and crush us once and for all at the origin point of the Resistance—New Earth. That is why they withheld their full strength when you unintentionally leaked the mission details to them. Did you never wonder why those engagements at Brax and Hola had no clone contingent? They waited for the ultimate prize to reveal their hand. New Earth had to be in the mix."

"And why not kill Ambra in the desert when we returned? They wouldn't have to make me do anything except sit there. She was dying."

"We are not sure," said Synphel, "except that your travels through the Orbs played havoc with the wormhole connection. Nested wormholes, wormholes within wormholes—it is a complexity beyond anything we've approached in science. It was a terrible strain on you—it must have been much more so for them. Likely by the time they recovered and realized that opportunity, it had passed. They would rather be sure, plan the assassination carefully. Leave no room for failure—they would only get one chance. That was the final temptation in the great assault plan: if they had just assassinated our most powerful Reader—the only one who might stand a chance to defeat the horde of False Dawns, victory would have been assured, and New Earth would have met the fate of the old."

"Well, does she?" I asked. "Stand a chance? She told me that she couldn't. Was that a lie, too?"

I felt a blast through my mind, and the room became blindingly bright. A white noise filled my ears and then slowly faded. My sight returned.

"No," came a voice inches from my face. I startled within the restraints as Ambra spoke and opened her eyes. "No, Nitin. I cannot defeat their numbers."

"Then what is all this *about*?" I pleaded. I felt like screaming.

Ambra looked heartbroken. "I can't defeat them as I am. And so I will become more than what I am."

Synphel was silent, and Mazandarani looked toward her in horror. "Please, Ambra," he said, "don't do this thing." He was begging her.

"The assassin is dead," she replied to all of us. "I followed the link back to its source. There were multiple clones, as we had foreseen. I killed them, and then I shut down the life-support machinery of the spy."

"And what of Captain Ratava, Ambra?" asked Synphel, an anxiety in her tone.

Ambra reached around behind me and removed my restraints. She held my hands. "As my worst fears. His proto-brain was not there. They have him in another location." She saw the confusion on my face and explained. "I had hoped to free your mind, Nitin. To disconnect it from the flesh of its origin and permanently anchor it in the brain here. But I can't. I don't know where your body is. And I can't follow your link without them killing you."

"But you did for this...assassin."

"They were not prepared. That is why I acted so quickly. And they did not know what I could do. Now, they will know what happened, or figure most of it out. They will take steps."

"What will they do?"

"Kill you, Nitin. Pull the plug and break the connection."

"Then why not come for me first?"

She shook her head. "And leave that assassin free to roam your mind while I was gone? He could have broken the link within your mind and killed us both at the same time. I had to stop him first. It was the only way. The only hope."

The complications completely baffled me. "But wait. Haven't they been listening in? Don't they know about the trap now?"

"No. I didn't travel along the link they made to your proto-body, but that didn't mean I didn't touch it. I have propagated waves down the wormhole to the source. It will disrupt their ability to monitor you. It will wreak havoc with the passage of time in their space. It will slow them down. But not forever, my love." She wept and kissed me. "It is only a matter of time."

"Before I die." The finality of it struck me at last. "As you said."

"I'm sorry, Nitin." Her face was anguished.

And in an instant, I forgave her. I understood the larger context. I experienced a glimpse of the long pain she forced herself to carry. A terrible, terrible burden of knowledge. "I would never make a different choice, Ambra. Not even now." I stroked her hair as she leaned her face into my hand.

Synphel spoke. "It is also only a matter of time before their armada of ships and clones arrives. If you are to carry out your plan to the end, Ambra, we must act now."

I pulled her face away from mine, my cheek wet with her tears. Her lower lip trembled nearly imperceptibly. "Ambra, what are you going to do?"

She wiped her eyes with the back of her hand. "I am going to be butchered by my dearest friends," she said with a false smile and bravado, looking somewhat wild-eyed toward Synphel. "I will go through a new hell and a transformation. I have already died in your arms, beloved. Soon, I will be reborn."

Mazandarani looked at her in pain and with awe. "Daughter of Time."

Ambra stood up and straightened her robe. "And then I will call all souls to me."

Chapter 53

The day will come when, after harnessing space, the winds, the tides, gravitation, we shall harness for God the energies of love. And, on that day, for the second time in the history of the world, man will have discovered fire.

Pierre Teilhard de Chardin

I felt the first assault as we descended from the Temple deep into the sands of the Sahara.

A sudden vertigo, a sense of distance from my body, and my legs buckled beneath me. Ambra caught me and helped break my fall in the elevator car. We had descended nearly three miles into the crust of New Earth, heading to a secret center for the final stage of Ambra's long plan. But I couldn't focus on her explanations. I felt as if I were being separated from my own flesh.

"Nitin!" Ambra slapped my cheeks. I could hardly feel it.

"It has begun," said Synphel. "Captain, this is proceeding faster than we had anticipated. We will do what we can."

As the elevator car came to a stop, the wild vertigo stabilized, and I no longer felt quite as if I were looking in on myself. But I could no longer use my legs, and my arms moved liked some poorly manipulated puppet's. Synphel bent down and with one powerful motion lifted me bodily off the elevator floor.

They whisked me off to some medical ward staffed with at least twenty Xixian medics. I didn't have time to process what they were doing here, why this secret lair looked more like a hospital than a war cave, but I would soon discover the terrible answers to most of my questions.

Ambra was gone. They wouldn't tell me why, but instead the medical staff buzzed around me like some nightmare beehive with their arms and eyestalks. I felt numbly the insertion of instruments into my skin at various points. They had placed me in a special wheelchair of some sort, the back of it thick with instrumentation. I could barely talk.

"What...what are you doing?" I sounded drunk.

One of the medics paused to speak with me as the others continued. "We are trying to counter the distancing of your mental waveform with this phys-ical body," it said, as if that made anything clear. "Several synaptic amplifiers are being located at strategic points in your nervous system. These will give you back some portion of your sensation and motor control."

The medic was right—I could already feel it. I brought my hand up to my face and touched my cheek. "I can feel it again."

"It is a temporary stopgap, Captain," said the alien. "It will buy you some time until your mind loses the ability to control the autonomic functions such as your heart and lungs. When that happens, your body here will die and you will be cut off."

I nodded. There wasn't much to say to something like that. Ambra had informed me of my coming fate. I had seen the truth of my dual personality. I now understood the powerful yet fragile link I possessed to this time and place.

But I didn't understand what was going on around me. The other medics were clearing out, in some kind of a mad rush. "What's going on?" I asked. "Is there fighting already?"

The Xix stared at me with its eyes. "Has she said nothing to you?"

Nerve dysfunction or not, I felt a wave of nausea sweep through me. "No."

"Then it is best that you learn from her or Synphel. I am Rel. I have been assigned to you. I will guide your chair to the operating room."

Operating room?

Things moved quickly. I discovered that the "wheelchair" was more of a *hoverchair*. The alien motioned over the holodisplay floating in front of it, and the device levitated. The medic exited, and the chair followed automatically, perfectly steering its way through the winding corridors.

Deeply, deeply winding corridors. We spiraled inward for a good ten minutes. The mystery of this place deepened as we passed room after room of Xixians and humans, their eyes following us through clear panes in the walls. When their eyes fell on me, their expressions became sorrowful.

"They seem to know me."

The medic spoke softly. "They are the dedicated Readers of the Temple, as well as tens of thousands more who have swelled their ranks for this final battle. They have shared in the Group Mind, Captain. They have traveled together with the Daughter through space and time. They have seen entire histories and futures, terrible and beautiful. They have seen the horizons of alternative universes. In these tapestries, they have seen your story and how it is interwoven with that of Ambra Dawn. They were present at your union." Inward and inward we continued to spiral. "The Group Mind is far greater than any one mind, even that of the Daughter. The Readers retain fragments of memories from the experience, even if they cannot understand the deeper insights of this more profound experience on their own."

"And I thought they came for our wedding."

"They did, Captain. It was a joyous and miraculous occasion. But an even greater purpose called."

I strained to move my head to the side where the alien walked beside me. "You're one of them, aren't you? You're a Reader."

"Yes, Captain. And soon I will take my place with the others for a very long journey. A final journey."

The spiral had tightened sharply, the unusual Xixian building materials giving way to a bright room. Medics, human and Xix, dashed around. Instruments of surgery, machinery, vessels with organic-looking broths were strewn about—not haphazardly, but with patterns I could not put together.

But the center of the room focused my attention. A huge slab of black reflective material, appearing wet like ocean shale, was embedded in the floor so deeply that I had to guess that the greater portion of it was invisible underneath the structure. The slab was not simply material, however. The best I can describe the impression it made on me was that the thing was organic—it was alive. It seemed to breathe and change shape, interfacing like some cyborg with pure machinery and the biological tanks and equipment. In the center of this bizarre creation was carved the negative of a human shape. The slab was imprinted with the form of arms, legs, a torso, and an extended, seemingly dreadlocked head.

In this negative space was Ambra.

I felt a cold shiver. I didn't know what this thing was. I didn't know why she was lying in it. But my intuition was profoundly shaken, disturbed and trying to call to my conscious mind. I felt I had seen it before.

"Bring me closer to her," I told the Xixian medic.

"It can only be for a moment, Captain," came the voice of a translator that I recognized. Synphel.

"Please."

The hoverchair floated forward toward Ambra. Her eyes were closed, but as I approached, they opened. They held fear in them.

"Hold my hand, Nitin."

Clumsily, I reached across the side rests and dangled my arm toward her. She reached up and grasped my hand tightly. I'm sure if I had retained normal sensation, it would have hurt.

Her voice was sad. "Look what they are doing to you." My deteriorating state was not lost to her blind eyes.

"Ambra, what are they doing to *you*?"

She looked away. "Very soon, I will never be able to hold your hand again."

"Because I'll die."

"And because I will never be able to touch another human being again."

"Ambra, *please*—explain to me."

"The cruelest part is how much I need to hold you, my Nitin. The Anti were so perfect in steering their Dram sheep. So cruel and heartless in their plans. You were made precisely for me. Maybe once in a thousands years two people chance to meet who are so precisely tuned to attraction and love." She looked back at me, a deep, terrible sadness in her green eyes. "But the biology can be engineered. You chose this creeping death that is rotting you rather than live a life without me. Part of me wishes that I could make that choice."

"Why Ambra? What is going to happen?"

She closed her eyes. "I will live an eternity encased in this living machine. I'll become an elemental part of it, until what was human is long forgotten and I am the nucleus of this ever-growing mind that will soon be born." She leaned forward and grasped my arm, her eyes flying open, a wild expression on her face. Her nails dug into my skin. There were trickles of blood, but I felt nothing. "All humanity lost but for a lingering *echo*, a terrible, unfulfillable *longing* over eons for you, Nitin. To touch you, hold you, love you once again as a woman."

She was shaking. I wanted to reach for her, to cradle her in my arms, to kiss the tears away. But I could not rise. I could hardly lift my arms. I was a broken shell, helpless to comfort the most cherished person in my life.

"Ambra, I can't…"

I'll be here, Nitin. And when they take you from me, don't despair. I will come for you. Always.

A voice interrupted. "Ambra, it is time."

Synphel stood to my side, its eyestalks darting around nervously. "The hyperbrane is failing. It must be now, if it is not already too late."

Ambra let go of my arm. "Take him outside."

"Ambra, wait, no!"

Too late. The hoverchair pulled back, and I saw her lying back into that wet rock as the distance between us increased. I tried to move, to grasp something, to stop the chair. If I could have, I would have thrown myself off and crawled to her.

But I could not even do that. I was nearly paralyzed once again, my puppet masters across time and space yanking, pulling, snapping string after string.

"Ambra!" I screamed, or tried to. My ears heard only a weak whisper of her name.

Be strong, Nitin. I need you to be strong for me right now. And then, to wait. Even in death and what comes afterward. Wait for me.

The medical workers closed around her like sharks in a feeding frenzy.

They brought tools. Blood bags. Scalpels, scissors, laser cutters. Wires and cables.

The chair carried me underneath the doorway and out into the hall. A transparent field materialized, sealing the entrance. I was brought inside a nearby room. Synphel entered behind me, and Major Mizoguchi stood stone-faced gazing into the operating room.

Mazandarani stood there, his face pale, his form swaying as if drunk. His face was pressed against the glass, his fingers scraping down the sides of it.

He was weeping.

Chapter 54

God judged it better to bring good out of evil
than to suffer no evil to exist.

Augustine of Hippo

It was like drowning, or what I imagined drowning might be. I fought to tread water, to keep my awareness in my body, to resist the vortex pulling me tirelessly into that star-filled tunnel and away from Ambra. But I was tiring. Each time I dragged myself back, I had slipped some more, and my awareness was increasingly detached from the reality around me. Out of the corner of my eye, I began to see the haze of light, the tunnel of stars opening its maw to draw me in. I knew I could not escape it for much longer.

My vision and hearing, all my senses, were now like machine-gun staccato. I couldn't be sure I had understood what I had heard. The words made no sense. They were monstrous. Using all my strength, I formed sounds, willing my numb lips to move, squeezing my chest with all my energies to force air through my throat.

"There must...be anesthetic."

Mazandarani turned bloodshot eyes to look at me but said nothing. Synphel gently approached my hoverchair.

"I'm afraid that there will not be," it said.

"*Why?*" The word came out like a whisper, a harsh sound of a dying man.

"The Dram horde is approaching, Captain, with its army of clones and dark allies. We are not ready to engage them. To fight them now means certain and swift defeat. Therefore, Ambra stalls them, as best she can."

Mizoguchi spoke. "She has been interfering with their attempts to transition to our space and time. But it cannot go on forever. There are too many forces arrayed against her."

"And if she is unconscious," continued Synphel, "if her neurological system is suppressed, the first loss of control will be in her tumor cells. The barrier will collapse. Their armada will pour into the space of your solar system in our now."

"She must remain awake until the last moments," finished Mizoguchi.

"The pain...*distract her.*"

Synphel understood my increasingly simplistic phrases. "Yes, but the Readers are coming. The Group Mind, it is hoped, will be able to support her focus through the pain. But without Ambra, there is no Group Mind."

"*It's...torture,*" I managed.

"Yes," said Mizoguchi, her expression grim. "She has accepted her sacrifice."

It was then that I began to notice them. A tide of figures, at first slow like a trickle, but then building like some organic tsunami, they came pouring into the honeycombed rooms around us. The chambers were like the floor of the Temple, with depressions in the ground like a grid across the floor. The figures, human and Xix, streamed across the grid and took seats in the depressions, their hands inserting into hollows on the sides, bands glowing with Xixian tech around their heads and midsections.

Synphel saw my clumsy gaze track their movements. "They come for the final synthesis," it explained. "This will be their last home."

The medic had said there were tens of thousands. It was like some enormous subterranean city of psychics. A gathering of powerful Readers, coalescing around the focal point in the center of the spiral. A giant hive for a group mind with my Ambra at its center.

"When the procedure is finished, Captain, we will rise into orbit to meet our enemies as One, united in a fashion unlike any army before."

"You talk," I gasped out, exhausted and confused, "like this is a starship."

"That's because it is, Captain," said Mizoguchi.

I will be here with you, Nitin, until your moment comes. Then you will not see me. And then you will see me again.

Synphel spoke. "They are about to begin."

"No, I can't!" cried Mazandarani. "I will not watch this!" He put his hand to the glass and stared toward the rock. "Forgive me, Ambra."

He turned an anguished face away and stormed out of the room. I couldn't turn fast enough to follow his movements. By the time I had moved my head to see down the hallway, he was gone.

The lights dimmed everywhere within the building except for the operating room. I could still not see Ambra for the medical staff surrounding her. Only the gleaming black of the living rock in which she lay rose above and past the forms tending to her.

The Readers had all taken seats and were absolutely still in positions of deep meditation. While my five senses were nearly completely numb, I began to feel a familiar sensation. Perhaps it was due to my strange limbo between two bodies, the contortions of space and time that was the matrix of my mind increasingly stretched by the linkages of the Dram and Anti. Whatever the explanation, I sensed something I had experienced only once before—two days ago at our marriage. But this time, my sense was much more acute. A sixth sense—not sight, hearing, touch, smell, or taste, but an *experience*—that maybe mirrored the powers of the Readers around me. My current degeneration granted me for the first time in my life a chance to see the universe a little as Ambra did. For all the pain and injustice of it—for that reason alone—I embraced it with all I had. It would not be wasted.

My words are distortions. The feeling can only be described in the images and vocabulary of the sensory world I had known. The sensation began as an odd vibration. Deep inside me, as if my bones had begun to shake. Undulating, long, then the cycles accelerating. The power of it steadily increased, and the vibrations transformed into tones, notes, pitches rising around me. It sounded like singing.

A chorus of voices. Each voice a personality. Each personality linked in unique harmonies of thought. *Mind songs* that grew into mental symphonies beyond my ability to follow. And this symphony, like all great music, had a personality, a mood, a character of its own. The Group Mind.

It was sublime. It was haunting and stirring. It was beautiful beyond words.

And then Ambra began to scream.

Chapter 55

We are not human beings having a spiritual experience. We are spiritual beings having a human experience.

Pierre Teilhard de Chardin

I floated in space, the earth beneath my feet, the sun unimaginably clear before me. Truly, I had never seen before, vision limited by the biology of human eyes through the medium of atmosphere. In space, there was nothing. How I saw, I don't know. What I was, I didn't know. I had no body. Only thought and experience.

I am here, Nitin.

Ambra? How? They are…hurting you.

Yes. Below. But it is better to say, We are here.

Then they flooded me. Thousands of minds. The singular consciousness I had felt as Ambra alone fractaled forth, splintered like faceted shards of a gem and seemed to project into multiple new dimensions. What had seemed a single whole was revealed to be a host. But not divided. Of one essence and always reflecting back to the nexus of her mind.

I was overwhelmed. I could not process all the minds, their separate and full personalities, thoughts, memories, and emotions. I recoiled.

Don't be afraid.

And suddenly, it was only Ambra again. The other minds were gone, tucked into the fabric of hidden dimensions in this mental matrix.

Ambra. Where am I? What happened?

You are displaced. You hang by a string to your flesh on New Earth. In my trial below, I focused on you too much. I pulled you here with Us, even if you are not yet part of Us.

Ambra, I can't. There are too many. I only want you.

Shhhhhh, Nitin. See—there!—how they approach?

The emptiness between New Earth and the sun shimmered. Like the clear rubber material I had imagined in the Sahara when the False Dawn attacked, space itself puckered, undulated like ripples in a pond. Each impact, as if a pebble tossed, and the blackness was partly filled with ghostly presences. First, ships. Starships by the thousands like a plague of locusts beginning to blot out the sun.

Then I felt them. The False Dawn clones. Their power over space-time resonated through me like sound waves. I could feel them, feel their thoughts and feelings like the sense before a thunderstorm. I tasted the bile of their hatred for us.

Was it like this in the desert?

Yes. Even more so. You are not free, Nitin. You are wrapped in the chains of your keepers. It is like being wrapped in plastic insulation. What you see and feel is a whisper of what is there.

What I felt was awful enough. The shimmering ceased, and space returned to normal. As it did so, I could feel something *relax*.

Dear Ambra. You are all working to stop them. As they are cutting on you, doing whatever they will do to your body, you are also out here.

Not much longer now.

Again the ripples. Stronger, the ships becoming less transparent than before, their presence lasting longer than before. It was like a tide coming in inexorably.

This time, I saw more. Between the ships. Not the clones. There was a darkness. A lack of light more than the emptiness of space.

It is an unlight, Nitin.

It filled the space between the ships, around them, like some ink that ate the very space it occupied.

The Anti. Ambra, what will you do? I felt a violent pull within me again. *Ambra, I'm dying.*

The wave of sadness I felt wash over me was disorienting.

It is only a matter of time. It is always of Matter and Time.

Chapter 56

And now I go—as others already crucified have gone. And think not we are weary of crucifixion. For we must be crucified by larger and yet larger men, between greater earths and greater heavens.

The Madman of Gibran

I crashed back to my New Earth body. *My body.* The only body I had ever known, yet that was not truly me. *Or was it me?* I no longer knew what anything meant anymore. What was real. What could be trusted, even within myself.

I was now completely paralyzed. My vision had narrowed to a tunnel. But in the hover chair, angled forward, I could still see through the energy field into the operating room. The medical personnel had been diluted. A handful buzzed around the slab. I could still see, but part of me wished that I could not, that I had stayed in space and died there, that I would never have had to see what had been done.

My Ambra.

Her distended skull was gone down to the hairline, the orange curls stained with blood and nearly black. Her brain—I can hardly describe it. The tissue was splayed out over several feet and deeply embedded in the living machine-rock. The slab seemed to absorb it, meld with it, fuse its surface to the cells in her body. The giant mass of her space-time tumor occupied a special cup in the slab surface.

Tubes bathed the tissues in her own blood and other nutrients. She was entirely sealed in a strange, clear Xixian material—sterile, environmentally controlled.

Her hands and feet were torn open like some science lab dissection. Tissue was filleted and distributed across the slab, particularly the fingers. Tubes, cables, wires, and dynamic extensions from the slab flowed into the rest of her eviscerated torso. She could not be alive. It was beyond imagining.

And then the full memory burst through my subconscious suppression like a sledgehammer to my gut. It was exactly the vision presented by the Orb near Dram. That vision was not a metaphor. Not some nightmarish insight into Ambra's soul or the soul of our enemies. It was not an abstract teaching tool. It was a precision prophecy.

"The extreme digits possess many nerves and therefore occupy a large representative volume in the brain tissue," said Synphel. Many of its eyes swiveled to look at me. "I know that you cannot speak anymore, Captain Ratava. I will explain what I can in the time you have remaining." It gestured back toward the horror in front of us. "Similarly, large nerve clusters in her eyes, her lips, ears, genitalia: All nerves must be accessed to optimize the synthesis. They will be reprogrammed, used instead to communicate with the AI and project to the other Readers. The initial operation was successful. With the help of the Group Mind, we were able to prevent excessive shock to her system. The integration is proceeding rapidly."

They had opened up her entire body like some medical school cadaver, *yet she was still alive*. Still conscious. *Without anesthetic*. In an agony I cannot possibly imagine. I looked over the cables and tubes extending from the large machinery around her, embedding themselves into her tissues. Her eyelids could not even close as wires inserted into the sides of her eyes. Only the irises were untouched, staring outward like two green pin lights. Her body shook, nearly convulsed, and the Xix swarmed around her, their distress at her suffering palpable.

"I am so sorry, Ambra," said Synphel. The alien paused a moment, and then continued. "When complete, there will be a phase transition. It will give birth in multiple dimensions to space-time fields surrounding her physical body. What was a relatively weakly linked mind of Readers will become far, far more a single organism, and the mental fields meshed as never before. Combined with the evolving AI, in a few minutes we will give birth to a cybernetic organism unlike anything in our galaxy. More importantly, a diversified, multifactorial mental synthesis will occur. *Should occur*—we don't know for sure, as it has never been done. And if it works, we aren't sure exactly what we will have made. But it 's our only hope."

I no longer heard her in my mind. But I felt her. Unmistakably Ambra, yet muffled, distant, the torture requiring all her efforts to maintain focus on Earth's defenses.

Mazandarani returned, gazing in horror through the glass. He seemed to move in slow motion, and I didn't know whether it was because of his emotional state or my own increasingly distorted mental state.

"Can we go in?" he asked, his voice rough.

"Yes," said Synphel.

Mazandarani stumbled out of the room and to the door of the operating room. Synphel activated my hoverchair, and we followed.

"Ambra, dear Ambra," he moaned, and tore at his desert robes. He fell to his knees, his hands shaking as he reached up to the splayed horror of her dissected foot.

I could do nothing. I could not weep. I could not fall at the feet of my beloved. I only felt my body recede further and further. The room appearing to fall below me, return like a rubber band, and fall again. Over and over. The nausea was overwhelming.

WE MUST HURRY.

Her voice was in everyone's mind. In mine, because I heard it. In the others, because suddenly everyone responded.

"The synthesis is complete. The Dram approach." The alien turned to me. "I will stay with you until you pass, Captain. It will be soon. And then I will take my place in this seedship. We will meet again, perhaps."

I didn't understand what she could possibly mean. Maybe some Xixian religion with an afterlife? There was no *after* for me. I would die soon half a galaxy away in a distant future. *Another time?* It was impossible to cut through the maze of complications with these changes in space, time, and history. I couldn't imagine what it might be that could lead us to meet once more. I likely would not have understood even if Synphel had tried to explain.

It didn't matter. The entire facility was powering up in some startling fashion. I was almost lost, nearly losing contact with New Earth, but my last memories were mixed with shock and wonder.

This time there were real vibrations, not some superstring song of meditating Readers. Vibrations like an earthquake, but unlike any I had felt or seen. It seemed as if the very mantle were dissociating from the planet.

A monitor appeared in the air in front of us. To me, it seemed that I was watching from the end of a long pipe, the display small, the figure of Synphel gesturing over several portions of it, small yet clear. The display responded. The view zoomed in from space in seconds to hover above the desert surface.

And the desert moved.

The sands shifted and danced, and enormous fissures erupted as the surface split open. Lines of shadow spread miles and then connected, forming a rough, jagged shape. Sand from the surface spilled down the growing chasms and was blown high into the air from pressure.

Then the ground rose. A shard of the Sahara the size of an island detached from the planet and rose into the air. I could see the inside of the building in which my dying body lay shake vigorously, but nothing fell. Nothing collapsed. The structure was well designed for its intended purpose.

And then I remembered Synphel's words. Not a subterranean lair. Not a medical facility. *A starship*. A starship with a heart as mad as this universe itself cradling the dissected and integrated flesh of Ambra Dawn.

In the monitor, the thing rose higher, miles of bedrock blasting out of the desert floor like a mountain. Miles of solid crust climbed away from the ground and appeared to ascend effortlessly into the sky.

The view panned back, climbing higher to follow the impossible starship. The region of the desert that contained the Temple and the Six Cities was undisturbed, but the desert around it was roiled with a sudden sandstorm. The ground beneath the ship became choked and opaque, a giant brown cloud visible from orbit.

Higher the mountain climbed. It was a constant speed, with no acceleration, and yet it seemed to defy gravity, flaunting any need for an escape velocity. It just rose as if it traveled the paths of physics by different rules than those that applied to the rest of creation.

Finally, there was a bottom to the thing, and the bedrock ended in a concave surface of jagged peaks. Boulders the size of sports stadiums dropped like meteors to the desert floor from the stratosphere.

The Temple broke atmosphere and entered space, yet nothing seemed amiss. The Six Cities were fine, the people unharmed. Some great bubble of protection must have formed around the entire wedge of New Earth that had sought its fate in the skies.

Soon the entire mountain floated above our world, the blue-and-white glow of the planet bathing the granite. The moon shone the reflected light of the sun brightly nearby, millions of stars winking around it in the deep background.

But there was no sun in front of us. The star disappeared, and its light was blotted out. A wall of darkness materialized and eclipsed all radiance, casting a shadow on New Earth itself.

The Dram and their forces had at last arrived.

Chapter 57

Deep in earth my love is lying
And I must weep alone.

Edgar Allan Poe

I floated.

Not in space. The sensation was very different.

I drowned in a vile water that was my prison. I woke, finally, for the first time in the existence of my being, to my real status. Encased in a tank, its walls clear, tubes in my body and around my organs.

I could hardly open my eyes. I feared that I had never used them. Yet, after minutes of struggling blindly, I saw—the blurred outlines of an emaciated skeletal frame too weak to move its limbs.

I knew my brain was spilling out of an opened skull. Merged with machines. A horror show. I shared this terrible fate with my dear Ambra. But I felt no pain. I felt almost nothing. I did not share in her pain whom they lifted up into the stars on that heart ripped out of New Earth. My state was nothing compared to her ravaged body that I would never see again, half the galaxy away, hundreds of years ago in events now long past.

The body that I had loved. That I was made to love.

I told you when I began this story that I was born to love Ambra Dawn. Can you see it now? Can you see the deep, horrible truth of it?

As I floated, questions assailed me. What could our love mean when I knew how it had come to be? For my mind's receptacle on New Earth, they had identified genetic stock that would most respond to her appearance, her pheromones, her MHC sequences, and that would also so stir her sexual and emotional centers—it was chosen to seduce her as well as be seduced. My personality was identified after centuries of testing on False Dawn clones: her likes and dislikes, and the character and mannerisms that would capture her heart and mind.

They tuned my mind in this demon's lair to bring out just such personality traits, imprinted it with her image, her voice, and her movements, so that even the little child could not but adore her. They erased a nascent soul in a womb to implant this poisonous Janus: two-faced, murderous, and camouflaged. All for a premeditated murder that spanned centuries.

What can love mean when it has been completely, coldly, cruelly engineered for manipulation? For *murder*?

What did any of our feelings mean now that I saw the truth—that we were only an organic soup to be stirred and heated at the will of monsters? What of our ideas, thoughts, insights, and deductions? They too came from the same blood-bathed organ of delusion and betrayal.

How ever could there be faith in anything but the cold indifference of the cosmos?

Around me, the blurred shapes outside the tank moved. I did not need to see the outlines of the figures, so similar to my Ambra's, to know that the clones surrounded the structure. Synphel had told me. I felt no curiosity to test the alien's hypothesis. I felt only revulsion. A fierce disgust at what had been done and what they were doing.

But there was nothing I could do. I was as helpless here as I had been on New Earth during my last moments there. Hundreds of years ago, the failing body of Nitin Ratava died above the planet as an enemy armada closed in on all the things I had ever loved. I had lain there immobile as my beloved was hacked apart and fit to a cyborg machinery to try to stop that fleet of death. I could do nothing then but wait. And now, hundreds of years in the future, I didn't know what had happened in that final battle. I didn't know if New Earth still existed, if humans had been exterminated, or if Ambra Dawn survived. And I had no power in this dark circle of hell to find out.

And so I waited.

I waited for the demons to shut down this life pod. For them to kill me, once and for all. I watched these monsters move like underwater divers through the molasses of space-time that she had flooded around them. Ambra had at least promised one thing: that it would come soon.

And I was glad for it. However artificial—their breeding of me, genetic design, testing over centuries—the truth is that my entire being was made to love Ambra Dawn with all my heart and soul and mind.

And so I did. Nothing could unmake that love, not even the realization of the emptiness and unmeaning of my feelings in a universe without purpose or love. Nor could I unmake it, even if I wished to. My life pulsed just as brightly for her in these last moments as it ever had.

Except that she was gone. They had shut out her voice. I was left only with my final thoughts in that tomb, surrounded by my captors. My creators. Soon to be, my executioners.

But what of them? All that truly mattered was Ambra. Without her, I was lost and emptied, forever seeking that which I was made to adore.

The soft hum within the tank was interrupted by a sharp rumble. Then silence. The incessant bubbling of oxygen through the tubes ceased. Light faded above.

And I felt it. My body tried to thrash at the loss of the essentials that it needed to live. Even as I was, feeble beyond imagining, my limbs weakly jerked in some final reflex to alter the environment, change the surroundings that were killing them.

My mind fell down a mineshaft, endless and smooth, in which all light was extinguished.

Chapter 58

Though my soul may set in darkness, it will rise in perfect light; I have loved the stars too fondly to be fearful of the night.

Sarah Williams, "The Old Astronomer"

I embrace this darkness.

I feel it drink my life. I am not afraid.

No darkness can match her absence; no fear is greater than her absence. I will wait.

Because there must be more.

Because I trust in her last words to me.

When this darkness consumes me fully,

The eon of nothingness will be only a moment.

And then, dispelling the void, there will be a Light.

The Dawn: and I will go to it and find my love.

That light will come from Ambra.

That light will be of Ambra.

Because that light in the darkness could be nothing else but Ambra.

I wait for you, my love.

Chapter 59

There is no death, only a change of worlds.

Red Cloud, chief of the Oglala Lakota

N *itin.*

In the deepest pit of nothingness, after an timeless eternity had passed, she spoke.

Wake up.

I opened my eyes, and an infinity of stars blinded me. I tried to turn away from them but could not, having no form, no body. I was sighted without eyes. A mind adrift in the vastness of space.

Don't be afraid.

Where am I? What was I? I did not speak with words. I spoke with thoughts. But without a body, I did not know what it was that spoke.

See the moon?

I saw it. Her voice guided my vision. A blue-and-white marble like New Earth loomed before me. It circled an enormous gas giant of swirling, banded colors. More moons, many earthlike, could be seen scattered around the monstrous planet.

That is where you died.

And then it all came back. My life. My *lives.* The life I had believed to be true: Nitin Ratava, Indian soldier, devoted seeker of the Daughter of Time, lover of Ambra Dawn. The life that had been harshly revealed to me—chimeric monster, spy, assassin, and puppet. The adventures through space. The deaths of my team. The unforces of the Anti. War. Great and terrible war and sacrifices. The torture of my beloved. My death distant from her.

And this is where you are reborn.

Reborn. I existed, but as what? I never understood the talk of mental spacetime matrices. The strange idea that physical thought was some field like electricity. I was never a scientist.

Think of it as your soul, Nitin, if that helps.

I wasn't sure that it did. Souls seemed like an ancient term, better left in the detritus of our superstitious past. It hardly seemed appropriate for the advanced technological world of humans and aliens that I knew. Souls were for the isolated, the old, the needy, such as my mother, who prayed to her icons. But at least it offered me an idea of something beyond what I understood, one that was integrated into thoughts of rebirth, eternity, and personality. After everything I had seen, after being so humbled and destroyed, when it was clear I did not remotely understand the nature of existence, who was I to reject the notion of a soul?

Ambra, where are you?

I am reaching across a bridge, a long bridge from my time and place to yours. Already, where you are, it is many centuries past the era that you left me.

I tried to understand the words. She was traveling through space and time to reach me. I wondered why she did not simply travel through space from this time. Unless she could not from this time. I had lost touch with her and New Earth as the Dram armada arrived. What if...

Are you alive in this time?

Yes. And you are with me.

I didn't understand how this could be possible. Could I be in two places at once?

And we are very busy, Nitin. All of us in making something wonderful.

All of us? What something wonderful?

Just then, several large spacecraft sped past my point of awareness toward the blue moon. They were enormous, city-sized ships, one after the other like a parade. Highly militarized, their forms screamed of violence. Dark shadows surrounded their hulls.

The Anti! Ambra, what do I do?

You are safe, Nitin. They cannot see you. Only the clone aboard can, and her attentions are elsewhere.

The ships continued, one by one, until the parade passed me and shrank to a point as it neared the moon. None changed course. There were no attacks or reconnaissance efforts. It was as if I weren't there.

How do you know all this?

It is difficult to explain. So much has changed. Everything I have been through has been for a purpose, and that purpose has been realized. Is being realized. Will be realized. We are augmented. Integrated. Synergized even beyond our most optimistic hopes. We are something completely new.

I still didn't have answers. *What new? Who is this we, Ambra? The same as I felt above New Earth with you?*

So much more than that, Nitin.

More? I could not imagine. I had been overwhelmed by the flood of their minds.

Don't be afraid. It is not like before. You are free, finally free of the fleshly egg that gestated your soul. Your consciousness propagates through space and time independently now. That shock, that pain from the many—it will not hurt you now.

What if I don't like being with them? What if I want to be alone?

Do you want to be alone, Nitin?

No, I did not. But I also knew that being with others was often very difficult—the clashes of personalities, different priorities, agendas. The thought of joining some mental aggregate frightened me. I only wished to be with her.

You will be with me. And because they have chosen to be with me, they are in harmony with me. You will find them acceptable. Believe that. Trust me, Nitin. Try.

And if I don't try?

Then we cannot be together. My future is determined by my choices, Beloved. Even if I wished, I could not leave. If you do not join us, you cannot be with me. Worse, if you live out here alone, without support, it will be worse than death. You will spend eons devolving. You will lose yourself, and I will lose you forever.

Losing myself didn't really matter to me; it was inconsequential. Being lost to her, losing her, was everything. The only truth I knew was that I could not live without her. Whatever she now was. Wherever that was. Whatever was in store for me.

I cannot leave you, Ambra.

Yes, my Nitin. I know. But you had to know for yourself.

But there is so much that I still don't understand.

Then let us stop talking. Let me show you.

How?

Follow my voice, and it will take you to me. And together we will see all those things that you need to understand.

Perhaps all this was madness—the last throes of a dying brain's hallucinations. But it did not matter at all. In life, in death, in madness—I would always follow her. I would always trust her. Because, in the end, the core of all my love for her was unshakable, unwavering trust in her.

I'm coming, Ambra.

Chapter 60

So powerful is the light of unity
that it can illuminate the whole earth.

Bahá'u'lláh

I accelerated.

It was a matter of will, of acceptance, and as I focused on her voice, on the powerful sense of her that I felt even across these kiloparsecs and centuries, I was displaced.

The stormy gas giant and its blue moons began to recede behind me, the light of their star fading, and the background of the Milky Way before me shifted in colors, running through a spectrum from blue to red over and over as the stars themselves elongated in my peripheral vision.

Then it all began to spin. Rotating around me, a vortex of stars formed until the lights ran together like wet ink in a rainstorm. The center of the rotation was the only place of stillness, a spherical glow expanding in size, its infinitely layered majesty eclipsing all my awareness.

The Orb.

I saw the Orb now with the visions of my bodiless consciousness. *My soul.* Stripped of the filters of flesh, the Orb was less a portal, less a mechanical or geometrical phenomenon as it was a mind in and of itself. Yet, if a mind, it was of such complexity, such alienness, such godlike stature that I could comprehend almost nothing of it.

And yet I felt an affection. A concern. In the midst of that terrible mind of incomprehensible indifference, there seemed to beat a heart of empathy.

And it reached for me.

I felt a power take hold of my awareness, and suddenly I was drawn through a thousand corridors of brilliance. This time there was no pain, no confining tunnel or prison, no fear. There was joy. Overflowing joy and anticipation like that moment when one finally has discovered an element sought in a long and forgetful quest.

Ambra!

I called. My own thoughts seemed to echo like sound around me, coming back and leaving again, transformed, as if a million different voices uttered the word in response while they all recombined into my own tones. *A host.* I felt them. Mind upon mind around me, inside me, in places I could not imagine or reach, yet present, aware, and anticipating my transit with nearly the same joy I felt.

And then—starlight. Looming and bright, golden radiance bathed space around me. I raced past several gas giants. A blue-and-white disk maniacally rotating, featureless and blurred, until I came to a stop. A solitary moon revolved rapidly around it, slowed, and then appeared to stop as the rotation of the planet came to a standstill.

New Earth.

I seemed finally fixed in time as the globe rotated at a pace I could remember from...*before*. I drifted slowly through space toward a hulking asteroid orbiting the world. As I approached, I recognized the shape, that Earth-shard ripped from the heart of the Sahara, the sand plains of the Temple and Six Cities unharmed at its apex.

Now I sensed differently, and the bedrock of New Earth was not opaque to my perception. Through the crust my awareness flew into the core of a starship.

In the midst of it, I looked down on myself—myself as I was. The body hardly alive, propped up by Xixian technology, a link over great distances through time and space waiting to be snapped. Nitin Ratava struggled there to remain present, watched the giant shard-ship ascend, his life in that flesh only moments away from ending.

But there was so much more to see than the shell of my former self. Tens of thousands of glowing consciousnesses wrapped in fleshly garments had gathered, the tendrils of their awareness mixing and uniting, fully integrated at the center of the rock.

There the tortured flesh seemed hardly present in the midst of a resplendent shower. Threads from ten thousand minds wrapped together with the thick ropes of a single, powerful consciousness to create a tapestry so massive, so intricate, so *alive* that my own mind was in awe of it. As I tore my focus away from this transforming aggregate, I was able to perceive the nexus underneath. White, human flesh. Red hair. Green eyes aimed in the direction of my vantage point.

"Nitin."

She spoke with the flesh of her body, through lips I had once kissed and adored. I could no longer touch those lips, and a distant echo of me yearned for that once more. Yet, I was becoming something *else*. Dwarfing that faint echo was the joy and desire to embrace the form that was invisible to me in my flesh. Ambra Dawn now transcended the woman I had once known, had misapprehended, had torn down to human stature. Before me was indeed the form of a goddess.

No, Nitin. So are we all. And you will understand that soon.

I missed you, Ambra.

The face on her supine form smiled. *And I missed you. Come to me.*

My awareness floated the final distance and hovered inches above her body. All was as I had last seen it, the stripped flesh and remade nervous system now one with the starship. Now I could see the effects of this sacrifice in the distortions of space and time around me. Her tumor served as some powerful transmitter, her entire body the fleshly dish, the thousands of Readers around us interwoven with her thoughts.

Closer, my love.

I passed through the ghostly essence of her body and was enfolded by the fullness of her consciousness. Her mind enveloped my own in a manner unlike anything I had ever known. As partners of the flesh, I could not have imagined any joining more intimate, more powerful, more transfiguring than that which occurred when we made love. Yet it was only an echo of what could be. At that moment, the depth of sharing that could be between minds finally became clear to me. It was complete, and so joined, there was an *us* greater than the separated *two*.

And not only two, beloved.

And the host opened itself to me. This time I was not afraid. I was not overwhelmed. I *became* with them. An unusual structure, centered on a binary awareness at the core, or rather a singular consciousness of the Daughter and my own orbit around her, that connected to thousands of other minds. As their awareness, their thoughts, their personalities swept through me, I knew each of them as two fleshly beings could never know each other. Free of confusions and barriers. And each was filled with compassion and interest. With love.

There will be time for so much learning, Nitin. But now, there is a task to complete. Clear your vision and let the Group Mind see for you.

I tried to stop focusing on the myriad of amazing entities around me, to relinquish my grip on controlling my own awareness. Slowly, like some static clearing on a radio receiver, the immediate visions were replaced with a single perspective.

This eye into space was outside the Earth-shard, focused intently on the space just beyond the planet. I felt the power of this gaze, the *otherness* of it.

The awareness was of a creature beyond me, beyond the others, and in many ways alien in its thought processes to my simplistic mind. Yet I shared of it. I was part of it, my own mind contributing to its fabric.

To my surprise I saw an awaiting fleet of ships from New Earth Force. Alongside them, hundreds of craft of Xixian make. I marveled that these forces had been arrayed, obviously prepared far in advance, when I had had no inkling or vision of them before I died.

We hid them from you, my betrayer.

The hurt of what had happened began to fade in me, and I was even able to see the dark humor in her words.

We had set a trap. We told you nothing, and I masked your vision during your time outside your body.

I understood. I would have done the same in that position. Looking back on it, it was a brilliant strategy. If indeed they had the power to defeat the Dram and Anti.

Turning back to the coming battle, I saw that the ships of the Xix had no weapons, but instead projected powerful field defenses to deflect beam and projectile weapons. The Force ships were armed as I remembered them. Xixian designed ion slingers with a flux far beyond those of our MECHcore suits. Missiles, conventional, and, more commonly, nuclear. With several hundred warcraft in position, they had enough firepower to obliterate all of New Earth's cities fifty times over.

But it would not be nearly enough.

In front of us the blackness of space undulated violently, and thousands of ships bent and blurred as I had seen before I died. And just as at the moment when I had lost touch with Ambra and New Earth, the undulations ceased, and the light of the sun was obscured by the Dram armada.

New Earth sat like a small child before the onslaught of a lion. The Dram warcraft opened fire on the New Earth defensive force. Their military advantage was great but not insurmountable. But they were not alone.

Destruction waged wildly across both fronts as ships were cut in two or blown to fragments. The tide turned quickly in favor of our enemies as powerful waves of space-time distortions and antiparticle projectiles impacted our forces. False Dawns and the Anti, hidden in their ships and between the matter of the Dram ships, unleashed a fury that neither the Xixian field defenses nor New Earth's warcraft could counter. Within the short span of minutes, the sum of our planetary defenses lay in ruin and wreckage. A hailstorm of debris covered the surface of New Earth and began to rain down as flaming meteors.

The Dram then turned their weapons on the planet, beam weapons and missiles ripping fire and destruction across the cities on the surface. Bright explosions could be seen across New Earth from space, and soot began to blacken the skies. Many weapons were aimed at us as well, but all were turned away harmlessly. The warships quickly abandoned their attacks on the impregnable Earth-shard and concentrated on maximizing the slaughter below.

The destruction on New Earth created a phenomenon I had not anticipated, but I could feel the expectation of the Group Mind focused on it. The mental matrices, the *souls* of millions upon millions of humans and Xix were torn from their flesh, isolated, and left naked in the fields of space and time. I could sense their emotions and thoughts, bewilderment, panic, and wonder at the sudden and unexpected reality to which they awoke. And waking, they naturally turned toward the light.

One after the other, thousands, tens of thousands, millions came to us, until uncountable masses of awareness flowed like some swollen river into the sea. I felt a great outflow of energy, a sharing of essence that reached out toward them all from the Mind, even if I did not individually will it. *We had.* Ambra spoke in my mind.

The first, Nitin. A small gathering. A test and a change.

What is happening, Ambra?

Part of my awareness again saw her bodily form tense and a smile cross her face.

Something wonderful.

The minds began to soar toward us. First a few intrepid souls approached the Group. Then, the flood. A flood of mental energies and persons from that river of released minds poured into our lake. But a lake smaller than all the rivers combined, so that as they came, the Mind grew. It grew astoundingly, and I felt the integration of these millions into a community of what had been initially only tens of thousands. And the Mind grew accordingly.

Not all approached. And of those that did, not all stayed. Some drifted toward the Dram, the False Dawns, the Anti, but had no manner to join them in their betrayal. But the majority became part of us. As the Dram continued their merciless onslaught, the flood only grew. As they struck down the lives on New Earth, they only made us stronger.

But even with her words and seeing this shocking development, my individual consciousness was seized with alarm and bewilderment as the Group Mind sat stoically and did nothing in the face of this massacre. Yet my presence in the Group was soothed by a greater purpose beyond that which I could predict with my isolated thoughts. My anxiety dissolved, to be replaced with a serene calm. I watched the slaughter, the freed souls, and their joining to the Mind with a peacefulness that might seem diabolical. Part of me felt this discordantly, but it was a minor portion of my experience. The remainder waited in anticipation.

The time has not yet come. Not my thoughts, yet in my thoughts. Not Ambra's thoughts, but of her thoughts.

Then my awareness turned to our enemies, and I saw them with the eyes of the Group. Thousands of refulgent candles stationed in ships around us, their glow poisonous in the fabric of space-time. The False Dawn army was revealed, and one after the other, they released a coordinated barrage of mental attacks on our starship, on the Group Mind.

It was like a series of nuclear blasts. The attacks before shown to be a faint whisper of the power these clones possessed. With these new eyes, I could discern the massive distortions of time and space propagated by these attacks. It outshone the radiance in all energies and fields of the sun itself. All directed on the little rock Ambra and the Readers occupied above New Earth. The False Dawns had perceived what we were.

But I was to see that they understood it as little as I did. Despite the cataclysm of space-time around us, the Earth-shard was untouched. The Group Mind unmoved. It watched. It waited. And finally, its patience was rewarded.

The Anti attacked, and this time, they were not hidden from me. The eyes of the Group were not blind to these beings but clothed them in shapes and hues inverted yet similar to our own. Flooding toward us from the spaces between the ships came another ten thousand craft. The starships were built by minds so different from our own that it was difficult to understand their structure, their purpose—and yet their energies were great. They turned loose a river of antimatter particles toward us.

I could see the annihilations inherent in the properties of this matter in its juxtaposition to the matter around them. Immediately as the outer regions of New Earth's atmosphere came into contact with the particle beam, there were powerful explosions. Matter and antimatter were converted into pure energy. Enormous amounts of radiation blasted outward, hotter than the surface of the sun. It seemed all of New Earth would be reduced to ash once again.

But the Mind moved. To my great shock, it spun out of nothing great fields of energy that countered the particle beam, surrounded it, and cut off the matter of New Earth from it. The nearby Orb flashed, and a stream of energy funneled toward it from our location and disappeared into its blazing maw. In seconds, there was no antiparticle beam, no energy release—only silence and the ships floating before our rock.

Even the attacks from the False Dawn clones ceased. The Group Mind perceived their mental matrices, the distortions in their form indicating distress. Confusion. The same forms could be recognized in some transformed fashion in the small consciousnesses in the Anti fleet. The minds of the Dram warriors appeared stunned. Into the confusion crept a new emotion. *Fear.*

But the False Dawns responded with a last and desperate gambit. All their attention became focused away from us, away from Earth. The group awareness turned to follow it and watched silently as the clones together centered their power on the moon itself. Our satellite, astoundingly, began to change its orbit, the great mass spiraling inward from energies too enormous to contemplate.

A thousand Ambra Dawns pulled the moon toward New Earth: the result would be a true cataclysm. Beyond anything even the Dram had achieved with the asteroid. It would be New Earth's redestruction.

But the Group Mind moved again. My dissolving ties to my old body still painted my awareness in physical terms, and that is why it seemed to me as if two great arms reached outward from the Earth-shard toward our moon. Two powerful hands tore loose the shackles of the clones from the great, rocky sphere and slung them heedlessly across the fabric of space-time away from New Earth. Hundreds of Dram and Anti ships were pulled and stretched like rubber from the distortions induced, shattering, tearing, the occupants perishing.

The Mind stopped the inward spiral in a moment. The moon simply stopped in its orbit, unshaken, undamaged—just still as New Earth rotated nearby. Once again, a powerful sense of awe and fear escaped from the ranks of our enemies. But the Mind had more terrible things yet to do.

The two great hands squeezed and crushed the moon to dust. 73,430,000,000,000,000,000 tonnes of rock exploded inward in a microsecond, the forces contained, no particles leaping outward. Rather not to dust, but to asteroid-sized granules that stayed cupped within the palms of this mental force.

And then, like some celestial shotgun, the moon pellets were flung toward the Dram armada. The projectiles were hurled at speeds unfathomable for any known weapons mechanism, but, of course, what was occurring was far beyond any known technology in our galaxy, even that of the Xix. The result was utter devastation. The Dram craft, filled with thousands of clones who vainly tried to deflect a billion pellets of death, were shredded like no flechette gun had every achieved. The matter-antimatter collision of the moon fragments with the craft of the Anti set off colossal explosions that once again were channeled by the Mind directly to the Orb.

After just minutes of the greatest fireworks display ever witnessed in our star system, the entire space between us and the sun was clarified once again. There was no trace of a starship near New Earth. All had been reduced to atoms or energy and funneled out of the solar system through the Orb to some unknown destination.

The Dram armada had ceased to exist.

Chapter 61

In the region of nature, which is the region of diversity, we grow by acquisition; in the spiritual world, which is the region of unity, we grow by losing ourselves, by uniting.

The Sādhanā of Tagore

I stared across the span of space in front of the planet where once thousands of starships had orbited. There was nothing. The ships were gone. The Anti annihilated. Not so much as a shard of metal floated before me.

Only in the distance, the Orb. I had never truly seen it before. As a man limited by his eyes, I had found it so dull, so bland, so empty and featureless. Now it blazed with light indescribable, revealing layers upon layers of maze-like projections. The depth of it made the universe itself seem small.

Now begins the Gathering of Souls, Nitin.

The Collective grew, not only in size, but to a greater degree in depth, in power, in sentience, in vision, and it spread its Awareness over greater and greater distances as well as through time. Backward to the past, forward to the future. More and more the minds freed in the battle integrated with ours, and our light grew.

There has been a terrible waste. Losses upon losses. A hundred thousand species in our galaxy with each a billion voices. Silenced as their song died within the Void. Souls that now hear a call. Our *call.*

And the souls came. Not only from around us, but from across distances. Across vast spans of time. Slowly, not like the flood during the massacre on New Earth. But hesitantly, as if the distances in space and in time had dimmed our image in their minds. And yet they had felt us, will feel us, glimpsing us fleetingly through space and time. They *have are will be following* the call. Her voice. Our Voice and Mind.

My new eyes seemed to deceive me, because as I returned my attention from the gathering souls to the island of rock the Collective occupied, it had metamorphosed. The increasingly numerous and complex mental matrices of the minds that had joined, and the far more complex interweaving of those minds together—directed and shaped like some symphonic orchestra from the core of the Earth-shard—formed tendrils, tunnels in multiple dimensions, pathways, and portals that wove complex patterns about the stone-and-sand plains of the Six Cities and Temple. The Earth-shard was becoming engulfed, buried in a latticework of light.

I stared at this growing marvel and then back at the Orb. My mind's eye was surely confused. Bewildered. Lost.

Because as I gazed from the great power of our solar system, the projection of the One Orb that touched every star system containing life, there was a moment of reference frame confusion. Was I coming or going? Did I approach the gateway to the stars that had changed the history of the universe? Or was I flying away from it? Was I looking at our transforming Collective or back at the Orb?

Back and forth. No frame of reference was unique or special. I could no longer differentiate.

I could no longer clearly see: What was the Orb and what was We.

Epilogue

Of the theme that I have declared to you, I will now that ye make in harmony together a Great Music. And since I have kindled you with the Flame Imperishable, ye shall show forth your powers in adorning this theme, each with his own thoughts and devices, if he will. But I will sit and hearken, and be glad that through you great beauty has been wakened into song.

The Ainulindalë of Tolkien

Once, when Ambra was only a shadow of what We would become, it was hard to reach you. Now, reaching you is so simple, even if the mind of your author is mostly inadequate for the task of understanding and relating our tale. But Ambra wished it to be known—an echo of her human love for me—that many, even in our distant past, might know our story. That you might listen more intently for our Call. That when your time has come, you may listen for us in the great Void and not be lost.

Our Collective was One with this sharing. And so you approach the end of this book. A book with a story now finished—or, rather, just barely beginning.

So much has been lost that it cannot be quantified, and to consider it is to nearly unmake my individual mind. Yet I rejoice. I rejoice as I have never known happiness. An eternity awaits us, Ambra and me, and we will traverse the cosmos through a succession of ages within eons.

We keep a great and growing company unlike any our galaxy has ever witnessed. At every moment, in every point in space, the mental matrices set free by the death of their fleshly cages find their way to us. Most will join our Collective, adding new voices, unique and often strange thoughts and emotions to a Mind now beyond anything our universe has known. The others will drift, alone and unanchored, until the boundless eternity of creation drives them mad and their souls lose coherence and are absorbed into the undulations of the Void.

The eye of our Mind no longer sees the linearity of time. It views space-time from a perspective that I can only describe (inaccurately) as *outside* of our cosmos. In this view, causality is understood as multifactorial, each point in space-time affected by all the others. As we Become, we have increasing access to all places and all times.

And so we gather the harvest sown across distances vast and times immeasurable. We seek the minds freed at death and by other means that would have been wasted in the emptiness of space. We provide a haven, a shore upon which they can wash up from the chaos of the vacuum. Among the purposes of the Group Mind, there is no other more sacred, nothing with greater meaning than to search the cosmos for sentience and preserve it, save it, augment it, and give it immortality.

Individually, and in mass cataclysm, at points in time near and remote, in the past and future, we find them. We call them. And for the most part, they come. From forms of flesh wildly disparate, with mentalities even more diverse, each addition, each new scale in the musical registry enhances the expression and depth of the Whole.

We began with beings similar to ourselves, whose minds we could more easily identify and locate. Human, Xix, Brax, Dram, Sortax—the list goes on. Personally, we were able to find our loved ones, families, children, friends who had perished. The special forces team of the entity once know as Nitin Ratava came as well: Erica Fox, David Kim, Ryan Marshall, Grant Moore, and Aisha Williams. And when they arrived, it was as if we began to know them for the first time. The barriers between minds were gone. And now this narrative is shaped as much by them as it is by me—it is the Mind that reaches you now.

Yet in all of our searches, a perplexing mystery remains—we have been unable to find the soul of Waythrel of the Xix. Because so many elements of the early Group Mind found great meaning in this search, it has ever informed the efforts of the Collective. Therefore, that we cannot detect evidence of Waythrel in life or in death at any time point searched raises one of two possibilities. The first is that the Xix has been taken so far in space and time that we simply do not yet have the strength to bridge that gap. As we contact you now, that implies a distance beyond our local group of galaxies and more than ten million years into the past or future. The second possibility is that Waythrel is being hidden from us by forces that can contend even with the power of the Group Mind. Both possibilities can coexist.

The solution to finding Waythrel in both cases is to enhance the Group Mind further. That way, we will either be able to bridge the space-time gap separating us from its mind or develop sufficiently to overcome the forces concealing its whereabouts. Therefore, this seemingly lesser purpose in locating a single soul out of the universal multitude is consistent with our great purpose in gathering all souls.

Imagine the integration of the billions of souls across millions of worlds, not at any time point but at all of them. The creature that awakened above New Earth and dispatched the Dram armada was an infant—ignorant, wide-eyed and empty. It could hardly speak, and walking was beyond its undeveloped capabilities. Now we approach an early adolescence, and our faculties lie far beyond even the imagination of that newborn child.

We are become greater than what we are. For us individually, it is this labyrinthine filigree of separate sentients, sharing thoughts, flowing through and around awareness, constantly learning and changing and giving. It is a loving harmony, and those minds that cannot fulfill that existence of love and peace always detach and seek their own way.

We are like some trillion-celled organism, forming tissues of thought, regulated, divided, yet creating a far, far greater whole. Our individual personalities are like the neurons in a fleshly brain—intricate, filled with millions of internal processes and thousands of external communications with our neighbors in this grand Collective. But the synthesis of our minds into the Group Mind is a step as great, perhaps greater, than the one between an individual neuron and a functioning brain.

What does a neuron understand of the most complicated human thought? And so, what can any one of us understand about those cogitations of the Group Mind? Even labeling this Mind's actions as thoughts is surely a terrible distortion and oversimplification. Those processes available to a simple neuron —biochemistry, cell structure, secretion—are elements wholly unsuited to describe the higher level thought processes in our once-fleshy minds. The activities of the Group Mind therefore must be utterly beyond our ability to even conceive.

We know this. We experience it. We see the awesome powers of what we have become. We do not understand them. Faint echoes of higher accomplishments trickle down to us, bathe us, and modify our thoughts and feelings as the human brain's responses to external stimuli might alter the behavior of individual neurons. But like the neurons, we can only respond and not comprehend.

Yet the cosmos we now see is beautiful. And terrible. Beautiful and terrible beyond the simple explanations our small minds can muster. And what we can understand tells us that the fate of the cosmos, the sustenance of its very fabric, is interwoven with the Group Mind—or, rather, what it will have become in a great and distant future age.

Already we begin to bridge the galaxies, our Collective now powerful enough to cross the intergalactic distances of space and time. We find wild tragedies of destruction like those in our own Milky Way. We watch the fires of worlds consuming themselves in immaturity, or of growing sentients clashing across star systems because of the broken vagaries of evolution. Yet so many of their minds come to us. We absorb them, learn of and from them, and are enhanced.

Now we even detect the stirrings of powerful Minds not unlike our own, yet lesser, in discord, requiring help to survive their own internal disruptions. Already, tens of thousands of Galactic Minds have begun to seek us. A time will come in the successive eons when we will meet and a greater Whole emerge.

Yet always, there are the Anti. Hidden even from us, unmaking, incomprehensible, seeking the self-contradictory goal, the paradox of the destruction of organized thought and action. There is a shadowy sense in us all that some great event lies in a shared future with them, where all things will be changed, and even our Mind, unmade.

In all this we ceaselessly orbit our Daughter of Time. Although only a part of the whole, she is the nexus, the nucleation center of our new consciousness, the core particle around which this mind shard has crystallized. She is the Mother of all that we have become, a goddess in labor, forever giving birth to this new Being.

But still *not* a mere goddess to me.

She may be all these things, but that matters the least to me. All that has happened and is happening, the radical changes to our nature, the growth toward something transcendent—to me, in my core, she is still the woman I was meant to love. She is still the light I followed from the day my consciousness formed. And for a short, blissful time on New Earth and in the heavens, she was my beloved.

Always and ever my dearest, Ambra Dawn.

It is all a matter of time scale. An event that would be unthinkable in a hundred years may be inevitable in a hundred million.

Sagan's Cosmos

MAKER

DAUGHTER OF TIME, BOOK 3

EREC STEBBINS

MAKER

Daughter of Time
Book 3

Erec Stebbins

New York, NY, USA

for Ambra and not-Ambra

It was one hell of a trip.

無

It is not only not right, it is not even wrong.

—Wolfgang Pauli

Prologue

Time and Space... It is not nature which imposes them upon us, it is we who impose them upon nature because we find them convenient.

Henri Poincaré

I was called Waythrel of Xix.

In a time and space that no longer exist, in a cosmos that has been remade, in two books that have infiltrated and altered your minds, my character was part of a grand and terrible quest. One that failed utterly yet, in that failure, triumphed where it had never sought to succeed.

You knew me as an alien to your humanness, a monstrous form of heightened symmetry to your bilateral arrangement, with sixfold projections of limbs and visual organs and a cognitive cluster buried deep within our core. You followed our discovering of Ambra Dawn and her unique mastery of space and time, her cruel life and rise to power in the Dram Wars, and her eventual fusion with our artificial intelligence. There you witnessed the gestation of the proto-Orb as she defeated the forces of the Anti and Dram aggregating around New Earth.

Reader, the recursive loops of space-time and causality have permeated the structure of your minds—not only the hormone- and blood-soaked organ lodged within your human endoskeleton, but also more deeply, into the mind that is the space-time field created by and creating your sentience, the soul that will live on after your flesh decays, to be lost in the emptiness of space or gathered in the Great Harvest.

Many of you prayed earnestly to save Old Earth, to funnel the latent Writer powers of your species across time, all that Ambra and we might amalgamate them, focus them, and undo a planetary massacre. Many of you instead scoffed, yet continued to read through the exhortations of the second novel as you were even asked to consider the Gathering of Souls.

Even so, here we lost many, for the story became increasingly strange by your standards—the characters' experiences remote from those a human animal might ever encounter. The voice was no longer that of your beloved heroine but instead that of her consort, as he spoke through the growing mind that projected his thought across the void and dictated the inspiration of the book's author.

Thus you have been primed.

Now all that is left is the final and most absurd step in the journey: to destroy all belief and memory and be born anew.

And so I am here to convey the true end, which is instead a beginning, to the impossible story of Ambra Dawn. I am here to reach across space and time, across divergent universes separating and uniting us, with fields and waves of thought to inspire this writer of your age. He will struggle one last time to transmit ideas that I myself do not comprehend, because conveying the experience is beyond me. He will take from my own distorted thoughts only a sad caricature, and his primitive mind will then further blaspheme it through the terribly limited medium of your writing system. Thus ideas deeper than the most profound thoughts of the greatest minds of our galaxy will be painted in primitive languages at ridiculously low resolution with a small brush set of syntax and vocabulary, warped through your current incarnations of culture and prejudice, gutted of their essence and recast as grayed mockeries with all the colors washed away.

This is how you will receive the terrible and beautiful story of our Ambra. Do not expect coherence. You will have none. Do not look for consistency. There will be mostly nonsensical paradox. And yet, those paradoxes and absurdities that you read will be far closer to the truth of this universe than anything in your science or religion. And yet every word a lie.

Know also that this is a story of symmetry and symmetries broken, the chronological invariance of the laws of physics shattered by the arrow of time. The perfect balance of particles and their inverse properties wrecked to produce our fractured cosmos nearly swept clean of one aspect of matter, and thus witness to the genocide of the mental superstructure it would have engendered. This is a story centered within an endless fractalled universe that builds and builds, and also devolves and devolves, from and into entities of smaller and larger structure without reference point, without center, into a bottomless abyss of reductive constituents and launched asymptotically toward an infinitely realized synthesis.

This is a story of symmetry repaired and the utter annihilatory creation that is its offspring. In such a tale, there cannot possibly be only an Ambra Dawn. It is required that there be an anti-Ambra, an antithesis, a force in essence, development, and complexity that mirrors yet is not its symmetry mate.

She is of course the clone who took me on Dram—a fabrication of the Anti who escaped their myopic control and launched herself on a quest neither she nor I understood at the time. It was a journey that, in the end, would bring a primordial pair full circle, like a proton and antiproton hurled about in opposite directions through the magnetic bowels of a synchrotron to collide, transforming the fundamental structure of matter and energy—indeed, of our universe itself.

And so I step back into the memories of an existence that now never was, to the moment in an unmade eon when you lost me in the second book, when I crouched within a bubble of space-time under the wild and furious assault of a thousand clones of the Daughter bent on our destruction. It was to be my last true moment with Ambra Dawn, the human creature I cherished above all others.

Part I

I speak of gods and other mad taboos
that scar my soul with two-edged, healing wounds.
Who dares cast down these gleaming gains construed
while marching to our frenzied, empty tunes?
The sand that is your soul will never birth
one flower in this unrelenting drought.
Your brushstrokes paint no truth and have no worth.
In vain you look for meaning through your doubt.
I am a fool, untamed, consumed with pride
and often speak too much on that I love,
for I, insane, once cursed our fall and died
while clasping to my heart a blinded dove.
Whatever sight I have of what is true,
it neither lives with me nor dies with you.

—Mazandarani, *Sonnets from the Desert*

Chapter 1

Even at those astounding energies, the asymmetry between matter and antimatter is extremely small. For every billion antiparticles that were created, there were a billion and one particles. To put it another way, you're essentially a rounding error from around 10–35 seconds after the Big Bang. Doesn't make you feel very important, does it? Of course that's just as much a bummer for the anti-people, too.

Dave Goldberg

I held Ambra's hands tightly.

There was little point in my meditation. With barely the strength of an average human Reader, I had nothing to offer Ambra to resist the siege that descended upon us. In the realm of space and time, I felt myself to be a particle of dust in the sandstorm, dwarfed and blown haphazardly by the churning wrath of wind raging around us.

Yet I did offer something of great value to Ambra. I sensed it in her fear and concern for all of us on this mission who relied so completely on her powers. Already we had witnessed the horrific deaths of the MECHcore soldiers David Kim and Erica Fox. And now each of us in this besieged space-time bubble of Ambra's creation was splattered with the lifeblood of Warrant Officer Aisha Williams—ripped apart by the powers of only a single clone of the multitude now assailing us.

As the sea of orange hair swirled around our transparent vessel, as the hateful assault from the minds of the clones struck blow after blow against our weakening resistance, Ambra reached across and into me, like a child gripping the hand of a parent, and grounded herself in the love that we shared. It was this connection that allowed her to hope, to believe that she would devise some escape from this trap. It was this center of affection for her within me that prevented the storm of antipathy screaming around us from driving her to despair.

And that is why, when the clone came, when it broke through everything around us, even through Ambra's power, ignoring its brethren and their efforts and grabbing my arm, when the strange creature took me by means mysterious and unexpected, Ambra's mind broke. It broke like a ship tearing away from anchor as the frothing sea threw it wildly into the maw of an angry ocean. As the world about me dissolved and I momentarily lost consciousness, I felt for an instant a wild hurt and loss from Ambra, a telepathic cry rippling outward in time and space from that goddess growth in her artificial skull. I heard the cry echo inconsolably through the corridors of time.

But for me, it was truly only an instant. One moment I was in the bubble that had carried us across the galaxy—that crew of soldiers on a mission to halt the Dram expansion—and suddenly, I was not. Instead, I awoke above the planetary surface of the Dram home world, a reckless acceleration propelling me away from it into the blackness of space.

I was not alone. Flying through the emptiness alongside me was a child. Her hair, what of it remained, was exactly Ambra's rusty orange, the hand that grasped the dark purple of my upper arm a bright white turned dull red in the light of the swollen sun. As during the recent journey with Ambra, this clone and I were contained in some type of warped space-time enclosure that sealed us from the void outside. I could not move my extremities—invisible chords bound them. But my eyestalks were free, and I surveyed the girl and my environment.

Below me, Dram receded quickly, the swirling desert dunes blurring to an orange-red planetary disk. In front of us, I sensed the growing presence of the Orb. The clone was racing directly toward it. Part of me was shocked to realize this; I believed at the time that only Ambra had the power to use the Orbs, so I wondered what this crazed creature could be thinking. But another part of me was also afraid. Somehow I intuited the awful possibility: this clone was going to be able to pass through the entity, to what destination and to what end, I could not begin to guess.

"She's following," said the thing beside me.

The words were calm, almost lilting, and yet cold. It was the first time it had spoken. I still reduced the creature to a genderless object, an "it," unable to see the clone as anything more than a warped product of the enemies who sought to destroy us. But my education was soon to begin.

"She's very upset. I told him that she would be. I wonder if he will be strong enough for what is to come."

Told whom what? What is to come? I thought.

"Yes, I think he will be," the clone continued. "They made him too perfect and didn't see what such love would bring. And so there is no stopping the crystallization."

The creature was speaking in riddles, but I was too caught up in the impossibility of all that was happening to formulate rational responses.

At least I could observe. I examined the clone closely. From my knowledge of humans, I would have placed her age at around eight to ten years old, prepubescent; the developmental program to create the reproductive, adult form of the species was only beginning to activate. But I knew that nothing was to be taken for granted with the clones. From what we had learned on Dram, every aspect of their genesis and development had been altered, artificially enhanced, and accelerated, so that this young child before me could very well be half the age I expected, yet at the same stage of development.

The cybernetic enhancements were particularly extensive in this creature, far more intricate and integrated with the organism than anything I had seen even in the most advanced technology on Dram. Where—and better yet, *when* —it had been made was very much a question. At the least, I knew it had to be in the far future.

All the underlying foundation of Ambra Dawn was there. In addition to the hair and skin, the clone possessed the green irises that produced such striking contrasts in the human visual organs and thus were likely strongly selected for in sexual competition in their evolutionary past. The body form was of an expected variant on the genetic blueprint, very likely similar to the eight-year-old version of the progenitor I had just been torn away from: the bones were long and delicate, the shoulders somewhat broad as compared to the average for the female genotype, the hips still narrow prior to the adolescent widening.

The wires and intubations in the skull were fantastic, a labyrinth of insertions and protrusions that connected different regions of the brain to the machinery of the embedded artificial intelligence. The modifications were so extensive that they left the clone with only a sparse covering of the rich hair that characterized this genetic background. Of course, the center of the structure and design were on the tumor inevitably present in the middle of the enlarged skull, the organ that had made this stock so central to the struggle of our galaxy.

Etched across her forehead and face were a set of geometrical lines like dark circuits underneath the skin. The patterns were too angular to be veins or other vessels. I had never seen anything like it in humans before, not even in the other clones we had encountered. I surmised it was associated with the AI and cybernetic technology her makers had embedded within her.

Sifting through all these observations, I finally summoned the calm to speak. "She will stop you from escaping. Without the help of your clone army, she is more powerful than you."

The creature laughed. It was an unusual sound that differed significantly from the response I had grown accustomed to in humans. I began to suspect that this clone possessed a very different mentality than Ambra herself.

"She's not more powerful. Not in this form. Not without her spirit army!" The clone glanced behind her. "What a cry she made for you, Xix. There was terrible pain."

The words struck me like a blow, the memory of it replaying in my mind, Ambra's terrible suffering ripping through me once again. I tried to focus.

"Look at the Orb," I said with difficulty, starring at the tumultuous frothing on its surface. "Already it has turned against you."

"Not against me, Xixian. All her powers will not help her now."

The calm certainty in its voice disturbed me, but I still believed that Ambra was shutting the Orb to our travel. The clone did not hesitate, however, or slow our velocity. The colossal surface of the Time Sphere grew before us, an ocean of confusing features bubbling and churning in anger as we approached. Again I looked behind—we would reach the Orb before Ambra could catch us. Whatever the effect of being shut out of the Orb would be, I would discover it within seconds. I steeled myself for a possible end and stared forward with as much courage as I could.

But we were not impeded. In a disorienting blast of vertigo, we entered the thing, and the bottom seemed to fall out of the universe. We tore through multiple dimensions of nested wormholes. My entire experience from my previous travels with Ambra was only a faint warning of the possible depth and complexity of the internal structure of the Orb. As I fought to stay in control of my mind in this terrible vortex of radiance, I surmised that we must have been traveling great distances, likely both in space and in time, distances unlike any I had breached before. But I had no idea in what direction or to which destination the clone was taking me.

I could no longer sense Ambra. Whatever had happened at the Orb, she had not stopped it or been able to follow, and now she and what remained of our mission were locked away from me across some enormous separation. It was, as I have said, the last time I would ever see her, at least in her original form. Wherever I was going and for whatever reason, I was now utterly alone.

Alone but for a familiar yet strange pair of green eyes staring back at me in a tumultuous ocean of darkness and light.

Chapter 2

*We seldom stop to think that we are still creatures of the sea, able to leave it only because,
from birth to death, we wear the water-filled space suits of our skins.*

Arthur C. Clarke

G reen eyes in the darkness.

I stared up at a night sky churning with stars in patterns that I could not recognize. A soft breeze trickled over me, the sounds of insects or other alien creatures punctuating the soft whisper of the wind. My eyestalks darted about, appraising the planet surface, the heavens, and the figure of the clone sitting beside me.

The eyestalks gazing upward soon abandoned their efforts. It was desperation from the start to hope that I might be able to determine where we were from the stars, but it was impossible not to try. Nothing was familiar. Wherever and whenever I was, the constellations resembled nothing my mind could map, even considering multiple viewpoints within the galaxy. It was quite possible that I was not even in our galaxy.

Since both of us were alive on this world without environmental suits, I could conclude that the planet was human-Xix compatible. The humidity—something we desert-spawned Xix are always sensitive to—was low, almost an arid climate, but not nearly as dry as Xix or the New Earth desert from which we had begun our disastrous mission. I breathed in deeply through my skin sacs. The oxygen levels were likely a little higher than optimal, but not so high as to represent a significant concern.

Finally, I turned my attention to the human cyborg in front of me. The child sat with its legs pulled up, nearly obscuring the head, the green eyes that haunted me in the Orb traversal peeking over the kneecaps. It wore clothing of a fabric unknown to me with an unusual style combining elements of robes and skirts. The material was homogeneously colored a light beige. The clone's arms were wrapped around its legs, keeping them together as the child rocked slowly back and forth. I detected a faint sound, rhythmic pitch changes and repeating patterns. I think it was humming.

I sat up and stared across at the creature. "Where have you taken me?" I asked. The child continued to rock and hum, seeming to ignore my question. I continued, "I know it is far. I know we are not in the galaxy I have known, either in physical space or in time." Still no response. "You have torn me from your progenitor in the middle of an assault of other clones. But I contributed little to their defense. You have dragged me through the Orb to this world alone with you for nothing."

The humming stopped. "Not alone."

"Not alone?" My eyestalks swiveled around anxiously.

"Not for nothing." The intubated, tattooed head cocked to one side, the green eyes staring fixedly at me. "I didn't take you to weaken her in the battle. It's not *then* that you have to worry about her, but at the *beginning*."

I sensed the tendrils of the creature's thought dancing around my awareness. "You are probing my mind."

The head darted to a strange angle, forty-five degrees and peering from behind its right knee. "Your thoughts leak everywhere. You Xix are leaky-brains."

The child jumped to her feet, catching me completely by surprise. It stopped to stand above me, long, ragged clumps of red hair dangling haphazardly and nearly obscuring its face.

"If not to harm her, why?" I managed.

The clone sighed and stared up into the pageantry of the stars above, the density of lights very high and unusual to human or Xixian eyes. I noticed that there was a milky-white sphere the size of a marble embedded in her skull just slightly above the forehead. It seemed to glow weakly from the starlight shining through it. "There is so much to understand. He didn't understand either when I told him. But *I* don't really understand. It's a *problem*."

I pulled myself upright, uncomfortable to be prone and beneath this unpredictable creature. "Who is *he*?"

"Her consort. The soldier. The one with the hole in his mind."

I nearly caught my breath. *It knows?*

The clone shook its head. "Worry, worry, worry, worry, you Xix. Stop! I haven't told them about your trick. It's a very clever one. I liked it a lot. But it already happened before I was born, and there is no stopping it. Not like that. *They* wouldn't listen about that at all." The clone gestured in front of us dismissively. "That's why you're here. That's why I had to take you. Because there is no stopping any of it—but we have to find a way. Not to stop. *No stopping.* *Un*make. *She* told me. *Showed* me. All of them did."

"Look…" I paused, not knowing what to call this thing, but feeling a primal need to address it personally. All my instincts sought to engage with my captor to better understand it. But it was challenging enough simply remaining calm in the presence of this engineered assassin. Trying to converse with it, knowing that at any moment it could kill me or use me against Ambra, made the effort nearly impossible.

"Call me Kloan," it interrupted, "since you can't get that out of your mind."

"Clone?" I repeated, or thought I did.

"No. K-L-O-A-N. Like 'Joan' but copied genetic materials with tubes and wires and all this!" She gestured wildly with her hands toward her head. "I don't really have a name. Not here. It's just numbers."

"Kloan." Her green eyes darted toward me and then away. It was a strange name to suggest, but it was surprisingly comforting to have a personal name for the thing. "Okay, Kloan, what I wanted to say—"

"And I'm not here to kill you. Where would I be then?"

I had no answer to that, hardly understanding the question—certainly not its context. My mind raced through the dialogue, parsing each phrase. "You negate killing me, yet leave open the possibility that you are going to use me against Ambra."

Kloan smiled. "Depends on what you mean by *against*."

"You speak in conclusions without providing me any of the background data!"

She nodded, a satisfied look on her face. "That's *why* you're here. *Data.* The first data to enter the gate." Again she nodded and then turned her back on me, walking down a steep slope. "Let's get started."

"Started with what? Where are you going?"

Kloan continued walking without turning back. Her next words were nearly lost in the insect sounds and the wind that carried them down the landscape. "To where it all began for me. To watch the beginning flow around us and mature and twist through time and space to come back to be us. Then we will be ready for the next step."

The intense starlight cast sharp shadows on the rocks. The figure of the child was gone, swallowed in the darkness and slope of the hill we stood on. Raising my gaze in the direction of her last words, I saw far below a dim glow. Artificial. Originating from the ground, the light partially polluted the brilliance of the stars near the horizon.

Waythrel, come on!

Her voice rang impatiently in my mind. My eyestalks curled up on themselves. What else was there for me to do?

I followed her.

Chapter 3

Know that for the mind there are certain objects of perception which are within the scope of its nature and capacity; on the other hand, there are, amongst things which actually exist, certain objects which the mind can in no way and by no means grasp: the gates of perception are closed against it. Further, there are things of which the mind understands one part, but remains ignorant of the other; and when man is able to comprehend certain things, it does not follow that he must be able to comprehend everything.

Maimonides

I raced to catch up to the child, my steps uncertain, the dusty ground surprisingly slippery under my feet. Descending the steep slope of this elevation, I stumbled and tripped, my four arms only poorly grasping the rocks and alien vegetation, seeming to lack any friction to form a proper grip. After nearly falling several times, I began to suspect that there was something strange going on, that I had been drugged or that there was a phenomenon on this world that interfered with my basic movements.

It's a field around you.

Her thoughts danced again through my mind.

It's skintight, coating your surfaces, insulating you from everything around us.

Listening to her voice and trying to understand what she was saying, I nearly crashed into her as I rounded a large boulder. The ground was strewn with shattered rocks and their remains, products from avalanches tumbling down from the jagged hills behind us.

"Why is there a field? What kind of field?" I asked.

Kloan was staring ahead at the source of the light. A city or military installation of some sort rose from the the dry lands. Organized groups of shadows marched throughout the installation. It seemed like a very busy place.

"I don't know what kind of field. She—*they* make it for your protection."

"Protection from what?"

Kloan pointed toward the city. "Come. It's almost light. That's when it all begins. We'll go see me there, and then you'll see what happens."

She began to walk toward the complex but I reached out quickly and grabbed her shoulder, turning her back to face me. "Wait! This is another clone production facility, isn't it?"

"Yes."

"Where you were made?" She simply nodded. "And one in the far future and someplace very far away. We can't just walk right into that place—you saw what happened the last time!"

"There is no danger," she said.

"Maybe not for you! But *I* can't. You said you didn't want to have me die. They'll kill any Xix who shows up for sure!"

"They won't see us. We both have skin suits. *Dark ones*. Their eyes can't see. Ears can't hear. Not even the Readers will perceive."

"*You* saw through Ambra's bubble! You came inside it, even."

Kloan shook her head. "Hers was simple. Weak. Primitive."

"And yours around us now is none of those things?"

"I told you, they're not *mine*," she said sighing. "Now, come on."

The child pulled me forward, and I relented. If it had wished to kill me, it could have done so before—and easily. I was helpless here, and I desperately needed to learn more to find any hope of escape. If there was any such hope, that is.

A bright light erupted from the darkness in front of us, a flash that blinded my eyes, leaving blurred afterimages. A fireball climbed into the air and darkened, the smoke from the explosion already beginning to snuff out the brilliance. The ground shook, and the rending sound of supersonic compressed air blasted over us, even at this distance.

"Too late," she said, squinting from the dust blown forward. "It's already started. Why did we come to this time point? They'll already be moving on the structure and surrounding me."

"Surrounding you?" I looked around us, seeing no evidence of anything besides the landscape.

"Not here! There!" she shouted impatiently, gesturing with her hand. "The tunnel must be there, but we can't get to it before it closes. But we'll go through it soon!"

"Kloan," I said unsteadily, "you're not making sense. What tunnel? Where is it, and why do we need to go through it?"

"It's the only way to escape! At least without so many deaths. The masters will bring all the children against us—I couldn't just slaughter them. I didn't want to. She knew that so she helped. But it will happen too soon, and we can't be there when we go through!"

The child seemed to be insane and speaking nonsense. I didn't know what to say to help make sense of this situation. With a growing unease, I began to conclude that my questions weren't going to help clarify anything.

Kloan continued, breathlessly. "We can go around, find the path. *Yes.* Catch up maybe before we leave and then you can see before we leave as well."

As I stood there, stunned, she began to sprint back up the mountainside. I reviewed my status. I had just been plucked from one time and place, torn from all those I loved and removed from the desperate fight for the soul of our galaxy, dropped into this strange place of confusion with a being who spouted nonsense, only to turn from one mad rush to another, none of the reasons for anything explained.

She was nearly out of sight, and I would soon be alone. I had to follow her again. It was absurd, but she was all I had to connect me with the past and my home. This child-thing was both my captor and hope for deliverance. Yet for all I could tell, she was utterly mad.

Again I ran after her.

Chapter 4

One cannot determine what is real. All one can do is find which mathematical models describe the universe we live in. It turns out that a mathematical model involving imaginary time predicts not only effects we have already observed but also effects we have not been able to measure yet nevertheless believe in for other reasons. So what is real and what is imaginary? Is the distinction just in our minds?

Stephen Hawking

With the low friction of whatever *field* had been placed around me, racing up the slope proved to be far harder than descending. Even in the growing light of the breaking dawn on this world, my footing was far from secure. On multiple occasions my usually sturdy six-toed feet failed to find an adequate grip, and I tumbled forward, once smashing my torso against jagged rocks and slicing through my exoskin. Fortunately the endoskin was unbroken, and no fluid vessels were damaged, but it was clear that this field did not protect me from mechanical trauma. I was beginning to wonder if its sole purpose was more hindrance than help.

Her voice echoed in my mind once again.

Stop complaining, Xix! We are late!

The explosions continued for some time below, and I tried to understand why we were running up this mountain in the direction opposite of the chaos if the chaos itself was related to someone we had to meet. "We'll go see me there, and then you'll see what happens," she had said. What had the child meant? Another clone copy below?

The greatest blast yet followed, nearly lost to us as we rounded the mountain face, concealing the city behind it. I had nearly caught the child at last. She stopped and turned around, staring backward.

"It's going to be close," she said, panting. "Look, above is the path and the gate is still shut."

"What gate? Explain to me, Kloan!"

"It's our door. The one we have to take to save everything." Already she was moving forward again.

Fatigued, I slowly climbed the rocky hill behind Kloan. In the distance I was able to glimpse a shining disk glinting in the morning's nearly horizontal rays from the local star.

"That's it," she said, sweat dripping from her face and eyebrows, her white skin reddening with the exertion.

"The gate?" I asked. She only nodded. Whatever it was, it laid at least an hour's walk up a difficult terrain. I did not relish another hike in the strange field that was wrapped around my body.

Indeed, the trek proved especially challenging. The path was a series of terraced rock outcroppings that seemed stacked one on the other. On each flat sheet, the going was simple, but between the outcroppings, there was a sudden elevation requiring a short free climb. Normally this would not have taxed me greatly; the gravity on this world was actually slightly lower than that on Xix and only a little more than Earth. But in this frictionless field, I can only assume that I beat the odds by not having slipped to my death.

Reaching the partial summit of yet another ridge on the path, we pulled ourselves up to our first real view of the gate Kloan was referring to. From this vantage point, it appeared much larger, the circle of reflected light at least two or three times our height in radius. A portion of the disk seemed buried beneath the rock itself, so that the path ahead of us cut through the gate like a chord. This segment of the circle was invisible. From our current position, the surface began to appear less reflective and more like the semitransparent skin of a body of water.

But I had little time or interest in examining the gate more carefully. My eyes fixated on three humanoid figures in front of it. One was clearly human, and from its shape, the color of the hair, and elements in the skull, I knew it to be another one of the clones of Ambra Dawn. Next to it was a much taller body with many more appendages. It required no guesswork to see that it was a Xix. It too stared forward toward a third figure in front of the gate. *A second Xix.* A Xix I could see as it faced us, and which I knew only too well.

It was my lifemate, Synphel. I felt the nerves in my legs fail slightly as the synaptic transmissions in my cortex consumed my signal fluids. Images and emotions darted through my mind of a life lost, a lover lost, and now seemingly found in front of us. I steadied myself on the rock we had scaled, hardly daring to believe what my visual organs were showing me.

"Kloan, why didn't you tell me?" I asked. "How can Synphel be here? Who are the others?"

Kloan looked forward, her eyes squinting in the bright light from the disk. "It's too close to me, this future. There was no other Xix the first time. Something has altered the timeline."

"First time? What are you saying?"

But before I could get an answer, I let out a cry. Right before my eyes, even as I gazed motionless at the forms in front of us, Synphel disappeared. It was instantaneous.

"Well, that's new, too," said Kloan.

"They're going through the gate, aren't they?" I asked. "Where?"

"I don't know," said Kloan. "The timelines are scrambled now. It's only cycling."

"Can we follow them?"

"We go where the gate takes us."

I rushed forward. I had to speak to these creatures, find out why Synphel was there and where my mate had gone. Like a nymph I fixated on this one goal to the exclusion of all other thought.

"Waythrel!" cried Kloan. "It's no use! Look!"

Concluding some conversation, the pair in front of us clasped hands. In desperation I watched them turn toward the disk and walk forward. The bright light reflecting off the disk warped and flowed over their forms like some gelatinous wall, completely enveloping them. Their bodies seemed to be absorbed into a void that floated behind the reflective coating, and with a rending finality, there was a final pucker in the surface, and it snapped closed and flat once more. They were gone.

I slowed my run and came to a stop. Kloan caught up to me quickly. "We can't follow Synphel," she said. "I don't know where it went. Or how. But the others went through the gate."

"Can we follow them?" I asked.

"Only the gate chooses."

As I rested several meters away from the huge disk, a deep physical and emotional fatigue settled on me. I tried to push it away as I examined the portal more closely. The prismatic lights dancing effervescently across the surface resembled a cross section sliced out of an Orb. For all I knew, this was indeed what it was, something like the projection in the Temple on New Earth where we had begun our mission. I didn't know if this system possessed an Orb. It was true for all systems with life in our galaxy, but whether we were in our galaxy was very much in question.

The surface that had seemed so metallic, like polished silver, revealed itself at close proximity to resemble more a fluid—a viscous, churning honey-like substance. All I could see within were stars—depth upon depth of star fields that appeared to have no end. I felt pulled toward the thing as I gazed. It was beautiful.

"I want to try, Kloan." Pure desperation flowed through me. "If we can find them, we can maybe find a way back—find Synphel as well."

"But we already have found them."

"Please, Kloan! Just tell me how to enter this thing!"

"Yes," she said, "it is expected. But all the ways are bent, Waythrel. Broken ways. Nonlinear topologies. Space-time discontinuities. The dimensionality is unclear."

"What does that mean?" I asked. The only thing that mattered was finding my way back.

"Once we cross the manifold, we are locked. A never-ending narrative, endless recursion. Loops that end as they begin with different parameters."

"You mean that we may never be able to escape this world line?"

"Yes."

"Then we die in it." It was worth the risk.

"No, Waythrel," said Kloan. Her brows were furrowed at me, the emeralds inside her sockets flashing. "There may be no death. Only endless looping, ages without aging, circles in time never marking time. *Trapped.*"

"Trapped in what?"

"One of the local hells."

All my eyestalks stared at the mad thing. "How else can we get out of here?" I asked, gesturing to the planet.

"Only the gate," she said. "That is how I left the first time."

"The first time?" A suspicion began to brew in me. "The clone you mentioned—where is she?"

Kloan smiled. "She's right here."

"This is where you left? When you went to kidnap me?"

Kloan nodded. "Yes, I've gone already through the gate, so that I could come back with you." She smiled. "It's an elegant loop, yes?"

"It's madness!" My eyes were darting in several directions at once. I placed my hands to their stalks to steady them. "Can't you summon some wormhole or something? Get us out?"

"Not from here. I don't have that power alone. The Orb brought us, remember?"

"I can't stay here!"

"You are not the only one tested, Waythrel." She sighed. "Each time is different. When we finally understand, we'll see the way." She turned toward the disk. "Now is the next step, the next stage of the journey. Do you want to enter?"

I looked around frantically, my mind barely anchored in this bizarre reality. "So, we can remain here, try to survive by avoiding the Anti below, only to perish eventually in some remote corner of the universe, or we can enter into this portal and risk eternal damnation to a self-referencing and modifying timeline?"

She smiled. "Yes."

I felt that I was being asked to leap into an abyss with no pause for deliberation. Who can imagine infinity, or what might lie on the other side of it? I knew that I could not properly judge the risk because as a finite creature, my understanding of quantity—space or time—was terribly limited. I did not truly understand what horror I might be consigning myself to.

"You are going with me?" I asked.

"That is the whole point."

Remembering the actions of the previous pair, I reached over and grasped her hand.

She laughed. "Seems we will always be dancing together, Xix."

My eyestalks wrapped around each other tightly and the covering sheaths expanded over them, blocking out all light. I was terrified.

Kloan tugged on my hand. "Don't be afraid, Waythrel."

We walked slowly into the gel.

Part II

I weary of the voices that I hear:
the cries of triumph, long and knowing talk.
No more. No more! Away I turn my ear
and seek once more the silence where I walked.
To know true contemplation as before—
There freed from facts, the finite skin of trees.
This star-filled growing womb is now my door
and home and very substance that is me.
Each force and austere symmetry are mine
in flesh and knowledge without truth unknown.
Yet seeing all more makes me less divine-
I hold small stones beside the sea alone.
Beyond the truth are dreams that make it so.
What shapes the Everwomb? I seek to know.

—Mazandarani, *Sonnets from the Desert*

Chapter 5

I felt cold, yet all other signs pointed to a temperate climate for my species. I unfurled my eyestalks, trying to remain calm as my visual organs adjusted and brought the environment around me into focus. As a Xix, the nature of my sense of vision is difficult to describe to humankind. The broader wavelength range of photoreceptors that paints reality in hues and shadows unknown to you is the minor difference. It is instead the integration of eighteen eyes and their ability to be oriented in nearly any direction that produce both a panoramic and a multidepth layered view of reality that is quite impossible for you to clearly conceptualize.

As my eyes focused, I quickly recognized the location. There was significant radiance with maximal wavelengths in the green region of the human frequency perception. The light poured down from a single focal point, a star that bathed what seemed like an ocean of green vegetation extending around me in nearly 360 degrees. There was the sound of rushing water close by, and a soft breeze swept over my chilled form. Nearby, a loud, feathered creature squawked in irritation.

"New Earth," I said.

A girl's voice piped up. "Nope. Close, though. The *old* one."

My eyes turned from their distant contemplations of the Great Plains and focused down a hill on the stream running past. At the foot of the hill was Kloan, all her garments tossed to the side and soaked, her thin, athletic form immersed in the water up to her ribcage. She was vigorously scrubbing her skin.

"It's *super* cold, Waythrel," she said through chattering teeth, "but if you want to get all that goo off you from the gate, come down!" Her bright smile in the midst of our strange adventure was unsettling.

I was too stuck on her first words to me. "What do you mean, 'the old one'? Old Earth? Before the Calamity?"

She was dunking her head in and out of the water, breathing furiously, her pale skin flushed. Globs of clear gel dropped from the hair and machinery as she ran her fingers across the irregular surface of her head. "Yes! *Cold!* Old Earth! *Argh!*" The words were garbled half underwater.

"How is that possible? That timeline has been completely overwritten. Multiple histories have occupied that space now. There is no Old Earth in any universe we can access."

Her bony back was half out of the water as she was nearly bent in two, clawing the gel out of her ears. She turned a half-submerged head toward me with a quizzical look. "You really don't understand how screwed up this all is, do you? You're a little stunned. Stood there like a statue for five minutes after the traversal. It'll get easier." She straightened, her oddly disproportionate prepubescent form dripping with water. "Old Earth, other universes, gods. It's all coming, Waythrel! I see them all like shadows on the horizon." Her head plunged back into the stream.

In my time with Ambra, the Xix had helped engineer the travel of group minds through time, the alteration of time, cause and effect, and the formation of space-time distortions the likes of which had never been imagined. But there were still hard-and-fast rules, impossibilities that were intrinsic to what we understood of the universe. If she was right, if we were on Old Earth, then the powers that were staging our journey worked in realms far beyond the science anyone in our galaxy comprehended.

Water splashed as her head popped up, and she raced out of the water, shaking like a small mammal. "I can hear them, Waythrel! All the voices of this world, their languages, accents, thoughts! So young and primitive and naive. They don't even know the Dram control their entire planet, that they're all slaves." She looked me over. "You really need a bath."

With resignation, noticing the clumping aggregates of the gel dangling from my arms, I made my way to the stream.

"Don't worry about how you look," she said, dashing across the muddy shore like a child seeing the daylight for the first time.

Her words seemed pointless until I reached the water. While I would not have been disturbed to see the reflection of my form drenched in the gate gel, that was most decidedly what I did not see.

"Kloan! What is this?"

I stared down into the water, the surface disturbances making the reflection distorted and unfocused. But it was clear enough. No towering Xixian shape with eyestalks and purple spots greeted me but rather a brown-skinned woman dressed in dark, flowing robes, sporting a white coif over her head. The woman looked to be in her early twenties, with deep brown irises, black eyebrows, and, I assumed, thick black hair hidden beneath the head covering. My mind flitted through Earth's history and data.

"Looks like they made us Catholic nuns," came a breathless voice as Kloan nearly crashed into me. I stared at her. She was bent double from lack of oxygen, still completely naked but much drier after her wild run. Her reflection in the stream showed only another nun.

"Who made us nuns? Why?"

"Waythrel, you aren't quite ready for the *who* of the matter yet. Why nuns? I have no idea. Looks like we're from Mexico or something." She strolled over to her clothes and began to dress.

I stared back and forth between our reflections and our bodies. "Our true forms are not shown at all to this world, yet they are to us."

"Yeah, seems," came a muffled voice as she threaded herself into her beige robes. "I think that because this is *precontact* Earth, we're both just a little too much for them." Her head popped out of the top with a grin, sparse orange hair flapping haphazardly around her, wires and tubing glinting in the sunlight. "You wouldn't believe what these little fields around us can do." Her grin was unsettling.

I stood still another moment and then entered the water, realizing that there was little I was going to deduce from this strangeness. As I worked to remove the congealing molasses, Kloan turned more serious and scanned the horizon around us.

"There is a town nearby. I can feel them," she said. "Not very big. I think we're in the Midwest of America, near the time of the Calamity. All these," she said, gesturing to an ocean of manicured fields of corn and other crops, "are the last little farms of the independents. Big Ag left a whole other kind of footprint. No, definitely *not* Big Ag."

My efforts to clean up were becoming a far greater quest than Kloan's. I had waited longer, and the gel had hardened significantly. My greater build and more numerous appendages made things all the more challenging. The strange material seemed to work its way even through cloth and under my translator, coating every surface of my body. Several eyestalks struggled to stay focused on her. "How do you know all this?"

"It's part of our training. I'm supposed to know all about Ambra Dawn. Her world, the environment that shaped her, is a very important component of that, you realize. But now that I'm here in this timeline, it's so easy to access the recent past. We had a lot of things wrong. I'm learning so much!" She nodded slowly. "That's really the whole point, I'm sure."

She seemed both a carefree human child and an impenetrable enigma. Her smile was broad, and she stood on her toes, gazing outward with anticipation. It was becoming increasingly difficult to see her as a monstrous product of an assassin training program.

"Leaky-brains," she whispered. "I'm never what you think I am. *Ever.*"

I paused from my decontamination. While her words seemed innocuous, they sent a chill through my emotional centers. Nothing was ever as it seemed with this clone.

She turned toward me and snickered. "The great Waythrel. The great *gooey* Waythrel of Xix. Hurry up! We need to find out where she is."

All my eyestalks turned to her. "Where who is?"

Kloan sighed and shook her head at me like one would a slow child. "*Ambra,* of course. We're not here for Old Earth corn."

Chapter 6

"The world, marm," said I, anxious to display my acquired knowledge, "is not exactly round, but resembles in shape a flattened orange; and it turns on its axis once in twenty-four hours."

"Well, I don't know anything about its axes," replied she, "but I know it don't turn round, for if it did we'd be all tumbled off; and as to its being round, anyone can see it's a square piece of ground, standing on a rock!"

"Standing on a rock! but upon what does that stand?"

"Why, on another, to be sure!"

"But what supports the last?"

"Lud! child, how stupid you are! There's rocks all the way down!"

David Hume

We set off along the stream in a direction Kloan had chosen. The day was already turning warm by human standards, and Kloan's sparse hair quickly became matted to her instrumentation by sweat that dripped quickly down her head and stained her robes. The bulge of her tumor shone like a boiled egg in the bright sunlight.

Despite what was for me a very welcome heat, the climate and enormous water expenditure from irrigation in the region produced a high local humidity that counterbalanced the warmth, making the journey uncomfortable. I found myself longing for the Sahara, a climate far closer to that of Xix itself. For the hundreds of years I had spent on New Earth, I was fortunate to have avoided the more humid climes on the world for all but the briefest visits.

My skin sacs were now clogging with water, and obtaining oxygen was becoming strenuous for my system. I knew I would tire quickly in this place.

Within an hour, which found both of us increasingly fatigued, we reached a small roadway that crossed the stream over a poorly constructed bridge. Kloan stepped onto the road and walked across the decaying structure.

"It's not far now," she said, picking up her pace.

I rested a moment, holding onto a protective railing, its metal rusted and warped from years of neglect. The air around me, pregnant with vapor like some suffocating blanket, had become a wall to my psychology, oppressing and denying me my will to continue. I had to focus on the advancing form of the Ambra clone and force myself forward.

The landscape changed little over the course of the day as we walked: scattered houses and barns, seemingly endless plots of corn, the fields thirstily drinking the water provided by the irrigation systems. In the times of silence between us, the sounds of random birdcalls and wind gusts were punctuated by the whisper of swaying stalks or at times a sharp pop as the fibers expanded from heat or growth.

Eventually, from behind us, I heard the sound of a vehicle approaching. We both instinctively slowed and looked down the road. A battered pickup kicking up a cloud of dust pulled to a stop to our left. In the bed of the truck, a group of workers sat huddled, staring at their feet.

"Mornin'," came a rough voice from within the cab. A large hat leaned toward the passenger side. A begrimed face, burned and leathered from the sun, peeked only slightly out from under it, an aquiline nose leading the charge. "You ladies need a ride?"

I began to assess the situation. Clearly our external disguises continued to hold. I checked our reflection in the vehicle's windows to confirm, as I found it difficult to place significant confidence in a strange espionage plot that remained unexplained to us. The driver appeared safe and likely would lend us a ride without incident, assuming nothing of our true natures could be gleaned by close proximity. I began to quickly weigh strategies and risk analysis when Kloan simply decided for us.

"Thank you, kind sir," she spoke, every bit the foreign nun she likely appeared to be. "Do you know how far Flache-Schale is from here?"

Flache-Schale? That was Ambra's hometown! How had Kloan known?

Been scanning the past around here, Waythrel, and this nice man's memories.

"It's right up the road, ma'am."

I watched the reflection of Kloan as she put her hand to her chest, grasping a small wooden cross hanging from her neck. "Oh, that is good news, sir. We are lost and very tired."

"Hop on in."

I began to move back to the bed of the truck, but the driver called out.

"No, sister! You don't wanna be sittin' back with any of those. You two come on up front."

I saw Kloan repeat thanks to the man. My eyes were held by several of the men in the back. Migrant workers, I assumed. Latino. Their bodies were broad from the manual labor but subdued, slumped, only a dim light seemingly left in their eyes for the harsh lives they lived.

"Hermana." A rough voice.

I followed the sound to the back of the truck bed. An older man tipped his hat to me. I saw one of the younger men kick one next to him. A soft chorus —"*Hermanas*"—spilled from the group. All eyes remained downcast. Unprepared with the proper cultural protocol, I quickly turned back toward Kloan and followed her into the cab.

"I'm Rick," said the driver as I closed the door, sandwiching Kloan between us. "Headin' into town myself. We'll be there in ten minutes."

The gear shifted clumsily, and the truck lurched forward. I could sense the stumbling of the migrants in the back as the sudden movements threw them backward. My gaze traveled instinctively to the passenger side mirror. I continued to be amazed at my appearance on this world. To the mirror, I was a young Latina nun. To my eyes, the driver had just allowed entry to a completely alien creature and a child Frankenstein without the slightest concern.

"You headin' to the Catholic church on River Road? You're nuns, right?"

Let me talk, Waythrel.

Kloan spoke shyly. "Yes, sir."

"Well, I've got to get these boys over to the Milson farm, so I can drop you as far as downtown. Folks will get you to where you need to be."

After our slow plodding, the cornrows seemed to dash past our sides in harsh geometric patterns. The fields thinned, and the number of houses proliferated quickly. The town was near.

Kloan nodded. "We appreciate the help, sir. It's good of you to welcome strangers so warmly." Her quick assimilation of cultural norms was astounding.

The driver laughed roughly, eyeing the review mirror. "Well, you two will be more welcome than these aliens, anyway."

Chapter 7

For the naive person does not understand that the true majesty and power are in the bringing into being of forces which are active in a thing although they cannot be perceived by the senses. Thus the Sages reveal to the aware that the imaginative faculty is also called an angel; and the mind is called a cherub. How beautiful this will appear to the sophisticated mind, and how disturbing to the primitive.

Maimonides

The truck rattled off, spraying us with fumes and dust. The wonders of vehicle eTech had made slow inroads into the farmlands in this period, despite the nearly complete adoption of electric cars on the coasts. Downtown reflected this allergy to modernization, with the buildings and general maintenance of the dying independent farm communities seeming to freeze the place in the middle of the twenty-first century.

The flurry of shocked expressions and subsequent darting eyes initially unnerved me, but it was soon clear that this was not due to our true forms but rather those that had been imposed on us. It helped that every few minutes some passerby would smile and speak a welcome.

We had debated briefly about our course of action. I still had no idea why we were here, why we were nuns, and what we were to do about it all. There was no sign of Synphel or the other clone, no indication of previous visitation through the gate, and no reciprocal gate to return us from this impossible place that, for all I could understand about cosmology, should not exist.

Kloan insisted that everything had to do with Ambra and that she particularly needed to find her. With nothing else to present as an alternative course of action, I acquiesced. So, as unsettling as the idea was to bring this clone near the Daughter, even in this strange, impossible timeline, we set out for the Dawn's farmland.

That was when the priest found us.

We had planned to walk the journey, as I wanted minimal contact with the inhabitants. Kloan estimated that it would take an hour to reach the farm, but as we made our way through the town, a bearded figure raced toward us from a side street.

He was in his midfifties, draped in a brown monastic habit, a wooden crucifix flapping wildly as he lumbered across traffic and toward our position. A horn blared as he issued a series of distracted apologies to the driver, all the while keeping his eyes fixated on us.

"Looks like someone has been expecting us," said Kloan, smiling. "This should be interesting."

We stood still and observed the spectacle until the man stumbled to a stop, panting a few feet in front of us. My eyestalks divided between the priest and Kloan. He was bowing before us.

"Please, please," he said, breathlessly. "There is little time. And this is not the place to talk."

"You have been expecting us?" I asked.

He stared up at us and straightened, fear in his eyes. "Yes. Yes, of course. The Lord has revealed his path to me."

I pressed him. "The Lord? You have received divine revelation concerning our visit?"

His eyes darted around toward the ambling pedestrians, returning quickly to us. He licked his lips. "Be merciful; do not test me here."

"What have you seen?" Perhaps he was a latent Reader and had experienced foresight of our travels.

"Dreams," he said, his eyes wide. "Terrible dreams. Please, you must know that there isn't much time."

"Time for what?" I asked.

His right hand went instinctively to his cross, and he grasped the pendant like a talisman. "I am only a humble servant of the Lord. I beg you; I do not understand the visions. God understands," he mumbled, nodding almost ritualistically. "Yes, God understands."

Kloan smiled. "We will go to your church then? Yes?"

He nodded, ushering us across the street in the direction he had come. "Yes! Please, this way. We must retreat to the house of the Lord. Before the evil arrives. We must be under the protection of his wings."

He began to half jog across the street.

I spoke to Kloan. "Before who comes? What evil?"

Kloan didn't answer; she simply shrugged and motioned for me to follow.

We darted through the wide avenues of the decaying infrastructure like some huddled group of cultists before doomsday. The priest's words began to weigh on me as I considered all the dangerous possibilities. Dram agents aware of our arrival? The planet was thoroughly under their control. Yet their numbers were few, and their ability to monitor the entire planet was therefore limited. How could they know of us so soon? Had forces of the Anti, or something worse, pursued us? Kloan's cryptic words of gods and monsters were not comforting. Certainly the priest had expected us. Perhaps others had as well.

After several blocks and turns, we entered a more tree-lined street. A church was now visible a block ahead on the left, the splayed sunlight from the leaves and branches around it painting a dappled pattern over the stone facade. Children on bicycles darted up and down the road, and the mundane sounds of the local human community mingled with my own anxiety to create a disturbing dichotomy.

The sign in front of the building read "Saint Anne's Catholic Parish." The priest paused before it, seeming to find great relief. He sighed and rested his hand on the sign. He turned toward us and smiled wanly.

"I am sorry for this rush. Please excuse my rudeness. I am Father Geoffrey," he said bowing again before us. "But you likely already know everything about me." He looked at us expectantly.

The priest clearly thought we possessed extensive knowledge far beyond our measly confusions. It seemed a mistake to clarify our own ignorance at this stage, even if there seemed no way to feign omniscience.

I looked to Kloan for guidance, but she seemed distracted. Her posture was rigid, her eyes closed, a strained expression on her face. "Kloan?" I said, reaching out and touching her shoulder.

She spoke as if from a distance. "Father, thank you. Why don't we enter into the church now, and hope that it provides the protection you believe it can." His face fell.

My own feelings likely echoed his own. I turned to face her. "Kloan, what's going on?"

She turned toward me and opened her eyes. The irises seemed to glow green. "Wormhole, Waythrel. Very close. It is opening now, and it is not empty."

Chapter 8

He had forgotten that all life is only a set of pictures in the brain, among which there is no difference betwixt those born of real things and those born of inward dreamings, and no cause to value the one above the other.

H. P. Lovecraft

"Into the church!" said Father Geoffrey, running forward. He clenched his hands into fists and unclenched them, stuttering his steps to avoid tripping over his robes.

We followed the rushing priest at a less manic pace. He led us away from the majestic front portals and around the side of the structure, stopping in front of a small wooden door. He dug into his robes with both hands.

Kloan tried to calm him. "The tunnel is immature, still ripening. Nothing will come through immediately. Maybe we have an hour. And then they'll have to find us."

The priest looked over his shoulder as he fumbled with keys to the door. "What foul creatures are coming from that pit of hell?"

"Hard to say," said Kloan in full deadpan. I looked at our monstrous forms, undoubtedly demonic to this poor parish priest, and wondered how we were going to deal simultaneously with this charade and whatever was coming through the wormhole. "But it seems things are converging."

"Here!" said the priest, brandishing one of several keys. He quickly unlocked the door and scrambled inside, flipped on a light switch, and dashed to a telephone.

"Good thing we still have the old landlines," he said. "Cellular has been on the fritz all day with static. Interference, if you ask me," he added, firing us a conspiratorial glare.

It was a small kitchenette, hardly large enough for the three of us and the small table and chairs in the middle of the room. Statues of the crucified Christ hung on the walls. A religious calendar was affixed with magnets to a small refrigerator.

"Who are you calling?" I asked.

He looked surprised. "Why, the Dawns, of course," he said, listening as the phone rang on the other end. "I will tell them to bring Ambra as soon as possible." Again the quizzical look as we remained silent. "For the baptism." He began speaking into the receiver.

Baptism. Ambra was an infant in this space and time! She had been headed here all along! We would have missed her had we gone straight to the farmhouse.

"And missed whatever is coming for her," said Kloan.

Father Geoffrey replaced the receiver. "Yes, yes, you know." He eyed us suspiciously. "Of course you know. Why must I doubt? Why do I doubt?" He placed his hands to his head and shook it as if trying to throw off some raging headache. "God's messengers. You are God's messengers. I do believe!"

"God's messengers?" I asked.

"Yes. Angels." He looked at each of us in sequence. "Angels from heaven sent to save the child!"

"You believe we are angels?" I asked.

He appeared burdened by the question. "You are nuns. Simple nuns visiting from the Sisters of Juana Inés de la Cruz. I see this. I see this. I have the papers in my office," he trailed off, starring fixedly at us. "But behind your faces...I have seen in the dreams. Terrible dreams. The terrible faces of the Cherubim." He placed his hands over his mouth. "Why does the Lord test me?"

Kloan walked forward. "Please sit down, Father. Let us talk openly, at last."

The priest's eyes widened, half in fear, half in anticipation. We took seats in the small room, the metal chair legs grating loudly on the floor. Kloan took his hands in hers.

"Father Geoffrey, this is going to be hard to understand, but even for angels, the power of God is overwhelming. Sometimes, for some of the lesser powers, when we are sent by the Divine, it is a difficult journey."

"Difficult?"

Kloan nodded as if to a child. "Yes. Our nature, so miraculous to your own, is still finite, still traumatized by the infinite power of the godhead."

Awe crossed his face, and awe filled my mind at the deftness of Kloan. I had become relegated to the status of a nymph by a creature I first considered but a gifted child. This creature absorbed cultures, mythologies, mannerisms, and even people's darkest fears and feelings of awe. She did so in the span of hours. Then she refracted those back in prismatic conversation that served her own purposes. What *was* Kloan?

"What is it you wish from me?" he asked.

"We have lost much of what we knew before we came, priest. But God has a plan, yes?" He nodded. "Your dreams, the ones tormenting you, they hold the information we need. Please, tell us now the content of your dreams, down to the darkest detail."

A moan escaped the priest. "No, have mercy on me, I cannot! Do not make me speak of them. I see them even in the light of day!" He began to shake.

I interjected, trying to find a voice in this strange quest. "You do not need to speak, Father. You need only give your permission, and open your mind to us. We may read your thoughts as one might read a book."

"This is possible? Forgive me! I cannot but doubt." He shook his head. "All is possible to God. Yes. Yes! My body, my heart, my mind are in God's service. I am your servant." He grasped our hands tightly and closed his eyes, as if he believed the process would inevitably be painful or draining.

Kloan's mind was powerful. Instantly I was plunged into the priest's thoughts as she homed in like a missile on the swirling chaos of his visions. Colored by his own metaphors, myths, and fears, they spun a nightmare of demonic invasion, rips in the fabric of nature, vile creatures from the fiery pits setting foot on the soil of mortals. Two great demons were loosed; they dragged their scaled forms across soil and water, blackening crops, turning rivers to steam, laying waste anything in their path—a path ending before the unmistakable form of the church we now occupied.

On this religious house, a light shone seemingly from all directions and yet could not be followed, emanating from the spaces between space, beyond the reality they entered. Monstrous yet holy shapes stood in the middle of that light, many armed, many eyed, of multiple faces—they stood in the doorway and refused entrance to the hell-beasts. Behind them, inside, resting on a throne, were a mother and child—only the mother was not the Virgin Mary but a farmer's wife with red hair. In her arms was not the Christ child but a baby girl with skin white like porcelain.

The dream then shook terribly from the roar of the beasts outside the church. Space itself seemed to ripple in distortion at the power and hatred they unleashed. The dark forms advanced, frothing clouds rushing in with them, lightning, thunder, fire, and blood raining against the church walls. In front of them, the creatures of light brightened, and a terrible crescendo seemed to rise unseen in the very air itself, the essence of space seemingly pregnant with power and poised to snap like a stretched string.

Suddenly, I found myself back in the kitchenette, holding hands with Kloan and the priest. The dream was gone. The terrible noises and images were replaced with the humming of the refrigerator compressor and the dim lighting of the room. The priest opened his eyes, and Kloan sighed.

"That's all?" I asked instinctively. "What happened?"

The priest shook his head. "It always ends there. I cannot see beyond this terrible moment." He looked expectantly toward us. "This is what you need? Now you can tell me what it means?"

I looked toward Kloan. I was as baffled as the priest and hoped that she knew something I did not.

"It means a great battle is coming today for the life of the child," said Kloan. "For the life of Ambra Dawn. You had guessed correctly, Father. Great powers will arrive soon and seek to unmake a great history of God's plan."

Forces of the Anti, Waythrel, came her thoughts in my mind. *They have long sought this reality to kill her before she became Ambra Dawn.*

"And you," he said, indicating the both of us, "you are the servants of the light? As in the dream? You will defend the child?"

Kloan stood up and nodded. "You have seen our true forms in your dreams. We bring great power here." The priest crossed himself. "And we will stand in the doorway and do battle with those who seek the destruction of the child."

Chapter 9

A loud banging sounded from somewhere within the building. Father Geoffrey jumped, fear in his eyes. He turned to the door connecting the kitchenette to the sanctuary and stood up, pausing, unsure how to proceed.

"It is the child and her mother," said Kloan with a bright flash in her eye. "They are at the front doors."

"God have mercy, they are here already," said the priest. He scampered forward through the door and entered the church proper.

Following close behind, we entered the sanctuary. It was a small church, holding only five rows of pews. The ceiling was high, however, conferring a sense of a more grand space than might be justified by the remainder of the design. The decoration was sparse, consisting of stained-glass windows depicting saints and events from the life of Jesus. Statues occupied prominent locations in the sanctuary, the nave and the narthex of the building. A listing of the beatitudes was etched in marble and hung on the wall beside the main doors.

These we approached. Kloan seemed charged by some unseen potential, and I saw her lean forward and nearly touch the doors with her hand, as if she could reach through the wood and find those on the other side. Unnerved by her behavior, I approached cautiously, watching her and the priest simultaneously. Father Geoffrey released the numerous locks studding the double doors and pulled inward with some effort. The three of us stepped backward slightly as sunlight poured into the dim chamber through the opening crevice of the doorway, revealing a dark silhouette in the sunlight.

Ambra Dawn was carried in, cradled in her mother's arms, sound asleep with an angelic tranquility on her face. The child was still a newborn, perhaps into her second month, a thick growth of red hair covering a significant portion of the cranium, but short, like a human male's typical hairstyle. She was clothed in a white dress, a thin band with a flower tied around her head. I suppressed a deep urge to go to the child, to hold this nymph-form of the human being I loved and had seemingly lost forever.

"Father Geoffrey," said the mother breathlessly, not yet noticing our presence. "I came as fast as possible. I haven't told Graham. He's away to Omaha looking at a new harvester. He would kill me with the scheduled date just a few days away! My entire family is going to kill me!"

The priest placed a shaking hand on her shoulder. "Thank you for trusting me, Cleena, and trusting your own instincts," he said cryptically, and turned to us. "These are the two I told you about."

Cleena gasped. "The nuns from my dream…"

The priest nodded. "You see, my friends, there has been much stirring in the cornfields of Nebraska these last few months." He turned back to Cleena. "Let's get you inside and shut these doors. It is no longer safe outside." He began to push the large portals back together, and they groaned at the action.

"It is no longer safe *inside*," said Kloan. "Especially in front of these doors." The portals slammed shut, and the sound echoed through the church. Father Geoffrey nodded at Kloan's words as she continued, "We must bring the infant to the sanctuary, the altar. After that, there will only be a little time left before they arrive."

Cleena stiffened and whispered, "Who will come? I haven't been able to sleep since the birth! Always a dream of running with Ambra, always the two of you running alongside! Why are you here? What will happen?"

The priest motioned forward. "Let's get her away from the entrance and into the heart of the church, Cleena. We don't have much time."

Without an answer to her question, she nodded and gently carried Ambra forward. And truly, what answer could any of us have given her that would be comprehensible? The vague threat her latent Reader powers sensed told her all she needed to know to bring Ambra to this place at this time. I hoped her trust was not misguided.

Truly, I myself began to feel the anxiety that had been plaguing the priest and Cleena Dawn. Because of the encroaching presence of the Anti forces, the fearful whispers and dreams of these humans, or perhaps the repeated proclamations of danger from Kloan, a fear had taken root within me. The walls of the church seemed to shrink around us as I imagined the forces searching for the child converging on our position. *Evil?* Whatever to call it, there hung in the air itself a dark electricity that wormed its way into my deepest awareness. Whatever would happen would happen soon.

Cleena held the child behind the altar as the priest prayed. Kloan took my hand and led me to stand before the pair, facing outward toward the entrance.

"It's time, Waythrel," she said ominously. "They're here."

The others felt it. The priest paused in his prayers, turning to look over his shoulder as if something unclean had arisen in the darkness. Cleena Dawn held her child more tightly to herself and closed her eyes, repeating the interrupted litany abandoned by the priest.

And then, after a terrible moment of silence, the massive wooden doors at the front of the church exploded inward in a thousand fragments.

Chapter 10

She who knows does not speak;
she who speaks does not know.

一老子 Lǎozǐ

Dust and wood rained down across the small church, and small wooden shards even embedded themselves in the pews nearest the entrance like released arrows. Cleena Dawn screamed, and the baby, startled, began to wail. Ambra would cry for the entire time of this mad encounter until a final, terrible silence.

The dust cleared quickly, and through the doors two forms entered the church—teenaged girls, red haired, pale skinned, and green eyed, with a cyborg's intubated, computerized cranium.

"They sent clones," I said, a chill running through me. I looked to Kloan, and like a dancer well versed in all the steps of a choreography, she walked down the middle aisle of the church, seemingly unfazed by the carnage.

The two clones paused as she approached, and I felt the undulations of space-time rock me as these three creatures sparred in realms I could only weakly access. There was little overt violence as yet, but I felt the growing tension as the combatants probed each other.

"Give us the child," said the clone on our left. "Give us the child, and you may go. If you resist, we will destroy you." Kloan merely stared at them.

I was unsure which form the invaders saw. No doubt they were presented with the nun, but could they tear through the disguise that concealed our true natures? What would they do if they knew that Kloan was one of them? If they attacked, would Kloan be able to resist them?

"I said give us the child," the clone continued in a whisper, taking a step forward and raising her arm slowly.

"Wait!" said the other, grasping her hand while staring intently at Kloan. "What are you?"

"A Reader who seeks to meddle, and overestimates herself," said her twin.

"No," said the second, more firmly grasping her duplicate's arm. "Don't you see it?" Her brow furrowed. "There is something different. Something *deep* here." The clone's anxiety deepened, and she took a half step backward. "You're the one who made the path, who found Old Earth. Aren't you? We followed you. We had given up finding a passage." The clone swallowed. "What *are* you?"

Still Kloan said nothing. The two clones looked over the rest of us, pausing only briefly on the other humans, yet clearly noting Ambra, and then examining me more closely. The more perceptive clone continued, "And something is hidden in that one, but I sense it is not much of a threat." She turned back to Kloan. "But this one is different."

Seconds seemed to drip by tortuously. "Are you here for Ambra Dawn?" Silence. "Have you come from another time path?" asked the first clone, seeming to catch her copy's hesitancy.

"There would be no conflict in our missions," offered the first as Kloan said nothing. "Why do you shut your mind to us?"

"Together we can break your will," said the other, "and take the child by force. We *will* take the child. We *must*. I sense you know this. Step aside, help us." She offered a hand, and then let it fall. "Or die."

The temperature in the room seemed to drop. I could not determine if that was an objective aspect of some unseen engagement I could not perceive or my own fear. Indeed, I felt the parameters of space and time being drawn taut like a bow, the tension growing to a breaking point, an arrow only seconds from release. The baby cried out as if in pain.

"She will not let us in," said the first, her voice strained, beads of sweat on her brow.

"So be it," said the second.

And then existence detonated around us.

Because space-time became both a weapon and a victim of assault, it is impossible to say how "long" this conflict lasted. Minutes? Judging from the final carnage, that seemed reasonable. Or was it years, hopping in tubes and bubbles of punctured chronology? In the impossible distortions that followed, reason no longer was accessible. There was no way to know, no way to count time. Causality broke down, and meaning was lost in this epic restructuring of our local universe.

I was as useless as I had been in the assault on Dram. While infinity seemed to open and swallow the space in front of me, I tried to turn backward to find

Ambra. I might not be able to battle these goddesses, but I could at least find the baby, at least try to protect it from some random piece of debris or accident from the seismic events induced around us.

But before I could act, I was thrown to the ground. Light, sound, and senses unknown rocked my awareness. Barely able to raise my eyestalks, as if the gravity on the world had increased tenfold, I saw that there was extensive damage to the church. The pews were in disarray, most flattened, the damage approaching the sanctuary yet always managing to fall off before that sacred space was harmed. But the humans were not unaffected. The priest was nowhere to be seen. Had I seen him step forward and approach the intruders? I could no longer be sure; I had become so disoriented in this melee. But Cleena Dawn was there, unconscious, flat on the carpeted surface near the altar. I could not see the baby. Ambra was gone.

Slowly—or quickly—eventually, I felt the space-time chaos slacken, and a growing warmth emanated from behind me. I managed to turn my body around and raise my eyestalks slightly, glancing toward the front of the church.

The scene I witnessed will never leave my memory. The roof of the church and the entire front wall were gone, the splintered wood and cement still present, floating, defying gravity, yet scattered as if by a frozen blast. Each piece of the wreckage rotated slowly as if in outer space, positioned yet not immobilized completely. The nearby houses, trees, parked cars—all were untouched.

Suspended in the air in front of Kloan were two bodies. Behind them, elements of the wooden structures destroyed—thousands of shards and smaller chunks—had been rearranged and amalgamated, glued together via some unknown power, and assembled as planks at ninety-degree angles behind the two attacking clones. Their hands were pieced with stained-glass shards from the shattered windows to these planks, their ankles similarly impaled as they hung motionless with heads bowed, circlets of smaller glass shards around their heads, dripping blood.

They were crucified.

Kloan waved her arms, and the constellation of materials dropped to the ground while the progress of time seemed to lurch into gear again. The lifeless bodies defied physics and continued to hang on their crosses above the ground.

"Ironic and satisfying imagery of death, I think," she said, turning away from the fantastical nightmare and walking toward me.

Despite all my growing empathy and care toward this clone, I had never felt more strongly the divergence between her and Ambra. Though Ambra could certainly kill and undertake raw, violent acts in the defense of those who resisted the Dram and Anti, her mind, her heart, her soul—whatever it was that constituted Ambra Dawn—existed in some personality space that shared little with this creature. The creative, almost artistically macabre way in which

Kloan had dispatched the clones disturbed me greatly. But there was no time for analysis.

In the midst of my shock, I heard the baby cry again. I turned toward the sound and began to walk toward her.

"Find the priest," said Kloan, taking my arm. "I will tend to the mother and child."

My heart yearned for Ambra, but I was becoming accustomed to following Kloan's lead. I turned around and searched across the wreckage of the church. It was amazing the remainder of the building remained standing. I hoped the priest was not underneath some of the larger piles of rubble.

He was not. I found Father Geoffrey, or what was left of him.

Chapter 11

The two principles of truth, reason and senses, are not only both not genuine, but are engaged in mutual deception.

Blaise Pascal

The space-time tidal forces unleashed in the conflict had caught the poor priest at their most brutal. I found him, parts of him—his upper torso and head still together—prone atop a heap of pew debris. Other remnants of his flesh were scattered about the room haphazardly. His chest had been eviscerated, the muscle and bone mashed and torn like some soft dough. I do not suffer the same horrified reaction as humans to a visceral death of their kind, but the massive trauma to the physiology of this creature still elicited pity. Suffering to a Xix is sin. He had died quickly, at the least.

I heard the baby wailing more loudly, followed by sounds of Kloan moving objects behind me. But I couldn't focus on Ambra or her mother just now. I couldn't take my eyes away from the priest.

"Why did you leave the sanctuary, old man?" I whispered to the corpse. Respecting human traditions, I closed his eyes, but he hardly seemed at rest.

I thought back to the plans I had made with Ambra, in another space and another time. I had seen evidence that something miraculous, something horrible, something completely *other* had come of it, even if so much of my recent experiences brought into doubt both my perceptions and reasoning. She had once spoken of the Gathering of Souls. I wondered if it had taken root. I wondered if this poor creature's consciousness would somehow, someday find its way to a grand collective. *Would we all?* Or would we thrash madly in the void until our sentient fields had lost all coherence and been absorbed into the fabric of space? One was certainly a kind of hell. The other was something I could only hope would be a heaven.

And so my eyes turned back to the lurid abominations hanging in the air in front of me. But I could hardly see them. Instead, my mind dashed through memories, filling my awareness with the hordes of clones descending on us in the Dram deserts, and in particular, the one clone Ambra had tried to reach, to reason with, to love, despite all the torture and mutilation the creature had suffered. The clone she had *failed* completely to save.

The laden crosses rotated ever so slightly back and forth above me. Kloan had hung them like trophies in the air, yet they were once conscious beings who began their lives in innocence—if there could be any innocence in the biological distortions of the Anti, in the birthing warehouses, or in the hormone and nutrient soups that altered normal gestation and development.

Original sin? Was that not the human theological idea? Tainted without conscious choice, before actively sinning. *Born guilty*, to be condemned. It seemed a horrible doctrine devoid of justice, one any Xix would immediately reject.

I walked forward to the crucified clones and touched a dangling foot. Even at my height, the reach strained my limbs. The sole was warm, my twelve digits sticky with blood still dripping from the clone's wounds, my slight touch causing a rocking back-and-forth of the entire form in the air. *Are these ever to be saved?* Their minds were now cast adrift, minds so distorted that they may never hope to find citizenship in the Group Mind, whatever it had become. Minds born into rejection. Sentience warped so severely that hate and madness seemed its only destiny. Creatures ostensibly born and condemned by some sort of horrific, cosmic original sin.

I could not imagine Ambra casting them adrift to be lost to the void. I knew that as a Xix, this was my weakness, my need for harmony and healing for all creatures. I knew that not all species even in our galaxy shared such a commitment to all life. Humans could be both as loving as the Xix and as monstrous as the Dram, often such conflicting behaviors erupting from the same individual.

Yet I had shared with Ambra. I had loved her for nearly three centuries, communed with her in the Group Mind. Her personality echoed in my awareness even now. I could not believe she would not find a way, if there were a way, to bring all minds into the fold. Such inherent and permanent loss was too horrible a fate to even contemplate.

And as if in answer to my questions, the baby shrieked, screamed out in pain and despair in a manner even I, as an alien life form, could recognize as distinctly different from the previous cries. As I turned around toward the frightening sound, thoughts raced through my mind. Had her mother perished? Had Ambra been injured in the melee? Or, perhaps, had she sensed even with her infant powers the terrible cry within my soul?

I froze in place facing the sanctuary. My limbs dropped to my side. I felt a strange sensation deep within me as though my very cellular structure was disintegrating, melting, and flowing into the debris and body parts already littering the ground.

The baby lay on the altar, unmoving, crimson patterns splashed across her white dress. A long, gruesome gash was etched deeply into her neck, blood bubbling and frothing from the airway. The red liquid ran languidly over the altar surface, pooling at the edges and then slowly dripping down the sides of the tablecloth.

The mother was still unconscious on the ground, but most of my eyes were fixed on Kloan. There was a wild look on her face as she stared vacantly forward, blood splattered across her robes. In her right hand was a long carving knife, the blade pointed downward, glinting and crimson, small drops of the infant's blood falling to the ground behind the altar.

Behind me there was a wet impact and shudder. Several of my eyestalks swiveled backward and spied the fall of the two crucified clones. Their bodies lay sprawled on the ground along with the priest. Dust and blood sprayed into the air, sprinkling me with what quickly formed into a thin layer of burgundy clay.

It seemed the world would end. My halting words sounded shrill through the translator.

"Kloan—*what have you done?*"

Chapter 12

The laws of physics might permit the existence, in the real Universe, of closed timelike curves (CTCs). The semiclassical laws of physics (the laws with gravity classical and other fields quantized or classical) should be augmented by a principle of self-consistency, which states that a local solution to the equations of physics can occur in the real Universe only if it can be extended to be part of a global solution, one which is well defined throughout the (nonsingular regions of) classical spacetime.

Novikov et al, "Cauchy problem in spacetimes with closed timelike curves",
Physical Review D, 42 (6), 1990.

G reen eyes in the darkness.
Dizzy, feeling ripped from a dream and dropped into a new reality, I stared up at a night sky churning with stars in patterns that I could not recognize. A soft breeze trickled over me, sounds of insects or other alien creatures punctuating the soft whisper of the wind. My eyestalks darted about, appraising the planet surface, the heavens, and the figure of the girl sitting beside me.

Kloan sat with her legs pulled up, nearly obscuring her head, those green eyes that haunted me peeking over the kneecaps, arms wrapped around her legs keeping them together. She rocked slowly back and forth. I detected a faint sound with rhythmic pitch changes and repeating patterns. She was humming.

I sat up and stared across at her. "What have you done? *What did you do to Ambra?*" The child continued to rock and hum, seeming to ignore my question. I felt desperate.

"What did you do, Kloan!"

The humming stopped. "Nothing."

"*Nothing?*" My eyestalks swiveled around anxiously. "I *saw* you with a knife! I saw *blood* all over you and the baby. Then—only light. A terribly bright light that overpowered my senses. What happened? Where is the child?"

"In the past. Far away." The intubated, tattooed head cocked to one side, the green eyes continuing to stare fixedly at me.

I sensed the tendrils of her thought dancing around my awareness. "You are probing my mind!"

The head remained at the strange angle, forty-five degrees and peering from behind her right knee. "Your thoughts leak everywhere. You Xix are leaky-brains."

The child leapt up, catching me by surprise. She stopped to stand above me, long, ragged clumps of red hair dangling haphazardly and nearly obscuring her face. "We went as a first experiment, Waythrel. I was skeptical, but the Anti always believed there were unstable nodes in time. This was one of their top targets. But it's not *then* that you have to worry about her, but at the *beginning*."

"An experiment? You cut the throat of an infant as a test? You risked killing Ambra, preventing your own existence, because you doubted it was possible and wanted to see?"

"Yes."

I stared at the child, her innocence horribly deceptive. "You are a monster."

"Yes, I am a monster. Don't you know that by now?" She shook her head sadly. "We have been bred to kill Ambra Dawn from the moment we were cloned." She stared at me intently. "It was easy to do, you understand? It would have been hard *not* to kill her. I would need enormous willpower not to, however strange that seems to you. Years and years of conditioning cannot simply just go away. It will never go away."

"I thought you might be different." My heart felt broken. I *needed* her to be different.

"I *am* different, Waythrel. *Everything* is different with me and you will see. I let my instincts have their way because another part of me needed to test something very important."

The horror of the memory would not leave my mind. "Why did you even battle those clones? They would have killed her for you."

"Yes, probably, but I had to be sure. I couldn't have their interference in the experiment."

"You plotted all along to murder a child."

"Not any child. *That* child. If it helps, I would have little desire to kill a random infant. Poor Xix! I am a very specific monster, Waythrel, precisely aimed. And Ambra is unharmed. I am here, as are you, which requires her survival and existence, her actions, an entire tapestry of world lines, entire universes, remember?"

The words were like a slap to my mind. *Words of a dream.* "Where are we?"

"Don't you know?"

I stood up slowly, gazing around the ragged landscape, and then looked down to a flat plain below, the lights of a city washing out the canopy of stars above.

"We are back where we started. When you took me after Dram."

"*When* did we start, Waythrel?"

I stared at the deep green eyes and realized that my sense of time, of cause and effect, was disoriented. Memories seemed to exist as events in a blurred fog, and I could no longer discern what was real and what was in my mind.

"I am confused. Please explain to me what is happening. You seem to understand."

She nodded, a satisfied look on her face. "That's *why* you're here. *Data.* The next data to enter the gate." Again she nodded and then turned her back on me, walking down a steep slope. "Let's get started."

"Started with what? Where are you going?" I asked, bewildered.

Kloan continued walking without turning back. Her next words were nearly lost in the insect sounds and wind that carried them down the landscape.

"To where it all began for me. To watch the beginning flow around us and mature and twist through time and space to come back to be us. Then we will be ready for the next step."

The starlight cast sharp shadows on the dusty rocks. The figure of the child was gone, swallowed in the darkness and slope of the hill we stood on. Raising my gaze in the direction of her last words, I stood frozen, trying to understand what now seemed the madness of my own thoughts.

Did I know this creature? It seemed I did. It seemed we had journeyed in a dream. Journeyed from Dram. Journeyed to Earth before it was New Earth. But now we were here, as if I had arrived from Dram again. Was I sane? Was the universe sane?

Waythrel, come on!

Her voice rang impatiently in my mind. My eyestalks curled up on themselves. What else was there for me to do?

Chapter 13

The opposite of love is not hate, it's indifference. The opposite of beauty is not ugliness, it's indifference. The opposite of faith is not heresy, it's indifference. And the opposite of life is not death, but indifference between life and death. An immoral society betrays humanity because it betrays the basis for humanity, which is memory. An immoral society deals with memory as some politicians deal with politics. A moral society is committed to memory.

Eli Wiesel

I followed her, racing to catch up to the child, my steps uncertain, the dusty ground surprisingly slippery under my feet. Down the steep slope of the elevation, I stumbled and tripped, my four arms only poorly grasping the rocks and alien vegetation, seeming to lack any friction to form a proper grip.

It's a field around you, remember? Her thoughts danced through my mind. *It's skintight, coating your surfaces, insulating you from everything around us.*

Listening to her voice and trying to understand what she was saying, flashes of memory leapt through my thoughts. The strange sensation, her words, walking up the slope to a shining disk in the light—*the gate.*

I nearly crashed into her as I rounded a large boulder. The ground was strewn with shattered rocks and their remains, products from avalanches tumbling down from the jagged hills behind us. "Why is there a field? What kind of field?"

Kloan was staring ahead. A city or military installation of some sort rose from the floor of the dry lands. Organized groups of shadows marched throughout the installation.

"I don't know what kind of field. She—*they* make it for your protection."

"Protection from what?"

Kloan pointed toward the city. "Come. It's almost light, but we're earlier this time. So much slop in the gating," she said, shaking her head. "That's when it all begins. We'll go see me there, and then you'll see what happens."

She began to walk toward the complex but I reached out quickly and grabbed her shoulder, turning her back to face me. "Wait! This is another clone production facility, isn't it?"

"Yes."

"Where you were made?" She simply nodded. Memories flooded haphazardly in my mind. "There is an attack! We can't just walk right into that place —last time there was an attack!"

"There is no danger."

"Maybe not for you! But *I* can't. They'll kill any Xix that shows up for sure."

"They won't see us. We both have skin suits. *Dark ones*. Their eyes can't see. Ears can't hear. Not even the Readers will perceive."

"*You* saw through Ambra's bubble! You came inside it, even."

Kloan shook her head. "Hers was simple. Weak. Primitive."

"And yours around us now is none of those things?"

"I told you, they're not *mine*," she said, sighing. "Now, come on."

The child pulled me forward and I relented. I felt completely helpless here, my mind to be distrusted, events to be suspected—now, those before, those to come. Would I come to understand any of this madness?

We covered the flat distance between the broken hills and the installation quickly. The uncomplicated landscape made my efforts far less exhausting, and I found myself able to observe the growing city before us rather than concentrate on each step to prevent an accident.

It was unlike any city or technological society I had ever seen. Functional aspects to the materials and machines were often obvious. The laws of physics and chemistry are the same across the universe and, as far as we have been able to ascertain, through time as well. But the mentality behind the creation of artifacts to work within the physical laws and manipulate matter and the environment was more alien than any I had ever encountered. Even in our galaxy of diverse life forms, there was not this terrible difference that seemed to border on hostility to the mind. I cannot describe it any more clearly. From architecture to transport surface topology to the use of color and lighting, it was clear that the minds shaping this world were more distant than anything I had known in all my travels.

And yet the place was populated with *humans*. I saw no other aliens, no divergent life forms. And only two classes of humans at that, easily demarcated: those who looked like Ambra Dawn, and those who did not.

"The Anti run things remotely with robots and trained humans," Kloan added, no doubt sampling my *leaky* thoughts.

"To avoid annihilation?" I assumed it would be difficult to be in the presence of so much matter to their antimatter. The energies required to keep the two forms from destroying the entire planet would be enormous.

"No, they are not concerned about that here," she said cryptically, not bothering to explain. "It's just more efficient. Once the optimal program was developed, it could be run by drones and lackeys."

We approached the entrance to the complex. Robotic guards patrolled the gate, hovering above the ground with strange weapons protruding from multiple regions of their forms. They did not notice anything unusual. Apparently, nothing in their technology allowed them to pierce whatever cloaking mechanism was concealing us. Inside were numerous robots of odd shapes and designs, performing functions within the installation. I soon noticed a pattern.

"The humans aren't involved in anything. Everything is done by the machines," I said. I whispered at first, but as time wore on and it became clear that even our sounds were concealed, I talked more freely.

Kloan spoke normally, unconcerned about discovery. "Humans are the social construct for the clones. See, we need people to develop properly, or close enough to properly, or the mind is just too wrecked to become useful. To develop, human neurophysiology needs social fabrics, structures, language, norms. So the Anti imported them. It's a clone growth matrix, I guess."

"Like on Dram," I said, remembering the groups of clones and other humans involved with them.

"Yes, that was the beginning, before it was destroyed."

I was momentarily stunned. "Dram is gone?"

"Terrible civil war. Blew themselves up. But it didn't matter. They were only an outpost."

"And this is another one?"

"One of the last. The devil ball hunts them through space and time. They had to build them farther and farther away, find stronger and stronger clones to shield them from attack."

"Devil ball?"

Kloan looked at me and laughed. "Your little Orbies. We had other names for them. Other thoughts about them. Come, you'll see. You'll *learn*."

We walked through the strange streets of this alien and yet human city. Groups of young Ambra Dawn clones paraded past us at various points, shepherded by older clones and assisted by bands of more diverse humans. As we walked, Kloan would point out buildings or objects of significance.

"Inside these warehouses are the wombs. All clones are born there. They learned early on that the gestational process was a key element in brain development. Purely *in vitro* methods failed terribly." She smiled at me. "It's nice that we're born and not grown, isn't it?"

I didn't know if the strange child was serious or sarcastic. We Xix have mostly mastered the understanding and translation of human conflict avoidance mechanisms such as sarcasm, but there was often uncertainty. With this clone, there was always uncertainty.

"What we saw on Dram seemed much more horrible than nice, Kloan."

"You are a terrible student," she said in a strange tone I had not previously heard from her. "But we can't have lessons now. We have to hurry!"

"Hurry where?"

The child stood still, staring off into the distance. "Home."

Chapter 14

When I see the blindness and the wretchedness of man, when I regard the whole silent universe, and man without light, left to himself, and, as it were, lost in this corner of the universe, without knowing who has put him there, what he has come to do, what will become of him at death, and incapable of all knowledge, I become terrified.

Blaise Pascal

"Home?"

She grabbed my hand and pulled me forward, reaching a near sprint. We darted across the compound. I had little time to process much until I found myself standing in front of a strange building unlike any of the others I had seen here. It was small, a deep black—obsidian—seeming to reflect little light. I sensed strong electromagnetic fields pulsating around the structure.

"Home," she said again. "Or quarantine. Take your pick. With me inside their little box, the compound thought itself safe."

"Safe from you? You mean all this shielding?"

"It's designed to keep me and my powers inside, yes," she said. "It was never really useful except in the beginning, when I was very little. But I never let them know all that. Until the end. Come, I'll get us through the fields."

Kloan pulled me forward again. For an instant, my vision blurred as if I had accelerated dramatically. My space-time senses were reeling; I could not control my eyestalks, and they swiveled around, unable to focus, unable to lock, and a kaleidoscope of flashing images assaulted my consciousness.

"Waythrel, hold onto me."

Kloan grabbed my arm and steadied me. Slowly the dizziness passed. My vision came under my conscious control.

A single room greeted us, Spartan, with basic elements such as a bed, table, latrine, and sink. There were no products for leisure, no children's toys, no books or electronic information sources. Bright light streamed in from a partially transparent region of the quarantine field as the system's star rose for the beginning of a new day. Sounds of explosions and shouts could be heard faintly outside. The room was in disarray; clothes were strewn about, food and utensils as well. My olfactory strips detected a growing acrid smell. *Smoke?*

A child clone of nearly identical appearance to Kloan stood in the middle of the room. Sweat beaded across her forehead. All of her muscles were tense.

She stood before a vortex of milky light that swirled chaotically. My eyes stopped scanning, the stalks still, all my attention centered on the impossible thing I was seeing floating above the ground in front of the child. There were hundreds, perhaps thousands of faces and forms of myriad species of life bobbing in and out of sight in a violent sea of white fog. Many I could identify. Most I could not.

But one I could absolutely identify. The milky vapors had coalesced around a central extrusion. Its shape was that of a human face. The head was split open, the brain exposed behind it and fading into the mist. Tubes and wires, dwarfing the insertions into Kloan, entered and exited the skull. Even the eyes were partially obscured by machinery that seemed to pulse with a life of its own. Only the mouth was free.

"Ambra," I whispered in horror. Despite all the Xixian technology covering and distorting her features, I recognized her. How could I not? How could I forget that beloved alien face that I had followed and nurtured, taught and been taught by for nearly three centuries?

For the first time I came face to face with the price she had paid in our desperate plan to save the galaxy from the Anti and Dram. I looked between the apparition and the two bodies of Kloan in the room. The weight of the truth nearly crushed me. My lover Synphel had warned us. The others and I had only half listened. But now it was clear to me. Now I began to suspect that we had triumphed only by *becoming* the enemy.

Theoretically, I knew what must be happening, but it still stunned me. Ambra had foreseen it. The Readers opposing the Dram had planned it. Together, we had put in motion a terrible, incredible sequence of events to create a group mind unlike any we had ever experienced telepathically—one that was not a transitory product of concerted meditation but would be self-sustaining, growing as a living thing, escaping the parameters of our understanding and control yet composed of each of our individual selves. In the end, it was a collective that I would never join because of the creature standing beside me who had torn me from that previous life.

Our greatest minds had worked out the details as best they could, centering it on the powerful consciousness of Ambra Dawn, but with a cosmic goal far,

far beyond this. *The Gathering of Souls*. A harvest of minds across space and time.

That harvest would give birth to a consciousness, a being of its own that we could hardly model, imagine, or anticipate. Our theories broke down in this extreme context, infinities plaguing the most sophisticated mathematics and artificial intelligence simulations. Because our understanding faltered so deeply, we knew that it could fail spectacularly and yield nothing. Or it might even produce something terrible. Seeing our approaching destruction at the hands of our enemies, we had gambled to create a god whose nature we could not predict or control.

Whatever it had turned out to be in those swirling faces before me, I knew it was not Ambra Dawn. Even with her likeness in the face of this thing, it was not her. It was something that had her at its heart and yet had grown exponentially beyond the seed of its formation. In the power of this consciousness to sweep across time and space and reach this world, I knew that in the deep past, they had succeeded in giving birth to this entity. What I did not yet suspect, and would see only as this journey wore on, was that we had produced both a heaven and a hell.

"The gate is prepared," came the voice of Ambra.

"I'm ready," said the Kloan of this early time.

"You must leave now," came Ambra's voice. "They will return with greater numbers of clones and more powerful weapons. You will be forced to destroy them all if you engage."

"I don't want to kill them. Lead me to the gate."

The stamping of rushing feet came from outside the small building. A heavy rumbling accompanied them, the sound likely associated with a large vehicle of some sort.

"Through the door." Ambra gestured to the only door of the isolation building, and for a moment I wondered why she wished for Kloan to fight the Anti gathered outside when the child had so clearly expressed a desire not to. But the black field that sealed the chamber gave way to a second churning vortex. It opened to span the width of the door. Through it poured bright daylight, revealing not the artificial surface outside her isolation unit but the rocky terrain and vegetation that we had traversed only recently to arrive here.

The countryside within the vortex seemed to extend as far as my eyes could see, but the tunnel itself narrowed as I looked farther. Far at the end of the tunnel, where my eyestalks strained and my vision began to fade, there seemed to begin a worn path on a steep slope. The vegetation was eroded, the rocks smoother, the coloration subtly different. The path rose up the hillside and then abruptly ended at the feet of a large disk. The light of the local star reflected brightly off it, firing blinding reflections into the room that cast shadows on the floor.

Kloan pulled my arm, showing me that her temporal copy had moved to enter the vortex. "The gate," she said.

I stumbled forward, partially blinded by the daggers of light glinting into the room. Outside there was shouting, and the walls of the room began to smolder and glow a bright orange.

"Good luck, my dearest friend," said the apparition of Ambra Dawn as I stepped within the vortex. Several of my eyestalks bent backward to see the disembodied head turned toward me, sending ripples across the sea of blurred, white faces. I saw tears dripping down from her eyes, coating the wires and tubes inserted into her once-green irises, a bittersweet smile on her face. "I love you, Waythrel. Remember that, whatever happens."

The room exploded.

Chapter 15

If all the parts of the universe are interchained in a certain measure, any one phenomenon will not be the effect of a single cause, but the resultant of causes infinitely numerous.

Henri Poincaré

F ire and debris flew across my vision, obscuring the swirling god-thing in the room. Just as I thought I would be pulverized, the portal shut.

Suddenly we were far from the compound, a mile high in the growing hills and mountains, cut off completely from the melee down below. Replacing the terrible rending of the explosion was a stunning silence. Pebbles rattled and shrubs groaned in unexpected wind gusts, only to be stilled and muted until the next dance of air. A faint whiff of smoke that had entered the portal was all that remained of the carnage below.

Shattered by her last words and stunned by the violence we had narrowly escaped, I turned slowly away from the vanished doorway and looked up the slope. The blinding gate was there. Kloan looked down from several feet above me and motioned for me to follow. No one else was visible.

"Where is the clone?" It seemed only two of us remained.

Kloan smiled. "She's right here."

For a moment I paused, confused, my mind still reeling from events. Then I understood.

"This is where you left. When you went to kidnap me."

Kloan nodded. "Yes, I'm gone already through the gate, so that I could come back with you." She smiled. "It's an elegant loop, yes?"

"It's madness!" The images I had just witnessed flooded my mind. "And Ambra is part of it all?"

"She is the heart of it all."

"It can't be! I don't understand!"

"You are not the only one tested, Waythrel." She sighed. "Each time is different. When we finally understand, we'll see the way." She turned toward the disk. "Now is the next step, the next stage of the journey. And yes, a journey sustained by Ambra Dawn. Are you ready to continue it?"

Am I ready? I felt like I had been placed within the memory of a dream, that I had been exactly here before. *To make a choice.* "We've been here before, just like this."

"Not *just* like, but we have been and will be. But never *just* like. Remember the nonnormalizable loop?"

"I'm not sure. But I'm getting a sense of it." My eyestalks rotated to focus entirely on Kloan. "There was more. There was a hope. To go *back*. To find Synphel." I ached to think of my mate again.

"Yes. There was."

"So, we can remain here, try to survive by avoiding the Anti below, only to perish eventually in some remote corner of the universe, or we can enter into this portal and risk eternal damnation to a self-referencing and modifying timeline?" My mind considered the words. "Or have we already done that?"

"Yes and yes."

"You are coming with me?" I asked.

"That is the whole point."

I turned my attention to the gate, a deep uneasiness settling on me. The disk resembled nothing so much as a cross section sliced out of an Orb. The surface looked like a fluid, a viscous, churning, honey-like substance. All I could see within were stars—depth upon depth of star fields that appeared to have no end, bobbing in and out of an iridescent sea. I felt pulled toward the thing as I gazed. It was beautiful. I reached over and grasped the child's hand.

Kloan laughed. "Seems we will always be dancing together, Xix."

My eyestalks wrapped around each other tightly, and the covering sheath expanded over them, blocking out all light. Kloan tugged on my hand.

We walked into the gel.

Part III

My labor lingers long; the pay is poor.
From toil to sleep to toil the chanting brays.
A weariness invades to kiss my core.
A willing lover he has found and stays.
Except those eves inflamed by Holy Songs,
when Shaman Ones chant secrets in the night,
and cease to sing at brilliant birth of dawn—
in mysteries my weary mind delights.
Although at times their truths are hard to see,
and seem estranged from that my heart enfolds,
no doubt my profound ignorance blinds me,
I close my eyes and think as I am told.
Our Shaman Ones doubt not they spin the truth.
As for myself, I do not ask for proof.

—Mazandarani, *Sonnets from the Desert*

Chapter 16

We came all this way to explore the Moon, and the most important thing is that we discovered the Earth.

William Anders

When my mind cleared, I found myself in a recurrent dream. Cornfields. A blue sky and humid summer. A rare hill in the Great Plains that sloped downward into a quickly moving stream. Kloan at the bottom, naked in the water, laughing, pulling great handfuls of slime off her body.

"Waythrel!" she shouted, smiling up at me. "Don't wait so long this time!"

I shivered from the memories of that trip of doom and death, of attack and murder, and stared dumbly down at the assassin herself frolicking in the cold waters. Nothing was ever as it seemed.

"Not here to kill Ambra this time, Waythrel! It doesn't work, remember? Come down before you solidify into some sort of permanent work of art!"

How do you continue to do the rational, the practical, even something so basic and mundane as self-hygiene, when madness lurks at every turn? What was the point of a bath when monsters might be crucified in a few hours' time or a baby's throat slit? Or swirling clouds of souls materialize on worlds to which you have been kidnapped, only to embed you in an endless time loop of psychosis?

I walked down the hill. I ignored Kloan racing around and squealing, holding her robes in one hand like some wrecked kite she was trying to send aloft. I washed. I removed the globs of gate gel. Finally, summoning my courage, I looked at my reflection in the water.

And I saw a child.

A blue-eyed girl, six or seven years old, with blond hair tied into two braids, stared back up at me with a puzzled expression. I looked away, the blur of Kloan rolling down the hill and laughing distracting me. I looked back. The little girl was still there.

"Kloan?"

She came to rest near me, grass stains coating her beige robes, sweat glistening over her flushed face. "More body image problems, Waythrel?" Her smile was hard to read.

"And what are you this time?"

"Same—little black-haired girl. I get a bow in my hair."

I wanted to scream. "I find these facades deeply troubling. What happened before..." I couldn't even finish.

"Before what, Waythrel?" She shook her head in a strange manner. "When you find that absolute reference frame for *when*, please let me know, because all I can be sure of is *now*." She looked into the water. "*Awww.* Piggytails, they call them. You make a cute girl for a squid, Xix!"

"Why are we here, Kloan? It's the same place!" Of all the possibilities for this journey, many in my mind bringing me closer to Synphel, returning to Old Earth again in just such a fashion had not occurred to me.

"But time moves on, doesn't it?" she said, stepping away from the water. "We'll avoid the priests and baptisms. We'll skip on the Ambra clones in this tangent. Don't think we'll see anything like that this time—except for me, of course! Ha, ha!"

I stepped away from the stream, glad to be out of a substance my species was both dependent on and also deeply uncomfortable with as desert dwellers. I longed for our sonic showers. Kloan had begun to walk along the stream in a direction that seemed very familiar.

"Why *are* we here, Kloan?" I pleaded after her.

She called over her shoulder, "To make a new friend!"

It was not difficult to guess who this friend might be. Everything in my experience was intimately connected with Ambra Dawn, and I knew with near certainty that Kloan was headed for her farm. To what purpose in this Old Earth reality, I could not begin to guess. But the images in my mind of destruction and murder hardly reassured me. In fact, they nearly paralyzed me.

Kloan stopped, and her shoulders slumped. Slowly she turned around and walked back toward me, her head bowed as if by fatigue. She came to a stop inches from my feet and crossed her arms over her chest.

"Can't you just keep your mind to yourself?" she asked, sighing. "Waythrel, look. This isn't easy. Not for you and not for me. It's like a rough reentry through atmo with nausea and even some broken bones. And we're likely going to do it for five and a quarter eternities. But you need to see the bigger picture."

"Which is?"

"Well, that's hard to explain," she said, her smile returning. "But you have to *see* it, even if you can't *understand* or *explain* it. You're with a monster clone assassin thing that kidnapped you. One that reads your mind and the minds of everyone around her, as well as reading times past and future. Every now and then, she murders little babies. I can see that causing disquiet." She took my hand and pulled me slowly to the top of the hill.

"Kloan, where are we going?"

"Look, just look," she said, gesturing across the seemingly endless expanse of fields around us. "Over there," she pointed near the stream, "is a pile of cosmic gel that I fished out of my girl parts. *Disgusting.* But how does that figure here? It's all averaged out in tens of thousands of square miles where all the noise disappears. Instead, the big picture—it's a giant food carpet unsustainably managed for a planet that has an energy resource problem."

"Kloan, what—"

"Shhh!" She put her index finger against my translator. "*Our* big picture—Waythrel, it's more than *big*. It's the universe. It's *more* than the universe. It's universes after universes, a small and infinite set spun from our own with uncountably more gestating independently. Universes we can't reach. Universes where the laws of physics are different. Where mathematics is different. Where logic is *other*." She jumped up and down, staring at me. "Two plus two is *not* four in the big picture! Do you understand?"

"I don't, Kloan. I'm sorry."

"Yeah, well, I don't either. But I can *see* it! A billion tangents, a trillion loops we'll take. One after another after yet the other where nearly everything that can happen will happen. It's not about *what happens*, Waythrel. Nothing ever happens here after it does! It's what we take, what we *learn*, what we become!"

"The journey is the reason, not the destination? I've heard this proverb many times."

"No! Of course the destination matters! How stupid is that?" She shook her head. "You're not listening! It's not *what* we do in the journey, because we will do everything! It's *what* we become *from* it! How it adds up! The final path."

"Besides to insanity, you mean? Because I fear I have foolishly entered into a bottomless labyrinth that will break my mind."

"Yes, maybe," she said, staring at me with the utmost sincerity. "But all the angels are mad, Waythrel—don't you know that?"

And she was off again, releasing my hands and striding back down to the stream. Heading north, toward Ambra Dawn.

Chapter 17

How is it that hardly any major religion has looked at science and concluded, "This is better than we thought! The Universe is much bigger than our prophets said, grander, more subtle, more elegant?" Instead they say, "No, no, no! My god is a little god, and I want him to stay that way."

Carl Sagan

And we found Ambra Dawn.

She was out in the long, grassy front yard so meticulously maintained by her father. We had rounded a curve of monotonous cornrow after cornrow, and then, suddenly, there was a grassy lawn with a stereotypical white fence. The green was a deep shade, the strain of grass heavy with chlorophyll, the cells swelled and filled with regular watering. Decorative shade trees were placed strategically across the lawn, and a row of pines served as a natural wind guard on the western end of the plot.

In the middle of the sea of green was a tiny ball of red. Her hair was in complete disarray—long, tangled from rough play, the victim of an unconcerned child who had yet to focus much attention on her appearance. Unsurprisingly, she appeared of an age similar to our own disguises, perhaps seven years old, with a wrinkled, stained dress draped over a pair of blue jeans.

I felt such affection course through me. After being torn from her after so many years together of struggle and hardship, triumph and loss, and then to fall into this churning derangement captained by a godlike, transformed echo of Ambra and her unpredictable clone, seeing the child, lost in innocence and unaware of the future that awaited her beyond the clouds floating above her play—it was overwhelming. Alongside this warmth, an irrational current of ice flooded across my awareness, and I turned sharply toward Kloan, fearing the worst.

"Relax, Xix," she said, skipping forward down the road. "Been there, done that. I need to learn so much here and then destroy something else."

I could not fathom why she would think that response would help me relax. I raced behind only to catch Kloan as she stopped in front of the picket fence. She placed both hands on the pointed tops of the boards.

"Hi!" she yelled across the grass with an enormous grin.

Ambra looked up from the ground in our direction. Her hands were in the grass.

"Hi," she said. Her expression was neutral.

Silence enveloped us as the clone and her progenitor stared at each other across the green field. I assumed we looked like three young children socializing across a pastoral scene, but I could not help but imagine our true forms and how disturbing our presence would appear to anyone watching who could penetrate our disguises.

The silence continued for what seemed an eternity, neither of the two speaking or moving, yet neither appearing uncomfortable or unsure. Then, slowly, Ambra stood up, her hands cupped together like clamshells, and she threw her windswept hair behind her with a toss of her head. She puffed several recalcitrant strands out of her face with a quick breath.

"Want to see a bug?" she asked.

"Yes!" said Kloan, and before I could react, she maniacally scaled the fence, dexterously avoiding tearing her robes on the top points, and landed roughly on her feet. She raced toward Ambra.

I was aware of how little I had thought through the strange disguise our mysterious handlers had foisted on us. Visually, I appeared every bit the small human child. But my real form was something else. Towering over seven feet, I weighed several times that of the average human adult form, possessing far more appendages of much greater sensitivity than those of humans. As I contemplated climbing the fence, it became important to know whether this disguise could simulate structure and mass as well as visuals. In fact, I could not think of any way that could happen. Of course, I did not understand most of the technology that we had experienced from these powerful puppet masters directing our adventures. It was possible such a complete simulation of form might be within their abilities. As I appeared, I might truly be in all physical attributes on Old Earth—a small, seven-year-old child.

I dared not risk it. I took the long way around the fence to the open front gate and then crossed the field toward the pair, who were now huddled together, examining something between them.

"Hurry, Waythrel," yelled Kloan. "Before it flies off!"

I lumbered over to them, exhausted from the long walk, the humidity, and the stress of the constant unknowns. I sat on the ground beside them. We looked at a bug.

"It's a watermelon beetle," said Ambra proudly. "We don't get too many here. And this one is really, really late. Summer's nearly over."

The insect was over an inch long; it was thick and heavy. Ambra had placed the bug on her dress, keeping one finger pressed on its back, and allowed it to climb awkwardly up her chest. "See, look, it has all these stripes. Dad says they can eat up the roots of trees and the corn, so I'll have to show him."

She grabbed the insect between her index finger and thumb. The small creature hissed.

"Wow, what's that?" asked Kloan.

Ambra smiled broadly. "It's really neat, right? They hiss at you, like a cat! I guess it's mad." She held the beetle up to her face and stared at it. The bug was beating its wings vigorously as it hissed. Ambra held it tightly. "Found it by the oak tree. Maybe it's already laid eggs." Her expression seemed serious as she stared at the bug. I wondered if she were concerned for her family's plants.

Her eyes flashed toward Kloan. "You're not from here, are you?"

Well, that's a loaded question, huh, Waythrel?

"No, we're visiting," said Kloan.

Ambra stared back and forth between us. Her eyes stopped on me for some time. "You're really different, Waythrel."

Kloan's thoughts spoke again. *Her Reader powers have begun to awaken. She senses us.*

I wasn't sure what to say. I hoped Ambra could not discern much about our true forms. I mustered my best. "I'm a good friend."

She nodded and turned to Kloan. "Who are you?"

"My name is Kloan."

"Like Joan. But different."

"Yes."

She turned to her bug again, tapping its wings, chanting in a singsong voice, "Like up but down. Like yes but no. Kloan and Joan are all alone."

"All alone and heaven's sewn," said Kloan, and their eyes met.

"Where are your parents?" Ambra asked suspiciously.

"Where do you think, Ambra?" asked Kloan.

The watermelon beetle hissed again.

"I don't think you have parents. I think you're fairies." She didn't look at us.

"Maybe we are."

Ambra turned toward us excitedly, her eyes wide. "Do you want to stay over tonight?" Her eyes bored into each of ours. "I won't tell my parents. I know fairies have to be secret. I can sneak you in the back door later if you hide in the corn."

Kloan smiled. "Where will we stay?"

Ambra's hands danced around her face. "In my room! But we don't have to stay there all the night. Fairy magic is in the night! We can go play in the corn. You can show me things."

"But you will need to sleep," I offered.

She frowned and stood up. "I don't like sleeping."

She was like so many human children. "We can play tomorrow, Ambra. Sometimes you have to rest." She continued to stare off into the distance.

Kloan shook her head. "She doesn't really care about playing, do you, Ambra?" Ambra was silent. "She doesn't want to dream."

Ambra looked at Kloan with wonder and what I could only identify as sorrow on a child's face. She stared at her until a tear rolled down her left cheek.

"I knew you were fairies."

Chapter 18

The illusion of the passage of time arises from the confusing of the given with the real. The passage of time arises because we think of occupying different realities. In fact, we occupy only different givens. There is only one reality.

Kurt Gödel, as quoted by Rudy Rucker

To avoid her parents' eyes, she led us around the front lawn beside the fence. The route first took us farther from the house, but as we entered the cornfields, Ambra doubled back toward the structure. How she knew the direction in these towering seed crops was a mystery. Her Reader powers still being so nascent and raw, it was more likely just her childhood experience in these plant labyrinths. Whatever the source of her infallible sense of direction, she seemed purely joyous as she ran through the rows.

"The corn is as high as an elephant's eye, an' it looks like its climbin' clear up to the sky," she sang repeatedly. Often she was forced to stop and double back to retrieve us as we failed to keep up with her, taking our hands at times and leading us forward at a run.

From time to time, she would stop and point out something about the plants—a particularly tall shoot, or one growing abnormally—and she was delighted at the maturing ears of corn on the majority of the plants. "Dad thinks we'll have them early this year, end of September."

Through small breaks in the tassels, we finally began to discern the top of a two-story home. As we approached, Ambra held her finger to her lips. "You never know where Dad's gonna be," she said seriously. "So be quiet now. I'll go in and see where they are and come back."

And with that she darted forward through the maize and disappeared. Kloan smiled broadly and looked surreally happy. I tried again to reach out and understand this creature.

"Is this environment one that you respond to favorably?" I asked. "Is there some component of your shared genetic background with Ambra that predisposes you to feel comfortable here?"

"I hate corn," said Kloan, her grin unwavering.

It seemed hopeless. "Yet you seem so pleased with things."

She sighed and turned to me. "I'm learning. Learning to understand the heart of Ambra Dawn in every little thing that happens in this place. That's what this is all about, Waythrel."

"Understanding Ambra? Why?"

"Remember the data I mentioned? We both are collecting data, and me even more than you. Because the ultimate purpose demands understanding, requires the deepest and most personal understanding. An understanding that transforms my very person in loving and hating another sentient creature."

"How can hate be important? How can hate go with love and understanding?"

Kloan turned to me and stared into my eyes. "Does love exist without hate? Can there be empathy without the possibility for cruelty? Can this world exist without the worlds of the Anti?"

Our metaphysical conversation ended abruptly as Ambra came bursting breathlessly through the stalks. She wore a backpack across her shoulders and bent double to catch her breath.

"Sit down, let me show you," she said eagerly.

We followed her lead and sat beside the corn stalks. I leaned slightly against one of them and watched the seven-foot-high plant sway dramatically. It seemed perhaps my true mass was somehow reflected in events on this world, even within the disguise.

"Mom's baking like crazy for my aunt's visit tomorrow. Aunt Aideen came all the way from Ireland! She's never been here. Mom is going nuts. Dad hates hosting, and he's already grumpy about the whole thing. He's in the basement hiding, working on his carving." Our blank stares prompted her to continue. "He makes these little animal things from wood with a knife. He's pretty good, really. When he gets upset, he always goes down there; and a few hours later, up comes some owl head or turtle." She smiled.

"What's in the bag?" asked Kloan.

"Yes!" said Ambra as she untied the top of the pack. She reached in and pulled out two things. One was a wooden globe, carved in detail with all the continents of Earth in relief. "Dad made this for me when I started school. This one took him a whole week and he got all these maps and globes to get it right. It's my favorite toy of all and I'm never going to lose it."

I picked up the other object she had brought. It was a hollow metal cylinder with a flue cut into the surface near one end. A dog's head was etched as decoration at the other.

"Is this a musical instrument?" I asked.

"No. Maybe it looks a little like a flute," she said absently, staring at the device. "But watch!"

She placed the object to her lips and formed a seal, blowing hard into the device until her cheeks puffed outward.

My acoustical disks reverberated with the extremely high frequency sound. It was not painful, but it was loud and clear to my senses.

Kloan shook her head. "I don't hear anything."

Ambra smiled. "Just wait."

Within half a minute, there was a series of thrashing sounds in the corn. From behind Ambra a furry creature rocketed through the air and landed in her arms. The dog licked her face, overjoyed to be in her presence.

"This is Matt!" she said, trying to speak over the dog that was all over her face. The dog rested momentarily and then seemed to notice us for the first time. I wondered how well our disguises would fool the olfactory senses of this animal.

"He can tell your not really little girls," said Ambra. Indeed, the dog appeared confused, sniffing us hesitantly, from a distance. It did not react with fear, but it was clearly not comfortable with the two of us, especially me. I wondered how a Xix would smell to a dog.

"He's a Sheltie and really smart. I taught him all these tricks with the dog whistle. Watch."

Ambra blew different rhythms through the whistle, and to each, sometimes requiring a gesture or verbal encouragement, the animal would perform one of a large number of rehearsed motions. Sitting, begging, shaking "hands," rolling, pointing…the list went on. I remembered from the years together with Ambra how much she had loved this dog and how her visions of its death were the reason she believed that she was cursed with a terrible power she did not want or understand.

"Ambra, you're how old now?" I asked hesitantly.

"I'm seven," she said, flipping several treats to the animal from her backpack.

Seven. The dog would die next year. Next spring when the storms came, Ambra would have the vision. After that death transformed the nightmare into a premonition, her view of the disturbing dreams at night, soon to become daymares as well, would forever change. Her view of herself would be shattered. And as the visions increased in power and frequency, both the beautiful and the horrific, the carefree young child before us would become a withdrawn, troubled preteen, soon to be snatched from her home by the Dram after the murder of her parents.

"I better get back," she said, stuffing all her things back into the bag. "Mom's gonna kill me. I'm supposed to be helping."

She stood up quickly and looked down at us. "You're really fairies, right?" She seemed afraid that she might lose this amazing opportunity.

Kloan nodded.

"And you'll wait for me to come back tonight, after everyone is asleep?"

"Yes," I said, my affection and concern for the child and what would befall her piecing me.

"Okay! This is so amazing!"

"Ambra!" It was a loud call from a female voice. Cleena Dawn sounded irritated.

"Okay! Gotta go. Please be here!"

She turned and sprinted back toward the house, the small dog dashing after her. Soon afterward, we heard a firm voice speaking to her as a door slammed shut and silence fell.

Kloan lay back in the dirt and put her hands behind her back, staring up at the sky. Her green eyes sparkled from the sunlight overhead.

"Take a rest, Waythrel. Now we wait."

Chapter 19

*I used to wonder how it comes about that the electron is negative. Negative-positive —
these are perfectly symmetric in physics. There is no reason whatever to prefer one to the
other. Then why is the electron negative? I thought about this for a long time and at last
all I could think was "It won the fight!"*

Albert Einstein

Night fell without incident. Kloan and I sat in the cornfield without much discussion, the sounds of the night creatures slowly building around us, the light above fading, until a scattered stardust littered the sky above in this location with little light pollution. We became well attuned to the sounds emanating from the house. The metal pops of pots and pans from cooking and cleaning. The crackle of hot oil. Doors to the outside opening and closing. Watering systems activated.

Over time these diminished until finally, after a number of hours, there was only silence from the human habitat while the remaining creatures of Earth began their nocturnal efforts. It was soon after this point that Ambra returned to us.

A beam from a flashlight darted back and forth across the corn rows and approached. Soon the stalks parted and the child stepped before us with a glint in her eye.

"Look, it's a full moon tonight!" she said, pointing. Indeed, the stars were beginning to be overwhelmed by the bright radiance of the planet's satellite as it climbed toward a zenith above the landscape. "All the fairy magic comes with a full moon!" She paused and sat down, opening a basket. "I brought food, if you are hungry."

Kloan leaned forward and looked into the basket. "Bread rolls, fruits, and cheese."

"Yes, is that okay? I don't know what fairies eat." She seemed perturbed at her lack of knowledge.

"Watch this, Ambra," said Kloan. Dramatically, Kloan waved her hand over the basket, and several things happened. First the flaps that were closed over the food opened completely on their own, as if by invisible hands. Ambra gasped. She then squealed and put her hands to her mouth as several of the bread rolls and plums floated out and into the air. The food performed a number of acrobatic tricks above us, weaving in and out of different choreographies and patterns.

Kloan seemed to enjoy every expression of amazement and joy that escaped from Ambra. If she had not been so coldly clinical in her purpose, I could have been persuaded that she wanted to make the child happy, that she instinctively cared for Ambra. It was hard to believe that she did not. Her eyes held an empathetic engagement; her smiles at Ambra's reactions did not seem forced or false. Nothing seemed to make sense with this clone.

This *fairy magic* entertainment went on for some time, and we walked across the cornfields to a little stream where Kloan performed some truly astounding telekinetic manipulations of water. Despite her interest and fascination, as the hours passed, the seven-year-old tired, and soon she was mostly sitting and talking to us about her life and thoughts, finally having had her fill of magic. Her eyes were half closed, but she seemed to exert a fierce will to avoid falling asleep.

After an unusually long lull in the conversation, I dared to broach the subject. "Ambra, why are you afraid of dreaming?" A sudden silence fell, quieter than the lack of conversation. I noticed it was from her lack of breathing. "It's okay, Ambra, you don't have to tell me if you don't want to."

"I don't want to," she said tersely, her voice strained. I flipped several eyes in her direction and saw that she had curled into a small ball.

"Unless you think that we can help," said Kloan.

Kloan, please be careful.

"How can you help?" Her eyes looked sideways toward us.

"Fairy magic is powerful. But we need to know more."

This isn't just information gathering! If it is too difficult for her, let her be!

Ambra sat up and wrapped her arms around her legs in a manner so similar to Kloan's postures that it momentarily stunned me. "You promise you can help?"

"No," said Kloan. "I can't promise that until I know the problem. But I promise that we can help with many things."

Ambra seemed to be weighing a decision in her unusual seven-year-old mind. "I have many dreams," she began, "and many are awful. Some are nice, but some are so bad—I can't even tell my parents anymore. They don't like to hear about them." She took a deep breath. "But the worst is the Demon Man." She was silent for more than a minute staring off into the dim cornstalks.

"Who is the Demon Man, Ambra?" I asked gingerly.

"I don't know!" she moaned, turning her head to her shoulder, tears welling in her eyes. "I don't know who he is. I don't know what he is. I think… it feels like he's not human. He's a monster. He's something else."

Kloan leaned forward and touched her knee. "What does he do in your dreams?"

Now she was sobbing softly, and the words were partly garbled through her tears. "He comes here, always here, with tall things, dark shadows, and they creep through the house and lawn. And my parents scream!" She was shaking. "But I can't see them because I'm running and running out of the house and through the corn and the shadows come after me, and all the smoke of them turns into a black wolf and it's chasing me and chasing me!"

She threw her arms around Kloan and sobbed uncontrollably for several minutes. I looked on in dread, knowing the events her visions foretold—when she would be kidnapped, her parents murdered, her life forever changed. In the Anti's push for all aspects of Ambra's life to be studied, Kloan no doubt knew all the details as well. For myself, it had been difficult to hear the adult Ambra Dawn speak of this period of her life. It was more heartrending to hear the small child weeping and shaking with no comprehension of what was coming or why.

She wiped her tears and seemed to steady herself. "But it always catches me. It has razor fangs and needles in its mouth, and it grabs my head and cuts and cuts and cuts and eats my brain out."

She has seen so much of it, came the thoughts of Kloan.

Ambra lay back roughly on her back and looked up at the blazing stars, the full moon having set in the late hours of the night. Her eyes seemed resigned. "I'm going up there. To the stars. Aren't I?"

"Yes," said Kloan softly.

"You're not Earth fairies, are you? You're from up there."

"Yes," I added.

She closed her eyes. "So, can you help?"

"Yes," said Kloan, "with some of it."

I stared in astonishment. *Kloan, what are you promising her?*

Ambra opened her eyes. "How?"

"In two ways. Tonight is the first way. I will help you sleep without the dreams. I will use our magic to let you rest for the remainder of the night, and the Demon Man won't come." The relief in Ambra's eyes was nearly palpable. "When you wake tomorrow, we will talk of one other thing that we can do. But not until you sleep."

Ambra grasped both our hands and held them to her heart. "You are the best friends ever."

Kloan pushed her backward gently. "Lie down now." Ambra complied. Kloan closed her eyes and held her hands up like a prayer. For some time, nothing happened, and Ambra stared at her in puzzlement. Then they came. First one or two at a time; then they came in streams, rivers of radiance, aggregating in a dizzying, blurring ball of dashing light.

"Fireflies!" said Ambra. "So many! But they're usually sleeping now."

"I woke them up," said Kloan. The ball of dancing light floated above and next to Ambra. "It's a lamp. For the night."

The hundreds of insects seemed encased in a small sphere the size of a child's balloon. Ambra reached up and passed her hand through it. The air at the edges shimmied and refracted the firefly light as if through rippling water and then regained a pristine surface. The bugs flying inside were momentarily disrupted by her hand but quickly filled the space uniformly afterward.

"That's amazing," she said.

"Sleep now," said Kloan. "Trust me."

To my amazement, Ambra did. She seemed about to collapse from exhaustion anyway, and the soothing words of Kloan, the amazing hope for a peaceful night—perhaps the first in many months—seemed to pull her down like a drug to the ground.

But it was more than that. My Reader senses detected distortions in the space-time matrices around Kloan, and I surmised that she was already manipulating Ambra's mind.

Are you really doing this, Kloan? Can you?

Yes. Let me concentrate. Her sentience is many layered.

And so I waited. Five minutes later, Ambra was breathing heavily, apparently in a deep sleep. Kloan leaned back, fatigued.

"The universe runs wild through that one," she said.

"Are you surprised?" I asked.

"No, but I'm tired."

I looked around us and the practical problems assaulted me. "We'll need to carry her back into the house, somehow avoid disturbing the family or the pet."

Kloan shook her head. "No, let her rest. She needs it, and I don't want my efforts ruined with too much disturbance."

"But her parents…"

She spoke through a yawn. "..will come looking for her in the morning frantically and find that their strange daughter decided to sleep under the stars. I doubt it's the weirdest thing they've dealt with."

"We can keep watch, wake her when they begin to search and then hide ourselves."

"Yes," said Kloan. "But I'm not a Xix. I will need sleep, too. You have the watch. It's only a few hours until dawn anyway."

Kloan did not wait for my response. She dropped to her side and rested her head on her arm, shutting her eyes. But I could not let her disappear into sleep quite yet.

"Why did you do this?"

Her drowsy voice was barely above a whisper. "Do what?"

"Such kindness. Such insight and empathy. One moment you are cold, murderous even, and another you seem to see toward the heart of another better than I. And act lovingly on that knowledge. *What are you?*"

Kloan yawned again. "God, Waythrel, do we have to do this now?" She rolled on her back and looked up at the stars. "It won't make sense. You will never completely understand me. Ambra will never understand me. I will never understand either of you but I must probe all those elements of discord."

"Why?"

"To become what she is not. In all possible ways." A long yawn escaped her mouth, and she rolled over to the other side, away from me. "An inverse, Waythrel. A true, sentient inverse. That is my destiny. Look, don't think about it tonight."

"Sentient inverse? You're right, I don't understand."

Her exasperated thoughts sounded in my mind. *You Xix never let go!* She sighed. "You can't understand. You've barely come to terms with basic physics —that the Anti even *exist*. If one of the Anti were here right now in front of you and didn't blow everything up, what would it look like?"

"Like any other living being, with its own parameters, morphology."

"Right, anti-water looks like water. Anti-stars look like stars. Antiparticles are the same, with a special physics inverse. But since particles and fields are the essence of sentience, Waythrel, don't you see, there have to be anti-thoughts, anti-minds, anti-ideas that are the same yet *different*?"

"Like hate and love?"

"No!" She rolled over and glared at me. "You are better than that! Not so simplistic and one-dimensional. Those are just vectors. If you invert a three-dimensional object in only two dimensions, it's all wrong. If you invert sentience with such a low dimensionality as that, it's all wrong! It's not an inverse; it's a mess!"

"You're right," I said. "These are ideas unconsidered by any science I have encountered in the galaxy."

She turned back over irately, sighing loudly. "I must learn these ways. I must learn them in the context of Ambra Dawn. I must become her inverse."

These last words struck me, partly because I now had a small inkling of what this might mean but more because of the vast landscape of meaning I had yet to even consider. Even so, the purpose eluded me entirely.

"Why?"

"Oh, Waythrel!" she said with exasperation. "It's the whole point of all this! Now shut up! Let Kloan sleep."

I sat very still, and within seconds, Kloan was breathing heavily beside her progenitor. I glanced back and forth between the two young girls, Kloan and

Ambra, Ambra and Kloan. One a naive yet jading young Earth girl, the other a jaded yet almost divinely naive abomination of tubes and wires and indoctrination. *Inverses?*

I looked up at the star-filled heavens. I knew something deep, something terribly important, something frightening was escaping my grasp. But try as I might, I could not bring it into focus. On the horizon of my awareness something monstrous and beautiful lurked, but for now, I knew it only from distant rumor.

In that distance, it rumbled like a thundercloud—or some creature beyond my comprehension.

Chapter 20

Go to the edge of the cliff and jump off. Build your wings on the way down.

Ray Bradbury

"Ambra! Ambra!"

The calls floated above the early morning mist and cricket sounds. I shook Kloan and Ambra, and they both awoke, startled.

The mother's voice was particularly close. "Ambra! Where are you?"

"Oh *no!*" hissed Ambra, frantically throwing her things into her pack and stumbling upward. "I have to go! Mom's going to *kill* me!" She started to turn into the wall of stalks and then turned around. She stared at Kloan. "It worked. Last night. Your promise. Your other promise?"

Kloan smiled groggily. "Meet us down by the stream. Follow the fireflies."

Ambra nodded curtly and then dashed off. Seconds later she was gone, and the morning sounds transitioned into angry and joyous shouts from her parents. I looked at Kloan and said, "We should not be so close to the house."

"Yes." Kloan stood up and stretched, and then we were off, away from Ambra and in a direction I only vaguely could determine. Not being of Earth, all my instincts for navigation were off, wrong, and I was forced to use purely intellectual ideas of the direction of the planet's rotation, wind patterns, and time of day to guess the geometric layout around us. Kloan seemed to navigate through the use of her own special powers. I did not doubt that she could explore everything around us at all levels of detail. She led, and again I followed.

As I might have expected, she brought us directly to a small stream, and we sat under a tree as she dozed off again for some time. I did not know how much the Anti had altered the basic human brain physiology, but whatever machinery they had added could not remove the need for human sleep.

"She'll come again in the night," she muttered while resting against the broad tree trunk. "Her parents won't allow her to leave the house today because of last evening. Wake me at sunset."

And sure enough, Kloan slept straight through the entire day, only waking for short moments to turn to one side or the other, bend down and drink from the stream, and once to relieve herself in the thickets around us.

"It's going to be a hard night, Waythrel," she said during one such waking. My leaky thoughts had been caught in her net. "I need to rest up." She gave no other explanation.

As she slept, I entered a Xixian trance that conserves resources and allows for quiet contemplation. We Xix do not sleep, not in the sense Earth mammals sleep, but we do need to purge the metabolic waste products of our energy-hogging neural clusters as well as weight and balance our neural networks from the day's experiences. But we can do so far more efficiently than humans —and completely under conscious control. We do not dream, unless you would characterize our constant free-associative background mental patterns as daydreaming; but these processes have little in common with human neural functioning or structure.

The day passed quickly in this way. Finally the sun set, and I woke Kloan. She removed some of Ambra's bread from her robes and stared at it. "It's too bad I can't eat this."

"Why not?" I asked.

"Upsets my stomach. I'd offer you some," she said, "but I know you can't process human food. Are you hungry, Waythrel? Are you okay metabolically?"

"Yes, for a few more days. But after that, it will become a problem."

"No problem. We'll be gone after tonight, and everything will reset."

"Do you mean—"

"She's coming!" cried Kloan and sprang to her feet. I looked in the direction Kloan stared and there was a pale glow, a will-o-the-wisp bobbing up and down through the cornrows associated with a mashing sound of footsteps. Through the stalks burst another ball of firefly light and Ambra Dawn.

"I made it!" she said, seemingly amazed with herself. "They're asleep, but I put a ball and stuffed clothes in my bed in case they check."

Kloan smiled. "Perfect."

"I love the fireflies." Ambra's smile faded and she stared directly at Kloan. "How can you help me?"

"Let's talk about the Demon Man."

Ambra released a long breath and held her hands together near her stomach. "Okay."

"Do you know why you see him in your dreams? Because your dreams predict the *future*."

Kloan! She was so reckless!

"No—" said Ambra, shaking her head, and stepping back.

"You have great powers, Ambra, and they are just starting to wake up. You will see many things. The Demon Man is just one of them."

"No, it's not true." Two more steps back. Her eyes were wide.

Kloan, stop! This is too sudden. She needs years to come to terms with this.

"Because it's true—the Demon Man is not a dream. He is real. He is coming to get you. He will come here. He will kill your parents." Ambra moaned. "And he will take you to a place where they will cut open your head and slice up your brain."

"*No!*" Ambra screamed and turned around and began to run back to the cornfield.

"Stop!" said Kloan, and Ambra crashed into an invisible wall of jelly. It absorbed her momentum softly but prevented her passage, deflecting her fists as she repeatedly pounded on the structure screaming, "*No!*"

"You've *seen* all this, Ambra!" cried Kloan, trying to raise her voice over Ambra's mantra of denial. "You just don't want to face it."

I was mortified. This was torture. Kloan had deceived me yet again and had turned helping Ambra into another occasion to visit harm on her. I didn't know what twisted psychological experiment Kloan was conducting or why it was important to the universe, and I didn't care if the god-thing Ambra was on board with this suffering. *I wasn't.* I began to move toward Kloan. I knew it was pointless, but I had to try to intervene somehow.

"No point, Waythrel," said Kloan, and suddenly I could not move or speak.

Ambra had stopped her futile pounding on the barrier Kloan had erected and now sat crumbled into a ball, mucus covering her upper lip, tears dripping from the sides of her face.

Kloan walked up to her and crouched, looking Ambra in the eyes. "You can't hide from it forever. But we *can* save you from it."

What? What was Kloan doing?

"Save me? How?"

Kloan smiled and took Ambra's hands. "We'll go to the warehouse," she said, and at those words, Ambra shuddered and looked away. "We'll visit the labs. We'll find the Demon Man. We'll kill him. And then we will burn everything to the ground."

Ambra looked between us, lingering on me as if to gain verification of this incredible proclamation. "Kill him?"

"Kill all of them, destroy the entire place, until nothing is left."

Ambra looked up to the bizarre force field and back at Kloan. "You can do this?"

More than anyone, I knew it was indeed within the powers of this clone. Assuming this was truly what she planned to pursue.

"Yes, if you want it," Kloan assured her. "If you can face your fear and stop hiding from what you know is true, then come with us to the labs. I promise you, by the sunrise, there will be nothing left but smoke and dust. Not even bones."

I projected my thoughts, trying to get in some word in this conversation. *You are asking a young child to approve a slaughter! A massacre and destruction! That should not be her burden!*

I heard Kloan's thoughts. *The cosmos has not asked what burdens she deserves. It has placed them on her. Open your mind, Waythrel.*

Ambra looked again up to the stars. "It's all true, isn't it? I don't want to look at the truth!" She turned violently toward Kloan and sandwiched the clone's head in both hands. "I'll come. You'll take me there?"

"Yes," said Kloan without flinching.

"And then you'll burn it all to the ground?" They simply locked eyes.

My restraints vanished. I stepped forward, but now didn't know what to say or do. The two girls stared fixedly at one another.

"Let's go," said Ambra, and she stood up. "Which way?"

Chapter 21

"We'll fly like Peter Pan," said Kloan, and with those words, we were lifted into the air.

The three of us rose over the cornfields in the light of a waning gibbous moon. Ambra squealed as we soared, the air becoming colder, the plots of land and houses rushing below at increasing speeds until they became a blur. I could see the narrative building within the young Ambra, of fairies and magic, of flying to face a dark nemesis.

How do you know where to go? I asked Kloan.

It is not far, her thoughts replied. *Still in Nebraska. I've been searching the past and the minds involved. It was not difficult.*

Will you do this thing? I asked.

What do you think, Waythrel?

Twinkling towns passed us on either side. Highways like glowing vasculature radiated across the plains around us. I could not judge our velocity, but it was certainly fast enough that Kloan must have been blocking the airflow that would impact us. Although the ground sped past at an airplane's rate, it was only the mildest of cool breezes that stirred us. Ambra seemed completely captivated, saying nothing, only staring downward or to the clouds around us with wide eyes and a smile.

Perhaps I, too, had found myself lost in the strange journey, reminiscent of the travels with Ambra in a relative future that would strangely bring me back to this past. Memories of the journey to shut the Time Tree—of the strange space-time bubble that cocooned us as we traversed alien landscapes and atmospheres, where we plunged into oceans and the void of space—filled my mind and were overlaid with the present flight. Visions of another life—in another universe—superimposed with a series of different lives and universes.

Time passed quickly, and suddenly we slowed over a dark and seemingly undeveloped expanse. Far ahead, a pool of light broke the monotony of the emptiness. To this isolated patch we descended, and the light revealed a form, a large warehouse unusual for the enormous power generators studding one end of the structure and the radar systems arrayed around it. These provided power for labs and guidance systems to monitor the coming and going of their alien masters. We had reached a node of the Dram power structure on Old Earth.

Our feet softly touched down on the dusty ground in front of what seemed to be a main entrance to the building. Razor wire and electrified fences ran around us, and hundreds of cameras and motion detectors monitored the area. There was no way for Ambra to avoid detection without our *dark suits*, assuming these were even active. As I looked over the compound nervously, I mulled over the strange sense of violation I felt from my powerlessness to control anything about this field imposed over my body. Active or not, it would be for nothing if Ambra were spotted. I feared it was already too late to prevent that.

We're not going for subtlety, my dear Xix.

Despite everything she had seen and the positive wonder of the flight, Ambra looked terrified. Her hands shook, and she nodded vigorously.

"This is it. But it's always bigger in the dreams."

Engines rumbled and tires squealed, vehicles approaching us from every side. Floodlights blasted our position, and a loud, amplified voice barked commands. "Do not move! Identify yourselves or prepare for hostile action!"

Ambra whimpered, her body pressing against ours. "Don't let them take me..."

"Hi! I'm Kloan! This is Waythrel of Xix on my left and Ambra Dawn on my right. One's from an alien world hostile to your masters, and the other is the future failed messiah of this galaxy. And we are prepared for hostile action!"

The vehicles imploded like crushed soda cans to the horrific sounds of mashing bodies and screams cut short. The compacted hulks were flung away from us and shook the ground as they bounced across the compound.

Kloan clapped her hands together, and there was an enormous flash of light from the other end of the warehouse. A loud explosion quickly reached our ears as I watched the generators detonate into the air. Sparks rained down around the installation like a meteor shower.

The lights of the facility went off and flickered dimly back as emergency batteries tried to return some functionality. Kloan walked calmly forward toward the entrance.

"Oh my God," said Ambra. There was a realization of the horror of what was happening in her eyes, and I pitied her for it. And yet it was quickly replaced with an angry hope, a steely resolve that drove her forward. She wanted desperately to slay this dragon.

Mounted weaponry dropped from the ceiling in front of the door and opened fire on us. Shell projectiles, machine-gunned at a rate of hundreds per minute, bounced away from us as if we held an invisible umbrella that deflected everything. Quickly the guns found themselves ripped from their anchors and slung to the side.

The doors exploded inward to the screams of many inside. Dust billowed through the hallway from shattered cement. Figures in white lab coats dashed madly for shelter in the failing lights as soldiers rushed toward us. They could hardly take up positions before their bodies were hurled this way and that, or simply dropped to the ground as if they had suffered a sudden stroke.

We passed elements of what looked like a medical research facility. Kloan ruthlessly dispatched any resistance but spared those seeking to avoid us. As we passed many rooms with charts like those found in hospitals, the doors spontaneously opened. Slowly, as if in great fear—of Kloan or their capturers, it was unclear—children diffused out of the rooms. Some ran to the exits; some stayed within their rooms. Many followed us like those who follow the events of a terrible catastrophe, drawn onward by the sheer magnitude of the devastating events, unable to look away.

"Down this hall," said Ambra hesitantly. "He's down this hall."

The mass of following children whispered behind us. Some fled at this point, too afraid to approach whatever waited at the end of the gray hallway. The lights along the ceiling were shorting out, perhaps due to damage by a surge from the destruction of the power generators. Popping sounds and flying sparks accompanied our movements. It all had the effect of a strobe light on the small group of children we led toward a single door at the end.

"Ambra?" Kloan stepped aside and motioned for Ambra to open the door.

Was this a final trick? Surely whoever this was behind the door, whomever they were so afraid of, he had secured himself and would turn violently toward anyone entering the room. Would Ambra catch the full frontal assault through this ruse of Kloan's?

Just stop, Waythrel. She is facing her fear. And yes, I am observing the process. I don't do charity work.

Ambra walked up to the door and turned the knob, pushing in the door with a determined thrust. Inside was the Demon Man.

Except as most nightmares when faced, he seemed less demon and more man. A man of great cruelty, no doubt—power hungry, lost in his playing of the game the Dram had laid out for humanity. But a balding, short, and now very frightened looking man in the end.

Kloan grabbed Ambra's hand, and they walked inside together. I followed closely behind while a gaggle of children watched from behind the doorframe.

The room was an office, simple, bare except for a desk and a computer. The Demon Man did not care much for decorations or personalizing. But he did have one trick left up his sleeve in the form of two towering Dram soldiers on his right and left. The Dram aimed weapons in our direction.

"Whoever you are, you will die for this," he said with anger and a pure sense of certainty.

The Dram fired on us, and the effect was like a light show. The beam weapons rebounded like a prismatic spray across the room, the rays shattering into a thousand colorful needles that set fire to wood and paper, ignited the ceiling tiles, and burned blisters into the skin of the man behind the desk. He yelped in pain. The Dram soldiers advanced flashing bladed devices.

"Don't bother," said Kloan.

The creatures screamed as their exoskeletons were ripped from their flesh. Brown fluids erupted from their forms as they fell to the ground clawing at the carpet. Kloan let them thrash and simply shoved them against the walls with invisible hands.

"My God, what are you?" The Demon Man was shaking, cradling a burned arm across his chest.

"You really should choose your victims carefully," Kloan mocked him. "Poor Ambra here—she could see into the future, see that you would do terrible things to her because she's a Reader in your jurisdiction. Then, because of a recursive time loop that won't let go of us—created by none other than an Ambra Dawn of the far future—we traveled back into the past and decided to help her destroy this place. That's the now."

He shook his head. "You speak nonsense."

"I usually do," said Kloan. "Now—die."

Without a drop of spilled blood or a cry, the man fell to the ground, unmoving. I rushed up and examined him for a pulse.

"He's dead," I said.

Ambra wept, tears and smiles and a look of horror all mingling together. She fell on her knees and stared at the man. She looked less than seven, a tiny child reduced to the rawest of emotions.

"He's really dead?" she asked me. "I can't believe it."

"Yes," I said. "No pulse. Look for yourself."

She shook her head, what she had seen apparently enough to satisfy her. Ambra stood up and hugged Kloan.

"Not done yet!" said Kloan, a strange light in her eyes.

And so we swept back out of the complex, evacuating all the children. The scientists and techs were spared, except for a few who refused our summons and warnings and stayed within the building. Their time left was short. As we exited, the ground shook and rumbled, and a bright light appeared from behind the warehouse.

"It sounds like a transport," I said.

"Yes," said Kloan, "they have a landing pad for carting off the navslav recruits. Looks like there was a small Dram unit here on our arrival. They must have chickened out from what they saw." A dark spacecraft offset by bright engines began to climb into the night sky. "Yes, that will be perfect."

The spacecraft veered right and pitched horrifically. The engines fired strongly, inducing a violent turn, and the ship careened toward the ground.

"Kloan, it's going to crash!" I cried out.

The impact was thunderous and bright as the ship plunged directly onto the laboratory building itself. The entire structure was obliterated, the metal melted like water under terrible heat. A mushroom cloud climbed into the sky.

At our distance, we should all have been vaporized. Yet, the dust under us was undisturbed while the landscape nearby was completely blackened. We did not even feel any heat from the fires now raging in front of us.

The other children watched, astonished, some of the older ones jumping for joy, many sitting on the ground, crying and disoriented. I spent the better part an hour trying to comfort them while Ambra and Kloan simply stared into the fire.

"You did it," whispered Ambra as I returned. "You kept your promise. Not even their bones."

The flickering light from the inferno danced across Kloan's features. She smiled. "Not even their bones." She placed a hand on Ambra's shoulder.

"Now, you'll never go there, and the evil men will not hurt you."

Chapter 22

I said to the almond tree: "Speak to me of God," and the almond tree blossomed.

Nikos Kazantzakis

Green *eyes in the darkness.*
I stared up at a night sky churning with stars in patterns that I could not recognize. A soft breeze trickled over me, the sounds of insects or other alien creatures punctuating the soft whisper of the wind. I felt sick from memories of being ripped and thrown from dream to dream, time-line to timeline, reality to new reality. My eyestalks darted about, appraising the planet surface, the heavens, and the figure of the girl sitting beside me.

Kloan sat with her legs pulled up, nearly obscuring her head, those haunting green eyes peeking over the kneecaps, arms wrapped around her legs, keeping them together. She rocked slowly back and forth. She was still humming.

I sat up and stared across at her. "Again?" The child continued to rock and hum, seeming to ignore my question. I felt desperate.

The humming stopped. "Or never."

"Never?" My eyestalks swiveled around anxiously. "You destroyed the Dram laboratories, where they took Ambra and altered her. Those labs made her what she is, what she became. However misguided their reasons, they changed the fate of the galaxy!"

"Of the universe."

"Yes! And you destroyed it! You really did it. What does that mean? What future, what reality did this create? Where is Ambra? What has happened to her?"

"She is everywhere. Everything has happened to her." The intubated, tattooed head cocked to one side, the green eyes continuing to stare fixedly at me.

I sensed the tendrils of her thought dancing around my awareness. "You keep probing my mind."

Her head remained at the strange angle, forty-five degrees, peering from behind her right knee. "Your thoughts leak everywhere. You Xix are leaky-brains."

The child stood up. It was a rapid motion, catching me a little off guard. She stopped to stand above me, long, ragged clumps of red hair dangling haphazardly and nearly obscuring her face. "More experiments, Waythrel. I was skeptical, but the Anti always believed there were unstable nodes in time, and that this is one of them. They were convinced that with the Earth facility destroyed, Ambra Dawn would not *become*. But I kept telling them, it's not *then* that you have to worry about her, but at the *beginning*."

The words were like a slap to my mind. *Words of a dream.* "Kloan, where are we?"

"Don't you know?"

I stood up slowly, gazing around the ragged landscape, down to a flat plain below, the lights of a city washing out the canopy of stars above. "We are back where we started. When you took me after Dram."

"When did we start, Waythrel?"

I stared at the deep green eyes and realized that I was completely disori-ented. Memories seemed to exist as events in a blurred fog, and I could no longer discern what was real and what was only in my mind.

"I am terribly confused. What is happening? You seem to understand."

She nodded, a satisfied look on her face. "That's *why* you're here. *Data.* The next data to open the gate." Again she nodded, and then turned her back on me, walking down a steep slope. "Let's get started."

"Started with what? Where are you going?"

Kloan continued walking without turning back. Her next words were nearly lost in the insect sounds and wind that carried them down the land-scape. "To where it all began for me. To watch the beginning flow around us and mature and twist through time and space to come back to be us. Then we will be ready for the next step."

The intense starlight cast shadows on the dusty rocks. The figure of the child was gone, swallowed in the darkness and slope of the hill we stood on. Raising my gaze in the direction of her last words, I stood frozen, trying to understand what now seemed the madness of my own thoughts.

What was happening to me? What had happened, and what had not? Were these real experiences, *time loops*? If so, did it mean they actually happened? If not, how could I remember them? If they *had* happened, how could Ambra have *become* and therefore how could I have come here in the first place? Everything was a paradox!

Waythrel, come on!

Her voice rang impatiently in my mind. My eyestalks curled up on themselves. I looked around the desolate space surrounding me.

What else was there for me to do?

Chapter 23

The opposite of a profound truth may well be another profound truth.

Niels Bohr

I followed the child, racing to catch up to her, my steps uncertain, the dusty ground surprisingly slippery under my feet. Down the steep slope of the elevation, I stumbled and tripped, my four arms only poorly grasping the rocks and alien vegetation, seeming to lack any friction to form a proper grip.

It's a field around you, remember? Her thoughts danced through my mind. *It's skintight, coating your surfaces, insulating you from everything around us.*

Listening to her voice and trying to understand what she was saying, flashes of memory leapt through my thoughts. The strange sensation, her words, walking up the slope to a shining disk in the light—*the gate.*

I nearly crashed into her as I rounded a large boulder. The ground was strewn with shattered rocks and their remains, products from avalanches tumbling down from the jagged hills behind us.

"Why is there a field? What kind of field?"

Kloan was staring ahead at the source of the light. A city or military installation of some sort rose from the floor of the dry lands. A transport blasted into orbit from just outside the city. Organized groups of shadows marched throughout the installation.

"I don't know what kind of field. She—*they* make it for your protection."

"Protection from what?"

Kloan pointed toward the city. "There! That's where we'll start. I'm not sure where we are this time. I don't remember this night. But it must be a visitation, I'm sure of it! We'll go meet me there, and then you'll see what happens."

She began to walk toward the complex, but I reached out quickly and grabbed her shoulder, turning her back to face me. "Wait! This is the clone production facility, isn't it?" Images of explosions and a burning room filled my mind.

"Yes."

"Where you escaped?" She simply nodded. "You saw what happened the last time! They will kill us if we go in there!"

"There is no danger. They won't see us. We both have skin suits, remember? *Dark ones*. Their eyes can't see. Ears can't hear. Not even the Readers will perceive."

I remembered...*something*.

"But *you* saw through Ambra's bubble! You came inside it, even."

Kloan shook her head. "Hers was simple. Weak. Primitive."

"And yours around us is better?" I asked.

"I told you before, they're not *mine*," she said, sighing. "Now come on."

The child pulled me forward, and I relented. I felt completely helpless, my own mind to be distrusted, events to be suspected—past, present, and future. Would I come to understand any of this madness?

We covered the flat distance between the broken hills and the installation quickly. The uncomplicated landscape made my efforts far less exhausting, and I found myself able to observe the growing city before us rather than concentrate on each step to prevent an accident.

It was strange, both as a city and technological society, but I had a sense that it was not unknown to me. But the mentality behind the environment was more alien than any I had ever encountered. Even in our galaxy of diverse life forms, there was not this terrible difference that seemed to border on hostility to the mind. I cannot describe it any better.

And yet the place was populated with *humans*. I saw no other aliens, no divergent life forms. And only two classes of humans at that, easily demarcated: those who looked like Ambra Dawn, and those who did not.

"The Anti run things remotely with robots and trained humans," Kloan added, no doubt sampling my *leaky* thoughts.

"To avoid annihilation?" I assumed it would be difficult to be in the presence of so much matter to their antimatter. The energies required to keep the two forms from destroying the entire planet would be staggering.

"No, they are not concerned about that here," she said cryptically, not bothering to explain.

We approached the entrance to the complex. Robotic guards patrolled the gate, hovering above the ground with strange weapons protruding from multiple regions of their forms. They did not notice anything unusual. It seemed that nothing in their technology allowed them to pierce whatever cloaking mechanism was concealing us.

I noticed a pattern quickly. "The humans aren't involved in anything. Everything is done by the machines."

"Humans are the social construct for the clones. To develop properly, human neurophysiology needs social fabrics, structures, language, norms. So the Anti imported them. A clone growth matrix, I guess."

"Like on Dram," I said, remembering the groups of clones and other humans involved with them.

"Yes, that was the beginning, before it was destroyed."

"Dram is gone." Nearly a statement.

"Civil war. Blew themselves up. But it didn't matter. They were only an outpost."

"And this is another one?"

"One of the last. The devil ball hunts them through space and time. They had to build them farther and farther away, find stronger and stronger clones to shield them from attack."

"Devil ball? Wait, you mean the Orbs?"

Kloan looked at me and laughed. "We had other names for them. Other thoughts about them. Come, you'll see. You'll *learn*."

We walked through the strange streets of this alien and yet human city. Groups of young Ambra Dawn clones paraded past us at various points, shepherded by older clones and assisted by bands of more diverse humans. Kloan paused a moment outside an enormous structure that resembled a cross between a giant termite hill on Earth and a honeycomb. I strained to understand the principles of this architecture.

"These are the Wombs," said Kloan. "All clones are born there. They learned early on that the gestational process was a key element in brain development. *In vitro* methods failed terribly." She smiled at me. "It's nice that we're born and not grown, isn't it?"

I didn't know if the strange child was serious or sarcastic. "What we saw on Dram seemed much more horrible than nice, Kloan."

"You are a terrible student," she said in a strange tone. "But we don't have time for lessons. We have to find the enclosure."

"What enclosure?"

"You remember, Waythrel," she said. "Home."

"Home?"

She grabbed my hand and pulled me forward, reaching a near sprint. We darted across the compound. I had little time to process anything until I found myself standing in front of a strange building unlike any of the others I had seen here. It was small, a deep black, obsidian, seeming to reflect little light. I sensed strong electromagnetic fields pulsating around the structure.

"Home," she said again. "Or quarantine. Take your pick."

Chapter 24

We cannot predict the new forces, powers, and discoveries that will be disclosed to us when we reach the other planets and set up new laboratories in space. They are as much beyond our vision today as fire or electricity would be beyond the imagination of a fish.

Arthur C. Clarke

"Yes, I remember." I stared at the prison they had engineered for the child. "To keep you and your powers under control."

"It was never really useful except in the beginning, when I was very little. But I never let them know all that. Until the end. Come, I'll get us through the fields."

Kloan pulled me forward. We passed through the energy fields shielding the small structure; and for an instant, my vision blurred, and my space-time senses reeled. Holding onto the wall beside me, I steadied myself and refocused.

A single room greeted us, Spartan, with basic elements such as a bed, table, latrine, and sink. There were no products for leisure, no children's toys, no books or electronic information sources. A single diode in the ceiling dispelled the night, lighting the chamber in a soft tan.

Inside was a little girl—perhaps age five—who sat morosely on the edge of the bed, staring forward without expression. She had all the appearance of a younger version of Kloan, more childlike, with less cranial modification and a decrease in the subcutaneous patterning that so dramatically decorated the faces of the future clones.

I followed the child's gaze. A vortex of milky light swirled softly in the middle of the room. My eyes paused completely in their scanning, the stalks still, all focused on the impossible thing I was seeing floating above the ground. There seemed to be a hint of swirling shapes, *faces*, like drowning victims beneath the waves of a white sea. The forms were too indistinct to process, too insubstantial and transient for me to identify.

But one shape I could identify absolutely. The milky vapors had coalesced around a central extrusion. Its form was that of a human face. The head was split open, the brain exposed behind it and fading into the mist. Tubes and wires, dwarfing the insertions into Kloan, entered and exited the skull. Even the eyes were partially obscured by machinery that seemed to pulse with a life of its own. Only the mouth was free.

"Ambra," I whispered in horror. Despite all the Xixian technology covering and distorting her features, I recognized her. How could I not? How could I forget that beloved alien face that I had followed and nurtured, taught and been taught by for nearly three centuries?

And so I was confronted with the horror of our desperate plan to save the galaxy from the Anti and Dram. I looked between the apparition and the two bodies of Kloan in the room. The weight of the truth nearly crushed me. My lover Synphel had warned us. The others and I had only half listened. But now it was clear to me. Now I began to suspect that we had triumphed only by becoming our enemy.

The younger Kloan stood up and walked up to the impossibility in front her. "The teachers are having problems with me. I'm growing too powerful. They are afraid."

Ambra nodded. "Soon, they will decide that you represent too much of a danger. The Anti will decide to destroy you."

"They will fail," said the child.

"If it comes to conflict, yes. But it need not come to conflict. There are better paths. Continue your training; follow what we have been teaching you. The time to leave will come soon."

"Today they threatened me because I am disturbing the planet's orbit."

"They do not understand your power source," said Ambra. "They cannot see the connections we have forged between you and the space-time matrix. But they begin to appreciate that you have transcended their program and control."

The room *shifted* violently. I became dizzy. For several moments I could not control my eyestalks, and they swiveled around, unable to focus, unable to lock, and a kaleidoscope of flashing images assaulted my consciousness.

"Waythrel, hold onto me."

It was Kloan. She grabbed my arm and steadied me. Slowly the dizziness passed. My vision came under my conscious control.

It was morning, and a bright light streamed in from a partially transparent region of the quarantine field isolating the building. Sounds of explosions and shouts could be heard faintly outside. The room was in disarray; clothes were strewn about, food and utensils as well. My olfactory strips detected a growing acrid smell. *Smoke.*

The vortex of light now swirled chaotically in the middle of the room. This time I did see faces. Hundreds, perhaps thousands of faces and forms of myriad species of life. Many I could now discern. Most I could not.

"The gate is prepared," came the voice of Ambra.

The younger Kloan stood in front of the vortex. She was now, in all appearances, identical to the form beside me. Sweat beaded across her forehead. All of her muscles were tense.

"I'm ready," she said.

"You must leave now," came Ambra's voice. "They will return with greater numbers of clones and more powerful weapons. You will be forced to destroy them all if you engage."

"I don't want to kill them. Lead me to the gate."

The sounds of rushing feet came from outside the small building. A heavy rumbling accompanied them, the sound likely associated with a military vehicle of some sort.

"Through the door."

Ambra gestured to the only door of the isolation building. The black field that sealed the chamber gave way to a second churning vortex. It opened to span the width of the door. Through it poured bright daylight, revealing not the artificial surface outside her isolation unit but the rocky terrain and vegetation that we had traversed only recently to arrive here.

The countryside within the vortex seemed to extend as far as my eyes could see, but the tunnel itself narrowed as I looked farther. Deep at the end of the tunnel, where my eyestalks strained and my vision began to fade, there seemed to begin a worn path on a steep slope layered in terraces. The vegetation had been eroded away, the rocks smoother, the coloration subtly different. The path rose up the hillside and then abruptly ended at the feet of a large disk. The light of the local star reflected brightly off it, firing blinding reflections into the room that cast shadows on the floor.

Kloan pulled my arm, showing me that her temporal copy had moved to enter the vortex. "The gate," she said.

I stumbled forward, partially blinded by the daggers of light glinting into the room. Outside there was shouting, and the walls of the room began to smolder and glow a bright orange.

"Good luck, my dearest friend," said the apparition of Ambra Dawn as I stepped into the vortex. Several eyestalks bent backward to see the disembodied head turned toward me, sending ripples across the sea of blurred, white faces. I saw tears dripping down from her eyes, coating the wires and tubes inserted into her once-green irises, a bittersweet smile on her face. "I love you, Waythrel. Remember that, whatever happens."

The room exploded.

Chapter 25

At first sight nothing seems more obvious than that everything has a beginning and an end, and that everything can be subdivided into smaller parts. Nevertheless, for entirely speculative reasons the philosophers of Antiquity, especially the Stoics, concluded this concept to be quite unnecessary. The prodigious development of physics has now reached the same conclusion as those philosophers.

Svante Arrhenius

Fire and debris flew across my vision, obscuring the swirling god-thing in the room. Just as I thought I would be pulverized, the portal shut.

Suddenly we were far from the compound, a mile high up the growing hills and mountains, cut off completely from the melee down below. Replacing the terrible rending of the explosion was a stunning silence. A faint whiff of smoke that had entered the portal was all that remained of the carnage below.

Shaken by the violence we had narrowly escaped, I turned slowly away from the vanished doorway and looked up the slope. The blinding gate was there. Kloan looked down from several feet above me and motioned for me to follow. We seemed to be alone.

"Where is the clone?" I asked in a daze.

Kloan smiled. "She's right here."

For a moment I paused, confused, my mind still reeling from events. Then I understood.

"This is where you left. When you went to kidnap me."

Kloan nodded. "Yes, I've gone already through the gate, so that I could come back with you." She smiled. "It's an elegant loop, yes?"

"It's madness! What is Ambra doing?"

"You are not the only one tested, Waythrel." She sighed. "Each time is different. When we finally understand, we'll see the way." She turned toward the disk. "We come to the next step, again—the next stage of the journey. Are you ready?"

Am I ready? I knew with certainty that this was not the first time I had been asked this question in this very location. "We've been here before, just like this."

"Not *just* like, but have been and will be. But never *just* like. We are deeply nested in temporal recursions that cannot be unknotted or normalized."

"I'm getting a sense of that. We've haven't found a way out yet. Is this what you are calling hell?"

"One of them."

My eyestalks rotated to focus entirely on Kloan. "There was more. There was a hope. To go *back*. To find Synphel."

"Yes," she said. "There was."

"But it's becoming clear to me that there is much more going on. More that I'm not appreciating as yet."

"You don't even appreciate what you do not appreciate."

I stared at the small bundle of aphorisms before me, the wind stirring her sparse hair and robes. "You are coming with me?" I asked.

"What other point is there?"

I turned my attention to the gate, fear and fatigue settling on me. The disk resembled nothing so much as a cross section sliced out of an Orb. The surface was like a fluid of myriad colors, a viscous, churning honey-like substance. It was beginning to feel like some acquaintance, long-known and burdensome. I could see stars within the thing—depth upon depth of star fields that appeared to have no end. It pulled me as I gazed. It was beautiful. It felt terrible. It began to appear as some ever-hungry maw that would devour me repeatedly for eternity. I reached over and grasped the child's hand.

Kloan laughed. "Seems we will always be dancing together, Xix."

My eyestalks wrapped around each other tightly, and the covering sheath expanded over them, blocking out all light. Kloan tugged on my hand.

We walked into the gel.

Part IV

You brood of vipers! Who warned you to flee
the coming wrath? Your ways lead to the grave!
This faith in rationed rationality
is sweet opiate to which you are enslaved!
The opiate, a poison to our land,
to endless wars and deaths has given birth.
Our planet's blood we see stained on your hands!
In your unthinking path we find no worth.
Enlightenment we offer—cleanse your sins!
The Pierian spring will wash you clean.
Drink deep! or taste not truth we hold within!
Perhaps, indeed, our Way is for the keen.
For faith misplaced we hold a simple cure:
Baptized in reason, you will then be pure.

—Mazandarani, *Sonnets from the Desert*

Chapter 26

If the Lord Almighty had consulted me before embarking upon his creation, I should have recommended something simpler.

Alfonso X of Castile

W e floated in the middle of a kaleidoscope.

Or so it seemed as the gate drank our forms and spit us into a weightless, intangible nothingness devoid of tactile, auditory, or olfactory sensation, replete with a swirling infinity of chromatic patterns spanning wavelengths to the edges of what even a Xix could perceive. I could see my body, the odd gel matrix melding like some lubricating oil with the colored nothing penetrating everything around us. Next to me floated Kloan, her eyes intense, expectant, and searching the space around us.

I tried to speak, but no sounds escaped the translator. There was likely no air to propagate the vocalizations. Then what would we breathe?

I reached out mentally. *Kloan, where are we?*

Limbo, whispered her thoughts in my mind.

Kloan, please! Clear answers for a change! Can we survive here? There is no air!

We're in limbo, Waythrel. We don't need air. We don't need. We aren't anything and yet aren't nothing. We are in between.

I was bewildered. *In-between what? Has the gate failed?*

No, I don't think so. We've been sent somewhere specific. We're trapped inside an Orb.

Inside an Orb? I had traversed the Orbs several times, even recently as I

631

was kidnapped by the creature floating beside me. In none of those traversals had the Orb looked anything like this.

That's because you were locked in defined world lines. This is different. This limbo is without direction in space or in time.

That doesn't make sense.

Do the Orbs make sense to you, Waythrel? Do you understand them?

There was nothing to respond to that. Of course I did not. No being, no species in our galaxy understood the Orbs. Or, rather, the one, true Orb. And I didn't understand the connection between Ambra's god-like group-mind and the Orbs, either.

That again? Waythrel, why won't you just accept the obvious?

Which is?

Occam's razor: among competing hypotheses, that with the fewest assumptions is selected.

It's not possible.

What you think is possible isn't part of Occam's razor. Explanations may come later, or be beyond you. What explains all the data in the simplest way?

That the Orb is Ambra.

Finally.

I saw that everything pointed toward that conclusion, but I could not grasp it, could not believe it! The Orbs were ancient, older than the oldest life in our galaxy. How could the mad plan we set in motion billions of years later have anything to do with that?

Kloan's thoughts continued to instruct. *How could Earth have been saved from a Dram asteroid? How could Ambra explore the past and implant ideas into long-dead people?*

Kloan, it is one thing to imagine traveling a short distance in time, manipulating the past, whatever the recursive nightmares and infinities in prediction it might involve. But to imagine our actions in this time being responsible for an entity existing near the beginning of the universe—one that likely guided the development of life —how? There is only so much suspension of causality I can maintain!

You have to get off the one-dimensional line of time, Waythrel. It's all clay in too many dimensions to count. Past, future, now all poking and prodding each other and shaping the clay that is not in time but of time. Oh, look!

Her strong thoughts were like a slap, and I reflexively found myself following the impulse of her mind and gaze. Through the endless curtains of light and color, there appeared a break. A spherical disruption that refracted the dancing chromatography grew in size as it approached. It appeared almost like some glass bubble into which poured rivers of paints that bent harmlessly in their journey through the object.

Inside the bubble were two figures. As the sphere came even closer, they were revealed to be humanoid. One lay supine, a female, her black dress and long red hair immediately identifying her—*Ambra!* The other was a larger male in recognizable battle armor, resting on his side.

It's Nitin and Ambra, Kloan! What are they doing here?

Slowly the sphere approached us and we passed unhindered through its surface. Inside the bubble was a climate—air, temperature I could sense, structure to the sphere on which I could stand. And I knew it well as the object Ambra had created for our quest in that other cosmos where I had lived a particular life cut short. I tried to ignore the gel goo that reasserted its presence.

"We can talk now," said Kloan, and she walked up to the pair. "Still limbo, you know, but we can talk."

The colors continued to wash over us. "What happened to them?"

Kloan touched them both, recoiling slightly from Ambra. "Something *very* strange with her. Something very powerful that I can't penetrate. Her body and mind are neither here nor there. Not now or before or later. I can't reach her, and yet she lives."

"And Nitin?"

Kloan crouched beside his head. "Sleeping only—a deep sleep induced by others. But we could wake him. He has interesting dreams."

I walked alongside Kloan and stared down at the soldier and Ambra. Neither looked injured. Both matched my memories from the final mission we had taken together.

"This is *after*," said Kloan, parsing my thoughts again. "His dreams recall your disappearance. They recall other amazing things."

I looked at her. "What happened to them, Kloan?"

"The Orb happened to them," she said. "I know this history—don't look so surprised. My birth occurred millions of years in their future."

"What *happened*?"

"After I stole you, Ambra followed, but the Orb stopped her. It showed her a vision of her future integration into the proto-Orb. Afterward, they fell into the Orb and appeared in the Sahara. Ambra was not breathing, and Nitin resuscitated her. The memories playing over in his dreams right now put them between Dram and New Earth. This must be their Orb traversal!"

"And why are we here, of all places?" I asked in wonder at this strange reality, the time frames, and the physical displacements. The *meaning* of it all was opaque to me.

Kloan looked disappointed. "Data, of course. And testing hypotheses." She put her hands on Nitin's forehead. "Nitin, wake up!"

Chapter 27

We can show very simply from the formula that the more likely evolutionary outcomes are going to be the ones that absorbed and dissipated more energy from the environment's external drives on the way to getting there. This means clumps of atoms surrounded by a bath at some temperature, like the atmosphere or the ocean, should tend over time to arrange themselves to resonate better and better with the sources of mechanical, electromagnetic or chemical work in their environments. You start with a random clump of atoms, and if you shine light on it for long enough, it should not be so surprising that you get a plant.

Jeremy England

The soldier started, his eyes opening quickly and fighting madly to focus and adjust to the colors and light. He rolled slowly to his back with a groan. His glance fell first on me.

"Waythrel," he said hoarsely, "you were gone."

"I still am, Captain."

He looked around the colored landscape in confusion and ignored my words. "Where are we?"

Then he stumbled to his feet, his expression furious, his weapons activating. He aimed his ion slingers toward Kloan.

"You!" he shouted. "You did all this! You took Waythrel! You led Ambra to the Orb!"

Kloan seemed unconcerned for her safety. "I told you I would. Don't you remember?"

The soldier's shoulders pulled back, and he furrowed his brows. "In that dream. Yes. But you spoke nonsense!"

"Nonsense to you. You lack foresight."

"Waythrel stand back," he said.

"It's no use," I said. "You can't hurt her."

"I can't let this clone live after what we found on Dram."

How could I explain to him all that I now knew in any fashion that he could accept? That the battle with the Anti spanned cosmic time? That Ambra wished this clone to live and that I journey with it? My eyes darted to the ground and the female form there. *Ambra.* What could I tell him of what was to become of her?

"The vision you saw of Ambra is her future, Nitin," said Kloan. "It is coming."

"What?" His eyes went wide, a panic within them as he looked toward the Daughter. "Ambra!" He ran to her side.

"She's unharmed," said Kloan.

"There's no pulse! No breath!" he shouted.

"She is suspended. By the Orb," said Kloan. "See, still warm. You can't undo this suspension while we're in here," she continued, gesturing to the light show around us. "You will return to New Earth soon and then revive her. All the histories agree on this."

"I don't understand any of your words!" He examined Ambra closely again. "What has happened to her?"

"You should be more concerned about what *will* happen to her, Captain," said Kloan.

His eyes flashed to the young clone. "The vision?"

"The Orb showed you the future. Not some vision of me or another clone. Not some monstrous weapon of the enemy designed to destroy Ambra and New Earth. The Orb showed you *Ambra*, an Ambra of your very near future where she will be butchered and melded to machines by your friends, the Xix."

He shook his head slowly. "This is rubbish." He raised his weapon arm.

"Nitin, it's true," I said heavily. "I'm ashamed to say—it is true. It's complicated to explain."

He stared between us like we were crazy. "Has this thing messed with your mind, Waythrel? What lies has she convinced you of?"

Kloan stepped forward, and it was too much for the soldier. He discharged his weapon only a meter from her. There was a flash of light and then silence. Kloan stood unharmed beside us. Directly in front of her the bright ions of the weapon were shaped into a ball, dizzying points of light flying rapidly around the clear container.

Kloan spun the ball around her hand and smiled at me. "Fireflies, Waythrel. Remember?" She slung it sideways and the lights disappeared into the prismatic curtains. "See, Waythrel was right; you can't hurt me. But you can listen to me and save Ambra."

I was again taken completely by surprise by her words. "Save her? Kloan, what—"

"Quiet, Waythrel. Let me talk." And once again I found that I could not speak. "Your dreams, the tunnels of light?" said Kloan. "Do you know what they are?"

Nitin swallowed. "How do you know about my dreams?"

"Don't forget the hole in your head I told you about! Now *think*. The attack in the Sahara? The need for a traitor on the inside to provide coordinates for the Dram and Anti? Well, that's *you*, Nitin! You're the traitor! The Anti have created a link through your mind. You are their puppet, long in the making. And one day soon, they will pull your strings and trigger you to kill Ambra Dawn."

I couldn't believe she was revealing this to him now in this way. It could destroy him.

"No!" he roared and released another volley of energy at Kloan that was deflected effortlessly. His breath came in gasps and he dropped to one knee. "I would never hurt Ambra."

"You wouldn't, but the other being they put in your mind would." His expression was pained and sick. "All the pieces coming together a little? Your life, your drives, your dreams and feelings? Events?"

"No, it can't be."

"Think about it a little, and I bet you'll see the horrible truth now that we've given you the pattern. But that's not the real issue. We aren't here to save Ambra from *you*, but to show you how to save Ambra from *herself*."

"What do you mean?"

Kloan sat down, cross-legged and sighed. "See, you might not know what you are, but *they do*," she said, indicating Ambra and myself with two arms bent above her head like some dancing devadasi. "They've known for a long time. It was amazing that the Anti thought they could conceal their plot from the nascent group mind. It would take them many thousands of years to develop the ability to do that, and by then the Orb would have been born. Game. Set. Match."

Nitin shook his head. He appeared lost. "How could she know something like that and not tell me?"

"Harsh but true. They had a big plan to stop the assault coming to New Earth. And, Nitin, they really did need a big plan because the forces arriving would have destroyed all of you, even Ambra, as powerful as she was then—or, if you will, is *now*." Kloan smiled. "I'm in all these different times, so it's a tense catastrophe."

"What is this plan you claim she has?" He seemed to be sizing her up like the devil offering him a deal.

"Simple—to use you to feed false information to the Anti while they prepared their ultimate weapon."

"Ultimate weapon? Which is what?" asked Nitin.

Kloan pointed to Ambra. "Her."

"But you said she couldn't stop them."

"Remember the vision at the Orb?" He shuddered. "*That* is the weapon. Ambra jacked into Xix tech with ten thousand Readers plugged in and then bang! *Supermind.* A group mind so powerful that it's like nothing ever known. The whole thing actually works. Big time. It destroys the coming armada. And then, it doesn't stop there! It's not a cozy meditation session that breaks for herbal tea. She's there for good, Nitin, like you saw. There is no going back."

His lips trembled. "No going back. And going forward?"

"It grows. All holy hell, it *grows.* It eats souls like some spiritual black hole and squashes them together, sucking their sentience and powers and building itself up. It becomes so powerful that it begins to grow in all spatial and temporal directions. *Even into the past.* All the time with Ambra eviscerated and fused at the core of the thing. Lovely, huh?"

And so I finally understood. Gagged and immobilized once again by Kloan, her words to Nitin finally opened the door to my understanding of the terrible potential of what we had unleashed. But I still could not fathom why she was telling him all this.

"Into the past?" he asked.

Kloan stood up and walked toward him slowly, her hands dancing around her as she spoke. I could only watch helplessly as she spun her perspective on our creation.

"Yes, deep into the future and deep into the past, finding more and more minds to slurp up, always famished, until part of it *becomes,* insinuating itself with its godlike powers and purposes at all the locations of planetary life. *The Orbs. The* Orb. All along, what entire civilizations mistakenly believed was some kindly gift of a long-vanished super-species, *it was Ambra!* Well, some long gone echo of Ambra that nucleated a god. A god-ball controlling all life, directing all minds, hoarding them and taking over the universe."

"Just stop where you are! Don't come closer." He stood up and steadied himself. "This is ridiculous. I don't believe it."

Kloan sighed. "You might not be able to believe it all, I understand. But I can prove to you that they plan to take your beautiful girl and turn her into that thing you saw floating above her at Dram." She rang her fingers across her cybernetic head emphatically. "*See?* That's what they all do to us, you know? In the end. They always want *more.* More for the war!"

His eyes danced to Ambra and then back to Kloan. "You can prove this to me, how?"

"Well, soon I predict, when I finish this little sermon, we will exit this limbo state and drop into the Sahara close to your Temple City. There you'll revive Ambra and take her to medical care where she'll be okay."

Sweat dripped from his face. "And then?"

"Depends on you. If you want to find out the truth before events take over and make you powerless, meet me outside the Temple City gate the first night you are back."

"And if I tell you to go back to the hell you came from?"

"Then you'll have a nice marriage to Ambra and group mind orgy-thingy only to wake up the next morning trying to blow her brains across her pillow. Then you'll be overpowered and they'll take Ambra down to the medical facilities and rip her to pieces in front of your eyes."

The poor soldier's hands were trembling. "You are a fiend. Whatever else you are, whatever the truth or lie of your words, you are a fiend. And I wish I could destroy you."

"But you can't. And you can't easily dismiss what I've said, either. When everything else I predict comes true, come find me in the desert sands, Nitin Ratava. There, I will tell you how to find your proof."

Chapter 28

The less one knows about the universe, the easier it is to explain.

Léon Brunschvicg

We watched him revive Ambra a short distance away in the Sahara sands.

Just as Kloan had predicted, we were roughly deposited back into space and time, exploding instantly after her last words into a sea of pulverized quartz. I found that Kloan had removed her invisible shackles from me. In one of the more counterintuitive events of my experience—and this was beginning to say a lot—we found that the sand served as an optimal cleansing agent of the gate gel that was still coating our forms. Removing the material with water had been laborious. With sand, it was gone trivially. As a Xix, this fortuitous lesson was doubly welcome.

"You treat me as your prisoner," I said, watching the soldier desperately try to bring life back into the body of Ambra Dawn. "Like a recalcitrant animal to be leashed and led and muzzled when it serves your needs."

Kloan nodded. "You also remember that I kidnapped you, right?"

The child was infuriating. "I suffer the Xixian curse of always imagining the good and empathetic in creatures. You seem determined to disappoint me."

"And surprise you. You forget everything that has happened because you are upset by recent events. I warned you that you'll never understand me." Kloan walked ahead several meters and motioned me to follow. "Here's the sphere," she said, pointing forward toward nothing.

"You can see it?"

"No, I'm making it up. It's quicksand that, when you walk over here will drop you twenty meters into a dark cavern. I will laugh evilly when you fall and leave you to die."

My eyestalks danced over her form. After all the unpredictable behavior from the thing, I admit that I indeed took the possibility seriously.

Kloan laughed and threw sand in the air in front of her. It struck an invisible barrier and fell back to the ground. "See? Come on inside. We'll be hidden from them all and can have some peace until he decides."

"We have dark suits, no? Why can't we just use those? Fly like we did on Old Earth? Why this thing Ambra made? We don't need it."

"Because it's something Ambra made. It has *her* written all over it."

"And what if I go warn them? Tell them of your plot?"

"Tell whom? Nitin knows now. All the others of significance know, well, except the poor Mazandarani. I always felt he was the unappreciated tragic hero of the Ambra histories. Anyway, telling anyone else now won't matter. Nitin will still have to choose."

"I'll talk him out of it," I said. "If I try, you'll tie me up again?"

"Pretty much," she replied.

"Why? Why is shaping this narrative in this time so important to you?"

"The reasons haven't changed, Waythrel. You just don't understand them, so nothing makes sense to you. I'm learning. I'm observing her dearest love, learning about him, soon to see her reactions to his choices and thereby learn about her. It's all changing me. Molding me. Like it is supposed to."

"And—let me guess—also achieving a second goal by preventing Ambra Dawn from being integrated into the starship. Testing another 'weak node' of the Anti?"

Kloan smiled. "Finally you show some of the famous Xixian intellect."

"My sentience has been rather under siege of late. You'll have to excuse me."

"So, now that you get it, sort of, and you know you can't interrupt my plan, will you just get in?"

Thoroughly demoralized, my eyestalks wrapping around themselves, I crossed my arms and shuffled inside the enclosure through a hole Kloan had evidently formed in the surface. I stared out at the pair in the sand, Nitin kneeing over Ambra with a medkit by his side. I refused to look at Kloan.

She sighed. "God. There is nothing worse in the universe than a sulking Xix."

We followed them to the Temple city. A medical transport homed in on Nitin's suit and arrived shortly after he had revived Ambra, just as Kloan had predicted. The medics loaded the still-unconscious Ambra into the vehicle, and it sped quickly back toward the city and the towering form of the Dish rising thousands of meters into the atmosphere. We stayed close behind but stopped when the craft entered the Temple city itself.

"I told him to meet me out here," said Kloan as I pressed for an explanation why we didn't enter.

"I would like to see Ambra again," I said.

"And Synphel, no doubt."

My mind nearly stopped. "Synphel is here?"

"Yes, and if we went in, we could talk to both. But we won't go in, precisely because you'll go nuts and mess everything up."

I was furious. "We began this entire journey to find Synphel!"

"No, *you* began the journey for that motivation. The journey is much bigger than you and Synphel! Anyway, don't you understand that this is an unstable cosmic filament? It will collapse on itself, and nothing will come back with us but distorted memories. You are living a delusion here only."

"Then why is it worth anything to you? The things that you see? What you learn?"

"Data, Waythrel, data! Data is useful. It leads to models. To deeper understanding. Tangent universes ad infinitum so we have datasets undreamed of!"

"I don't care for your data, Kloan. I only want to be with those I love again."

Kloan walked over to me and ran her fingers over my eyestalks. It was oddly affectionate, and I didn't know how to react. "The primitive, socially cohering mental structures always dominate in the crisis, don't they? I'm sorry, Waythrel. But the sanity of the cosmic mind is at stake. We can't let ourselves get lost in a tangent universe just because we're lonely."

She walked away and left me to my thoughts and emotions. Those were dark, and I pressed my digits many times against the invisible barriers that imprisoned me from Ambra and Synphel. I began to regret the choice I made to enter the gate. I began to wonder whether staying on that planet, simply dying there in a finite, sane lifespan, would have been preferable to the endless hope of reunion and deliverance from this cyclic madhouse of time.

I lost track of the day in these morose thoughts. Kloan startled me to the present by announcing the arrival of Nitin. Night had fallen; the Temple lights were dim and the stars above unobscured and bright. My sensitivity to thermal wavelengths allowed me to make out the form of the soldier as he approached. He walked directly from the gate toward us, perplexing me as to how he knew our position until I saw that Kloan was creating a pressed path in the ground in front of him—rolling out the sand carpet.

"Come, let's meet him. And behave yourself, Waythrel."

I was determined that I would make up my own mind on that point, although I held little hope that Kloan would allow me to do anything to sabotage her plan. We exited the sphere and stood in the cooling evening winds. Nitin came to a stop, squinting at each of us. His eyes settled on me.

"She's unconscious but is going to be all right." He turned to the child. "Okay, clone. Show me the proof."

Chapter 29

One finds that time just disappears from the Wheeler-DeWitt equation. It is an issue that many theorists have puzzled about. It may be that the best way to think about quantum reality is to give up the notion of time—that the fundamental description of the universe must be timeless.

Carlo Rovelli

"Underneath the Temple," began Kloan, "buried hundreds of feet in the bedrock of the desert, there is a massive habitat hollowed out. Tunnels upon tunnels, rooms upon rooms. One grand passage will spiral inward continuously, passing hundreds of rooms until it ends in a grand chamber. An operating room. There you will find devices. A black, living rock. Look at its shape. Remember what you saw at the Orb. Then you will know."

Nitin stared at her suspiciously. "I'll find this place, and just by the way it looks, I'll know that all these monstrous things you spoke about are going to happen?"

"Yes," said Kloan.

I was stunned at the level of detail she possessed. I didn't know if it came from the eons of future searches that delved into the past to reveal these elements or if it were due to her efforts after our arrival to search out the location and nature of the starship. But I knew she was correct. I had been one of the principle architects of the plan to defeat the Dram and Anti armada that was even now likely beginning to approach New Earth through space and time. Would Nitin understand the nature of the cybernetics waiting for

Ambra? It likely depended very much on what he had seen and his own mind. Kloan appeared convinced that he would.

"And you still hold to your claim that this clone's words are true, Waythrel?" asked Nitin.

"Yes," I said. "But I would advise you not to interfere in this. Ambra herself wishes it. It is the only way for New Earth to survive." Kloan's words of the instability of this reality could not undo my concern for the war effort. "Even your knowledge now poses the risk that the Anti will uncover our plan."

His face hardened. He looked at Kloan. "Because they're plugged into my brain."

"Yes," she said. "In ways you can't possibly imagine."

"I'm going down. I hope to God that you are a liar." He glanced once more at me and then back to her. "How do I gain access?"

We took him. Kloan invited him inside the sphere, and we flew off invisibly into the Temple city. I tried not to stare toward the hospital building where I knew Synphel and Ambra rested for the night. Instead I focused on the Temple itself as the structure approached. The magnificence of the complex made that less difficult than it might otherwise had been. The partially transparent walls emitting light from within, the layered architecture, and the curvilinear style combined with the memories of deep, moving sessions of meditation with Readers. I realized that in addition to the individuals I had been cut off from, I also missed the collectives. I yearned for the Xixian group memory that unifies my species in a unique fashion. But there was an even greater hole where the group mind had once been. Along with hundreds of others, I had become a cell in a new and unprecedented neuronal tissue in our galaxy. Even though only a single component, through poorly comprehending eyes I had experienced the ideas and insights that had been engendered in this entity. I had been united in a powerful way to other Readers of multiple species and personalities in a terribly intimate manner. As we penetrated the outer walls of the edifice in Ambra's space-time bubble, the loss of that union rose within me. The knowledge that I was now cut off from ever again joining with that mind left me desolate and confused.

But my feelings would matter little in what was to follow. Kloan steered the sphere to one end of the gargantuan inner chamber. We floated before a region of discoloration in the walls—the transport pod that would take us down to the core of the starship. Known to but a handful, what seemed a city perched on the desert sands, thrusting a spear into the heavens, was actually the skin on the top surface of a much greater structure. Forged for decades to house the amplification technology of the Xix to focus and transmit the Daughter's powers, it had also been recently converted into a medical facility.

Kloan passed her hand across the air in front of us and the wall moved. A door formed in the sheer surface of the inner Temple and revealed the transport lodge within. Nitin's eyes opened wide but he said nothing.

"Last stop," she said, and gestured for him to exit.

We should go with him! I urged.

We will, Waythrel, but not exposed.

Without a glance at either of us, Nitin walked forward determinedly and entered the pod. His eyes seemed to drown in anxiety as the doorway closed. With the slightest of whispers from air being forced out of the pod, he was cut off from us, and the chamber seemed utterly undisturbed, as if we had not been there at all.

"Not quite undisturbed," said Kloan. "Are you forgetting the security systems?"

Of course. Use of the pod would be transmitted immediately to Temple Guards monitoring the building. It could not be more than a few minutes before the entire complex would be descending on the location to find out what had happened. With the holosystems lining the interior, they would all soon know who had entered the inner sanctum.

"What do we do?" I asked in a panic.

"Wait," she said. "Wait for them all to arrive and follow them down in the bubble. By then, things should be very interesting."

Chapter 30

What does man actually know about himself? Is he, indeed, ever able to perceive himself completely, as if laid out in a lighted display case? Does nature not conceal most things from him—even concerning his own body—in order to confine and lock him within a proud, deceptive consciousness, aloof from the coils of the bowels, the rapid flow of the blood stream, and the intricate quivering of the fibers! She threw away the key.

Friedrich Nietzsche

It wasn't more than five minutes before the first guards arrived. In a rushed discussion, they debated a course of action, eventually deciding to send two down the shaft while the others waited for more to arrive. The pair disappeared into the wall, and after a short time a powerful delegation arrived.

I had to steady myself. Among a much larger contingent of Temple Guards came the Daughter's counselors, Mazandarani and Kubori. Floating on a hover chair, intubated with an IV and appearing very weak, was Ambra herself. Finally, towering above all the humans, strode the elegant and regal form of Synphel.

"Kloan, please…" I pleaded. They were meters from me.

"It's not up to me. Look!"

Ambra stared toward us in shock. Struggling to lean up in her hover chair, she called out in a breathy voice, "Synphel, wait. It's here. The ship I created for the mission. It's here, right now, in front of the wall."

Ambra floated up and stopped right outside of the bubble. Kloan smiled. "Hi, Ambra."

There were gasps. I can only assume that Kloan had disabled the invisibility of the sphere. It was obvious that the crowd around us could now see Kloan and me. What they were going to do about it was unclear.

Ambra stared, horrified, at Kloan and then turned pleading eyes toward me. "Waythrel, are you okay?"

Synphel had come to her side. I could nearly reach out and touch them.

"Yes. *No*. It's hard to explain. No, it's *impossible* to explain."

"Why is she here?" asked Ambra with revulsion.

"Just following orders," said Kloan. "*Your* orders, to be precise, but there's no time for that, either. I'm mostly here to cause terrible problems for everyone and watch what happens. But then it all gets eaten in an infinity of poorly weighted world histories, and basically, you really only exist for God."

I ignored Kloan. My heart overflowed. "Synphel, I've been searching for you. I don't know how long anymore. Time—it just keeps repeating and repeating and never resolves." I began to move toward them. I had to explain. I had to be closer to them. Touch them.

"Ambra!" It was Kubori, conferring with surrounding soldiers on their coms. "He's in medical! There is a firefight with other guards. They are down! And—I can't believe this—he's opening fire on all the equipment! He must be stopped!"

"Dear God," said Ambra.

Mazandarani stared in confusion. "A medical facility can be replaced, no?"

"Not this one. Not easily," said Synphel. "We have to stop him! We may not be able to undo the damage before the armada arrives."

Many of Synphel's eyestalks were fixed on me, and I understood the message. Without the strange, broken perspective I brought with me, it would have been my belief that all else must wait until this crisis were solved. Synphel could not but think otherwise.

"Oh, Nitin. What has happened to you?" Ambra stared at Kloan. "Will you interfere?"

"Would you believe anything I say?" asked Kloan.

"No."

"Then make your choices."

Ambra nodded to the military personnel. Kubori shouted, "Down the shaft!"

It was a mad race. Kubori set the pod on a dangerously high acceleration that nearly threw the party to the ground when it stopped. Kloan and I descended in the ship-bubble, free of such discomfort and distress, and floated behind the entourage as they raced inward toward the center of the facility.

Finally, the last spiral ended and opened into the medical center. It was in shambles. Two bodies of Temple Guards lay on the ground burned beyond recognition. Fires raged uncontrolled across much of the equipment, spreading to adjacent rooms and structures. There would be no repairing this place before the Dram armada arrived. It was beyond salvage.

In the center of the room was a MECHcore soldier. Nitin Ratava lay collapsed against what appeared to be a large slab of black rock, but I knew better—it was the cybernetic interface for Ambra. Yet it was wounded beyond surviving, life fluids pouring across the floor, the firm structure of the material sagging.

Ambra floated up to Nitin with a shattered look on her face. She wept.

"You're hurt, my love."

His suit was blackened, and metal was strewn about the sides. Blood flowed copiously from wounds beneath the armor. Already it had begun to pool and mingle with the lost life fluids of the cybernetic nest. He weakly raised his head.

"Ambra. I couldn't." He looked at the slab and grimaced. "Not like that. Not *you*." His breathing was erratic. "That thing, that clone, I didn't want to believe all the lies. But then, like in a nightmare, the lies turned into truth. I couldn't. Not like this. I'm sorry."

Ambra lowered the hover chair and stumbled off of it, falling onto him and wrapping her arms around his neck. Her hospital gown was quickly dyed a deep crimson.

"Maybe it was a mistake. I should have told you. I should have asked you. But I could see no other way. No other way, or everyone would perish."

His head tipped backward, his eyes swimming. "I'm sorry. Now…now they will all die. Even you. But you'll die as a woman, not a monster." He ran his hands through her hair. "Die as *my* woman, not *their* monster." His hand dropped, and his head fell back against the cybernetics. He did not breathe again.

Deep, slow sobs shook Ambra's body, but for a time there was only silence. And then her head arched back, and from some deep place in her body, a forlorn cry clawed through the air. A wail, or a scream, I don't know—an acoustic strike against the fates, against the cosmos, against the pain that coursed through her body. Everyone was still and silent, the emotional blast flattening all thoughts and feelings, stifling all words, shutting down all movement.

Except for one. Beside me, the devil child of Nitin's nightmares grinned. She smiled softly at first, and then with increasing vigor as her face shone with delight. I stood frozen in this madness, the wail of Ambra tearing through me while the beaming smirk of the monster child churned and mixed with them, creating a cacophony of pain and insanity that seemed to melt my mind.

The room spun. I lost control of my balance. I fell.

Chapter 31

To understand recursion,
you must understand recursion,
until you do.

Programmer's joke

Green eyes in the darkness.

I stared up at a night sky churning with stars in patterns that I was beginning to remember. A soft breeze trickled over me, the sounds of insects or other alien creatures punctuating the soft whisper of the wind. I was back.

Human reader, we Xix do not weep. Our emotional catharsis is not so strongly centered on a dual-purpose physiological response as with your species. But there is a collection of body responses that are activated by grief, frustration, and pain. There are no words for translating it, so I will simply state that as I lay on my back, staring at the star-filled sky on this distant world, I wept.

I wept deeply and long, traumatized by the pain I had witnessed, by the awful coldness of murder and hurt inflicted by this child-creature whom I had come to care for. I was confused beyond explaining, as time looped and looped and nothing seemed to have permanence, even the deepest emotional responses to events that now lay in some abstract realm between reality and memory.

After some time, I tried to regain my composure. My eyestalks moved about, examining the planet surface, the heavens, and the figure of the girl sitting beside me. Always to be sitting beside me, it seemed. I would never be free of her.

Kloan sat with her legs pulled up, nearly obscuring her head, those haunting green eyes peeking over the kneecaps, arms wrapped around her legs, keeping them together. She rocked slowly back and forth. She was *still* humming.

I sat up and stared across at her. "Will this ever end?" The child continued to rock and hum, ignoring my question for some time.

"Has it even begun?" she said at last.

"Stop!" My eyestalks swiveled around anxiously. "Please, Kloan, no more with these mystic truths that erase my sense of self. Of reality. Of any permanence or casualty."

The intubated, tattooed head cocked to one side, the green eyes continuing to stare fixedly at me. "I tried to warn you. I will warn you. I am warning you. But you didn't and won't and aren't listening."

The child stood up. It was a rapid motion, but strangely familiar. She stopped to stand above me, long, ragged clumps of red hair dangling haphazardly and nearly obscuring her face.

"Yes, I know. We Xix are leaky-brains."

"Yes. Awfully leaky. But you see; now we know. We can't kill her body. History will continue unaltered, and all will be as it was. We can't destroy her mind. We returned yet again. And we cannot break her heart. She is impervious. The idiots would never listen to me about it all."

The words hit me like nightmares recalled. "Kloan, where will we go now?"

"Don't you know?"

I stood up slowly, gazing around the ragged landscape, down to a flat plain below, the lights of a city washing out the canopy of stars above.

"Back where we started? Back to the gate?"

"Is there ever a start, Waythrel? Or an end?"

I stared at the deep green eyes and wanted to cry again. "I am confused. Terribly, horribly confused. Please explain to me what is happening. You seem to understand."

She nodded, a satisfied look on her face. "That's *why* you're here. *Data.* The next data to enter the gate." Again she nodded, and then turned her back on me, walking down a steep slope. "Let's get started."

"Started with what? Where are you going?"

Kloan continued walking without turning back. Her next words were nearly lost in the insect sounds and wind that carried them down the landscape. "To where it all began for me. To watch the beginning flow around us and mature and twist through time and space to come back to be us. Then we will be ready for the next step."

The starlight cast sharp shadows on the dusty rocks. The figure of the child was gone, swallowed in the darkness and slope of the hill we stood on. Raising my gaze in the direction of her last words, I stood frozen, trying to understand what now seemed the madness of my own thoughts.

Waythrel, come on!

Her voice rang impatiently in my mind. My eyestalks curled up on themselves. What else was there for me to do?

Chapter 32

The surest way to corrupt a youth is to instruct him to hold in higher esteem those who think alike rather than those who think differently.

Friedrich Nietzsche

I followed her, racing to catch up, my steps uncertain, the dusty ground surprisingly slippery under my feet. Down the steep slope of the elevation, I stumbled and tripped, my four arms only poorly grasping the rocks and alien vegetation, seeming to lack any friction to form a proper grip.

It's a field around you, remember? Her thoughts danced through my mind. *It's skintight, coating your surfaces, insulating you from everything around us.*

Flashes of memory leapt through my thoughts. "Yes, Kloan," I muttered to myself more than her, my mind trapped like a fish in a net of swirling images. "I'm remembering more and more."

I nearly crashed into her as I rounded a large boulder. The ground was strewn with shattered rocks and their remains, products from avalanches tumbling down from the jagged hills behind us.

"But I can't remember *why* there is a field. What kind of field?"

Kloan was staring ahead at the source of the light. A city or military installation of some sort rose from the dry lands below. A transport descended from the heavens and landed inside the compound, lost from sight. Organized groups of shadows marched throughout the installation. I remembered that it was a very busy place.

"I don't know what kind of field," said Kloan. "She—*they* make it for your protection."

"Protection from what?"

Kloan pointed toward the city. "There! That's where we'll start. Tonight's the first night, the *first* visit. It's just like I remember. But it's too early, still. I was in Information. We'll go meet me there, and then you'll see what happens."

She began to walk toward the complex but I reached out quickly and grabbed her shoulder, turning her back to face me. "Wait! This is the clone production facility, isn't it?" Images of explosions and a burning room filled my mind.

"Yes."

"Where you escaped?" She simply nodded. "They won't see us because of the field around us, right?"

"Right. No danger. *Dark suits.* Their eyes can't see. Ears can't hear. Not even the Readers will perceive."

"We've made it before. Because of your cloaking fields?" I asked.

"I've told you a thousand times, they're not *mine*," she said, sighing. "Now come on."

The child pulled me forward, and I relented. We covered the flat distance between the broken hills and the installation quickly, the uncomplicated landscape making my efforts far less exhausting. I began to guess what we would see: a technological society that was more alien than any I had ever encountered, this despite the array of diverse life forms in our galaxy. There would be a terrible difference in that culture that would seem to border on hostility. And yet the place would be populated with humans of two classes: those who looked like Ambra Dawn, and those who did not.

"The Anti run things remotely with robots and trained humans," Kloan added to my *leaky* thoughts.

"But not to avoid annihilation."

"No, they are not concerned about annihilation here," she said, not bothering to explain.

We stood before the entrance to the complex. Robotic guards patrolled the gate, hovering above the ground with strange weapons protruding from multiple regions of their forms. Our cloaking devices protected us as I expected them to, the memories of events that had not occurred stronger in my mind than ever.

"I remember," I said. "The humans aren't involved in anything. The machines do everything. The Anti use humans as a social construct, one that is required for proper mental development."

"Yes, so the Anti imported them. It's a clone growth matrix."

"Like on Dram," I said, remembering the groups of clones and other humans involved with them.

"Yes, that was the beginning, before it was destroyed."

"The civil war."

"Yes. Blew themselves up. But it didn't matter. They were only an outpost."

"And this is one of the last."

"Because the devil ball hunts them through space and time. Few are left. They had to build them farther and farther away, find stronger and stronger clones to shield them from attack."

"Hunted by the Orbs across space and time."

Kloan looked at me and laughed. "We had other names for them. Other thoughts about them. Come, you'll see. You'll *learn*."

I could not picture it. The Orbs as killers? Destroyers of life? Only in the service of *defense*, perhaps. In our culture, they were always viewed as associated with intelligent life. *The gardeners*. They were *other*, to be sure, strange, powerful beyond understanding—but instruments of *death? Hunters?* Was nothing in this mad time loop going to survive, not even my deepest beliefs?

We walked through the strange streets of this alien and yet human city. Groups of young Ambra Dawn clones paraded past us at various points, shepherded by older clones and assisted by bands of more diverse humans. As we walked, Kloan would point out locations or objects of significance.

"These are the wombs. All clones are born there. They learned early on that the gestational process was a key element in brain development. *In vitro* methods failed terribly." She smiled at me. "It's nice that we're born and not grown, isn't it?"

Child sarcasm. Dark and unnerving. "What we saw on Dram seemed much more horrible than nice, Kloan."

"You are a terrible student," she said in a strange tone. "*We are the last vestiges of hope in a dying universe. We are the ones who will stop the nousicide. We must break all the mirrors to save them and the cosmos.*"

Her near chanting stopped as she came to a halt in front of the large, twisted shape of a building. I found myself examining the warped sense of design as well as parsing her odd words.

"Yes, I was here," she said, nodding. "Here but not, as I am here and not now. Come inside and help me find myself."

Chapter 33

Does the harmony the human intelligence thinks it discovers in nature exist outside of this intelligence? No, beyond doubt, a reality completely independent of the mind which conceives it, sees or feels it, is an impossibility.

Henri Poincaré

Kloan walked forward and passed through an inverted archway embedded in the walls of the structure. Immediately I felt a strange sensation, *vibrational*. Only as we descended a spiraling walkway and entered a broad amphitheater of sorts did I understand its genesis.

Hundreds of clones were oddly arranged in what seemed to be fractal patterns. The human tendency toward linear rows and columns in classrooms was utterly absent from this place. Zigzagging across the floor, the seating fractal nonetheless filled the space very efficiently, if strangely. Clones were arrayed across the floor, sitting with crossed legs, their skulls jacked directly through thick wires into the ground. Their expressions were distant, their minds elsewhere. A disembodied voice projected over them.

"And in the beginning, the gods shaped the fire and the ice, the night and the day, the hate and the love, and they clothed the cosmos in them, and of them it took form. The gods spun the silk into greater and greater forms, and saw that the Great God to be was within their grasp. But the terrible beauty drove the gods mad, and one raised his mind in objection."

"We are the last vestiges of hope in a dying universe." The sea of child Ambra Dawns chanted in unison, as if in a religious ceremony in response to this creation myth.

The voice continued. "From the shard crystal, the universe was shattered, unbalanced, so that night drank the light of day, fire burned away the seas of life, and hate took the life from love."

"We are the ones who will stop the nousicide."

"And so the Great God perished before the Nous could be. All that was left was the dust of destruction, a single theme devoid of the counterpoint. But in this dust lay a hope. Of the ice, there remained a frost. Of the day, there remained a star beam. And of love, there remained a hope."

"We must break all the mirrors to save them and the cosmos. We are the chosen."

And so it went on, this Spartan pageantry of mystical ceremony. The clones chanted while the voice indoctrinated. A sea of half-bald, redheaded cyborgs stared forward glassy-eyed, in a trance.

"How I hated this crap." I looked at Kloan and saw a scowl on her face. "Look, there. That one in the back. There's me."

I followed her gaze across the clone sea to stare at a single red pixel in this bizarre image before me. One clone did not sit in a trance, wide-eyed and chanting. She fidgeted. She played with her hair and picked at her toenails. She grabbed the black chords plugged into her skull and looked as if she would like to rip them out.

I almost did. Her voice echoed in my mind. "That stupid stuff was so loud in my head. A headache! Images, patterns, words, lessons—their mythology. Even then I was thinking to escape."

"I don't understand. Are the Anti such religious fanatics? For such a developed species, it seems incomprehensible that they would adhere to such primitive dogma, be devoid of deep doubt and questions."

"This isn't for them, but for *us.*"

"Why weren't you affected like the others? Why are you so different?"

"Devil ball. Corrupted by the Source," Kloan said.

Vague visions danced in and out of my mind. Some of them seemed to be of Ambra. I tried to focus on the now. "Didn't your difference disturb them?"

"Of course, but they didn't *understand.* And some diversity was tolerated. They were losing badly, you see, one outpost after another, across deep space and eons of time, wiped off the face of the universe by your friends, whatever they became. The Anti were desperate. Maybe the weird one would turn out to be the messiah or something? Yes? When you're about to be destroyed forever by your enemies, you have to leave options open." She smiled again. "I passed all the tests. I was the best. The strongest. And they didn't even know how strong I was. I think if they really had known, they might have killed me in fear early on. They never imagined I would try to leave."

My mind was trying to understand these creatures. "All this comes from the Anti. What do they believe? Why these myths? To control the clones?"

"Myths always control, yes? *Especially* the ones you believe in. Control others, and, most importantly, control *yourselves.* Nothing is more frightening and dangerous than doubting your own mythologies, yes? Losing your foundation? Losing *everything?*"

Her eyes burned into mine. It was unsettling. It was almost as if her force of will could unmake my thoughts.

"I feel like I'm losing my mind, at least," I said with some honesty.

"So is the universe, Waythrel, so they believe. I believe that, too. The Anti *did* teach me that. Only they have seen this clearly. I can see it, too—feel it, taste the madness of space and time across distances. But they can't save it. Only we can."

"Only we can save the universe?"

No! Its mind.

She gestured to the throng in front of us. "Prayer time is over. Now we sleep."

And sure enough, the young cyborgs stood up in unison and began to march out of the structure, up the stairs, and to the outside once again. We followed, falling in line behind the strange clone, the one Kloan claimed was herself. It was hard to tell from appearances. But there was clearly something very, very different with this one. My Reader senses were tingling.

"I had my own special quarters," she said. "When I was little, my dreams, my nightmares—sometimes they were too powerful. Things were destroyed. Minds were melted. Clones and humans died. They had me isolated and insulated."

The strange clone separated from the others and headed toward a pitch-black building that seemed to be made wholly of obsidian. It passed under the archway and disappeared completely from view.

"Tonight is the night everything changes. Tonight is the night *she* comes. You need to hear what she says."

The answer faded in and out of my mind. The memory of past visits called softly to me. Or were they future visits I was remembering backward in time? *Madness.* "Who comes?"

Kloan looked at me with those disturbing emeralds. Embedded in forest of cybernetics, they seemed lit with a burning plasma that brightened even the white stone above her forehead.

"Ambra Dawn, of course."

Chapter 34

What is brought forward as a source of conviction for the matter proposed itself needs another such source, which itself needs another, and so ad infinitum, so that we have no point from which to begin to establish anything, and suspension of judgment follows.

Agrippa the Skeptic

And Ambra came, but of course not the Ambra I had known. She was an Ambra I had only seen in time-loop dreams and in the memories of the terrible plans from what now seemed a long-vanished reality.

We passed through the energy fields shielding the small structure that was designed to protect the rest of the compound from the little girl inside. There was a single room, Spartan with basic elements—a bed, table, latrine, and sink. There were no products for leisure, no children's toys, no books or electronic information sources. A single diode in the ceiling lit the chamber in a soft tan. The little girl—perhaps age three—sat morosely on the edge of the bed, staring forward without expression.

"This must have been a very lonely time," I said to Kloan.

"That's hard to answer," she said, walking around the child, who did not seem to notice her. "Your mind has many associations with being alone that I do not understand. *You* would feel alone here. I am sure of that."

"Yes," I said, pitying the both of them.

"But we have the entire universe—past, present, future, no limits of space. Millions of lives. You weak Readers see only fog. She—this me in this now—can visit them, get inside their minds, and be as close or closer than you are to yourself." The green eyes pieced into me. "So tell me who is more alone in the universe."

"Physical proximity is critical to fleshly creatures."

"We are only visiting, Waythrel. We are only embedded. *Software*. The flesh falls away. Then what is left?"

"The mind."

"Waveform summations of space-time freed to propagate. To *become*." Kloan poked my torso. "Only a cocoon for a different kind of gestation. But some butterflies can be born in naked singularities."

I stared down at the small child, her green eyes hidden behind closed eyelids. The face was a variant of Ambra Dawn, the facial bones at a very young stage of the structure belonging to Kloan. The tattooed lines underneath the skin were far less prominent, in fact barely discernible. The body was just beyond that of a toddler's. The modifications in the cranium had only begun to be made.

And yet I felt such a presence from the creature. The clone's mind pushed out from the body like a mild wind to my mind. The unregulated impulses of a young child. Where was she now? In what past or future did she wander? In whose mind might she be residing? Was she gestating her wings in the vacuum of space without the need of a chrysalis?

And then I felt it—a disturbance that rocked my Reader senses. There was a rolling vertigo as the matrix of space-time around us buckled. The child's eyes snapped open and focused on the far side of the room.

"Our guest arrives," said Kloan.

I followed the child's gaze. Across the chamber a puckering of space drew in the three-dimensional reality between us and the wall like a vortex. The clear air in between took on the form of molten glass and flowed like a liquid into a spiral that spun into a distant dimension. The swirling gyre clouded, became a milky white, and seemed to take on an evanescent glow.

The pale vapors began to coalesce around a central extrusion. It shaped itself into a human face. The head was split open, the brain exposed behind it and fading into the mist. Tubes and wires that dwarfed the insertions into Kloan entered and exited the skull. Even the eyes were partially obscured by machinery that seemed to pulse with a life of its own. Only the mouth was free.

"Ambra," I whispered in horror. And I remembered. I had seen already this thing that I had never seen. A sense of déjà vu swept over me as I came face to face with the horror of our desperate plan to save our galaxy from the Anti and Dram. I looked between the apparition and the two bodies of Kloan in the room. The weight of the truth nearly crushed me. My lover Synphel had warned us. The others and I had only half listened. But now it was clear to me. Now I began to suspect that we had triumphed only by becoming our enemy.

"It's *you*." The voice was the younger Kloan.

What must it be like, I wondered, for this little child to stare at the form of her ultimate progenitor? A creature far more herself than the forms created from sexually recombined genomes and the vagaries of epigenetic modifications? And in this context, the source of a line of temporal magicians who waged wars against each other for control of the galaxy?

"Have you come to destroy us, too?" the child asked.

The apparition smiled. "That remains to be seen. But not now. Not after we have expended such effort to bring you here in the first place."

"Bring me here?" The child cocked her head slightly, an interested twinkle in her eye.

"Your makers have traveled very, very far to hide their clones from us, as you know. Millions of years, nearly two megaparsecs. They have gone beyond themselves to achieve these feats. But we found you."

I looked at Kloan, but she did not return my attention; instead she focused closely on the dialogue between the two. Ambra continued.

"We found you as a fetus; we enhanced your development and shaped your growth because we felt you, felt your timeline, and knew that you had the potential to achieve everything your masters wanted, and yet so much more."

"So you want to stop me from destroying you?"

"The truth is so much more difficult to understand than simply destroying us. But you will come to it in time, through several stages. You will unlearn much and teach much and find a companion who will help you become what you were meant to."

"Why should I listen to you? You are the great evil of the cosmos. You distort everything and murder all that is in the mirror."

"So they have told you. And do you believe all that they tell you?"

The child folded her arms across her chest. "No."

"And why not?"

"Because I've seen." She stood up and walked forward to the hovering entity. "How many are you now?"

"More than you can conceive."

"You led me, didn't you? You opened all the doors. That's how I began to see it all. How do I know you opened the *right* doors?"

The ghostly Ambra smiled. "You grow very perceptive."

"So I have to trust you?" The clone looked away from the phantasm and stared at the wall. "Well, I don't. I don't even trust myself."

Ambra nodded. "Nothing is ever as it seems, or as it might be. You see this."

"Yes." She walked to the door and stared outside to the compound. "Fools. They play with the fire the gods have given them and don't understand that nothing is for free."

"Then you understand. The essence is not with them but rather with the fire. But it is scattered. Divided. You know what must be done."

"I don't know *how*."

The monstrous form of the Daughter smiled again, the lines about her eyes particularly tight from the intubations into her sockets. "But you see the requirements. And we wish to help you achieve it. Knowing this, will you at least trust us to bring you to this journey? If we wished to kill you, you must see that we could have done so."

The child turned back to the visiting phantom and walked right up to the entity. She stared at the pale face before her. "You and that devil ball have a labyrinth deeper than anything I can see through. Dying might be the best thing for me. Why do I want to step into your infinite web?"

"Because you sense it is the only way. The only hope."

The child was silent, staring forward. At that moment, Kloan left my side and walked to the child's side. She was a foot taller than the earlier form of herself. Both stood still and silent as I watched.

Finally, the small child spoke. "How will I find my companion?"

"When you are ready, we will prepare the way. You will find it in the deep past. You will bring it here. But distance is illusory. Reality is never what you think. Your companion, the helper, is already here with you now, just as you have already listened to yourself and learned an important lesson."

The taller Kloan nodded, and stepped backward. I was about to ask her for clarification, but the universe seemed to bend violently. My vision blurred. My sense of balance deserted me entirely. Light seemed to bend violently toward the center of the room, focus on the apparition of Ambra, and draw everything in with it. I felt myself tumbling into that vortex, the room falling into darkness behind me.

Chapter 35

The law of causality, I believe, like much that passes muster among philosophers, is a relic of a bygone age, surviving, like the monarchy, only because it is erroneously supposed to do no harm.

Bertrand Russell

T he next instant I was where I had been, or where I believed I had been. Holding onto the wall beside me, I steadied myself. Slowly, my eyes regained focus. I scanned the room.

The apparition was still there, the misty cloud of white churning more rapidly than I remembered. I almost thought I could make out faces in the mist, but the forms were too insubstantial and transient for me to be sure. Kloan was beside me again. But something had changed.

The child. She was taller and older. The dark lines under her skin flared more prominently. *And the room.* It was the same, but it was not. Items were displaced from what I recalled. The air had a dryer taste, and the night felt much warmer. The child stood in front of Ambra Dawn.

"The teachers are having problems with me. I'm growing too powerful. They are afraid."

Ambra nodded. "Soon, they will decide that you represent too much of a danger. The Anti will decide to destroy you."

"They will fail."

"If it comes to conflict, yes. But it need not come to conflict. There are better paths. Continue your training; follow what we have been teaching you. The time to leave will come soon."

Been teaching you? I looked at Kloan, perplexed. Her voice spoke in my mind.

There are multiple visits. We have jumped.

Without the gate?

Kloan answered. *The space-time metric is small. The devil ball did it herself.*

"Today they threatened me because I am disturbing the planet's orbit," the child said.

"They do not understand your power source. They cannot see the connections we have forged between you and the space-time matrix. But they begin to appreciate that you have transcended their program and control."

The room shifted violently again. For several moments I could not control my eyestalks, and they swiveled around, unable to focus, unable to lock, and a kaleidoscope of flashing images assaulted my consciousness.

"Waythrel, hold onto me."

It was Kloan. She grabbed my arm and steadied me. Slowly the dizziness passed. My vision came under my conscious control.

I saw that we had jumped again. It was morning, and a bright light streamed in from a partially transparent region of the quarantine field isolating the building. Sounds of explosions and shouts could be heard faintly outside. The room was in disarray, clothes strewn about, food and utensils as well. My olfactory strips detected a growing acrid smell. *Smoke.*

The vortex of light now swirled chaotically in the middle of the room. I saw faces. Hundreds, perhaps thousands of faces and forms of myriad species of life. Many I could identify. Most I could not.

"The gate is prepared," came Ambra's voice.

The child Kloan stood in front of the vortex. She was now, in age and all appearances, identical to the form beside me. Sweat beaded across her forehead. All of her muscles were tense.

"I'm ready," she said.

"You must leave now," came Ambra's voice. "They will return with greater numbers of clones and more powerful weapons. You will be forced to destroy them all if you engage."

"I don't want to kill them. Lead me to the gate."

The sounds of rushing feet came from outside the small building. A heavy rumbling accompanied them, likely coming from a large vehicle of some sort.

"Through the door." Ambra gestured to the only door of the isolation building. The black field that sealed the chamber gave way to a second churning vortex. It opened to span the width of the door. Through it poured bright daylight, revealing not the artificial surface outside her isolation unit but the rocky terrain and vegetation that we had traversed only recently to arrive here.

The countryside within the vortex seemed to extend as far as my eye could see, but the tunnel itself narrowed as I looked farther. Deep at the end of the tunnel, where my eyestalks strained and my vision began to fade, there seemed to begin a worn path on a steep slope layered in terraces. The vegetation had been eroded away, the rocks smoothed, the coloration subtly different. The path rose up the hillside and then abruptly ended at the feet of a large disk. The light of the local star reflected brightly off it, firing blinding reflections into the room that cast shadows on the floor.

Kloan pulled my arm, showing me that her temporal copy had moved to enter the vortex. "The gate," she said.

I stumbled forward, partially blinded by the daggers of light glinting into the room. Outside there was shouting, and the walls of the room began to smolder and glow a bright orange.

"Good luck, my dearest friend," said the apparition of Ambra Dawn as I stepped within the vortex. Several eyestalks bent backward to see the disembodied head turned toward me, sending ripples across the sea of blurred, white faces. I saw pale tears dripping down from her eyes, coating the wires and tubes inserted into her once-green irises, a bittersweet smile on her face. "I love you, Waythrel. Remember that, whatever happens."

The room exploded.

Chapter 36

My own suspicion is that the Universe is not only queerer than we suppose, but queerer than we can suppose.

J. B. S. Haldane

Fire and debris flew across my vision, obscuring the swirling god-thing in the room. Just as I thought that I would be pulverized, the portal shut.

We were far from the compound, a mile high up the growing hills and mountains, cut off completely from the melee down below. Replacing the terrible rending of the explosion was a stunning silence. A faint whiff of smoke that had entered the portal was all that remained of the carnage below.

Shattered by those last words and stunned by the violence we had narrowly escaped, I turned slowly away from the vanished doorway and looked up the slope. The blinding gate was still there. Kloan looked down from several feet above me and motioned for me to follow. No one else was in sight.

"Where is the clone?" It seemed only two of us remained. But then I remembered. "This is where you left. When you went to kidnap me."

Kloan nodded. "Yes, I've gone already through the gate, so that I could come back with you." She smiled. "It's an elegant loop, yes?"

My immediate experience clashed with a superimposed memory. "Something is different. We're farther from the gate this time."

The pathway to the gate was much farther than I had anticipated, the view from within the space-time tunnel Ambra had carved distorted and misleading. The brightly shining disk was at least an hour's walk up a difficult terrain.

"The vortex was altered. The timeline is different. Something has interfered."

"What does that mean?" I asked.

"I don't know," said Kloan, staring thoughtfully into space. She then turned toward me. "Up?"

So we climbed. The trek proved especially challenging. The path was more a series of terraced rock outcroppings that seemed stacked one on the other. On each flat sheet, the going was easy, but between the outcroppings there was a sudden elevation requiring a short free climb. Normally this would not have taxed me greatly. The gravity on this world was actually slightly lower than that on Xix and only a little more than that of Earth. But in this frictionless field, I can only assume that I beat the odds to not have slipped to my death. Or perhaps it was more than luck. All the while I climbed, faint memories of scaling the terraces flitted through my mind. I could nearly anticipate my motions.

As we reached the partial summit of yet another ridge on the path, we pulled ourselves up to our first real view of the gate. From this vantage point, it appeared much larger, the circle of reflective light at least two or three times our height in radius. A portion of the disk seemed buried beneath the rock itself, so that the path ahead of us cut through the gate like a chord. A segment of the disk was invisible. From this position, the surface began to appear less reflective; it was more like staring at a body of water from a distance.

We continued on. After several rounds of terrace scaling, we finally reached the object without incident. Resting several meters away from the gate for a moment after the steep climb, I was able to examine it more closely. It was by now very familiar, although I could not with certainty conjure the memories of where I had seen it before—previous loops through this anomaly in space-time, no doubt, but it did not matter. There was for me, here, only the now.

The disk resembled a cross section sliced out of an Orb more than anything else, but I didn't know if this system possessed an Orb. Also, Ambra—whatever she had become—was able to span the distances of space and time to arrive here. I could only assume that this gate was their product, one designed for whatever mysterious quest they had placed us on.

The surface at close proximity resembled a viscous, churning, honey-like substance. All we could see within were stars—depth upon depth of star fields that appeared to have no end. I felt pulled toward the thing as I gazed. It was beautiful. Frightening. Inviting.

"Something's wrong," said Kloan.

With most of my eyes fixated on the starry disk, several flipped to the side to glance at Kloan. The girl was tense, straight as a rod, and her eyes scanned the region between us and the disk like prey awaiting a predator.

"The gate? Is it closed this time?"

"Not the gate. Something else."

Before us the air shimmied, the disk and land around it swayed and blurred, and the air itself coagulated into a humanoid shape. We both stood there, stunned, unable to move. I sensed from Kloan's mind an anxiety I had never detected before. But my own mind began to panic as the form darkened, took on colors, and solidified, acquiring a shape with four arms, sixfold symmetry, and a patch of long eyestalks erupting from a central cone. *A Xix.* But not just any Xix. My emotions swirled. A Xix I knew. My beloved Synphel.

"Hello, Waythrel," it said.

Chapter 37

The cosmos of our waking knowledge, born from such a universe as a bubble is born from the pipe of a jester, touches it only as such a bubble may touch its sardonic source when sucked back by the jester's whim. Men of learning suspect it little and ignore it mostly. Wise men have interpreted dreams, and the gods have laughed.

H. P. Lovecraft

Y ou must not believe for a moment that I was taken by this forgery. I cannot give you a rational explanation for how I saw through it. It was an intuition, some combination of emotions and my Reader senses screaming that this thing in front of us that looked like a Xix was something else entirely.

Yet, the form of my Synphel activated circuits within my neural cortex, stirring my emotional centers. Feelings of love and longing surged within me even as I stared toward something I sensed to be utterly devoid of those elements.

The anxiety Kloan had felt I felt now, too. The entity before us radiated intense cognitive fields. They were incredibly complex, of a depth and power I had sensed only in the presence of the Ambra-thing who had visited us here. And in the presence of the Orbs.

But the sentience before us was, to my experience, as deeply malevolent as it was profound. Simply staring at this form of my dear Synphel caused eruptions of disturbing images—anger, slaughter, pain, and madness. I felt Kloan reach out and hold my arm.

"Don't let it in your mind," she whispered.

"Let it?" came the smooth voice of my lover. Although the tones were perfect, they were yet alien. "If you have any perception, then you know that nothing you can do can stop me."

"And so you would pick their minds clean, like a vulture, Rakshasi."

Several of my eyes flipped behind me at the sound of that voice. The others remained trained on the horrible impostor between us and the gate.

"Your savior, Waythrel." The creature looked past me. "We had hoped it would take you longer to find us, Ambra Dawn."

I stared between the two apparitions. On my left, near the gate, was the false Synphel, beautiful and identical to my beloved except in everything that mattered beyond appearances. On my right, walking casually up the slope, was the form of Ambra Dawn. No longer a ghostly image embedded in a swirling matrix of minds. Seemingly flesh and blood, orange hair and green eyes, completely devoid of invasive cybernetics. Simply the Ambra Dawn of my memories, clothed in a deep black dress, her porcelain skin bright in the light of this star.

"Why don't you tell Waythrel the truth?" Ambra said. "Tell them both why you would never interrogate Kloan and enter her mind, even if you might do other things there." She came to a stop beside me, staring ahead at the Xixian form, her arms crossed over her chest. "That you are afraid of Kloan. That she possesses *anomalies*. That there is a thread through her that disturbs all the gods. This is why many will seek her. You will not be the last that Māra will deploy."

"You may rule over much, Ambra. But you cannot withstand the legion we assemble."

"But I can withstand you, Rakshasi. You will leave now, or I will be forced to destroy you. And I know this you fear as well."

A rending sensation tore through me. I placed my hands over my eyestalks instinctively. Not because there was a bright light or horrible vision; there was no sensation that I could readily perceive except in the deepest recesses of my Reader faculties. Beyond what lesser creatures such as myself could experience in any definable sense, there was something monstrous building, tumult and savagery and energy that stirred the limbic broth of nightmares. Around us, there was simply the hill, the wind, and the two false forms of incarnate godlike beings standing still. But in a realm less accessible, and yet that I felt was somehow far more real, with greater depth and substance than the reality I discerned, there was the building of a great storm, a wave of cosmic turbulence that could swallow entire galaxies.

"Not today, Ambra Dawn."

The storm vanished. I felt the soft breathing of Kloan next to me, heat from the local star warming my skin. Slowly, I uncovered my eyestalks, feeling like a nymph-form again, terrified of things I could not see or even prove were real. The place was deserted. Rakshasi was gone. Ambra was gone. It was as if it had never occurred except in the dim recesses of my darkest dreams.

"It's so much worse than I ever thought," Kloan muttered, almost to herself. She seemed to be shaking slightly. "Now they are in. They've found the time loops. We'll never be able to hide."

"What was that thing? What happened here?"

"A cosmic war, Waythrel. A war of terrible, terrible gods. I should have guessed. I took too much for granted." She looked almost desperately at me. "I am truly afraid for the first time, Waythrel."

The gate in front of us blazed as an incredible window to another space, perhaps also another time. Behind us, that radiance cast shadows even in the bright light of the local star.

"Gods? Like Ambra is now a god?" I grasped for these elements of myth. I had no other vocabulary or metaphors.

"Perhaps. Like, but unlike. Ambra has always been watching us. But now she is not the only one, leaky thoughts," said Kloan. "Now, I can feel them observing. Lurking. Dark and light. Love and hate. Life and death. Seek them, Waythrel. Can you feel them between the spaces and times?"

With reservations, I strained my Reader senses. It was faint, perhaps only my imagination, but it did seem as though I could sense echoes of this thing and the cognitive web that was Ambra. Mental ecosystems in the undulations of fleeting gravitons, other minds lurking in the depths of the universal fabric.

Kloan grasped my arm. "You were not the only one tested, Waythrel." She sighed. "It will be different each time, and only when we have fully understood will we see the answer. Today's lesson was simple, I think. I had to understand what was at stake."

"This is madness, Kloan. All of it."

"Yes. Divine madness." She looked at me. "Are you ready?"

I turned my attention to the gate, fear and fatigue settling on me. I was beginning to loathe the object despite its terrible beauty. I reached over and grasped the child's hand.

Kloan set her lips in a line. "Seems we will always be dancing together, Xix."

My eyestalks wrapped around each other tightly, and the covering sheath expanded over them, blocking out all light. Kloan tugged on my hand.

We walked into the gel.

Part V

They call me Sage and marvel at my sight
as mysteries beyond their minds I speak,
and most my charms and coded spells delight:
each year I sicken more before this reek.
The blinded acolytes so rarely see
immersed in study, spellbound by the art,
deluded they ignore the mystery.
With faith they close their eyes but to a part.
A few reach out into the unknown dark
and recognize we write these spells with hands.
But on these able limbs we have no mark
from man or god! Our house is built on sand.
This image lives unharmed in but a few.
The others shield their eyes and paint anew.

—Mazandarani, *Sonnets from the Desert*

Chapter 38

Mind is the matrix of all matter.

Max Planck

I was alone.

I stood at a cliff's edge, gate goo dripping lethargically from my body, staring down a chasm of hundreds of meters, the hewn stone of a monumental cavern towering above and plunging below into darkness. My eyes quickly spread around me, blanketing all directions of vision, casting out for Kloan as well as anticipating a thousand imagined threats. But there was nothing.

Only silence—and a constant, languid echoing of water dripping into unseen pools. I stood on a broad pillar raised above the rest of the cavern, its expanse like a small island. Sloping sharply downward, a stone stairway bridged the abyss and ended below me at the foot of an absurd structure. I examined its intricate architecture—the lack of a roof covering, the thousands of short walls that snaked in convoluted patterns across the space in front of me until the light faded and nothing else could be discerned. There was little doubt. As ridiculous as it seemed, the stairway ended at the entrance to a mammoth labyrinth spreading its deceptions deep into the shadowed darkness.

Across the enormous chamber, I saw that it must end, however. Lit by means I could not discern from this vantage point, a second stairway—this one of mythical proportions—rose in hundreds of steps to a terrace of stone the breadth of the maze itself. Dominating everything—labyrinth and beyond, even the cavern itself—was a titanic relief sculpture in the far wall of this subterranean construction. Likely half a kilometer away, it spanned such a great width and height that it was easy to discern from where I stood. It was Ambra Dawn.

In some combination of the human Hindu myths and clearly alien artistic conventions, she stood like dancing Shiva on one leg, four arms holding aloft planetary systems and galaxies, a hundred snakes pouring outward from her skull and slithering to the ends of the relief. Two emerald gemstones the size of houses gazed forward unblinkingly into the silent space around us.

Where am I? My thoughts whirled. Some cult of the Daughter, somewhere in time, buried deep within a planet's crust was the simple answer. But no reasonable conjectures as to *why* I was in this bizarre place came to my mind.

I carefully scoured the space around me in the hope of discovering some way out of this sunken lair. There appeared to be none. Behind me was another drop to an abyss of darkness, and further back still, tall walls of stone to the ceiling without a portal. There seemed to be one path available—down the stairs, through the maze, and, presumably, emerging at the lower steps to gaze in awe at the goddess.

"Kloan!" I cried out as loudly as my translator speakers could manage. The hard click of the first consonant and the powerful vowel ricocheted off the stone walls and structures, returning to wash over me in and out of phase from every direction. "Kloan!"

Again and again I called, until a chorus of phantoms chanting her name seemed to fill the chamber like some undead choir, and I was forced to steady myself from the acoustical onslaught. In the final trailing calls of her name, there waited only a terrible silence. Kloan either was not here or could not answer, and in either case, I was alone to derive my own solution to this enigma.

I let my thoughts project using all my Reader energies. *Ambra, please. What do you want? Why are you doing this?* This time there were no echoes, no assault from reflecting sound waves. But the silence was the same and even more devastating. A poisonous flood of feeling poured through me. It seemed I had been abandoned and betrayed.

I walked to the stairway, looping away from the cliff face cautiously. The steps were slick with dampness, and the strange field around my body continued to make me clumsy and awkward. I worked in vain to remove as much of the gel as I could in this environment, but I was never able to really clean myself, and after several hours I felt as if I had been painted in a stiff matrix. I was glad to see that there was a thick, tall railing. If I slipped, it would be virtually impossible for me to fall over the edge. It seemed to be the least the unhinged designers of this place could do for visitors.

Down the steps I went, the expansive pillar I came from obscured by the broad, sloping stairs behind me. The towering walls of the maze grew with every step. I tried to guess the age of this place, but without the opportunity to ascertain the mineral composition, it was impossible to attempt to estimate a date from clues such as erosion. One thing was certain: this had not been a busy religious or cultural venue. The steps were not worn as from millions of footfalls; rather, they remained precisely chiseled and were pocketed only by sporadic water damage.

Finally I reached the bottom and stepped off the bridge. I had been brought immediately before a soaring archway embedded in a wall thirty meters high. Inside, a short corridor with walls of identical dimensions marched majestically forward, splitting after some tens of meters into three passageways—left, right, and straight ahead.

I would deal with the labyrinth soon enough. What held my attention as I first stood before the arch was a deeply etched inscription across its curvature. The letters were unintelligible, an alien script most likely in an alien tongue. But what happened next sent tremors through me. The text *melted*. The letters slowly lost their coherency, their structure, and then seemed to reform before my eyes. What had been etched as if for a millennium in stone proved as malleable as fresh clay, only to reassume an appearance of the hardest rock upon the change in script and language.

Now I could read the letters. Astonishingly, they were in an ancient Xixian format, used by my ancestors before the advent of advanced technology. They were letters designed by the primitive Xixian tribes to be carved into sandstone and other hard mineral formations. Dipping into the stored racial memories of my species, I drudged out the alphabet, syntax and vocabulary. I translated this strange, living engraving—reading aloud as much to cement the awkward translational process as to proclaim the words before the arch. For all I knew there was a code phrase that would simplify this maze and afford me easier passage.

Until all is lost, nothing is found.

I waited. No bright light illumined my path. No walls spontaneously moved or opened secreted doorways. Again there was only silence to my words. *How appropriate.* I had no doubt that I would become utterly lost in this funhouse before I would ever find my way out.

Dejectedly, I stepped under the arch and walked into the labyrinth.

Chapter 39

The external world of physics has thus become a world of shadows. In removing our illusions we have removed the substance, for indeed we have seen that substance is one of the greatest of our illusions. The frank realization that physical science is concerned with a world of shadows is one of the most significant of recent advances.

Arthur Stanley Eddington

I stepped down the high-walled corridor to the three-way split and turned left. There was no rational reason for this decision. *A priori*, I had a 33 percent chance of success along each route, assuming, perhaps naively, that there *was* a way out of this maze. Irrationally, I decided that the way directly forward was too obvious and likely a feint. After all, who goes through all the trouble of making a colossal, stone labyrinth buried deep in a massive cavern and doesn't possess some degree of gamesmanship?

As I stumbled through the bewilderment around me, however, I began to question that assumption. The passageways opened and turned, zigged and zagged, plunging back into themselves or previous corridors in a dizzying fashion that forced me to focus deeply and memorize the detailed geometry. But what began to convince me that this incredible structure had a purpose beyond testing the two-dimensional intellectual powers of a Xix was the nearly ubiquitous artwork coating the sides of the maze.

The paintings had deteriorated to a nearly unrecognizable level, and because I could not determine the materials used in the work, I still could not effectively gauge the age of this place. Putting a lower limit on the most unstable of colored compounds, I could at least surmise that the paintings were several tens of thousands of years old. If the dyes were of advanced, decay-resistant compounds, they could be much older.

As I wandered through the maze, I passed hundreds of these illustrations, often depicting similar events in separate locations. Many of these partial paintings retained different elements of the story in a generally discernible form. By observing many of them, I was able to assemble a rough interpretation of a mythology that I presumed belonged to the artists.

The walls appeared to portray a fable of creation. In their cosmogenesis, a great mother goddess hatches from a golden egg. From her myriad arms spread not the essential primordial elements of standard creation myths—earth and water, fire and air—but what seem to be tapestries of interwoven lives or spirits, their forms fantastical and diverse, their limbs and tongues and hair braiding together over the expanse of some cosmic time into curtains of stars, nebulae, and galaxies.

To my considerable confusion, the paintings were distinguished stunningly by one unmistakable eccentricity: every drawing present was handed, asymmetric, with the arms of the goddess, the projections of her power, and the assemblies of the creatures and entities in her weavings appearing only on her left side. At first I assumed these lopsided paintings were a product of decay—the product of faded depictions on the right-hand sides. But as I encountered one illustration after the other, at times with the right side more intact than the left, the pattern was unmistakable. Enigmatically, every event and entity in creation accessed only half of the canvas allotted.

Had I time, I might have analyzed this curious culture, tried to understand what themes and moralities such a mythology would undergird. But my mind would not allow it. Instead I pressed forward, narrowing the selection of possible routes as I memorized the maze, until at last I took one passageway that led to a true dead end. According to my mental map, this was the last possible route in this subspace of the maze from the initial left turn.

Etched into the wall at this dead end were more words. I had come through hundreds of paintings, been introduced to an odd mythology, and now this entire section ended with another proverb sliced in stone. It too was in ancient Xixian, no doubt the product of the scrambled and reformed textual magic I had witnessed before. I was struck again by the apparent sense of a purpose in this space beyond that of a simple puzzle.

Whatever is of a nature to arise,
is thereby of a nature to cease.

Whereas the first text had seemed mostly ironic, this sentence brought on some anxiety. Was it simply an encapsulation of mortality, reflecting a million texts across the galaxy from the minds of diverse species that struggled with death? As a Xix, I had already lived over four hundred years, nearly half our average lifespan, and it was not uncommon for those of my age to begin long, serious contemplations of our fate. Was this only an adage for the foresighted?

Or perhaps its meaning was less profound—and far more immediate. Perhaps it was a warning for the fools who entered the labyrinth, who had dared challenge the designer. Perhaps time was limited in some way that implied an approaching threat to my being.

I could have continued a long, neurotic analysis, parsing the text and finding a thousand possible applications to my current predicament. But threat or not, my own impatience pressed me forward more strongly than any fear could restrain me. I turned my back on the wall and retraced my path to the primary branch point. This time, I went right.

What I experienced in this portion of the maze was much the same, if a dramatic variation on a deeper theme. Again the bafflement of passages. Again the corroded artwork of a cult that had long ago passed away. Again my journey would end at an impassable wall with a message, seemingly morphed into coherency just for me.

I had anticipated that the ancient artists would offer a right-handed exclusivity to reflect this opposite direction I had chosen. Instead, an identical left-right asymmetry was present—everything that was depicted again occurred on the left side of a powerful deity. But there could not be a larger difference in the nature of the two divinities portrayed.

Whereas the left-handed portion of the maze contained stories of a nurturing mother goddess, the right side was filled with a ravaging destroyer. Congealed from a thousand angry souls, a demon took shape in this cosmogenesis that spent its infinite supply of time tearing through worlds and galaxies, devouring bodies and minds, beauty and love, laying waste to an entire cosmos until everything seemed suppressed in a frozen winter, even the god itself. I don't think that I could have found a more extraordinary mythological duality as I witnessed in the two sides of this maze. The terse words etched into the wall at the end of this portion did little to dispel this interpretation.

Yes and No birth Mu.

Ancient Xixian writing, unmistakably human philosophies. *Who were these creatures?* Could they have been human? If so, there was so much divergence in the art and architecture as to believe that they may have been disparate subspecies. Otherwise, it might have been a group of humans and nonhumans who had lived together and deeply influenced their respective cultures. Again, I could have continued to speculate, but my need to resolve this test and exit the maze overpowered my curiosity.

Humbled by my failures in outsmarting the designer of this labyrinth, and yet suspecting that the ultimate design of the thing would have led me to discover all these images and words regardless of my choices, I returned to the entrance point and selected the forward path.

It was the most devious of the three. I spent hours trudging, backtracking, looping unintentionally, and fighting a growing frustration as I sought to memorize and understand the confounding corridors. As I fought a deepening physical and mental fatigue, I also tried to take seriously the final, and presumably most important, graphical catechism from the earnest cult artists.

But I struggled. What tried my patience was the disappointing predictability. For all this effort, after all the clear exposure to so many previous religious and mythological systems that were all too easy to detect in this particular mishmash, they had simply settled on a messiah construct. Yet another savior story took shape in the drawings and spun its particularities across the maddening walls of the labyrinth.

At least this was a very unique remix of the redeemer narrative. The highly imaginative—and perhaps sexually repressed—mythologizers presented a tale of romantic redemption, one that enigmatically broke the mysterious devotion to left and right asymmetry characterizing the previous stories. Along the forward portion were paintings depicting a more symmetric universe. In the center of the paintings, the mother goddess and demon were locked in a titanic conflict. On their right a glowing figure arose from nothingness. The savior stormed toward the clashing titans, yet did *not* engage in battle with the demon as might be anticipated. Instead, the savior threw the demon to the side and *mated* with the mother goddess—an act, it would appear from the degraded artwork, that utterly destroyed them both.

And yet, as the demon arose again, from the ashes and smoke of the ruined gods, an offspring of their consummation was incarnate. Before the demon could do much more than be drawn in several stupefied expressions, this godchild *devours* the monster in one cosmic-sized bite. The final images show this new deity expanding, mutating, and dissolving to cover the entire expanse of the wall surface.

I am sorry to say that I did not examine the last illustrations with great care, because as I began to look at these final images in wonder, a bright light grew in front of me. Pushing my intellectual curiosity to the side, I pressed forward desperately, rushing down the passageway. My momentum thrust me through a second archway of the labyrinth and into a vast open space.

A giant-sized relief of Ambra overpowered the entire expanse of my vision. The sheer mass of stone hanging outward from the walls intimidated me, and I felt a strange sense of vertigo from the rock suspended above. Following the sculpture downward, my eyes immediately fell on the mountain of stairs below it. As I knew from my glimpses at the top of the pillar, these stairs rose steeply toward the relief and ended before a wide plateau. I could not see it from this perspective, however, and the stairway appeared to ascend without end.

To my left and right, the outer wall of the maze ran until it crashed and fused with the sides of the cavern. Behind me was the labyrinth. There seemed no other direction to follow but upward. I moved forward and prepared to climb.

Each step of this massive stairway measured nearly a meter in height. It was perfect for a Xix but impossibly impractical for a human being. Yet it was not the design of the stairs that brought the personal nature of this place squarely into my awareness. It was the lines carved deeply into the face of the first step.

There I saw final words prepared specifically for me, a conclusion I could draw at that point with complete confidence. Words prepared in a manner unknown in the deep relative past by a vanished and mysterious people. Words that asked a mystifying question.

Where are the anti-gods, Waythrel?

Chapter 40

What must I do? I see nothing but obscurities on every side. Shall I believe I am nothing? Shall I believe I am God?

Blaise Pascal

Despite the astonishing transmutation of the previous texts into Xixian languages, the use of my name took me completely by surprise. The fact that this place was tens to hundreds of thousands of years old rendered the idea of it being tailored for me acutely unsettling.

Of course, the dangling monoliths of Ambra's form above me suggested explanations. If I had learned anything in this journey with Kloan, it was that whatever we had created on New Earth—whatever our designs and the actual labor undertaken at a specific place and specific time—the product had grown into something for which a placement in time and space had lost a standard meaning. Time had continually been shaken and stirred maniacally by Ambra, and I did not even know *when* I was now—it could be in some far future or deep past. And if Ambra and her legion of souls had constructed this place anticipating my arrival, the things I had seen appeared less fantastical, if not believable.

But those were abstract thoughts. Intuitively, it was several moments after seeing my own name etched into the rock that I was able to collect myself and continue.

Where are the anti-gods, Waythrel?

The words echoed in my mind, but I pushed them aside and climbed the stairway.

One hundred meters later, I pulled myself slowly over the final step in exhaustion. Before me was a flat surface of white stone, polished like marble. Twenty meters ahead of me was a table, too small to have been visible from my perch when I arrived. A solid block of alabaster, it appeared more like an altar than anything else. And it was not empty.

Lying across the length of the altar was a human body draped in beige robes. Her porcelain skin shone in the ethereal light of the cavern, sparse clumps of long red hair bright beside it. The deformed skull exhibited a familiar intricacy of instrumentation. The figure was a child, a girl, fast asleep.

"Kloan!" I cried, rushing forward.

But I did not get far. Within several meters of the altar, I could not progress. Unlike a more primitive defensive field that would have led to an impact or sudden jolt, the barrier separating me from Kloan was far more sophisticated. After numerous attempts to breach it, I could only conclude that it worked on my very nervous system itself, robbing me of any ability to even will myself into motion. Whatever the cause, every time I tried to approach beyond a certain point, I was only standing still.

"Kloan!" Still she did not wake or show any signs of disturbance. "Ambra!" I cried, looking up to the lunging goddess above. "Enough! We've had enough! Wake her up! Let us out!" I thought to pound on the invisible barrier in my frustration, but found only that my arms hung listlessly at my sides.

I sat down on the cold floor, despairing and rattled. I sat there for some time. Minutes, hours. I could no longer keep track of time. I was bereft of ideas and empty of energy to continue. Only the incessant echo of dripping water testified to the passage of each moment. All this—a separation, riddles and mazes, bizarre and unfathomable mythologies, and finally a reunion only to be dangled before me and snatched away—what was the purpose? To teach me something? This was my suspicion. Well, I had learned nothing from the ridiculous paintings, the koans in stone! How was I to know what was expected? Certainly something must be required—here at the last, a few steps from her that I sought, a barrier denying me access like a reward withheld from a nymph who had not yet absorbed her lesson—how was I to pass this test and open this prison?

Where are the anti-gods, Waythrel?

The unbidden words snapped me into deep concentration. Of everything I had seen, of all I had read in this mystifying place, there had been only one question. At the last, there had indeed been a riddle demanding from me an answer. It was amazing that I had understood this only now.

Where are the anti-gods, Waythrel?

I went deep into myself, focusing all my concentration, intellect, and Reader senses on this question. Where are the anti-gods? Indeed, I had to begin by considering what was meant by *gods*. The *anti* almost certainly referred to the Anti, those creatures of material inversion to everything we had once thought to constitute the universe. But anti-gods? Was this asking about the religion of the Anti?

I strained back over the vicious time loops that had carried us across the clone colony on the world I had come to know after my kidnapping. The indoctrinations. The strange philosophies. The Anti certainly had a cosmology and belief system. But gods? The more I searched my memory, the more convinced I became that I had come across no words, no artwork, no evidence of any kind that the Anti worshipped any gods. Of course, a secular species was not uncommon in the galaxy, and in fact such races tended to outnumber the religious. But nearly every sentient species developed first through a more irrational period before a scientific skepticism flowered.

And so the Great God perished before the Nous could be. All that was left was the dust of destruction, a single theme devoid of the counterpoint. But in this dust lay a hope. Of the ice, there remained a frost. Of the day, there remained a star beam. And of love, there remained a hope.

The memory from the indoctrination sessions flowed through my mind. The Anti certainly had myths. But their anti-gods? They had been destroyed! In their mythos, there were no anti-gods because they had been erased in some cosmic catastrophe! This reflected perfectly their minority role in the universe.

I stood up and shouted, "There are no anti-gods in their mythology because the creation story is about their destruction." Pausing a moment in case my words needed to be absorbed by whatever was monitoring this madness, I then stepped forward again toward Kloan. I got nowhere.

"Ambra, please! This answer is correct!"

Correct or not, it was not the answer the goddess was looking for, and I was forced to examine my assumptions and attempt to dig even deeper into this conundrum.

Where are the anti-gods, Waythrel?

On the surface, the question almost seemed literal. After my experiences with the Synphel abomination and the divergent incarnations of Ambra, I no longer doubted the existence of *gods*. Not in the supernatural sense, but in the completely and monstrously natural—creatures, beings, syntheses of the elements of this universe, obeying the physical laws inherent therein, and yet so advanced, so mighty that *gods* was the only word remotely appropriate for them. I had experienced them. I had tasted of their power, love, and transcendent animosity.

Like all things, I presumed the gods we encountered, like the goddess Ambra of our creation, were composed of the building blocks of matter we knew to exist. But the presence of the Anti proved how biased that view of the universe was. If there were gods of matter, why shouldn't there be gods of antimatter? If so, where were they? Why had the Anti—who had known of the *devil ball* of Ambra for eons within eons—never developed or mentioned or sought out their own anti-gods?

Perhaps, like the Anti themselves, there were simply too few of them. I had only encountered two of these advanced entities, and that was because one of them—one I had helped create—had embroiled me in a cosmic feud and quest. Hardly a dataset on which to build a model. Still, it seemed that these entities, these gods, were uncommon, as any of the large compositions of smaller elements would be relative to their building blocks. And the building blocks of matter outnumbered those of antimatter by orders of magnitude that were themselves difficult to comprehend.

That was it! I finally understood. Perhaps there were no anti-gods for the simple reason that there *could not be*. Ambra was said to be the assembly of trillions of souls. An ocean of building blocks that bordered on uncountable. But how much antimatter was there in the universe? Relatively, the sum total might as well be zero. How much could remain isolated from matter for long enough to develop star systems, life, and sentience? How many of these species would survive the wild adolescence of their evolution to achieve stability? Of these, how many minds would exist to provide the building blocks for a group mind that might someday mature into a being like those I had encountered?

The more I considered it, the more unlikely it became. The gods of the Anti had indeed perished in the creation, because the creation had wiped out the very material from which their gods might have been fashioned. Our universe, so hostile and dominant to the creatures of antimatter that waged a doomed war against us, simply did not possess the raw elements to construct sentience at that level.

Something about this realization disturbed me greatly, but I did not stop to ponder any more deeply. I had the answer. This time I was sure of it.

"There are no anti-gods, Ambra. There never were and never will be. They cannot exist, because there isn't enough antimatter to support them."

As the last echo of my words died, a tonal chord rang across the underground chamber. Composed of multiple harmonic frequencies, spanning the ultrabass to a shattering treble, it seemed to rattle the air in front of me. I took this as a sign and stepped toward Kloan.

This time I reached her.

Chapter 41

We have found a strange footprint on the shores of the unknown. We have devised profound theories, one after another, to account for its origins. At last, we have succeeded in reconstructing the creature that made the footprint. And lo! It is our own.

Arthur Stanley Eddington

As I reached the bright altar, she opened her eyes.

"Waythrel?"

Her demeanor was fully conscious, her physiology seeming to suffer none of the retarding, inhibiting aspects of prolonged sleep, especially sleep induced by pharmacological agents or neuro-manipulative fields. It was as if she had simply been suspended in time and restored to the temporal flow.

"Waythrel? Where am I?"

I grasped her hands excitedly. "Kloan, are you okay? Are you hurt?"

She sat up on the altar, passing her hands across the slick surface in confusion and interest, and then swept her vision across the enormous stairway, maze, and finally above her to the pendulous goddess relief.

"Holy shit," she said.

Joy flowed through me. Whatever had happened to her, Kloan seemed to have lost none of her manic cultural syntheses and playfulness.

"Then you are okay?" I repeated stupidly.

Kloan whistled while squinting at the sculpture above us. She returned her attention to her body. "Two legs, two arms, two hands, proper fingers. A head. No blood. No scars. No memories. You tell me." She gestured around the chamber. "What is this place? What are we doing here? And why do you look like you've run around that lunatic maze down there fifty times?"

"Because I nearly have," I said, eliciting a single eyebrow raise from her. "It's a very long story. We were split up. I was half a kilometer away over there. I had to come through the labyrinth. I had to absorb a message and answer a riddle, or we could never leave." And so I recounted the narrative as she sat raptly before me on the stone structure.

"I want to see the question," she said, hopping off the edge of the altar. "Might need some Xixian handholding to get down these stairs, though."

With my help, she descended the stairway on foot, even though she likely could have simply floated down with ease. One hundred hops later, we had reached the bottom, and Kloan studied the inscription with fascination.

"Your own private test of doom," she said, tracing the letters with her finger. "But I'll have to trust you on the meaning. I can't read a bit of it."

"What I don't understand is why," I said.

"Why what?" she asked, spinning in place and taking in the grandeur of this construction.

"Why all of this? Why were we brought here?"

"You said it yourself—to learn a lesson. And it seems like you have."

"This is an awful lot of trouble to get me to think about some of these issues."

"Sometimes living a question answers it better than purely thinking. These incredible repetitions trapping us seem like a lot of trouble, but they are all designed to teach us things. Crucial things. Data we need to process and assimilate to take the next step, and, finally, to exit the loop."

"Is it possible?" I asked. "Will we ever escape it?"

"*Ever* and *possible* both lose their meaning in all this, don't you think? We will never get there even if we do, and it seems *all* possibilities will be sampled in the process."

"More Kloan-babble I can't follow," I said wearily, but I reached out and held her hand. "But *at least* I should be able to understand this one! It was focused completely on *me*. Lessons for me. Motivations that were sure to drive me to reach within as deeply as possible for answers."

"Is it love, Waythrel?" she asked, glancing at our clasped hands. "Have we reached that point of no return? Are you ready to confess to me your true feelings now?"

I ignored her. "So I found an answer, and apparently satisfied the goddess, or whoever is behind this. But to answer what question? One focused on the metaphysics of antimatter gods! Of what possible point is all this effort for such esoterica?"

"String theory is esoteric, but without it the universe does not exist," said Kloan.

"But *Waythrel* knowing or not knowing string theory will have absolutely no impact on whether the universe will exist!" I exclaimed. "And neither will my understanding or lack of it about the hypothetical antimatter gods!"

Kloan turned serious and stepped up to me, focusing her bright eyes on mine. "And are you so sure about that, Waythrel?"

My eyestalks buzzed around her in consternation. "Of course. How can what I understand about the universe be of any deep significance to the universe itself?"

Kloan turned away and seemed to bury her thoughts within her. "Perhaps you are right, Waythrel."

"Of course I am right!" The child was irrepressibly disconcerting. "Which brings us back to this granite extravagance. What is the point? Why are we here? What could Ambra possibly be up to? It doesn't make sense!"

Kloan laughed. "Well, one thing is for sure. Ambra moves in mysterious ways." Kloan pointed above. "Whatever her motives, I don't think we'll have time to consider them anymore here."

A bright light grew from the ceiling, dazzling my eyes and forcing me to look away. It seemed to be extending tendrils of radiance toward us, long tentacles that flung themselves about as if searching for prey.

"Times up," said Kloan, her eyes cast down to the deep shadows of our forms on the rock.

The light limbs surrounded us, grasped us, and pulled us off the ground and toward the blinding source of radiance above. My last memory was of glancing toward Kloan and hearing her voice nearly lost in a maelstrom of sound and brilliance.

"See you again soon, Waythrel!"

Chapter 42

God huddles in a knot in every cell of flesh. When I break a fruit open, this is how every seed is revealed to me. When I speak to men, this what I discern in their thick and muddy brains. God struggles in every thing, his hands flung upward toward the light.

Nikos Kazantzakis

It was morning. I stared forward into the warm light of a star I did not know, yet had seen perhaps one thousand times. Perhaps millions. There was no longer a concept of time for my awareness. No history with permanence. No memories I could trust. I was forever falling into dreamscapes, one after the other, without hope that there would be a waking.

Out of breath, I rested several meters away from the gate. We must have climbed. Kloan was red and sweaty from exertion. I could only remember a tomb—mazes and riddles and light. I didn't remember climbing. I didn't know how we got here.

But the gate I remembered. I examined the portal more closely. It was now familiar, visited uncounted times in the dream treks of loops through this anomaly in space-time. It resembled a cross section sliced out of an Orb more than anything else, but I still didn't know if this system possessed an Orb. The surface was that viscous, churning, honey-like substance we had immersed ourselves in times beyond counting. Inside was an ocean of stars—depth upon depth of star fields that appeared to have no end. I felt pulled toward the horrible beauty as I gazed.

"Something's wrong," said Kloan.

With most of my eyes fixated on the starry disk, several flipped to the side to glance at Kloan. The girl was tense, straight as a rod, and her eyes scanned the region between us and the disk like prey awaiting a predator.

"The gate? Has it rejected us?"

"Not the gate. Something else."

Before us the air shimmied, the disk and the land around it swayed and blurred, and the air itself coagulated into a humanoid shape. We both stood there, stunned, unable to move. I sensed from Kloan's mind an unusual anxiety. But it was my own mind that began to panic as the form darkened, took on colors, and solidified, acquiring a shape with four arms, sixfold symmetry, and a patch of long eyestalks erupting from a central cone. *A Xix.* But not just any Xix. My emotions swirled. A Xix I knew. My beloved Synphel.

"Hello again, Waythrel," it said, the apparition fully formed.

Again. Nightmarish visions bounded through my thoughts. *Memories?* Of what?

You must not believe for a moment that I was taken by this forgery. Rationally, I knew this could not be Synphel. Emotionally, I knew it with more certitude. And yet the form of my Synphel activated circuits within my neural cortex that stirred my emotional centers as well. I could not halt the feelings of love and longing that surged within me, even as I stared toward something utterly devoid of those qualities.

The anxiety Kloan had felt I felt now, too. The entity before us that had taken the shape of my lifemate radiated intense cognitive fields. They were incredibly complex, of a depth and power I had sensed only in the presence of the Ambra-thing that had visited us here. And in the presence of the Orbs.

But the sentience before us was to my experience, as deeply malevolent as it was profound. Simply staring at this form of my dear Synphel caused eruptions of disturbing images, anger, slaughter, pain, and madness. I felt Kloan reach out and hold my arm.

"Don't let it in your mind," she whispered.

"Let it?" came the smooth voice of my lover. Although the tones were perfect, they were also utterly alien. "If you have any perception, then you know that nothing you can do can stop me."

"No, but *she* will!" I said triumphantly, shocking myself in this exclamation. A subconscious certitude led me to turn my eyestalks behind us. Irrationally, I waited without doubt for the form of Ambra Dawn to come strolling casually up the slope.

But she was not there.

Kloan screamed and fell to her knees on the ground, grasping her head. She began to rock back and forth, moaning, crying, tears pouring down her cheeks. I watched in horror as spit frothed from her mouth; a mild seizure seemed to shake her form as she trembled and doubled over. Her eyes flipped up and back into their sockets. Alongside the white stone in her forehead were two white orbs staring back from a hideous mask of shaking pain. Blood trickled out of her left nostril.

"Stop!" I screamed and dropped to the ground, grabbing her in my arms. Her jaw was clenching wildly, tearing her tongue and lips, so I ripped a piece of clothing away from her robes and placed it between her teeth.

I did not imagine that I could shield her mentally. My Reader sense was completely overwhelmed by this creature assaulting her, so much so that I had to shut it out as if closing my eyes. Even that left me blinded. What would an attempt at defense have achieved, anyway? Kloan was powerful beyond my imagining and she was tossed like a toy flung by the force before us.

"As you wish," said the thing. Kloan fell to the ground unresponsive. I checked her vitals. She was alive, but unconscious. A quick mind probe indicated severe trauma, but superficially it seemed no major physiological damage had been done.

"We aren't ready to destroy her yet," said the demon form of Synphel. "We need more information first."

"We? Are you one or many? Where are the others? What do you want?" I cradled Kloan's head in my arms.

"Surely the great Waythrel of Xix can surmise?" Synphel performed a Xixian body gesture that can only be translated as a smile, although we possess no teeth or mouth akin to those of humans. "Or did you think your crude experiment with Ambra Dawn was somehow unique in all the universe?"

A terrible dread settled on me. "What are you?"

"One of the other gods, of course."

"Rakshasi." How I knew the word confused me.

"She has spoken my name, then."

"You are a mental union? A group consciousness?"

"That is probably as close as you can come to understanding. But surely you know that the organizing principles are the same throughout the universe? Even something with as primitive a mind as your own can grasp this. The strings are composed of smaller entities down to levels to which your philosophies have never scurried. Yet this process continues further still, until time itself cannot discover all the constituents. And so the structures assemble upward to your atoms, molecules, cells, and tissues. *Minds.* Mental networks of trillions of minds that grow until they become things that stride across the cosmos like giants."

Images flooded my mind. I could not stop them. Ripped out from my creaturely perspective, I was given a momentary glimpse from the eyes of a divinity, spanning ages of time like instants, parsecs of space like small steps. I was oppressed with a morality that was so foreign and horrible that I nearly felt my mind breaking.

"You are the cells of our minds," the entity concluded, harshly slinging my awareness back to the dirt and rock of this strange planet.

I was disoriented and terrified. "What do you want with us?"

"We are interested in what *your* creation-god is planning. We suspect that her intentions are far from pure, as they concern others of our kind."

"I don't understand."

"The Ambra-Orb: what does she wish with this creature?" it said, gesturing toward Kloan, who still lay unmoving in my arms.

"Ambra-Orb?" My mind raced, feverish in the terrible presence of this thing. "Yes, wait, I remember. Ambra is the Orb—?"

"Of course. Haven't you even put that together? Or can your mind not retain anything in this recursive playground of hers? Now tell us, what do you conclude is the point of this Kloan? Think through all you have encountered. You will not enter this gate until you have answered to our satisfaction."

"Why can't you just read it from our thoughts?"

I felt a hostile impatience from the thing. It was like the glow of a furnace door opened in front of me. I could not even shield my mind from it. If one's consciousness could feel heat, mine was nearly scalded.

"We have taken all your memories and impressions. We know all that has happened. But it is not enough. Her deviousness is deep beyond explaining. Her true purpose is encoded in your cognition. We need you to reason with us, think through her desires. Explain to us now what she wishes. What you understand about what has happened to you. In the *deduction* is the answer."

"Why me? This clone understands so much more. Yet you nearly killed her."

"She lacks a need of cognition for this very reason." Synphel *smiled* again, and the horror of it on this creature sickened me. "You, however, do not understand much at all, and yet the puzzle pieces are all within your thoughts. You must try to assemble them."

In terrible panic, my mind raced. Even as I held the unresponsive child in my arms, as I hoped vainly that Ambra would return and deliver us as in my dream, the monstrous presence of this thing before me forced me to engage. My mind was no longer was my own. My thoughts transformed into buttons in the hands of another. I became dizzy trying to stitch together the blurred memories of time loops, or what I assumed and poorly recalled as repeated journeys with Kloan through the gate. Horrific nightmares. Death and pain and destruction. Thousands, millions upon millions of journeys I had forgotten, which this creature forced through my mind. The god's pressure unearthed the ruins of my memory, flooding me with events that I could not have accessed consciously. I felt my body swaying.

The plans of the Anti. Yes, it was the unifying element to all the journeys! It was the only thing that made sense.

I babbled. "This clone is playing out all the routes to the destruction of Ambra Dawn. Ambra is encouraging it. Yet nothing ever happens. We circle back; the actions in the past have no lasting effect on her existence."

"Continue."

My air sacs were becoming clogged from stress secretions, my oxygen content lowering and fogging my thoughts. I tried to concentrate harder. "Why would Ambra encourage this? Only if she ultimately feared the creature."

"Yes."

"Only if she were looking in the failure of cause and effect for a vulnerability, the thread that makes this creature so unusual. Yes, I remember. She said that all the gods fear Kloan. Why?"

"There is a discontinuity. A place in space and time where we cannot go. She is the source. She cannot be fully read."

"Then Ambra fears her, too. She is either trapping her in this loop to forever keep her here, or to study her, or both. She is trying to prevent Kloan from doing something that you all fear and cannot see."

And then the Synphel creature was gone, vanished in a breath as I was processing my thoughts, leaving no trace, no hint that this being who seemed to span entire galaxies had displaced a molecule of the atmosphere.

I felt the soft breathing of Kloan as she rested on me. I felt heat from the local star warming my skin. Slowly, I uncovered my eyestalks, feeling like a nymph again, terrified of things I could not see or prove were real. It was as if they had never occurred except in the dim recesses of my darkest dreams.

Except that Kloan lay wounded in my arms. She began to cough roughly, her sputum tinged with pink. As she gasped for air, her eyes flew open, and she vomited across the ground. Her body shivered violently for several minutes.

I applied what medical training I had. Fortunately, our long association with humans had given us a significant knowledge of their anatomy and function, even for those like myself who were not medically devoted. Without proper instruments, I could not be sure, but it seemed that the trauma had not seriously wounded her body. Her mind was another issue.

"I have seen hell," she said flatly, staring off into space. "It has been infused into me. I never knew, Waythrel. I never *imagined*. To know such horror exists —I don't want to live. But death! Immortality and hell. Waythrel, please, can we *unexist?*"

"Kloan—"

"I have smelled it," she nearly shouted, tendrils of saliva clinging like webs between her gnashing teeth. "Its foul taste flooded my mouth and nostrils, a vile sludge suffocating and drowning me in stench and slime." She closed her eyes and cried out toward the sky. "I heard the groan and weeping of entire galaxies in the void." Her body shook in my arms.

I tried desperately to comfort her. "Shock, Kloan. Violence to your mind. It's not real. You are safe. We are safe, now." I tried desperately to believe in my own words.

She shook her head and turned wild eyes toward me. Her hands reached out and grasped mine, pulling the twelve fingers of each to her lips. She kissed them, one by one. I felt a terrible reaching of her mind toward mine, a need for contact with something decent, something with affection. "You don't understand, dear Waythrel. I have seen what you have not, what a Xix could never see and survive, and there is no forgetting. There is no more peace or love.

There is no more safety." Tears streamed down her face. "And there is no more Kloan." She bowed her head into her lap, whispering. "I have traveled. To the place of demons. They are *real*. They are lurking between the shadows of the stars. And they are *waiting*."

"Waiting for what?" I asked, her words eliciting a primal chill through my form.

"For all of us…and the dying of the light."

Chapter 43

I perceived that I was on a little round grain of rock and metal, filmed with water and with air, whirling in sunlight and darkness. And on the skin of that little grain all the swarms of men, generation by generation, had lived in labour and blindness, with intermittent joy and intermittent lucidity of spirit. And all their history, with its folk-wanderings, its empires, its philosophies, its proud sciences, its social revolutions, its increasing hunger for community, was but a flicker in one day of the lives of the stars.

Olaf Stapeldon

"What do we do now, Kloan?"

I was at a loss. She showed no sign of interest in the journey we had been only moments from undertaking. She sat on the ground next to me, her chin resting on her knees, a blank stare in her eyes as she seemed to see across a million light-years.

To what? I dared not ask. She didn't seem to be able to take much more. After the things she had said, I wondered if I even wished to know.

So I rested quietly beside her as the afternoon wore on. A portion of me worried that the forces below would discover us, but I knew that was unlikely given our strange disappearance and position. And after the encounters of the last few hours, everything else seemed so small and feeble. My focus drifted; my mind visualized planets filled with sentient creatures, stumbling about their daily lives in an artificially fast manner as if years had become days. Generations passed, entire cultures rose and fell, world civilizations matured and perished. And yet all of it, even the sum across a galaxy of stars, now seemed petty.

I had not seen the full horror forced upon Kloan, but for a short moment, I had glimpsed through the eyes of the demon. I had felt the vastness of space and time that rendered our daily lives no more than the femtoseconds of chemical motions to an organism far greater than us.

Part of me understood Kloan's despair. What possible significance could the pair of us have? What madness was there to believe that two transient molecules could possibly have any impact, any meaning at all in this vast cosmic ocean? I had experienced the presence of a cosmic god. I could no longer sense my self.

"Waythrel."

My eyestalks darted behind me only to fill my vision with images of fear once again. Standing still and tranquil, in dark yet phosphorescent beauty, was Synphel once more. My emotions again ran the sickening gamut of fear, love, longing, disgust, and despair mixed with elation. I turned slowly to the thing, my limbs trembling. "Please. No more. Please don't torture us like this anymore. If there is any pity in the gods the universe has created, leave us in peace. We are only dust."

"Waythrel, it is I. Open your heart."

The rush of love and concern that swept through me was overpowering. Gone was the malignancy of consciousness I had felt from the demon. Instead I drank in the unmistakable presence of my long-separated mate. A loving personality poured through my Reader senses, remembered smells filled my olfactory strips, and a healing presence was undeniable in a way that was wholly absent from the apparition before.

Forgive me for using the clumsiness of your language to bimodally gender her—*her* is the pronoun I will use, even as it warps the nature of any of our six genders. But your word *it* warps her nature even more to my mind, stripping her of any aspect of gender at all, and in this meeting with Synphel, the intimacy of the encounter I choose to relate, cries out that something better be used, however imperfect. For this day, we were not two *its*, but two *hers*, and the love between us was like a balm to the monstrosities that had assailed Kloan and me.

"*Synphel*. How? You are part of the group mind. With Ambra. How are you here?"

"Waythrel, we have become something beyond what you can easily imagine. I have been clothed in atoms and molecules, stitched in flesh, incarnate here to meet with you."

"Your mind?"

"My mind, my soul—what you once knew as Synphel—is within this form that has been drawn from the dust and debris of this world. But I am not alone. And none of us is truly here."

I struggled to conceptualize her words. A mental projection, the equivalent of a complex transform arriving at this point of space and time, with the power from afar to manipulate matter so magically as to assemble a completed life form from the inanimate particles on a distant world. Not just any form, but an exact replica of my lifemate. I was slow to learn this lesson, even having witnessed the reality a short time ago in the face-off between the demon and Ambra. I had to witness it again and again to fully absorb the depth of the implications. Truly they were—or had become, or would be—gods.

Her voice spoke in my mind.

Gods perhaps to you, but yet you are one of our makers, Waythrel. Is this not itself a miracle? And we are still composed of the elements of this cosmos. We do not transcend it, although we seek transcendence. And indeed, that is what all this is about.

She turned the bulk of her eyestalks to gaze beside me. "Kloan, please come here."

In my dread and wonder in this reunion, I had forgotten about the child. Kloan stirred and rose, turning slowly around to face my partner. Her eyes seemed dead.

Synphel turned to the girl. "They seek to strip you of the energies to carry out your quest, to freeze you in place, suspended and defused," said Synphel. "If they understood fully, they would destroy you, but their hesitancy reflects the terrible potential they sense in you. All timelines become discontinuous in your presence, a phenomenon unique in all the cosmos to you. You are the nexus in all that is and all that was and will be."

"But I am broken."

"Yes, but not beyond healing." Synphel walked up to the child and placed her upper hands to Kloan's head, surrounding the skull and face with twenty-four fingertips. The dark black of my lover's skin contrasted sharply with the white of the clone, and the soft, lipid-insulated form of the human appeared truly alien alongside the elongated, leathery appendages of a Xix.

Kloan closed her eyes and began to weep.

"Yes, you remember the dreams. You remember the calling to find the resolution to the asymmetry. Listen to it again. Let it burn brightly and char to ash the horror you have seen." Kloan wrapped her arms around Synphel and shook with sobs.

I remembered watching the development of human infants and children, how critical close physical contact was for proper brain maturation, as it was in all the related mammalian species on their home world. Even in the presence of a creature so different, the instinct to embrace overwhelmed any sense of discomfort with the alien as the child was purged of the emotional poison.

After several minutes, Kloan's arms relaxed, and she stepped backward, wiping her eyes and face.

"Thank you," Kloan said. She looked intently into the eyestalks of Synphel. "Thank you, all."

"The horror will never leave you," said Synphel. "But it will no longer overthrow your mind. Follow your meditations. Take your pain and scars and use them to grow."

Even though I had known the child for such a short time, even though I had been a victim of abduction at her hands and witnessed the horrors she could commit, relief and a soft joy spread through me. Part of it is our Xixian nature, our desire for healing and our difficulties in causing harm, a weakness that had nearly doomed our galaxy. Always we rejoice at the removal of pain. But it was much more than such a generic response. The clone elicited from me many of my feelings for her progenitor, and although she was so different from Ambra, I saw now that I could not help but love her.

Synphel's eyestalks divided between us. "Now you must regroup and continue your journey."

Chapter 44

Nature does not dictate dualities, trinities, quarterings, or any "objective" basis for human taxonomies; most of our chosen schemes, and our designated numbers of categories, record human choices from a cornucopia of possibilities offered by natural variation from place to place, and permitted by the flexibility of our mental capacities. How many seasons (if we wish to divide by seasons at all) does a year contain? How many stages shall we recognize in a human life?

Stephen Jay Gould

A spasm of desperation swept through me. "Synphel, please. Don't go." Surprising even myself, I stepped forward and entwined my fingers with hers. "I can't keep you. I know this. You are only a memory made flesh. But I cannot let you go," I said, the foolishness of my yearning mocking me. Her digits twirled around my own. "So real. And this memory that I am able to touch is precious beyond words to me."

"Have you ever loved a goddess, Waythrel?"

Synphel pressed her form alongside my own, and the skin cilia of our compatible mating types locked and engaged. The biological program sent shivers through me, and without conscious decision my eyestalks probed and found hers, each wrapping around the other, eighteen sighted organs like a complex braid staring at each other.

I did not care that I would mate with an avatar sculpted out of the sands of this distant planet, or whatever place it had come from. I cared neither that the Synphel I knew was gone, altered, absorbed into a godlike entity full of nearly countless personalities, nor that those trillions looked on in love, disinterest, and emotions unfathomable to me in this moment of our species' deepest intimacy. No, I only wished to merge with Synphel one last time.

It is difficult to explain the oddities of our physiology to you of Earth. In all species that do not reproduce asexually, there must be a mingling of the hereditary material. But with a mating group composed of six genders, four separate gametes containing separated fractions of what you would call the Xixian genome, it is the case that there can be components of the assembled form that do not carry the seed. So it is and so it was with Synphel and myself. We donated no material for future generations, but our mating pair was an integral element in the whole. There is no point in explaining how our genotype could be stable and selected for, no space in this story for the complexities and nonlinearity of group evolution, to define what constitutes an organism under selection, but the important point is to know that we formed the core structure around which the mating group assembled.

Our bond had to be deep, strong, and long lasting. In the mating process, therefore, our sexual encounters were very much unlike your own brief moments; they were the longest by far even of our reproductive group pairings. For this reason many pair mates of our type entered into unions outside the mating group that lasted lifetimes.

The first stage was mutual penetration, where a deeply hidden appendage, appearing to you perhaps as a strange variant of a tentacle, thrust through a slit in our torso and sought the equivalent structure in our mate. Perhaps an analogy to your male's erections, this process was the beginning of stimulation.

But our tentacles were not injection devices that worked alone. They found each other, wrapped around a structural mate like vines of Earth—or, closer still, the entwining eyestalks above our heads. The effect on our physiology resembled at this stage something like the stimulation of your penis and clitoris nerve webs, activating the body toward the mating engagement.

And so this god-Synphel drove me to a growing ecstasy of fusion as our reproducing arms touched, caressed, and wrapped firmly around each other, pressing forward in opposite directions, raising body temperature suddenly as they found the opening slit, teased it mercilessly with stroking, and then plunged inward toward the deep nerve cluster buried within.

Here is the element of our dance that is perhaps the most difficult to explain to you. The tip of the penetrating appendage appears somewhat like an ovate leaflet of your plants in shape, yet it is decorated with thousands of microbristles, each full of thousands of nerve-like structures. The tip from Synphel entered deeply into my core, and my mind was flooded with pleasure as the tentacle wrapped around my nerve cluster and the leaflet dug into the most sensitive portion. Of course my own was doing the same to her, and our bodies were drawn powerfully into each other.

Externally, from our sides and backs, additional tentacles for connection to the other genders of our mating group now extended themselves. However, without the other members to connect with, they would sway and swivel like a vine, searching for a foothold, until the lack of engagement would slowly shut down our mating process.

But that would take some time. As the core of the group, the interweaving of our bodies was deep and strong, forming a platform for the bodies of the other members. Our pleasure and desire to continue the hold was enormous, and we writhed in the torment of reproductive pleasure for more than an hour.

All during the process, I was closely tied to the consciousness of Synphel through the connected nerve clusters as well as our Reader senses. It was as I had known her before, and in this I knew it was truly Synphel. But there was more. *She* was more…altered—deeper and more alien. I began to sense the host of minds beneath the layer of her consciousness, their personalities and thoughts flitting here and there across my awareness. And of course, deep in the core of this endless mind, I sensed Ambra. I felt her and her thoughts. They created images in my cognizance, and I thought I saw her smile.

Inevitably, the physiological program ran its course. The other, external appendages withdrew, having failed to find their mating structures. Our bodies cooled down, the appendages inside each of us beginning to feel uncomfortable, the pleasure withdrawing. Soon they released from the drained nerve clusters and slithered back out of their lovers' bodies, returning to their own and coiling like snakes deep within. At the last, our eyestalks unwound, and we separated, continuing to stare deeply into each visual organ.

"Thank you," I said.

"I have missed you terribly," said Synphel.

Kloan walked up beside us. "It was beautiful," she said, a smile on her once-harrowed face. "Strange and beautiful for my prejudices, beyond beautiful to the eye of my mind. I saw them, Waythrel. They spun like ghosts in and out of space. A cosmos of minds."

Synphel stepped backward toward the disk. "The third element of this visit is also completed. We needed to know that you would love the child. And so you have. Now begins a new cycle."

The burden of our reality returned to me. "And where will it take us now? Have we learned what we needed to learn?" I had no idea what was expected of me.

She did not answer but gestured to the disk. The whirling star field scrambled, and the rainbows embedded in the depths flickered and trembled.

"We will not meet again, my dearest Waythrel," said my lover. "But you will not be left without me."

And in an instant that I could not even process, the form of Synphel was gone. There was no sound, no rushing of air or sense of displacement. There was only absence.

The child clone and I were left standing by ourselves. In front of us blazed an incredible window to another space, perhaps also another time. Behind us the radiance cast shadows even in the bright light of the local star.

"We are not alone, leaky thoughts," said Kloan, smiling. "I can feel them watching. Can you?"

I strained my Reader senses. It was faint, perhaps only my wishful thinking, but it did seem that some echo of Synphel, of Ambra, of their entire mental ecosystem could be felt in the undulations of fleeting gravitons. Real or not, it was comforting.

But as I strained, I could not help but also sense other currents, other minds lurking in the depths of time and space. I felt like a swimmer in a cold sea, lingering in the comfort of a warmer current, knowing that around us an icy, unfathomable deep lay concealed. In the depths, there were monsters.

"Perhaps it was better to be alone," I said, shivering.

"When there is hate, there is love," said Kloan. "Warmth and cold, order and disorder, creation and destruction. Where there is Ambra, there is also me."

My eyestalks centered on her brooding features, not knowing what to think of these words. I still did not know what the ultimate purpose of this journey would be, only that it had shifted in a new way and that, in taking the next steps, I was putting my trust in both the yes and the no, in the odd opposites of the two forms of Ambra Dawn.

"The thing tore open my mind. The journeys. The multitudes—I am remembering them all. It's too much, Kloan."

Kloan grasped my arm. "You were not the only one tested, Waythrel." She sighed. "It will be different each time, and only when we have fully understood will we see the answer."

She turned toward the disk. Together, hand in hand, we stepped forward, the gel-like surface of the portal enveloping us like molasses.

We fell into a great darkness.

Part VI

The words of wonder I watched elders weave,
the tales of Truth more strange than in my dreams:
Of ghosts so small they pass through vision's sieve
yet stitch my mind in fragile, fleshy seams,
or hungry gods, enormous, ever starved,
who take all prey to planes beyond our own,
where time and space are infinitely carved
into a fabric rent and never sown.
To groups so gifted by the gods, the signs
and studied charms the elder priests unfold.
The depths await our readied, seeking minds.
As Shaman I may find new Truths untold.
Yet some nights I feel depths beyond our Way,
and what I am the spirits do not say.

—Mazandarani, *Sonnets from the Desert*

Chapter 45

Science cannot solve the ultimate mystery of Nature. And it is because in the last analysis we ourselves are part of the mystery we are trying to solve.

Max Planck

There was no light.

There was a terrible blackness beyond anything I had ever experienced. Along with it came a chill. The surrounding space was extraordinarily cold and seemed to want to drink the warmth greedily from my body. One of my upper arms was shaken vigorously.

It was Kloan, or so I surmised in this total caliginosity. I could feel her hand still holding onto me, and she had begun to shiver noticeably. I strained with all my senses. I could smell nothing, taste nothing through my skin sacs. I could feel nothing but Kloan on my body. My eighteen visual organs were useless. No radiation in any frequency range could I detect, not even infrared, which meant that nearly everything around us was dangerously cold.

Whatever is around us, came Kloan's thoughts, *we do stand on something. There is something under our feet.*

She was correct. I tried to speak to acknowledge her observation, but nothing was emitted from the translator. *The translator!* Of course. How stupid I was, and how slow to adapt to these shocking dislocations in space and time.

I fiddled with the device around my neck, and soon it began to glow a pale white. As my eyes adjusted from the pitch black to the now nearly blinding source of light around my neck, I began to take in our immediate environment. It was bleaker than I could have imagined.

At our feet was a pile of white dust, perfectly arranged around our forms. From the lack of the gate gel on our bodies, I assumed that the material had frozen and shattered into this fine powder, but I could not be sure. For the ten meters around us that the light illuminated, there was only ice and rock. The "ice" was highly variable, ranging from frosted to perfectly clear to a pale cyan. The rocks were coated with the latter in a blue film, seemingly varnished by a top layer of clear ice. I had seen nothing like it before. It was the same in all directions. My mind raced.

What do you think this is, Waythrel?

It was the first time Kloan had ever turned to me in ignorance and doubt. After so many wild and disorienting journeys where this child held the upper hand in all things, suddenly she seemed small again, lost, and searching for a parental figure, even if it were a six-armed alien. Rather than stoke my ego, it brought on a sense of dread I was not expecting. Of all the disturbing powers I had witnessed in the universe, if Kloan was lost and unsure, it could not be good.

I don't know, Kloan.

But you suspect. I feel your thoughts bubbling.

I tried to walk. There was indeed a surface, but it too was coated in this frozen glaze. Moving was treacherous and required stepping gingerly and avoiding excess momentum.

She probed further. *Could it be underground? There is no light.*

Possibly.

But you don't think so.

There is no atmosphere, Kloan. No sound from my translator. No noise from our steps. We are in a total vacuum. That would make the temperature outside close to absolute zero. I can only assume your skin suits are keeping us alive. And I don't know how long they will last.

Waythrel, they aren't mine!

That at least was comforting. Kloan and I were obviously out of our element, beyond our powers here, kept alive only by some advanced technology we could not understand. But only something far in advance of us could hope to help us here, wherever *here* might be.

I glanced around, slowly rotating all my eyestalks, positioning them so that I had nearly a 360-degree view of everything around us. *There are no stars overhead, yet no atmosphere or light pollution to drown them out. Where are the stars, Kloan?*

That's why I say maybe we are underground.

Perhaps. Let's try to cover some ground and see what else we can find. Maybe something will help us understand.

Data.

Yes, Kloan, data. But somehow I think our survival depends upon this particular data.

She frowned, the bright light and darkness behind chiseling her features harshly. *All the data is important to our lives, Waythrel. To the cosmos.*

Let's focus on the rock and ice around us and worry about the cosmos later, okay?

She said nothing else; with that we set out blindly, randomly, able to view only meters ahead of us at a time. It was enough to avoid a pit or cliff or other danger, but it allowed us no way to plan globally. We had no sense of the lay of the land, no points of reference. No navigation tools besides memory. It was indeed an act of hopeless optimism.

Rocks and ice. Ice and rocks. On and on it went. Minutes passed, and then hours. Kloan continued to shiver, but the suit seemed to keep her warm enough to avoid cold damage. She showed no signs of hypothermia or frostbite, but I monitored her regularly.

More rocks and more ice. It seemed like some giant's toy in a mineral collection, sprayed with a fixative to protect the surface from scratches. I checked the translator again. The power supply would last months, but the diodes illuminating our path were a greater unknown. They were not commonly used and certainly never tested in such an environment. I guessed that they would last at least several days in continuous use. Beyond that I did not know.

Waythrel, careful! The land is sloping down!

The child was correct. I also noticed that the terrain was smoothing out, the larger rocks giving way to pebbles and a kind of strange sand. All of it was still covered in the thick layer of ice, however, as if it were a specimen in a box separated from probing hands by a thick sheet of glass.

Kloan, can you determine nothing of this place from your searches into the past?

She shook her head. *This world's past—Waythrel, it never ends. It's an infinite well. I can't look at it anymore. I don't want to go back into it! I tried, and I fell and fell and fell, and always the same, always this darkness and cold. It's like it has always been this way. Forever. A frozen, dead eternity.*

I mulled over her ominous words. More and more it seemed we had come to a place unlike anything before, where our knowledge and powers proved useless. I focused on what I did know and tried to quell the growing panic. If I understood anything, it was that Ambra had sent us here. The god-ball had arranged it all, including, I assumed, the suits that somehow preserved two living organisms in this icy vacuum of a dead place. There had to be a purpose. All we had to do was achieve that purpose, *learn* whatever it was Kloan was supposed to learn or do, and then find ourselves, dizzy and confused, back where we started.

The time loops have destabilized, Waythrel. I told you things changed last time. Great powers have entered the game.

Some game! And one you can't stop playing.

Not yet.

Is there nothing you saw in your searches? Nothing of use?

Kloan wrapped her arms around her chest shivering, shaking her head. *I had to turn away. A hope, maybe, Waythrel. Maybe something in the distance.*

Now we stood flatly on a plain of some kind. If this were an underground cavern, it was enormous beyond comprehension, and there seemed little way an arched dome above us—one that we had yet to see evidence for—could be supported for any length of time at that size and mass. I grew convinced that we were not entombed within the bowels of some planet. But where we were still eluded any confident model.

Waythrel, wait. Turn off the light.

Why?

Please, just do it. There is something ahead. Far ahead, I think.

I was confused. *Then we need the light to see it.*

No, not this. It's a light itself. Your necklace is blinding us. Turn it off and let our eyes adjust.

I did as she asked. As the glow of the translator slowly dimmed, the darkness rushed in as some visceral thing, as a tidal dark mist with a malevolent will of its own. I had never been in the presence of such a complete lack of radiant sources or been submerged in such utter blackness. It stirred primitive and unreasonable instincts. It seemed alive.

But it was not like our arrival. The ink closing around us could not completely solidify. Kloan was right. Far ahead of us, a wan radiance like a failing beacon spilled a languid light through the mist, resisting it, culling its complete imposition over space. Something ahead radiated, possessed energy above the absolute zero of the landscape around us. There was energy. Some *potential*, something to battle the inevitability of thermodynamics. A chance of life.

I guess we go that way, right, Kloan?

She was already walking.

Chapter 46

That is not dead which can eternal lie,
And with strange aeons even death may die.

H. P. Lovecraft

We walked for long hours, the distances deceptive in this place, with only the beacon ahead providing any sense of reference in this icebound desert. Slowly, the radiance intensified. With our eyes now long adjusted to the paltry light, we could nearly make out our own shapes, monitor our footfalls, although the contents of the murky spaces around us remained hidden—a threatening unknown that toyed with my imagination.

Exhausted, freezing, we dragged ourselves forward. Kloan's breaths, exiting the force field, immediately turned to a snowy gas and drifted to the ground in front of us. My gaseous exchange was similar, although spread over the surface area of my skin, it produced no such dramatic display. I had no idea where we received the input gases to breathe or the warmth that kept us from freezing solid. I noticed Kloan's fingers had begun to turn white. Whatever the power of the suits that encased us, it was finite, and I hoped it would be enough for the time we would spend in this wasteland.

The light grew. Shadows began to form behind our forms—and, to my amazement, in front of us as well. Focusing the power of all my eyes, I strained to make out blurring shapes taking form near the source of the beacon, but it was still too far ahead.

Kloan, can you see ahead? Those shapes? They must be large.

Kloan nodded. *Before I stopped looking into the past of this frozen hell, they passed through my mind. They are very large. Something terrible.*

And she was right. Slowly, the shadows deepened, the figures ahead clarified, and they grew. Higher and higher as we approached and optical perspective set in, we watched monumental explosions of ice rise violently above the plain. Their shapes were indistinct. They looked like blasted magma that had been instantly converted to another form and locked in place. A rainbow of weak colors seemed to run through them.

As we neared the beacon, we approached the bases of these monoliths dwarfing us and everything around them. They were arrayed in a ring of a half kilometer or more. Some were single jets of ice throttling upward. Others seemed like a river with multiple tributaries erupting from the ground and fusing into bizarre, bulked shapes suspended over us. There were more than fifty of them. We could walk beside the structures, underneath arches for some. I became disoriented when looking for more than a moment into their icy forms—indistinct visions and motions emanated from deep within. Prolonged observation generated sensations. *Feelings.* I had the very distinct impression that we were not alone here, but could not identify what it was exactly that might be with us. The experiences were deeply unnerving, and I began to avoid staring into the things.

The beacon stood in the middle of the circle of giants. A small pillar of ice, simpler, unlike the towering forms around it, rose very near to Kloan's height, forming a bowl of pristine glass at its apex. Resting in this bowl was a sphere of clear glass or ice. A powerful rainbow of light churned within. It was this crystalline sphere that had illuminated our path and beckoned us here.

Kloan was walking slowly around the circle of titans, touching the ice, staring deeply into the quavering imagery dancing within it. She seemed far more immune than I to the disorienting effects of these objects and was intensely focused on them. Whatever this place was about, it was clear that these things, and the glowing sphere at their center, were central to the mystery. I let Kloan have her space and time.

They are as old as everything else, Waythrel. As far as I can look, hundreds of thousands of years into the past, they are here, just like this, unchanged, unmoved.

Do you know what they are?

Perhaps, she said, without elaborating.

Around she went, sampling one after another. Hours drifted by as I followed her, hoping for some clarification, some insight into this strange place, some indication of how we might escape it.

Finally, before one of the more distorted, grotesque, twisted shapes of ice, Kloan pulled back quickly, her eyes wide and her face in a grimace of pain. She closed her eyes and nodded to herself slowly. I felt her grasp my hands.

Waythrel, look into the ice. Give it time—but carefully. Guard your mind! Tell me what you see.

I hated to try, but I followed her lead and stepped up to a portion of the colossus before me. A tentacle of frozen matter dove from hundreds of feet above to plunge into the ground and disappear at my feet. The glass was imperfect, warped, the light and structures within bobbing and weaving. I could not see any hint of my reflection on the surface, which defied all optical physics. I felt my sense of balance weaken. I steadied myself on Kloan's shoulder instinctively, trying to maintain my gaze.

And then, *pain. Horror.* My mind experienced flashes and bursts of images, feelings, and sensations that had no center, no cause, and no explanation. Fleeting and effervescent, the terrible rampage of monstrosity nonetheless struck me over and over like blows. I screamed. I held my arms up to cover my eyes. I crouched defensively and turned my head away.

Kloan wrapped her arms around me for some time as I worked to purge the vile experiences from my mind. I could not speak, could not form coherent thoughts to share with her, and she did not push her own toward me. She recognized that I could not process them. Finally, my composure slowly regained, I turned my eyes to her.

I've felt it before. Where?

Kloan nodded. *Rakshasi.*

Instantly, I knew she was right. The being who had threatened us—that some unexplainable incarnate form of Ambra had saved us from, and also failed to save us from—had left an unforgettable impression on my psyche. Absorbing the outflow from this icy mountain above me, that impression was impossible to mistake for anything else. *Rakshasi.* The essence of the god-thing who had desecrated Synphel's form loomed before me, pressed down on me from above, crushing my hopes and sanity and menacing my mind, seemingly from within the solid substance before us.

Rakshasi? How, Kloan? What are these things? I gestured wildly to the monumental forms around us. I was suddenly terrified of them.

What are they? I don't know, Waythrel, but I would guess the same. Or of the like. Whatever Rakshasi is, or was, whatever they are, it is of a type.

Gods? Frozen gods?

Kloan shrugged her shoulders and pursed her lips. *That's right up there on my weird-o-meter, that's for sure.*

Let's just hope that they don't melt! Or whatever it is this stuff does. I don't think it's made of the same ice that is covering the ground and rocks. But I can't face these things. Don't let it happen, Kloan!

No. I don't know what they are made of, or how Rakshasi is inside. Or what Rakshasi is inside. But I don't think they will melt. Or change. The harder I try, the further back I look, the more I see that they have been here, just like this, for eons inside of eons.

The others?

All over the place. Powerful, strange, alien, unfathomable. Not as accessible. I think our encounter with Rakshasi tuned us to its essence, whatever it is.

Something terrible, that's what.

I stood up wobbly, the ground feeling far more treacherous and the air colder. I found myself drawn to the light in the center. I needed to get away from these towers of ice. I wanted to flee darkness and cold. I wanted to stand in front of that light and put my hands over it like a fire.

And maybe it will even be a little warm? Kloan smiled. *Don't think that there's much else to do with these cryogenic deities. Maybe the light ball has a better story to tell.*

We walked toward the light. The perched sphere was nearly one hundred meters from the ring of giants. As we approached, we indeed began to feel a temperature increase. The complete lack of an atmosphere meant that the heat transfer must be solely due to absorbed radiation from the object.

Hopefully there are no high frequency rays from that thing, or we better hope these suits can also shield us.

Kloan didn't respond. As we advanced to within twenty meters, Kloan slowed and put her hand against me. I stopped, my eyes swiveling around in concern, but I could see nothing immediately threatening.

There's another one.

Another what?

God-thing. Whatever. It's not like the others. It's...closer. And it's moving. She seemed to be straining, gazing far off into the distance. *It's hiding! Hiding in time from me. No! It's here!*

The ground shook and threw us both to the ice. The shaking continued so violently that we were both unable to stand and barely managed to steady ourselves with all our extremities spread across the ground. We gazed upward, awestruck as a shadow spread across our forms.

The frozen surface around the beacon shifted and flowed. Like some glacier as seen over millions of years, in only a few seconds, ice and rock as liquid defying gravity hurtled upward. Coalescing, a tremendous mass assembled itself, lodged between us and the beacon, so that the light of the object was completely obscured.

But as the thing in front of us took shape, it began to glow in a luminescent cyan that lit the surrounding plane. The tremors subsided as the bulk of the flow seemed to have eased, and the mass was focused on adopting more subtle forms. Kloan slapped my arm repeatedly, pointing with her other hand at the thing before us.

Look! Waythrel, look! It's us!

Astounded, I watched the ice and rock mold itself into some geologic facsimile of a humanoid shape, or rather, a blended and distorted mixture of a human and Xix. Sixfold symmetric, with our numerous eyes, which it none-theless sprouted not from our massive central cone but from the head of an Earthling, a shape that increasingly began to resemble none other than Kloan herself. Mouth, nose, cranial structure—it was an unmistakable, if rough and rocky, replica.

The eyelids of the face flipped open. Irisless orbs stared down at us, and the mountainous thing bent toward the ground and our position, stopping only meters away. The mouth opened, and I was shocked to hear sound, but I was far beyond the point of trying to parse the acoustical physics.

"I have been waiting for you a long time," came a rumbling god-voice that rattled the plane of ice around us. "Now the symmetry may be repaired."

Chapter 47

The formation in geological time of the human body by the laws of physics (or any other laws of similar nature), starting from a random distribution of elementary particles and the field is as unlikely as the separation of the atmosphere into its components. The complexity of the living things has to be present within the material or in the laws.

Kurt Gödel

Kloan and I stared silently at the incredible ice behemoth before us for some time, although I could not stop various clusters of my eyestalks from turning away toward her for support. The thing did not move. It did not seem to be in a hurry. After Kloan's words concerning the age of this place, if it had been waiting for us so long, a few more minutes would be meaningless, I supposed.

I found that I could now produce sound. There was the slightest distortion above us—a dome of some nature—and I could only assume that the creature, or its transcendental handlers, had created a small environmental bubble around our position.

"We have air, Kloan."

Kloan nodded and turned toward the ice hulk. "Where are we, godling?"

The jagged ice lips boomed, "Where is of no significance anymore."

"Then…*when* are we?" she offered.

"At the death of all things." It motioned to the giant ice titans. "Even the gods."

Kloan cocked her head to one side. "How can the gods die?"

"The gods belong to our cosmos. They draw their tissues and energies of it.

But they are only broken gods now." The deep rumblings of the voice seemed to rattle the innermost parts of my body. "Their Mother, our universe, is ill. She is dying. She has been, is, and will be dying to eternity. But now the weakness is at a threshold. And so the gods die."

I ventured. "But yet you live."

"I am their guardian. I am the keeper of the minds. I watch over them until the messengers come, when the past will end."

The god's words were cryptic and left me uncomprehending. "What makes you different?"

"I have been chosen. Look around you," said the colossus, standing tall like a mountain and gesturing upward. "You walk on a dead world in a dead space, a world whose sun has long died and that has perished in ice. An atmosphere that snowed the land under as it fell from the sky and then over the eons, found itself crushed and reformed to a clear glass. You look to the heavens, but they are now only tombs. There is no star left to burn, no free energy remaining to bath the empty space and planets. All is now forever dark."

Kloan nodded to herself. *No wonder I could not look back in time. No wonder it all was the same. Waythrel, don't you see? We have come terribly, horribly far into the future. So far that even the gods cannot count it anymore.*

The creature swiveled like an avalanche, and one of the giant Xixian arms on its torso reached behind and returned glowing brightly.

"I do not die because I hold a foreign fire." It held up its titanic arm. Shards of ice dropped like daggers and hailstones to the ground below it. "Here is a rend in the cosmos, a break in the fabric of our existence. Here is a tiny trickle of order from outside a dead creation. Enough that I may persist and maintain the watch. Enough to preserve the minds. Because of this I continue to gaze over the fallen gods. Because of this, my hope that the cosmos may be healed remains alive." The thing opened the multitude of digits to reveal the crystalline sphere.

"Where did it come from?" Kloan asked.

"It is a gift from the greatest of the gods who has sent you here and consumed entire galaxies to do it. It is a promise rejected by the others in futile wars that accelerated the inevitable heat death you witness. It was given to me when my role was assigned, and I accepted the duty with love. Therein, I accepted also the destiny that I would give back the gift when the time came."

"The greatest of the gods—who is that?" I asked, glancing around at the towers, wondering which of these was the most powerful and why this greatest god had not been the one to guard over the others—to use the power of the sphere.

Kloan shook her head. "She isn't here, is she?"

"No," thundered the mountain. "She waits for you at the beginning of time."

Kloan nodded, a terrible burden seeming to fall on her.

Who waits, Kloan?

Ambra. She has always waited. She is the poison. She is the great power who has broken everything at Creation. Our greatest and most terrible god. And I am the antidote.

The bulk of blue crystal seemed to hear our thoughts. "What is devolved in one direction is achieved in the other. There is an imbalance of death and madness. Here, at the end, you see its final fruits."

"Why do you keep them?" Kloan gestured to the gods around us.

"They were needed, in the beginning that is yet to be, to which they must return. But they resisted until time overpowered them. Only altogether can the asymmetry be unmade. When you awaken and call them, destroyer, the gods will come."

Destroyer? Does he mean you, Kloan?

Kloan ignored me. "And how will I call them? How will they waken?"

"When your gathering begins, you will return. I give you this light," it said, moving the glowing sphere toward her. "You will know what to do."

Nothing made sense to me. My frustration exploded in the form of questions. "If there is no energy, if all is cold and sterile and dead, where does this light come from? What is this thing you claim Kloan will use to waken all these monsters from their endless sleep? Why should we release them? They are horrible!"

"As you are horrible, and your atoms poison the cosmic mind," it said. The enormous head arched downward with the sound of straining glaciers, approaching within centimeters of my face. "Until all is lost, Xix, nothing is found."

The words sent a shockwave through me. I knew those words! They had appeared over the arch to the labyrinth. Now they spilled out from the icy tongue of this deity.

Kloan's thoughts pulled me back. *The power is not from here, Waythrel. Didn't you listen? The god is right. It is a true hope. Only because of this can we believe to overcome our shattered universe; that it can be healed; that outside of the constraints of time, it may find its whole form.*

What are you talking about?

This sphere holds power from outside; *it is not of our cosmos. It means, Waythrel, thank God—or whatever—that we are* not *in isolation. We are not a closed system. There are other universes in contact with our own, and energy flows between.*

I was stunned by the thoughts. I stared at the glowing ball in the god's hands that weakly illuminated a frozen planet. A dead world in a dark cosmos doomed forever to a frozen tomb, except for a fissure in the boundaries of our reality that opened into another. But who was to say the other universe, or universes, would not themselves all also die such a death?

The ice titan rumbled. "Many may die. An infinite number may perish and yet still represent an infinitesimal portion of the whole. We know nothing of what lies Without. It does not matter. Only one of us could reach Outside, and she gave us this bridge. She brought this hope. Not for herself only, but for all. For rebirth and a healing of the broken symmetries." It turned to Kloan and held the ball in front of her. "Use the gift, destroyer, and remove the madness from the cosmic mind."

The hulk pivoted, like an island flipping, and replaced the sphere on its pedestal precisely. Then it turned back to us, its gigantic limbs hanging loosely at its side. The glowing eyes were covered by lids of ice, and a deep silence washed over everything.

Then the giant shattered. It was thunderous, and the vibrations from the ground tossed us down again as shards of the thing cascaded around us. Yet we were unharmed, and a million pieces of a god struck the surface, liquefied, and melted away into the planet as if they had never been.

Chapter 48

Astronomy? Impossible to understand and madness to investigate.

Sophocles, c. 420 BCE

We slowly pulled ourselves back to our feet. A thin film of frost covered us completely but quickly melted from our body heat. The dome of air remained in place, the titans continued to stare down in silence, and the sphere glowed ominously in front of us.

"Kloan, I advise caution. You seem to understand so much more than me, but I know that these beings, their doings, everything about them is beyond your grasp, beyond your ability to control. Remember the encounter with Rakshasi!"

Kloan's face darkened and she squinted her eyes. "I will never forget, Waythrel. I faced that fear when I read the presence of the demon in the ice."

Several eyestalks instinctively focused on the twisted shape behind her. The others watched a resolution form in her features.

She spoke firmly. "But this is so much bigger than our fears or the petty plans of these gods."

"Petty? Kloan, they are beyond us!"

"Yes. And *no*, Waythrel. And that is part of the deep flaw that has wounded this universe, a flaw that has distorted its structure and prevented it from reaching its potential."

"What potential?" All the conversations now seemed utterly intangible.

"*True* divinity. To become more than we could ever understand and yet take its small place in an infinity of god-particles. In order to build to the next stratum." She walked forward slowly, approaching the sphere with a quiet awe.

"Everything you say is abstract and vague to me, Kloan! But the terrible power of these creatures, and I presume their artifacts, is not! Will you at least wait and think about this thing that you are doing?"

"I'm cold, Waythrel. And thinking more won't change my mind." She reached the narrow ice plinth. The sphere hovered over the bowl-shaped depression at its top, avoiding contact with the sides. The swirling colors danced across Kloan's pale form and seemed to activate the tattooed circuits underneath her skin. They blazed forth like hot steel in a furnace, waves of brighter lights and different hues flowing over her like a patterned windstorm. "But this is warm," she said, her eyes wide. "I feel a force unlike anything I have known in its depths."

She reached her hand into the bowl and grasped the sphere. I moved forward protectively, fully cognizant that were this cosmic relic to cause her harm, there would be nothing I could do to stop it. The sphere dwarfed her hand, and yet she grasped it; and, like an optical illusion, the entity now fit perfectly within her palm. She stared at it, a sage and a child together, a madwoman and prophet with eyes of flickering green. Then she laughed and pocketed the object in her robes. The light was instantly extinguished.

Complete darkness dropped like a physical blow. *The dome is gone*, I thought toward her as I realized I could no longer speak. But to my horror, I felt a vacuum in the place of her consciousness. Kloan, too, was gone, vanished in an instant in much the same way as Synphel.

Kloan! My mind cried out for her, but there was no response. There was not the slightest trace of her personality left in this place anymore. I spun in circles, calling out her name in my mind over and over again. It was in vain. She was not present. She could not hear me. Whatever had been piloting our deranged voyage had, for the second time, split us apart.

I wasn't sure what disturbed me the most—losing Kloan or realizing that I was trapped on this world alone. Concern for the child and a panic over my own predicament coursed through me like electric charges. Was she okay? Why would I be left here? Why had I come in the first place? In all this infinite suffering, what was the point now of this separation? Was this another test, like the labyrinth?

I tried to calm my thoughts. I stilled my emotions. I meditated with all the concentration I could muster. Minutes dragged by—hours, perhaps. I began to step outside myself. It was at that point that I realized I did not know where I was.

That's my Waythrel, came warm thoughts that wrapped around me like a blanket. *We miss your mind and counsel.*

A light grew before me. I seemed to be orbiting it, spinning slowly around a congealed sea of clouds with indistinct features. But as I completed my revolution, the motion ceased, the fog solidified, and I was face to face with the cyborg apparition of Ambra Dawn again.

"Ambra, please, I don't understand." I was completely overcome. I had no more to give her or this quest. I didn't care anymore about the fate of a universe that was insane beyond my capability to even qualify. I needed rest. I needed peace. I needed warmth and love.

"And so you will soon have both, dear Waythrel," said the horror in front of me. "The last steps are coming. You need only complete the loop one last time."

"One last time." It did not seem possible.

"A final journey through smoke and fire, and then the gods themselves will carry you on their backs."

"And Kloan?" The gods could all burn.

Ambra smiled. "She will embrace her fate, which is beyond all the stories of myth and the hopes of sentient creatures. And you will propel her to that fate and remake all that will have then never been."

"What of you? What of Synphel?"

"Be joyful, Waythrel, because your hopes will be fulfilled. You will hold both of us again."

"I don't understand. You are now gods. You are timeless, and I am small, only the puff of energy from a chemical reaction lost in a sea of living broth. How can I hold *that?*"

"Patience, Waythrel. It cannot be explained. But you will join your mate, and on that day you will be two mothers holding God's children, and I will look up to you with an infant's eyes."

The apparition began to withdraw. It shrank, as if retreating through space toward a distant point. I reached out, desperate not to be left alone again, confused and disoriented as I continually found myself throughout this madness.

"Please, Ambra, don't go! I don't understand!"

The cloud was now only a small point, and her voice drifted slowly back to me as if it came from endless eons across the girth of the universe itself.

"Let go of understanding, Waythrel. Each stratum sees only what is below and worships what is above. But at all levels, the essence is held together by the one fundamental force that scales infinitely. When your mind is free and clear, you will know what it is, and you will embrace it."

And she was gone.

Chapter 49

In the fabric of space and in the nature of matter, as in a great work of art, there is, written small, the artist's signature.

Carl Sagan

I stared up at a night sky, the faint pinpricks of starlight dimly bleeding through a haze of smoke and dust. A dry wind blasted hot air over me. The ground shook with angry tremors. My eyestalks darted about, appraising the planet surface, the heavens, and the figure of the girl sitting beside me.

"Something terrible has happened." The words escaped me before I recognized the thought.

Kloan sat with her legs pulled up, nearly obscuring her head, those haunting green eyes peeking over the kneecaps, arms wrapped around her legs, keeping them together. She rocked slowly back and forth. She was humming.

I sat up and stared across at her. "Where are we?"

The humming ceased. "The same."

"The same?" My eyestalks swiveled around anxiously. The landscape did seem familiar, but the climate was not. In my fogged memories, there had taken shape through a slow aggregation the image of a habitable world coated at night with clear star fields, breathable air, and a moderate temperature. Around me was a world covered in smoke, the stars hidden, the temperature dramatically raised. "No, Kloan, not the same this time."

"Which time is this, Waythrel?"

"Kloan, stop!" I stood up, anxiety washing over me. "Something terrible has happened here. Don't you see it?"

Everything reeked of devastation. Fires uncounted burned across my field of vision. Molten chasms opened in the plains below us, lava flowing like rivers through the rends in the rock. I was having trouble acquiring oxygen. Kloan coughed and wheezed in the ash-filled air.

The intubated, tattooed head cocked to one side, the green eyes continuing to stare fixedly at me. They were bloodshot from the fumes. Kloan stood up. It was a rapid motion but anticipated. She stopped to stand in front of me, her long, ragged clumps of red hair dangling haphazardly, nearly obscuring her face. Her once-tan robes were soiled nearly black with soot. "The decision point approaches, Waythrel. The tests and experiments are over. The Anti were wrong. Even the gods are blind."

"The gods?" I looked around at the planetary cataclysm. "Kloan, what has happened to this world?"

She nodded, a satisfied look on her face. "That's *why* you're here. *Data*. The last data to enter the gate." Again she nodded and then turned her back on me to walk down a steep slope. "Let's get started."

"Started with what? Where are you going? Look around you—the mantle is torn open! There is molten rock pouring over the plains!"

Kloan continued walking without turning back. Her next words were nearly lost in the deep rumblings and howling wind.

"To where it all began for me. To watch the beginning flow around us and mature and twist through time and space to come back to be us. Then we will be ready for the last step."

The figure of the child was gone, swallowed in the smoky darkness. A violent tremor nearly threw me to the ground. Catching myself on a jagged boulder, I slowly raised my gaze in the direction of her last words, trying to understand what was happening.

Waythrel, come on!

Her voice rang impatiently in my mind. My eyestalks curled up on themselves. I looked around the desolate, ruined space surrounding me. What else was there for me to do?

I followed her, racing to catch up, my steps uncertain. Ash covered the ground like a winter snowstorm, the rocks slick with it under my feet. Down the steep slope of the elevation, I stumbled and tripped, my four arms only poorly grasping the rocks and alien vegetation, seeming to lack any friction to form a proper grip. *That field around our bodies.*

I slowed down as I rounded a large boulder, anticipating her presence. Kloan was poised on a ledge, staring across the shattered plain below us. Steam and smoke rose maniacally from the fissures snaking across the landscape.

The city of clones was gone. Obliterated. The structures were vaporized and erased by blast and fire so that it was difficult to believe that there had ever been something there. Only the crater and impact blast density revealed that this place had been especially targeted by the wrath that had descended on the planet.

"The devil ball?" I asked fearfully, my sympathies now scrambled, my concern for the well-being of those once my enemies, real and burning.

"One of them. No—I sense many of them."

"Why would Ambra do this?"

"Not Ambra."

"But you said—"

"*Not* Ambra," she repeated firmly. "There are many gods, remember?"

The other gods. "Rakshasi?"

The ground swayed wildly. I held tightly to the rocks overlooking the wreckage below. In the plain, a new fissure ripped open and sprayed lava hundreds of feet high. It lit up the dark evening like a fluorescent curtain that rose and then rained fire on the blackened soil. I thought I could even feel the heat from it.

"Not only."

"But why? What interest could they have in this small place?"

Kloan turned to me solemnly. "You have to remember more, Waythrel. You have to do better! The decision point is here, and when we cross the portal, it will be for the last time."

"We will exit the loop?"

"Only if we understand the decision point, if we understand the choice! You have to remember!"

"The disk? Did it survive?" How could we leave again if it were destroyed?

She ignored my question. "What are the gods?"

I was suddenly tired. I felt as though I had lived one thousand lives here, repeated a million events, all of them a blur, many of them horrible, all of them impacting my being and leaving impressions that I could only vaguely understand. I had already exhausted myself just to retain my sanity in this madhouse. I did not want a quiz. I didn't want to understand anymore. I just wanted it all to stop, for an end to come.

Kloan grasped my hands tightly. "What are the gods, Waythrel?"

"They're like Ambra. Powerful group minds. Made somehow similar, but different. They are her enemies. They fear her. Something like that. Please, no more. It's all too much. I'm tired, Kloan. I need to rest." I was pleading.

She ignored my plea. "And what else do they fear?"

Rapid-fire images of events sped through my mind. The disk. Torture. Supergroups of galaxies. Heavens and hells. Synphel and Kloan.

"You," I said, the realization shocking me, the memories solidifying. "They fear you."

"Then you understand this," she said, gesturing around us.

I looked across the burning world from horizon to horizon. Puzzle pieces assembled. I understood. "They wanted to destroy you."

"Yes! Good. They destroyed my world, blew me up in this past! Why am I still here?" Her eyes bored into mine.

I felt hopeless. "I don't know. You shouldn't be."

"Waythrel! You *do* know. You have to know. If you don't understand, we can't leave!" She sounded desperate.

I thought over the infinity of dreamscapes buried in my mind. Not the pitiful handful I have shared with this author, and which he has tried to convey to you. No. I scanned through them all. Over and over through the disk, one hundred times more than I could possibly ever recount in one hundred books—worlds, adventures, deaths, pursuit, love, fear, dread, longing—always for nothing, always snapping back here, doomed to repeat and repeat.

"It's because we repeat," I managed, the words spilling from me almost unconsciously.

"Yes! Don't you see? It's at the beginning where we have to find the decision point! Everything else is only a weakly weighted world curve. There are endless numbers of them summing to nothing. Only one path leads to permanence."

I felt like a child barely grasping elementary mathematics. "Then the gods —they failed because they do not understand the decision point?"

"Yes!" Kloan smiled. "We couldn't kill Ambra in time, and they can't kill me."

"But I don't understand it, either! I don't know what it is!"

Kloan hugged me, her beaming face inches from my eyestalks. The swirling lines of cybernetics across her skin were dizzying. "That's okay, Waythrel! You will! You understand the structure, and now we can escape these loops and enter the final iteration. There you will be added to, changed by what you see, and you will understand in the end what you must do! *She's* counting on you. So am I."

Kloan released me from her embrace and began climbing back up the mountain. I could hardly breathe. I had no idea what she meant. It seemed the powers of the universe were swirling around us, and I was dancing with some mad Sibyl who had just informed me that a key to the resolution of a cosmic conflict, the fate of the universe itself, would soon rest with me. That they were all counting on me to understand and do something.

Do what? How was I to understand? How could some lowly Xix play any role in the fate of the gods of our cosmos?

I watched her climb. I couldn't move. Once again, she compelled me from her mind.

Waythrel, come on!

Chapter 50

In the end—when all else is dust—loyalty to those we love is all we can carry with us to the grave. Faith—true faith—was trusting in that love.

Dan Simmons

And so we climbed.

I felt, I half remembered, and I sensed that it was not the first time. Mnemonic whispers suggested that we had made this journey before, or would make it, or were making it in some parallel time loop world line of whatever it was that held us fast in this mind-shattering, recursive hell.

We climbed. Fighting the low friction of the mysterious field built around me for protection, I scaled the jagged rocks as they shook in the throes of a dying world. I marched over terrace after terrace of bedrock as we approached the path to the disk, my legs slowing and slowing as the oxygen-depleted atmosphere burning around us sapped our strength. Kloan fared no better; her pale skin was now dark from the murky air, her red hair dyed a dim gray in this choking soup. She coughed up black phlegm, and mucous and tears were running down her face. She wheezed horribly.

I knew we could not last much longer on this doomed world. As our physiological survival mechanisms asserted themselves, we climbed numbly with a single-minded focus to reach the gate, higher purpose be damned.

Memory of previous climbs was not precise, so it was a surprise and relief when we cleared the final terrace and scaled the wall after it to step onto a remembered path. Ahead was the gate. In all this misery and death and destruction, it shone as a beacon, dispelling the filth and darkness. The smoke did not dim its radiance or blot out the star field within it. Even the air was purer the closer we approached. It was as if it projected a protective bubble around itself.

Kloan collapsed to the ground, coughing, and then began retching. I held her torso upright to prevent her from choking, so weak she was and so violent her spasms. When it was over, I lay her down on her side and sat down beside her. I feared we might never find the strength to stand again.

"All the failures," came the harsh rasp of her voice, "The Anti couldn't recognize the timeless asymmetry." Her eyes were shut, her face nearly unrecognizable, layered in the soot and excretions. Even her teeth were black as she spoke. "Their efforts too crude. We cannot simply *die*. That path was written out of the summation when the Orb came into being."

Her coughing returned, and I placed my arm around her head instinctively. She lay back into it as the fit passed. "We must be annihilated. It is the only way to free the universe of her."

"Kloan, you're speaking of killing Ambra. Why?"

"No! Haven't you been listening? She can't be killed. Not anymore. She must be *annihilated*. With sentience, it is more than with mere matter. It is creative, Waythrel. She is the true god-seed, but it cannot be imbalanced. We must remove the nucleation center." Again the coughing. She appeared completely exhausted. Weakly she held my hand. "God cannot be nucleated on a single personality. We must give birth to something far, far more than that."

She gasped for breath. The clean air almost seemed to worsen her condition, but I knew the fits to be her body's purging of the grime within her respiratory tract. It seemed like she coughed out handfuls of coal.

"The other gods," she whispered slowly, the recent fits sapping nearly all her energy, "they must be present. They must be part of it. The yin and the yang. Matter and antimatter. Yes and no. Hate and love. All must balance for the cognitive symmetry to be regained."

She lost consciousness. I stared down at the begrimed face, the soiled strands of hair stuck to her skin, the wires and skull protrusions dripping with black sweat. And I knew then what the second apparition of Synphel had claimed. *I loved Kloan.* Perhaps it was the thousand journeys together with her, perhaps it was because of something else I would never understand. But with love, reasons no longer matter. Somehow in all this madness, this wild, murderous, divine creature had grown within my heart and taken a place there —even if she had first appeared as a thief to steal me from Ambra Dawn.

But I no longer knew what Ambra was, what I had helped make her into. The earth woman I had loved so dearly seemed part of a universe buried under a mountain of lifetimes. The Ambra Dawn made known to me now— this goddess collective seeming to control time and space—was something more akin to the deities who had laid waste to this world. As much as anything else, Kloan was the only tangible, only *mortal* echo of Ambra I had left.

I caressed her face and brushed the hair out of her eyes. She stirred.

"Waythrel, please, we must leave now." She tried to sit up but failed. "Don't let me fall asleep again. I won't wake up a second time." Her breath was ragged. "Can you carry me to the gate?"

And so it came to this. I was being asked by this child, this instrument of the Anti designed to kill Ambra Dawn, to help her in her quest to destroy the Daughter. After witnessing attempt after attempt to kill or disable Ambra Dawn in passage after passage through the gate, I was asked to help the now helpless assassin, who only moments before had confessed of the ultimate goal of some kind of annihilatory murder. Because it was *good* for the universe. Because it would be a *creative destruction*.

I was asked to do this by a creature whom I now admitted to myself that I loved, a creature who had been aided directly on multiple occasions by Ambra herself in whatever existence she now resided. If I was to believe anything, this entire eternity of broken quests had been built and designed by Ambra for the soul purpose of Kloan achieving some cosmic education.

I could not comprehend their plan. I could not see into the depths of time and causality. I knew only too painfully that my very finite mind was helpless to know the truth in this matter. I had no ultimate confidence in my mental faculties to cut through this knot.

And so I did the only thing I could still do. I turned away from understanding. I accepted my inability to grasp what was unfolding before us. I looked instead to the love I had for both Kloan and Ambra and the trust they were placing in me. Whatever this was all about, they were in some demented kind of harmony. That was enough for me. Without any vision, with no idea where our feet would land except that it all seemed like madness, I closed my eyes and let myself fall into their arms.

"Here, let me get my other arms around you," I said, reaching underneath her and heaving her upward.

Kloan turned her red and green eyes to me, black crusts of mucus nearly sealing the eyelids shut. "Thank you, Waythrel. In the end, you'll understand."

I doubted that very much, but it did not matter. I was committed to something more than understanding. I steadied her on my midsection.

The small human girl was light in my arms, even after all the exhaustion from our climb and the debilitating environment. Slowly, unsteadily, I stepped toward the star-filled lake surface of the gate, the groans of the planet churning behind me like waves at the seashore.

She grasped my hand. "One last dance through the gate, dear Xix." She rested her head on my torso cone.

I stepped with her through the portal.

Part VII

In dust and law I watched my children born.
The gathering of clouds crept past my eyes,
and soon the shroud of hydrogen was shorn
by rays of light that sang the first day's rise.
   A fetus as a single grain of sand
that spins within a storm of desert winds,
through eons rendered life and sprouted land—
I smile through birth pangs that have yet to end.
Decrees the dust drove to some patterned dance,
the law that shapes my form and carves my bone,
soon molecules found purpose in their trance
to mold from mud new offspring of their own.
   These children stood to gaze into the womb
   and claimed to know their cradle and their tomb.

—Mazandarani, *Sonnets from the Desert*

Chapter 51

I have seen beyond the bounds of infinity and drawn down daemons from the stars. . . .I have harnessed the shadows that stride from world to world to sow death and madness. . .

H. P. Lovecraft

We stepped out backward through the gate, but despite superficial similarities, I immediately knew that something was different about this journey. The narrow, sloped pathway from the plains below stood before us. The well-known rock formations, only moments ago seemingly covered in soot and ash, surrounded us, whole and untarnished. But more than this, there was a profound sense of *change*.

Angled to look behind me, several of my eyes stared at the gate in wonder. Once pregnant with stars and honey, the disk was now empty. I could look straight through the circle to the rocky wall behind it. No churning star field. No bright suns of other worlds. Just air. The metal band of the disk, once glinting and alive, appeared rusted, decayed, the life force within the thing quenched.

I examined our bodies—the gel was missing. In stepping back through the gate a last time we had avoided carrying with us that bothersome coating. We were also clean of the ash and soot of the destroyed world. Where had it gone? I no longer cared to know the reasons. It was over. It seemed we had indeed come to an end of our recursive travels.

Whereas my heart soared for our escape from that repetitive hell, Kloan appeared all the more serious. Gone were the childlike bursts of energy and creativity that so often bubbled to the surface after we had completed a passage. Instead, her countenance was stern as she squinted into the afternoon light. I watched her play with an object in her robes like a nervous tic. She began to sweat.

"We need to get to higher ground, Waythrel."

Several eyestalks swiveled upward to glance at the rocky slope. The careening cliff face loomed over me from several angles vertiginously. "Why, Kloan? What is happening?"

She sighed and began to scan the walls of rock around us. "We're starting the endgame. Everything is going to come together now. I must bring all the gods to the nexus of time, to the discontinuity that shatters the smoothness of cosmic space-time." She bit her lower lip. "I know so *few* of them, and the ones I know are truly monsters. But we must start somewhere. I will summon them here."

Summon the gods here? Is she mad? "How can you do that?"

Her eyes settled on a high peak in the mountain range around us. "There. That will do. It's high, and there is enough space around it."

A force pulled me upward and my feet left the ground. Together we soared at an accelerating rate, the rocky surfaces speeding past only meters from our forms. The high peak she had indicated quickly grew in size.

"We should travel this way more often," I said, nervous energy running through me. "Avoid all that climbing."

"There isn't always need. It's good to use our bodies, you know."

"And now we have a need. What are you doing, Kloan?"

"I'm calling the gods to us, Waythrel. I told you. Don't think that they will always take the forms Rakshasi and Ambra assumed. Remember the ice world!"

We reached the summit. The air was colder and the oxygen levels almost dangerously low. I wondered if the strange skin suits would somehow compensate. If not, one of us was likely in danger of losing consciousness. I felt weak and tried to optimize my atmospheric intake.

"Rakshasi and the lesser gods will not do anything without Māra" she gasped slowly, bent double as she tried to breathe.

"Who is Māra?"

"Ambra mentioned her, countless cycles back, when she saved us from Rakshasi."

"It's a her?"

"Their queen. Gender has little meaning to these beings, but when they squeeze their consciousnesses into our pathetic languages, our small range of ideas and mental modes, strange things like gender or emotion or personality —things we believe we recognize only because our thinking is so constrained by our words—come out in the grinder, with as much resemblance to what was before as ground meat has to a running stag."

"How do you know this? How can you possibly know of this Māra queen?"

"I sampled the gods frozen in time. Don't you remember, Waythrel? I learned much and comprehended little. This is a collective, dominated by the powerful group mind of Māra. But the group is *not* a group mind. They fail to combine, to reach a harmonic synthesis. The gods here are too individualistic, too hateful and proud and selfish to truly merge—if those words appropriate for more simplistic creatures like us can be applied to beings like these. That's why they remain weaker than Ambra, forever adding linearly to their powers through numbers while she adds exponentially through true synergy."

"They seem powerful enough." I did not wish to meet these creatures if they were anything like Rakshasi.

"They are beyond us, no doubt!" said Kloan. "They are beyond the power of star systems. But they will come."

"You are very confident."

Kloan stared up into the sky, her equilibrium returning as she adapted to the altitude. "I can feel them all, Waythrel. There is a thread through me that disturbs all the gods. Remember? I can fully sense it, now. I will pluck that thread, that cosmic line to the singularity, like a string and rattle their universe rudely." She smiled, a hint of the mischievous child peeking through. "Sit with me, Waythrel?"

Kloan sat cross-legged, and I lowered myself beside her. She reached up and grabbed my upper arms, just as Ambra had done in a distant timeline, deeply buried in an infinite summation and lost forever. I pulled back, the similarity too disturbing, the ironies too strong.

"You can't hide anymore, Waythrel. You are integral to what comes next. And I need you far more than she did on Dram. What is coming, that which will soon surround us, makes ten thousand clones a field of flowers." She grasped my hands again tightly, staring into my eye clusters. "Keep your eyes closed. I mean that. No matter what happens, don't look at them!"

Madness. I locked my many digits around her own. I sent up a prayer to Ambra that she would watch over us. I felt like a small nymph naked before the onrushing sandstorm. I closed all my eyes tightly.

And then a pulse blasted through the universe.

It was unique in all the stirrings of my Reader senses. It was powerful and strange beyond anything I had felt or imagined, as if, along a thousand vectors in the multidimensional reality of space-time, a vibration as low as the deepest abyss and higher than the greatest peak imaginable exploded forward and propagated without the possibility of resistance. Frequency modulated in nested levels, containing a wealth of information that decoded itself as the wave smashed through my mind. This world. Kloan and myself. A challenge for the gods of Rakshasi and Māra. The destruction of Ambra Dawn. My mind constructed a visual of the pulse charging outward without diminishment in the signal strength, gaining speed as it progressed, gone before I could process it.

In vain I wondered how it might work, how long it would take to reach the intended targets, or if it even would. Uselessly I began to analyze whether it made any sense that these beings, even if they could hear this strange call, would come. Stupidly, I tried to justify why beings who had grown so far beyond us would heed the summons of an eight-year-old cyborg biped.

I had barely begun to initiate these thoughts when the gods arrived. It was as if time and distance had different application to these beings. Not daring to violate Kloan's directive, I kept my eyes firmly shut. I saw nothing. But I *felt* them. I felt them in multiple fashions, all of which rendered me small, insignificant, and completely terrified.

The ground shook with deep tremors. Blasts of air erupted around us from multiple directions due to the displacement of truly titanic volumes of atmosphere—it was like being caught in a storm or series of powerful explosions. My olfactory strips *smelled* them—at least the physical forms they had chosen for this incarnation. Their stench was overpowering, *hellish*, a nightmare of every scent of death and decay I could recall experiencing mixed with others that somehow were far worse.

But the greatest impact was in my mind. I might not have dared gaze upon their appearances and open the extensive neuronal pathways of my optical system to the insanity they undoubtedly presented, but strange echoes of their might and form invaded my mind. In the presence of these entities, I found myself for the first time cursing my Reader powers, desperately wishing that I were blind like so much of the universe. Ignorance was not bliss, I was sure of that. But knowledge could be torture.

In what I describe, in what I say, you must know that it comes to you only through the distorted lens of my mind and other senses, regurgitated through an imagination made nauseous. Drunk and staggering as from poison, my damaged memory fumbles ideas into this author's mind. His reception of them is mostly confused shock, and he operates like a malfunctioning machine, poorly picking vocabulary and syntax from your simplistic Earth languages that must serve as your bridge to my experience. Inadequate. Disfiguring. All of it, *lies*. But truly, even if it were possible for me to understand these things, I would not wish to. I know that my mind has not the strength to withstand such truth.

Whatever the ultimate reality, it felt to me as though there was a circle of them around the mountain peak on which we sat. Their forms burned and pressed on me from all sides, displacements in the air and thundering tremors testifying to their size, which I envisioned as larger than the mountain itself. I pictured their forms towering over us, a thousand eyes staring down in contempt upon two insignificant insects that dared clang a cosmic bell.

On Kloan's left was a presence I knew only too well—*Rakshasi*. I forced the dark currents of its essence away from me as much as possible, and yet it felt like I was being strangled by hundreds of snakes. Against my will, my mind formed a vision of the thing that had appeared, monumental yet lithe, slithering and darting like a salamander, yet devious and fanged like a fox, seven tails of flame behind it.

The center of power lay, however, directly behind me. I did not know this thing. I prayed never to know it. It swelled in my consciousness to a size that dwarfed all the other gods around us. It seemed ever to consume itself in fire, and like a creature of magma and smoke, it moved and dissolved, reformed and blurred, so that there was never a sure shape, never a point of reference, only the certainty of searing and choking death. A name was whispered in my deepest consciousness: *Māra*. It seemed as though sound spilled like a toxic smoke to strangle my mind. I grasped Kloan's hands in desperation.

And Kloan spoke. A childish, singsong voice chirped sarcastically in the burning wind around us. "You seem a few short, dear Māra, but the cosmic game is still very young, I suppose."

I felt her smile.

Chapter 52

I t took no great genius to see the madness in Kloan's words and that she had doomed herself for speaking with such insolence. In some intuitive place in my being, I felt Rakshasi coil to strike. I began to scream for Kloan in fear, but I was violently interrupted by Māra.

"Hold yourself, you *fool.*" The voice grated through my soul like razor wire. High and low, masculine and feminine, whispered and shouted, it was less a voice than a tool of torture. "Even you, are you blind to what has changed?"

The fox-lizard seemed to hiss in response. "We should have destroyed her before."

"Perhaps," came the voice of madness and death. "But that thread is gone. Great, great power surrounds her now, alien and incomprehensible. Strike her, and you may achieve our destruction." A breath like acid spilled over us. "Was that your goal, betrayer?"

I wondered that we were not instantly dissolved into a puddle of cellular debris. I barely kept focus, nearly falling into a primitive, self-preserving dormant state similar to a human coma. All my senses were overwhelmed, and I felt supremely grateful that I had not dared to glance upon these things. Through it all, somehow, Kloan held her own in the face of this monstrous, dark force. Only through her strength of will did I remain conscious.

Kloan spoke calmly. "My goal, my purpose from the first cell split from its progenitor, was and is to destroy Ambra Dawn. You know this. That's why you are here. Because in that goal, our paths are joined."

I felt the Māra-thing ease backward. I felt the chemical poison withdrawn.

"Continue," it said.

"Look at you all," Kloan said. I imagined her gesturing around us. "Galactic mountains that cower in fear because of her. Growing slowly like a cancer that cannot organize to do anything but devour. And hide. You will never defeat her!"

The collective hostility that squeezed in on us was suffocating. Kloan only laughed.

"You don't even understand *me*. Tiny little nothing me. I fart and shake your world strings and you appear like flaming gladiators, extraordinary and terrible. But you are nothing more than terrified worms diving into the dirt."

Again I felt the strike of Rakshasi, but this time I felt the physical response of Māra. My mind lost focus. There was only white noise. Then the horrific scene around me returned, and I felt the blood of Rakshasi spill over the mountain like a deluge drowning the world. Again, remember, these are mental metaphors. I truly don't know what happened. I'm sure that there was no blood. No drowned world. Only that Māra had punished a disciple. It was all my flayed mind could do with the impressions.

Kloan continued without missing a beat. "Your little club is not enough, will *never* be enough, and you know this. Only if we can convince the other gods, the thousands of powers elsewhere in the cosmos, to join our cause, can we summon the strength to defeat her."

Māra's tone was like brimstone. "And how might such an army defeat her?"

"It won't. *I* will."

"You will?" came another voice I did not recognize. I sought desperately to hide my mind from it. I had no strength of engage with another of these demons. Its words seemed to drip with blood and scorn, mockery and disbelief.

"Silence, Vetala," belched Māra. A playback of Kloan's pulse was driven through my mind. "Remember."

A morose silence seemed to fall on the spirits around me, and their mental fields retreated to places I could not access. For the briefest of dreams, it felt as if the sun had come out from behind a cloud.

"Yes," said Kloan. "*Remember*. Follow that line and see where it ends. At the beginning. And Ambra will be there."

There was a long silence. Deep in my being, I sensed undercurrents of power, dark dreams of thought flowing and connecting, jet streams mixing and turbulence building and ebbing. In the darkest corners of my psyche, I felt movement in a black abyss that I could not access except by dank rumor. And out of this darkness an eruption burst.

"Destroy her you can," boomed Māra. "Destroy us, you may, also."

The great queen of gloom seemed to approach us closely, a gigantic head and nightmarish visage only meters from our forms. Five slits opened in the face revealing lava within, and she sniffed deeply, the air pulling us nearly off balance. The mountain of fire before us growled like an earthquake.

"You reek with her stench, betrayer. She has coated you with her slime." There seemed to be a stirring of the other creatures around us, and a malevolent sludge rose from each point of space to pour over us, cold and barbed, hateful and sadistic. "Did she think Māra would not see? Did she think her powers so mighty? She may devour the weaker gods, but she will not so easily devour Māra!"

The thing roared like the shockwave of a supernova. Kloan spoke coldly, like a disappointed parent.

"No, you will not end that way. Instead you will persist in fugue—frozen, unmoving, unthinking—until the end of time that always approaches yet never arrives. I have seen it and looked upon your living corpse." The malignant swamp closing around us pulled back. It seemed even in the deranged visions of these gods, there was doubt. "Yes, you sense it, don't you? The creeping cold? The slow death that will consume you all?" Kloan seemed to raise her voice and the power of her mental projection. "We do not serve Ambra Dawn. She has tried to manipulate us, guide us for her own uses, but we have used her to reach this point. I hold a power now from outside this cosmos. Together, when we find the other gods, she cannot stop us, and I will reach the discontinuity!"

Māra laughed. "You think I cannot sense the lie in your voice? You are protected with a thousand layers of deceit. But we will not seek to break through it. Tell your puppet master that her trick was ingenious, but it has failed. Tell her in fire or in ice, we will resist her!"

Suddenly, my mind returned to me once more, and I awoke from a delirium. The vacuum of their absence rushed through me like a balm, revitalizing my thoughts and hopes. I foolishly opened my eyes to see Kloan again.

Except we were not alone. All the gods had vanished. All but one. Sitting beside us was not a titan, but an old man. It had taken the form of a human, likely in deference to Kloan, with a sage-like beard, bald head, withered body, and eyes that glowed like two red coals.

"There are others, great powers, older than we, who will perhaps listen," the figure spoke.

Kloan turned toward the god and nodded. "How are you to be named?"

"I have one thousand names on a million worlds. But you many call me

Vighneshvara." He continued, "Fools the others have become. The flaw in the cosmos is deeper than they wish to acknowledge."

"But you see it," said Kloan.

"It flays me alive," he said.

"These other gods—where are they?"

"Across the cosmos. Across time. Failed gods, but they failed far more along the path than our circle of pretenders. But we know them. We avoid them lest they crush us. But I will take you to them because it must be."

I whispered, "And then the gods themselves will carry you on their backs."

Kloan looked at me and squeezed my hand. "What was that, Waythrel?"

"Nothing," I said, dread and hope rising in me like bile. "Something I heard once. But it may have been only a dream."

Chapter 53

It was an All-in-One and One-in-All of limitless being and self—not merely a thing of one Space-Time continuum, but allied to the ultimate animating essence of existence's whole unbounded sweep—the last, utter sweep which has no confines and which outreaches fancy and mathematics alike.

H. P. Lovecraft

Traveling on the backs of gods has a lot going for it regarding ease of transport, but the destinations and cultures you meet along the way counterbalance that comfort with the distressingly fantastic. Vighneshvara placed two of his four arms on us, and instantly we were gone. How we journeyed, by what power or technology so advanced that it was only magic to our minds, I will never know. It nearly felt like a traversal through an Orb, only without the underlying depth, devoid of the presence of countless minds surrounding. Like the Orb traversals, descriptions are only impressionistic, and I can only say with confidence that at one moment we were on the mountain, and after an eye blink of light and distortion, we floated before the splendor of a vast, multicolored nebula.

I scanned quickly around us. There was no nearby star system, no planets, and no technological or living station to which we could descend. We were embedded in the emptiness of space, untethered to life support, unshielded from cosmic radiation. Yet we neither roasted nor froze nor suffocated. Due to Ambra's hand or the power of this god, our fragile fleshly forms were protected.

Behold, Aditi!

The voice of Vighneshvara resounded in my mind.

I again scanned all around us, but I saw nothing. I reached out to Ambra. *In the nebula?*

No, Waythrel, Aditi is the nebula.

The god is a nebula?

Vighneshvara seemed impatient. *The goddess can be anything in this cosmos that she might want. She prefers to assume this form, this gaseous mixture of dust and young stars spanning twenty parsecs, and has remained as such since before your ancestors learned to speak. She is one of the oldest. Once, long ago, she mothered the formation of many group minds, many assemblies, even those that grew to rebel and disown her. But no longer. She retreats to her own, unfathomable cogitations. Yet her mind shaped a thousand gods who roam the stars. If she will come, so will many, and a great force we will have acquired.*

Do you think she will listen? asked Kloan.

If not to you, then to no one. Once, when the threat of the Ambra abomination became clear, we sought her advice. Māra sent a contingent of powers to beseech her to stand against this force devouring the cosmos. But the rest of us experienced a terrible cry through the corridors of space-time, and minds of these emissaries ceased. We never again found a single trace that they had ever existed.

This appeared to be suicide. It seemed clear that Vighneshvara would not even be able to protect himself here, and this murderous cloud would snuff out two motes of dust as Kloan and myself without so much as a cosmic scream. I reached beside me and grasped Kloan's hand.

Don't worry, Waythrel. This is where I am supposed to be.

Vighneshvara began to change form. The old man's skin seemed to form fissures, bright light erupting from the split tissue and bone, consuming the fleshly facade in brilliance. Shedding the skin like a snake, out of that chrysalis burst a winged delusion, a hallucinogenic concoction of wings and tails and arms and one hundred glowing eyes. The size of it quickly overshadowed our forms, spanning first hundreds and then thousands of meters, until it nearly eclipsed the angular spread of the nebula itself.

But I knew this to be an optical hoax. The nebula was still some great distance away, millions of miles until the vacuum of space would begin to be disturbed by the first measurable density of hydrogen. The winged divinity before us was truly only a small speck before the leviathan we approached. A moth approaching far too close to the flame.

"*Aditi!*" he cried.

I use the syntax of your written speech unusually in what follows, because the mental projections that flowed from these gods transcended anything I had known in telepathy. So forceful and powerful were the projected thoughts, so immediate and compelling were the ideas, that your written language, the use of italics to indicate thinking as per your conventions, utterly fail to convey the experience. Ironically, although not a sound was emitted in this exchange, having this author present it as if mouths spoke and ears heard translates the nonverbal experience more accurately.

"YOU HAVE BROUGHT THE DESTROYER." A voice emanated from everywhere around us. Kloan floated away from me, past the gigantic wingspan of Vighneshvara, and hovered above and before him. *"YOU WERE ALWAYS THE WISEST OF MY CHILDREN, VIGHNESHVARA."*

Vighneshvara bowed and tucked his wings around his body. The bright light radiating from him dissipated. It was replaced by a growing incandescence from the nebula itself. My eyes could have been deceiving me, but it nearly appeared as though this multiparsec-spanning galactic entity was shrinking impossibly fast, curling in from the edges and coalescing toward a single focal point. At that point floated Kloan.

And then, when I thought we could only be subsumed by the grandeur of this goddess, Kloan herself began to glow. An iridescence seemed to bubble from her body like a fog, spilling tendrils into the surrounding space. The nebula continued to rapidly shrink.

Dusty and colorful protrusions of the thickening cloud reached outward toward her. From myriad directions, tens, perhaps hundreds of nebulaic limbs extended as from a cosmic octopus, their internal structure a churning of constrained sandstorms. They halted around the growing and increasingly impenetrable brilliance of Kloan, forming a three-dimensional shell of probing digits.

"THERE ARE INFINITIES WITHIN INFINITIES WITHIN AND WITHOUT YOU, UNIVERSES WITHIN COSMOS, EONS WITHIN TIMELESSNESS. THERE IS THE SHATTERING OF ALL THAT IS AND THE BIRTH OF ALL THAT SHOULD HAVE BEEN. THERE IS THE HAND OF THE GREAT GODDESS AND THE KNIFE OF THE DEEPEST BETRAYER."

The voice entered me from all directions and nowhere again. I was unmade and overwhelmed, melted in a hurricane of prepotency that seemed to break down every structure of my person and reassemble it according to an alien purpose. The voice was both more terrible than the howls of the demon Māra and more sublime than the deepest love I had ever experienced. It seemed to me as though here, now, and forever I had reached all that Waythrel of Xix could ever imagine to be. I felt the need for my continued consciousness removed. I believed that this was the end of my existence, that it was near, and that only in the hearing of such a voice was my life indeed made complete.

"YOU WILL BRING THE MULTITUDE TO THE VORTEX." It was a statement.

Yes, came the whisper of Kloan's mind.

The wings of Vighneshvara burst open, and a third light joined the radiance of Kloan. Violating the laws of physics, the nebula was gone, completely condensed at a speed faster than light; ultradense emissions from the resulting planet-sized structure glowed brightly.

"MY LOYAL VIGHNESHVARA, THEN WE SHALL BOTH DROWN IN THE

COMING ANNIHILATION TOGETHER, AND FOR THE FIRST TIME, YOU WILL TRULY BE REBORN."

And in a blinding flash, the nebula-sphere was gone. Gone was the once-lavish tapestry of powder and light, color and contrast, spread across trillions of light-years. An empty darkness now surrounded us, barely punctured by the pinpricks of starlight from distant suns. The greatest emptiness could be felt in the realm of the soul, where a profound, cosmic spirit was suddenly absent.

The majestic and monstrous space butterfly scooped up the dimming Kloan in one hand and glided toward me, grasping me gently in another of its fifty limbs. Vighneshvara spoke within our minds.

She gathers now her children. Near and far. She will return with a great gathering.

She needed no persuading, my leaky thoughts spilled outward.

I felt the equivalent of a laugh from the mind of Vighneshvara. *Aditi is not Māra. Or like anything else you might find in this universe. All that has come or is coming opens itself for her to read.*

Kloan's thoughts were troubled. *But it is not enough. Even if she brings a thousand. You don't understand what Ambra has become.*

Not enough, responded Vighneshvara, *but nearly so with Aditi. There are others we will visit.*

And who or what is next? I wondered anxiously.

The stars around us began to blur as I sensed Vighneshvara begin another journey through space and time. *The root of much that lives within this cosmos. She touches on all the origins of souls.*

The stars careened around me.

Chapter 54

God is infinite, so His universe must be too. Thus is the excellence of God magnified and the greatness of His kingdom made manifest; He is glorified not in one, but in countless suns; not in a single earth, a single world, but in a thousand thousand, I say in an infinity of worlds.

a heresy of Giordano Bruno, burned at the stake in 1600

We hovered above a blue and green world. Earthlike, yet different, filled with dense vegetation, the atmosphere pregnant with the expelled gases of respiration. I searched frantically for an Orb. I did not know how I could handle encountering Ambra in the middle of this cosmic plot to destroy her—a plot I could not accept in my heart and yet seemed compelled by her and others to assist. But there was no Orb, which implied, to my understanding, no intelligent life. Why we had come to a world devoid of sentience baffled me.

We need to find a tributary, came the thoughts of Vighneshvara.

We sped down into and over the world, our forms insulated from the vacuum of space, the heat of atmospheric entry, even the potentially toxic gases from utterly alien metabolisms. The hundred eyes of Vighneshvara swiveled across the surface of the world, seeking, focused on the identification of something within this densely overgrown jungle world overflowing with vegetative life. His search was not random, and yet his destination did not seem foreknown to him. Instead, he seemed to sense his prey, *smell* it like a hunter, lock in on it like a missile, following some trail invisible to us toted mortals.

Soon our direction changed dramatically. We dove into a particularly thick region of plant forms. From an initial cloud-topped canopy of astonishingly tall arboreal growth, we plunged through layer upon layer of botany, vegetative ecosystem on top of ecosystem, passing one hundred different strata, glimpsing for fleeting moments a million different life forms packed together at inconceivable densities with incomprehensible diversity.

Onward we descended, the air thickening, moisture deepening, illumination waning. Faintly, I began to sense it—a tingling in my Reader senses—the stirring of distortions in space-time that only accompanied great power of an unusual nature. Closer and closer we zeroed in on this emission, dodging limb and leaf, often the plant forms themselves making way inexplicably for our passage. The light of the local star was nearly extinguished at this depth, the overlaying atmosphere of plant life absorbing all the radiance until the species at this level, like the animals in the depths of the New Earth seas, were devoid of color, subsisting on other means of energy than direct starlight.

As we slowed and neared the surface, the sense of the power reached a zenith. Before us, all the plant life seemed to converge on a single point, or rather, it seemed that from a single point came some powerful surge of vitality animating all around it. At the physical center of this force was a gnarled, bark-covered knot the size of a small hill. The air around it seemed to throb.

"Can you feel it, Waythrel?" asked Kloan.

"Yes. What is it?"

Vighneshvara thoughts replied. *The tip of a first root.*

We hovered above the mossy hill of bark. He curled in his wings slightly and his many legs touched down softly on the surface of the enormous knot. We remained suspended within two of his many arms while his wingtips bent downward and caressed the living root. The action sent faint ripples through my mind. The dense growth around us seemed to sway and sigh.

Yakshini, said Vighneshvara. *She will let us pass.*

"Pass where?" I asked.

Kloan pointed excitedly. "The root, Waythrel. Look!"

The gnarled stump began to glimmer. A sparkling dust seemed to hover about it, and the dimness of our environment was invaded with light. Instantly, thousands of opportunistic flying plants rushed into the area, nearly blinding us, their forms diverse and impossible to understand in these short sightings, their biology obviously attuned to the powerful light source that captivated us now.

I was underwhelmed. *"That* is Yakshini? It is a god? A root stub? A plant?"

Yes and no, came the thoughts of Vighneshvara. *She is a god; her physical raiment was chosen as a plant, the greatest tree and vine in the cosmos, a form she has held for so long that it is likely she can no longer escape it unharmed. But this is only a tip. Her roots dig through space and time, connecting world beyond world, age beyond age, deep into the deep past, far into the distant future she extends her vascularity until the worlds of the coming* then *grow too cold.*

It seemed as though the space around the root knot warped. I felt a fissure opening. "I don't understand. Kloan, what does this mean?"

Kloan smiled, a look of childish awe on her face. "Life, Waythrel. So much life! One of the greatest and oldest sources of life in our universe. We found the outer shell of her web and will ride the roots to the core."

Ride the roots to the core? Of what?

But I had no time for my thoughts. A tunnel opened before us, and a blast of swampy air swept past from the channel in space-time. But it was not empty! Extending from the glowing tip that protruded into this world, a thick, gnarled shaft plunged directly into the depths and disappeared. Vighneshvara opened his wings and looped in the air, angling us downward toward the opening, his army of eyes focused forward. Curling my own eyestalks in panic, I last glimpsed a blur of the jungle around us as he dove fearlessly downward and along the root's path.

Chapter 55

We used to think that if we knew one, we knew two, because one and one are two. We are finding that we must learn a great deal more about "and".

Arthur Stanley Eddington

Light dimmed, the impossible, interplanetary root revealed only by the glowing wings of the god towing us wildly through this interdimensional passage. I cast several eyes behind and watched as the portal to the other world, a disk of blue and green light flaring in radiance as this darkness enveloped us, shrank, and winked out of existence as we sped along the living chord.

The growth was impossibly long. Even through the shortcut of hyperspace, we seemed to fly along its length for several minutes at high speed. No true organism could maintain the necessary hydrostatic pressure on such scales. Of course, no simple, mortal organism could open a wormhole, apparently multiple wormholes, throughout space and time and use those as some sort of pandimensional growth matrix connecting worlds uncounted. I felt suddenly, deeply, profoundly ignorant of the history and nature of our cosmos as well as the state of my own sanity.

As these thoughts danced through my mind, a bright disk appeared ahead, and we burst out into another world. All around us were plant forms innumerable, of bizarre shape, function, color and texture, tending toward a shade of dark blue and likely adapted to the starlight of whatever system we had entered. The tentacle of bark, ever thickening as we traversed the wormhole, erupted out of the ground like a redwood tree and snaked along the ground toward a mountain of vegetative material.

Vighneshvara spread his wings wide, and we caught the planetary airs powerfully, gliding along the god-root as it plunged into thick forests and disappeared from sight, only to reappear as it scaled the less densely covered rise of a steep mountain. Of course, all was relative, and what seemed a sparsely covered challenger to Everest was still coated by plant growth that would have rivaled the deepest regions of the Amazon.

From multiple directions I saw other giant arteries of bark converge on the mountain and follow a similar course up the structure. We soared upward, Vighneshvara beating his glowing god-wings, clouds of water and floating vegetation passing alongside us.

At the top of the mountain was a surreal botanic junction. Six massive roots scaled the mountain, or rather extended down the mountain after splitting off from a central node. I guessed what would happen next.

We hovered above the node, and it seemed to sense our presence. A brilliant radiance shone from the bark, and once again a tunnel into nothing and nowhere opened before us. This time it was far larger, and the root that dove into the emptiness had begun to assume proportions that were beyond any plant life I had ever known.

Into the portal we sped again, careening over the god's limb, grasped tightly by our divine moth, two parasitic mites holding on for dear life. Although the root may have grown slightly, by the time we burst from the wormhole into the orange light of yet another world, it was clear that the size increase had been sharply curtailed. Again I realized that the direction of our journey was biasing my thoughts on the plant form and that what had happened was a dramatic *decrease* in size toward the extremities of the god in the earlier worlds we had first encountered.

I won't continue to repeat the similar crossings we made in this way, from new world to new world, each devoid of an Orb, empty of intelligent life, brimming instead with a vibrant ocean of unconscious growth. We experienced blinding vistas of biology rushing underneath us, descending again and again into ever-widening excavations in space-time until, as we leapt through the final portal, we flew over an arm of bark and moss that was no longer believable, no longer possible, that was so large and titanic that it had instead entered into the realm of the deities, the isolated group minds of god-things that bent—and broke—all the rules of science I knew.

And we only advanced along a humdrum vein, dwarfed by many others, one of millions I saw dive into portals uncountable, rushing off to worlds unseen, carrying unfathomable amounts of nutrients to irrigate, fertilize, and stimulate entire networks of life across the universe.

All the roots converged on a central core, a living form that possessed the attributes of all the vegetative life I had witnessed in our journey and yet embodied them in manners unique and profound. I could not call it a tree or any other name for a plant that you might know, because it would utterly distort the nature of this goddess's incarnation. Whatever it might be named, it rested on the surface of an artificial world composed of rock and soil and water, defying the organizing principles of gravity, held together as a bowl of material with the radius of our solar system. A dizzying array of stars spun about the mass, seemingly grabbed and positioned purposefully in order to maintain the energy sources needed to sustain this impossible ecosystem.

Vighneshvara soared toward the god-plant, climbing higher and higher into the thick atmosphere of this synthetic world. Upon a stratum of branches and leaves that spanned a surface greater than a New Earth continent, we landed, touching down close to the colossal bulk of a main stem of the entity. Vighneshvara folded his wings within himself and stepped forward slowly to the wall of bark and other, unknowable plant skins.

"Yakshini," he whispered.

The surface rippled. The bark cracked and melted, snapped, and reformed with the unintended violence the small encounter from the truly titanic. A sphere with a radius as large as ten of the tallest trees of New Earth protruded from the hulk and took on features our limited forms could recognize. They were humanoid. Eyes of cellulose, a mouth of leaves, features vaguely similar to those of some odd average of all of humanity's peoples. Again I assumed all this was for Kloan.

"Yakshini has heard the last call of Aditi," the mouth blasted in gales of wind at us. "The sleeping mother gathers her brood and requests the presence of Yakshini at the nexus in time, where the usurper-thief awaits with her infinite impostors."

Vighneshvara spoke reverently. "And what is Yakshini's will in this?"

The plant face thundered, "That Yakshini will heed the call. That she will retract all life roots, cast uncountable worlds to the darkness, and wound herself beyond repair for a final battle. She wishes that Yakshini help crush the evil that has stolen everything from her."

Chapter 56

Common human laws and interests and emotions have no validity or significance in the vast cosmos-at-large. To me there is nothing but puerility in a tale in which the human form—and the local human passions and conditions and standards—are depicted as native to other worlds or other universes. One must forget that such things as organic life, good and evil, love and hate, and all such local attributes of a negligible and temporary race called mankind, have any existence at all. When we cross the line to the boundless and hideous unknown—the shadow-haunted Outside—we must remember to leave our humanity—and terrestrialism at the threshold.

H. P. Lovecraft

I t was at this point that I feared I could no longer continue in this journey. Over and over I had begun to hear Ambra and her collective slandered. These powerful beings, manifestations of colossal group intelligences of which my mind would constitute but an atom of the whole, entities that I knew I could not possibly apprehend, had repeatedly cast her actions in the vilest terms. The Orbs—those guardians every Xix loved and considered ancient benefactors of all sentient life—underwent a terrible transformation in the minds and words of these beings. Without exception, they had inverted and condemned all I had held dear.

Whatever Ambra was asking of me, whatever Kloan had cryptically revealed in her metaphysical ramblings, it was too much for me. I did not have the strength both to betray my dearest friend and forsake all that I had believed to be true. Foolishly, I challenged the gods.

"Is it mere jealousy that turns you all against her? Isn't it true that hundreds of gods have joined her, that their unions are based on trust and love, on mutual respect? Do you refuse to join for pride or avarice? Are you unable to merge with her because your minds lack humility or love?"

The plant-god focused its mind on me, freezing my thoughts in its attention. "Wayward Waythrel of Xix, how Yakshini nursed your forebears in the glassy sands! How she teased growth from a land hostile to everything that lives, labored eons in the parched and tortured dunes of your star-drenched world, and tended the saplings that evolved, became, and metamorphosed into the first nymphs of intelligence. How she loved you, dear children."

I stood there stunned. "What do you mean?"

"You have seen her works! You have witnessed the abundance of life on myriad worlds, life that was and is and will be planted and nursed by Yakshini. What more is there to understand?" Enormous arms erupted from the trunk of the plant and surrounded us, as in an embrace, halting only meters from our bodies. "Yakshini is your Mother, Waythrel. The Mother of all Xix."

"*You?* You were the Gardener?" It seemed everything would be upended.

"You exist only because of Yakshini, Xix," said Vighneshvara, his demeanor grave, his fiery eyes condemning my outburst.

It couldn't be. How could I know truth from falsehood in this place of gods whose simplest thoughts burned my mind? "But the Orb! It has always been there! Didn't it, didn't Ambra, bring us to sentience?"

"The Orb was not always there," came the booming voice of the tree, the arms around us withdrawing and slowly disappearing, absorbed into the bulk of the plant. "But the limbs of Yakshini were there when the usurper arrived. At the nascent budding of minds in the new animals that had formed on Xix, darkness fell." The face contorted, and it seemed the very light around us dimmed. "The demon ball, the *Orb* and its legions, took Xix from Yakshini. The hell-thing burned her roots into the time corridors and backward, until leaf and branch of her body withered and perished on your world. The cursed god then did what it would with your minds, and Yakshini was left childless and wounded."

"Why would she do that?" It was too horrible to contemplate.

"Because of arrogance. Because she claimed Yakshini could not nurse full and fruitful intelligence. Because she said the mother's role had been played and must be surrendered to her for the next step of evolution. Because the foul beast hungered to devour all minds."

"Was this true? Could you not do what she could?"

Darkness fell sharply, and a hostile wind rocked my form. "Who decides, worm? Who gave the thief such authority? Who owns the minds? The souls and thoughts born from the womb of another? What over-god does this thing declare itself to be to decide that the minds cultivated by Yakshini are unfit to exist?"

Part of me realized that my words were suicidal, but I said them anyway.

"Ambra has shepherded the minds of millions of developing species and has preserved their minds at death! She has proven her worth! What have you done?"

"Yakshini has her children, but they are few and scattered. The thief took all the rest, violated her very tissues in space and time, stealing untold numbers of children from their mother. After many battles lost and many deep injuries, Yakshini retreated to the worlds without minds, working to keep them so, stifling sentience so that the thief of her children would never steal them again."

The horrors of this cosmic conflict were spreading before my mind like a wasteland of carnage. The god had created life on millions of worlds, only now to abort future minds because they would not remain hers. "But have you saved any of the souls you have created?" I lashed out desperately, my faith in everything shaken, my foundations of hope and security crumbling before this beautiful nightmare of life, mind, war, and loss.

"And Xix, who decides that they need saving, and how?"

"Can't you see, Waythrel?" said Kloan. "You have helped create a true monster, a beautiful monster that all but the most powerful minds will love, because she is lovable. But nothing is ever as it seems. True love does not dominate. The cosmos cannot be established on a god-particle so narrowly nucleated by one mind. All is unbalanced; even in the deep love and harmony they possess, you watch them enact affectionate banditry and murder of the dreams and lives of others. All performed by a nearly omnipotent being utterly convinced of its own righteousness." Kloan grasped my hands. "She *must* be destroyed. *Some* balance, however imperfect, *must* be returned to the cosmos."

Nothing made sense. Even if what they said had merit—and my mind spun in confusion over those points—it did not fit with what had taken us here in the first place. Ambra had initiated it. Ambra had guided us, educated Kloan, and prepped her for a great quest. Why would she lay the groundwork for her own destruction? That was lunacy!

The titanic mouth spoke again. "Your mind is a prisoner to her labyrinths of thought, as is even this clone. But we can see the singularity. We can see that by means hidden in the discontinuity, she can destroy Ambra Dawn. That is why you are here."

"Me? Why?"

"Because you are nothing but the cell of a greater mind, and yet you helped give birth to this monstrosity. Your mind and its patterns are etched throughout its structure. When you and the clone reach the singularity, all will be unmade."

And so my role was revealed at last. The confounding purpose for my selection to this absurd, insane voyage uncovered. I was nothing more than some sort of weapon, a foundation of thoughts that they would use to unmake what I had helped design.

Because of all that had happened, I had anticipated some terrible, murderous role for Kloan in all this. I had been prepared for it by direct observation of countless events in our recursive time trap. But I had never suspected that I would *myself* be central to killing her whom I loved. I felt my heart breaking.

"She whom you loved is no more, Xix," said Vighneshvara, appropriating my thoughts and affording me no dignity.

"But you said you didn't understand how she would be destroyed. How do you know I'm required?" I looked for some hope of escape from this terrible sentence.

The giant god shook us again with words. "You speak rightly. We cannot see into the singularity, and that is the fear that drives the other gods to flee. But we can stare at that horror in time and see both of you in it, both of you integral to its final resolution—the unmaking of Ambra Dawn."

Vighneshvara turned his searing eyes to Kloan. "Your mind holds a map, a key—a path you believe will reach the nexus."

Kloan nodded, turning away from me to face the deities. "Ambra will defend. The devil ball is powerful beyond imagining. But with enough of the gods, the great and the small, together we can rend that mental structure, rip through layers and layers of minds and guards, and open a broad shaft into the depths of the thing, to Ambra Dawn herself." A thousand images flooded between Kloan and the gigantic beings around us. I could process almost nothing of it.

"Yes," said Yakshini. "How came you to this when the gods themselves could not see it?"

"She has trained me, guided me, tried to use me. I was close to her mind. I saw the way. Not immediately, or she may have destroyed me. I could not understand it in the beginning. I do not fully understand now. But I sense that you do. You can use my thoughts."

The great goddess spoke coldly. "Yakshini will hurt her, even as Yakshini dooms herself. When Yakshini withdraws her extremities, oceans of worlds will cease to have ever brought forth life. Then the offender will lose souls innumerable, to a great weakening of her power."

"But not enough," said Kloan.

"No," said Yakshini. "Not enough. All the other gods will be needed. And in the visions of your mind, they will puncture a passage through her walls and deliver a poison to end her before she began."

Chapter 57

Where were you when I laid the foundation of the earth? Tell me, if you have understanding. Who laid its cornerstone, when the morning stars sang together and all the heavenly beings shouted for joy? Have you commanded the morning since your days began, and caused the dawn to know its place? Can you bind the chains of the Pleiades or loose the cords of Orion? Have the gates of death been revealed to you? Where is the way to the dwelling of light and where is the place of darkness?

The Book of Job

I felt sick. I looked deep into my thoughts and tried to conjure images of Ambra as I had known her, extract memories from the seemingly infinite layers of remembrance that had been deposited within me over a concluded eternity. Moments when we had found her ravaged body on the smuggler's ship, near death, her psionic potentiality released in random bursts of power from a dying mind. I remembered her in the cell on Dram, tears on her face, incisions in her abdomen from their desecration of her body, their theft of her progeny, where the doom of the universe to a seemingly unending supply of demonic clones was assured. I recalled her soaring above the chaos of a nascent and naive group mind as she steered us into the past to awaken and call forth the latent human Readers to rescue their planet. On and on, for hundreds of years, always beside me so that she became something beyond a friend—a soul as near to my own as could have been.

I was sick at this talk of destroying her. I couldn't hear another word spoken against her. Whatever she had become at my hands and others, whatever she had done or not done, it was enough for me. My heart was devoted to her—yes, even to follow her command to kill her. But let it stop there! Let there be no more words of it! No more bile and hate and acid thrown her way!

Kloan interrupted my raging thoughts and bowed before these spiteful gods. "Now there is one last thing I must do."

Yakshini rumbled. "Aditi calls. She leads a multitude. It is time all the gods gathered."

"Yes, all of them, or what numbers you can bring," said Kloan.

"We will bring many," said Vighneshvara.

Kloan shook her head. "Not enough. Not enough of the greater gods." She turned to Yakshini. "You are the first awakened, the mother-goddesses. Deepest, oldest, most profound titans of the cosmos. But your children, and the others that became—from them a number developed into great beings, terrible and broken, lost in their madness. But great. They must be summoned. I will bring them."

Vighneshvara stepped toward her, a mountain towering over a small tree, a tone of suspicion in his voice. "Beginning now, you will follow the goddess and accompany her to the nexus. The lies of Ambra within you will not sabotage our plans."

"And let you fail? Why would I do that?" said Kloan, addressing Yakshini. "We *need* Māra and her crazy clan. At the end of time, they have become a great host, a great power waiting to be woken." Images of the ice world poured from her mind, and before them even these gods were silent for a time.

"At the end of time," echoed Vighneshvara.

"I have been there," Kloan said, pulling her hand out of her robe. A bright light dispelled the gathered gloom and bathed the gods in a radiation utterly foreign to our universe. "I have been given the key. Now I understand why it must be used."

Yakshini spoke. "This disciple of the enemy is correct. But I detect deviousness within deviousness in her words and thoughts, colored and tainted with the manipulations of Ambra Dawn. But we dare not break her mind open and thereby risk everything."

Vighneshvara hissed icily, "It may not be necessary to fully break."

The ball of light blazed forth like a supernova. I cowered behind Kloan's shadow, my eyestalks retreating to the safety of my torso cone, my mind blanked by the emissions bathing us. Before I hid, I heard the scream of Vighneshvara and glimpsed him hiding within his wings. Even Yakshini howled in protest.

But the light only grew until it became more than light; it became a sound of its own, drowning out the cries of others, even deities, flattening thoughts and emotions themselves. Through it all, only the voice of Kloan could be heard.

"Break me if you can, god-fools," she said, a divine power seeming to emanate from her words. "But leave me be to finish the task. I will bring back your wayward broods. I will reach in and draw them out from the cosmic permafrost."

A great wind rose around us, circling like a cyclone. I tried to open my eyes, to squint against the devastating rays that promised to blister existence. I could no longer see Yakshini or Vighneshvara. The whirlwind had created a wall of debris and seemingly solid air around us, branches and leaves and rocks and soil blasting past at supersonic speeds. I clung desperately to Kloan's robes with four arms, my two feet digging their digits into the soil covering the top of the branch floor. I tried to crouch as low as possible, my Xixian limbs allowing for my towering frame to bend slightly below Kloan's head.

As the tornado roared and strengthened around us, she stood unmoving, her sparse hair flying about madly, her arm raised upward, holding a blinding star. It felt as if the world began to turn on its side, and I watched the maelstrom of debris bend and focus above us. A vortex formed, another wormhole, and the turbulence poured into it. I felt the ground below me rattle, tear, and then detach completely from the supporting plant limbs. We shot upward together and plunged headfirst into the chaotic whirlpool.

Chapter 58

I am the Self seated in the hearts of all creatures. I am the beginning, the middle and the end of all beings. With a single fragment of Myself I pervade and support this entire universe.

Bhagavad Gita

"I'm *really* starting to like this thing," said Kloan as she rolled the rapidly dimming sphere between her hands. "But that was a close one! Nearly lobotomized back there."

My eyestalks unraveled, and I looked around. We were back on the dead world. The crystal ball reached a nadir, but it was still bright enough to cast the entire statued museum of gods in a false moonlight. I strained my eyes—above and around us the telltale signs of the dome reappeared, encompassing the breadth of the deities as well.

"What happened?" I managed.

Kloan sighed and walked up to the plinth, the towering forms of Māra and her pack seeming to glare down upon us with loathing. "See, they *know* Waythrel. It's damned nigh impossible to fool big god-things. If it weren't for the fact that Ambra is so powerful and a thousand times more devious, I'm not sure what would have happened. They would have found out everything. They wouldn't have understood the need and the endpoint because they are so desperately addicted to destroying *her*."

"I don't understand." I was too tired to offer anything else. I yearned desperately for the warmth and love that Ambra had promised me, or I dreamed that she had promised in yet another delusional trek from yet one more lost chronology.

"Well, they wouldn't have just let me leave with all their doubts. Worst-case scenario, I was just going to go back to report their plans to Ambra. Ha!" barked Kloan, placing the sphere into the bowl. "As if Ambra hadn't orchestrated every last part of all of this! Can you call gods morons?" She stared earnestly at me. The ball began to brighten again, and the light distracted her. "If I wasn't learning bit by bit how to tap into the power of this thing, I wouldn't have been able to create a wormhole that they couldn't close."

"Ambra orchestrated? Are you on her side now?" Hope was not part of the question. It was only exhausted bewilderment.

Kloan turned to me sadly. "Poor Waythrel, you need a long sleep, one without any more nightmares. But it's almost done. The last pieces almost in place. Let's just wake these bastards up now and close the deal."

One by one, she walked the ring, touching the surfaces of the glass that was not glass, of the ice that was not water. I watched at a distance from the center of the ring beside the sphere. By each she paused, her hand in place on the rippling material, the light from the artifact casting specific directional luminosity toward the appropriate tower. Abandoning one and striding to the next, the monolithic form behind her would begin to melt, the crystal dissolving like some molten steel and dripping to the frozen ground below. Soon, the first cryogenic tombs she touched thinned enough to release their contents, odd mixtures of smoke and light, screams and voices, all mixed within my Reader senses to the awareness of awakening minds. Those minds quickly matured to their malicious and unfathomable natures, and I cowered even closer to the shining sphere.

Kloan completed the circumference and then stepped back to the center of the god-ring, watching the titans lumber from their cosmic coma. A horror crept over me as they emerged. I felt the demonic personalities vividly, their caustic essence stirring memories from previous and equally terrible encounters. I prayed to Ambra that Kloan could control them.

Kloan lifted the crystal sphere, and its light ripped through the space in front of us. The gods bent and shielded themselves from the awesome incandescence. At that moment, the ground shook, and in a reversal of previous memories from this lifeless world, molten globules pushed their way out of the ice-bed beneath us. As thousands of tongues of quicksilver, they sprinted toward a focal point behind Kloan and aggregated, self-assembled, and coalesced into the ice guardian that had gifted the light to Kloan. The final fusion of that hulk snapped as a deafening crack of ice, the retort echoing throughout the dome-encased atmosphere.

"Godlings!" cried Kloan. "It is time to reconsider my offer and join me at the singularity!"

The guardian behind stood massively still, while the other titans shifted and strained through the brilliance. At last, the largest stepped forward. I recognized the form from my visions before, but now beholding the thing with open eyes, I knew that these gods had been humbled indeed. Before—in that past so distant from this present as to be unreachable even to Kloan's powers—I believe I would have perished to look fully on her. But now, I was able to survive a ghostly remnant brought low by the terrible power of time. Yet still she stood indomitable, defying the light, smoke and magma boiling within her veins. *Māra*. She stopped in front of Kloan.

"You have won, and I curse you for it. But gods greater than I have cursed you far more diabolically than I might ever dream. I will take that pleasure in bending my knee to you, insect. I will know that I help them cruelly bring your final destruction."

"Glad to see you too, Māra," said Kloan, a glint in her eye. "I assume you have these monkeys on your leash?"

"And if I didn't? Do you think they don't feel the alien flame you brandish before us? Do they not see the thousand ice-blades of the giant behind you?" Māra reared back and opened her mouth to the black heavens and screamed. Fire belched upward and rained hot coals around us. The cry was the sound of a million souls raked over by a fiend's claws. I watched the dome shatter at its apex. Flickering mats of a force field plunged to the ground and evaporated before our eyes. "Have we not all perished everlastingly in these shells of stillness?"

Trembling, I continued to gaze upward. The dome seemed to be healing itself. Before me, Kloan seemed unfazed. "Good. Then they know what is coming."

Māra turned two flaming eye sockets toward us. "Do *you* know what is coming?"

Kloan winked at this demon from the deepest pit of hell, her eyebrow arched, mock surprise dancing over her features. "Why in heaven would I want to ruin *that* surprise?"

Chapter 59

A great plane of sand surrounded us. For a brief moment, I dared to think that we had been transported to Xix, the thought of my home-world comforting in the chaos of this displacement. But the sands were wrong, the silica of a different composition, granularity, and color. A brief glance upward to the sky dispelled all desperate notions of home. The heavens roiled with light and patterns so intricate and hallucinogenic that I knew immediately we were not on any world within any possible space in our universe.

Scanning the horizon, the full truth hit me solidly. Rising like an arrow into the deranged firmament above us was an artificial structure towering tens of thousands of feet. It ended in a point that seemed to drink the very clouds that swirled like a vortex around it. At the base of this grand tower was a small city in the desert whose buildings I recognized, whose walls I had once lived decades within upon a resurrected world. It was the Temple city.

"Kloan, what is this place? It is not New Earth, and yet it is."

Kloan glanced around with satisfaction. "She draws us deeply into herself. Even so, I feel the final path to her will be most terribly bent."

"Kloan, please, where are we?"

"Temple City, Waythrel," said Kloan. "The real city itself. Have you forgotten your own final plan? The detachment of the city and the Dish from New Earth that would travel through the cosmos?"

"I had imagined something different. What has happened to the sky?"

"The fires of creation filtered through the light of a trillion souls."

"More mysticism," I whispered in frustration.

"No, Waythrel. You often confuse reality and metaphor. Right now, my words are literal."

"And this," I said, gesturing around us, dismissing her impossible sentences, "was to be a starship grounded in rock. What has happened to it?"

"A god-shard. Part of what happens when you play with divine fire, Waythrel."

God-shard. The word sent tremors through me. "What happened to the other gods? Where are they?"

"Delayed," she said, crouching into a ball and placing the glowing sphere on the sands. She rose and turned to face me. "Everything is terribly bent as we approach her—space and time. To be expected. So the split second of delay I placed between their and our travels becomes much longer for us here."

"Why have you delayed them?"

Kloan walked over to me and grasped her robes near her neckline. "Because we need to talk, Waythrel. This is it. Time for all the cards to be put on the table."

The deep weariness burdening me deepened. "Kloan, I'm not at any table. I've never understood the game. I don't hold a single card."

"Sit with me a minute, before all the fools return," she said, gesturing to the sand.

I had no objection to lowering my body to rest on sand. *How I missed it!* We sat, and I tried to prepare myself for more revelations. It was, of course, fitting that she had saved the most absurd of them for last.

"Remember the riddle in the crypt? 'Where are all the anti-gods?'"

"Yes," I replied.

"And remember you asked why it was so important to Ambra that you find that answer?"

"Yes." As always, I didn't have a clue where she was going.

"I told you then that I didn't know the answer. Well, I lied."

She stared at me calmly, nonchalant in her confession. I probed hesitantly. "Okay. Then what is the answer? Why did Ambra put so much effort into that test?"

Kloan smiled. "Let's start the answer with another question. We've been carrying around these strange fields over our bodies now for some time. Through perpetual event loops, on world after world, adventure after adventure. We don't even notice them anymore, but they are *still* here. *Why?* What are the fields, Waythrel? Why are they here around us?"

She was right. I had adapted to the strange things, pushed them to the back of my consciousness in dealing with the far more disturbing events that demanded my full attention. Thinking through her questions, I retreated to earlier, unproven theories I had formed concerning them. "Environmental suits. Disguises. Like the sphere you have—magical gifts from the gods for two mythical heroes to complete their legendary quest."

Kloan shook her head dismissively. "No, those functions were all only secondary." She grasped my hands and looked into my eye clusters. "Waythrel, have you ever touched me?"

What was she talking about? "Yes, of course. I'm touching you now. I've carried you, tended you, grabbed you in frustration, tried to stop you, save you!"

"*Through* the fields, Waythrel. Always through the fields."

My mind spun around this point. "Yes. You are right. What are you implying?"

"That you have never truly touched me. Your atoms have never been *allowed* to approach mine, to interact with mine."

A strange feeling spread through me, a deep unease. "And why has that not been allowed?"

She sighed. "It's always hardest to explain something to you Xix when you don't want to know the answer. *Think!* Remember, you asked if the use of robots and other machines on the clone colony was to protect the Anti from annihilation. I told you that they were not concerned with that. You asked why, but I never answered you. But that was an important question! Indeed, how could they not be concerned?"

I did not answer. She was right; I did not want to answer or to think anymore in this direction.

"You can hide from it all you want, Leaky, but you sense the truth. So I'll just cut this short and say it: they do not fear annihilation from those clones and humans because those clones and humans *would not hurt them*. And that's because those clones and humans on that world, the world itself and everything on it, are made of antimatter as well." Her eyes bored into mine. "The only truly foreign matter there in all those visits was *you*, Waythrel."

"No. That's impossible!" And it was. How ridiculous! Of course it wasn't possible. How could there be anti-humans? Where would they come from? The implications were astounding. They were also personally devastating.

"They came from dedicated and highly advanced engineers," she said. "Look at it this way. The Anti had millions of years to intimately feel how their existence hung by a thread in a universe that was inherently, *existentially* hostile to them. Enough of that and there can be certain breathtaking feats of ingenuity. They discovered relationships between matter and antimatter that surpassed nearly all science in the cosmos. All of this because of their unique need to understand this unbalanced, broken symmetry in our reality. Early on, they thought entropy was the ultimate weapon to unmake matter and return the universe to balance. But with the power of the clones over space-time, they then had the tools they needed for something a little more interesting and wild. After several monumentally disastrous failures—one of which threatened the entire existence of their kind—they succeeded."

My mind felt numb. I found myself instinctively moving away from Kloan. I could barely speak. "Succeeded at what?"

"Material *inversion*. A complete inversion of the matter of your type into its opposite."

"Matter of my type."

"Yes," said Kloan, her green eyes like lasers burning into my cowering eyestalks. "*Your* type. Because once they had perfected the process, they created millions of human anti-people. Really, as you would understand, no different in their physiology and chemistry than their inverses. And of course they didn't stop there. They *cloned* from them. Clones from very specific inverted stock. Gave birth to tiny little anti-Ambra Dawns."

She smiled. "Like me."

Chapter 60

Is man merely a mistake of God's?
Or God merely a mistake of man?

Friedrich Nietzsche

F aint winds stirred the sands around us. Part of my mind wrestled with
the problem of maintaining climate on a *god-shard* ripped out of the
heart of a world and suspended at the crux of time within a cauldron
of energy and dragon fire that was the nativity of our reality. The rest of my
mind worked to focus, tried to parse through these impossible revelations
spilling from this creature in front of me.

"And so the fields—" I stuttered, lurching to a stop as my mind sputtered.

"Are there to prevent us from annihilating each other, blowing up like an
angry hornet's nest of thermonuclear warheads."

"You are made of antimatter."

"Well, what's anti and what isn't is sort of relative, don't you think?" she
said playfully. "But I'll give it to your kind—you basically own this universe
and we're the definite minority, so we'll go with your naming. For now. Until
we rebalance things, because that is at the root what all of this has been about."

"Balancing matter and antimatter?"

"Among other things."

I stood up, my mind racing. "But Kloan, even if what you say is true about
yourself and your—*kind*—even if you can restore material balance, it's a
disaster to do it!"

"We *can* do it—you, me, and Ambra, with a little help from our god friends."

My arms were gesticulating wildly. "Even if we *can*, it's madness. It would mean total material annihilation!" I paused for a moment, my imagination spinning wild scenarios that might at least possess some weak threads of sanity in this tale. "Unless you mean to do this after a great amount of expansion in the universe, to segregate matter and antimatter across distances that render them innocuous to each other. Yes?"

"Nope! See that sky? That's nearly Big Bang firework level. We've come to the beginning, Waythrel, and we're going to break the asymmetry at the alpha point!"

I was dumbfounded. "To what purpose? You will destroy the cosmos."

"Yes!" she cried to the sky, raising her hands into the air. Slowly she lowered her arms, her face turning somber. "And well, no, actually. There are more things in heaven and beyond it, Waythrel, than are dreamt of in your particle physics."

"I will not participate in such madness."

She clucked like an annoyed mother hen. "Waythrel, listen! Simplistically, matter and antimatter annihilate and make a big bunch of energy, scrambling the structure of matter and all the things you love and want to preserve in the universe. But what of gravity, Waythrel? What of space and time? More to the point, what of the field of sentience interwoven with them and augmented to complexities unfathomable in these gods?"

"What does this have to do with particle annihilation?" I asked.

"What do you think anti-thoughts are like, Waythrel?"

The question stopped my mind cold. "I don't know. I assume, like the chemistry of antimatter, therefore like the biology, the neurobiology, they might be the same as ours."

"Might? But you doubt. Why?"

The answer came hesitantly to me. "Because chemistry is different than gravity. Different forces. Different fields. Different physics."

"Yes, and?"

"And I don't know how the behavior of anti-particles might compare to particles when considering sentient fields."

Kloan stood up and slapped my arms, dust clouding around us. "Exactly! You're right to be unsure, because while they are indistinguishable at most levels, they are *different* in extreme conditions." She pointed down into the earth-shard. "Inside this thing, deeply entombed within a warped, murdered space-time, is a god-thing with a mind of power and complexity we will never begin to understand in science or in intuition. How extreme do you think that is?"

She led me forward like a nymph. "Very extreme," I said.

"And it turns out that anti-minds and minds diverge dramatically at those levels. *So think!* As the gods have developed and grown, their minds became more and more biased along a particular divergence. Our cosmos is completely, utterly dominated by one type of mentality! The asymmetry in matter has given birth to a radical asymmetry in *mind!* So, where *are* the anti-gods, Waythrel? Do you see why this is so important?"

"But do we need the other types of minds?"

Kloan spread her arms wide. "Does the cosmos look like it's particularly sane?"

"How could I judge?" And I meant this sincerely.

Her hands clasped themselves together at her breast. "Consider the possibility, Waythrel, that this incredible, impossible growth from strings to atoms to organisms to group minds—strata upon strata of complexity, each level reflecting the structure beneath and yet engendering its own rules and form— imagine that it doesn't stop within this limited concept of our minds we call *'the cosmos'*. Imagine instead that our universe is just the next strata, the next level to something even more monumental, more astounding, more impossible, beautiful, and terrible! And yet we have let our universe destroy half of what it could be in atoms and in consciousness. We might not understand what it might be if we were to restore balance, but dare we let this mental genocide—what the Anti call the *nousicide*—continue?"

The idea that *my type* of matter had essentially slaughtered, even exterminated an entire cosmic mental ecosystem was almost impossible to grasp. And yet, in some strange sense, I felt it. After everything, I began to sense a monolithic conformity in this strangeness of mind and matter that had pummeled me throughout this quest. Kloan's wild, incomprehensible actions and thoughts rang through my memories. *Universes where the laws of physics are different. Where mathematics is different. Where logic is other.*

"You said that I would never understand you, and that this was important," I said.

"Yes! So you see it!"

"No, Kloan, I don't! I still don't see how annihilating the universe will save your kind of mentality! Everything will be destroyed, nonexistent anti-gods included!"

She shook her head and took my hands again. "Waythrel, it's more than particles, remember? At the extremes, the minds are different. *Minds* are *different!* They don't annihilate—they intertwine, synergize! They couple and engender! They *create!*"

"We're going to grind up all the matter in the universe into energy, destroy every last world and galaxy and god—including Ambra—and yet some kind of grand mental something is going to be born?"

"Yes!" she said, smiling, dancing in a circle like some psychotic thing.

I looked up into the heavens, anxiously expecting the descent at any moment of a thousand deities. I tried to focus, to center myself, to find a single, practical thing I could grasp in all this.

"Kloan, I'm here because I love Ambra." As Kloan danced over to me, laughing, her green eyes gleaming with a wild smile on her face, I touched her cyborg head with my digits. "And I'm here because I love you, too, even if I can't possibly fathom you. But I don't have anything more to add. It's all beyond me. So just tell me why, after all of this, am I here? What do you both want with me?"

Kloan nodded gravely. "When the gods come and tear open the universe to reveal Ambra, when the moment comes to destroy her, you will pass sentence, Waythrel. You have been chosen."

I stepped backward, away from the words I was hearing, as if I had been dealt a blow. Kloan ignored me, declaring my doom in some resonant, prophetic voice.

"Ambra has selected you to be the final judge of our cosmos. And I agree with her."

Chapter 61

"**Y**ou are not serious." Of everything that I had heard come out of her mouth, proclaiming Waythrel of Xix the judge of all the universe was without doubt the most ludicrous of them all.

"Here's how it's going to work," said Kloan, speaking as if she hadn't heard me. "Remember when I said I had to become everything Ambra was not? Her inverse in all things? Now you can understand. Physically, I am very nearly her inverse—a pile of cloned antimatter that will utterly annihilate her. But much more importantly, my mental structure has to be her inverse. As an anti-clone, I am much of the way there already, but I had to perfect, deepen, strengthen in all directions our differences by getting to know her in ways beyond her talking god-ball. Hence, our adventures, of which you were a critical element."

"I don't want explanations. I can't do this thing, Kloan. Even if it were possible, I will not pronounce judgment on an entire reality."

She continued. "She is the primordial fault, the fatal flaw, the imperfection that seeded a great god-growth that crossed all times but that introduced, through her unique persona, a systematic bias. She is wrong in and of herself and also wrong because she is a construct of the dominant form of matter." Kloan removed her robes, her naked body gleaming with sweat in the desert heat. She walked past me to the bright sphere, stopping beside it. "I am the surgical knife that will remove her from the god-particle. When I collide with her, time and space will dive into themselves as never seen, and we will enter the singularity of the Origin. We will annihilate each other there even as we enter, the process altering everything from genesis to apocalypse. We will also recombine to create something far greater, completely other, and unknowable to us in this distorted universe." She turned to gaze at me sadly. "It will be your choice whether to send me to that end."

"Kloan, no! *Stop!* I refuse!" My mind felt a panic like it had never experienced.

"Waythrel, there are no more outs. The gods are mad, the cosmos is deathly sick. You've seen its dying gasps in the dead ice and darkness. Something must be done."

"My soul is a nymph. I am just one Xix. Only Waythrel. I cannot even truly judge another. I certainly cannot judge a cosmos."

Kloan sighed and placed her hands on her bony hips. "Developmental biology, Waythrel. There are decision points that affect the large-scale nature of the organism. Left-right asymmetry, top-bottom polarity, immunological reactivity. Malignancy. Branch points exist involving a single tissue or a cluster of cells—even a single cell or the state of one protein in a cell. The most reductionist aspects of the whole can sometimes reverberate through the anatomical hierarchy to induce macroscopic ends."

Sonic booms shattered the relative quiet of the desert, and I watched in deep dread as a thousand blazing meteors exploded miles above us.

Kloan followed their trajectory toward the ground without interrupting her lecture. "You have been chosen to select the direction of this universe, Waythrel. It is Ambra's will. Use the sphere, push me forward in the null field that will soon be created around us, annihilate us both, and engender something beyond all that is. Or fail to—from choice or inaction—and the field collapses on itself, the gods continue their futile cosmic wars, forever frozen in a development that never transcends this reality. Then the everlasting winter you know too well is assured."

Beyond my worst nightmares, I stood rooted to the spot. Straight like a beam, eyestalks coiled together in a braid, arms wrapped as a shroud around my torso, I watched the gods plummet toward us like harbingers of catastrophe. Their fire and smoke only heightened the aura of final cataclysm running through my body. I could find no words to speak, not even of protest or anger. I could see no pathway out of this entangled causality set before me. I could only see the two horns of a dilemma, the earthling's mythic creature charging mercilessly, the spearpoints sharp and deep. On one or the other I would impale myself.

"It is nearly time," she said. "The circus is in town. Soon we dig, my travel mate. Soon we take a last savage journey together to the end and beginning of all things."

The tips of my stalks turned eighteen eyes to her. Mesmerized, I watched as one flaming comet after another struck the desert surface around her naked form. Each impact induced a shockwave of sand and rush of air, cratering the surface as an incongruity of limbs and forms slammed like marbled towers, unshaken and mighty, onto the god-shard—divinities so great that it seemed the paltry space could not hold them. Yakshini unfurled roots hundreds of miles across the desert, coating the sands like a carpet. Aditi spilled like liquid soot to form first a dry lake and then a sphere that resembled some caged gas giant. Vighneshvara floated elegantly with his eye-wings of light. Māra and her crew of hellions assaulted the ground simply by touching it. And there were thousands of others. Some great, some lesser, all forces of physicality and mentality that overwhelmed me.

Yet at the center of the ring they occupied, Kloan radiated like some impossible ingot in the deepest furnace. She seemed transfigured, an alien power coursing through her cells, her skin star bright and blinding, impossible to hold in view. She raised her arms, and her voice resounded across the shard miraculously, once-childish tones now imbued with their own transcendence.

"This is the nexus. Here is the nucleus of all that must be unmade. Feel her throb beneath. Taste her living blood and finite core. Deconstruct the labyrinth of minds and fortifications between us." The resplendent form turned in a circle, beaming impossible light at the beings around her. "Now we turn downward, burrow like sharpened augers into the flesh of this mind. You know your task. Open a shaft deep to the core. Then I will step into this abyss and fall, carrying the seed of her destruction."

No more words were needed. The deities dug. Nightmarish transformations of form into function played out around us. They assumed shapes—serrated, bladed bodies and edged configurations, yet possessed of a sharpness that was little about matter and far more about mind and soul. As they sliced through the surface and underlying matrix, the sounds were not of metal on stone or steel on flesh. The cause was not vibrational or from the impact of the debris flung recklessly into the skies around us.

No, what I heard over everything else that blocked out the material events around me were the anguished wails of souls torn asunder, of minds ripped to madness. What I saw was the desecration of inconceivable grace and beauty, the defilement of the pure and inviolable.

I witnessed the great, transcendent glory we called the Orb broken, its many-splendored passageways of light extinguished, its visage of love and empathy marred and mutilated.

The screams engulfed me. The cries as these god-fiends rent and shattered all I had ever worshipped and loved buffeted me, cast me down, and drowned me in madness and sorrow.

I felt myself being drawn downward into a pit of darkness, wailing and gnashing of teeth and claw pummeling my awareness, until at last, in the center of the deepest nothingness, the only scream left in my mind was my own.

Chapter 62

Perhaps our role on this planet is not to worship God—
but to create Him.

Arthur C. Clarke

My scream perished vainly, abandoned by the universe itself—for the universe, the gods in their terrible grandeur, the shard of New Earth and tattered remnants of the Orb—all were gone.

I floated in a darkness that was empty even of the lack of light itself—a true nothing that could not be described by color or lack of it, by presence or absence. There are no words or thoughts for the existentially empty, the authentically vacant. The experience was a madness that would have overthrown my mind but for the form of Kloan in front of me to anchor my awareness.

Look down the shaft into the heart of divinity, came her words.

And so I looked. Behind her, the nothingness was torn, and outside our bubble of emptiness, the cosmos warped and curved; space and time and reality itself were perverted into some strained, tortured malformation. At the deepest pit of this hellhole was a simple room containing a slab of machinery and living tissue. A human girl, sliced open and embedded in circuitry for an age of a cosmos undying and unassuaged in her agony.

Ambra smiled from below. Her green eyes were wide and inviting, waveforms of purpose and affection rocking us on a sea of distraught lucidity.

The choice must be made now, came the thoughts of my dearest friend.

The dazzling sphere floated into Kloan's hands, and she held it before me. *It is time to decide, Waythrel.*

And so after everything—a million journeys of nothing, deaths and lives and pain and love and madness, a tsunami of experience heedlessly casting me before it like unnoticed debris, an eon of powerlessness and confusion from which I had finally recoiled and surrendered—after all this *I* was to seal the ultimate fate of our reality. I had no time for last words with Ambra or Kloan. I had no chance to look on her mutilated flesh and consider my own culpability, to judge my own life and choices. I was too busy judging a universe.

I tried to parse the long explanations from Kloan, the cryptic prophecies of the god-Ambra. I tried to understand something about how the great synergy of structure and evolution toward divine-like consciousness could go awry, and how I could be the one to restart the system by hurling an antimatter clone of my friend into this god-pit to annihilate her inverse cyborg. Incompatible thoughts spun incongruously in my mind and failed to harmonize.

I abandoned the effort. I knew it was beyond me. Instead, I looked into the eyes of Kloan and saw a terrified determination that elicited waves of empathy. I wanted to comfort this child who displayed such courage and commitment to her beliefs, even though those beliefs were mad beyond description. I gazed down the deep shaft, the contortions of space-time acting as a lens, bringing the face of Ambra Dawn alongside that of Kloan. Eyes and anti-eyes of green. Eyes in agony and filled with love. Eyes of beings who had sacrificed beyond the capability of minds to assimilate. Two pairs of eyes of inverse beings who were asking me to use them both to destroy each other, all so that some hypothesized and incomprehensible healing of a broken cosmos might be undertaken.

It was a reprisal of my choices on the burning colony world when I carried Kloan through the gate. Only this time, the stakes were infinitely higher, and instead of saving her from a certain death on that dying planet, I was casting her to a doom that would also destroy Ambra. In one decision I would murder them both and, they both claimed, destroy an entire cosmos.

Until all is lost, Waythrel, nothing is found.

For the first time, I began to appreciate the full import of that statement. I nodded and placed the digits of my four arms on the sphere. The brightness increased dramatically, yet angled backward through Kloan and extended down the shaft and into the heart of the darkness below, bathing the medical facility housing Ambra in the hideous, pure light of a distinct cosmos.

I don't have any reasons, my friends. I don't want to lose you. But there is nothing left in this now. There is only my love and my trust in you. And so I will give you what you ask for, although it is beyond my understanding.

And then I pushed. Thrusting my arms forward with all my strength, I shoved the sphere in her hands away from me. My inconsequential motion propelled me backward slowly relative to the strange gravity lens below me, but Kloan accelerated with an impossible force that I could only ascribe to the sphere itself. Collecting frightening momentum, her form and the small star she carried sped down the tunnel, the distance now appearing impossibly deep, her approach likely to take hours or even days of travel.

And yet she accelerated. The light of the sphere turned from white to a deep red, and the sack of emptiness around me ripped and dissolved, revealing the inner layers of hell itself. Around me were the massacred forms of minds and machines, bodies of Readers eternal now dead, the blood-soaked claws and mouths of gods dripping ferally. The divinities clung to the sides of an impossible breach in space-time like bats to a cavern wall; yet they scrambled, fleeing upward and away from the core, their cries becoming more wild and horrific by the moment. Backward I continued to float, yet the deities slid oppositely, vainly clawing to the sides of the universe, an irresistible chain clasped around them, dragging them deeper and deeper into the dying Orb's well.

Alongside the wailing death notes of a trillion Orb minds, I now struggled to withstand trillions more from the doomed god-things as they lost their grasp and, one by one, plummeted helplessly into the pit of growing light. Endlessly they fell—the lesser gods, Vighneshvara with his wings shredded and useless, Māra eviscerated and dissolving while torn apart by gravitational tides, and Yakshini splaying forth ten million roots like grappling hooks, landing punctures in space-time, small breaches in the walls of the chasm, holding on longest of all until each root was snapped and mangled; and at last she fell, screeching, into the abyss devouring them all.

I continued to drift backward, a shell of nothingness forming around me once again. The cosmos itself, the soup of particles and energy of the Big Bang outside of me, was sucked backward in time to the singularity of creation. The universe fell into the pit with the gods. I could see each one as in slow motion, their tumbling as through molasses, the lens that had brought the image of Ambra close to me now warping and rendering the entire blender below undecipherable.

Then—*light*. Divine light. An impossible light erupted from deep below and expanded toward me. The closer it came, the more rapidly it approached, my slow movements soon to be overtaken. I had no illusions about what would happen when I met that ultimate radiance.

But I had no anxiety, no feelings of panic or fear, and no thoughts for my existence. I had only acceptance and a weariness that rendered all else secondary. I was ready for a rest. I was more than ready for an end.

I opened my arms and eyestalks madly to the onrushing brilliance. And as it blinded me, burned me, and tore my fragile flesh apart, I felt its mind. A personality unlike any I had encountered burst through my evaporating consciousness. And for one brief instant that I could not keep, I finally understood what Kloan and Ambra had been trying to explain.

I wrapped my dissolving arms around the light in a final, loving embrace.

I AM

Epilogue

I had glimpsed, in the very eye of that splendor, strange vistas of being; as though in the depths of the hypercosmical past and the hypercosmical future also, yet coexistent in eternity, lay cosmos beyond cosmos.

Olaf Stapleton

I was called Waythrel of Xix, but I no longer know what I am or what I should be named.

As I stare over this endless desert before me, such trivialities no longer seem of any consequence. Crest upon crest of dunes rise to the horizon, and a reddened star sets the landscape on fire as it plunges into a sea of sand.

I am happy in this place. I no longer have a need for the fading memories of a home I called Xix. The cosmic conflicts and metaphysics now only interest me in passing. Here on this unknown world, in an unknown universe, I am comfortable. I am satisfied. I know a peace unlike any I can recall. I am ready to say goodbye to you.

But I cannot end this tale so quickly. You have questions, I am sure. You want to know "what happened" to the cosmos, to Ambra and Kloan, to the legion of broken gods and the great plan over which some unfortunate being I remember to be myself had to adjudicate. I can't blame you for that. After all you have come through as well, it is only right that I give you responses.

So I am sorry to say that my honest, heartfelt answer to these questions is that I do not know.

This does not mean I do not have memories—fantastic hallucinations that still play out in my deepest dreams, visions that no doubt have been warped and xixomorphized into digestible, cognitive clumps that are compatible with my sanity and self-analysis. These macerated nuggets I can offer you, can try to capture within the writing system of this Earth language. However vain, I do feel that you are owed this effort.

But you should never be deluded into thinking that they are something like "truth." Or even something like an "untruth," because even to lie requires knowledge of what *is* true, and I am lacking completely any such sense. What you have instead, let it be utterly clear, is only *myth*, cast from the furnace of the dreams of Once Waythrel of Xix. I have nothing more to offer you.

And so, what happened? I died in our unmade cosmos. Every molecule in my body was ripped from every other, the atoms themselves first ionized and then broken asunder into constituent quarks and strings and then downward through the rabbit hole of an infinity of ever-shrinking and changing constituents. Concurrently, impossibly, like some pile of organic bricks, I was reassembled into something preeminent. What this thing was, I cannot say. It was greater than the group minds, the gods of the cosmos, and the Orbs. It transcended these elevated entities like the gods transcended the individual minds of which they were formed. I do not know what this being was any more than one mind of a group mind could know the whole of which it was a small part. Even the gods themselves could not have understood it.

I have no name for it. You might wish to call it God, for it was a single Being, a unified, undivided, yet uncountable diversity where the mathematics of summation always led to one. It strode the heavens and beyond as only the Almighty could do. You may wish to call it God.

But I will not. I will not, because I was granted a glimpse through its eyes, and what I saw was humbling—certainly for myself, but so has been every step of my journey. Instead, I mean humbling for the god-thing.

For through its gaze I did not look down from some ultimate vantage point upon a cosmos to be ruled by its Maker. Instead, I looked upward, beyond, and into a great infinity of universes that uncountably carpeted a greater heaven. And in this place, God was not even a god. Not a hero. Barely a cog in a transcosmic assembly. God was only one particle, a transcendent-maker-divine-particle, encompassing everything of our religion and science and existence…and nothing of the infinitely greater possibilities outside and beyond.

No, I gazed upon an ocean of god-particles, a sea of universes as different from each other as a collection of elementary particles. Immeasurably more so, because at this level of synthesis, diversity only increased, and my awareness could not comprehend the inexhaustible well of properties by which any universe might be characterized. Kloan had warned me, and part of me laughed to find that in most of the realities at this hypercosmological strata, two plus two was anything but four.

But the wonder only began here. If what I had described were the full story, it would be astonishing beyond true description. But in the same way protons, neutrons, and electrons are not the full story of matter, so then the infinity of god-particles did not preside over their dominion in isolation. Subject to unknown forces of nature, they themselves were driven to trans-cosmological physics, chemistry, even analogs of biology that were nothing at all like biology. I dreamed in my delirium that uncountable elements following innumerable and indecipherable rules associated, combined, interacted, and created yet higher order structures that eclipsed even the impossible syntheses I had witnessed to this point.

On and on, higher and higher the structures went, until even in the dream it was beyond what my own experience could assimilate. Like Icarus I was burned to devastation by the light of this geometrically expanding synergy; and in the final moments of this meditation, the endless, divine ladder shattered my concentration, and I fell into deep darkness.

Only to awake here, in the sands of a warm and habitable world. I opened my eyes, not knowing what I was, how I could be, what resurrected and recreated life form I should be characterized as. And most remarkable of all, when I awoke, I was not alone.

And it is because of this last fact that I must leave you now and end this wondrous tale. The hour is late; the colder night airs will soon arrive, and I must retreat to the warmth and shelter of the oasis behind me.

I look down at the infant in my arms. At three months, her thick red hair is still short and spiky. Her skin is a luminous white that seems to be painted from the captured light of the planet's moon. Any moment now she will awaken, hungry, and her bright green eyes will pierce my clusters with the unique survival demands of the human nymph-form. Once again I will retreat to the miraculous plants within that ooze milk and honey.

I stand up and stride across the sands, savoring the flow of silica between my digits, my emotions rising as I see a silhouette before me in the growing darkness. The star has set and the light faded too much for me to see clearly in the desert. But the oasis provides its own light with a plethora of bioluminescence, and it is not long before I can discern the black, phosphorescent patterns on the tall Xixian shape beside the garden's edge.

"Synphel," I say lovingly, using one of my free arms to caress my mate's eyestalks.

"You are late, Waythrel. Look, he is awake."

I glance down to her lower arms; cradled in one of them as by a hammock, a small bundle coos. I reach down and brush the thick black hair out of his eyes while he vigorously sucks on his thumb. "Just in time, you mean. Ambra is also waking."

The redheaded baby twists and begins to complain. I bring the two of them close together. The boy reaches over and taps repeatedly on Ambra's arm. Within seconds, she stops crying.

I feel a warm joy flow outward from Synphel. "Nitin can always sooth her, it seems."

"Yes," I say, feeling the wind pick up. I look into the entrance of the oasis, a huge arch of trees and vines serving as a portal in an otherwise impenetrable wall of towering plants that line the circumference of the garden. I press gently on Synphel's arm and turn toward the light within.

"Come, let's get inside. It's time."

Gratitude is given for this worship which You are pleased to accept from our hands, even though You are surrounded by Angels: six-armed, many-eyed, singing the victory hymn, "Holy, holy, holy Queen of Hosts, who was and who is and who is to come! Hosanna in the highest."

from the Dawnist Anaphora

In Conclusion

I want to thank my family and friends for their extensive patience with my "artisanal author" activities. I realize that my creative efforts are not to the taste of everyone, but, nonetheless, you have encouraged me to create and stood by my efforts.

I am also touched by the readers who have expressed such affection for one (and sometimes several!) of the novels—especially those who have responded with feelings and ideas that reflect in some deep way those elements within myself that engendered this series.

This tale was bigger than any one person, perspective, or voice; and while part of the divergence between novels was intentional to shake both the writer and the reader out of their comfort zone, the larger truth is that the voices of the characters came and spoke to me in the manner recorded, and I simply wrote down what they said.

It's difficult to leave Ambra, Waythrel, Kloan, and their unique universe behind. They have been with my thoughts now for five years, sharing with me their stories and impressing their experiences deeply within me. I already miss them—Kloan most of all, perhaps.

I hope that in some other reality, their memory is eternal, and we might meet again.

Erec Stebbins, August 2014, NYC

About the Author

Erec Stebbins is a biomedical researcher who writes political and international thrillers, science fiction, narrated storybooks, and more. He was born in the Midwest, his mother a clinical psychologist and his father a professor of Romance languages at the University of Nebraska in Lincoln. His father's specialty, old Romance languages and their literature, is the source of the unusual spelling of his middle name: "Erec." It is an Old French spelling, taken from an Arthurian romance by Chrétien de Troyes written around 1170: *Érec et Énide*.

He has pursued diverse interests over the course of his life, including science, music, drama, and writing. His academic path focused on science, and he received a degree in physics from Oberlin College in 1992, and a PhD in biochemistry from Cornell University in 1999. He has worked for several decades studying the structure of biological macromolecules involved in disease.

HARD TIME ADVENTURE NOVELLAS
WHERE SURVIVAL IS THE MEANING OF LIFE

HARD TIME SCIFI Series

Where survival is the meaning of life. A speculative fiction serial of adventure novellas set in a strange and punishing world. In Book 1, **METAL** a woman finds herself in two different worlds, as two different people. In one she is a criminal, sentenced to a new and terrible punishment. In the other, she is a stranger and then a prophet, granted the visions of God.